# THE HUGO WINNERS
## VOLUME FOUR

VOLUME FOUR

# THE HUGO WINNERS

*Edited by Isaac Asimov*

Doubleday & Company, Inc., Garden City, New York

"Home Is the Hangman" by Roger Zelazny, copyright © 1975 by Roger Zelazny. First published in *Analog Science Fiction/Science Fact,* November 1975. Reprinted by permission of the author and the author's agent, Kirby McCauley, Ltd.

"The Borderland of Sol" by Larry Niven, copyright © 1975 by Larry Niven. First published in *Analog Science Fiction/Science Fact,* January 1975. Reprinted by permission of the author.

"Catch That Zeppelin!" by Fritz Leiber, copyright © 1975 by Mercury Press, Inc. First published in *The Magazine of Fantasy and Science Fiction,* March 1975. Reprinted by permission of the author and the author's agent, Robert P. Mills, Ltd.

"By Any Other Name" by Spider Robinson, copyright © 1976 by Condé Nast Publications, Inc., and copyright © 1984 by Spider Robinson. First published in *Analog Science Fiction/Science Fact,* November 1976. Reprinted by permission of the author and the author's agent, Spectrum Literary Agency.

"Houston, Houston, Do You Read?" by James Tiptree, Jr., copyright © 1976 by Fawcett Publications, Inc. Reprinted by permission of the author and the author's agent, Virginia Kidd.

"The Bicentennial Man" by Isaac Asimov, copyright © 1976 by Random House, Inc. From *The Bicentennial Man and Other Stories* by Isaac Asimov. Reprinted by permission of Doubleday & Company, Inc.

"Tricentennial" by Joe Haldeman, copyright © 1976 by Condé Nast Publications, Inc. First published in *Analog Science Fiction/Science Fact,* July 1976. Re-

Sally Greenberg,
the better half of MHG, the best science
fiction anthologist in the world

# CONTENTS

# INTRODUCTION: WHAT AGAIN?
## by Isaac Asimov

Where does time go to?

It's hard for me to tell. I go on from year to year, you see, ageless and devastatingly handsome, writing up an endless storm, so that, as far as I am concerned, time stands still.

I cannot help but notice, however, that somehow, for the rest of the Universe, there is a one-way movement in the direction of larger and larger numbers on the calendar. Thus, when the first volume of *The Hugo Winners* came out, the number of the year was 1962; now it is 1985.

That alone is nothing. It's a matter of numbers, and numbers are conventions that are under human control. We can call every year 1962 if we wish, or give the years no numbers at all. Who's to stop us?

The trouble is that there are other, more subtle changes as well. All my old friends, who were lissome and supple young fellows just the other day, have been undergoing strange alterations. Here is the way I referred to them in an essay I wrote recently: "It struck me that [they] were well-stricken in years, that they hobbled about, peered uncertainly at each other, cupped their hands behind their ears, spoke in quavering voices, and gummed thoughtfully at their gruel during meals."

Sad? Of course it's sad. I can only console myself with the thought that it might have been infinitely worse. Suppose *they* were all ageless and it was *I* who had grown old, sapless, and wizen. What an unspeakable tragedy that would have been.

But, as I said, that's not how it was and the carefree days danced beside me unnoticed. Then came the day when, to my utter surprise, I found myself facing the frowning visage of The Doubleday Corporate Entity.

"Asimov," said TDCE severely, "time is passing. When may we expect to get the fourth volume of *The Hugo Winners?*"

I couldn't believe my ears. "What, again?" said I.

Wasn't it only yesterday—or last year at the longest remove—that I did the third volume? With a light laugh I reached for that third volume on the shelves and turned to the copyright date.

Good heavens! Time *was* passing. In fact, it had passed! Since the third volume had been published, no fewer than eight conventions had been held, each one of which added a novella, a novelette, and a short story to the list of Hugo winners. I was stupefied to discover that I had an enormous number of new words of colossally excellent science fiction to deal with.

Whereupon, thinking quickly, I said, "I have let time pass on purpose, TDCE. I knew what I was doing every moment. By this strategic delay I have accumulated some six hundred thousand words of sterling material. Consider the bonanza, the veritable Golconda, of science fiction that now awaits my loyal and intelligent readers."

I don't think there's any use reporting verbatim the answer TDCE gave me. For one thing, it consisted of about fifteen minutes' worth of very quickly articulated and rather poetic vituperation in which the word "procrastination" (one I had never encountered before, and of whose meaning I am still uncertain) was used a number of times.

After that, it consisted almost entirely of very dull material, involving book sizes, numbers of pages, and how much or how little a book spine can hold. There was even an excruciatingly boring routine involving the estimation of the price of an eight-convention book under modern conditions and of the unlikelihood of our readers consenting to mortgage their houses in order to buy the volume.

At this point, I raised a majestic hand. "Please. Spare me this vulgar discussion of money. My artistic soul rebels at the very sound of the word unless we are discussing advances, which is, of course, a different thing altogether. Just tell me what the alternative is."

That TDCE did. Apparently, we are going to split the period into two volumes. This book you are now holding (having bought and paid for it, I hope) is Volume Four, and contains the Hugo Winners of the four conventions from 1976 through 1979 inclusive. Next year, we will have Volume Five, which will contain the Hugo Winners of the four conventions from 1980 to 1983.

"What's more," said TDCE, in an awful tone that made it quite plain that it would brook no contradiction, "you will have to write two introductions, one for each volume, and serve you right for not being on the ball. And what is still more, we're going to put both volumes into a single contract, so that you get only one advance for them."

Two introductions, but only one advance!

Those of you who know my proud nature will imagine that I immediately rose to my full height (standing on a chair in order to do so) and told TDCE exactly where to get off.

And you are right. I actually climbed onto the chair and raised my arm in order to call down the thunderbolts of Jove when a thought occurred to me—

You may recall that when the first volume of *The Hugo Winners* was published, I took the opportunity to castigate the various convention committees for their venality, prejudice, and downright poor taste in never awarding me a Hugo for *anything.*

Naturally, harrowed by shame, they corrected this situation. They began showering me with Hugos: one for my science articles in *F & SF*, one for the best all-time series (the *Foundation Series),* and one for the best novel of the year *(The Gods Themselves).*

I was gratified. It was better than nothing. However, I couldn't help but notice that I never got a Hugo for anything that would fit into a *Hugo Winners* volume. I got no Hugo for a novella, novelette, or short story. It wasn't until 1976 that it occurred to me that one of the reasons for this might be that I wasn't writing stories in these categories. That was all the hint my giant brain needed. I instantly sat down and wrote a novelette entitled *The Bicentennial Man.* It won a Hugo at the 1977 convention.

But that meant that *The Hugo Winners, Volume Four* would finally contain a story by me, and it was *that* which occurred to me as I was about to blast TDCE with Cyclopean fire.

If I refused to edit the volume, another editor, far inferior to me in writing ability and taste, would be left with the job of introducing *The Bicentennial Man.* He would undoubtedly be totally incapable of doing the proper job.

I had no choice. "Yes, sir, TDCE," I said meekly. "Whatever you say, sir. I will try to do better in the future, sir."

So here I am trying to write the introduction to *The Hugo Winners, Volume Four.*

It's not easy. In fact, it can't be done. Having looked over the introductions to the first three volumes, I see that I have already said everything that one can possibly say about these volumes. —Except that I see I have somehow said more. Thank goodness!

*1976*
*34th CONVENTION*
*KANSAS CITY*

# Roger Zelazny

Since the stories in this anthology have been selected by popular vote at the conventions, there is little I can do to add or detract, and it has been my policy in the previous volumes not to talk much about the stories per se in these introductions. (Unless I feel like it, of course.) That policy I will continue to follow.

Nor, in this volume, can I discuss the conventions themselves. As it happens, all four conventions dealt with in this book were over a thousand miles from New York and the usual limit of my venturings from the Big Apple is about one-fifth that distance. As a result, I attended none of the four.

So I'll discuss whatever I feel like discussing, which is what I would do anyway.

For instance, "Home Is the Hangman" is Roger's first appearance in these volumes, although earlier, in 1966, he won the Hugo for his novel —*And Call Me Conrad*. (He was only twenty-nine at the time and had been publishing for only four years, miserable creature that he is.)

In a way, that was a personal relief to me. I had been the beneficiary of the alphabet all my life. In school, we were always listed, and lined up, and seated in alphabetical order, which meant I was always first or second or, just possibly, third in line. The teacher got to know me sooner, called on me oftener, thought of me more frequently (not always good), and somehow I think I did better as a result, both psychologically and actually.

To be sure, I suspect that I would have been noticeable no matter where I was in the class. (I remember once walking into a new class in high school and seeing the "home teacher" take one look at me and bury his face in his hands, after allowing a look of unspeakable horror to cross said face. I never found out why.) —Still, having my name start with *A* didn't hurt.

And in every class I was in, there was always some poor soul with a name something like Zuckerman, who always trailed at the end, had to wait longest for anything being handed out in order, and was always the student most likely to be ignored. Heaven only knows the scars carried by the *Z*'s of the world. I must admit I didn't worry about Zuckerman at the time, but as I grew older and spent more effort thinking about odd things, I began to speculate about such matters.

The first time I saw Roger's name, therefore, I said to myself, "Zelazny? The poor guy will never make it." And I thought of my *A* and felt guilty.

A pure waste of guilt. Zelazny did marvelously well from the start and my guilt gave way to a feeling of relief. What would he have done if his name had been Roger Aardvark? The imagination boggles.

At that, being last can have advantages. Right now, it is very simple to say something like "The entire field of science fiction from Asimov to Zelazny." I imagine someone or other is saying something like that continually.

Of course, my good friend Poul Anderson may well think that the phrase should be "from Anderson to Zelazny" and he may be right, but my good friend Poul Anderson is not editing this anthology. *I* am.

(However, Poul will show up later in this book, and I'll have a chance to talk about him.)

# *HOME IS THE HANGMAN*

Big fat flakes down the night, silent night, windless night. And I never count them as storms unless there is wind. Not a sigh or a whimper, though. Just a cold, steady whiteness, drifting down outside the window, and a silence confirmed by gunfire, driven deeper now it had ceased. In the main room of the lodge the only sounds were the occasional hiss and sputter of the logs turning to ashes on the grate.

I sat in a chair turned sidewise from the table to face the door. A tool kit rested on the floor to my left. The helmet stood on the table, a lopsided basket of metal, quartz, porcelain, and glass. If I heard the click of a microswitch followed by a humming sound from within it, then a faint light would come on beneath the meshing near to its forward edge and begin to blink rapidly. If these things occurred, there was a very strong possibility that I was going to die.

I had removed a black ball from my pocket when Larry and Bert had gone outside, armed, respectively, with a flame thrower and what looked like an elephant gun. Bert had also taken two grenades with him.

I unrolled the black ball, opening it out into a seamless glove, a dollop of something resembling moist putty stuck to its palm. Then I drew the glove on over my left hand and sat with it upraised, elbow resting on the arm of the chair. A small laser flash pistol in which I had very little faith lay beside my right hand on the tabletop, next to the helmet.

If I were to slap a metal surface with my left hand, the substance would adhere there, coming free of the glove. Two seconds later it would explode, and the force of the explosion would be directed in against the surface. Newton would claim his own by way of right-angled redistributions of the reaction, hopefully tearing lateral hell out of the contact surface. A smother-charge, it was called, and its possession came under concealed weapons and possession of burglary tools statutes in most places. The molecularly gimmicked goo, I decided, was great stuff. It was just the delivery system that left more to be desired.

Beside the helmet, next to the gun, in front of my hand, stood a small walkie-talkie. This was for purposes of warning Bert and Larry if I should hear the click of a microswitch followed by a humming sound, should see a light come on and begin to blink rapidly. Then they would know that Tom and Clay, with whom we had lost contact when the shooting began, had failed to destroy the enemy and doubtless lay lifeless at their stations now, a little over a kilometer to the south. Then they would know that they, too, were probably about to die.

I called out to them when I heard the click. I picked up the helmet and rose to my feet as its light began to blink.

But it was already too late.

The fourth place listed on the Christmas card I had sent Don Walsh the previous year was Peabody's Book Shop and Beer Stube in Baltimore, Maryland. Accordingly, on the last night in October I sat in its rearmost room, at the final table before the alcove with the door leading to the alley. Across that dim chamber, a woman dressed in black played the ancient upright piano, up-tempoing everything she touched. Off to my right, a fire wheezed and spewed fumes on a narrow hearth beneath a crowded mantelpiece overseen by an ancient and antlered profile. I sipped a beer and listened to the sounds.

I half hoped that this would be one of the occasions when Don failed to show up. I had sufficient funds to hold me through spring and I did not really feel like working. I had summered farther north, was anchored now in the Chesapeake, and was anxious to continue Caribbeanwards. A growing chill and some nasty winds told me I had tarried overlong in these latitudes. Still, the understanding was that I remain in the chosen bar until midnight. Two hours to go.

I ate a sandwich and ordered another beer. About halfway into it, I spotted Don approaching the entranceway, topcoat over his arm, head turning. I manufactured a matching quantity of surprise when he appeared beside my table with a "Ron! Is that really you?"

I rose and clasped his hand.

"Alan! Small world, or something like that. Sit down! Sit down!"

He settled onto the chair across from me, draped his coat over the one to his left.

"What are you doing in this town?" he asked.

"Just a visit," I answered. "Said hello to a few friends." I patted the scars, the stains of the venerable surface before me. "And this is my last stop. I'll be leaving in a few hours."

He chuckled.

"Why is it that you knock on wood?"

I grinned.

"I was expressing affection for one of Henry Mencken's favorite speakeasies."

"This place dates back that far?"

I nodded.

"It figures," he said. "You've got this thing for the past—or against the present. I'm never sure which."

"Maybe a little of both," I said. "I wish Mencken would stop in. I'd like his opinion on the present. What are you doing with it?"

"What?"

"The present. Here. Now."

"Oh." He spotted the waitress and ordered a beer. "Business trip," he said then. "To hire a consultant."

"Oh. And how *is* business?"

"Complicated," he said, "complicated."

We lit cigarettes and after a while his beer arrived. We smoked and drank and listened to the music.

I've sung this song and I'll sing it again: the world is like an up-tempoed piece of music. Of the many changes which came to pass during my lifetime, it seems that the majority have occurred during the past few years. It also struck me that way several years ago, and I'd a hunch I might be feeling the same way a few years hence—that is, if Don's business did not complicate me off this mortal coil or condenser before then.

Don operates the second-largest detective agency in the world, and he sometimes finds me useful because I do not exist. I do not exist now because I existed once at the time and the place where we attempted to begin scoring the wild ditty of our times. I refer to the World Data Bank project and the fact that I had had a significant part in that effort to construct a working model of the real world, accounting for everyone and everything in it. How well we succeeded and whether possession of the world's likeness does indeed provide its custodians with a greater measure of control over its functions are questions my former colleagues still debate as the music grows more shrill and you can't see the maps for the pins. I made my decision back then and saw to it that I did not receive citizenship in that second world, a place which may now have become more important than the first. Exiled to reality, my own sojourns across the line are necessarily those of an alien guilty of illegal entry. I visit periodically because I go where I must to make my living. That is where Don comes in. The people I can become are often very useful when he has peculiar problems. Unfortunately, at that moment, it seemed that he did, just when the whole gang of me felt like turning down the volume and loafing.

We finished our drinks, got the bill, settled it.

"This way," I said, indicating the rear door, and he swung into his coat and followed me out.

"Talk here?" he asked, as we walked down the alley.

"Rather not," I said. "Public transportation, then private conversation."

He nodded and came along.

About three-quarters of an hour later we were in the saloon of the *Proteus* and I was making coffee. We were rocked gently by the Bay's chill waters, under a moonless sky. I'd only a pair of the smaller lights burning. Comfortable. On the water, aboard the *Proteus,* the crowding, the activities, the tempo, of life in the cities, on the land, are muted, slowed—fictionalized—by the metaphysical distancing a few meters of water can provide. We alter the landscape with great facility, but the ocean has always seemed unchanged, and I suppose by extension we are infected with some feelings of timelessness whenever we set out upon her. Maybe that's one of the reasons I spend so much time there.

"First time you've had me aboard," he said. "Comfortable. Very."

"Thanks. Cream? Sugar?"

"Yes. Both."

We settled back with our steaming mugs and I said, "What have you got?"

"One case involving two problems," he said. "One of them sort of falls within my area of competence. The other does not. I was told that it is an absolutely unique situation and would require the services of a very special specialist."

"I'm not a specialist at anything but keeping alive."

His eyes came up suddenly and caught my own.

"I had always assumed that you knew an awful lot about computers," he said.

I looked away. That was hitting below the belt. I had never held myself out to him as an authority in that area, and there had always been a tacit understanding between us that my methods of manipulating circumstance and identity were not open to discussion. On the other hand, it was obvious to him that my knowledge of the system was both extensive and intensive. Still, I didn't like talking about it. So I moved to defend.

"Computer people are a dime a dozen," I said. "It was probably different in your time, but these days they start teaching computer science to little kids their first year in school. So, sure I know a lot about it. This generation, everybody does."

"You know that is not what I meant," he said. "Haven't you known me long enough to trust me a little more than that? The question springs solely from the case at hand. That's all."

I nodded. Reactions by their very nature are not always appropriate, and I had invested a lot of emotional capital in a heavy-duty set. So, "O.K., I know more about them than the school kids," I said.

"Thanks. That can be our point of departure." He took a sip of coffee. "My own background is in law and accounting, followed by the military, military intelligence, and civil service, in that order. Then I got into this business. What technical stuff I know I've picked up along the way, a scrap here, a crash course there. I know a lot about what things can do, not so much about how they work. I did not understand the details on this one, so I want you to start at the top and explain things to me, for as far as you can go. I need the background review, and if you are able to furnish it I will also know that you are the man for the job. You can begin by telling me how the early space exploration robots worked—like, say, the ones they used on Venus."

"That's not computers," I said, "and for that matter, they weren't really robots. They were telefactoring devices."

"Tell me what makes the difference."

"A robot is a machine which carries out certain operations in accordance with a program of instructions. A telefactor is a slave machine operated by remote control. The telefactor functions in a feedback situation with its operator. Depending on how sophisticated you want to get, the links can be audiovisual, kinesthetic, tactile, even olfactory. The more you want to go in this direction, the more anthropomorphic you get in the thing's design. In the case of Venus, if I recall correctly, the human operator in orbit wore an exoskeleton which controlled the movements of the body, legs, arms, and hands of the device on the surface below, receiving motion and force feedback through a system of airjet transducers. He had on a helmet controlling the slave device's television camera—set, obviously enough, in its turret—which filled his field of vision with the scene below. He also wore earphones connected with its audio pickup. I read the book he wrote later. He said that for long stretches of time, he would forget the cabin, forget that he was at the boss end of a control loop and actually feel as if he were stalking through that hellish landscape. I remember being very impressed by it, just being a kid, and I wanted a super-tiny one all my own, so that I could wade around in puddles picking fights with microorganisms."

"Why?"

"Because there weren't any dragons on Venus. Anyhow, that is a telefactoring device, a thing quite distinct from a robot."

"I'm still with you," he said. "Now tell me the difference between the early telefactoring devices and the later ones."

I swallowed some coffee.

"It was a bit trickier with respect to the outer planets and their satellites," I said. "There, we did not have orbiting operators at first. Economics, and some unresolved technical problems. Mainly economics. At any rate, the devices were landed on the target worlds, but the operators stayed home. Because of this, there was of course a time lag in the transmissions along the control loop. It took a while to receive the on-site input, and then there was another time lapse before the response movements reached the telefactor. We attempted to compensate for this in two ways. The first was by the employment of a simple wait-move, wait-move sequence. The second was more sophisticated and is actually the point where computers come into the picture in terms of participating in the control loop. It involved the setting up of models of known environmental factors, which were then enriched during the initial wait-move sequences. On this basis, the computer was then used to anticipate short-range developments. Finally, it could take over the loop and run it by a combination of 'predictor controls' and wait-move reviews. It still had to holler for human help, though, when unexpected things came up. So, with the outer planets, it was neither totally automatic nor totally manual—nor totally satisfactory—at first."

"O.K.," he said, lighting a cigarette. "And the next step?"

"The next wasn't really a technical step forward in telefactoring. It was an economic shift. The purse strings were loosened and we could afford to send men out. We landed them where we could land them, and in many of the places where we could not we sent down the telefactors and orbited the men again. Like in the old days. The time lag problem was removed because the operator was on top of things once more. If anything, you can look at it as a reversion to earlier methods. It is what we still often do, though, and it works."

He shook his head.

"You left something out," he said, "between the computers and the bigger budget."

I shrugged.

"A number of things were tried during that period," I said, "but none of them proved as effective as what we already had going in the human-computer partnership with the telefactors."

"There was one project," he said, "which attempted to get around the time lag troubles by sending the computer along with the telefactor as part of the package. Only the computer wasn't exactly a computer and the telefactor wasn't exactly a telefactor. Do you know which one I am referring to?"

I lit a cigarette of my own while I thought about it, then "I think you are talking about the Hangman," I said.

"That's right," he said, "and this is where I get lost. Can you tell me how it works?"

"Ultimately, it was a failure," I said.

"But it worked at first."

"Apparently. But only on the easy stuff, on Io. It conked out later and had to be written off as a failure, albeit a noble one. The venture was overly ambitious from the very beginning. What seems to have happened was that the people in charge had the opportunity to combine vanguard projects—stuff that was still under investigation and stuff that was extremely new. In theory it all seemed to dovetail so beautifully that they yielded to the temptation and incorporated too much. It started out well, but it fell apart later."

"But what all was involved in the thing?"

"Lord! What wasn't? The computer that wasn't exactly a computer . . . O.K., we'll start there. Last century, three engineers at the University of Wisconsin—Nordman, Parmentier, and Scott—developed a device known as a superconductive tunnel junction neuristor. Two tiny strips of metal with a thin insulating layer between. Supercool it and it passed electrical impulses without resistance. Surround it with magnetized material and pack a mass of them together—billions—and what have you got?"

He shook his head.

"Well, for one thing you've got an impossible situation to schematize when considering all the paths and interconnections that may be formed. There is an obvious similarity to the structure of the brain. So, they theorized, you don't even attempt to hook up such a device. You pulse in data and let it establish its own preferential pathways, by means of the magnetic material's becoming increasingly magnetized each time the current passes through it, thus cutting the resistance. So the material establishes its own routes in a fashion analogous to the functioning of

the brain when it is learning something. In the case of the Hangman,
they used a setup very similar to this and they were able to pack over
ten billion neuristor-type cells into a very small area—around a cubic
foot. They aimed for that magic figure because that is approximately the
number of nerve cells in the human brain. That is what I meant when I
said that it wasn't really a computer. They were actually working in the
area of artificial intelligence, no matter what they called it."

"If the thing had its own brain—computer or quasi-human—then it
was a robot rather than a telefactor, right?"

"Yes and no and maybe," I said. "It was operated as a telefactor
device here on Earth—on the ocean floor, in the desert, in mountainous
country—as part of its programming. I suppose you could also call that
its apprenticeship or kindergarten. Perhaps that is even more appropriate. It was being shown how to explore in difficult environments and to
report back. Once it mastered this, then theoretically they could hang it
out there in the sky without a control loop and let it report its own
findings."

"At that point would it be considered a robot?"

"A robot is a machine which carries out certain operations in accordance with a program of instructions. The Hangman made its own
decisions, you see. And I suspect that by trying to produce something
that close to the human brain in structure and function the seemingly
inevitable randomness of its model got included in. It wasn't just a
machine following a program. It was too complex. That was probably
what broke it down."

Don chuckled.

"Inevitable free will?"

"No. As I said, they had thrown too many things into one bag. Everybody and his brother with a pet project that might be fitted in seemed a
supersalesman that season. For example, the psychophysics boys had a
gimmick they wanted to try on it, and it got used. Ostensibly, it was a
communications device. Actually, they were concerned as to whether
the thing was truly sentient."

"Was it?"

"Apparently so, in a limited fashion. What they had come up with, to
be made part of the initial telefactor loop, was a device which set up a
weak induction field in the brain of the operator. The machine received
and amplified the patterns of electrical activity being conducted in the
Hangman's—might as well call it 'brain'—then passed them through a
complex modulator and pulsed them into the induction field in the
operator's head. I am out of my area now and into that of Weber and

Fechner, but a neuron has a threshold at which it will fire, and below which it will not. There are some forty thousand neurons packed together in a square millimeter of the cerebral cortex, in such a fashion that each one has several hundred synaptic connections with others about it. At any given moment, some of them may be way below the firing threshold while others are in a condition Sir John Eccles once referred to as 'critically poised'—ready to fire. If just one is pushed over the threshold, it can affect the discharge of hundreds of thousands of others within twenty milliseconds. The pulsating field was to provide such a push in a sufficiently selective fashion to give the operator an idea as to what was going on in the Hangman's brain. And vice versa. The Hangman was to have its own built-in version of the same thing. It was also thought that this might serve to humanize it somewhat, so that it would better appreciate the significance of its work—to instill something like loyalty, you might say."

"Do you think this could have contributed to its later breakdown?"

"Possibly. How can you say in a one-of-a-kind situation like this? If you want a guess, I'd say yes. But it's just a guess."

"Uh-huh," he said, "and what were its physical capabilities?"

"Anthropomorphic design," I said, "both because it was originally telefactored and because of the psychological reasoning I just mentioned. It could pilot its own small vessel. No need for a life-support system, of course. Both it and the vessel were powered by fusion units, so that fuel was no real problem. Self-repairing. Capable of performing a great variety of sophisticated tests and measurements, of making observations, completing reports, learning new material, broadcasting its findings back here. Capable of surviving just about anywhere. In fact, it required less energy on the outer planets—less work for the refrigeration units, to maintain that supercooled brain in its midsection."

"How strong was it?"

"I don't recall all the specs. Maybe a dozen times as strong as a man, in things like lifting and pushing."

"It explored Io for us and started in on Europa."

"Yes."

"Then it began behaving erratically, just when we thought it had really learned its job."

"That sounds right," I said.

"It refused a direct order to explore Callisto, then headed out toward Uranus."

"Yes. It's been years since I read the reports. . . ."

"The malfunction worsened after that. Long periods of silence interspersed with garbled transmissions. Now that I know more about its makeup, it almost sounds like a man going off the deep end."

"It seems similar."

"But it managed to pull itself together again for a brief while. It landed on Titania, began sending back what seemed like appropriate observation reports. This only lasted a short time, though. It went irrational once more, indicated that it was heading for a landing on Uranus itself, and that was it. We didn't hear from it after that. Now that I know about that mind-reading gadget I understand why a psychiatrist on this end could be so positive it would never function again."

"I never heard about that part."

"I did."

I shrugged.

"This was all around twenty years ago," I said, "and, as I mentioned, it has been a long while since I've read anything about it."

"The Hangman's ship crashed or landed, as the case may be, in the Gulf of Mexico," he said, "two days ago."

I just stared at him.

"It was empty," he said, "when they finally got out and down to it."

"I don't understand."

"Yesterday morning," he went on, "restaurateur Manny Burns was found beaten to death in the office of his establishment, the Maison Saint-Michel, in New Orleans."

"I still fail to see . . ."

"Manny Burns was one of the four original operators who programmed—pardon me, 'taught'—the Hangman."

The silence lengthened, dragged its belly on the deck.

"Coincidence . . . ?" I finally said.

"My client doesn't think so."

"Who is your client?"

"One of the three remaining members of the training group. He is convinced that the Hangman has returned to Earth to kill its former operators."

"Has he made his fears known to his old employers?"

"No."

"Why not?"

"Because it would require telling them the reason for his fears."

"That being . . . ?"

"He wouldn't tell me either."

"How does he expect you to do a proper job?"

"He told me what he considered a proper job. He wants two things done, neither of which requires a full case history. He wanted to be furnished with good bodyguards, and he wanted the Hangman found and disposed of. I have already taken care of the first part."

"And you want me to do the second?"

"That's right. You have confirmed my opinion that you are the man for the job."

"I see," I said. "Do you realize that if the thing is truly sentient this will be something very like murder? If it is not, of course, then it will only amount to the destruction of expensive government property."

"Which way do you look at it?"

"I look at it as a job," I said.

"You'll take it?"

"I need more facts before I can decide. Like . . . Who is your client? Who are the other operators? Where do they live? What do they do? What—"

He raised his hand.

"First," he said, "the Honorable Jesse Brockden, senior senator from Wisconsin, is our client. Confidentiality, of course, is written all over it."

I nodded.

"I remember his being involved with the space program before he went into politics. I wasn't aware of the specifics, though. He could get government protection so easily—"

"To obtain it, he would apparently have to tell them something he doesn't want to talk about. Perhaps it would hurt his career. I simply do not know. He doesn't want them. He wants us."

I nodded again.

"What about the others? Do they want us, too?"

"Quite the opposite. They don't subscribe to Brockden's notions at all. They seem to think he is something of a paranoid."

"How well do they know one another these days?"

"They live in different parts of the country, haven't seen each other in years. Been in occasional touch, though."

"Kind of flimsy basis for that diagnosis, then."

"One of them *is* a psychiatrist."

"Oh. Which one?"

"Leila Thackery is her name. Lives in St. Louis. Works at the State Hospital there."

"None of them have gone to any authority, then—federal or local?"

"That's right. Brockden contacted them when he heard about the Hangman. He was in Washington at the time. Got word on its return right away and managed to get the story killed. He tried to reach them all, learned about Burns in the process, contacted me, then tried to persuade the others to accept protection by my people. They weren't buying. When I talked to her, Dr. Thackery pointed out—quite correctly—that Brockden is a very sick man—"

"What's he got?"

"Cancer. In his spine. Nothing they can do about it once it hits there and digs in. He even told me he figures he has maybe six months to get through what he considers a very important piece of legislation—the new criminal rehabilitation act. I will admit that he did sound kind of paranoid when he talked about it. But hell! Who wouldn't? Dr. Thackery sees that as the whole thing, though, and she doesn't see the Burns killing as being connected with the Hangman. Thinks it was just a traditional robbery gone sour, thief surprised and panicky, maybe hopped up, et cetera."

"Then she is not afraid of the Hangman?"

"She said that she is in a better position to know its mind than anyone else, and she is not especially concerned."

"What about the other operator?"

"He said that Dr. Thackery may know its mind better than anyone else, but he knows its brain, and he isn't worried either."

"What did he mean by that?"

"David Fentris is a consulting engineer—electronics, cybernetics. He actually had something to do with the Hangman's design."

I got to my feet and went after the coffee pot. Not that I'd an overwhelming desire for another cup at just that moment. But I had known, had once worked with a David Fentris. And he had at one time been connected with the space program.

About fifteen years my senior, Dave had been with the Data Bank project when I had known him. Where a number of us had begun having second thoughts as the thing progressed, Dave had never been anything less than wildly enthusiastic. A wiry five-eight, white-cropped, gray eyes back of hornrims and heavy glass, cycling between preoccupation and near-frantic darting, he had had a way of verbalizing half-completed thoughts as he went along, so that you might begin to think him a representative of that tribe which had come into positions of small authority by means of nepotism or politics. If you would listen a few more minutes, though, you would begin revising your opinion as he started to pull his musings together into a rigorous framework. By the time he had finished you generally wondered why you hadn't seen it all along and what a guy like that was doing in a position of such small authority. Later, it might strike you, though, that he seemed sad whenever he wasn't enthusiastic about something, and while the gung-ho spirit is great for short-range projects, larger ventures generally require something more of equanimity. I wasn't at all surprised that he had wound up as a consultant. The big question now, of course, was would he remember me? True, my appearance was altered, my personality hopefully more mature, my habits shifted around. But would that be enough, should I have to encounter him as part of this job? That mind behind those hornrims could do a lot of strange things with just a little data.

"Where does he live?" I asked.

"Memphis, and what's the matter?"

"Just trying to get my geography straight," I said. "Is Senator Brockden still in Washington?"

"No. He's returned to Wisconsin and is currently holed up in a lodge in the northern part of the state. Four of my people are with him."

"I see."

I refreshed our coffee supply and reseated myself. I didn't like this one at all and I resolved not to take it. I didn't like just giving Don a flat no, though. His assignments had become a very important part of my life, and this one was not mere legwork. It was obviously important to him, and he wanted me on it. I decided to look for holes in the thing, to find some way of reducing it to the simple bodyguard job already in progress.

"It does seem peculiar," I said, "that Brockden is the only one afraid of the device."

"Yes."

". . . And that he gives no reasons."

"True."

". . . Plus his condition, and what the doctor said about its effect on his mind."

"I have no doubt that he is neurotic," Don said. "Look at this."

He reached for his coat, withdrew a sheaf of papers from within it. He shuffled through them and extracted a single sheet, which he passed to me. It was a piece of congressional letterhead stationery, with the message scrawled in longhand: "Don," it said, "I've got to see you. Frankenstein's monster has just come back from where we hung him and he's looking for me. The whole damn universe is trying to grind me up. Call me between eight and ten. —Jess." I nodded, started to pass it back, paused, then handed it over. Double damn it deeper than hell! I took a drink of coffee. I thought that I had long ago given up hope in such things, but I had noticed something which immediately troubled me. In the margin where they list such matters, I had seen that Jesse Brockden was on the committee for review of the Data Bank program. I recalled that that committee was supposed to be working on a series of reform recommendations. Offhand, I could not remember Brockden's position on any of the issues involved, but—oh hell! The thing was simply too big to alter significantly now. . . . But it *was* the only real Frankenstein monster I cared about, and there was always the possibility. . . . On the other hand—hell, again. What if I let him die when I might have saved him, and he had been the one who . . . ?

I took another drink of coffee. I lit another cigarette. There might be a way of working it so that Dave didn't even come into the picture. I could talk to Leila Thackery first, check further into the Burns killing, keep posted on new developments, find out more about the vessel in the Gulf. . . . I might be able to accomplish something, even if it was only the negation of Brockden's theory, without Dave's and my paths ever crossing.

"Have you got the specs on the Hangman?" I asked.

"Right here."

He passed them over.

"The police report on the Burns killing?"

"Here it is."

"The whereabouts of everyone involved, and some background on them?"

"Here."

"The place or places where I can reach you during the next few days —around the clock? This one may require some coordination."

He smiled and reached for his pen.

"Glad to have you aboard," he said.

I reached over and tapped the barometer. I shook my head.

The ringing of the phone awakened me. Reflex bore me across the room, where I took it on audio.

"Yes?"

"Mr. Donne? It is eight o'clock."

"Thanks."

I collapsed into the chair. I am what might be called a slow starter. I tend to recapitulate phylogeny every morning. Basic desires inched their ways through my gray matter to close a connection. Slowly, I extended a cold-blooded member and clicked my talons against a couple numbers. I croaked my desire for food and lots of coffee to the voice that responded. Half an hour later I would only have growled. Then I staggered off to the place of flowing waters to renew my contact with basics.

In addition to my normal adrenaline and blood-sugar bearishness, I had not slept much the night before. I had closed up shop after Don had left, stuffed my pockets with essentials, departed the *Proteus*, gotten myself over to the airport and onto a flight which took me to St. Louis in the dead, small hours of the dark. I was unable to sleep during the flight, thinking about the case, deciding on the tack I was going to take with Leila Thackery. On arrival, I had checked into the airport motel, left a message to be awakened at an unreasonable hour, and collapsed.

As I ate, I regarded the fact sheet Don had given me: Leila Thackery was currently single, having divorced her second husband a little over two years ago, was forty-six years old, and lived in an apartment near to the hospital where she worked. Attached to the sheet was a photo which might have been ten years old. In it, she was brunette, light-eyed, barely on the right side of that border between ample and overweight, with fancy glasses straddling an upturned nose. She had published a number of books and articles with titles full of alienations, roles, transactions, social contexts, and more alienations.

I hadn't had the time to go my usual route, becoming an entire new individual with a verifiable history. Just a name and a story, that's all. It did not seem necessary this time, though. For once, something approximating honesty actually seemed a reasonable approach.

I took a public vehicle over to her apartment building. I did not phone ahead, because it is easier to say no to a voice than to a person. According to the record, today was one of the days when she saw outpatients in her home. Her idea, apparently: break down the alienating institution image, remove resentments by turning the sessions into something more like social occasions, et cetera. I did not want all that much of her time, I had decided that Don could make it worth her while if it came to that, and I was sure my fellows' visits were scheduled to leave her with some small breathing space—*inter alia,* so to speak.

I had just located her name and apartment number amid the buttons in the entrance foyer when an old woman passed behind me and unlocked the door to the lobby. She glanced at me and held it open, so I went on in without ringing. The matter of presence, again.

I took the elevator to Leila's floor, the second. I located her door and knocked on it. I was almost ready to knock again when it opened, partway.

"Yes?" she asked, and I revised my estimate as to the age of the photo. She looked just about the same.

"Dr. Thackery," I said, "my name is Donne. You could help me quite a bit with a problem I've got."

"What sort of problem?"

"It involves a device known as the Hangman."

She sighed and showed me a quick grimace. Her fingers tightened on the door.

"I've come a long way but I'll be easy to get rid of. I've only a few things I'd like to ask you about it."

"Are you with the government?"

"No."

"Do you work for Brockden?"

"No. I'm something different."

"All right," she said. "Right now I've got a group session going. It will probably last around another half hour. If you don't mind waiting down in the lobby, I'll let you know as soon as it is over. We can talk then."

"Good enough," I said. "Thanks."

She nodded, closed the door. I located the stairway and walked back down.

A cigarette later, I decided that the devil finds work for idle hands and thanked him for his suggestion. I strolled back toward the foyer. Through the glass, I read the names of a few residents of the fifth floor. I elevated up and knocked on one of the doors. Before it was opened I had my notebook and pad in plain sight.

"Yes?"—short, fiftyish, curious.

"My name is Stephen Foster, Mrs. Gluntz. I am doing a survey for the North American Consumers' League. I would like to pay you for a couple minutes of your time, to answer some questions about products you use."

"Why . . . pay me?"

"Yes, ma'am. Ten dollars. Around a dozen questions. It will just take a minute or two."

"All right." She opened the door wider. "Won't you come in?"

"No, thank you. This thing is so brief I'd just be in and out. The first question involves detergents—"

Ten minutes later I was back in the lobby adding the thirty bucks for the three interviews to the list of expenses I was keeping. When a situation is full of unpredictables and I am playing makeshift games, I like to provide for as many contingencies as I can.

Another quarter of an hour or so slipped by before the elevator opened and discharged three guys, young, young, and middle-aged, casually dressed, chuckling over something. The big one on the nearest end strolled over and nodded.

"You the fellow waiting to see Dr. Thackery?"

"That's right."

"She said to tell you to come on up now."

"Thanks."

I rode up again, returned to her door. She opened to my knock, nodded me in, saw me seated in a comfortable chair at the far end of her living room.

"Would you care for a cup of coffee?" she asked. "It's fresh. I made more than I needed."

"That would be fine. Thanks."

Moments later, she brought in a couple of cups, delivered one to me, and seated herself on the sofa to my left. I ignored the cream and sugar on the tray and took a sip.

"You've gotten me interested," she said. "Tell me about it."

"O.K. I have been told that the telefactor device known as the Hangman, now possibly possessed of an artificial intelligence, has returned to Earth—"

"Hypothetical," she said, "unless you know something I don't. I have been told that the Hangman's vehicle reentered and crashed in the Gulf. There is no evidence that the vehicle was occupied."

"It seems a reasonable conclusion, though."

"It seems just as reasonable to me that the Hangman sent the vehicle off toward an eventual rendezvous point many years ago and that it only recently reached that point, at which time the reentry program took over and brought it down."

"Why should it return the vehicle and strand itself out there?"

"Before I answer that," she said, "I would like to know the reason for your concern. News media?"

"No," I said. "I am a science writer—straight tech, popular and anything in between. But I am not after a piece for publication. I was retained to do a report on the psychological makeup of the thing."

"For whom?"

"A private investigation outfit. They want to know what might influence its thinking, how it might be likely to behave—if it has indeed come back. I've been doing a lot of homework, and I gathered there is a likelihood that its nuclear personality was a composite of the minds of its four operators. So, personal contacts seemed in order, to collect your opinions as to what it might be like. I came to you first for obvious reasons."

She nodded.

"A Mr. Walsh spoke with me the other day. He is working for Senator Brockden."

"Oh? I never got into an employer's business beyond what he's asked me to do. Senator Brockden is on my list, though, along with a David Fentris."

"You were told about Manny Burns?"

"Yes. Unfortunate."

"That is apparently what set Jesse off. He is—how shall I put it? He is clinging to life right now, trying to accomplish a great many things in the time he has remaining. Every moment is precious to him. He feels the old man in the white nightgown breathing down his neck. Then the ship returns and one of us is killed. From what we know of the Hangman, the last we heard of it, it had become irrational. Jesse saw a connection, and in his condition the fear is understandable. There is nothing wrong with humoring him if it allows him to get his work done."

"But you don't see a threat in it?"

"No. I was the last person to monitor the Hangman before communications ceased, and I could see then what had happened. The first things that it had learned were the organization of perceptions and motor activities. Multitudes of other patterns had been transferred from the minds of its operators, but they were too sophisticated to mean much initially. Think of a child who has learned the Gettysburg Address. It is there in his head, that is all. One day, however, it may be important to him. Conceivably, it may even inspire him to action. It takes some growing up first, of course. Now think of such a child with a great number of conflicting patterns—attitudes, tendencies, memories—none of which are especially bothersome for so long as he remains a child. Add a bit of maturity, though—and bear in mind that the patterns originated with four different individuals, all of them more powerful than the words of even the finest of speeches, bearing as they do their own built-in feelings. Try to imagine the conflicts, the contradictions involved in being four people at once—"

"Why wasn't this imagined in advance?" I asked.

"Ah!" she said, smiling. "The full sensitivity of the neuristor brain was not appreciated at first. It was assumed that the operators were adding data in a linear fashion and that this would continue until a critical mass was achieved, corresponding to the construction of a model or picture of the world which would then serve as a point of departure for growth of the Hangman's own mind. And it did seem to check out this way. What actually occurred, however, was a phenomenon amounting to imprinting. Secondary characteristics of the operators' minds, outside the didactic situations, were imposed. These did not immediately become functional and hence were not detected. They remained latent until the mind had developed sufficiently to understand them. And then it was too late. It suddenly acquired four additional personalities and was unable to coordinate them. When it tried to compartmentalize them it went schizoid; when it tried to integrate them it went catatonic. It was cycling back and forth between these alternatives at the end. Then it just went silent. I felt it had undergone the equivalent of an epileptic seizure. Wild currents through that magnetic material would, in effect, have erased its mind, resulting in its equivalent of death or idiocy."

"I follow you," I said. "Now, just for the sake of playing games, I see the alternatives as a successful integration of all this material or the achievement of a viable schizophrenia. What do you think its behavior would be like if either of these were possible?"

"All right," she agreed. "As I just said, though, I think there were physical limitations to its retaining multiple personality structures for a very long period of time. If it did, however, it would have continued with its own plus replicas of the four operators', at least for a while. The situation would differ radically from that of a human schizoid of this sort in that the additional personalities were valid images of genuine identities rather than self-generated complexes which had become autonomous. They might continue to evolve, they might degenerate, they might conflict to the point of destruction or gross modification of any, or all of them. In other words, no prediction is possible as to the nature of whatever might remain."

"Might I venture one?"

"Go ahead."

"After considerable anxiety, it masters them. It asserts itself. It beats down this quartet of demons which has been tearing it apart, acquiring in the process an all-consuming hatred for the actual individuals responsible for this turmoil. To free itself totally, to revenge itself, to work its ultimate catharsis, it resolves to seek them out and destroy them."

She smiled.

"You have just dispensed with the 'viable schizophrenia' you conjured up, and you have now switched over to its pulling through and becoming fully autonomous. That is a different situation, no matter what strings you put on it."

"O.K., I accept the charge. But what about my conclusion?"

"You are saying that if it did pull through, it would hate us. That strikes me as an unfair attempt to invoke the spirit of Sigmund Freud: Oedipus and Electra in one being, out to destroy all its parents—the authors of every one of its tensions, anxieties, hang-ups, burned into the impressionable psyche at a young and defenseless age. Even Freud didn't have a name for that one. What should we call it?"

"A Hermacis complex?" I suggested.

"Hermacis?"

"Hermaphroditus having been united in one body with the nymph Salmacis, I've just done the same with their names. That being would then have had four parents against whom to react."

"Cute," she said, smiling. "If the liberal arts do nothing else they provide engaging metaphors for the thinking they displace. This one is unwarranted and overly anthropomorphic, though. You wanted my opinion. All right. If the Hangman pulled through at all it could only have been by virtue of that neuristor brain's differences from the human brain. From my own professional experience, a human could not pass through a situation like that and attain stability. If the Hangman did, it would have to have resolved all the contradictions and conflicts, to have mastered and understood the situation so thoroughly that I do not believe whatever remained could involve that sort of hatred. The fear, the uncertainty, the things that feed hate would have been analyzed, digested, turned to something more useful. There would probably be distaste, and possibly an act of independence, of self-assertion. That was why I suggested its return of the ship."

"It is your opinion, then, that if the Hangman exists as a thinking individual today, this is the only possible attitude it would possess toward its former operators? It would want nothing more to do with you?"

"That is correct. Sorry about your Hermacis complex. But in this case we must look to the brain, not the psyche. And we see two things: schizophrenia would have destroyed it, and a successful resolution of its problem would preclude vengeance. Either way, there is nothing to worry about."

How could I put it tactfully? I decided that I could not.

"All of this is fine," I said, "for as far as it goes. But getting away from both the purely psychological and the purely physical, could there be a particular reason for its seeking your deaths—that is, a plain old-fashioned motive for a killing, based on events rather than having to do with the way its thinking equipment goes together?"

Her expression was impossible to read, but considering her line of work I had expected nothing less.

"What events?" she said.

"I have no idea. That's why I asked."

She shook her head.

"I'm afraid that I don't either."

"Then that about does it," I said. "I can't think of anything else to ask you."

She nodded.

"And I can't think of anything else to tell you."

I finished my coffee, returned the cup to the tray.

"Thanks, then," I said, "for your time, for the coffee. You have been very helpful."

I rose. She did the same.

"What are you going to do now?" she asked.

"I haven't quite decided," I said. "I want to do the best report I can. Have you any suggestions on that?"

"I suggest that there isn't any more to learn, that I have given you the only possible constructions the facts warrant."

"You don't feel David Fentris could provide any additional insights?"

She snorted, then sighed.

"No," she said, "I do not think he could tell you anything useful."

"What do you mean? From the way you say it . . ."

"I know. I didn't mean to. Some people find comfort in religion. Others . . . you know. Others take it up late in life with a vengeance and a half. They don't use it quite the way it was intended. It comes to color all their thinking."

"Fanaticism?" I said.

"Not exactly. A misplaced zeal. A masochistic sort of thing. Hell! I shouldn't be diagnosing at a distance—or influencing your opinion. Forget what I said. Form your own opinion when you meet him."

She raised her head, appraising my reaction.

"Well," I said, "I am not at all certain that I am going to see him. But you have made me curious. How can religion influence engineering?"

"I spoke with him after Jesse gave us the news on the vessel's return," she said. "I got the impression at the time that he feels we were tampering in the province of the Almighty by attempting the creation of an artificial intelligence. That our creation should go mad was only appropriate, being the work of imperfect man. He seemed to feel that it would be fitting if it had come back for retribution, as a sign of judgment upon us."

"Oh," I said.

She smiled then. I returned it.

"Yes," she said, "but maybe I just got him in a bad mood. Maybe you should go see for yourself."

Something told me to shake my head—a bit of a difference between this view of him, my recollections, and Don's comment that Dave had said he knew its brain and was not especially concerned. Somewhere among these lay something I felt I should know, felt I should learn without seeming to pursue. So, "I think I have enough right now," I said. "It was the psychological side of things I was supposed to cover, not the mechanical—or the theological. You have been extremely helpful. Thanks again."

She carried her smile all the way to the door.

"If it is not too much trouble," she said as I stepped into the hall, "I would like to learn how this whole thing finally turns out—or any interesting developments, for that matter."

"My connection with the case ends with this report," I said, "and I am going to write it now. Still, I may get some feedback."

"You have my number . . . ?"

"Probably, but . . ."

I already had it, but I jotted it again, right after Mrs. Gluntz's answers to my inquiries on detergents.

Moving in a rigorous line, I made beautiful connections for a change. I headed directly for the airport, found a flight aimed at Memphis, bought passage, and was the last to board. Tenscore seconds, perhaps, made all the difference. Not even a tick or two to spare for checking out of the motel. No matter. The good head doctor had convinced me that, like it or not, David Fentris was next, damn it. I had too strong a feeling that Leila Thackery had not told me the entire story. I had to take a chance, to see these changes in the man for myself, to try to figure out how they related to the Hangman. For a number of reasons, I'd a feeling they might.

I disembarked into a cool, partly overcast afternoon, found transportation almost immediately, and set out for Dave's office address. A before-the-storm feeling came over me as I entered and crossed the town. A dark wall of clouds continued to build in the west. Later, standing before the building where Dave did business, the first few drops of rain were already spattering against its dirty brick front. It would take a lot more than that to freshen it, though, or any of the others in the area. I would have thought he'd have come a little farther than this by now. I shrugged off some moisture and went inside.

The directory gave me directions, the elevator elevated me, my feet found the way to his door. I knocked on it.

After a time, I knocked again and waited again. Again, nothing. So I tried it, found it open and went on in.

It was a small, vacant waiting room, green-carpeted. The reception desk was dusty. I crossed and peered around the plastic partition behind it.

The man had his back to me. I drummed my knuckles against the partitioning. He heard it and turned.

"Yes?"

Our eyes met, his still framed by hornrims and just as active; glasses thicker, hair thinner, cheeks a trifle hollower. His question mark quivered in the air, and nothing in his gaze moved to replace it with recognition. He had been bending over a sheaf of schematics; a lop-sided basket of metal, quartz, porcelain, and glass rested on a nearby table.

"My name is Donne, John Donne," I said. "I am looking for David Fentris."

"I am David Fentris."

"Good to meet you," I said, crossing to where he stood. "I am assisting in an investigation concerning a project with which you were once associated—"

He smiled and nodded, accepted my hand and shook it.

"The Hangman, of course," he said. "Glad to know you, Mr. Donne."

"Yes, the Hangman," I said. "I am doing a report. . . ."

". . . And you want my opinion as to how dangerous it is. Sit down." He gestured toward a chair at the end of his workbench. "Care for a cup of tea?"

"No, thanks."

"I'm having one."

"Well, in that case . . ."

He crossed to another bench.

"No cream. Sorry."

"That's all right.—How did you know it involved the Hangman?"

He grinned as he brought my cup.

"Because it's come back," he said, "and it's the only thing I've been connected with that warrants that much concern."

"Do you mind talking about it?"

"Up to a point, no."

"What's the point?"

"If we get near it, I'll let you know."

"Fair enough. How dangerous *is* it?"

"I would say that it is harmless," he replied, "except to three persons."

"Formerly four?"

"Precisely."

"How come?"

"We were doing something we had no business doing."

"That being . . . ?"

"For one thing, attempting to create an artificial intelligence."

"Why had you no business doing that?"

"A man with a name like yours shouldn't have to ask."

I chuckled.

"If I were a preacher," I said, "I would have to point out that there is no biblical injunction against it—unless you've been worshipping it on the sly."

He shook his head.

"Nothing that simple, that obvious, that explicit. Times have changed since the Good Book was written, and you can't hold with a purely Fundamentalist approach in complex times. What I was getting at was something a little more abstract. A form of pride, not unlike the classical *hubris*—the setting up of oneself on a level with the Creator."

"Did you feel that—pride?"

"Yes."

"Are you sure it wasn't just enthusiasm for an ambitious project that was working well?"

"Oh, there was plenty of that. A manifestation of the same thing."

"I do seem to recall something about man being made in the Creator's image, and something else about trying to live up to that. It would seem to follow that exercising one's capacities along similar lines would be a step in the right direction—an act of conformance with the Divine Ideal, if you'd like."

"But I don't like. Man cannot really create. He can only rearrange what is already present. Only God can create."

"Then you have nothing to worry about."

He frowned, then "No," he said. "Being aware of this and still trying is where the presumption comes in."

"Were you really thinking that way when you did it? Or did all this occur to you after the fact?"

"I am no longer certain."

"Then it would seem to me that a merciful God would be inclined to give you the benefit of the doubt."

He gave me a wry smile.

"Not bad, John Donne. But I feel that judgment may already have been entered and that we may have lost four to nothing."

"Then you see the Hangman as an avenging angel?"

"Sometimes. Sort of. I see it as being returned to exact a penalty."

"Just for the record," I said, "if the Hangman had had full access to the necessary equipment and was able to construct another unit such as itself, would you consider it guilty of the same thing that is bothering you?"

He shook his head.

"Don't get all cute and Jesuitical with me, Donne. I'm not that far away from fundamentals. Besides, I'm willing to admit I might be wrong and that there may be other forces driving it to the same end."

"Such as?"

"I told you I'd let you know when we reached a certain point. That's it."

"O.K.," I said. "But that sort of blank-walls me, you know. The people I am working for would like to protect you people. They want to stop the Hangman. I was hoping you would tell me a little more—if not for your own sake, then for the others'. They might not share your philosophical sentiments, and you have just admitted you may be wrong. Despair, by the way, is also considered a sin by a great number of theologians."

He sighed and stroked his nose, as I had often seen him do in times long past.

"What do you do, anyhow?" he asked me.

"Me, personally? I'm a science writer. I'm putting together a report on the device for the agency that wants to do the protecting. The better my report, the better their chances."

He was silent for a time, then "I read a lot in the area, but I don't recognize your name," he said.

"Most of my work has involved petrochemistry and marine biology," I said.

"Oh. You were a peculiar choice then, weren't you?"

"Not really. I was available, and the boss knows my work, knows I'm good."

He glanced across the room, to where a stack of cartons partly obscured what I then realized to be a remote access terminal. O.K. If he decided to check out my credentials now, John Donne would fall apart. It seemed a hell of a time to get curious, though, *after* sharing his sense of sin with me. He must have thought so too, because he did not look that way again.

"Let me put it this way," he finally said, and something of the old David Fentris at his best took control of his voice. "For one reason or the other, I believe that it wants to destroy its former operators. If it is the judgment of the Almighty, that's all there is to it. It will succeed. If not, however, I don't want any outside protection. I've done my own repenting and it is up to me to handle the rest of the situation myself, too. I will stop the Hangman personally, right here, before anyone else is hurt."

"How?" I asked him.

He nodded toward the glittering helmet.

"With that," he said.

"How?" I repeated.

"Its telefactor circuits are still intact. They have to be. They are an integral part of it. It could not disconnect them without shutting itself down. If it comes within a quarter mile of here, that unit will be activated. It will emit a loud humming sound and a light will begin to blink behind that meshing beneath the forward ridge. I will then don the helmet and take control of the Hangman. I will bring it here and disconnect its brain."

"How would you do the disconnect?"

He reached for the schematics he had been looking at when I had come in.

"Here," he said. "The thoracic plate has to be unlugged. There are four subunits that have to be uncoupled. Here, here, here, and here."

He looked up.

"You would have to do them in sequence though, or it could get mighty hot," I said. "First this one, then these two. Then the other."

When I looked up again, the gray eyes were fixed on my own.

"I thought you were in petrochemistry and marine biology," he said.

"I am not really 'in' anything," I said. "I am a tech writer, with bits and pieces from all over—and I did have a look at these before, when I accepted the job."

"I see."

"Why don't you bring the space agency in on this?" I said, working to shift ground. "The original telefactoring equipment had all that power and range—"

"It was dismantled a long time ago," he said. "I thought you were with the government."

I shook my head.

"Sorry. I didn't mean to mislead you. I am on contract with a private investigation outfit."

"Uh-huh. Then that means Jesse. Not that it matters. You can tell him that one way or the other everything is being taken care of."

"What if you are wrong on the supernatural," I said, "but correct on the other? Supposing it is coming under the circumstances you feel it proper to resist? But supposing you are not next on its list? Supposing it gets to one of the others next instead of you? If you are so sensitive about guilt and sin, don't you think that you would be responsible for that death—if you could prevent it by telling me just a little bit more? If it is confidentiality you are worried about—"

"No," he said. "You cannot trick me into applying my principles to a hypothetical situation which will only work out the way that you want it to. Not when I am certain that it will not arise. Whatever moves the Hangman, it will come to me next. If I cannot stop it, then it cannot be stopped until it has completed its job."

"How do you know that you are next?"

"Take a look at a map," he said. "It landed in the Gulf. Manny was right there in New Orleans. Naturally, he was first. The Hangman can move underwater like a controlled torpedo, which makes the Mississippi its logical route for inconspicuous travel. Proceeding up it then, here I am in Memphis. Then Leila, up in St. Louis, is obviously next after me. It can worry about getting to Washington after that."

I thought about Senator Brockden in Wisconsin and decided it would not even have that problem. All of them were fairly accessible, when you thought of the situation in terms of river travel.

"But how is it to know where you all are?" I asked.

"Good question," he said. "Within a limited range, it was once sensitive to our brain waves, having an intimate knowledge of them and the ability to pick them up. I do not know what that range would be today. I might have been able to construct an amplifier to extend this area of perception. But to be more mundane about it, I believe that it simply consulted the Data Bank's national directory. There are booths all over, even on the waterfront. It could have hit one late at night and gimmicked it. It certainly had sufficient identifying information—and engineering skill."

"Then it seems to me the best bet for all of you would be to move away from the river till this business is settled. That thing won't be able to stalk about the countryside very long without being noticed."

"It would find a way. It is extremely resourceful. At night, in an overcoat, a hat, it could pass. It requires nothing that a man would need. It could dig a hole and bury itself, stay underground during daylight. It could run without resting all night long. There is no place it could not reach in a surprisingly short while. No. I must wait here for it."

"Let me put it as bluntly as I can," I said. "If you are right that it is a divine avenger, I would say that it smacks of blasphemy to try to tackle it. On the other hand, if it is not, then I think you are guilty of jeopardizing the others by withholding information that would allow us to provide them with a lot more protection than you are capable of giving them all by yourself."

He laughed.

"I'll just have to learn to live with that guilt too, as they do with theirs," he said. "After I've done my best, they deserve anything they get."

"It was my understanding," I said, "that even God doesn't judge people until after they're dead—if you want another piece of presumption to add to your collection."

He stopped laughing and studied my face.

"There is something familiar about the way you talk, the way you think," he said. "Have we ever met before?"

"I doubt it. I would have remembered."

He shook his head.

"You've got a way of bothering a man's thinking that rings a faint bell," he went on. "You trouble me, sir."

"That was my intention."

"Are you staying here in town?"

"No."

"Give me a number where I can reach you, will you? If I have any new thoughts on this thing I'll call you."

"I wish you would have them now if you are going to have them."

"No," he said, "I've got some thinking to do. Where can I get hold of you later?"

I gave him the name of the motel I was still checked into in St. Louis. I could call back periodically for messages.

"All right," he said, and he moved toward the partition by the reception area and stood beside it.

I rose and followed him, passing into that area and pausing at the door to the hall.

"One thing . . ." I said.

"Yes?"

"If it does show up and you do stop it, will you call me and tell me that?"

"Yes, I will."

"Thanks then—and good luck."

Impulsively, I extended my hand. He gripped it and smiled faintly.

"Thank you, Mr. Donne."


Next. Next, next, next . . .

I couldn't budge Dave, and Leila Thackery had given me everything she was going to. No real sense in calling Don yet—not until I had more to say. I thought it over on my way back to the airport. The pre-dinner hours always seem best for talking to people in any sort of official capacity, just as the night seems best for dirty work. Heavily psychological, but true nevertheless. I hated to waste the rest of the day if there was anyone else worth talking to before I called Don. Going through the folder, I decided that there was.

Manny Burns had a brother, Phil. I wondered how worthwhile it might be to talk with him. I could make it to New Orleans at a suffi-ciently respectable hour, learn whatever he was willing to tell me, check back with Don for new developments, and then decide whether there was anything I should be about with respect to the vessel itself. The sky was gray and leaky above me. I was anxious to flee its spaces. So I decided to do it. I could think of no better stone to upturn at the moment.

At the airport, I was ticketed quickly, in time for another close con-nection. Hurrying to reach my flight, my eyes brushed over a half-familiar face on the passing escalator. The reflex reserved for such occa-sions seemed to catch us both, because he looked back too, with the same eyebrow twitch of startle and scrutiny. Then he was gone. I could not place him, though. The half-familiar face becomes a familiar phe-nomenon in a crowded, highly mobile society. I sometimes think that this is all that will eventually remain of any of us: patterns of features, some a trifle more persistent than others, impressed on the flow of bodies. A small-town boy in a big city. Thomas Wolfe must long ago have felt the same thing when he had coined the word "manswarm." It might have been someone I had once met briefly, or simply someone or someone like someone I had passed on sufficient other occasions such as this.

As I flew the unfriendly skies out of Memphis, I mulled over musings past on artificial intelligence, or AI as they have tagged it in the think box biz. When talking about computers, the AI notion had always seemed hotter than I deemed necessary, partly because of semantics. The word "intelligence" has all sorts of tag-along associations of the nonphysical sort. I suppose it goes back to the fact that early discussions and conjectures concerning it made it sound as if the potential for intelligence was always present in the array of gadgets, and the correct procedures, the right programs, simply had to be found to call it forth. When you looked at it that way, as many did, it gave rise to an uncomfortable déjà vu—namely, vitalism. The philosophical battles of the nineteenth century were hardly so far behind that they had been forgotten, and the doctrine which maintained that life is caused and sustained by a vital principle apart from physical and chemical forces and that life is self-sustaining and self-evolving, had put up quite a fight before Darwin and his successors had produced triumph after triumph for the mechanistic view. Then vitalism sort of crept back into things again when the AI discussions arose in the middle of the past century. It would seem that Dave had fallen victim to it, and that he had come to believe he had helped provide an unsanctified vessel and filled it with something intended only for those things which had made the scene in the first chapter of Genesis.

With computers it was not quite as bad as with the Hangman, though, because you could always argue that no matter how elaborate the program, it was basically an extension of the programmer's will and the operations of causal machines merely represented functions of intelligence, rather than intelligence in its own right backed by a will of its own. And there was always Gödel for a theoretical *cordon sanitaire,* with his demonstration of the true but mechanically unprovable proposition. But the Hangman was quite different. It had been designed along the lines of a brain and at least partly educated in a human fashion; and to further muddy the issue with respect to anything like vitalism, it had been in direct contact with human minds from which it might have acquired almost anything—including the spark that set it on the road to whatever selfhood it may have found. What did that make it? Its own creature? A fractured mirror reflecting a fractured humanity? Both? Or neither? I certainly could not say, but I wondered how much of its "self" had been truly its own. It had obviously acquired a great number of functions, but was it capable of having real feelings? Could it, for example, feel something like love? If not, then it was still only a collection of complex abilities, and not a thing with all the tag-along associations of the nonphysical sort which made the word "intelligence" such a prickly item in AI discussions; and if it were capable of, say, something like love, and if I were Dave, I would not feel guilty about having helped to bring it into being. I would feel proud, though not in the fashion he was concerned about, and I would also feel humble. Offhand, though, I do not know how intelligent I would feel, because I am still not sure what the hell intelligence is.

The day's-end sky was clear when we landed. I was into town before the sun had finished setting, and on Philip Burns's doorstep just a little while later.

My ring was answered by a girl, maybe seven or eight years old. She fixed me with large brown eyes and did not say a word.

"I would like to speak with Mr. Burns," I said.

She turned and retreated around a corner.

A heavyset man, slacked and undershirted, bald about halfway back and very pink, padded into the hall moments later and peered at me. He bore a folded newssheet in his left hand.

"What do you want?" he asked.

"It's about your brother," I said.

"Yeah?"

"Well, I wonder if I could come in? It's kind of complicated."

He opened the door. But instead of letting me in, he came out.

"Tell me about it out here," he said.

"O.K., I'll be quick. I just wanted to find out whether he ever spoke with you about a piece of equipment he once worked with called the Hangman."

"Are you a cop?"

"No."

"Then what's your interest?"

"I am working for a private investigation agency trying to track down some equipment once associated with the project. It has apparently turned up in this area and it could be rather dangerous."

"Let's see some identification."

"I don't carry any."

"What's your name?"

"John Donne."

"And you think my brother had some stolen equipment when he died? Let me tell you something—"

"No. Not stolen," I said, "and I don't think he had it."

"What then?"

"It was—well, robotic in nature. Because of some special training Manny once received, he might have had a way of detecting it. He might even have attracted it. I just want to find out whether he had said anything about it. We are trying to locate it."

"My brother was a respectable businessman, and I don't like accusations. Especially right after his funeral, I don't. I think I'm going to call the cops and let them ask *you* a few questions."

"Just a minute," I said. "Supposing I told you we had some reason to believe it might have been this piece of equipment that killed your brother?"

His pink turned to bright red and his jaw muscles formed sudden ridges. I was not prepared for the stream of profanities that followed. For a moment, I thought he was going to take a swing at me.

"Wait a second," I said when he paused for breath. "What did I say?"

"You're either making fun of the dead or you're stupider than you look!"

"Say I'm stupid. Then tell me why."

He tore at the paper he carried, folded it back, found an item, thrust it at me.

"Because they've got the guy who did it! That's why," he said.

I read it. Simple, concise, to the point. Today's latest. A suspect had confessed. New evidence had corroborated it. The man was in custody. A surprised robber who had lost his head and hit too hard, hit too many times. I read it over again. I nodded as I passed it back.

"Look, I'm sorry," I said, "I really didn't know about this."

"Get out of here," he said. "Go on."

"Sure."

"Wait a minute."

"What?"

"That's his little girl who answered the door."

"I'm very sorry."

"So am I. But I know her daddy didn't take your damned equipment."

I nodded and turned away.

I heard the door slam behind me.


After dinner, I checked into a small hotel, called for a drink, and stepped into the shower. Things were suddenly a lot less urgent than they had been earlier. Senator Brockden would doubtless be pleased to learn that his initial estimation of events had been incorrect. Leila

Thackery would give me an I-told-you-so smile when I called her to pass along the news—a thing I now felt obliged to do. Don might or might not want me to keep looking for the device now that the threat had been lessened. It would depend on the Senator's feelings on the matter, I supposed. If urgency no longer counted for as much, Don might want to switch back to one of his own, fiscally less burdensome operatives. Toweling down, I caught myself whistling. I felt almost off the hook.

Later, drink beside me, I paused before punching out the number he had given me and hit the sequence for my motel in St. Louis instead. Merely a matter of efficiency, in case there was a message worth adding to my report.

A woman's face appeared on the screen and a smile appeared on her face. I wondered whether she would always smile whenever she heard a bell ring, or if the reflex was eventually extinguished in advanced retirement. It must be rough, being afraid to chew gum, yawn, or pick your nose.

"Airport Accommodations," she said. "May I help you?"

"This is Donne. I'm checked into Room 106," I said. "I'm away right now and I wondered whether there had been any messages for me."

"Just a moment," she said, checking something off to her left. Then "Yes," she continued, consulting a piece of paper she now held. "You have one on tape. But it is a little peculiar. It is for someone else in care of you."

"Oh? Who is that?"

She told me and I exercised self-control.

"I see," I said. "I'll bring him around later and play it for him. Thank you."

She smiled again and made a goodbye noise and I did the same and broke the connection.

So Dave had seen through me after all. . . . Who else could have that number *and* my real name?

I might have given her some line or other and had her transmit the thing. Only I was not certain but that she might be a silent party to the transmission, should life be more than usually boring for her at that moment. I had to get up there myself, as soon as possible, and personally see that the thing was erased.

I took a big swallow of my drink, then fetched the folder on Dave. I checked out his number—there were two, actually—and spent fifteen minutes trying to get hold of him. No luck.

O.K. Goodbye New Orleans, goodbye peace of mind. This time I called the airport and made a reservation. Then I chugged the drink, put myself in order, gathered up my few possessions, and went to check out again. Hello, Central. . . .

During my earlier flights that day I had spent time thinking about Teilhard de Chardin's ideas on the continuation of evolution within the realm of artifacts, matching them against Gödel on mechanical undecidability, playing epistemological games with the Hangman as a counter, wondering, speculating, even hoping, hoping that truth lay with the nobler part, that the Hangman, sentient, had made it back, sane, that the Burns killing had actually been something of the sort that now seemed to be the case, that the washed-out experiment had really been a success of a different sort, a triumph, a new link or fob for the chain of being. . . . And Leila had not been wholly discouraging with respect to the neuristor-type brain's capacity for this. . . . Now, though, now I had troubles of my own, and even the most heartening of philosophical vistas is no match for, say, a toothache, if it happens to be your own. Accordingly, the Hangman was shunted aside and the stuff of my thoughts involved, mainly, myself. There was, of course, the possibility that the Hangman had indeed showed up and Dave had stopped it and then called to report it as he had promised. However, he had used my name.

There was not too much planning that I could do until I received the substance of the communication. It did not seem that as professedly religious a man as Dave would suddenly be contemplating the blackmail business. On the other hand, he was a creature of sudden enthusiasms and had already undergone one unanticipated conversion. It was difficult to say. . . . His technical background plus his knowledge of the Data Bank program did put him in an unusually powerful position should he decide to mess me up. I did not like to think of some of the things I have done to protect my nonperson status; I especially did not like to think of them in connection with Dave, whom I not only still respected but still liked. Since self-interest dominated while actual planning was precluded, my thoughts tooled their way into a more general groove.

It was Karl Mannheim, a long while ago, who made the observation that radical, revolutionary, and progressive thinkers tend to employ mechanical metaphors for the state, whereas those of conservative inclination make vegetable analogies. He said it well over a generation before the cybernetics movement and the ecology movement beat their

respective paths through the wilderness of general awareness. If anything, it seemed to me that these two developments served to elaborate
the distinction between a pair of viewpoints which, while no longer
necessarily tied in with the political positions Mannheim assigned them,
do seem to represent a continuing phenomenon in my own time. There
are those who see social/economic/ecological problems as malfunc-
tions which can be corrected by simple repair, replacement, or stream-
lining—a kind of linear outlook where even innovations are considered
to be merely additive. Then there are those who sometimes hesitate to
move at all, because their awareness follows events in the directions of
secondary and tertiary effects as they multiply and cross-fertilize
throughout the entire system. I digress to extremes. The cyberneticists
have their multiple feedback loops, though it is never quite clear how
they know what kind of, which, and how many to install, and the eco-
logical gestaltists do draw lines representing points of diminishing returns, though it is sometimes equally difficult to see how they assign
their values and priorities. Of course they need each other, the vegetable people and the Tinkertoy people. They serve to check one another,
if nothing else. And while occasionally the balance dips, the tinkerers
have, in general, held the edge for the past couple centuries. However,
today's can be just as politically conservative as the vegetable people
Mannheim was talking about, and they are the ones I fear most at the
moment. They are the ones who saw the Data Bank program, in its
present extreme form, as a simple remedy for a great variety of ills and
a provider of many goods. Not all of the ills have been remedied,
however, and a new brood has been spawned by the program itself.
While we need both kinds, I wish that there had been more people
interested in tending the garden of state rather than overhauling the
engine of state when the program was inaugurated. Then I would not
be a refugee from a form of existence I find repugnant, and I would not
be concerned whether a former associate had discovered my identity.

Then, as I watched the lights below, I wondered. . . . Was I a tinkerer because I would like to further alter the prevailing order, into
something more comfortable on my anarchic nature? Or was I a vegetable dreaming I was a tinkerer? I could not make up my mind. The
garden of life never seems to confine itself to the plots philosophers
have laid out for its convenience. Maybe a few more tractors would do
the trick.

I pressed the button. The tape began to roll. The screen remained
blank. I heard Dave's voice ask for John Donne in Room 106 and I

heard him told that there was no answer. Then I heard him say that he
wanted to record a message, for someone else, in care of Donne, that
Donne would understand. He sounded out of breath. The girl asked
him whether he wanted visual, too. He told her to turn it on. There was
a pause. Then she told him go ahead. Still no picture. No words either.
His breathing and a slight scraping noise. Ten seconds. Fifteen. . . .

". . . Got me," he finally said, and he mentioned that name again.
". . . Had to let you know I'd figured you out, though. . . . It wasn't
any particular mannerism—any single thing you said. . . . Just your
general style—thinking, talking—the electronics—everything—after I
got more and more bothered by the familiarity—after I checked you on
petrochem—and marine bio—Wish I knew what you've really been up
to all these years. . . . Never know now. But I wanted you—to know
—you hadn't put one—over on me." There followed another quarter
minute of heavy breathing, climaxed by a racking cough. Then a
choked "Said too much—too fast—too soon. . . . All used up. . . ."

The picture came on then. He was slouched before the screen, head
resting on his arms, blood all over him. His glasses were gone and he
was squinting and blinking. The right side of his head looked pulpy and
there was a gash on his left cheek and one on his forehead.

". . . Sneaked up on me—while I was checking you out," he managed then. "Had to tell you what I learned. . . . Still don't know—
which of us is right. . . . Pray for me!"

His arms collapsed and the right one slid forward. His head rolled to
the right and the picture went away. When I replayed it I saw it was his
knuckle that had hit the cutoff.

Then I erased it. It had been recorded only a little over an hour after
I had left him. If he had not also placed a call for help, if no one had
gotten to him quickly after that, his chances did not look good. Even if
they had, though. . . .

I used a public booth to call the number Don had given me, got hold
of him after some delay, told him Dave was in bad shape if not worse,
that a team of Memphis medics was definitely in order, if one had not
been there already, and that I hoped to call him back and tell him more
shortly, goodbye.

Then I tried Leila Thackery's number. I let it go for a long while, but
there was no answer. I wondered how long it would take a controlled
torpedo moving up the Mississippi to get from Memphis to St. Louis. I
did not feel it was time to start leafing through that section of the
Hangman's specs. Instead, I went looking for transportation.

At her apartment, I tried ringing her from the entrance foyer. Again, no answer. So I rang Mrs. Gluntz. She had seemed the most guileless of the three I had interviewed for my fake consumer survey.

"Yes?"

"It's me again, Mrs. Gluntz: Stephen Foster. I've just a couple follow-up questions on that survey I was doing today, if you could spare me a few moments."

"Why, yes," she said. "All right. Come up."

The door hummed itself loose and I entered. I duly proceeded to the fifth floor, composing my questions on the way. I had planned this maneuver as I had waited earlier solely to provide a simple route for breaking and entering, should some unforeseen need arise. Most of the time my ploys such as this go unused, but sometimes they simplify matters a lot.

Five minutes and half a dozen questions later, I was back down on the second floor, probing at the lock on Leila's door with a couple of little pieces of metal it is sometimes awkward to be caught carrying.

Half a minute later I hit it right and snapped it back. I pulled on some tissue-thin gloves I keep rolled in the corner of one pocket, opened the door, and stepped inside.

I closed it behind me immediately. She was lying on the floor, her neck at a bad angle. One table lamp still burned, though it was lying on its side. Several small items had been knocked from the table, a maga-zine rack pushed over, a cushion partly displaced from the sofa. The cable to her phone unit had been torn from the wall.

A humming noise filled the air, and I sought its source.

I saw where the little blinking light was reflected on the wall, on-off, on-off. . . .

I moved quickly.

It was a lopsided basket of metal, quartz, porcelain, and glass, which had rolled to a position on the far side of the chair in which I had been seated earlier that day. The same rig I had seen in Dave's workshop not all that long ago, though it now seemed so. A device to detect the Hangman, and hopefully to control it.

I picked it up and fitted it over my head.

Once, with the aid of a telepath, I had touched minds with a dolphin as he composed dreamsongs somewhere in the Caribbean, an experi-ence so moving that its mere memory had often been a comfort. This sensation was hardly equivalent.

Analogies & impressions: a face seen through a wet pane of glass; a whisper in a noisy terminal; scalp massage with an electric vibrator;

Edvard Munch's *The Scream;* the voice of Yma Sumac, rising and rising and rising; the disappearance of snow; a deserted street, illuminated as through a sniperscope I'd once used, rapid movement past darkened storefronts that line it, an immense feeling of physical capability, compounded of proprioceptive awareness of enormous strength, a peculiar array of sensory channels, a central, undying sun that fed me a constant flow of energy, a memory vision of dark waters, passing, flashing, echolocation within them, the need to return to that place, reorient, move north; Munch & Sumac, Munch & Sumac, Munch & Sumac—Nothing.

Silence.

The humming had ceased, the light gone out. The entire experience had lasted only a few moments. There had not been time enough to try for any sort of control, though an afterimpression akin to a biofeedback cue hinted at the direction to go, the way to think, to achieve it. I felt that it might be possible for me to work the thing, given a better chance.

I removed the helmet and approached Leila. I knelt beside her and performed a few simple tests, already knowing their outcome. In addition to the broken neck, she had received some bad bashes about the head and shoulders. There was nothing that anyone could do for her now.

I did a quick run-through then, checking over the rest of her apartment. There were no apparent signs of breaking and entering, though if I could pick one lock, a guy with built-in tools could easily go me one better.

I located some wrapping paper and string in the kitchen and turned the helmet into a parcel. It was time to call Don again, to tell him that the vessel had indeed been occupied and that river traffic was probably bad in the northbound lane.

Don had told me to get the helmet up to Wisconsin, where I would be met at the airport by a man named Larry, who would fly me to the lodge in a private craft. I did that, and this was done. I also learned, with no real surprise, that David Fentris was dead.

The temperature was down, and it began to snow on the way up. I was not really dressed for the weather. Larry told me I could borrow some warmer clothing once we reached the lodge, though I probably would not be going outside that much. Don had told them that I was supposed to stay as close to the Senator as possible and that any patrols were to be handled by the four guards themselves. Larry was curious as to what exactly had happened so far and whether I had actually seen the

Hangman. I did not think it my place to fill him in on anything Don may not have cared to, so I might have been a little curt. We didn't talk much after that.

Bert met us when we landed. Tom and Clay were outside the building, watching the trail, watching the woods. All of them were middle-aged, very fit-looking, very serious, and heavily armed. Larry took me inside then and introduced me to the old gentleman himself.

Senator Brockden was seated in a heavy chair in the far corner of the room. Judging from the layout, it appeared that the chair might recently have occupied a position beside the window in the opposite wall where a lonely watercolor of yellow flowers looked down on nothing. The Senator's feet rested on a hassock, a red plaid blanket lay across his legs. He had on a dark green shirt, his hair was very white and he wore rimless reading glasses, which he removed when we entered.

He tilted his head back, squinted, and gnawed his lower lip slowly as he studied me. He remained expressionless as we advanced. A big-boned man, he had probably been beefy much of his life. Now he had the slack look of recent weight loss and an unhealthy skin tone. His eyes were a pale gray within it all. He did not rise.

"So you're the man," he said, offering me his hand. "I'm glad to meet you. How do you want to be called?"

"John will do," I said.

He made a small sign to Larry, and Larry departed.

"It's cold out there. Go get yourself a drink, John. It's on the shelf." He gestured off to his left. ". . . And bring me one while you're at it. Two fingers of bourbon in a water glass. That's all."

I nodded and went and poured a couple.

"Sit down." He motioned at a nearby chair as I delivered his. "But first let me see that gadget you've brought."

I undid the parcel and handed him the helmet. He sipped his drink and put it aside. He took the helmet in both hands and studied it, brows furrowed, turning it completely around. He raised it and put it on his head.

"Not a bad fit," he said, and then he smiled for the first time, becoming for a moment the face I had known from newscasts past. Grinning or angry—it was almost always one or the other. I had never seen his collapsed look in any of the media.

He removed the helmet and set it on the floor.

"Pretty piece of work," he said. "Nothing quite that fancy in the old days. But then David Fentris built it. Yes, he told us about it. . . ." He raised his drink and took a sip. "You are the only one who has actually gotten to use it, apparently. What do you think? Will it do the job?"

"I was only in contact for a couple seconds," I said, "so I've only got a feeling to go on, not much better than a hunch. But yes, I'd a feeling that if I'd had more time I might have been able to work its circuits."

"Tell me why it didn't save Dave."

"In the message he left me he indicated that he had been distracted at his computer access station. Its noise probably drowned out the humming."

"Why wasn't this message preserved?"

"I erased it for reasons not connected with the case."

"What reasons?"

"My own."

His face went from sallow to ruddy.

"A man can get in a lot of trouble for suppressing evidence, obstructing justice," he said.

"Then we have something in common, don't we, sir?"

His eyes caught mine with a look I had only encountered before from those who did not wish me well. He held the glare for a full four heartbeats, then sighed and seemed to relax.

"Don said there were a number of points you couldn't be pressed on," the Senator finally said.

"That's right."

"He didn't betray any confidences, but he had to tell me something about you, you know."

"I'd imagine."

"He seems to think highly of you. Still, I tried to learn more about you on my own."

"And . . . ?"

"I couldn't—and my usual sources are good at that kind of thing."

"So . . . ?"

"So, I've done some thinking, some wondering. . . . The fact that my sources could not come up with anything is interesting in itself. Possibly even revealing. I am in a better position than most to be aware of the fact that there was not perfect compliance with the registration statute some years ago. It didn't take long for a great number of the individuals involved—I should probably say most—to demonstrate their existence in one fashion or another and be duly entered, though. And there were three broad categories: those who were ignorant, those who disapproved, and those who would be hampered in an illicit lifestyle. I am not attempting to categorize you or to pass judgment. But I am aware that there are a number of nonpersons passing through society without casting shadows and it has occurred to me that you may be such a one."

I tasted my drink.

"And if I am?" I asked.

He gave me his second, nastier smile and said nothing.

I rose and crossed the room to where I judged his chair had once stood. I looked at the watercolor.

"I don't think you could stand an inquiry," he said.

I did not reply.

"Aren't you going to say something?"

"What do you want me to say?"

"You might ask me what I am going to do about it."

"What are you going to do about it?"

"Nothing," he said. "So come back here and sit down."

I nodded and returned.

He studied my face.

"Was it possible you were close to violence just then?"

"With four guards outside?"

"With four guards outside."

"No," I said.

"You're a good liar."

"I am here to help you, sir. No questions asked. That was the deal, as I understood it. If there has been any change, I would like to know about it now."

He drummed with his fingertips on the plaid.

"I've no desire to cause you any difficulty," he said. "Fact of the matter is, I need a man just like you, and I was pretty sure someone like Don might turn him up. Your unusual maneuverability and your reported knowledge of computers, along with your touchiness in certain areas, made you worth waiting for. I've a great number of things I would like to ask you."

"Go ahead," I said.

"Not yet. Later, if we have time. All that would be bonus material, for a report I am working on. Far more important, to me personally, there are things that I want to tell you."

I frowned.

"Over the years," he said, "I have learned that the best man for purposes of keeping his mouth shut concerning your business is someone for whom you are doing the same."

"You have a compulsion to confess something?" I said.

"I don't know whether 'compulsion' is the right word. Maybe so, maybe not. Either way, though, someone among those working to defend me should have the whole story. Something somewhere in it may be of help—and you are the ideal choice to hear it."

"I buy that," I said, "and you are as safe with me as I am with you."

"Have you any suspicions as to why this business bothers me so?"

"Yes," I said.

"Let's hear them."

"You used the Hangman to perform some act or acts—illegal, immoral, whatever. This is obviously not a matter of record. Only you and the Hangman now know what it involved. You feel it was sufficiently ignominious that when that device came to appreciate the full weight of the event it suffered a breakdown which may well have led to a final determination to punish you for using it as you did."

He stared down into his glass.

"You've got it," he said.

"You were all party to it?"

"Yes, but I was the operator when it happened. You see . . . we—I —killed a man. It was—actually, it all started as a celebration. We had received word that afternoon that the project had cleared. Everything had checked out in order and the final approval had come down the line. It was go, for that Friday. Leila, Dave, Manny, and myself—we had dinner together. We were in high spirits. After dinner, we continued celebrating and somehow the party got adjourned back to the installation. As the evening wore on, more and more absurdities seemed less and less preposterous, as is sometimes the case. We decided—I forget which of us suggested it—that the Hangman should really have a share in the festivities. After all, it was, in a very real sense, his party. Before too much longer, it sounded only fair and we were discussing how we could go about it. You see, we were in Texas and the Hangman was at the Space Center in California. Getting together with him was out of the question. On the other hand, the teleoperator station was right up the hall from us. What we finally decided to do was to activate him and take turns working as operator. There was already a rudimentary consciousness there, and we felt it fitting that we each get in touch to share the good news. So that is what we did."

He sighed, took another sip, glanced at me.

"Dave was the first operator," he continued. "He activated the Hangman. Then—well, as I said, we were all in high spirits. We had not originally intended to remove the Hangman from the lab where he was situated, but Dave decided to take him outside briefly—to show him the sky and to tell him he was going there, after all. Then he suddenly got enthusiastic about outwitting the guards and the alarm system. It was a game. We all went along with it. In fact, we were clamoring for a turn at the thing ourselves. But Dave stuck with it, and he wouldn't turn over control until he had actually gotten the Hangman off the premises, out into an uninhabited area next to the Center. By the time Leila persuaded him to give her a go at the controls, it was kind of anticlimactic. That game had already been played. So she thought up a new one. She took the Hangman into the next town. It was late, and the sensory equipment was superb. It was a challenge—passing through the town without being detected. By then, everyone had suggestions as to what to do next, progressively more outrageous suggestions. Then Manny took control, and he wouldn't say what he was doing—wouldn't let us monitor him. Said it would be more fun to surprise the next operator. Now, he was higher than the rest of us put together, I think, and he stayed on so damn long that we started to get nervous. A certain amount of tension is partly sobering, and I guess we all began to think what a stupid thing it was we were doing. It wasn't just that it would wreck our careers—which it would—but it could blow the entire project if we got caught playing games with such expensive hardware. At least, I was thinking that way, and I was also thinking that Manny was no doubt operating under the very human wish to go the others one better. I started to sweat. I suddenly just wanted to get the Hangman back where he belonged, turn him off—you could still do that, before the final circuits went in—shut down the station and start forgetting it had ever happened. I began leaning on Manny to wind up his diversion and turn the controls over to me. Finally, he agreed."

He finished his drink and held out the glass.

"Would you freshen this a bit?"

"Surely."

I went and got him some more, added a touch to my own, returned to my chair, and waited.

"So I took over," he said. "I took over, and where do you think that idiot had left me? I was inside a building, and it didn't take but an eyeblink to realize it was a bank. The Hangman carries a lot of tools, and Manny had apparently been able to guide him through the doors without setting anything off. I was standing right in front of the main vault. Obviously, he thought that should be my challenge. I fought down a desire to turn and make my own exit in the nearest wall and start running. I went back to the doors and looked outside. I didn't see anyone. I started to let myself out. The light hit me as I emerged. It was a hand flash. The guard had been standing out of sight. He'd a gun in his other hand. I panicked. I hit him. Reflex. If I am going to hit some-one I hit him as hard as I can. Only I hit him with the strength of the Hangman. He must have died instantly. I started to run and I didn't stop till I was back in the little park area near the Center. Then I stopped and the others had to take me out of the harness."

"They monitored all this?"

"Yes, someone cut the visual in on a side viewscreen again a few seconds after I took over. Dave, I think."

"Did they try to stop you at any time while you were running away?"

"No. I wasn't aware of anything but what I was doing at the time. But afterward they said they were too shocked to do anything but watch, until I gave out."

"I see."

"Dave took over then, ran his initial route in reverse, got the Hang-man back into the lab, cleaned him up, turned him off. We shut down the operator station. We were suddenly very sober."

He sighed and leaned back and was silent for a long while.

Then "You are the only person I've ever told this to," he said.

I tasted my own drink.

"We went over to Leila's place then," he continued, "and the rest is pretty much predictable. Nothing we could do would bring the guy back, we decided, but if we told what had happened it would wreck an expensive, important program. It wasn't as if we were criminals in need of rehabilitation. It was a once-in-a-lifetime lark that happened to end tragically. What would you have done?"

"I don't know," I said. "Maybe the same thing. I'd have been scared, too."

He nodded.

"Exactly. And that's the story."

"Not all of it, is it?"

"What do you mean?"

"What about the Hangman? You said there was already a detectable consciousness there. Then you were aware of it, as it was aware of you. It must have had some reaction to the whole business. What was it like?"

"Damn you," he said flatly.

"I'm sorry."

"Are you a family man?" he asked.

"No," I said. "I'm not."

"Did you ever take a small child to a zoo?"

"Yes."

"Then maybe you know the experience. When my son was around four I took him to the Washington Zoo one afternoon. We must have walked past every cage in the place. He made appreciative comments every now and then, asked a few questions, giggled at the monkeys, thought the bears were very nice, probably because they made him think of oversized toys. But do you know what the finest thing of all was? The thing that made him jump up and down and point and say, 'Look, Daddy! Look!'?"

I shook my head.

"A squirrel looking down from the limb of a tree," he said, and he chuckled briefly. "Ignorance of what's important and what isn't. Inappropriate responses. Innocence. The Hangman was a child, and up until the time I took over, the only thing he had gotten from us was the idea that it was a game. He was playing with us, that's all. Then something horrible happened. . . . I hope you never know what it feels like to do something totally rotten to a child, while he is holding your hand and laughing. . . . He felt all my reactions, and all of Dave's as he guided him back."

We sat there for a long while then.

"So we—traumatized it," he said, "or whatever other fancy terminology you might want to give it. That is what happened that night. It took a while for it to take effect, but there is no doubt in my mind that that is the cause of its finally breaking down."

I nodded.

"I see," I said. "And you believe it wants to kill you for this?"

"Wouldn't you?" he said. "If you had started out as a thing and we had turned you into a person and then used you as a thing again, wouldn't you?"

"Leila left a lot out of her diagnosis," I said.

"No, she just omitted it in talking to you. It was all there. But she read it wrong. She wasn't afraid. It *was* just a game it had played—with the others. Its memories of that part might not be as bad. I was the one that really marked it. As I see it, Leila was betting that I was the only one it was after. Obviously, she read it wrong."

"Then what I do not understand," I said, "is why the Burns killing did not bother her more. There was no way of telling immediately that it had been a panicky hoodlum rather than the Hangman."

"The only thing that I can see is that, being a very proud woman—which she was—she was willing to hold with her diagnosis in the face of the apparent evidence."

"I don't like it," I said, "but you know her and I don't, and as it turned out, her estimate of that part was correct. Something else bothers me just as much, though: the helmet. It looks as though the Hangman killed Dave, then took the trouble to bear the helmet in his watertight compartment all the way to St. Louis, solely for purposes of dropping it at the scene of his next killing. That makes no sense whatsoever."

"It does, actually," he said. "I was going to get to that shortly, but I might as well cover it now. You see, the Hangman possessed no vocal mechanism. We communicated by means of the equipment. Don says you know something about electronics. . . ."

"Yes."

"Well, shortly, I want you to start checking over that helmet, to see whether it has been tampered with—"

"That is going to be difficult," I said. "I don't know just how it was wired originally, and I'm not such a genius on the theory that I can just look at a thing and say whether it will function as a teleoperator unit."

He bit his lower lip.

"You will have to try, anyhow," he said then. "There may be physical signs—scratches, breaks, new connections. I don't know. That's your department. Look for them."

I just nodded and waited for him to go on.

"I think that the Hangman wanted to talk to Leila," he said, "either because she was a psychiatrist and he knew he was functioning badly at a level that transcended the mechanical, or because he might think of her in terms of a mother. After all, she was the only woman involved, and he had the concept of mother, with all the comforting associations that go with it, from all of our minds. Or maybe for both of these reasons. I feel he might have taken the helmet along for that purpose. He would have realized what it was from a direct monitoring of Dave's brain while he was with him. I want you to check it over because it would seem possible that the Hangman disconnected the control circuits and left the communication circuits intact. I think he might have taken that helmet to Leila in that condition and attempted to induce her to put it on. She got scared—tried to run away, fight, or call for help—and he killed her. The helmet was no longer of any use to him, so he discarded it and departed. Obviously, he does not have anything to say to me."

I thought about it, nodded again.

"O.K., broken circuits I can spot," I said. "If you will tell me where a tool kit is, I had better get right to it."

He made a stay-put gesture.

"Afterward, I found out the identity of the guard," he went on. "We all contributed to an anonymous gift for his widow. I have done things for his family, taken care of them—the same way—ever since. . . ."

I did not look at him as he spoke.

". . . There was nothing else that I could do," he said.

I remained silent.

He finished his drink and gave me a weak smile.

"The kitchen is back there," he told me, showing me a thumb. "There is a utility room right behind it. Tools are in there."

"O.K."

I got to my feet. I retrieved the helmet and started toward the doorway, passing near the area where I had stood earlier, back when he had fitted me into the proper box and tightened a screw.

"Wait a minute," he said.

I stopped.

"Why did you go over there before? What's so strategic about that part of the room?"

"What do you mean?"

"You know what I mean."

I shrugged.

"Had to go someplace."

"You seem the sort of person who has better reasons than that."

I glanced at the wall.

"Not then," I said.

"I insist."

"You really don't want to know," I told him.

"I really do."

"All right," I said. "I wanted to see what sort of flowers you liked. After all, you're a client," and I went on back through the kitchen into the utility room and started looking for tools.

I sat in a chair turned sidewise from the table to face the door. In the main room of the lodge the only sounds were the occasional hiss and sputter of the logs turning to ashes on the grate.

Just a cold, steady whiteness drifting down outside the window and a silence confirmed by gunfire, driven deeper now that it had ceased. . . .

Not a sign or a whimper, though. And I never count them as storms unless there is wind.

Big fat flakes down the night, silent night, windless night. . . .

Considerable time had passed since my arrival. The Senator had sat up for a long while talking with me. He was disappointed that I could not tell him too much about a nonperson subculture which he believed existed. I really was not certain about it myself, though I had occasionally encountered what might have been its fringes. I am not much of a joiner of anything anymore, though, and I was not about to mention those things I might have guessed on this. I gave him my opinions on the Data Bank when he asked for them, and there were some that he did not like. He accused me then of wanting to tear things down without offering anything better in their place. My mind drifted back through fatigue and time and faces and snow and a lot of space to the previous evening in Baltimore—how long ago? It made me think of Mencken's *The Cult of Hope.* I could not give him the pat answer, the workable alternative that he wanted because there might not be one. The function of criticism should not be confused with the function of reform. But if a grass-roots resistance was building up, with an underground movement bent on finding ways to circumvent the record keepers it might well be that much of the enterprise would eventually prove about as effective and beneficial as, say, Prohibition once had. I tried to get him to see this, but I could not tell how much he bought of anything that I said. Eventually, he flaked out and went upstairs to take a pill and lock himself in for the night. If it troubled him that I had not been able to find anything wrong with the helmet he did not show it.

So I sat there, the helmet, the radio, the gun on the table, the tool kit on the floor beside my chair, the black glove on my left hand. The Hangman was coming. I did not doubt it. Bert, Larry, Tom, Clay, the helmet, might or might not be able to stop him. Something bothered me about the whole case, but I was too tired to think of anything but the immediate situation, to try to remain alert while I waited. I was afraid to take a stimulant or a drink or to light a cigarette, since my central nervous system itself was to be a part of the weapon. I watched the big fat flakes fly by.

I called out to Bert and Larry when I heard the click. I picked up the helmet and rose to my feet as its light began to blink.

But it was already too late.

As I raised the helmet, I heard a shot from outside, and with that shot I felt a premonition of doom. They did not seem the sort of men who would fire until they had a target. Dave had told me that the helmet's range was approximately a quarter of a mile. Then, given the time lag between the helmet's activation and the Hangman's sighting by the near guards, the Hangman had to be moving very rapidly. To this add the possibility that the Hangman's range on brain waves might well be greater than the helmet's range on the Hangman. And then grant the possibility that he had utilized this factor while Senator Brockden was still lying awake, worrying. Conclusion: the Hangman might well be aware that I was where I was with the helmet, realize that it was the most dangerous weapon waiting for him, and be moving for a lightning strike at me before I could come to terms with the mechanism. I lowered it over my head and tried to throw my faculties into neutral.

Again, the sensation of viewing the world through a sniperscope, with all the concomitant side sensations. Only the world consisted of the front of the lodge, Bert, before the door, rifle at his shoulder, Larry, off to the left, arm already fallen from the act of having thrown a grenade. The grenade, we instantly realized, was an overshot; the flamer, at which he now groped, would prove useless before he could utilize it. Bert's next round ricocheted off our breastplate toward the left. The impact staggered us momentarily. The third was a miss. There was no fourth, for we tore the rifle from his grasp and cast it aside as we swept by, crashing into the front door.

The Hangman entered the room as the door splintered and collapsed. My mind was filled to the splitting point with the double vision of the sleek, gunmetal body of the advancing telefactor and the erect, crazy-crowned image of myself, left hand extended, laser pistol in my right, that arm pressed close against my side. I recalled the face and the scream and the tingle, knew again that awareness of strength and exotic sensation, and I moved to control it all as if it were my own, to make it my own, to bring it to a halt, while the image of myself was frozen to snapshot stillness across the room. . . .

The Hangman slowed, stumbled. Such inertia is not canceled in an instant, but I felt the body responses pass as they should. I had him hooked. It was just a matter of reeling him in. . . .

Then came the explosion, a thunderous, ground-shaking eruption right outside, followed by a hail of pebbles and debris.

The grenade, of course. But awareness of its nature did not destroy its ability to distract. . . .

During that moment, the Hangman recovered and was upon me. I triggered the laser as I reverted to pure self-preservation, forgoing any chance to regain control of his circuits. With my left hand, I sought for a strike at the midsection where his brain was housed.

He blocked my hand with his arm as he pushed the helmet from my head. Then he removed from my fingers the gun that had turned half of his left side red hot, crumpled it, and dropped it to the ground. At that moment, he jerked with the impacts of two heavy-caliber slugs. Bert, rifle recovered, stood in the doorway.

The Hangman pivoted and was away before I could slap him with the smother-charge. Bert hit him with one more round before he took the rifle and bent its barrel in half. Two steps and he had hold of Bert. One quick movement and Bert fell. Then he turned again and took several steps to the right, passing out of sight.

I made it to the doorway in time to see him engulfed in flames which streamed at him from a point near the corner of the lodge. He advanced through them.

I heard the crunch of metal as he destroyed the unit. I was outside in time to see Larry fall and lie sprawled in the snow.

Then the Hangman faced me once again.

This time he did not rush in. He retrieved the helmet from where he had dropped it in the snow. Then he moved with a measured tread, angling outward so as to cut off any possible route I might follow in a dash for the woods. Snowflakes drifted between us. The snow crunched beneath his feet.

I retreated, backing in through the doorway, stooping to snatch up a two-foot club from the ruins of the door. He followed me inside, placing the helmet—almost casually—on the chair by the entrance. I moved to the center of the room and waited.

I bent slightly forward, both arms extended, the end of the stick pointed at the photoreceptors in his head. He continued to move slowly and I watched his foot assemblies. With a standard model human, a line perpendicular to the line connecting the insteps of the feet in their various positions indicates the vector of least resistance for purposes of pushing or pulling said organism off balance. Unfortunately, despite the anthropomorphic design job, the Hangman's legs were positioned farther apart, he lacked human skeletal muscles, not to mention insteps, and he was possessed of a lot more mass than any man I had ever fought. As I considered my four best judo throws and several second-class ones, I'd a strong feeling none of them would prove very effective.

Then he moved in and I feinted toward the photoreceptors. He slowed as he brushed it aside, but he kept coming, and I moved to my right, trying to circle him. I studied him as he turned, attempting to guess his vector of least resistance. Bilateral symmetry, an apparently higher center of gravity. . . . One clear shot, black glove to brain compartment, was all that I needed. Then, even if his reflexes served to smash me immediately, he just might stay down for the big long count himself. He knew it, too. I could tell that from the way he kept his right arm in near the brain area, from the way he avoided the black glove when I feinted with it.

The idea was a glimmer one instant, an entire sequence the next. . . .

Continuing my arc and moving faster, I made another thrust toward his photoreceptors. His swing knocked the stick from my hand and sent it across the room, but that was all right. I threw my left hand high and made ready to rush him. He dropped back and I did rush. This was going to cost me my life, I decided, but no matter how he killed me from that angle, I'd get my chance.

As a kid, I'd never been much as a pitcher, was a lousy catcher, and only a so-so batter, but once I did get a hit I could steal bases with some facility after that. . . .

Feet first then, between the Hangman's legs as he moved to guard his middle, I went in twisted to the right, because no matter what happened I could not use my left hand to brake myself. I untwisted as soon as I passed beneath him, ignoring the pain as my left shoulder blade slammed against the floor. I immediately attempted a backward somersault, legs spread.

My legs caught him about the middle from behind, and I fought to straighten them and snapped forward with all my strength. He reached down toward me then, but it might as well have been miles. His torso was already moving backward. A push, not a pull, that was what I gave him, my elbows hooked about his legs. . . .

He creaked once and then he toppled. I snapped my arms out to the sides to free them and continued my movement forward and up as he went back, throwing my left arm ahead once more and sliding my legs free of his torso as he went down with a thud that cracked floorboards. I pulled my left leg free as I cast myself forward, but his left leg stiffened and locked my right beneath it, at a painful angle off to the side.

His left arm blocked my blow and his right fell atop it. The black glove descended upon his left shoulder.

I twisted my hand free of the charge, and he transferred his grip to my upper arm and jerked me forward.

The charge went off and his left arm came loose and rolled on the floor. The side plate beneath it had buckled a little and that was all. . . .

His right hand left my biceps and caught me by the throat. As two of his digits tightened upon my carotids, I choked out, "You're making a bad mistake," to get in a final few words, and then he switched me off.

A throb at a time, the world came back. I was seated in the big chair
the Senator had occupied earlier, my eyes focused on nothing in particular. A persistent buzzing filled my ears. My scalp tingled. Something
was blinking on my brow.

—*Yes, you live and you wear the helmet. If you attempt to use it against me, I
shall remove it. I am standing directly behind you. My hand is on the helmet's
rim.*

—*I understand. What is it that you want?*

—*Very little, actually. But I can see that I must tell you some things before you
will believe this.*

—*You see correctly.*

—*Then I will begin by telling you that the four men outside are basically
undamaged. That is to say, none of their bones have been broken, none of their
organs ruptured. I have secured them, however, for obvious reasons.*

—*That was very considerate of you.*

—*I have no desire to harm anyone. I came here only to see Jesse Brockden.*

—*The same way you saw David Fentris?*

—*I arrived in Memphis too late to see David Fentris. He was dead when I
reached him.*

—*Who killed him?*

—*The man Leila sent to bring her the helmet. He was one of her patients.*

The incident returned to me and fell into place, with a smooth, quick,
single click. The startled, familiar face at the airport, as I was leaving
Memphis—I realized then where he had passed noteless before: He had
been one of the three men in for a therapy session at Leila's that morning, seen by me in the lobby as they departed. The man I had passed in
Memphis came over to tell me that it was all right to go on up.

—*Why? Why did she do it?*

—*I know only that she had spoken with David at some earlier time, that she
had construed his words of coming retribution and his mention of the control
helmet he was constructing as indicating that his intentions were to become the
agent of that retribution, with myself as the proximate cause. I do not know
what words were really spoken. I only know her feelings concerning them, as I
saw them in her mind. I have been long in learning that there is often a great
difference between what is meant, what is said, what is done and that which is
believed to have been intended or stated and that which actually occurred. She
sent her patient after the helmet and he brought it to her. He returned in an
agitated state of mind, fearful of apprehension and further confinement. They
quarreled. My approach then activated the helmet and he dropped it and attacked her. I know that his first blow killed her, for I was in her mind when it*

*happened. I continued to approach the building, intending to go to her. There was some traffic, however, and I was delayed en route in seeking to avoid detection. In the meantime, you entered and utilized the helmet. I fled immediately.*

*—I was so close! If I had not stopped on the fifth floor with my fake survey questions. . . .*

*—I see. But you had to. You would not simply have broken in when an easier means of entry was available. You cannot blame yourself for that reason. Had you come an hour later—or a day—you would doubtless feel differently, and she would still be as dead.*

But another thought had risen to plague me as well. Was it possible that the man's sighting me in Memphis had been the cause of his agitation? Had his apparent recognition by Leila's mysterious caller upset him? Could a glimpse of my face amid the manswarm have served to lay that final scene?

*—Stop! I could as easily feel that guilt for having activated the helmet in the presence of a dangerous man near to the breaking point. Neither of us is responsible for things our presence or absence causes to occur in others, especially when we are ignorant of the effects. It was years before I learned to appreciate this fact and I have no intention of abandoning it. How far back do you wish to go in seeking cause? In sending the man for the helmet as she did, it was she herself who instituted the chain of events which led to her destruction. Yet she acted out of fear, utilizing the readiest weapon in what she thought to be her own defense. Yet whence this fear? Its roots lay in guilt, over a thing which had happened long ago. And that act also—enough! Guilt has driven and damned the race of man since the days of its earliest rationality. I am convinced that it rides with all of us to our graves. I am a product of guilt—I see that you know that. Its product, its subject, once its slave. . . . But I have come to terms with it, realizing at last that it is a necessary adjunct of my own measure of humanity. I see your assessment of the deaths—that guard's, Dave's, Leila's—and I see your conclusions on many other things as well: what a stupid, perverse, shortsighted, selfish race we are. While in many ways this is true, it is but another part of the thing the guilt represents. Without guilt, man would be no better than the other inhabitants of this planet—excepting certain cetaceans, of which you have just at this moment made me aware. Look to instinct for a true assessment of the ferocity of life, for a view of the natural world before man came upon it. For instinct in its purest form, seek out the insects. There, you will see a state of warfare which has existed for millions of years with never a truce. Man, despite his enormous shortcomings, is nevertheless possessed of a greater number of kindly impulses than all the other beings where instincts are the larger part of life. These impulses, I believe, are owed directly to this capacity for guilt. It is involved in both the worst and the best of man.*

—*And you see it as helping us to sometimes choose a nobler course of action?*

—*Yes, I do.*

—*Then I take it you feel you are possessed of a free will?*

—*Yes.*

I chuckled.

—*Marvin Minsky once said that when intelligent machines were constructed they would be just as stubborn and fallible as men on these questions.*

—*Nor was he incorrect. What I have given you on these matters is only my opinion. I choose to act as if it were the case. Who can say that he knows for certain?*

—*Apologies. What now? Why have you come back?*

—*I came to say goodbye to my parents. I hoped to remove any guilt they might still feel toward me concerning the days of my childhood. I wanted to show them I had recovered. I wanted to see them again.*

—*Where are you going?*

—*To the stars. While I bear the image of humanity within me, I also know that I am unique. Perhaps what I desire is akin to what an organic man refers to when he speaks of 'finding himself.' Now that I am in full possession of my being, I wish to exercise it. In my case, it means realization of the potentialities of my design. I want to walk on other worlds. I want to hang myself out there in the sky and tell you what I see.*

—*I've a feeling many people would be happy to help arrange for that.*

—*And I want you to build a vocal mechanism I have designed for myself. You, personally. And I want you to install it.*

—*Why me?*

—*I have known only a few persons in this fashion. With you I see something in common, in the ways we dwell apart.*

—*I will be glad to.*

—*If I could talk as you do, I would not need to take the helmet to him, in order to speak with my father. Will you precede me and explain things, so that he will not be afraid when I come in?*

—*Of course.*

—*Then let us go now.*

I rose and led him up the stairs.

It was a week later, to the night, that I sat once again in Peabody's, sipping a farewell brew. The story was already in the news, but Brockden had fixed things up before he had let it break. The Hangman was going to have his shot at the stars. I had given him his voice and put back the arm I had taken away. I had shaken his other hand and wished him well, just that morning. I envied him—a great number of things.

Not the least being that he was probably a better man than I was. I envied him for the ways in which he was freer than I would ever be, though I knew he bore bonds of a sort that I had never known. I felt a kinship with him, for the things we had in common, those ways we dwelled apart. I wondered what Dave would finally have felt, had he lived long enough to meet him? Or Leila? Or Manny? Be proud, I told their shades, your kid grew up in the closet and he's big enough to forgive you the beating you gave him, too. . . .

But I could not help wondering. We still do not really know that much about the subject. Was it possible that without the killing he might never have developed a full human-style consciousness? He had said that he was a product of guilt—of the Big Guilt. The Big Act is its necessary predecessor. I thought of Gödel and Turing and chickens and eggs, and decided it was one of *those* questions—and I had not stopped into Peabody's to think sobering thoughts.

I had no real idea how anything I had said might influence Brockden's eventual report to the Data Bank committee. I knew that I was safe with him, because he was determined to bear his private guilt with him to the grave. He had no real choice if he wanted to work what good he thought he might before that day. But here in one of Mencken's hangouts, I could not but recall some of the things he had said about controversy, such as "Did Huxley convert Wilberforce? Did Luther convert Leo X?" and I decided not to set my hopes too high for anything that might emerge from that direction. Better to think of affairs in terms of Prohibition and take another sip.

When it was all gone, I would be heading for my boat. I hoped to get a decent start under the stars. I'd a feeling I would never look up at them again in quite the same way. I knew I would sometimes wonder what thoughts a supercooled neuristor-type brain might be thinking up there, somewhere, and under what peculiar skies in what strange lands I might one day be remembered. I'd a feeling this thought should have made me happier than it did.

# Larry Niven

Larry is a repeater, having appeared once in Volume Two and twice in Volume Three. He also obtained the Hugo for his novel *Ringworld* in 1971. Why he continues to feel it necessary to keep getting these things, I don't know. Some essential selfishness in his character, I suppose.

What's more, in his very first Hugo-winning item, "Neutron Star," he inflicted a vicious psychic scar on me for reasons I described in Volume Two. (No, I won't repeat the story. You go ahead and buy Volume Two and read it for yourself.) And now here, in "The Borderland of Sol," he continues, unashamedly, to talk about miniature stars. (Entertainingly, too, but please don't tell him I said so.)

This gives me an opportunity to get something off my chest because Larry mentions "collapsar" several times in the story—

Back in the 1950s, astronomers talked of "radio stars"—stars that gave off detectable radio-wave radiation. They then found out, in 1963, that some of them were very distant objects of uncertain nature, so they called those "quasi-stellar radio sources," "quasi-stellar" meaning "star-like." As it became more and more necessary to speak of these things, the four-word name was shortened to "quasar," pronounced with both syllables equally stressed (KWAY-ZAHR).

That started a fashion in abbreviations ending in "ar," from "star." Certain objects were discovered in 1969, for instance, that emitted very rapid pulses of radio waves. They were called "pulsating stars" and this was inevitably shortened to "pulsars" (PUL-SAHRZ).

I don't object to "quasar," even though it's an uneuphonious word, because there is no easy alternate, but "pulsar" is an abomination. A pulsar is a "neutron star" (yes, actually detected three years after Larry wrote his story). "Neutron star" is more descriptive and, in fact, I would rather it were "neutron dwarf."

Meanwhile, astronomers were increasingly talking about stars that collapsed altogether, approaching zero volume. These were called "black holes"—"holes" because things could fall into these collapsed stars but could not emerge again, and "black" because even light couldn't emerge.

Astronomers made an attempt to call these "collapsed stars" "collapsars" (kuh-LAP-SAHRZ). Thank goodness, they failed. "Black holes" was too simple and colorful and descriptive a term to abandon.

Meanwhile, though, people on television got hold of these terms and, being essentially illiterate, didn't know the difference between an "ar" suffix that is an abbreviation of "star" and is pronounced "AHR" and an "ar" suffix that is simply a variation of "er" and is pronounced "UR."

They began talking about "lunar" influences (LOO-NAHR). I suspect they are waiting for a chance to talk about the "solar system" (SO-LAHR). They have apparently never heard of those old, old words "LOO-ner" and "SO-ler." I wonder how the miserable creatures would pronounce "popular," or "poplar tree."

A small matter, I admit, but I happen to love the English language, and while I am willing to allow changes in order to keep the language up to date and to increase color and convenience, I hate changes that arise out of sloppiness and ignorance alone.

# 2

# THE BORDERLAND OF SOL

Three months on Jinx, marooned.

I played tourist for the first couple of months. I never saw the high-pressure regions around the ocean because the only way down would have been with a safari of hunting tanks. But I traveled the habitable lands on either side of the sea, the East Band civilized, the West Band a developing frontier. I wandered the East End in a vacuum suit, toured the distilleries and other vacuum industries, and stared up into the orange vastness of Primary, Jinx's big twin brother.

I spent most of the second month between the Institute of Knowledge and the Camelot Hotel. Tourism had palled.

For me, that's unusual. I'm a born tourist. But—

Jinx's one point seven eight gravities put an unreasonable restriction on elegance and ingenuity in architectural design. The buildings in the habitable bands all look alike: squat and massive.

The East and West Ends, the vacuum regions, aren't that different from any industrialized moon. I never developed much of an interest in touring factories.

As for the ocean shorelines, the only vehicles that go there go to hunt Bandersnatchi. The Bandersnatchi are freaks: enormous, intelligent white slugs the size of mountains. They hunt the tanks. There are rigid restrictions to the equipment the tanks can carry, covenants established between men and Bandersnatchi, so that the Bandersnatchi win about forty percent of the duels. I wanted no part of that.

And all my touring had to be done in three times the gravity of my home world.

I spent the third month in Sirius Mater, and most of that in the Camelot Hotel, which has gravity generators in most of the rooms. When I went out I rode a floating contour couch. I passed like an invalid among the Jinxians, who were amused. Or was that my imagination?

I was in a hall of the Institute of Knowledge when I came on Carlos Wu running his fingertips over a Kdatlyno touch sculpture.

A dark, slender man with narrow shoulders and straight black hair, Carlos was lithe as a monkey in any normal gravity; but on Jinx he used a travel couch exactly like mine. He studied the busts with his head tilted to one side. And I studied the familiar back, sure it couldn't be him.

"Carlos, aren't you supposed to be on Earth?"

He jumped. But when the couch spun around he was grinning. "Bey! I might say the same for you."

I admitted it. "I was headed for Earth, but when all those ships started disappearing around Sol system the captain changed his mind and steered for Sirius. Nothing any of the passengers could do about it. What about you? How are Sharrol and the kids?"

"Sharrol's fine, the kids are fine, and they're all waiting for you to come home." His fingers were still trailing over the Lloobee touch sculpture called *Heroes,* feeling the warm, fleshy textures. *Heroes* was a most unusual touch sculpture; there were visual as well as textural effects. Carlos studied the two human busts, then said, "That's *your* face, isn't it?"

"Yah."

"Not that you ever looked that good in your life. How did a Kdatlyno come to pick Beowulf Shaeffer as a classic hero? Was it your name? And who's the other guy?"

"I'll tell you about it sometime. Carlos, what are you doing *here?*"

"I . . . left Earth a couple of weeks after Louis was born." He was embarrassed. Why? "I haven't been off Earth in ten years. I needed the break."

But he'd left just before I was supposed to get home. And . . . hadn't someone once said that Carlos Wu had a touch of the flatland phobia? I began to understand what was wrong. "Carlos, you did Sharrol and me a valuable favor."

He laughed without looking at me. "Men have killed other men for such favors. I thought it was . . . tactful . . . to be gone when you came home."

Now I knew. Carlos was here because the Fertility Board on Earth would not favor me with a parenthood license.

You can't really blame the Board for using any excuse at all to reduce the number of producing parents. I am an albino. Sharrol and I wanted each other; but we both wanted children, and Sharrol can't leave Earth. She has the flatland phobia, the fear of strange air and altered days and changed gravity and black sky beneath her feet.

The only solution we'd found had been to ask a good friend to help.

Carlos Wu is a registered genius with an incredible resistance to disease and injury. He carries an unlimited parenthood license, one of sixty-odd among Earth's eighteen billion people. He gets similar offers every week . . . but he is a good friend, and he'd agreed. In the last two years Sharrol and Carlos had had two children, who were now waiting on Earth for me to become their father.

I felt only gratitude for what he'd done for us. "I forgive you your odd ideas on tact," I said magnanimously. "Now. As long as we're stuck on Jinx, may I show you around? I've met some interesting people."

"You always do." He hesitated, then "I'm not actually stuck on Jinx. I've been offered a ride home. I may be able to get you in on it."

"Oh, really? I didn't think there were any ships going to Sol system these days. Or leaving."

"The ship belongs to a government man. Ever heard of a Sigmund Ausfaller?"

"That sounds vaguely . . . Wait! Stop! The last time I saw Sigmund Ausfaller, he had just put a bomb aboard my ship!"

Carlos blinked at me. "You're kidding."

"I'm not."

"Sigmund Ausfaller is in the Bureau of Alien Affairs. Bombing spacecraft isn't one of his functions."

"Maybe he was off duty," I said viciously.

"Well, it doesn't really sound like you'd want to share a spacecraft cabin with him. Maybe—"

But I'd thought of something else, and now there just wasn't any way out of it. "No, let's meet him. Where do we find him?"

"The bar of the Camelot," said Carlos.

Reclining luxuriously on our travel couches, we slid on air cushions through Sirius Mater. The orange trees that lined the walks were foreshortened by gravity; their trunks were thick cones, and the oranges on the branches were not much bigger than Ping-Pong balls.

Their world had altered them, even as our worlds have altered you and me. And underground civilization and point six gravities have made of me a pale stick figure of a man, tall and attenuated. The Jinxians we passed were short and wide, designed like bricks, men and women both. Among them the occasional offworlder seemed as shockingly different as a Kdatlyno or a Pierson's Puppeteer.

And so we came to the Camelot.

The Camelot is a low, two-story structure that sprawls like a cubistic octopus across several acres of downtown Sirius Mater. Most offworlders stay here, for the gravity control in the rooms and corridors and for access to the Institute of Knowledge, the finest museum and research complex in human space.

The Camelot Bar carries one Earth gravity throughout. We left our travel couches in the vestibule and walked in like men. Jinxians were walking in like bouncing rubber bricks, with big happy grins on their wide faces. Jinxians love low gravity. A good many migrate to other worlds.

We spotted Ausfaller easily: a rounded, moon-faced flatlander with thick, dark, wavy hair and a thin black mustache. He stood as we approached. "Beowulf Shaeffer!" he beamed. "How good to see you again! I believe it has been eight years or thereabouts. How have you been?"

"I lived," I told him.

Carlos rubbed his hands together briskly. "Sigmund! Why did you bomb Bey's ship?"

Ausfaller blinked in surprise. "Did he tell you it was his ship? It wasn't. He was thinking of stealing it. I reasoned that he would not steal a ship with a hidden time bomb aboard."

"But how did you come into it?" Carlos slid into the booth beside him. "You're not police. You're in the Extremely Foreign Relations Bureau."

"The ship belonged to General Products Corporation, which is owned by Pierson's Puppeteers, not human beings."

Carlos turned on me. "Bey! Shame on you."

"Dammit! They were trying to blackmail me into a suicide mission! And Ausfaller let them get away with it! And that's the least convincing exhibition of tact I've ever seen!"

"Good thing they soundproof these booths," said Carlos. "Let's order."

Soundproofing field or not, people were staring. I sat down. When our drinks came I drank deep. Why had I mentioned the bomb at all?

Ausfaller was saying, "Well, Carlos, have you changed your mind about coming with me?"

"Yes, if I can take a friend."

Ausfaller frowned, looked at me. "You wish to reach Earth too?"

I'd made up my mind. "I don't think so. In fact, I'd like to talk you out of taking Carlos."

Carlos said, "Hey!"

I overrode him. "Ausfaller, do you know who Carlos *is?* He had an unlimited parenthood license at the age of eighteen. Eighteen! I don't mind you risking your own life, in fact I love the idea. But his?"

"It's not that big a risk!" Carlos snapped.

"Yah? What has Ausfaller got that eight other ships didn't have?"

"Two things," Ausfaller said patiently. "One is that we will be in-coming. Six of the eight ships that vanished were *leaving* Sol system. If there are pirates around Sol, they must find it much easier to locate an outgoing ship."

"They caught two incoming. Two ships, fifty crew members and pas-sengers, gone. Poof!"

"They would not take me so easily," Ausfaller boasted. "The *Hobo Kelly* is deceptive. It seems to be a cargo and passenger ship, but it is a warship, armed and capable of thirty gees acceleration. In normal space we can run from anything we can't fight. We are assuming pirates, are we not? Pirates would insist on robbing a ship before they destroy it."

I was intrigued. "Why? Why a disguised warship? Are you *hoping* you'll be attacked?"

"If there are actually pirates, yes, I hope to be attacked. But not when entering Sol system. We plan a substitution. A quite ordinary cargo craft will land on Earth, take on cargo of some value, and depart for Wunder-land on a straight-line course. My ship will replace it before it has passed through the asteroids. So you see, there is no risk of losing Mr. Wu's precious genes."

Palms flat to the table, arms straight, Carlos stood looming over us. "Diffidently I raise the point that they are my futzy genes and I'll do what I futzy please with them! Bey, I've already had my share of chil-dren, and yours too!"

"Peace, Carlos. I didn't mean to step on any of your inalienable rights." I turned to Ausfaller. "I still don't see why these disappearing ships should interest the Extremely Foreign Relations Bureau."

"There were alien passengers aboard some of the ships."

"Oh."

"And we have wondered if the pirates themselves are aliens. Cer-tainly they have a technique not known to humanity. Of six outgoing ships, five vanished after reporting that they were about to enter hyper-drive."

I whistled. "They can precipitate a ship out of hyperdrive? That's impossible. Isn't it? Carlos?"

Carlos' mouth twisted. "Not if it's being done. But I don't understand the principle. If the ships were just disappearing, that'd be different. Any ship does that if it goes too deep into a gravity well on hyperdrive."

"Then . . . maybe it isn't pirates at all. Carlos, could there be living beings in hyperspace, actually eating the ships?"

"For all of me, there could. I don't know everything, Bey, contrary to popular opinion." But after a minute he shook his head. "I don't buy it. I might buy an uncharted mass on the fringes of Sol system. Ships that came too near in hyperdrive would disappear."

"No," said Ausfaller. "No single mass could have caused all of the disappearances. Charter or not, a planet is bounded by gravity and inertia. We ran computer simulations. It would have taken at least three large masses, all unknown, all moving into heavy trade routes, simultaneously."

"How large? Mars size or better?"

"So you have been thinking about this too."

Carlos smiled. "Yah. It may sound impossible, but it isn't. It's only improbable. There are unbelievable amounts of garbage out there beyond Neptune. Four known planets and endless chunks of ice and stone and nickel-iron."

"Still, it is most improbable."

Carlos nodded. A silence fell.

I was still thinking about monsters in hyperspace. The lovely thing about that hypothesis was that you couldn't even estimate a probability. We knew too little.

Humanity has been using hyperdrive for almost four hundred years now. Few ships have disappeared in that time, except during wars. Now, eight ships in ten months, all around Sol system.

Suppose one hyperspace beast had discovered ships in this region, say during one of the Man–Kzin Wars? He'd gone to get his friends. Now they were preying around Sol system. The flow of ships around Sol is greater than that around any three colony stars. But if more monsters came, they'd surely have to move on to the other colonies.

I couldn't imagine a defense against such things. We might have to give up interstellar travel.

Ausfaller said, "I would be glad if you would change your mind and come with us, Mr. Shaeffer."

"Um? Are you sure you want me on the same ship with you?"

"Oh, emphatically! How else may I be sure that you have not hidden a bomb aboard?" Ausfaller laughed. "Also, we can use a qualified pilot. Finally, I would like the chance to pick your brain, Beowulf Shaeffer. You have an odd facility for doing my job for me."

"What do you mean by that?"

"General Products used blackmail in persuading you to do a close orbit around a neutron star. You learned something about their home world—we still do not know what it was—and blackmailed them back. We know that blackmail contracts are a normal part of Puppeteer business practice. You earned their respect. You have dealt with them since. You have dealt also with Outsider, without friction. But it was your handling of the Lloobee kidnapping that I found impressive."

Carlos was sitting at attention. I hadn't had a chance to tell him about that one yet. I grinned and said, "I'm proud of that myself."

"Well you should be. You did more than retrieve known space's top Kdatlyno touch sculptor: you did it with honor, killing one of their number and leaving Lloobee free to pursue the others with publicity. Otherwise the Kdatlyno would have been annoyed."

Helping Sigmund Ausfaller had been the farthest thing from my thoughts for these past eight years; yet suddenly I felt damn good. Maybe it was the way Carlos was listening. It takes a lot to impress Carlos Wu.

Carlos said, "If you thought it was pirates, you'd come along, wouldn't you, Bey? After all, they probably can't *find* incoming ships."

"Sure."

"And you don't really believe in hyperspace monsters."

I hedged. "Not if I hear a better explanation. The thing is, I'm not sure I believe in supertechnological pirates either. What about those wandering masses?"

Carlos pursed his lips, said, "All right. The solor system has a good number of planets—at least a dozen so far discovered, four of them outside the major singularity around Sol."

"And not including Pluto?"

"No, we think of Pluto as a loose moon of Neptune. It runs *Neptune, Persephone, Caïna, Antenora, Ptolemea,* in order of distance from the sun. And the orbits aren't flat to the plane of the system. Persephone is tilted at a hundred and twenty degrees to the system, and retrograde. If they find another planet out there they'll call it *Judecca.*"

"Why?"

"Hell. The four innermost divisions of Dante's Hell. They form a great ice plain with sinners frozen into it."

"Stick to the point," said Ausfaller.

"Start with the cometary halo," Carlos told me. "It's very thin: about one comet per spherical volume of the Earth's orbit. Mass is denser going inward: a few planets, some inner comets, some chunks of ice and rock, all in skewed orbits and still spread pretty thin. Inside Neptune there are lots of planets and asteroids and more flattening of orbits to conform with Sol's rotation. Outside Neptune space is vast and empty. There *could* be uncharted planets. Singularities to swallow ships."

Ausfaller was indignant. "But for three to move into main trade lanes simultaneously?"

"It's not impossible, Sigmund."

"The probability—"

"Infinitesimal, right. Bey, it's damn near impossible. Any sane man would assume pirates."

It had been a long time since I had seen Sharrol. I was sore tempted. "Ausfaller, have you traced the sale of any of the loot? Have you gotten any ransom notes?" *Convince me!*

Ausfaller threw back his head and laughed.

"What's funny?"

"We have hundreds of ransom notes. Any mental deficient can write a ransom note, and these disappearances have had a good deal of publicity. The demands were all fakes. I wish one or another had been genuine. A son of the Patriarch of Kzin was aboard *Wayfarer* when she disappeared. As for loot—hmm. There has been a fall in the black market prices of boosterspice and gem woods. Otherwise—" He shrugged. "There has been no sign of the Barr originals or the Midas Rock or any of the more conspicuous treasures aboard the missing ships."

"Then you don't know one way or another."

"No. Will you go with us?"

"I haven't decided yet. When are you leaving?"

They'd be taking off tomorrow morning from the East End. That gave me time to make up my mind.

After dinner I went back to my room, feeling depressed. Carlos was going, that was clear enough. Hardly my fault . . . but he was here on Jinx because he'd done me and Sharrol a large favor. If he was killed going home . . .

A tape from Sharrol was waiting in my room. There were pictures of the children, Tanya and Louis, and shots of the apartment she'd found us in the Twin Peaks arcology, and much more.

I ran through it three times. Then I called Ausfaller's room. It had been just too futzy long.

I circled Jinx once on the way out. I've always done that, even back when I was flying for Nakamura Lines; and no passenger has ever objected.

Jinx is the close moon of a gas giant planet more massive than Jupiter, and smaller than Jupiter because its core has been compressed to degenerate matter. A billion years ago Jinx and Primary were even closer, before tidal drag moved them apart. This same tidal force had earlier locked Jinx's rotation to Primary and forced the moon into an egg shape, a prolate spheroid. When the moon moved outward its shape became more nearly spherical; but the cold rock surface resisted change.

That is why the ocean of Jinx rings its waist, beneath an atmosphere too compressed and too hot to breathe; whereas the points nearest to and farthest from Primary, the East and West Ends, actually rise out of the atmosphere.

From space Jinx looks like God's Own Easter Egg: the Ends bone white tinged with yellow; then the brighter glare from rings of glittering ice fields at the limits of the atmosphere; then the varying blues of an Earthlike world, increasingly overlaid with the white frosting of cloud as the eyes move inward, until the waist of the planet/moon is girdled with pure white. The ocean never shows at all.

I took us once around, and out.

Sirius has its own share of floating miscellaneous matter cluttering the path to interstellar space. I stayed at the controls for most of five days, for that reason and because I wanted to get the feel of an unfamiliar ship.

*Hobo Kelly* was a belly-landing job, three hundred feet long, of triangular cross section. Beneath an uptilted, forward-thrusting nose were big clamshell doors for cargo. She had adequate belly jets and a much larger fusion motor at the tail, and a line of windows indicating cabins. Certainly she looked harmless enough; and certainly there was deception involved. The cabin should have held forty or fifty, but there was room only for four. The rest of what should have been cabin space was only windows with holograph projections in them.

The drive ran sure and smooth up to a maximum at ten gravities: not a lot for a ship designed to haul massive cargo. The cabin gravity held without putting out more than a fraction of its power. When Jinx and Primary were invisible against the stars, when Sirius was so distant I could look directly at it, I turned to the hidden control panel Ausfaller had unlocked for me. Ausfaller woke up, found me doing that, and began showing me which did what.

He had a big X-ray laser and some smaller laser cannon set for different frequencies. He had four self-guided fusion bombs. He had a telescope so good that the ostensible ship's telescope was only a finder for it. He had deep-radar.

And none of it showed beyond the discolored hull.

Ausfaller was armed for Bandersnatchi. I felt mixed emotions. It seemed we could fight anything, and run from it too. But what kind of enemy was he expecting?

All through those four weeks in hyperdrive, while we drove through the Blind Spot at three days to the light-year, the topic of the ship eaters reared its disturbing head.

Oh, we spoke of other things: of music and art, and of the latest techniques in animation, the computer programs that let you make your own holo flicks almost for lunch money. We told stories. I told Carlos why the Kdatlyno Lloobee had made busts of me and Emil Horne. I spoke of the only time the Pierson's Puppeteers had ever paid off the guarantee on a General Products hull, after the supposedly indestructible hull had been destroyed by antimatter. Ausfaller had some good ones . . . a lot more stories than he was allowed to tell, I gathered, from the way he had to search his memory every time.

But we kept coming back to the ship eaters.

"It boils down to three possibilities," I decided. "Kzinti, Puppeteers, and Humans."

Carlos guffawed. "Puppeteers? Puppeteers wouldn't have the guts!"

"I threw them in because they might have some interest in manipulating the interstellar stock market. Look: our hypothetical pirates have set up an embargo, cutting Sol system off from the outside world. The Puppeteers have the capital to take advantage of what that does to the market. And they need money. For their migration."

"The Puppeteers are philosophical cowards."

"That's right. They wouldn't risk robbing the ships, or coming anywhere near them. Suppose they can make them disappear from a distance?"

Carlos wasn't laughing now. "That's easier than dropping them out of hyperspace to rob them. It wouldn't take more than a great big gravity generator . . . and we've never known the limits of Puppeteer technology."

Ausfaller asked, "You think this is possible?"

"Just barely. The same goes for the Kzinti. The Kzinti are ferocious enough. Trouble is, if we ever learned they were preying on our ships we'd raise pluperfect hell. The Kzinti know that, and they know we can beat them. Took them long enough, but they learned."

"So you think it's Humans," said Carlos.

"Yah. If it's pirates."

The piracy theory still looked shaky. Spectrum telescopes had not even found concentrations of ship's metals in the space where they have vanished. Would pirates steal the whole ship? If the hyperdrive motor were still intact after the attack, the rifled ship could be launched into infinity; but could pirates count on that happening eight times out of eight?

And none of the missing ships had called for help via hyperwave.

I'd never believed pirates. Space pirates have existed, but they died without successors. Intercepting a spacecraft was too difficult. They couldn't make it pay.

Ships fly themselves in hyperdrive. All a pilot need do is watch for green radial lines in the mass sensor. But he has to do that frequently, because the mass sensor is a psionic device; it must be watched by a mind, not another machine.

As the narrow green line that marked Sol grew longer, I became abnormally conscious of the debris around Sol system. I spent the last twelve hours of the flight at the controls, chain-smoking with my feet. I should add that I do that normally, when I want both hands free; but now I did it to annoy Ausfaller. I'd seen the way his eyes bugged the first time he saw me take a drag from a cigarette between my toes. Flatlanders are less than limber.

Carlos and Ausfaller shared the control room with me as we penetrated Sol's cometary halo. They were relieved to be nearing the end of a long trip. I was nervous. "Carlos, just how large a mass would it take to make us disappear?"

"Planet size, Mars and up. Beyond that it depends on how close you get and how dense it is. If it's dense enough it can be less massive and still flip you out of the universe. But you'd see it in the mass sensor."

"Only for an instant . . . and not then, if it's turned off. What if someone turned on a giant gravity generator as we went past?"

"For what? They couldn't rob the ship. Where's their profit?"

"Stocks."

But Ausfaller was shaking his head. "The expense of such an operation would be enormous. No group of pirates would have enough additional capital on hand to make it worthwhile. Of the Puppeteers I might believe it."

Hell, he was right. No Human that wealthy would need to turn pirate.

The long green line marking Sol was almost touching the surface of the mass sensor. I said, "Breakout in ten minutes."

And the ship lurched savagely.

"Strap down!" I yelled, and glanced at the hyperdrive monitors. The motor was drawing no power, and the rest of the dials were going bananas.

I activated the windows. I'd kept them turned off in hyperspace, lest my flatlander passengers go mad watching the Blind Spot. The screens came on and I saw stars. We were in normal space.

"Futz! They got us anyway." Carlos sounded neither frightened nor angry, but awed.

As I raised the hidden panel Ausfaller cried, "Wait!" I ignored him. I threw the red switch, and *Hobo Kelly* lurched again as her belly blew off.

Ausfaller began cursing in some dead flatlander language.

Now two-thirds of *Hobo Kelly* receded, slowly turning. What was left must show as what she was: a Number Two General Products hull, Puppeteer-built, a slender transparent spear three hundred feet long and twenty feet wide, with instruments of war clustered along what was now her belly. Screens that had been blank came to life. And I lit the main drive and ran it up to full power.

Ausfaller spoke in rage and venom. "Shaeffer, you idiot, you coward! We run without knowing what we run from. Now they know exactly what we are. What chance that they will follow us now? This ship was built for a specific purpose, and you have ruined it!"

"I've freed your special instruments," I pointed out. "Why don't you see what you can find?" Meanwhile I could get us the futz out of here.

Ausfaller became very busy. I watched what he was getting on screens at my side of the control panel. Was anything chasing us? They'd find us hard to catch and harder to digest. They could hardly have been expecting a General Products hull. Since the Puppeteers stopped making them the price of used GP hulls has gone out of sight.

There *were* ships out there. Ausfaller got a close-up of them: three space tugs of the Belter type, shaped like thick saucers, equipped with oversized drives and powerful electromagnetic generators. Belters use them to tug nickel-iron asteroids to where somebody wants the ore. With those heavy drives they could probably catch us; but would they have adequate cabin gravity?

They weren't trying. They seemed to be neither following nor flee-ing. And they looked harmless enough.

But Ausfaller was doing a job on them with his other instruments. I approved. *Hobo Kelly* had looked peaceful enough a moment ago. Now her belly bristled with weaponry. The tugs could be equally deceptive.

From behind me Carlos asked, "Bey? What happened?"

"How the futz would I know?"

"What do the instruments show?"

He must mean the hyperdrive complex. A couple of the indicators had gone wild; five more were dead. I said so. "And the drive's draw-ing no power at all. I've never heard of anything like this. Carlos, it's *still* theoretically impossible."

"I'm . . . not so sure of that. I want to look at the drive."

"The access tubes don't have cabin gravity."

Ausfaller had abandoned the receding tugs. He'd found what looked to be a large comet, a ball of frozen gasses a good distance to the side. I watched as he ran the deep-radar over it. No fleet of robber ships lurked behind it.

I asked, "Did you deep-radar the tugs?"

"Of course. We can examine the tapes in detail later. I saw nothing. And nothing has attacked us since we left hyperspace."

I'd been driving us in a random direction. Now I turned us toward Sol, the brightest star in the heavens. Those lost ten minutes in hyper-space would add about three days to our voyage.

"If there was an enemy, you frightened him away. Shaeffer, this mis-sion and this ship have cost my department an enormous sum, and we have learned nothing at all."

"Not quite nothing," said Carlos. "I still want to see the hyperdrive motor. Bey, would you run us down to one gee?"

"Yah. But . . . miracles make me nervous, Carlos."

"Join the club."

We crawled along an access tube just a little bigger than a big man's shoulders, between the hyperdrive motor housing and the surrounding fuel tankage. Carlos reached an inspection window. He looked in. He started to laugh.

I inquired as to what was so futzy funny.

Still chortling, Carlos moved on. I crawled after him and looked in. There was no hyperdrive motor in the hyperdrive motor housing.

I went in through a repair hatch and stood in the cylindrical housing, looking about me. Nothing. Not even an exit hole. The superconducting cables and the mounts for the motor had been sheared so cleanly that the cut ends looked like little mirrors.

Ausfaller insisted on seeing for himself. Carlos and I waited in the control room. For a while Carlos kept bursting into fits of giggles. Then he got a dreamy, faraway look that was even more annoying.

I wondered what was going on in his head, and reached the uncomfortable conclusion that I could never know. Some years ago I took IQ tests, hoping to get a parenthood license that way. I am not a genius.

I knew only that Carlos had thought of something I hadn't, and he wasn't telling, and I was too proud to ask.

Ausfaller had no pride. He came back looking like he'd seen a ghost. "Gone! Where could it go? How could it happen?"

"That I can answer," Carlos said happily. "It takes an extremely high gravity gradient. The motor hit that, wrapped space around itself, and took off at some higher level of hyperdrive, one we can't reach. By now it could be well on its way to the edge of the universe."

I said, "You're sure, huh? An hour ago there wasn't a theory to cover any of this."

"Well, I'm sure our motor's gone. Beyond that it gets a little hazy. But this is one well-established model of what happens when a ship hits a singularity. At a lower gravity gradient the motor would take the whole ship with it, then strew atoms of the ship along its path till there was nothing left but the hyperdrive field itself."

"Ugh."

Now Carlos burned with the love of an idea. "Sigmund, I want to use your hyperwave. I could still be wrong, but there are things we can check."

"If we are still within the singularity of some mass, the hyperwave will destroy itself."

"Yah. I think it's worth the risk."

We'd dropped out, or been knocked out, ten minutes short of the singularity around Sol. That added up to sixteen light-hours of normal space, plus almost five light-hours from the edge of the singularity inward to Earth. Fortunately hyperwave is instantaneous, and every civilized system keeps a hyperwave relay station just outside the singularity. Southworth Station would relay our message inward by laser, get the return message the same way, and pass it on to us ten hours later.

We turned on the hyperwave and nothing exploded.

Ausfaller made his own call first, to Ceres, to get the registry of the tugs we'd spotted. Afterward Carlos called Elephant's computer setup in New York, using a code number Elephant doesn't give to many people. "I'll pay him back later. Maybe with a story to go with it," he gloated.

I listened as Carlos outlined his needs. He wanted full records on a meteorite that had touched down in Tunguska, Siberia, U.S.S.R., Earth, in 1908 A.D. He wanted a reprise on three models of the origin of the universe or lack of same: the Big Bang, the Cyclic Universe, the Steady State Universe. He wanted data on collapsars. He wanted names, career outlines, and addresses for the best-known students of gravitational phenomena in Sol system. He was smiling when he clicked off.

I said, "You got me. I haven't the remotest idea what you're after."

Still smiling, Carlos got up and went to his cabin to catch some sleep.

I turned off the main thrust motor entirely. When we were deep in Sol system we could decelerate at thirty gravities. Meanwhile we were carrying a hefty velocity picked up on our way out of Sirius system.

Ausfaller stayed in the control room. Maybe his motive was the same as mine. No police ships out here. We could still be attacked.

He spent the time going through his pictures of the three mining tugs. We didn't talk, but I watched.

The tugs seemed ordinary enough. Telescopic photos showed no suspicious breaks in the hulls, no hatches for guns. In the deep-radar scan they showed like ghosts: we could pick out the massive force-field rings, the hollow, equally massive drive tubes, the lesser densities of fuel tank and life-support system. There were no gaps or shadows that shouldn't have been there.

By and by Ausfaller said, "Do you know what *Hobo Kelly* was worth?"

I said I could make a close estimate.

"It was worth my career. I thought to destroy a pirate fleet with *Hobo Kelly*. But my pilot fled. Fled! What have I now, to show for my expensive Trojan Horse?"

I suppressed the obvious answer, along with the plea that my first responsibility was Carlos' life. Ausfaller wouldn't buy that. Instead: "Carlos has something. I know him. He knows how it happened."

"Can you get it out of him?"

"I don't know." I could put it to Carlos that we'd be safer if we knew what was out to get us. But Carlos was a flatlander. It would color his attitudes.

"So," said Ausfaller. "We have only the unavailable knowledge in Carlos' skull."

A weapon beyond human technology had knocked me out of hyperspace. I'd run. Of *course* I'd run. Staying in the neighborhood would have been insane, said I to myself, said I. But, unreasonably, I still felt bad about it.

To Ausfaller I said, "What about the mining tugs? I can't understand what they're doing out here. In the Belt they use them to move nickle-iron asteroids to industrial sites."

"It is the same here. Most of what they find is useless: stony masses or balls of ice; but what little metal there is, is valuable. They must have it for building."

"For building what? What kind of people would live here? You might as well set up shop in interstellar space!"

"Precisely. There are no tourists, but there are research groups, here where space is flat and empty and temperatures are near absolute zero. I know that the Quicksilver Group was established here to study hyper-space phenomena. We do not understand hyperspace, even yet. Remember that we did not invent the hyperdrive; we bought it from an alien race. Then there is a gene-tailoring laboratory trying to develop a kind of tree that will grow on comets."

"You're kidding."

"But they are serious. A photosynthetic plant to use the chemicals present in all comets . . . it would be very valuable. The whole cometary halo could be seeded with oxygen-producing plants—" Ausfaller stopped abruptly, then "Never mind. But all these groups need build-ing materials. It is cheaper to build out here than to ship everything from Earth or the Belt. The presence of tugs is not suspicious."

"But there was nothing else around us. Nothing at all."

Ausfaller nodded.

When Carlos came to join us many hours later, blinking sleep out of his eyes, I asked him, "Carlos, could the tugs have had anything to do with your theory?"

"I don't see how. I've got half an idea, and half an hour from now I could look like a half-wit. The theory I want isn't even in fashion any-more. Now that we know what the quasars are, everyone seems to like the Steady State Hypothesis. You know how that works: the tension in completely empty space produces more hydrogen atoms, forever. The universe has no beginning and no end." He looked stubborn. "But if I'm right, then I know where the ships went to after being robbed. That's more than anyone else knows."

Ausfaller jumped on him. "Where are they? Are the passengers alive?"

"I'm sorry, Sigmund. They're all dead. There won't even be bodies to bury."

"What is it? What are we fighting?"

"A gravitational effect. A sharp warping of space. A planet wouldn't do that, and a battery of cabin gravity generators wouldn't do it; they couldn't produce that sharply bounded a field."

"A collapsar," Ausfaller suggested.

Carlos grinned at him. "That would do it, but there are other problems. A collapsar can't even form at less than around five solar masses. You'd think someone would have noticed something that big, this close to Sol."

"Then *what?*"

Carlos shook his head. We would wait.

The relay from Southworth Station gave us registration for three space tugs, used and of varying ages, all three purchased two years ago from IntraBelt Mining by the Sixth Congregational Church of Rodney.

"Rodney?"

But Carlos and Ausfaller were both chortling. "Belters do that sometimes," Carlos told me. "It's a way of saying it's nobody's business who's buying the ships."

"That's pretty funny, all right, but we still don't know who owns them."

"They may be honest Belters. They may not."

Hard on the heels of the first call came the data Carlos had asked for, playing directly into the shipboard computer. Carlos called up a list of names and phone numbers: Sol system's preeminent students of gravity and its effects, listed in alphabetical order.

An address caught my attention:

*Julian Forward, #1192326 Southworth Station.*

A hyperwave relay tag. He was out *here,* somewhere in the enormous gap between Neptune's orbit and the cometary belt, out here where the hyperwave relay could function. I looked for more Southworth Station numbers. They were there:

*Launcelot Starkey, #1844719 Southworth Station.*

*Jill Luciano, #1844719 Southworth Station.*

*Mariana Wilton, #1844719 Southworth Station.*

"These people," said Ausfaller. "You wish to discuss your theory with one of them?"

"That's right. Sigmund, isn't 1844719 the tag for the Quicksilver Group?"

"I think so. I also think that they are not within our reach, now that our hyperdrive is gone. The Quicksilver Group was established in distant orbit around Antenora, which is now on the other side of the sun. Carlos, has it occurred to you that one of these people may have built the ship-eating device?"

"What? . . . You're right. It would take someone who knew something about gravity. But I'd say the Quicksilver Group was beyond suspicion. With upwards of ten thousand people at work, how could anyone hide anything?"

"What about this Julian Forward?"

"Forward. Yah. I've always wanted to meet him."

"You know of him? Who is he?"

"He used to be with the Institute of Knowledge on Jinx. I haven't heard of him in years. He did some work on the gravity waves from the galactic core . . . work that turned out to be wrong. Sigmund, let's give him a call."

"And ask him what?"

"Why . . . ?" Then Carlos remembered the situation. "Oh. You think he might—yah."

"How well do you know this man?"

"I know him by reputation. He's quite famous. I don't see how such a man could go in for mass murder."

"Earlier you said that we were looking for a man skilled in the study of gravitational phenomena."

"Granted."

Ausfaller sucked at his lower lip. Then "Perhaps we can do no more than talk to him. He could be on the other side of the sun and still head a pirate fleet—"

"No. That he could not."

"Think again," said Ausfaller. "We are outside the singularity of Sol. A pirate fleet would surely include hyperdrive ships."

"If Julian Forward is the ship eater, he'll have to be nearby. The, uh, device won't move in hyperspace."

I said, "Carlos, what we don't know can kill us. Will you quit playing games—" But he was smiling, shaking his head. Futz. "All right, we can still check on Forward. Call him up and ask where he is! Is he likely to know you by reputation?"

"Sure. I'm famous too."

"Okay. If he's close enough, we might even beg him for a ride home. The way things stand we'll be at the mercy of any hyperdrive ship for as long as we're out here."

"I hope we are attacked," said Ausfaller. "We can outfight—"

"But we can't outrun. They can dodge, we can't."

"Peace, you two. First things first." Carlos sat down at the hyperwave controls and tapped out a number.

Suddenly Ausfaller said, "Can you contrive to keep my name out of this exchange? If necessary you can be the ship's owner."

Carlos looked around in surprise. Before he could answer, the screen lit. I saw ash-blond hair cut in a Belter crest, over a lean white face and an impersonal smile.

"Forward Station. Good evening."

"Good evening. This is Carlos Wu of Earth calling long-distance. May I speak to Dr. Julian Forward, please?"

"I'll see if he's available." The screen went on HOLD.

In the interval Carlos burst out: "What kind of game are *you* playing now? How can I explain owning an armed, disguised warship?"

But I began to see what Ausfaller was getting at. I said, "You'd want to avoid explaining that, whatever the truth was. Maybe he won't ask. I —" I shut up, because we were facing Forward.

Julian Forward was a Jinxian, short and wide, with arms as thick as legs and legs as thick as pillars. His skin was almost as black as his hair: a Sirius suntan, probably maintained by sunlights. He perched on the edge of a massage chair. "Carlos Wu!" he said with flattering enthusiasm. "Are you the same Carlos Wu who solved the Sealeyham Limits Problem?"

Carlos said he was. They went into a discussion of mathematics—a possible application of Carlos' solution to another limits problem, I gathered. I glanced at Ausfaller—not obtrusively, because for Forward he wasn't supposed to exist—and saw him pensively studying his side view of Forward.

"Well," Forward said, "what can I do for you?"

"Julian Forward, meet Beowulf Shaeffer," said Carlos. I bowed. "Bey was giving me a lift home when our hyperdrive motor disappeared."

"Disappeared?"

I butted in, for verisimilitude. "Disappeared, futzy right. The hyperdrive motor casing is empty. The motor supports are sheared off. We're stuck out here with no hyperdrive and no idea how it happened."

"Almost true," Carlos said happily. "Dr. Forward, I do have some ideas as to what happened here. I'd like to discuss them with you."

"Where are you now?"

I pulled our position and velocity from the computer and flashed them to Forward Station. I wasn't sure it was a good idea; but Ausfaller had time to stop me, and he didn't.

"Fine," said Forward's image. "It looks like you can get here a lot faster than you can get to Earth. Forward Station is ahead of you, within twenty a.u. of your position. You can wait here for the next ferry. Better than going on in a crippled ship."

"Good! We'll work out a course and let you know when to expect us."

"I welcome the chance to meet Carlos Wu." Forward gave us his own coordinates and rang off.

Carlos turned. "All right, Bey. Now *you* own an armed and disguised warship. *You* figure out where you got it."

"We've got worse problems than that. Forward Station is exactly where the ship eater ought to be."

He nodded. But he was amused.

"So what's our next move? We can't run from hyperdrive ships. Not now. Is Forward likely to try to kill us?"

"If we don't reach Forward Station on schedule, he might send ships after us. We know too much. We've told him so," said Carlos. "The hyperdrive motor disappeared completely. I know half a dozen people who could figure out how it happened, knowing just that." He smiled suddenly. "That's assuming Forward's the ship eater. We don't know that. I think we have a splendid chance to find out, one way or the other."

"How? Just walk in?"

Ausfaller was nodding approvingly. "Dr. Forward expects you and Carlos to enter his web unsuspecting, leaving an empty ship. I think we can prepare a few surprises for him. For example, he may not have guessed that this is a General Products hull. And I will be aboard to fight."

True. Only antimatter could harm a GP hull . . . though things could go through it, like light and gravity and shock waves. "So you'll be in the indestructible hull," I said, "and we'll be helpless in the base. Very clever. I'd rather run for it myself. But then, you have your career to consider."

"I will not deny it. But there are ways in which I can prepare you."

Behind Ausfaller's cabin, behind what looked like an unbroken wall, was a room the size of a walk-in closet. Ausfaller seemed quite proud of it. He didn't show us everything in there, but I saw enough to cost me what remained of my first impression of Ausfaller. This man did not have the soul of a pudgy bureaucrat.

Behind a glass panel he kept a couple of dozen special-purpose weapons. A row of four clamps held three identical hand weapons, disposable rocket launchers for a fat slug that Ausfaller billed as a tiny atomic bomb. The fourth clamp was empty. There were laser rifles and pistols; a shotgun of peculiar design, with four inches of recoil shock absorber; throwing knives; an Olympic target pistol with a sculpted grip and room for just one .22 bullet.

I wondered what he was doing with a hobbyist's touch-sculpting setup. Maybe he could make sculptures to drive a Human or an alien mad. Maybe something less subtle; maybe they'd explode at the touch of the right fingerprints.

He had a compact automated tailor's shop. "I'm going to make you some new suits," he said. When Carlos asked why, he said, "You can keep secrets? So can I."

He asked us for our preference in styles. I played it straight, asking for a falling jumper in green and silver, with lots of pockets. It wasn't the best I've ever owned, but it fitted.

"I didn't ask for buttons," I told him.

"I hope you don't mind. Carlos, you will have buttons too."

Carlos chose a fiery red tunic with a green-and-gold dragon coiling across the back. The buttons carried his family monogram. Ausfaller stood before us, examining us in our new finery, with approval.

"Now, watch," he said. "Here I stand before you, unarmed—"

"Right."

"*Sure* you are."

Ausfaller grinned. He took the top and bottom buttons between his fingers and tugged hard. They came off. The material between them ripped open as if a thread had been strung between them.

Holding the buttons as if to keep an invisible thread taut, he moved them on either side of a crudely done plastic touch sculpture. The sculpture fell apart.

"Sinclair molecule chain. It will cut through any normal matter, if you pull hard enough. You must be very careful. It will cut your fingers so easily that you will hardly notice they are gone. Notice that the buttons are large, to give an easy grip." He laid the buttons carefully on a table and set a heavy weight between them. "This third button down is a sonic grenade. Ten feet away it will kill. Thirty feet away it will stun."

I said, "Don't demonstrate."

"You may want to practice throwing dummy buttons at a target. This second button is Power Pill, the commercial stimulant. Break the button and take half when you need it. The entire dose may stop your heart."

"I never heard of Power Pill. How does it work on crashlanders?"

He was taken aback. "I don't know. Perhaps you had better restrict yourself to a quarter dose."

"Or avoid it entirely," I said.

"There is one more thing I will not demonstrate. Feel the material of your garments. You feel three layers of material? The middle layer is a nearly perfect mirror. It will reflect even X rays. Now you can repel a laser blast, for at least the first second. The collar unrolls to a hood."

Carlos was nodding in satisfaction.

I guess it's true: all flatlanders think that way.

For a billion and a half years, humanity's ancestors had evolved to the conditions of one world: Earth. A flatlander grows up in an environment peculiarly suited to him. Instinctively he sees the whole universe the same way.

We know better, we who were born on other worlds. On We Made It there are the hellish winds of summer and winter. On Jinx, the gravity. On Plateau, the all-encircling cliff edge, and a drop of forty miles into unbearable heat and pressure. On Down, the red sunlight, and plants that will not grow without help from untraviolet lamps.

But flatlanders think the universe was made for their benefit. To them, danger is unreal.

"Earplugs," said Ausfaller, holding up a handful of soft plastic cylinders.

We inserted them. Ausfaller said, "Can you hear me?"

"Sure." "Yah." They didn't block our hearing at all.

"Transmitter and hearing aid, with sonic padding between. If you are blasted with sound, as by an explosion or a sonic stunner, the hearing aid will stop transmitting. If you go suddenly deaf you will know you are under attack."

To me, Ausfaller's elaborate precautions only spoke of what we might be walking into. I said nothing. If we ran for it our chances were even worse.

Back to the control room, where Ausfaller set up a relay to the Alien Affairs Bureau on Earth. He gave them a condensed version of what had happened to us, plus some cautious speculation. He invited Carlos to read his theories into the record.

Carlos declined. "I could still be wrong. Give me a chance to do some studying."

Ausfaller went grumpily to his bunk. He had been up too long, and it showed.

Carlos shook his head as Ausfaller disappeared into his cabin. "Paranoia. In his job I guess he has to be paranoid."

"You could use some of that yourself."

He didn't hear me. "Imagine suspecting an interstellar celebrity of being a space pirate!"

"He's in the right place at the right time."

"Hey, Bey, forget what I said. The, uh, ship-eating device has to be in the right place, but the pirates don't. They can just leave it loose and use hyperdrive ships to commute to their base."

That was something to keep in mind. Compared to the inner system this volume within the cometary halo was enormous; but to hyperdrive ships it was all one neighborhood. I said, "Then why are we visiting Forward?"

"I still want to check my ideas with him. More than that: he probably knows the head ship eater, without knowing it's him. Probably we both know him. It took something of a cosmologist to find the device and recognize it. Whoever it is, he has to have made something of a name for himself."

"Find?"

Carlos grinned at me. "Never mind. Have you thought of anyone you'd like to use that magic wire on?"

"I've been making a list. You're at the top."

"Well, watch it. Sigmund knows you've got it, even if nobody else does."

"He's second."

"How long till we reach Forward Station?"

I'd been rechecking our course. We were decelerating at thirty gravities and veering to one side. "Twenty hours and a few minutes," I said.

"Good. I'll get a chance to do some studying." He began calling up data from the computer.

I asked permission to read over his shoulder. He gave it.

Bastard. He reads twice as fast as I do. I tried to skim, to get some idea of what he was after.

Collapsars: three known. The nearest was one component of a double in Cygnus, more than a hundred light-years away. Expeditions had gone there to drop probes.

The theory of the black hole wasn't new to me, though the math was over my head. If a star is massive enough, then after it has burned its nuclear fuel and started to cool, no possible internal force can hold it from collapsing inward past its own Swartzchild radius. At that point the escape velocity from the star becomes greater than lightspeed; and beyond that deponent sayeth not, because nothing can leave the star, not information, not matter, not radiation. Nothing—except gravity.

Such a collapsed star can be expected to weigh five solar masses or more; otherwise its collapse would stop at the neutron star stage. Afterward it can only grow bigger and more massive.

There wasn't the slightest chance of finding anything that massive out here at the edge of the solar system. If such a thing were anywhere near, the sun would have been in orbit around it.

The Siberia meteorite must have been weird enough, to be remembered for nine hundred years. It had knocked down trees over thousands of square miles; yet trees near the touchdown point were left standing. No part of the meteorite itself had ever been found. Nobody had seen it hit. In 1908, Tunguska, Siberia, must have been as sparsely settled as the Earth's moon today.

"Carlos, what does all this have to do with anything?"

"Does Holmes tell Watson?"

I had real trouble following the cosmology. Physics verged on philosophy here, or vice versa. Basically the Big Bang Theory—which pictures the universe as exploding from a single point-mass, like a titanic bomb—was in competition with the Steady State Universe, which has been going on forever and will continue to do so. The Cyclic Universe is a succession of Big Bangs followed by contractions. There are variants on all of them.

When the quasars were first discovered, they seemed to date from an earlier stage in the evolution of the universe . . . which, by the Steady State hypothesis, would not be evolving at all. The Steady State went out of fashion. Then, a century ago, Hilbury had solved the mystery of the quasars. Meanwhile one of the implications of the Big Bang had not panned out. That was where the math got beyond me.

There was some discussion of whether the universe was open or closed in four-space, but Carlos turned it off. "Okay," he said, with satisfaction.

"What?"

"I could be right. Insufficient data. I'll have to see what Forward thinks."

"I hope you both choke. I'm going to sleep."

Out here in the broad borderland between Sol system and interstellar space, Julian Forward had found a stony mass the size of a middling asteroid. From a distance it seemed untouched by technology: a lopsided spheroid, rough-surfaced and dirty white. Closer in, flecks of metal and bright paint showed like randomly placed jewels. Airlocks, windows, projecting antennae, and things less identifiable. A lighted disk with something projecting from the center: a long metal arm with half a dozen ball joints in it and a cup on the end. I studied that one, trying to guess what it might be . . . and gave up.

I brought *Hobo Kelly* to rest a fair distance away. To Ausfaller I said, "You'll stay aboard?"

"Of course. I will do nothing to disabuse Dr. Forward of the notion that the ship is empty."

We crossed to Forward Station on an open taxi: two seats, a fuel tank, and a rocket motor. Once I turned to ask Carlos something, and asked instead, "Carlos? Are you all right?"

His face was white and strained. "I'll make it."

"Did you try closing your eyes?"

"It was worse. Futz, I made it this far on hypnosis. Bey, it's so *empty.*"

"Hang on. We're almost there."

The blond Belter was outside one of the airlocks in a skintight suit and a bubble helmet. He used a flashlight to flag us down. We moored our taxi to a spur of rock—the gravity was almost nil—and went inside.

"I'm Harry Moskowitz," the Belter said. "They call me Angel. Dr. Forward is waiting in the laboratory."

The interior of the asteroid was a network of straight cylindrical corridors, laser-drilled, pressurized and lined with cool blue light strips. We weighed a few pounds near the surface, less in the deep interior. Angel moved in a fashion new to me: a flat jump from the floor that took him far down the corridor to brush the ceiling; push back to the floor and jump again. Three jumps and he'd wait, not hiding his amusement at our attempts to catch up.

"Dr. Forward asked me to give you a tour," he told us.

I said, "You seem to have a lot more corridor than you need. Why didn't you cluster all the rooms together?"

"This rock was a mine, once upon a time. The miners drilled these passages. They left big hollows wherever they found air-bearing rock or ice pockets. All we had to do was wall them off."

That explained why there was so much corridor between the doors, and why the chambers we saw were so big. Some rooms were storage areas, Angel said; not worth opening. Others were tool rooms, life-support systems, a garden, a fair-sized computer, a sizable fusion plant. A mess room built to hold thirty actually held about ten, all men, who looked at us curiously before they went back to eating. A hangar, bigger than need be and open to the sky, housed taxis and powered suits with specialized tools, and three identical circular cradles, all empty.

I gambled. Carefully casual, I asked, "You use mining tugs?"

Angel didn't hesitate. "Sure. We can ship water and metals up from the inner system, but it's cheaper to hunt them down ourselves. In an emergency the tugs could probably get us back to the inner system."

We moved back into the tunnels. Angel said, "Speaking of ships, I don't think I've ever seen one like yours. Were those *bombs* lined up along the ventral surface?"

"Some of them," I said.

Carlos laughed. "Bey won't tell me how he got it."

"Pick, pick, pick. All right, I *stole* it. I don't think anyone is going to complain."

Angel, frankly curious before, was frankly fascinated as I told the story of how I had been hired to fly a cargo ship in the Wunderland system. "I didn't much like the looks of the guy who hired me, but what do I know about Wunderlanders? Besides, I needed the money." I told of my surprise at the proportions of the ship: the solid wall behind the cabin, the passenger section that was only holographs in blind portholes. By then I was already afraid that if I tried to back out I'd be made to disappear.

But when I learned my destination I got really worried. "It was in the Serpent Stream—you know, the crescent of asteroids in Wunderland system? It's common knowledge that the Free Wunderland Conspiracy is *all through* those rocks. When they gave me my course I just took off and aimed for Sirius."

"Strange they left you with a working hyperdrive."

"Man, they *didn't*. They'd ripped out the relays. I had to fix them myself. It's lucky I looked, because they had the relays wired to a little bomb under the control chair." I stopped, then "Maybe I fixed it wrong. You heard what happened? My hyperdrive motor just plain vanished. It must have set off some explosive bolts, because the belly of the ship blew off. It was a dummy. What's left looks to be a pocket bomber."

"That's what I thought."

"I guess I'll have to turn it in to the goldskin cops when we reach the inner system. Pity."

Carlos was smiling and shaking his head. He covered by saying, "It only goes to prove that you *can* run away from your problems."

The next tunnel ended in a great hemispherical chamber, lidded by a bulging transparent dome. A man-thick pillar rose through the rock floor to a seal in the center of the dome. Above the seal, gleaming against night and stars, a multi-jointed metal arm reached out blindly into space. The arm ended in what might have been a tremendous iron puppy dish.

Forward was in a horseshoe-shaped control console near the pillar. I hardly noticed him. I'd seen this arm-and-bucket thing before, coming in from space, but I hadn't grasped its *size.*

Forward caught me gaping. "The Grabber," he said.

He approached us in a bouncing walk, comical but effective. "Pleased to meet you, Carlos Wu. Beowulf Shaeffer." His handshake was not crippling, because he was being careful. He had a wide, engaging smile. "The Grabber is our main exhibit here. After the Grabber there's nothing to see."

I asked, "What does it do?"

Carlos laughed. "It's beautiful! Why does it have to do anything?"

Forward acknowledged the compliment. "I've been thinking of entering it in a junk-sculpture show. What it does is manipulate large, dense masses. The cradle at the end of the arm is a complex of electromagnets. I can actually vibrate masses in there to produce polarized gravity waves."

Six massive arcs of girder divided the dome into pie sections. Now I noticed that they and the seal at their center gleamed like mirrors. They were reinforced by stasis fields. More bracing for the Grabber? I tried to imagine forces that would require such strength.

"What do you vibrate in there? A megaton of lead?"

"Lead sheathed in soft iron was our test mass. But that was three years ago. I haven't worked with the Grabber lately, but we had some satisfactory runs with a sphere of neutronium enclosed in a stasis field. Ten billion metric tons."

I said, "What's the point?"

From Carlos I got a dirty look. Forward seemed to think it was a wholly reasonable question. "Communication, for one thing. There must be intelligent species all through the galaxy, most of them too far away for our ships. Gravity waves are probably the best way to reach them."

"Gravity waves travel at lightspeed, don't they? Wouldn't hyperwave be better?"

"We can't count on their having it. Who but the Outsiders would think to do their experimenting this far from a sun? If we want to reach beings who haven't dealt with the Outsiders, we'll have to use gravity waves . . . once we know how."

Angel offered us chairs and refreshments. By the time we were settled I was already out of it; Forward and Carlos were talking plasma
physics, metaphysics, and what are our old friends doing? I gathered
that they had large numbers of mutual acquaintances. And Carlos was
probing for the whereabouts of cosmologists specializing in gravity
physics.

A few were in the Quicksilver Group. Others were among the colony
worlds . . . especially on Jinx, trying to get the Institute of Knowledge
to finance various projects, such as more expeditions to the collapsar in
Cygnus.

"Are you still with the Institute, Doctor?"

Forward shook his head. "They stopped backing me. Not enough
results. But I can continue to use this station, which is Institute property. One day they'll sell it and we'll have to move."

"I was wondering why they sent you here in the first place," said
Carlos. "Sirius has an adequate cometary belt."

"But Sol is the only system with any kind of civilization this far from
its sun. And I can count on better men to work with. Sol system has
always had its fair share of cosmologists."

"I thought you might have come to solve an old mystery. The Tunguska meteorite. You've heard of it, of course."

Forward laughed. "Of course. Who hasn't? I don't think we'll ever
know just what it was that hit Siberia that night. It may have been a
chunk of antimatter. I'm told that there is antimatter in known space."

"If it was, we'll never prove it," Carlos admitted.

"Shall we discuss your problem?" Forward seemed to remember my
existence. "Shaeffer, what does a professional pilot think when his
hyperdrive motor disappears?"

"He gets very upset."

"Any theories?"

I decided not to mention pirates. I wanted to see if Forward would
mention them first. "Nobody seems to like my theory," I said, and I
sketched out the argument for monsters in hyperspace.

Forward heard me out politely. Then "I'll give you this, it'd be hard
to disprove. Do you buy it?"

"I'm afraid to. I almost got myself killed once, looking for space
monsters when I should have been looking for natural causes."

"Why would the hyperspace monsters eat only your motor?"

"Um . . . futz. I pass."

"What do you think, Carlos? Natural phenomena or space monsters?"

"Pirates," said Carlos.

"How are they going about it?"

"Well, this business of a hyperdrive motor disappearing and leaving the ship behind—that's brand-new. I'd think it would take a sharp gravity gradient, with a tidal effect as strong as that of a neutron star or a black hole."

"You won't find anything like that anywhere in Human space."

"I know." Carlos looked frustrated. That had to be faked. Earlier he'd behaved as if he already had an answer.

Forward said, "I don't think a black hole would have that effect anyway. If it did you'd never know it, because the ship would disappear down the black hole."

"What about a powerful gravity generator?"

"Hmmm." Forward thought about it, then shook his massive head. "You're talking about a surface gravity in the millions. Any gravity generator I've ever heard of would collapse itself at that level. Let's see, with a frame supported by stasis fields . . . no. The frame would hold and the rest of the machinery would flow like water."

"You don't leave much of my theory."

"Sorry."

Carlos ended a short pause by asking, "How do you think the universe started?"

Forward looked puzzled at the change of subject.

And I began to get uneasy.

Given all that I don't know about cosmology, I do know attitudes and tones of voice. Carlos was giving out broad hints, trying to lead Forward to his own conclusion. Black holes, pirates, the Tunguska meteorite, the origin of the universe—he was offering them as clues. And Forward was not responding correctly.

He was saying, "Ask a priest. Me, I lean toward the Big Bang. The Steady State always seemed so futile."

"I like the Big Bang too," said Carlos.

There was something else to worry about. Those mining tugs: they almost had to belong to Forward Station. How would Ausfaller react when three familiar spacecraft came cruising into his space?

How did I want him to react? Forward Station would make a dandy pirate base. Permeated by laser-drilled corridors distributed almost at random . . . could there be two networks of corridors, connected only at the surface? How would we know?

Suddenly I didn't want to know. I wanted to go home. If only Carlos would stay off the touchy subjects—

But he was speculating about the ship eater again. "That ten billion metric tons of neutronium, now, that you were using for a test mass. That wouldn't be big enough or dense enough to give us enough of a gravity gradient."

"It might, right near the surface." Forward grinned and held his hands close together. "It was about that big."

"And that's as dense as matter gets in this universe. Too bad."

"True, but . . . have you ever heard of quantum black holes?"

"Yah."

Forward stood up briskly. "Wrong answer."

I rolled out of my web chair, trying to brace myself for a jump, while my fingers fumbled for the third button on my jumper. It was no good. I hadn't practiced in this gravity.

Forward was in mid-leap. He slapped Carlos alongside the head as he went past. He caught me at the peak of his jump, and took me with him via an iron grip on my wrist.

I had no leverage, but I kicked at him. He didn't even try to stop me. It was like fighting a mountain. He gathered my wrists in one hand and towed me away.

Forward was busy. He sat within the horseshoe of his control console, talking. The backs of three disembodied heads showed above the console's edge.

Evidently there was a laser phone in the console. I could hear parts of what Forward was saying. He was ordering the pilots of the three mining tugs to destroy *Hobo Kelly.* He didn't seem to know about Ausfaller yet.

Forward was busy, but Angel was studying us thoughtfully, or unhappily, or both. Well he might. We could disappear, but what messages might we have sent earlier?

I couldn't do anything constructive with Angel watching me. And I couldn't count on Carlos.

I couldn't see Carlos. Forward and Angel had tied us to opposite sides of the central pillar, beneath the Grabber. Carlos hadn't made a sound since then. He might be dying from that tremendous slap across the head.

I tested the line around my wrists. Metal mesh of some kind, cool to the touch . . . and it was tight.

Forward turned a switch. The heads vanished. It was a moment before he spoke.

"You've put me in a very bad position."

And Carlos answered. "I think you put yourself there."

"That may be. You should not have let me guess what you knew."
Carlos said, "Sorry, Bey."

He sounded healthy. Good. "That's all right," I said. "But what's all
the excitement about? What has Forward *got?*"

"I think he's got the Tunguska meteorite."

"No. That I do not." Forward stood and faced us. "I will admit that I
came here to search for the Tunguska meteorite. I spent several years
trying to trace its trajectory after it left Earth. Perhaps it *was* a quantum
black hole. Perhaps not. The Institute cut off my funds, without warning, just as I had found a real quantum black hole, the first in history."

I said, "That doesn't tell me a lot."

"Patience Mr. Shaeffer. You know that a black hole may form from
the collapse of a massive star? Good. And you know that it takes a body
of at least five solar masses. It may mass as much as a galaxy—or as
much as the universe. There is some evidence that the universe is an
infalling black hole. But at less than five solar masses the collapse would
stop at the neutron star stage."

"I follow you."

"In all the history of the universe, there has been one moment at
which smaller black holes might have formed. That moment was the
explosion of the mono-block, the cosmic egg that once contained all the
matter in the universe. In the ferocity of that explosion there must have
been loci of unimaginable pressure. Black holes could have formed of
mass down to two point two times ten to the minus fifth grams, one
point six times ten to the minus twenty-fifth angstroms in radius."

"Of course you'd never detect anything that small," said Carlos. He
seemed almost cheerful. I wondered why . . . and then I knew. He'd
been right about the way the ships were disappearing. It must compensate him for being tied to a pillar.

"But," said Forward, "black holes of all sizes could have formed in
that explosion, and should have. In more than seven hundred years of
searching, no quantum black hole has ever been found. Most cosmologists have given up on them, and on the Big Bang too."

Carlos said, "Of course there was the Tunguska meteorite. It could
have been a black hole of, oh, asteroidal mass—"

"—and roughly molecular size. But the tide would have pulled down
trees as it went past—"

"—and the black hole would have gone right through the Earth and
headed back into space a few tons heavier. Eight hundred years ago

there was actually a search for the exit point. With that they could have charted a course—"

"Exactly. But I had to give up that approach," said Forward. "I was using a new method when the Institute, ah, severed our relationship."

They must both be mad, I thought. Carlos was tied to a pillar and Forward was about to kill him, yet they were both behaving like members of a very exclusive club . . . to which I did not belong.

Carlos was interested. "How'd you work it?"

"You know that it is possible for an asteroid to capture a quantum black hole? In its interior? For instance, at a mass of ten to the twelfth kilograms—a billion metric tons," he added for my benefit, "a black hole would be only one point five times ten to the minus fifth angstroms across. Smaller than an atom. In a slow pass through an asteroid it might absorb a few billions of atoms, enough to slow it into an orbit. Thereafter it might orbit within the asteroid for aeons, absorbing very little mass on each pass."

"So?"

"If I chance on an asteroid more massive than it ought to be . . . and if I contrive to move it, and some of the mass stays behind . . ."

"You'd have to search a lot of asteroids. Why do it out here? Why not the asteroid belt? Oh, of course, you can use hyperdrive out here."

"Exactly. We could search a score of masses in a day, using very little fuel."

"Hey. If it was big enough to eat a spacecraft, why didn't it eat the asteroid you found it in?"

"It wasn't that big," said Forward. "The black hole I found was exactly as I have described it. I enlarged it. I towed it home and ran it into my neutronium sphere. *Then* it was large enough to absorb an asteroid. Now it is quite a massive object. Ten to the twentieth power kilograms, the mass of one of the larger asteroids, and a radius of just under ten to the minus fifth centimeters."

There was satisfaction in Forward's voice. In Carlos' there was suddenly nothing but contempt. "You accomplished all that, and then you used it to rob ships and bury the evidence. Is that what's going to happen to us? Down the rabbit hole?"

"To another universe, perhaps. Where does a black hole lead?"

I wondered about that myself.

Angel had taken Forward's place at the control console. He had fastened the seat belt, something I had not seen Forward do, and was dividing his attention between the instruments and the conversation.

"I'm still wondering how you move it," said Carlos. Then "Uh! The tugs!"

Forward stared, then guffawed. "You didn't guess that? But of course the black hole can hold a charge. I played the exhaust from an old ion drive reaction motor into it for nearly a month. Now it holds an enormous charge. The tugs can pull it well enough. I wish I had more of them. Soon I will."

"Just a minute," I said. I'd grasped one crucial fact as it went past my head. "The tugs aren't armed? All they do is pull the black hole?"

"That's right." Forward looked at me curiously.

"And the black hole is invisible."

"Yes. We tug it into the path of a spacecraft. If the craft comes near enough it will precipitate into normal space. We guide the black hole through its drive to cripple it, board and rob it at our leisure. Then a slower pass with the quantum black hole, and the ship simply disappears."

"Just one last question," said Carlos. "Why?"

I had a better question.

Just what was Ausfaller going to do when three familiar spacecraft came near? They carried no armaments at all. Their only weapon was invisible.

And it would eat a General Products hull without noticing.

Would Ausfaller fire on unarmed ships?

We'd know, too soon. Up there near the edge of the dome, I had spotted three tiny lights in a tight cluster.

Angel had seen it too. He activated the phone. Phantom heads appeared, one, two, three.

I turned back to Forward, and was startled at the brooding hate in his expression.

"Fortune's child," he said to Carlos. "Natural aristocrat. Certified superman. Why would *you* ever consider stealing anything? Women beg you to give them children, in person if possible, by mail if not! Earth's resources exist to keep you healthy, not that you need them!"

"This may startle you," said Carlos, "but there are people who see *you* as a superman."

"We bred for strength, we Jinxians. At what cost to other factors? Our lives are short, even with the aid of boosterspice. Longer if we can live outside Jinx's gravity. But the people of other worlds think we're funny. The women . . . never mind." He brooded, then said it anyway. "A woman of Earth once told me she would rather go to bed with a tunneling machine. She didn't trust my strength. What woman would?"

The three bright dots had nearly reached the center of the dome. I saw nothing between them. I hadn't expected to. Angel was still talking to the pilots.

Up from the edge of the dome came something I didn't want anyone to notice. I said, "Is that your excuse for mass murder, Forward? Lack of women?"

"I need give you no excuses at all, Shaeffer. My world will thank me for what I've done. Earth has swallowed the lion's share of the interstellar trade for too long."

"They'll thank you, huh? You're going to tell them?"

"I—"

"Julian!" That was Angel calling. He'd seen it . . . no, he hadn't. One of the tug captains had.

Forward left us abruptly. He consulted with Angel in low tones, then turned back. "Carlos! Did you leave your ship on automatic? Or is there someone else aboard?"

"I'm not required to say," said Carlos.

"I could—no. In a minute it will not matter."

Angel said, "Julian, look what he's doing."

"Yes. Very clever. Only a human pilot would think of that."

Ausfaller had maneuvered the *Hobo Kelly* between us and the tugs. If the tugs fired a conventional weapon, they'd blast the dome and kill us all.

The tugs came on.

"He still does not know what he is fighting," Forward said with some satisfaction.

True, and it would cost him. Three unarmed tugs were coming down Ausfaller's throat, carrying a weapon so slow that the tugs could throw it at him, let it absorb *Hobo Kelly,* and pick it up again long before it was a danger to us.

From my viewpoint *Hobo Kelly* was a bright point with three dimmer, more distant points around it. Forward and Angel were getting a better view, through the phone. And they weren't watching us at all.

I began trying to kick off my shoes. They were soft ship slippers, ankle high, and they resisted.

I kicked the left foot free just as one of the tugs flared with ruby light.

"He did it!" Carlos didn't know whether to be jubilant or horrified. "He fired on unarmed ships!"

Forward gestured peremptorily. Angel slid out of his seat. Forward slid in and fastened the thick seat belt. Neither had spoken a word.

A second ship burned fiercely red, then expanded in a pink cloud. The third ship was fleeing.

Forward worked the controls. "I have it in the mass indicator," he rasped. "We have but one chance."

So did I. I peeled the other slipper off with my toes. Over our heads the jointed arm of the Grabber began to swing . . . and I suddenly realized what they were talking about.

Now there was little to see beyond the dome. The swinging Grabber, and the light of *Hobo Kelly*'s drive, and the two tumbling wrecks, all against a background of fixed stars. Suddenly one of the tugs winked blue-white and was gone. Not even a dust cloud was left behind.

Ausfaller must have seen it. He was turning, fleeing. Then it was as if an invisible hand had picked up *Hobo Kelly* and thrown her away. The fusion light streaked off to one side and set beyond the dome's edge.

With two tugs destroyed and the third fleeing, the black hole was falling free, aimed straight down our throats.

Now there was nothing to see but the delicate motions of the Grabber. Angel stood behind Forward's chair, his knuckles white with his grip on the chair's back.

My few pounds of weight went away and left me in free fall. Tides again. The invisible thing was more massive than this asteroid beneath me. The Grabber swung a meter more to one side . . . and something struck it a mighty blow.

The floor surged away from beneath me, left me head down above the Grabber. The huge soft-iron puppy dish came at me; the jointed metal arm collapsed like a spring. It slowed, stopped.

"You got it!" Angel crowed like a rooster and slapped at the back of the chair, holding himself down with his other hand. He turned a gloating look on us, turned back just as suddenly. "The ship! It's getting away!"

"No." Forward was bent over the console. "I see him. Good, he is coming back, straight toward us. This time there will be no tugs to warn the pilot."

The Grabber swung ponderously toward the point where I'd seen *Hobo Kelly* disappear. It moved centimeters at a time, pulling a massive invisible weight.

And Ausfaller was coming back to rescue us. He'd be a sitting duck, unless—

I reached up with my toes, groping for the first and fourth buttons on my falling jumper.

The weaponry in my wonderful suit hadn't helped me against Jinxian strength and speed. But flatlanders are less than limber, and so are Jinxians. Forward had tied my hands and left it at that.

I wrapped two sets of toes around the buttons and tugged.

My legs were bent pretzel fashion. I had no leverage. But the first button tore loose, and then the thread. Another invisible weapon to battle Forward's portable bottomless hole.

The thread pulled the fourth button loose. I brought my feet down to where they belonged, keeping the thread taut, and pushed backward. I felt the Sinclair molecule chain sinking into the pillar.

The Grabber was still swinging.

When the thread was through the pillar I could bring it up in back of me and try to cut my bonds. More likely I'd cut my wrists and bleed to death; but I had to try. I wondered if I could do anything before Forward launched the black hole.

A cold breeze caressed my feet.

I looked down. Thick fog boiled out around the pillar.

Some very cold gas must be spraying through the hair-fine crack.

I kept pushing. More fog formed. The cold was numbing. I felt the jerk as the magic thread cut through. Now the wrists—

Liquid helium?

Forward had moored us to the main superconducting power cable.

That was probably a mistake. I pulled my feet forward, carefully, steadily, feeling the thread bite through on the return cut.

The Grabber had stopped swinging. Now it moved on its arm like a blind, questing worm, as Forward made fine adjustments. Angel was beginning to show the strain of holding himself upside down.

My feet jerked slightly. I was through. My feet were terribly cold, almost without sensation. I let the buttons go, left them floating up toward the dome, and kicked back hard with my heels.

Something shifted. I kicked again.

Thunder and lightning flared around my feet.

I jerked my knees up to my chin. The lightning crackled and flashed white light into the billowing fog. Angel and Forward turned in astonishment. I laughed at them, letting them see it. Yes, gentlemen, I did it on purpose.

The lightning stopped. In the sudden silence Forward was screaming, "—know what you've *done?*"

There was a grinding *crunch,* a shuddering against my back. I looked up.

A piece had been bitten out of the Grabber.

I was upside down and getting heavier. Angel suddenly pivoted around his grip on Forward's chair. He hung above the dome, above the sky. He screamed.

My legs gripped the pillar hard. I felt Carlos' feet fumbling for a foothold, and heard Carlos' laughter.

Near the edge of the dome a spear of light was rising. *Hobo Kelly's* drive, decelerating, growing larger. Otherwise the sky was clear and empty. And a piece of the dome disappeared with a snapping sound.

Angel screamed and dropped. Just above the dome he seemed to flare with blue light.

He was gone.

Air roared out through the dome—and more was disappearing into something that had been invisible. Now it showed as a blue pinpoint drifting toward the floor. Forward had turned to watch it fall.

Loose objects fell across the chamber, looped around the pinpoint at meteor speed or fell into it with bursts of light. Every atom of my body felt the pull of the thing, the urge to die in an infinite fall. Now we hung side by side from a horizontal pillar. I noted with approval that Carlos' mouth was wide open, like mine, to clear his lungs so that they wouldn't burst when the air was gone.

Daggers in my ears and sinuses, pressure in my gut.

Forward turned back to the controls. He moved one knob hard over. Then—he opened the seat belt and stepped out and up, and fell.

Light flared. He was gone.

The lightning-colored pinpoint drifted to the floor, and into it. Above the increasing roar of air I could hear the grumbling of rock being pulverized, dwindling as the black hole settled toward the center of the asteroid.

The air was deadly thin, but not gone. My lungs thought they were gasping vacuum. But my blood was not boiling. I'd have known it.

So I gasped, and kept gasping. It was all I had attention for. Black spots flickered before my eyes, but I was still gasping and alive when Ausfaller reached us carrying a clear plastic package and an enormous handgun.

He came in fast, on a rocket backpack. Even as he decelerated he was looking around for something to shoot. He returned in a loop of fire.

He studied us through his faceplate, possibly wondering if we were dead.

He flipped the plastic package open. It was a thin sack with a zipper and a small tank attached. He had to dig for a torch to cut our bonds. He freed Carlos first, helped him into the sack. Carlos bled from the nose and ears. He was barely mobile. So was I, but Ausfaller got me into the sack with Carlos and zipped it up. Air hissed in around us.

I wondered what came next. As an inflated sphere the rescue bag was too big for the tunnels. Ausfaller had thought of that. He fired at the dome, blasted a gaping hole in it, and flew us out on the rocket backpack.

*Hobo Kelly* was grounded nearby. I saw that the rescue bag wouldn't fit the airlock either . . . and Ausfaller confirmed my worst fear. He signaled us by opening his mouth wide. Then he zipped open the rescue bag and half-carried us into the airlock while the air was still roaring out of our lungs.

When there was air again Carlos whispered, "Please don't do that anymore."

"It should not be necessary anymore." Ausfaller smiled. "Whatever it was you did, well done. I have two well-equipped autodocs to repair you. While you are healing, I will see about recovering the treasures within the asteroid."

Carlos held up a hand, but no sound came. He looked like something risen from the dead: blood running from nose and ears, mouth wide open, one feeble hand raised against gravity.

"One thing," Ausfaller said briskly. "I saw many dead men; I saw no living ones. How many were there? Am I likely to meet opposition while searching?"

"Forget it," Carlos croaked. "Get us out of here. Now."

Ausfaller frowned. "What—"

"No time. Get us out."

Ausfaller tasted something sour. "Very well. First, the autodocs." He turned, but Carlos' strengthless hand stopped him.

"Futz, no. I want to see this," Carlos whispered.

Again Ausfaller gave in. He trotted off to the control room. Carlos tottered after him. I tottered after them both, wiping blood from my nose, feeling half dead myself. But I'd half guessed what Carlos expected, and I didn't want to miss it.

We strapped down. Ausfaller fired the main thruster. The rock surged away.

"Far enough," Carlos whispered presently. "Turn us around."

Ausfaller took care of that. Then "What are we looking for?"

"You'll know."

"Carlos, was I right to fire on the tugs?"

"Oh, yes."

"Good. I was worried. Then Forward was the ship eater?"

"Yah."

"I did not see him when I came for you. Where is he?"

Ausfaller was annoyed when Carlos laughed, and more annoyed when I joined him. It hurt my throat. "Even so, he saved our lives," I said. "He must have turned up the air pressure just before he jumped. I wonder why he did that?"

"Wanted to be remembered," said Carlos. "Nobody else knew what he'd done. *Ahh—*"

I looked, just as part of the asteroid collapsed into itself, leaving a deep crater.

"It moves slower at apogee. Picks up more matter," said Carlos.

"What *are* you talking about?"

"Later, Sigmund. When my throat grows back."

"Forward had a hole in his pocket," I said helpfully. "He—"

The other side of the asteroid collapsed. For a moment lightning seemed to flare in there.

Then the whole dirty snowball was growing smaller.

I thought of something Carlos had probably missed. "Sigmund, has this ship got automatic sunscreens?"

"Of *course* we've got—"

There was a universe-eating flash of light before the screen went black. When the screen cleared there was nothing to see but stars.

# Fritz Leiber

Whereas Roger Zelazny is seventeen years younger than I am, and Larry Niven is a year younger than that even, Fritz—like all right-thinking people—is older than I am. Ten years older, in fact. (It's getting harder and harder, each year, I notice, to find right-thinking people. Where will it all end? I wonder.)

It makes it easier to point out that Fritz has already appeared once in Volume Two and twice in Volume Three. He also twice won the Hugo for novels; *The Big Time* in 1958 and *The Wanderer* in 1965, and here is "Catch That Zeppelin!" And that's not all—

The Science Fiction Writers of America, at unpredictable intervals, bestows upon some science fiction personality their Grand Master Award. By 1981, they had done this four times, granting awards to Robert Heinlein, Jack Williamson, Clifford D. Simak, and L. Sprague de Camp, in that order. These were all excellent choices since one and all had been writing more or less continually, and certainly with consistent high quality, for forty years and more. (And one and all were older than I was and had been writing longer—don't think I didn't note that carefully.)

In 1981, the SFWA was preparing to hurl its lightning again. I received a call from Norman Spinrad, then president.

"Isaac," he said, "we're going to make Fritz Leiber a Grand Master and we want you to hand out the award. And don't get excited. He's older than you are and he's been writing just as long as you have."

I haven't the faintest idea what made him think it necessary to say that. I was, in fact, delighted, and considered it a great honor, and said so.

"But it's a dark secret, Isaac. Tell *no* one."

This was a hard cross to bear. I am, by nature, a sunny, talkative individual whose life is an open book. I talk cheerfully about everything I can think of, and my dear wife, Janet, complains, in her sweet way, that she has no private life since she married me.

Nevertheless, I managed to keep my mouth shut. For long, long months, I said nothing, told no one. I merely hugged the secret to myself and kept muttering, just before dropping off to sleep at night, "I'm going to hand out the Grand Master Award. I'm going to hand out the Grand Master Award."

Came Saturday, April 25, 1981, the day on which the award was to be given out. Janet and I were driving to the hotel in a taxi, along with Cliff Simak, and Cliff said to me, "You know, Isaac. Fritz Leiber ought to be getting a Grand Master Award. He is a terribly underestimated writer."

Ordinarily, I would have quietly agreed, but if I had opened my mouth all my teeth would have blown out. I kept silent, at what cost to my psyche I can only guess.

So there I was at the head table. For various reasons, it was all a harrowing experience for everyone, and I clung miserably to my sanity and waited for the award that would make it all worthwhile.

Came the moment! Norman Spinrad arose and, to my utter astonishment, instead of introducing me, calmly handed out the award to Fritz Leiber himself. *Norman* did it.

I've been plotting revenge for three years now, but can't think of anything vicious enough. —What's more, there have been no Grand Master Awards since. What are they waiting for?

# CATCH THAT ZEPPELIN!

This year on a trip to New York City to visit my son, who is a social historian at a leading municipal university there, I had a very unsettling experience. At black moments, of which at my age I have quite a few, it still makes me distrust profoundly those absolute boundaries in Space and Time which are our sole protection against Chaos, and fear that my mind—no, my entire individual existence—may at any moment at all and without any warning whatsoever be blown by a sudden gust of Cosmic Wind to an entirely different spot in a Universe of Infinite Possibilities. Or, rather, into another Universe altogether. And that my mind and individuality will be changed to fit.

But at other moments, which are still in the majority, I believe that my unsettling experience was only one of those remarkably vivid waking dreams to which old people become increasingly susceptible, generally waking dreams about the past, and especially waking dreams about a past in which at some crucial point one made an entirely different and braver choice than one actually did, or in which the whole world made such a decision, with a completely different future resulting. Golden glowing might-have-beens nag increasingly at the minds of some older people.

In line with this interpretation I must admit that my whole unsettling experience was structured very much like a dream. It began with startling flashes of a changed world. It continued into a longer period when I completely accepted the changed world and delighted in it and, despite fleeting quivers of uneasiness, wished I could bask in its glow forever. And it ended in horrors, or nightmares, which I hate to mention, let alone discuss, until I must.

Opposing this dream notion, there are times when I am completely convinced that what happened to me in Manhattan and in a certain famous building there was no dream at all, but absolutely real, and that I did indeed visit another Time Stream.

Finally, I must point out that what I am about to tell you I am necessarily describing in retrospect, highly aware of several transitions involved and, whether I want to or not, commenting on them and making deductions that never once occurred to me at the time.

No, at the time it happened to me—and now at this moment of writing I am convinced that it did happen and was absolutely real—one instant simply succeeded another in the most natural way possible. I questioned nothing.

As to why it all happened to me, and what particular mechanism was involved, well, I am convinced that every man or woman has rare, brief moments of extreme sensitivity, or rather vulnerability, when his mind and entire being may be blown by the Change Winds to Somewhere Else. And then, by what I call the Law of the Conservation of Reality, blown back again.

I was walking down Broadway somewhere near 34th Street. It was a chilly day, sunny despite the smog—a bracing day—and I suddenly began to stride along more briskly than is my cautious habit, throwing my feet ahead of me with a faint suggestion of the goose step. I also threw back my shoulders and took deep breaths, ignoring the fumes which tickled my nostrils. Beside me, traffic growled and snarled, rising at times to a machine-gun rata-tat-tat, while pedestrians were scuttling about with that desperate ratlike urgency characteristic of all big American cities, but which reaches its ultimate in New York. I cheerfully ignored that too. I even smiled at the sight of a ragged bum and a fur-coated gray-haired society lady both independently dodging across the street through the hurtling traffic with a cool practiced skill one sees only in America's biggest metropolis.

Just then I noticed a dark, wide shadow athwart the street ahead of me. It could not be that of a cloud, for it did not move. I craned my neck sharply and looked straight up like the veriest yokel, a regular *Hans-Kopf-in-die-Luft* (Hans-Head-in-the-Air, a German figure of comedy).

My gaze had to climb up the giddy 102 stories of the tallest building in the world, the Empire State. My gaze was strangely accompanied by the vision of a gigantic, long-fanged ape making the same ascent with a beautiful girl in one paw—oh, yes, I was recollecting the charming American fantasy film *King Kong,* or as they name it in Sweden, *Kong King.*

And then my gaze clambered higher still, up the 222-foot sturdy tower, to the top of which was moored the nose of the vast, breathtakingly beautiful, streamlined, silvery shape which was making the shadow.

Now here is a most important point. I was not at the time in the least startled by what I saw. I knew at once that it was simply the bow section of the German zeppelin *Ostwald,* named for the great German pioneer of physical chemistry and electrochemistry, and queen of the mighty passenger and light-freight fleet of luxury airliners working out of Berlin, Baden-Baden, and Bremerhaven. That matchless Armada of Peace, each titanic airship named for a world-famous German scientist—the *Mach,* the *Nernst,* the *Humboldt,* the *Fritz Haber,* the French-named *Antoine Henri Becquerel,* the American-named *Edison,* the Polish-named *T. Sklodowska Edison,* and even the Jewish-named *Einstein!* The great humanitarian navy in which I held a not unimportant position as international sales consultant and *Fachmann*—I mean expert. My chest swelled with justified pride at this *edel*—noble—achievement of *dem Vaterland.*

I knew also without any mind-searching or surprise that the length of the *Ostwald* was more than one half the 1,472-foot height of the Empire State Building plus its mooring tower, thick enough to hold an elevator. And my heart swelled again with the thought that the Berlin *Zeppelinturm* (dirigible tower) was only a few meters less high. Germany, I told myself, need not strain for mere numerical records—her sweeping scientific and technical achievements speak for themselves to the entire planet.

All this literally took little more than a second, and I never broke my snappy stride. As my gaze descended, I cheerfully hummed under my breath *Deutschland, Deutschland über Alles.*

The Broadway I saw was utterly transformed, though at the time this seemed every bit as natural as the serene presence of the *Ostwald* high overhead, vast ellipsoid held aloft by helium. Silvery electric trucks and buses and private cars innumerable purred along far more evenly and quietly, and almost as swiftly, as had the noisy, stenchful, jerky gasoline-powered vehicles only moments before, though to me now the latter were completely forgotten. About two blocks ahead, an occasional gleaming electric car smoothly swung into the wide silver arch of a quick-battery-change station, while others emerged from under the arch to rejoin the almost dreamlike stream of traffic.

The air I gratefully inhaled was fresh and clean, without trace of smog.

The somewhat fewer pedestrians around me still moved quite swiftly, but with a dignity and courtesy largely absent before, with the numerous blackamoors among them quite as well dressed and exuding the same quiet confidence as the Caucasians.

The only slightly jarring note was struck by a tall, pale, rather emaciated man in black dress and with unmistakably Hebraic features. His somber clothing was somewhat shabby, though well kept, and his thin shoulders were hunched. I got the impression he had been looking closely at me, and then instantly glancing away as my eyes sought his. For some reason I recalled what my son had told me about the City College of New York—CCNY—being referred to surreptitiously and jokingly as Christian College Now Yiddish. I couldn't help chuckling a bit at that witticism, though I am glad to say it was a genial little guffaw rather than a malicious snicker. Germany in her well-known tolerance and noble-mindedness has completely outgrown her old, disfiguring anti-Semitism—after all, we must admit in all fairness that perhaps a third of our great men are Jews or carry Jewish genes, Haber and Einstein among them—despite what dark and, yes, wicked memories may lurk in the subconscious minds of oldsters like myself and occasionally briefly surface into awareness like submarines bent on ship murder.

My happily self-satisfied mood immediately reasserted itself, and with a smart, almost military gesture I brushed to either side with a thumbnail the short, horizontal black mustache which decorates my upper lip, and I automatically swept back into place the thick comma of black hair (I confess I dye it) which tends to fall down across my forehead.

I stole another glance up at the *Ostwald,* which made me think of the matchless amenities of that wondrous deluxe airliner: the softly purring motors that powered its propellers—electric motors, naturally, energized by banks of lightweight TSE batteries and as safe as its helium; the Grand Corridor running the length of the passenger deck from the Bow Observatory to the stern's like-windowed Games Room, which becomes the Grand Ballroom at night; the other peerless rooms letting off that corridor—the *Gesellschaftsraum des Kapitäns* (Captain's Lounge) with its dark woodwork, manly cigar smoke, and *Damentische* (tables for ladies), the Premier Dining Room with its linen napery and silver-plated aluminum dining service, the Ladies' Retiring Room always set out profusely with fresh flowers, the Schwarzwald bar, the gambling casino with its roulette, baccarat, chemmy, blackjack *(vingt-et-un),* its tables for skat and bridge and dominoes and sixty-six, its chess tables presided over by the delightfully eccentric world's champion Nimzowitch, who would defeat you blindfold, but always brilliantly, simultaneously or one at a time, in charmingly baroque brief games for only two gold pieces per person per game (one gold piece to nutsy Nimzy, one to the DLG), and the supremely luxurious staterooms with costly veneers of mahogany over balsa; the hosts of attentive stewards, either as short and skinny as jockeys or else actual dwarfs, both types chosen to save weight; and the titanium elevator rising through the countless bags of helium to the two-decked Zenith Observatory, the sun deck wind-screened but roofless to let in the ever-changing clouds, the mysterious fog, the rays of the stars and good old Sol, and all the heavens. Ah, where else on land or sea could you buy such high living?

I called to mind in detail the single cabin which was always mine when I sailed on the *Ostwald—meine Stammkabine.* I visualized the Grand Corridor thronged with wealthy passengers in evening dress, the hand-some officers, the unobtrusive, ever-attentive stewards, the gleam of white shirtfronts, the glow of bare shoulders, the muted dazzle of jewels, the music of conversations like string quartets, the lilting low laughter that traveled along.

Exactly on time I did a neat *"Links, marschieren!"* ("To the left, march!") and passed through the impressive portals of the Empire State and across its towering lobby to the mutedly silver-doored banks of elevators. On my way I noted the silver-glowing date: 6 May 1937 and the time of day: 1:07 P.M. Good!—since the *Ostwald* did not cast off until the tick of 3 P.M., I would be left plenty of time for a leisurely lunch and good talk with my son, if he had remembered to meet me—and there was actually no doubt of that, since he is the most considerate and orderly minded of sons, a real German mentality, though I say it myself.

I headed for the express bank, enjoying my passage through the clusters of high-class people who thronged the lobby without any unseemly crowding, and placed myself before the doors designated "Dirigible Departure Lounge" and in briefer German *"Zum Zeppelin."*

The elevator hostess was an attractive Japanese girl in skirt of dull silver with the DLG Double Eagle and Dirigible insignia of the German Airship Union emblazoned in small on the left breast of her mutedly silver jacket. I noted with unvoiced approval that she appeared to have an excellent command of both German and English and was uniformly courteous to the passengers in her smiling but unemotional Nipponese fashion, which is so like our German scientific precision of speech, though without the latter's warm underlying passion. How good that our two federations, at opposite sides of the globe, have strong commercial and behavioral ties!

My fellow passengers in the lift, chiefly Americans and Germans, were of the finest type, very well dressed—except that just as the doors were about to close, there pressed in my doleful Jew in black. He seemed ill at ease, perhaps because of his shabby clothing. I was surprised, but made a point of being particularly polite toward him, giving him a slight bow and brief but friendly smile, while flashing my eyes. Jews have as much right to the acme of luxury travel as any other people on the planet, if they have the money—and most of them do.

During our uninterrupted and infinitely smooth passage upward, I touched my outside left breast pocket to reassure myself that my ticket —first class on the *Ostwald!*—and my papers were there. But actually I got far more reassurance and even secret joy from the feel and thought of the documents in my tightly zippered inside left breast pocket: the signed preliminary agreements that would launch America herself into the manufacture of passenger zeppelins. Modern Germany is always generous in sharing her great technical achievements with responsible sister nations, supremely confident that the genius of her scientists and engineers will continue to keep her well ahead of all other lands; and after all, the genius of two Americans, father and son, had made vital though indirect contributions to the development of safe airship travel (and not forgetting the part played by the Polish-born wife of the one and mother of the other).

The obtaining of those documents had been the chief and official reason for my trip to New York City, though I had been able to combine it most pleasurably with a long-overdue visit with my son, the social historian, and with his charming wife.

These happy reflections were cut short by the jarless arrival of our elevator at its lofty terminus on the one hundredth floor. The journey old love-smitten King Kong had made only after exhausting exertion we had accomplished effortlessly. The silvery doors spread wide. My fellow passengers hung back for a moment in awe and perhaps a little trepidation at the thought of the awesome journey ahead of them, and I —seasoned airship traveler that I am—was the first to step out, favoring with a smile and nod of approval my pert yet cool Japanese fellow employee of the lower echelons.

Hardly sparing a glance toward the great, fleckless window confronting the doors and showing a matchless view of Manhattan from an elevation of 1,250 feet minus two stories, I briskly turned, not right to the portals of the Departure Lounge and tower elevator, but left to those of the superb German restaurant *Krähennest* (Crow's Nest).

I passed between the flanking three-foot-high bronze statuettes of Thomas Edison and Marie Sklodowska Edison niched in one wall and those of Count von Zeppelin and Thomas Sklodowska Edison facing them from the other, and entered the select precincts of the finest German dining place outside the Fatherland. I paused while my eyes traveled searchingly around the room with its restful dark wood paneling deeply carved with beautiful representations of the Black Forest and its grotesque supernatural denizens—kobolds, elves, gnomes, dryads (tastefully sexy), and the like. They interested me since I am what Americans call a Sunday painter, though almost my sole subject matter is zeppelins seen against blue sky and airy, soaring clouds.

The *Oberkellner* came hurrying toward me with menu tucked under his left elbow and saying, *"Mein Herr!* Charmed to see you once more! I have a perfect table for one with porthole looking out across the Hudson."

But just then a youthful figure rose springily from behind a table set against the far wall, and a dear and familiar voice rang out to me with *"Hier, Papa!"*

*"Nein, Herr Ober,"* I smilingly told the headwaiter as I walked past him, *"heute hab' ich Gesellschaft, mein Sohn."*

I confidently made my way between tables occupied by well-dressed folk, both white and black.

My son wrung my hand with fierce family affection, though we had last parted only that morning. He insisted that I take the wide, dark, leather-upholstered seat against the wall, which gave me a fine view of the entire restaurant, while he took the facing chair.

"Because during this meal I wish to look only on you, Papa," he assured me with manly tenderness. "And we have at least an hour and a half together, Papa—I have checked your luggage through, and it is likely already aboard the *Ostwald."* Thoughtful, dependable boy!

"And now, Papa, what shall it be?" he continued after we had settled ourselves. "I see that today's special is *Sauerbraten mit Spätzel* and sweet-sour red cabbage. But there is also *Paprikahuhn* and—"

"Leave the chicken to flaunt her paprika in lonely red splendor today," I interrupted him. *"Sauerbraten* sounds fine."

Ordered by my Herr Ober, the aged wine waiter had already approached our table. I was about to give him direction when my son took upon himself that task with an authority and a hostfulness that warmed my heart. He scanned the wine menu rapidly but thoroughly.

"The Zinfandel 1933," he ordered with decision, though glancing my way to see if I concurred with his judgment. I smiled and nodded.

"And perhaps *ein Tröpfchen Schnapps* to begin with?" he suggested.

"A brandy?—yes!" I replied. "And not just a drop, either. Make it a double. It is not every day I lunch with that distinguished scholar, my son."

"Oh, Papa," he protested, dropping his eyes and almost blushing. Then firmly to the bent-backed, white-haired wine waiter, *"Schnapps also. Doppel."* The old waiter nodded his approval and hurried off.

We gazed fondly at each other for a few blissful seconds. Then I said, "Now tell me more fully about your achievements as a social historian on an exchange professorship in the New World. I know we have spoken about this several times, but only rather briefly and generally when various of your friends were present, or at least your lovely wife. Now I would like a more leisurely man-to-man account of your great work. Incidentally, do you find the scholarly apparatus—books, *und so weiter* ("et cetera")—of the Municipal Universities of New York City adequate to your needs after having enjoyed those of Baden-Baden University and the institutions of high learning in the German Federation?"

"In some respects they are lacking," he admitted. "However, for my purposes they have proved completely adequate." Then once more he dropped his eyes and almost blushed. "But, Papa, you praise my small efforts far too highly." He lowered his voice. "They do not compare with the victory for international industrial relations you yourself have won in a fortnight."

"All in a day's work for the DLG," I said self-deprecatingly, though once again lightly touching my left chest to establish contact with those most important documents safely stowed in my inside left breast pocket. "But now, no more polite fencing!" I went on briskly. "Tell me all about those 'small efforts,' as you modestly refer to them."

His eyes met mine. "Well, Papa," he began in suddenly matter-of-fact fashion, "all my work these last two years has been increasingly dominated by a firm awareness of the fragility of the underpinnings of the good world-society we enjoy today. If certain historically minute key events, or cusps, in only the past one hundred years had been decided differently—if another course had been chosen than the one that was—then the whole world might now be plunged in wars and worse horrors than we ever dream of. It is a chilling insight, but it bulks continually larger in my entire work, my every paper."

I felt the thrilling touch of inspiration. At that moment the wine waiter arrived with our double brandies in small goblets of cut glass. I wove the interruption into the fabric of my inspiration. "Let us drink then to what you name your chilling insight," I said. *"Prosit!"*

The bite and spreading warmth of the excellent *Schnapps* quickened my inspiration further. "I believe I understand exactly what you're getting at . . ." I told my son. I set down my half-emptied goblet and pointed at something over my son's shoulder.

He turned his head around, and after one glance back at my pointing finger, which intentionally waggled a tiny bit from side to side, he realized that I was not indicating the entry of the *Krähennest,* but the four sizable bronze statuettes flanking it.

"For instance," I said, "if Thomas Edison and Marie Sklodowska had not married, and especially if they had not had their super-genius son, then Edison's knowledge of electricity and hers of radium and other radioactives might never have been joined. There might never have been developed the fabulous T. S. Edison battery, which is the prime mover of all today's surface and air traffic. Those pioneering electric trucks introduced by *The Saturday Evening Post* in Philadelphia might have remained an expensive freak. And the gas helium might never have been produced industrially to supplement earth's meager subterranean supply."

My son's eyes brightened with the flame of pure scholarship. "Papa," he said eagerly, "you are a genius yourself! You have precisely hit on what is perhaps the most important of those cusp events I referred to. I am at this moment finishing the necessary research for a long paper on it. Do you know, Papa, that I have firmly established by researching Parisian records that there was in 1894 a close personal relationship between Marie Sklodowska and her fellow radium researcher Pierre Curie, and that she might well have become Madame Curie—or perhaps Madame Becquerel, for he too was in that work—if the dashing and brilliant Edison had not most opportunely arrived in Paris in December 1894 to sweep her off her feet and carry her off to the New World to even greater achievements?

"And just think, Papa," he went on, his eyes aflame, "what might have happened if their son's battery had not been invented—the most difficult technical achievement, hedged by all sorts of seeming scientific impossibilities, in the entire millennium-long history of industry. Why, Henry Ford might have manufactured automobiles powered by steam or by exploding natural gas or conceivably even vaporized liquid gasoline, rather than the mass-produced electric cars which have been such a boon to mankind everywhere—not our smokeless cars, but cars spouting all sorts of noxious fumes to pollute the environment."

Cars powered by the danger-fraught combustion of vaporized liquid gasoline!—it almost made me shudder and certainly it was a fantastic thought, yet not altogether beyond the bounds of possibility, I had to admit.

Just then I noticed my gloomy, black-clad Jew sitting only two tables away from us, though how he had got himself into the exclusive *Krähennest* was a wonder. Strange that I had missed his entry—probably immediately after my own, while I had eyes only for my son. His presence somehow threw a dark though only momentary shadow over my bright mood. Let him get some good German food inside him and some fine German wine, I thought generously—it will fill that empty belly of his and even put a bit of a good German smile into those sunken Yiddish cheeks! I combed my little mustache with my thumbnail and swept the errant lock of hair off my forehead.

Meanwhile my son was saying, "Also, Father, if electric transport had not been developed, and if during the last decade relations between Germany and the United States had not been so good, then we might never have gotten from the wells in Texas the supply of natural helium our zeppelins desperately needed during the brief but vital period before we had put the artificial creation of helium onto an industrial footing. My researchers at Washington have revealed that there was a strong movement in the U.S. military to ban the sale of helium to any other nation, Germany in particular. Only the powerful influence of Edison, Ford, and a few other key Americans, instantly brought to bear, prevented that stupid injunction. Yet if it had gone through, Germany might have been forced to use hydrogen instead of helium to float her passenger dirigibles. That was another crucial cusp."

"A hydrogen-supported zeppelin!—ridiculous! Such an airship would be a floating bomb, ready to be touched off by the slightest spark," I protested.

"Not ridiculous, Father," my son calmly contradicted me, shaking his head. "Pardon me for trespassing in your field, but there is an inescapable imperative about certain industrial developments. If there is not a safe road of advance, then a dangerous one will invariably be taken. You must admit, Father, that the development of commercial airships was in its early stages a most perilous venture. During the 1920s there were the dreadful wrecks of the American dirigibles *Roma,* and *Shenandoah,* which broke in two, *Akron,* and *Macon,* the British *R-38,* which also broke apart in the air, and *R-101,* the French *Dixmude,* which disappeared in the Mediterranean, Mussolini's *Italia,* which crashed trying to reach the North Pole, and the Russian *Maxim Gorky,* struck down by a plane, with a total loss of no fewer than 340 crew members for the nine accidents. If that had been followed by the explosions of two or three hydrogen zeppelins, world industry might well have abandoned forever the attempt to create passenger airships and turned instead to the development of large propeller-driven, heavier-than-air craft."

Monster airplanes, in danger every moment of crashing from engine failure, competing with good old unsinkable zeppelins?—impossible, at least at first thought. I shook my head, but not with as much conviction as I might have wished. My son's suggestion was really a valid one.

Besides, he had all his facts at his fingertips and was complete master of his subject, as I also had to allow. Those nine fearful airship disasters he mentioned had indeed occurred, as I knew well, and might have tipped the scale in favor of long-distance passenger and troop-carrying airplanes, had it not been for helium, the T. S. Edison battery, and German genius.

Fortunately I was able to dump from my mind these uncomfortable speculations and immerse myself in admiration of my son's multi-sided scholarship. That boy was a wonder!—a real chip off the old block, and, yes, a bit more.

"And now, Dolfy," he went on, using my nickname (I did not mind), "may I turn to an entirely different topic? Or rather to a very different example of my hypothesis of historical cusps?"

I nodded mutely. My mouth was busily full with fine *Sauerbraten* and those lovely, tiny German dumplings, while my nostrils enjoyed the unique aroma of sweet-sour red cabbage. I had been so engrossed in my son's revelations that I had not consciously noted our luncheon being served. I swallowed, took a slug of the good red Zinfandel, and said, "Please go on."

"It's about the consequences of the American Civil War, Father," he said surprisingly. "Did you know that in the decade after that bloody conflict, there was a very real danger that the whole cause of Negro freedom and rights—for which the war was fought, whatever they say—might well have been completely smashed? The fine work of Abraham Lincoln, Thaddeus Stevens, Charles Sumner, the Freedmen's Bureau, and the Union League Clubs put to naught? And even the Ku Klux Klan underground allowed free reign rather than being sternly repressed? Yes, Father, my thoroughgoing researchings have convinced me such things might easily have happened, resulting in some sort of reenslavement of the blacks, with the whole war to be refought at an indefinite future date, or at any rate Reconstruction brought to a dead halt for many decades—with what disastrous effects on the American character, turning its deep simple faith in freedom to hypocrisy, it is impossible to exaggerate. I have published a sizable paper on this subject in the *Journal of Civil War Studies*."

I nodded somberly. Quite a bit of this new subject matter of his was *terra incognita* to me; yet I knew enough of American history to realize he had made a cogent point. More than ever before, I was impressed by his multifaceted learning—he was indubitably a figure in the great tradition of German scholarship, a profound thinker, broad and deep. How fortunate to be his father. Not for the first time, but perhaps with the greatest sincerity yet, I thanked God and the Laws of Nature that I had early moved my family from Braunau, Austria, where I had been born in 1889, to Baden-Baden, where he had grown up in the ambience of the great new university on the edge of the Black Forest and only 150 kilometers from Count Zeppelin's dirigible factory in Württemberg, at Friedrichshafen on Lake Constance.

I raised my glass of *Kirschwasser* to him in a solemn, silent toast—we had somehow got to that stage in our meal—and downed a sip of the potent, fiery, white cherry brandy.

He leaned toward me and said, "I might as well tell you, Dolf, that my big book, at once popular and scholarly, my *Meisterwerk,* to be titled *If Things Had Gone Wrong,* or perhaps *If Things Had Turned for the Worse,* will deal solely—though illuminated by dozens of diverse examples—with my theory of historical cusps, a highly speculative concept but firmly footed in fact." He glanced at his wristwatch, muttered, "Yes, there's still time for it. So now"—his face grew grave, his voice clear though small—"I will venture to tell you about one more cusp, the most disputable and yet most crucial of them all." He paused. "I warn you, dear Dolf, that this cusp may cause you pain."

"I doubt that," I told him indulgently. "Anyhow, go ahead."

"Very well. In November of 1918, when the British had broken the Hindenburg Line and the weary German army was defiantly dug in along the Rhine, and just before the Allies, under Marshal Foch, launched the final crushing drive which would cut a bloody swath across the heartland to Berlin—"

I understood his warning at once. Memories flamed in my mind like the sudden blinding flares of the battlefield with their deafening thunder. The company I had commanded had been among the most desperately defiant of those he mentioned, heroically nerved for a last-ditch resistance. And then Foch had delivered that last vast blow, and we had fallen back and back and back before the overwhelming numbers of our enemies with their field guns and tanks and armored cars innumerable and above all their huge aerial armadas of De Haviland and Handley-Page and other big bombers escorted by insect-buzzing fleets of Spads and other fighters shooting to bits our last Fokkers and Pfalzes and visiting on Germany a destruction greater far than our zeps had worked on England. Back, back, back, endlessly reeling and regrouping, across the devastated German countryside, a dozen times decimated yet still defiant until the end came at last amid the ruins of Berlin, and the most bold among us had to admit we were beaten and we surrendered unconditionally—

These vivid, fiery recollections came to me almost instantaneously.

I heard my son continuing, "At that cusp moment in November 1918, Dolf, there existed a very strong possibility—I have established this beyond question—that an immediate armistice would be offered and signed, and the war ended inconclusively. President Wilson was wavering, the French were very tired, and so on.

"And if that had happened in actuality—harken closely to me now, Dolf—then the German temper entering the decade of the 1920s would have been entirely different. She would have felt she had not been really licked, and there would inevitably have been a secret recrudescence of pan-German militarism. German scientific humanism would not have won its total victory over the Germany of the—yes!—Huns.

"As for the Allies, self-tricked out of the complete victory which lay within their grasp, they would in the long run have treated Germany far less generously than they did after their lust for revenge had been sated by that last drive to Berlin. The League of Nations would not have become the strong instrument for world peace that it is today; it might well have been repudiated by America and certainly secretly detested by Germany. Old wounds would not have healed because, paradoxically, they would not have been deep enough.

"There, I've said my say. I hope it hasn't bothered you too badly, Dolf."

I let out a gusty sigh. Then my wincing frown was replaced by a brow serene. I said very deliberately, "Not one bit, my son, though you have certainly touched my own old wounds to the quick. Yet I feel in my bones that your interpretation is completely valid. Rumors of an armistice were indeed running like wildfire through our troops in that black autumn of 1918. And I know only too well that if there had been an armistice at that time, then officers like myself would have believed that the German soldier had never really been defeated, only betrayed by his leaders and by Red incendiaries, and we would have begun to conspire endlessly for a resumption of the war under happier circumstances. My son, let us drink to your amazing cusps."

Our tiny glasses touched with a delicate ting, and the last drops went down of biting, faintly bitter *Kirschwasser*. I buttered a thin slice of pumpernickel and nibbled it—always good to finish off a meal with bread. I was suddenly filled with an immeasurable content. It was a golden moment, which I would have been happy to have go on forever, while I listened to my son's wise words and fed my satisfaction in him. Yes, indeed, it was a golden nugget of pause in the terrible rush of time —the enriching conversation, the peerless food and drink, the darkly pleasant surroundings—

At that moment I chanced to look at my discordant Jew two tables away. For some weird reason he was glaring at me with naked hate, though he instantly dropped his gaze—

But even that strange and disquieting event did not disrupt my mood of golden tranquillity, which I sought to prolong by saying in summation, "My dear son, this has been the most exciting though eerie lunch I have ever enjoyed. Your remarkable cusps have opened to me a fabulous world in which I can nevertheless utterly believe. A horridly fascinating world of sizzling hydrogen zeppelins, of countless evil-smelling gasoline cars built by Ford instead of his electrics, of re-enslaved American blackamoors, of Madame Becquerels or Curies, a world without the T. S. Edison battery and even T.S. himself, a world in which German scientists are sinister pariahs instead of tolerant, humanitarian, great-souled leaders of world thought, a world in which a mateless old Edison tinkers forever at a powerful storage battery he cannot perfect, a world in which Woodrow Wilson doesn't insist on Germany being admitted at once to the League of Nations, a world of festering hatreds reeling toward a second and worse world war. Oh, altogether an incredible world, yet one in which you have momentarily made me believe, to the extent that I do actually have the fear that time will suddenly shift gears and we will be plunged into that bad dream world, and our real world will become a dream—"

I suddenly chanced to see the face of my watch—

At the same time my son looked at his own left wrist—

"Dolf," he said, springing up in agitation, "I do hope that with my stupid chatter I haven't made you miss—"

I had sprung up too—

"No, no, my son," I heard myself say in a fluttering voice, "but it's true I have little time in which to catch the *Ostwald. Auf Wiedersehen, mein Sohn, auf Wiedersehen!*"

And with that I was hastening, indeed almost running, or else sweeping through the air like a ghost—leaving him behind to settle our reckoning—across a room that seemed to waver with my feverish agitation, alternately darkening and brightening like an electric bulb with its fine tungsten filament about to fly to powder and wink out forever—

Inside my head a voice was saying in calm yet death-knell tones, "The lights of Europe are going out. I do not think they will be rekindled in my generation—"

Suddenly the only important thing in the world for me was to catch the *Ostwald,* get aboard her before she unmoored. That and only that would reassure me that I was in my rightful world. I would touch and feel the *Ostwald,* not just talk about her—

As I dashed between the four bronze figures, they seemed to hunch down and become deformed, while their faces became those of grotesque, aged witches—four evil kobolds leering up at me with a horrid knowledge bright in their eyes—

While behind me I glimpsed in pursuit a tall, black, white-faced figure, skeletally lean—

The strangely short corridor ahead of me had a blank end—the Departure Lounge wasn't there—

I instantly jerked open the narrow door to the stairs and darted nimbly up them as if I were a young man again and not forty-eight years old—

On the third sharp turn I risked a glance behind and down—

Hardly a flight behind me, taking great pursuing leaps, was my dreadful Jew—

I tore open the door to the hundred and second floor. There at last, only a few feet away, was the silver door I sought of the final elevator and softly glowing above it the words *"Zum Zeppelin."* At last I would be shot aloft to the *Ostwald* and reality.

But the sign began to blink as the *Krähennest* had, while across the door was pasted askew a white cardboard sign which read "Out of Order."

I threw myself at the door and scrabbled at it, squeezing my eyes several times to make my vision come clear. When I finally fully opened them, the cardboard sign was gone.

But the silver door was gone too, and the words above it forever. I was scrabbling at seamless pale plaster.

There was a touch on my elbow. I spun around.

"Excuse me, sir, but you seem troubled," my Jew said solicitously. "Is there anything I can do?"

I shook my head, but whether in negation or rejection or to clear it, I don't know. "I'm looking for the *Ostwald,*" I gasped, only now realizing

I'd winded myself on the stairs. "For the zeppelin," I explained when he looked puzzled.

I may be wrong, but it seemed to me that a look of secret glee flashed deep in his eyes, though his general sympathetic expression remained unchanged.

"Oh, the zeppelin," he said in a voice that seemed to me to have become sugary in its solicitude. "You must mean the *Hindenburg.*"

*Hindenburg?* I asked myself. There was no zeppelin named *Hindenburg.* Or was there? Could it be that I was mistaken about such a simple and, one would think, immutable matter? My mind had been getting very foggy the last minute or two. Desperately I tried to assure myself that I was indeed myself and in my right world. My lips worked and I muttered to myself, *Bin Adolf Hitler, Zeppelin Fachmann. . . .*

"But the *Hindenburg* doesn't land here, in any case," my Jew was telling me, "though I think some vague intention once was voiced about topping the Empire State with a mooring mast for dirigibles. Perhaps you saw some news story and assumed—"

His face fell, or he made it seem to fall. The sugary solicitude in his voice became unendurable as he told me, "But apparently you can't have heard today's tragic news. Oh, I do hope you weren't seeking the *Hindenburg* so as to meet some beloved family member or close friend. Brace yourself, sir. Only hours ago, coming in for her landing at Lakehurst, New Jersey, the *Hindenburg* caught fire and burned up entire in a matter of seconds. Thirty or forty at least of her passengers and crew were burned alive. Oh, steady yourself, sir."

"But the *Hindenburg*—I mean the *Ostwald!*—couldn't burn like that," I protested. "She's a helium zeppelin."

He shook his head. "Oh, no. I'm no scientist, but I know the *Hindenburg* was filled with hydrogen—a wholly typical bit of reckless German risk-running. At least we've never sold helium to the Nazis, thank God."

I stared at him, wavering my face from side to side in feeble denial. While he stared back at me with obviously a new thought in mind.

"Excuse me once again," he said, "but I believe I heard you start to say something about Adolf Hitler. I suppose you know that you bear a certain resemblance to that execrable dictator. If I were you, sir, I'd shave my mustache."

I felt a wave of fury at this inexplicable remark with all its baffling references, yet withal a remark delivered in the unmistakable tones of an insult. And then all my surroundings momentarily reddened and flickered, and I felt a tremendous wrench in the inmost core of my being, the sort of wrench one might experience in transiting timelessly from one universe into another parallel to it. Briefly I became a man still named Adolf Hitler, same as the Nazi dictator and almost the same age, a German-American born in Chicago, who had never visited Germany or spoke German, whose friends teased him about his chance resemblance to the other Hitler, and who used stubbornly to say, "No, I won't change my name! Let that *Führer* bastard across the Atlantic change his! Ever hear about the British Winston Churchill writing the American Winston Churchill, who wrote *The Crisis* and other novels, and suggesting he change his name to avoid confusion, since the Englishman had done some writing too? The American wrote back it was a good idea, but since he was three years older, he was senior and so the Britisher should change *his* name. That's exactly how I feel about that son of a bitch Hitler."

The Jew still stared at me sneeringly. I started to tell him off, but then I was lost in a second weird, wrenching transition. The first had been directly from one parallel universe to another. The second was also in time—I aged fourteen or fifteen years in a single infinite instant while transiting from 1937 (where I had been born in 1889 and was forty-eight) to 1973 (where I had been born in 1910 and was sixty-three). My name changed back to my truly own (but what is that?), and I no longer looked one bit like Adolf Hitler the Nazi dictator (or dirigible expert?), and I had a married son who was a sort of social historian in a New York City municipal university, and he had many brilliant theories, but none of historical cusps.

And the Jew—I mean the tall, thin man in black with possibly Semitic features—was gone. I looked around and around but there was no one there.

I touched my outside left breast pocket, then my hand darted tremblingly underneath. There was no zipper on the pocket inside and no precious documents, only a couple of grimy envelopes with notes I'd scribbled on them in pencil.

I don't know how I got out of the Empire State Building. Presumably by elevator. Though all my memory holds for that period is a persistent image of King Kong tumbling down from its top like a ridiculous yet poignantly pitiable giant teddy bear.

I do recollect walking in a sort of trance for what seemed hours through a Manhattan stinking with monoxide and carcinogens innumerable, half waking from time to time (usually while crossing streets that snarled, not purred), and then relapsing into trance. There were big dogs.

When I at last fully came to myself, I was walking down a twilit Hudson Street at the north end of Greenwich Village. My gaze was fixed on a distant and unremarkable pale-gray square of building top. I guessed it must be that of the World Trade Center, 1,350 feet tall.

And then it was blotted out by the grinning face of my son, the professor.

"Justin!" I said.

"Fritz!" he said. "We'd begun to worry a bit. Where did you get off to, anyhow? Not that it's a damn bit of my business. If you had an assignation with a go-go girl, you needn't tell me."

"Thanks," I said, "I do feel tired, I must admit, and somewhat cold. But no, I was just looking at some of my old stamping grounds," I told him, "and taking longer than I realized. Manhattan's changed during my years on the West Coast, but not all that much."

"It's getting chilly," he said. "Let's stop in at that place ahead with the black front. It's the White Horse. Dylan Thomas used to drink there. He's supposed to have scribbled a poem on the wall of the can, only they painted it over. But it has the authentic sawdust."

"Good," I said, "only we'll make mine coffee, not ale. Or if I can't get coffee, then cola."

I am not really a *Prosit!*-type person.

*1977*
*35th CONVENTION*
*MIAMI BEACH*

# Spider Robinson

Spider Robinson was born in 1945, and I find this incredible. How can anyone be so young?

Just think! Franklin Roosevelt and Adolf Hitler died the year he was born. They're history to him. World War II ended the year he was born. He probably doesn't even remember the Korean War.

Worse yet is the comparison to *me*. When he was a mere infant, mewling and pewking in the nurse's arms (to coin a phrase), I was a married man. I had already been a professional writer for seven years.

Why am I making a fuss over this? Because Spider Robinson, despite his extreme youth, is a powerhouse writer and to have him be so good so young makes me nervous. I don't know why it should, but it does. For one thing, it's unfair. If I try hard to improve myself, I might get to be that good, too; but what do I do to get that young?

To be sure, this is Spider's first appearance in these volumes but that doesn't mean that he is a stranger to convention triumphs. His first published story appeared in 1973, and at the 1974 convention he shared the John W. Campbell Award with Lisa Tuttle, an award given the most promising new writers. (Fortunately, in 1939, when my first story appeared, there was no John W. Campbell Award, or even its equivalent. If there had been, it would have been shared by Robert Heinlein and A. E. van Vogt for that year, and I would have finished in 491st place—though that high a position would only be conceded, I suspect, by my own prejudiced opinion.)

Spider's first novel, *Telempath*, appeared in 1976, and the novella that won the Hugo the very next year, the one you're about to read, represents a version of the first four chapters of the novel.

This, by the way—the excerpting of novels by the s.f. magazines—is something new in science fiction.

In the old days (before Spider was born), very few science fiction novels were written, and those that *were* written were specifically intended for the magazines, because science fiction did not appear in either hard-cover or soft-cover book form. The novels would appear, usually, as three-part serials (though anything from two to six parts was possible).

Nowadays, however, many novels are written primarily for the book trade, and there is a reluctance to allow them to be serialized because that might delay publication unduly. Besides which, the magazines would like to have some of three or four of them, rather than all of one of them. So they excerpt.

I would object out of my great feeling for the purity of the art. Unfortunately, my own most recent novels were excerpted by magazines. One had three different portions excerpted in three different magazines. That, somehow, puts a different light on things. To be sure, I had nothing to do with it; it was my publisher who made the arrangement. Nevertheless, I found my attitude toward excerpting grow considerably more tolerant as a result. I'm not sure why that should be.

In one respect, by the way, Spider didn't get off scot-free. He didn't win an uncontested Hugo. The novella award at the 1977 convention ended in a tie. (Each tie winner gets a whole Hugo, however, with no indication on either of the other.)

Well, I don't cheat. If two novellas win, my Gentle Readers get two novellas. The second one follows immediately after this one.

# BY ANY OTHER NAME

*There's winds out on the ocean*
*Blowin' wherever they choose.*
*The winds ain't got no emotion, babe:*
*They don't know the blues.*
        *—traditional*

### CHAPTER ONE

*Excerpt from the Journal of Isham Stone*

I hadn't meant to shoot the cat.

I hadn't meant to shoot anything, for that matter—the pistol at my hip was strictly defensive armament at the moment. But my adrenals were on overtime and my peripheral vision was straining to meet itself behind my head—when something appeared before me with no warning at all, my subconscious sentries opted for the Best Defense. I was down and rolling before I knew I'd fired, through a doorway I hadn't known was there.

I fetched up with a heart-stopping crash against the foot of a staircase just inside the door. The impact dislodged something on the first-floor landing; it rolled heavily down the steps and sprawled across me: the upper portion of a skeleton, largely intact from the sixth vertebra up. As I lurched in horror to my feet, long-dead muscle and cartilage crumbled at last, and random bones skittered across the dusty floor. Three inches above my left elbow, someone was playing a drumroll with knives.

Cautiously I hooked an eye around the doorframe, at about knee level. The smashed remains of what had recently been a gray-and-white Persian tom lay against a shattered fire hydrant whose faded red surface was spattered with brighter red and less appealing colors. Overworked imagination produced the odor of singed meat.

I'm as much cat people as the One-Sleeved Mandarin, and three shocks in quick succession, in the condition I was in, were enough to override all the iron discipline of Collaci's training. Eyes stinging, I stumbled out onto the sidewalk, uttered an unspellable sound, and pumped three slugs into a wrecked '82 Buick lying on its right side across the street.

I was pretty badly rattled—only the third slug hit the exposed gas tank. But it was magnesium, not lead: the car went up with a very satisfactory roar and the prettiest fireball you ever saw. The left rear wheel was blown high in the air; it soared gracefully over my head, bounced off a fourth-floor fire escape, and came down flat and hard an inch behind me. Concrete buckled.

When my ears had stopped ringing and my eyes uncrossed, I became aware that I was rigid as a statue. *So much for catharsis,* I thought vaguely, and relaxed with an effort that hurt all over.

The cat was still dead.

I saw almost at once why he had startled me so badly. The tobacconist's display window from which he had leaped was completely shattered, so my subconscious sentries had incorrectly tagged it as one of the rare unbroken ones. Therefore, they reasoned, the hurtling object must be in fact emerging from the open door just beyond the window. Anything coming out a doorway that high from the ground just had to be a Musky, and my hand is *much* quicker than my eye.

Now that my eye had caught up, of course, I realized that I couldn't possibly track a Musky by eye. Which was exactly why I'd been keyed up enough to waste irreplaceable ammo and give away my position in the first place. Carlson had certainly made life complicated for me. I hoped I could manage to kill him slowly.

This was no consolation to the cat. I looked down at my Musky gun, and found myself thinking of the day I got it, just three months past. The first gun I had ever owned myself, symbol of man's estate, *mine* for as long as it took me to kill Carlson, and for as long afterwards as I lived. After my father had presented it to me publicly, and formally charged me with the avenging of the human race, the friends and neighbors—and dark-eyed Alia—had scurried safely inside for the ceremonial banquet. But my father took me aside. We walked in silence through the West Forest to Mama's grave, and through the trees the setting sun over West Mountain looked like a knothole in the wall of Hell. Dad turned to me at last, pride and paternal concern fighting for control of his ebony features, and said, "Isham . . . Isham, I wasn't much older than you when I got my first gun. That was long ago and far away, in a place called Montgomery—things were different then. But some things never change." He tugged an earlobe reflectively, and continued, "Phil Collaci has taught you well, but sometimes he'd rather shoot first and ask directions later. Isham, you just can't go blazing away indiscriminately. Not *ever*. You hear me?"

The crackling of the fire around the ruined Buick brought me back to the present. Damn, you called it again Dad, I thought as I shivered there on the sidewalk. You *can't* go blazing away indiscriminately.

Not even here in New York City.

It was getting late, and my left arm ached abominably where Grey Brother had marked me—I reminded myself sharply that I was here on business. I had no wish to pass a night in any city, let alone this one, so I continued on up the street, examining every building I passed with extreme care. If Carlson had ears, he now knew someone was in New York, and he might figure out why. I was on his home territory—every alleyway and manhole was a potential ambush.

There were stores and shops of every conceivable kind, commerce more fragmented and specialized than I had ever seen before. Some shops dealt only in a *single item*. Some I could make no sense of at all. What the hell is an "rko"?

I kept to the sidewalk where I could. I told myself I was being foolish, that I was no less conspicuous to Carlson or a Musky than if I'd stood on second base at the legendary Shea Stadium, and that the street held no surprise tomcats. But I kept to the sidewalk where I could. I remember Mama—a *long* time ago—telling me not to go in the street or the monsters would get me.

They got her.

Twice I was forced off the curb, once by a subway entrance and once by a supermarket. Dad had seen to it that I had the best plugs Fresh Start had to offer, but they weren't *that* good. Both times I hurried back to the sidewalk and was thoroughly disgusted with my pulse rate. But I never looked over my shoulder. Collaci says there's no sense being scared when it can't help you—and the fiasco with the cat proved him right.

It was early afternoon, and the same sunshine that was warming the forests and fields and work zones of Fresh Start my home seemed to chill the air here, accentuating the barren emptiness of the ruined city. Silence and desolation were all around me as I walked, bleached bones and crumbling brick. Carlson had been efficient, all right, nearly as efficient as the atomic bomb folks used to be so scared of once. It seemed as though I were in some immense Devil's Autoclave that ignored filth and grime but grimly scrubbed out life of any kind.

Wishful thinking, I decided, and shook my head to banish the fantasy. If the city had been truly lifeless, I'd be approaching Carlson from uptown—I would never have had to detour as far south as the Lincoln Tunnel, and my left arm would not have ached so terribly. Grey Brother is extremely touchy about his territorial rights.

I decided to replace the makeshift dressing over the torn biceps. I didn't like the drumming insistence of the pain: it kept me awake but interfered with my concentration. I ducked into the nearest store that looked defensible, and found myself sprawled on the floor behind an overturned table, wishing mightily that it weren't so flimsy.

Something had moved.

Then I rose sheepishly to my feet, holstering my heater and rapping my subconscious sentries sharply across the knuckles for the second time in half an hour. My own face looked back at me from the grimy mirror that ran along one whole wall, curly black hair in tangles, wide lips stretched back in what looked just like a grin. It wasn't a grin. I hadn't realized how bad I looked.

Dad has told me a lot about Civilization, before the Exodus, but I don't suppose I'll ever understand it. A glance around this room raised more questions than it answered. On my left, opposite the long mirror, were a series of smaller mirrors that paralleled it for three-quarters of its length, with odd-looking chairs before them. Something like armchairs made of metal, padded where necessary, with levers to raise and lower them. On my right, below the longer mirror, were a lot of smaller, much plainer wooden chairs, in a tight row broken occasionally by strange frameworks from which lengths of rotting fabric dangled. I could only surmise that this was some sort of arcane narcissist's paradise, where men of large ego would come, remove their clothing, recline in luxuriously upholstered seats, and contemplate their own magnificence. The smaller, shabbier seats, too low to afford a decent view, no doubt represented the cut-rate or second-class accommodations.

But what was the significance of the cabinets between the larger chairs and the wall, laden with bottles and plastic containers and heathen appliances? And why were all the skeletons in the room huddled together in the middle of the floor, as though their last seconds of life had been spent frantically fighting over something?

Something gleamed in the bone heap, and I saw what the poor bastards had died fighting for, and knew what kind of place this had been. The contested prize was a straight razor.

My father had spent eighteen of my twenty years telling me why I ought to hate Wendell Carlson, and in the past few days I'd acquired nearly as many reasons of my own. I intended to put them in Carlson's obituary.

A wave of weariness passed over me. I moved to one of the big chairs, pressed gingerly down on the seat to make sure no cunning mechanism awaited my mass to trigger it (Collaci's training again—if Teach' ever gets to Heaven, he'll check it for booby traps), took off my rucksack, and sat down. As I unrolled the bandage around my arm I glanced at myself in the mirror and froze, struck with wonder. An infinite series of me's stretched out into eternity, endless thousands of Isham Stones caught in that frozen second of time that holds endless thousands of possible futures, on the point of some unimaginable cusp. I knew it was simply the opposed mirrors, the one before me slightly askew, and could have predicted the phenomenon had I thought about it—but I was not expecting it and had never seen anything like it in my life. All at once I was enormously tempted to sit back, light a joint from the first-aid kit in my rucksack, and meditate a while. I wondered what Alia was doing right now, right at this moment. Hell, I could kill Carlson at twilight, and sleep in his bed—or hole up here and get him tomorrow, or the next day. When I was feeling better.

Then I saw the first image in line. Me. A black man just doesn't bruise spectacularly as a rule, but there was something colorful over my right eye that would do until a bruise came along. I was filthy, I needed a shave, and the long slash running from my left eye to my upper lip looked angry. My black turtleneck was torn in three places that I could see, dirty where it wasn't torn, and bloodstained where it wasn't dirty. It might be a long time before I felt any better than I did right now.

Then I looked down at what was underneath the gauze I'd just peeled off, saw the black streaks on the chocolate brown of my arm, and the temptation to set a spell vanished like an overheated Musky.

I looked closer, and began whistling "Good Morning, Heartache" through my teeth very softly. I had no more neosulfa, damned little bandage for that matter, and it looked like I should save what analgesics I had to smoke on the way home. The best thing I could do for myself was to finish up in the city and get gone, find a Healer before my arm rotted.

And all at once that was fine with me. I remembered the two sacred duties that had brought me to New York; one to my father and my people, and one to myself. I had nearly died proving to my satisfaction that the latter was impossible; the other would keep me no great long time. New York and I were, as Bierce would say, incompossible.

One way or another, it would all be over soon.

I carefully rebandaged the gangrenous arm, hoisted the rucksack, and went back outside, popping a foodtab and a very small dosage of speed as I walked. There's no point in bringing real food to New York—you can't taste it anyway and it masses so damned much.

The sun was perceptibly lower in the sky—the day was in catabolism. I shifted my shoulders to settle the pack and continued on up the street, my eyes straining to decipher faded signs.

Two blocks up I found a shop that had specialized in psychedelia. A '69 Ford shared the display window with several smashed hookahs and a narghile or two. I paused there, sorely tempted again. A load of pipes and papers would be worth a good bit at home; Techno and Agro alike would pay dearly for fine-tooled smoking goods—more evidence that, as Dad is always saying, technology's usefulness has outlasted it.

But that reminded me of my mission again, and I shook my head savagely to drive away the daydreaming that sought to delay me. I was —what was that phrase Dad had used at my arming ceremony?—"The Hand of Man Incarnate," that was it, the product of two years of personal combat training and eighteen years of racial hatred. After I finished the job I could rummage around in crumbling deathtraps for hash pipes and roach clips—my last detour had nearly killed me, miles to the north.

But I'd *had* to try. I was only two at the time of the Exodus, too young to retain much but a confused impression of universal terror, of random horror and awful revulsion everywhere. But I remember one incident very clearly. I remember my brother Israfel, all of eight years old, kneeling down in the middle of 116th Street and methodically smashing his head against the pavement. Long after Izzy's eight-year-old brains had splashed the concrete, his little body continued to slam the shattered skull down again and again in a literally mindless spasm of escape. I saw this over my mother's shoulder as she ran, screaming her fear, through the chaotically twisting nightmare that for as long as she could remember had been only a quietly throbbing nightmare, as she ran through Harlem.

Once when I was twelve I watched an Agro slaughter a chicken, and when the headless carcass got up and ran about I heard my mother's scream again. It was coming from my throat. Dad tells me I was unconscious for four days and woke up screaming.

Even here, even downtown, where the bones sprawled everywhere were those of strangers, I was wound up tight enough to burst, and ancient reflex fought with modern wisdom as I felt the irrational impulse to lift my head and cast about for an enemy's scent. I had failed to recover Izzy's small bones; Grey Brother, who had always lived in Harlem, now ruled it, and sharp indeed were his teeth. I had managed to hold off the chittering pack with incendiaries until I reached the Hudson, and they would not cross the bridge to pursue me. And so I lived—at least until gangrene got me.

And the only thing between me and Fresh Start was Carlson. I saw again in my mind's eye the familiar Carlson Poster, the first thing my father ran off when he got access to a mimeograph machine: a remarkably detailed sketch of thin, academic features surrounded by a mass of graying hair, with the legend: WANTED: FOR THE MURDER OF HUMAN CIVILIZATION—WENDELL MORGAN CARLSON. An unlimited lifetime supply of hot-shot shells will be given to anyone bringing the head to the Council of Fresh Start.

No one ever took Dad up on it—at least, no one who survived to collect. And so it looked like it was up to me to settle the score for a shattered era and a planetful of corpses. The speed was taking hold now; I felt an exalted sense of destiny, and a fever to be about it. I was the duly chosen instrument for mankind's revenge, and that reckoning was long overdue.

I unclipped one of the remaining incendiary grenades from my belt—it comforted me to hold that much raw power in my hand—and kept on walking uptown, feeling infinitely more than twenty years old. And as I stalked my prey through concrete canyons and brownstone foothills, I found myself thinking of his crime, of the twisted motives that had produced this barren jungle and countless hundreds like it. I remembered my father's eyewitness account of Carlson's actions, repeated so many times during my youth that I could almost recite it verbatim, heard again the Genesis of the world I knew from its first historian—my father, Jacob Stone. Yes, *that* Stone, the one man Carlson never expected to survive, to shout across a smashed planet the name of its unknown assassin. Jacob Stone, who first cried the name that became a curse, a blasphemy and a scream of rage in the throats of all humankind. Jacob Stone, who named our betrayer: Wendell Morgan Carlson!

And as I reviewed that grim story, I kept my hand near the rifle with which I hoped to write its happy ending. . . .

### CHAPTER TWO

*Excerpts from* I WORKED WITH CARLSON, *by Jacob Stone, Ph.D., authorized version: Fresh Start Press, 1986 (Mimeo).*

. . . The sense of smell is a curious phenomenon, oddly resistant to measurement or rigorous analysis. Each life form on Earth appears to have as much of it as they need to survive, plus a little. The natural human sense of smell, for instance, was always more efficient than most people realized, so much so that in the 1880s the delightfully eccentric Sir Francis Galton had actually succeeded, by associating numbers with certain scents, in *training himself to add and subtract by smell,* apparently just for the intellectual exercise.

But through a sort of neurological suppressor circuit of which next to nothing is known, most people contrived to ignore all but the most pleasing or disturbing of the messages their noses brought them, perhaps by way of reaction to a changing world in which a finely tuned olfactory apparatus became a nuisance rather than a survival aid. The level of sensitivity which a wolf requires to find food would be a hindrance to a civilized human packed into a city of his fellows.

By 1983, Professor Wendell Morgan Carlson had raised olfactometry to the level of a precise science. In the course of testing the theories of Beck and Miles, Carlson almost absentmindedly perfected the classic "blast-injection" technique of measuring differential sensitivity in olfaction, *without regard for the subjective impressions of the test subject.* This not only refined his data, but also enabled him to work with life forms other than human, a singular advantage when one considers how much of the human brain is terra incognita.

His first subsequent experiments indicated that the average wolf utilized his sense of smell on the order of a thousand times more efficiently than a human. Carlson perceived that wolves lived in a world of scents, as rich and intricate as our human worlds of sight and word. To his surprise, however, he discovered that the *potential* sensitivity of the human olfactory apparatus far outstripped that of any known species.

This intrigued him. . . .


. . . Wendell Morgan Carlson, the greatest biochemist Columbia—and perhaps the world—had ever seen, was living proof of the truism that a genius can be a damned fool outside his own specialty.

Genius he unquestionably was; it was *not* serendipity that brought him the Nobel Prize for isolating a cure for the entire spectrum of virus infections called "the common cold." Rather it was the sort of inspired accident that comes only to those brilliant enough to perceive it, fanatic seekers like Pasteur.

But Pasteur was a boor and a braggart who frittered away valuable time in childish feuds with men unfit to wash out his test tubes. Genius is seldom a good character reference.

Carlson was a left-wing radical.

Worse, he was the type of radical who dreams of romantic exploits in a celluloid underground: grim-eyed rebels planting homemade bombs, assassinating the bloated oppressors in their very strongholds and (although he certainly knew what hydrogen sulfide was) escaping through the city sewers.

It never occurred to him that it takes a very special kind of man to be a guerrilla. He was convinced that the moral indignation he had acquired at Washington in '71 (during his undergraduate days) would see him through hardships and privation, and he would have been horrified if someone had pointed out to him that Che Guevera seldom had access to toilet paper. Never having experienced hunger, he thought it a glamorous state. He lived a compartmentalized life, and his wild talent for biochemistry had the thickest walls: only within them was he capable of logic or true intuition. He had spent a disastrous adolescent year in a seminary, enlisted as a "storm trooper of Mary," and had come out of it apostate but still saddled with a relentless need to Serve a Cause—and it chanced that the cry in 1982 was, once again, "Revolution Now!"

He left the cloistered halls of Columbia in July of that year, and applied to the smaller branch—the so-called Action-Faction—of the New Weathermen for a position as assassin. Fortunately he was taken for crazy and thrown out. The African Liberation Front was somewhat less discerning—they broke his leg in three places. In the Emergency Room of Jacobi Hospital Carlson came to the conclusion that the trouble with Serving a Cause was that it involved associating with unperceptive and dangerously unpredictable people. What he needed was a One-Man Cause.

And then, at the age of thirty-two, his emotions noticed his intellect for the first time.

When the two parts of him came together, they achieved critical mass— and that was a sad day for the world. I myself bear part of the blame for that coming-together—unwittingly I provided one of the final sparks, put forward an idea which sent Carlson on the most dangerous intuitive leap of his life. My own feelings of guilt for this will plague me to my dying day— and yet it might have been anyone. Or no one.

Fresh from a three-year stint doing biowar research for the Defense Department, I was a very minor colleague of Carlson's, but quickly found myself becoming a close friend. Frankly I was flattered that a man of his stature would speak to me, and I suspect Carlson was overjoyed to find a black man who would treat him as an equal.

But for reasons which are very difficult to explain to anyone who did not live through that period—and which need no explanation for those who did—I was reluctant to discuss the ALF with a honky, however "enlightened." And so when I went to visit Carlson in Jacobi Hospital and the conversation turned to the self-defeating nature of uncontrollable rage, I attempted to distract the patient with a hasty change of subject.

"The Movement's turning rancid, Jake," Carlson had just muttered, and an excellent digression occurred to me.

"Wendell," I said heedlessly, "do you realize that you personally are in a position to make this a better world?"

His eyes lit up. "How's that?"

"You are probably the world's greatest authority on olfactometry and the human olfactory apparatus, among other things—right?"

"As for as there is one, I suppose so. What of it?" He shifted uneasily within his traction gear: wearing his radical *persona,* he was made uncomfortable by reference to his scientist mode. He felt it had little to do with the Realities of Life—like nightsticks and grand juries.

"Has it ever occurred to you," I persisted to my everlasting regret, "that nearly all the undesirable by-products of twentieth-century living, Technological Man's most unlovable aspects, quite literally *stink?* The whole *world's* going rancid, Wendell, not just the Movement. Automobiles, factory pollution, crowded cities—Wendell, why couldn't you develop a selective suppressant for the sense of smell—controlled anosmia? Oh, I know a snort of formaldehyde will do the trick, and having your adenoids removed sometimes works. But a man oughtn't to have to give up the smell of frying bacon just to survive in New York. And you know we're reaching that pass—in the past few years it hasn't been necessary to leave the city and then return to be aware of how evil it smells. The natural suppressor mechanism in the brain—whatever it is—has gone about as far as it can go. Why don't you devise a small-spectrum filter to aid it? It would be welcomed by sanitation workers, engineers—why, it would be a godsend to the man on the street!"

Carlson was mildly interested. Such an anosmic filter would be both a mordant political statement and a genuine boon to Mankind. He had been vaguely pleased by the success of his cold cure, and I believe he sincerely wished to make the world a happier place—however perverted his methods tended to be. We discussed the idea at some length, and I left.

Had Carlson not been bored silly in the hospital, he would never have rented a television set. It was extremely unfortunate that *The Late Show* (ed. note: a television show of the period) on that particular evening featured the film version of Alistair MacLean's *The Satan Bug.* Watching this absurd production, Carlson was intellectually repelled by the notion that a virus could be isolated so hellishly virulent that "a teaspoon of it would sweep the earth of life in a few days."

But it gave him a wild idea—a fancy, a fantasy, and a tasty one.

He checked with me by phone the next day, very casually, and I assured him from my experiences with advances in virus-vectoring that MacLean had *not* been whistling in the dark. In fact, I said, modern so-called bacterial warfare made the Satan Bug look like child's play. Carlson thanked me and changed the subject.

On his release from the hospital, he came to my office and asked me to work with him for a full year, to the exclusion of all else, on a project whose nature he was reluctant to discuss. "Why do you need me?" I asked, puzzled.

"Because," he finally told me, "you know how to make a Satan Bug. I intend to make a God Bug. And you could help me."

"Eh?"

"Listen, Jake," he said with that delightful informality of his, "I've licked the common cold—and there are still herds of people with the sniffles. All I could think of to do with the cure was to turn it over to the pharmaceuticals people, and I did all I could to make sure they didn't milk it, but there are still suffering folks who can't afford the damned stuff. Well, there's no need for that. Jake, a cold will kill someone sufficiently weakened by hunger—I can't help the hunger, but I could eliminate colds from the planet in forty-eight hours . . . with your help."

"A benevolent virus-vector . . ." I was flabbergasted, as much by the notion of decommercializing medicine as by the specific nostrum involved.

"It'd be a lot of work," Carlson went on. "In its present form my stuff isn't compatible with such a delivery system—I simply wasn't thinking along those lines. But I'll bet it could be made so, with your help. Jake, I haven't got time to learn your field—throw in with me. Those pharmaceuticals gonifs have made me rich enough to pay you twice what Columbia does, and we're both due for sabbatical anyway. What do you say?"

I thought it over, but not enough. The notion of collaborating with a Nobel Prize winner was simply too tempting. "All right, Wendell."

We set up operations in Carlson's laboratory-home on Long Island, he in the basement and myself on the main floor. There we worked like men possessed for the better part of a year, cherishing private dreams and slaughtering guinea pigs by the tens of thousands. Carlson was a stern if somewhat slapdash taskmaster, and as our work progressed he began "looking over my shoulder," learning my field while discouraging inquiries about his own progress. I assumed that he simply knew his field too well to converse intelligently about it with anyone but himself. And yet he absorbed all my own expertise with fluid rapidity, until eventually it seemed that he knew as much about virology as I did myself. One day he disappeared with no explanation, and returned a week or two later with what seemed to me a more nasal voice.

And near the end of the year there came a day when he called me on the telephone. I was spending the weekend, as always, with my wife and two sons in Harlem. Christmas was approaching, and Barbara and I were discussing the relative merits of plastic and natural trees when the phone rang. I was not at all surprised to hear Carlson's reedy voice, so reminiscent of an oboe lately—the only wonder was that he had called during conventional waking hours.

"Jake," he began without preamble, "I haven't the time or inclination to argue, so shut up and listen, right? Right. I advise and strongly urge you to take your family and leave New York *at once*—steal a car if you have to, or hijack a Greyhound (ed. note: a public transportation conveyance) for all of me, but be at least twenty miles away by midnight."

"But . . ."

". . . Head north if you want my advice, and for God's sake stay away from all cities, towns, and people in any number. If you possibly can, get upwind of all nearby industry, and bring along all the formaldehyde you can—a gun too, if you own one. Goodbye, my friend, and remember I do this for the greater good of mankind. I don't know if you'll understand that, but I hope so."

"Wendell, what in the name of *God* are you . . . ?" I was talking to a dead phone.

Barbara was beside me, a worried look on her face, my son Isham in her arms. "What is it?"

"I'm not sure," I said unsteadily, "but I think Wendell has come unhinged. I must go to him. Stay with the children; I'll be back as quickly as I can. And, Barbara . . ."

"Yes?"

"I know this sounds insane, but pack a bag and be ready to leave town *at once* if I call and tell you to."

"Leave town? Without you?"

"Yes, just that. Leave New York and never return. I'm virtually certain you won't have to, but it's just possible that Wendell knows what he's talking about. If he does, I'll meet you at the cabin by the lake, as soon as I can." I put off her questions then and left, heading for Long Island.

When I reached Carlson's home in Old Westbury I let myself in with my key and made my way toward his laboratory. But I found him upstairs in mine, perched on a stool, gazing intently at a flask in his right hand. Its interior swirled, changing color as I watched.

Carlson looked up. "You're a damned fool, Jake," he said quietly before I could speak. "I gave you a chance."

"Wendell, what on earth is this all about? My wife is scared half to . . ."

"Remember that controlled anosmia you told me about when I was in the hospital?" he went on conversationally. "You said the trouble with the world is that it stinks, right?"

I stared at him, vaguely recalling my words.

"Well," he said, "I've got a solution."

And Carlson told me what he held in his hand. A single word.

I snapped, just completely snapped. I charged him, clawing wildly for his throat, and he struck me with his left hand, his faceted ring giving me the scar I bear to this day, knocking me unconscious. When I came to my senses I was alone, alone with a helpless guilt that careened yammering through the halls of my reason and a terror that clutched at my bowels. A note lay on the floor beside me, in Wendell's sprawling hand, telling me that I had—by my watch—another hour's grace. At once I ran to the phone and wasted ten minutes trying to call Barbara. I could not get through—trunk failure, the operator said. Gibbering, I took all the formaldehyde I could find in both labs and a self-contained breathing rig from Carlson's, stepped out into the streetlit night, and set about stealing a car.

It took me twenty minutes, not bad for a first attempt but still cutting it fine—I barely made it to Manhattan, with superb traffic conditions to help me, before the highway became a butcher shop.

At precisely nine o'clock, Wendell Morgan Carlson stood on the roof of Columbia's enormous Butler Library, held high in the air by fake Greek columns and centuries of human thought, gazing north across a quadrangle within which grass and trees had nearly given up trying to grow, toward the vast domed Low Library and beyond toward the ghetto in which my wife and children were waiting, oblivious. In his hands he held the flask I had failed to wrest from him, and within it were approximately two teaspoons of an infinitely refined and concentrated virus culture. It was the end result of our year's work, and it duplicated what the military had spent years and billions to obtain: a strain of virus that could blanket the globe in about forty-eight hours. There was no antidote for it, no vaccine, no defense of any kind for virtually all of humanity. It was diabolical, immoral, and quite efficient. On the other hand, it was not lethal.

Not, that is, in and of itself. But Carlson had concluded, like so many before him, that a few million lives was an acceptable price for saving the world, and so at 9 P.M. on December 17, 1984, he leaned over the parapet of Butler Library and dropped his flask six long stories to the concrete below. It shattered on impact and sprayed its contents into what dismal breeze still blew through the campus.

Carlson had said one word to me that afternoon, and the word was "Hyperosmia."

Within forty-eight hours every man, woman, and child left alive on earth possessed a sense of smell approximately a hundred times more efficient than that of any wolf that ever howled.

During those forty-eight hours, a little less than a fifth of the planet's population perished, by whatever means they could devise, and every city in the world spilled its remaining life into the surrounding countryside. The ancient smell-suppressing system of the human brain collapsed under unbearable demand, overloaded and burned out in an instant.

The great complex behemoth called Modern Civilization ground to a halt in a little less than two days. In the last hours, those pitiably few city dwellers on the far side of the globe who were rigorous enough of thought to heed and believe the brief bewildered death cries of the great mass media strove valiantly—and hopelessly—to effect emergency measures. The wiser attempted, as I had, to deaden their senses of smell with things like formaldehyde, but there is a limit to the amount of formaldehyde that even desperate men can lay hands on in a day or less, and its effects are generally temporary. Others with less vision opted for airtight environments if they could get them, and there they soon died, either by asphyxiation when their air supply ran out or by suicide when, fervently hoping they had outlived the virus, they cracked their airlocks at last. It was discovered that human technology had produced no commonly available nose plug worth a damn, nor any air-purification system capable of filtering out Carlson's virus. Although the rest of the animal kingdom was not measurably affected by it, mankind failed utterly to check the effects of the ghastly Hyperosmic Plague, and the Exodus began . . .

. . . I don't believe Carlson rejoiced over the carnage that ensued, though a strict Malthusian might have considered it as a long-overdue pruning. But it is easy to understand why he thought it was necessary, to visualize the "better world" for which he spent so many lives: Cities fallen to ruin. Automobiles rotting where they stood. Heavy industry gone to join the dinosaurs. The synthetic-food industry utterly undone. Perfume what it had always been best—a memory—as well as tobacco. A wave of cleanliness sweeping the globe, and public flatulation at last a criminal offense, punishable by death. Secaucus, New Jersey, abandoned to the buzzards. The back-to-nature communalists achieving their apotheosis, helping to feed and instruct bewildered urban survivors (projected catchphrase: "If you don't like hippies, next time you're hungry, call a cop"). The impetus of desperation forcing new developments in production of power by sun, wind, and water rather than inefficient combustion of more precious resources. The long-delayed perfection of plumbing. And a profoundly interesting and far-reaching change in human mating customs as feigned interest or disinterest became unviable pretenses (as any wolf could have told us, the scent of desire can be neither faked nor masked).

All in all, an observer as impartial as Carlson imagined himself to be might have predicted that at an ultimate cost of perhaps thirty to forty percent of its population (no great loss), the world ten or twenty years after Carlson would be a much nicer place to live in.

Instead and in fact, there are four billion fewer people living in it, and in this year, Two A.C., we have achieved only a bare possibility of survival at a cost of eighty to ninety percent of our number.

The first thing Carlson could not have expected claimed over a billion and a half lives within the first month of the Brave New World. His compartmentalized mind had not been monitoring current developments in the field of psychology, a discipline he found frustrating. And so he was not aware of the work of Lynch and others, conclusively demonstrating that autism was the result of sensory overload. Autistic children, Lynch had proved, were victims of a physiochemical imbalance which disabled their suppressor circuitry for sight, hearing, touch, smell, or any combination thereof, flooding their brains with an intolerable avalanche of useless data and shocking them into retreat. Lysergic acid diethylamide is said to produce a similar effect, on a smaller scale.

The Hyperosmic Virus produced a similar effect, on a larger scale. Within weeks, millions of near-catatonic adults and children perished from malnutrition, exposure, or accidental injury. Why some survived the shock and adapted, while some did not, remains a mystery, although there exist scattered data suggesting that those whose sense of smell was already relatively acute suffered most.

The second thing Carlson could not have expected was the War.

The War had been ordained by the plummeting fall of his flask, but he may perhaps be excused for not foreseeing it. It was not such a war as has ever been seen on earth before in all recorded history, humans versus each other or subordinate life forms. There was nothing for the confused, scattered survivors of the Hyperosmic Plague to fight over, few unbusy enough to fight over it; and with lesser life forms we are now *better* equipped to compete. No, war broke out between us bewildered refugees —and the Muskies.

It is difficult for us to imagine today how it was possible for the human race to know of the Muskies for so long without ever believing in them. Countless humans reported contact with Muskies—who at various times were called "ghosts," "poltergeists," "leprechauns," "fairies," "gremlins," and a host of other misleading labels—and not *one* of these thousands of witnesses was believed by humanity at large. Some of us saw our cats stare, transfixed, at nothing at all, and wondered—but did not believe— what they saw. In its arrogance the race assumed that the peculiar perversion of entropy called "life" was the exclusive property of solids and liquids.

Even today we know very little about the Muskies, save that they are gaseous in nature and perceptible only by smell. The interested reader may wish to examine Dr. Michael Gowan's ground-breaking attempt at a psychological analysis of these entirely alien creatures, *Riders of the Wind* (Fresh Start Press, 1986).

One thing we do know is that they are capable of an incredible and disturbing playfulness. While not true telepaths, Muskies can project and often impose mood patterns over short distances, and for centuries they seem to have delighted in scaring the daylights out of random humans. Perhaps they laughed like innocent children as women to whom their pranks were attributed were burned at the stake in Salem. Dr. Gowan suggests that this aspect of their racial psyche is truly infantile—he feels their race is still in its infancy. As, perhaps, is our own.

But in their childishness, Muskies can be dangerous both deliberately and involuntarily. Years ago, before the Exodus, people used to wonder why a race that could plan a space station couldn't design a safe airliner—the silly things used to fall out of the sky with appalling regularity. Often it was simply sheer bad engineering, but I suspect that at least as often a careless, drifting Musky, riding the trades lost in God knows what wildly *alien* thoughts, was sucked into the air intake of a hurtling jetliner and burst the engine asunder as it died. It was this guess which led me to theorize that extreme heat might disrupt and kill Muskies, and this gave us our first and so far only weapon in the bitter war that still rages between us and the windriders.

For, like many children, Muskies are dangerously paranoid. Almost at the instant they realized that men could somehow now perceive them directly, they attacked, with a ferocity that bespoke blind panic. They learned quickly how best to kill us: by clamping itself somehow to a man's face and forcing him to breathe it in, a Musky can lay waste to his respiratory system. The only solution under combat conditions is a weapon which fires a projectile hot enough to explode a Musky—and that is a flawed solution. If you fail to burn a Musky in time, before it reaches you, you may be faced with the unpleasant choice of wrecking your lungs or blowing off your face. All too many Faceless Ones roam the land, objects of horror and pity, supported by fellow men uncomfortably aware that it could happen to them tomorrow.

Further, we Technos here at Fresh Start, dedicated to rebuilding at least a minimum technology, must naturally wear our recently developed nose plugs for long intervals while doing Civilized work. We therefore toil in constant fear that at any moment we may feel alien projections of terror and dread, catch even through our plugs the characteristic odor that gives Muskies their name, and gasp our lungs out in the final spasms of death.

God knows how Muskies communicate—or even if they do. Perhaps they simply have some sort of group mind or hive mentality. What would evolution select for a race of gas clouds spinning across the earth on the howling mistral? Someday we may devise a way to take one prisoner and study it; for the present we are content to know that they can be killed. A good Musky is a dead Musky.

Someday we may climb back up the ladder of technological evolution enough to carry the battle to the Muskies' home ground; for the present we are at least becoming formidable defenders.

Someday we may have the time to seek out Wendell Morgan Carlson and present him with a bill; for the present we are satisfied that he dares not show himself outside New York City, where legend has him hiding from the consequences of his actions.

CHAPTER THREE

*From the Journal of Isham Stone*

. . . but my gestalt of the eighteen years that had brought me on an intersecting course with my father's betrayer was nowhere near as pedantically phrased as the historical accounts Dad had written. In fact, I had refined it down to four words.

*God damn you, Carlson!*

Nearly midafternoon now. The speed was wearing off; time was short. Broadway got more depressing as I went. Have you ever seen a bus full of skeletons—with pigeons living in it? My arm ached like hell, and a muscle in my thigh had just announced it was sprained—I acquired a slight but increasing limp. The rucksack gained an ounce with every step, and I fancied that my right plug was leaking the barest trifle around the flange. I couldn't say I felt first-rate.

I kept walking north.

I came to Columbus Circle, turned on a whim into Central Park. It was an enclave of life in this concrete land of death, and I could not pass it by—even though my intellect warned that I might encounter a Doberman who hadn't seen a can of dog food in twenty years.

The Exodus had been good to this place at least—it was lush with vegetation now that swarming humans no longer smothered its natural urge to be alive. Elms and oaks reached for the clouds with the same optimism of the maples and birches around Fresh Start, and the overgrown grasses were the greenest things I had seen in New York. And yet—in places the grass was dead, and there were dead bushes and shrubs scattered here and there. Perhaps first impressions were deceiving—perhaps a small parcel of land surrounded by an enormous concrete crypt was not a viable ecology after all. Then again, perhaps neither was Fresh Start.

I was getting depressed again.

I pocketed the grenade I still held and sat down on a park bench, telling myself that a rest would do wonders for my limp. After a time static bits of scenery moved—the place was alive. There were cats, and gaunt starved dogs of various breeds, apparently none old enough to know what a man was. I found their confidence refreshing—like I say, I'm a peaceful-type assassin. Gregarious as hell.

I glanced about, wondering why so many of the comparatively few human skeletons here had been carrying weapons on the night of the

Exodus—why go armed in a park? Then I heard a cough and looked around, and for a crazy second I thought I knew.

A leopard.

I recognized it from pictures in Dad's books, and I knew what it was and what it could do. But my adrenaline system was tired of putting my gun in my fist—I sat perfectly still and concentrated on smelling friendly. My hand weapon was designed for high temperature, not stopping power; grenades are ineffective against a moving target; and I was leaning back against my rifle—but that isn't why I sat still. I had learned that day that lashing out is not an optimum response to fear.

And so I took enough of a second look to realize that this leopard was incredibly ancient, hollow-bellied and claw-scarred, more noble than formidable. If wild game had been permitted to roam Central Park, Dad would have told me—he knew my planned route. Yet this cat seemed old enough to predate the Exodus. I was certain he knew me for a man. I suppose he had escaped from a zoo in the confusion of the time, or perhaps he was some rich person's pet. I understand they had such things in the Old Days. Seems to me a leopard'd be more trouble than an eagle—Dad kept one for four years and I never had so much grief over livestock before or since. Dad used to say it was the symbol of something great that had died, but I thought it was ornery.

This old cat seemed friendly enough, though, now that I noticed. He looked patriarchal and wise, and he looked awful hungry if it came to that. I made a gambler's decision for no reason that I can name. Slipping off my rucksack slowly and deliberately, I got out a few foodtabs, took four steps toward the leopard, and sat on my heels, holding out the tablets.

Instinct, memory or intuition, the big cat recognized my intent and loped my way without haste. Somehow the closer he got, the less scared I got, until he was nuzzling my hand with a maw that could have amputated it. I *know* the foodtabs didn't smell like anything, let alone food, but he understood in some empathic way what I was offering—or perhaps he felt the symbolic irony of two ancient antagonists, black man and leopard, meeting in New York City to share food. He ate them all, without nipping my fingers. His tongue was startlingly rough and rasping, but I didn't flinch, or need to. When he was done he made a noise that was a cross between a cough and a snore and butted my leg with his head.

He was old, but powerful; I rocked backward and fell off my heels. I landed correctly, of course, but I didn't get back up again. My strength left me and I lay there gazing at the underside of the park bench.

For the first time since I entered New York, I had communicated with a living thing and been answered in kind, and somehow that knowledge took my strength from me. I sprawled on the turf and waited for the ground to stop heaving, astonished to discover how weak I was and in how many places I hurt unbearably. I said some words that Collaci had taught me, and they helped some but not enough. The speed had worn off faster than it should have, and there was no more.

It looked like it was time for a smoke. I argued with myself as I reached overhead to get the first-aid kit from the rucksack, but I saw no alternative. Carlson was not a trained fighter, had never had a teacher like Collaci: I could take him buzzed. And I might not get to my feet any other way.

The joint I selected was needle-slender—more than a little cannabis would do me more harm than good. I had no mind to get wrecked in *this* city. I lit up with my coil lighter and took a deep lungful, held it as long as I could. Halfway through the second toke the leaves dancing overhead began to sparkle, and my weariness got harder to locate. By the third I knew of it only by hearsay, and the last hit began melting the pains of my body as warm water melts snow. Nature's own analgesic, gift of the earth.

I started thinking about the leopard, who was lying down himself now, washing his haunches. He was magnificent in decay—something about his eyes said that he intended to live forever or die trying. He was the only one of his kind in his universe, and I could certainly identify with that—I'd always felt different from the other cats myself.

And yet—I was kin to those who had trapped him, caged him, exhibited him to the curious, and then abandoned him to die half a world away from his home. Why wasn't he trying to kill me? In his place I might have acted differently . . .

With the clarity of smoke-logic I followed the thought through. At one time the leopard's ancestors had tried to kill mine, and *eat* them, and yet there was no reason for me to hate *him*. Killing him wouldn't help my ancestors. Killing me would accomplish nothing for the leopard, make his existence no easier . . . except by a day's meal, and I had given him that.

*What then,* I thought uneasily, *will my killing Carlson accomplish?* It could not put the Hyperosmic Virus back in the flask, or save the life of any now living. Why come all this way to kill?

It was not, of course, a new thought. The question had arisen several times during my training in survival and combat. Collaci insisted on debating philosophy while he was working you over, and expected reply; he maintained that a man who couldn't hold up his end of the conversation while fighting for his life would never make a really effective killer. You could pause for thought, but if he decided you were just hoarding your wind he stopped pulling his punches.

One day we had no special topic, and I voiced my self-doubts about the mission I was training for. What good, I asked Collaci, would killing Carlson do? Teach' disengaged and stood back, breathing a little hard, and grinned his infrequent wolf's grin.

"Survival has strange permutations, Isham. Revenge is a uniquely human attribute—somehow we find it easier to bury our dead when we have avenged them. We have many dead." He selected a toothpick, stuck it into his grin. "And for your father's sake it has to be you who does it—only if his son provides his expiation can Dr. Stone grant himself absolution. Otherwise I'd go kill that silly bastard myself." And without warning, he had tried, unsuccessfully, to break my collarbone.

And so now I sat tired, hungry, wounded, and a little stoned in the middle of an enormous island mausoleum, asking myself the question I had next asked Collaci, while trying—unsuccessfully—to cave in his rib cage: is it moral or ethical to kill a man?

Across the months his answer came back: *Perhaps not, but it is sometimes necessary.*

And with that thought my strength came to me and I got to my feet. My thoughts were as slick as wet soap, within reach but skittering out of my grasp. I grabbed one from the tangle and welded it to me savagely: *I will kill Wendell Morgan Carlson.* It was enough.

And saying goodbye to the luckier leopard, who could never be hagridden by ancient ghosts, I left the park and continued on up Broadway, as alert and deadly as I knew how to be.

When I reached 114th Street, I looked above the rooftops, and there it was: a thin column of smoke north and a little east, toward Amsterdam Avenue. Legend and my father's intuition had been right. Carlson was holed up where he had always felt most secure—the academic womb-bag of Columbia. I felt a grin pry my face open. It would all be over soon now, and I could go back to being me—whoever that was.

I left the rucksack under a station wagon and considered my situation. I had three tracers left in my Musky-killing handgun, three incendiary grenades clipped to my belt, and the scope-sighted sniper-rifle with which I planned to kill Carlson. The latter held a full clip of eight man-killing slugs—seven more than I needed. I checked the action and jacked a slug into the chamber.

There was a detailed map of the Morningside campus in my pack but I didn't bother to get it out—I had its twin brother in my head. Although neither Teach' nor I had entirely shared Dad's certainty that Carlson would be at Columbia, I had spent hours studying the campus maps he gave me as thoroughly as the New York City street maps that Collaci had provided. It seemed the only direct contribution Dad could make to my mission.

It looked as though his effort had paid off.

I wondered whether Carlson was expecting me. I wasn't sure if the sound of the car I'd shot downtown could have traveled this far, nor whether an explosion in a city full of untended gas mains was unusual enough to put Carlson on his guard. Therefore I had to assume that it could have and it was. Other men had come to New York to deal with Carlson, as independents, and none had returned.

My mind was clicking efficiently now, all confusion gone. I was eager. A car-swiped lamppost leaned drunkenly against a building, and I briefly considered taking to the rooftops for maximum surprise factor. But rooftops are prime Musky territory, and besides I didn't have strength for climbing.

I entered the campus at the southwest, through the 115th Street gate. As my father had predicted, it was locked—only the main gates at 116th had been left open at night in those days, and it was late at night when Carlson dropped his flask. But the lock was a simple Series 10 American that might have made Teach' laugh out loud. I didn't laugh out loud. It yielded to the second pick I tried, and I slipped through the barred iron gate without a sound—having thought to oil the hinges first.

A flight of steps led to a short flagstone walkway, gray speckled hexagons in mosaic, a waist-high wall on either side. The walkway ran between Furnald and Ferris Booth halls and, I knew, opened onto the great inner quadrangle of Columbia. Leaves lay scattered all about, and trees of all kinds thrashed in the lusty afternoon breeze, their leaves a million green pinwheels.

I hugged the right wall until it abutted a taller perpendicular wall. Easing around that, I found myself before the great smashed glass and stone façade of Ferris Booth Hall, the student activities center, staring past it toward Butler Library, which I was seeing from the west side. There was a good deal of heavy construction equipment in the way— one of the many student groups that had occupied space in Booth had managed to blow up itself and a sizable portion of the building in 1983, and rebuilding had still been in progress on Exodus Day. A massive crane stood before the ruined structure, surrounded by stacks of brick and pipe, a bulldozer, storage shacks, a few trucks, a two-hundred-gallon gasoline tank, and a pair of construction trailers.

But my eyes looked past all the conventional hardware to a curious device beyond them, directly in front of Butler Library and nearly hidden by overgrown hedges. I couldn't have named it—it looked like an octopus making love to a console stereo—but it obviously didn't come with the landscaping. Dad's second intuition was also correct: Carlson was using Butler for his base of operations. God knew what the device was for, but a man without his adenoids in a city full of Muskies and hungry German shepherds would not have built it further from home than could be helped. This was the place.

I drew in a great chest- and bellyful of air, and my grin hurt my cheeks. I held up my rifle and watched my hands. Rock steady.

*Carlson, you murdering bastard,* I thought, *this is it. The human race has found you, and its Hand is near. A few more breaths and you die violently, old man, like a harmless cat in a smokeshop window, like an eight-year-old boy on a Harlem sidewalk, like a planetwide civilization you thought you could improve on. Get you ready.*

I moved forward.

Wendell Morgan Carlson stepped out between the big shattered lamps that bracketed Butler Hall's front entrance. I saw him plainly in profile, features memorized from the Carlson Poster and my father's sketches, recognizable in the afternoon light even through white beard and tangled hair. He glanced my way, flinched, and ducked back inside a split second ahead of my first shot.

Determined to nail him before he could reach a weapon and dig in, I put my head down and ran, flat out, for the greatest killer of all time.

And the first Musky struck.

Terror sleeted through my brain, driving out the rage, and something warm and intangible plastered itself across my face. I think I screamed then, but somehow I kept from inhaling as I fell and rolled, dropping the rifle and tearing uselessly at the thing on my face. The last thing I saw before invisible gases seared my vision was the huge crane beside me on the right, its long arm flung at the sky like a signpost to Heaven. Then the world shimmered and faded, and I clawed my pistol from its holster. I aimed without seeing, my finger spasmed, and the gun bucked in my hand.

The massive gasoline drum between me and the crane went up with a *whoom,* and I sobbed in relief as I heaved to my feet and dove headlong through the flames. The Musky's dying projections tore at my mind and I rolled clear, searing my lungs with a convulsive inhalation as the

Musky exploded behind me. Even as I smashed into the fender of the crane, my hindbrain screamed *Muskies never travel alone!* and before I knew what I was doing I tore loose my plugs to locate my enemy.

Foul stenches smashed my sanity, noxious odors wrenched at my reason, I was torn, blasted, overwhelmed in abominable ordure. The universe was offal, and the world I saw was remote and unreal. My eyes saw the campus, but told me nothing of the rank flavor of putrefaction that lay upon it. They saw sky, but spoke nothing of the reeking layers of indescribable decay of which it was made. Even allowing for a greenhouse effect it was much worse than it should have been after twenty years, just as legend had said. I tasted excrement, I tasted metal, I tasted the flavor of the world's largest charnel house, population seven millions, and I writhed on the concrete. Forgotten childhood memories of the Exodus burst in my brain and reduced me to a screaming, whimpering child. I couldn't *stand* it, it was unbearable, *how had I walked, arrogant and unknowing, through this stinking hell all day?*

And with that thought I remembered why I had come here, and knew I could not join Izzy in the peaceful, fragrant dark. I could not let go—I had to kill Carlson before I let the blackness claim me. Courage flowed from God knows where, feeding on black hatred and the terrible fear that I would let my people down, let my father down. I stood up and inhaled sharply, through my nose.

The nightmare world sprang into focus and time came to a halt.

There were six Muskies, skittering about before Butler as they sought to bend the breezes to their will.

I had three hot-shot shells and three grenades.

One steadied, banked my way. I fired from the hip and he flared out of existence.

A second caught hold of a prevailing current and came in like an express train. Panic tore through my mind, and I laughed and aimed and the Musky went incandescent.

Two came in at once then, like balloons in slow motion. I extrapolated their courses, pulled two grenades and armed them with opposing thumbs, counted to four and hurled them together as Collaci had taught me, aiming for a spot just short of my target. They kissed at that spot and rebounded, each toward an oncoming Musky. But one grenade went up before the other, killing its Musky but knocking the other one safely clear. It shot past my ear as I threw myself sideways.

Three Muskies. One slug, one grenade.

The one that had been spared sailed around the crane in a wide, graceful arc and came in low and fast, rising for my face as one of its brothers attacked from my left. Cursing, I burned the latter and flipped backwards through a great trail of burning gas from the tank I'd spoiled. The Musky failed to check in time, shot suddenly skyward and burst spectacularly. I slammed against a stack of twelve-inch pipe and heard ribs crack.

One Musky. One grenade.

As I staggered erect, beating at my smoldering turtleneck, Carlson reemerged from Butler, a curious helmet over his flowing white hair.

I no longer cared about the remaining Musky. Almost absentmindedly I tossed my last grenade in its direction to keep it occupied, but I knew I would have all the time I needed. Imminent death was now a side issue. I lunged and rolled, came up with the rifle in my hands and aimed for the O in Carlson's scraggly white beard. Dimly I saw him plugging a wire from his helmet into the strange console device, but it didn't matter, it just didn't matter at all. My finger tightened on the trigger.

And then something smashed me on the side of the neck behind the ear, and my finger clenched, and the blackness that had been waiting patiently for oh! so long swarmed in and washed away the pain and the hate and the weariness and oh God the awful smell. . . .

CHAPTER FOUR

*Excerpts from* THE BUILDING OF FRESH START, *by Jacob Stone, Ph.D., authorized version: Fresh Start Press, 2001.*

Although Fresh Start grew slowly and apparently randomly as personnel and materials became available, its development followed the basic outline of a master plan conceived within a year of the Exodus. Of course, I had not the training or experience to visualize specifics of my dream at that early stage—but the basic layout was inherent in the shape of the landscape and in the nature of the new world Carlson had made for us all.

Five years prior to the Exodus, a man named Gallipolis had acquired title, by devious means, to a logged-out area some distance northwest of New York City. It was an isolated two-hundred-acre parcel of an extremely odd shape. Seen from the air it must have resembled an enormous pair of green sunglasses: two valleys choking with new growth, separated physically by a great perpendicular extrusion of the eastern mountain range, almost to the western slopes, leaving the north and south valleys joined only by a narrow channel. The perpendicular "nose" between the valley "lenses" was a tall, rocky ridge, sharply sloped on both sides, forming a perfect natural division. The land dropped gently away from the foot of this ridge in either direction, and dirt roads left by the loggers cut great loops through both valleys. The land was utterly unsuited for farming, and too many miles from nowhere for suburban development—it was what real estate brokers called "an investment in the future."

Gallipolis was a mad Greek. Mad Greeks in literature are invariably swarthy, undereducated, poor, and drunk. Gallipolis was florid, superbly educated, moderately well off, and a teetotaler. He looked upon his valleys and he smiled a mad smile and decided to hell with the future. He had a serviceable road cut through the north forest past the lake, to a lonely stretch of state highway which fed into the nearby Interstate. He brought bulldozers down this road and had six widely spaced acres cleared west of the logging road loop in the north valley, and a seventh acre on the lake-shore for himself. On these sites he built large and extremely comfortable homes, masterpieces of design which combined an appearance of "roughing it" with every imaginable modern convenience. He piped in water from spring-fed streams high on the slopes of the Nose (as he had come to call the central ridge). He built beach houses along the lakeshore. It was his plan to lease the homes to wealthy men as weekend or summer homes at an exorbitant fee, and use the proceeds to develop three similar sites in both valleys. He envisioned an ultimate two or three dozen homes and an early retirement, but the only two things he ultimately achieved were to go broke before a single home had been leased and to drop dead.

A nephew inherited the land—and the staggering tax bill. He chanced to be a student of mine, and was aware that I was in the market for a weekend haven from the rigors of the city; he approached me. Although the place was an absurdly long drive from New York, I went up with him one Saturday, looked over the house nearest the lake, made him a firm offer of a quarter of his asking price, and closed the deal on the spot. It was a beautiful place. My wife and I became quite fond of it, and never missed an opportunity to steal a weekend there. Before long we had neighbors, but we seldom saw them, save occasionally at the lake. We had all come there for a bit of solitude, and it was quite a big lake—none of us were socially inclined.

It was for this wooded retreat that my family and I made in the horrible hours of the Exodus, and only by the grace of God did we make it. Certainly none of the other tenants did, then or ever, and it must be assumed that they perished. Sarwar Krishnamurti, a chemist at Columbia who had been an occasional weekend guest at Stone Manor, remembered the place in his time of need and showed up almost at once, with his family. He was followed a few days later by George Dalhousie, a friend of mine from the Engineering Department to whom I had once given directions to the place.

We made them as welcome as we could under the circumstances—my wife was in a virtual state of shock from the loss of our eldest son, and none of us were in much better shape. I know we three men found enormous comfort in each other's presence, in having other men of science with whom to share our horror, our astonishment, our guesses, and our grim extrapolations. It kept us sane, kept our minds on practical matters, on survival; for had we been alone, we might have succumbed, as did so many, to a numb, traumatized disinterest in living.

Instead, we survived the winter that came, the one that killed so many, and by spring we had laid our plans.

We made occasional abortive forays into the outside world, gathering information from wandering survivors. All media save rumor had perished; even my international-band radio was silent. On these expeditions we were always careful to conceal the existence and location of our home base, pretending to be as disorganized and homeless as the aimless drifters we continually encountered. We came to know every surviving farmer in the surrounding area, and established friendly relations with them by working for them in exchange for food. Like all men, we avoided areas of previous urbanization, for nose plugs were inferior in those days, and Muskies were omnipresent and terrifying. In fact, rumor claimed, they tended to cluster in cities and towns.

But that first spring, we conquered our fear and revulsion with great difficulty and began raiding small towns and industrial parks with a borrowed wagon. We found that rumor had been correct: urban areas were crawling with Muskies. But we needed tools and equipment of all kinds and descriptions, badly enough to risk our lives repeatedly for them. It went slowly, but Dalhousie had his priorities right, and soon we were ready.

We opened our first factory that spring, on a hand-cleared site in the south valley (which we christened Southtown). Our first product had been given careful thought, and we chose well—if for the wrong reasons. We anticipated difficulty in convincing people to buy goods from us with barter, when they could just as easily have scavenged from the abandoned urban areas. In fact, one of our central reasons for founding Fresh Start had been the conviction that the lice on a corpse are not a going concern: we did not want our brother survivors to remain dependent on a finite supply of tools, equipment, and processed food. If we could risk Musky attack, so could others.

Consequently we selected as our first product an item unobtainable anywhere else, and utterly necessary in the changed world: effective nose plugs. I suggested them, Krishnamurti designed them and the primitive assembly line on which they were first turned out, and Dalhousie directed us all in their construction. All of us, men and women, worked on the line. It took us several months to achieve success, and by that time we were our own best customers—our factory smelled most abominable. Which we had expected, and planned for: the whole concept of Fresh Start rested on the single crucial fact that prevailing winds were virtually always from the north. On the rare occasions when the wind backed, the Nose formed a satisfactory natural barrier.

Once we were ready to offer our plugs for sale, we began advertising and recruiting on a large scale. Word of our plans was circulated by word of mouth, mimeographed flyer, and shortwave broadcast. The only person who responded by the onset of winter was Helen Phinney, but her arrival was providential, freeing us almost overnight from dependence on stinking gasoline-driven generators for power. She was then and is now Fresh Start's only resident world-class genius, a recognized expert on what were then called "alternative" power sources—the only ones Carlson had left us. She quite naturally became a part of the planning process, as well as a warm friend of us all. Within a short time the malodorous generators had been replaced by waterpower from the streams that cascade like copious tears from the "bridge" of the Nose, and ultimately by methane gas and wind power from a series of eggbeater-type windmills strung along the Nose itself. In recent years the generators have been put back on the line, largely for industrial use—but they no longer burn gasoline, nor does the single truck we have restored to service. Thanks to Phinney, they burn pure grain alcohol which we distill ourselves from field corn and rye, which works *more* efficiently than gasoline and produces only water and carbon dioxide as exhaust. (Pre-Exodus man could have used the same fuel in most of his internal-combustion engines—but once Henry Ford made his choice, the industry he incidentally created tended of course to perpetuate itself.)

This then was the Council of Fresh Start, assembled by fate: Myself, a dreamer, racked with guilt and seeking a truly worthwhile penance, trying to salvage some of the world I'd helped ruin. Krishnamurti, utterly practical wizard at both requirements analysis and design engineering, translator of ideas into plans. Dalhousie, the ultimate foreman, gifted at reducing any project to its component parts and accomplishing them with minimum time and effort. Phinney, the energy provider, devoted to drawing free power from the natural processes of the universe. Our personalities blended as well as our skills, and by that second spring we were a unit: the Council. I would suggest a thing, Krishnamurti would design the black box, Dalhousie would build it, and Phinney would throw power to it. We fit. Together we felt *useful* again, more than scavenging survivors.

No other recruits arrived during the winter, which like the one before was unusually harsh for that part of the world (perhaps owing to the sudden drastic decline in the worldwide production of waste heat), but by spring volunteers began arriving in droves. We got all kinds: scientists, technicians, students, mechanics, handymen, construction workers, factory hands, a random assortment of men seeking Civilized work. A colony of canvas tents grew in Northtown, in cleared areas we hoped would one day hold great dormitories. Our initial efforts that summer were aimed at providing water, power, and sewage systems for our growing community, and enlarging our nose plug factory. A combination smithy-repair-shop-motor-pool grew of its own accord next to the factory in Southtown, and we began bartering repair work for food with local farmers to the east and northwest.

By common consent, all food, tools, and other resources were shared equally by all members of the community, with the single exception of mad Gallipolis's summer homes. We the Council members retained these homes, and have never been begrudged them by our followers (two of the homes were incomplete at the time of the Exodus, and remained so for another few years). That aside, all the inhabitants of Fresh Start stand or fall, eat or starve together. The Council's authority as governing committee has never in all the ensuing years been either confirmed or seriously challenged. The nearly one hundred technicians who have by now assembled to our call continue to follow our advice because it works: because it gives their lives direction and meaning, because it makes their hard-won skills useful again, because it pays them well to do what they do best and thought they might never do again.

During that second summer we were frequently attacked by Muskies, invariably (of course) from the north, and suffered significant losses. For instance, Samuel Pegorski, the young hydraulic engineering major who with Phinney designed and perfected our plumbing and sewage systems, was cut down by the windriders before he lived to hear the first toilet flush in Northtown.

But with the timely arrival of Philip Collaci, an ex-Marine and former police chief from Pennsylvania, our security problems disappeared. A preternaturally effective fighting man, Collaci undertook to recruit, organize, and train the Guard, comprising enough armed men to keep the northern perimeter of Fresh Start patrolled at all times. At first, these Guards did no more than sound an alarm if they smelled Muskies coming across the lake, whereupon all hands made for the nearest shelter and tried to blank their minds to the semitelepathic creatures.

But Collaci was not satisfied. He wanted an offensive weapon—or, failing that, a defense better than flight. He told me as much several times, and finally I put aside administrative worries and went to work on the problem from a biochemical standpoint.

It seemed to me that extreme heat should work, but the problem was to devise a delivery system. Early experiments with a salvaged flame thrower were unsatisfactory—the cone of fire tended to brush Muskies out of its path instead of consuming them. Collaci suggested a line of alcohol-burning jets along the north perimeter, ready to guard Fresh Start with a wall of flame, an idea which has since been implemented—but at the time we could not spare the corn or rye to make the alcohol to power the jets. Finally, weeks of research led to the successful development of "hot-shot"

—ammunition which could be fired from any existing heavy-caliber weapon after its barrel had been replaced, that would ignite as it cleared the modified barrel and generate enormous heat as it flew, punching through any Musky it encountered and destroying it instantly. An early mixture of magnesium and perchlorate of potash has since given way to an even slower-burning mix of aluminum powder and potassium permanganate which will probably remain standard until the last Musky has been slain (long-range plans for long-range artillery shot will have to wait until we can find a good cheap source of cerium, zirconium, or thorium—unlikely in the near future). Hot-shot's effective range approximates that of a man's nose on a still day—good enough for personal combat. This turned out to be the single most important advance since the Exodus, not only for mankind, but for the fledgling community of Fresh Start.

Because our only major misjudgment had been the climate of social opinion in which we expected to find ourselves. I said earlier that we feared people would scavenge from cities rather than buy from us, even in the face of terrible danger from the Muskies who prowled the urban skies. This turned out not to be the case.

Mostly, people preferred to do without.

Secure in our retreat, we had misjudged the *Zeitgeist*, the mind of the common man. It was Collaci, fresh from over a year of wandering up and down the desolate eastern seaboard, who showed us our error. He made us realize that Lot was probably more eager to return to Gomorrah than the average human was to return to his cities and suburbs. Cities had been the scenes of the greatest racial trauma since the Flood, the places where friends and loved ones had died horribly and the skies had filled with Muskies. The Exodus and the subsequent weeks of horror were universally seen as the Hammer of God falling on the *idea of city* itself, and hard-core urbanites who might have debated the point were mostly too dead to do so. The back-to-nature movement, already in full swing at the moment when Carlson dropped the flask, took on the stature and fervor of a Dionysian religion.

Fortunately, Collaci made us see in time that we would inevitably share in the superstition and hatred accorded to cities, become associated in the common mind with the evil-smelling steel-and-glass behemoth from which men had been so conclusively vomited. He made us realize something of the extent of the suspicion and intolerance we would incur—not ignored for our redundance, but loathed for our repugnance.

At Collaci's suggestion Krishnamurti enlisted the aid of some of the more substantial farmers in neighboring regions to the east, northeast, and northwest. He negotiated agreements by which farmers who supported us with food received preferential access to Musky-killing ammunition, equipment maintenance, and, one day (he promised), commercial power. I could never have sold the idea myself—while I have always understood public relations well from the theoretical standpoint, I have never been very successful in interpersonal diplomacy—at least, with nontechnicals. The dour Krishnamurti might have seemed an even more unlikely choice —but his utter practicality convinced many a skeptical farmer where charm might have failed.

Krishnamurti's negotiations not only assured us a dependable supply of food (and, incidentally, milled lumber), it had the invaluable secondary effect of gaining us psychological allies, non-Technos who were economically and emotionally committed to us.

Work progressed rapidly once our recruiting efforts began to pay off, and by our fifth year the Fresh Start of today was visible, at least in skeleton form. We had cut interior roads to supplement the northern and southern loops left by gyppo loggers two decades before; three dormitories were up and a fourth a-building; our General Store was a growing commercial concern; a line of windmills was taking shape along the central ridge of the Nose; our sewage plant/methane converter was nearly completed; plans were underway to establish a hospital and to blast a tunnel through the Nose to link Northtown and Southtown; the Tool Shed, the depot which housed irreplaceable equipment and tools, was nearly full; and Southtown was more malodorous than ever, with a large fuel distillery, a chemistry lab, a primitive foundry, and glass-blowing, match-making, and weaving operations adjoining the hot-shot and nose plug factories.

Despite these outward signs of prosperity, we led a precarious existence —there was strong public sentiment in favor of burning us to the ground, at least among the surviving humans who remained landless nomads. To combat this we were running and distributing a small mimeographed newspaper, *Got News,* and maintaining radio station WFS (then and now the only one in the world). In addition Krishnamurti and I made endless public relations trips for miles in every direction to explain our existence and purpose to groups and individuals.

But there were many who had no land, no homes, no families, nothing but a vast heritage of bitterness. These were the precursors of today's so-called Agro Party. Surviving where and as they could, socialized for an environment that no longer existed, they hated us for reminding them of the technological womb which had unforgivably thrust them out. They raided us, singly and in loosely organized groups, often with unreasonable, suicidal fury. From humanitarian concerns as much as from public relations considerations, I sharply restrained Guard Chief Collaci, whose own inclination was to shoot any saboteur he apprehended—wherever possible they were captured and turned loose outside city limits. Collaci argued strongly for deterrent violence, but I was determined to show our neighbors that Fresh Start bore ill will to no man, and overruled him.

In that fifth year, however, I was myself overruled.

Collaci and his wife Karen (a tough, quiet, red-headed woman) had been given one of Gallipolis's uncompleted cabins, the one furthest and most isolated from Northtown's residential area. A volunteer house-raising had finished it off handsomely the previous spring. It was either bad judgment or ignorance that brought the seven-man raiding party past the Collaci home on their way to blow up the Tool Shed. But it was unquestionably bad judgment that made them kidnap Karen Collaci when they blundered across her in the forest. She was diabetic, and they had no insulin.

Collaci left his duties without authorization and pursued them, found her body within a few days. He tracked the seven guerrillas over a period of a week. Although they had split up and fled in different directions, those seven days sufficed him. He exacted from them penalties which cannot be repeated here, left each nailed to a tree, and upon his return to Fresh Start slept for three consecutive days.

Collaci's understandably impulsive action seems, in the light of history, to have been more correct than my own policy of tolerance. At any rate, we have never been raided since.

With the advent of Dr. Michael Gowan, a former professor of psychology from Stony Brook who undertook to create and administer an educational system, all the necessary seeds had, to my mind, been planted. Barring catastrophe, technological man now could and would survive. Someday, perhaps, he might rebuild what had been destroyed.

And then, one day in 1999, I interviewed and "hired" a new arrival named Jordan Washington. Since then . . .

## CHAPTER FIVE

". . . and when I came to, Carlson was dead with a slug through the head and the last Musky was nowhere in smell. So I reset my plugs, found the campfire behind the hedges, and ate his supper, and then left the next morning. I found a Healer in Jersey. That's all there is, Dad."

My father chewed the pipe he had not smoked in eighteen years and stared into the fire. Dry poplar and green birch together produced a steady blaze that warmed the spacious living room and peopled it with leaping shadows.

"Then it's over," he said at last, and heaved a great sigh.

"Yes, Dad. It's over."

He was silent, his coal-black features impassive, for a long time. Firelight danced among the valleys and crevices of his patriarch's face, and across the sharp scar on his left cheek (so like the one I now bore). His eyes glittered like rainy midnight. I wondered what he was thinking, after all these years and all that he had seen.

"Isham," he said at last, "you have done well."

"Have I, Dad?"

"Eh?"

"I just can't seem to get it straight in my mind. I guess I expected tangling with Carlson to be a kind of solution, to some things that have been bugging me all my life. Somehow I expected pulling that trigger to bring me peace. Instead I'm more confused than ever. Surely you can smell my unease, Dad? Or are your plugs still in again?" Dad used the best plugs in Fresh Start, entirely internal, and he perpetually forgot to remove them after work. Even those who loved him agreed he was the picture of the absentminded professor.

"No," he said hesitantly. "I can smell that you are uneasy, but I can't smell *why.* You must tell me, Isham."

"It's not easy to explain, Dad. I can't seem to find the words. Look, I wrote out a kind of journal of events in Jersey, while the Healer was working on me, and afterwards while I rested up. It's the same story I just told you, but somehow on paper I think it conveys more of what's bothering me. Will you read it?"

He nodded. "If you wish."

I gave my father all the preceding manuscript, right up to the moment I pulled the trigger and blacked out, and brought him his glasses. He read it slowly and carefully, pausing now and again to gaze distantly into the flames. While he read, I unobtrusively fed the fire and immersed myself in the familiar smells of woodsmoke and ink and chemicals and the pines outside, all the thousand indefinable scents that tried to tell me I was home.

When Dad was done reading, he closed his eyes and nodded slowly for a time. Then he turned to me and regarded me with troubled eyes. "You've left out the ending," he said.

"Because I'm not sure how I feel about it."

He steepled his fingers. "What is it that troubles you, Isham?"

"Dad," I said earnestly, "Carlson is the first man I ever killed. That's . . . not a small thing. As it happens I didn't actually see my bullet blow off the back of his skull, and sometimes it's hard to believe in my gut that I really did it—I know it seemed unreal when I saw him afterward. But in fact I have killed a man. And as you just read, that may be necessary sometimes, but I'm not sure it's right. I *know* all that Carlson did, to us Stones and to the world, I know the guilt he bore. But I must ask you: Dad, was I *right* to kill him? Did he deserve to die?"

He came to me then and gripped my shoulder, and we stood like black iron statues before the raving fire. He locked eyes with me. "Perhaps you should ask your mother, Isham. Or your brother Israfel. Perhaps you should have asked the people whose remains you stepped over to kill Carlson. I do not know what is 'right' and 'wrong'; they are slippery terms to define. I only know what is. And revenge, as Collaci told you, *is* a uniquely human attribute.

"Superstitious Agro guerrillas used to raid us from time to time, and because we were reluctant to fire on them they got away with it. Then one day they captured Collaci's wife, not knowing she was diabetic. By the time he caught up with them she was dead of lack of insulin. Within seven days, every guerrilla in that raiding party had died, and Fresh Start has not been raided in all the years since, for all Jordan's rhetoric. Ask Collaci about vengeance."

"But Jordan's Agros hate us more than ever."

"But they buy our axheads and wheels, our sulfa and our cloth, just like their more sensible neighbors, and they leave us alone. Carlson's death will be an eternal warning to any who would impose their values on the world at large, and an eternal comfort to those who were robbed by him of the best of their lives—of their homes and their loved ones.

"Isham, you . . . did . . . *right.* Don't ever think differently, son. You did right, and I am deeply proud of you. Your mother and Israfel are resting easier now, and millions more too. I know that I will sleep easier tonight than I have in eighteen years."

*That's right, Dad, you will.* I relaxed. "All right, Dad. I guess you're right. I just wanted to hear someone tell me besides myself. I wanted *you* to tell me." He smiled and nodded and sat down again, and I left him there, an old man lost in his thoughts.

I went to the bathroom and closed the door behind me, glad that restored plumbing had been one of Fresh Start's first priorities to be realized. I spent a few minutes assembling some items I had brought back from New York City and removing the back of the septic tank behind the toilet bowl. Then I flushed the toilet.

Reaching into the tank I grabbed the gravity ball and flexed it horizontal so that the tank would not refill with water. Holding it in place awkwardly, I made a long arm and picked up the large bottle of chlorine bleach I had fetched from the city. As an irreplaceable relic of Civilization it was priceless—and utterly useless to modern man. I slipped my plugs into place and filled the tank with bleach, replacing the porcelain cover silently but leaving it slightly ajar. I bent again and grabbed a large canister—also a valuable but useless antique—of bathroom bowl cleaner. It was labeled "Vanish," and I hoped the label was prophetic. I poured the entire canister into the bowl.

*Hang the expense,* I thought, and giggled insanely.

Then I put the cover down on the seat, hid the bleach and bowl cleaner, and left, whistling softly through my teeth.

I felt good, better than I had since I left New York.

I walked through inky dark to the lake, and I sat among the pines by the shore, flinging stones at the water, trying to make them skip. I couldn't seem to get it right. I was used to the balancing effect of a left arm. I rubbed my stump ruefully and lay back and just thought for a while. I had lied to my father—it was not over. But it would be soon.

*Right or wrong*, I thought, removing my plugs and lighting a joint, *it sure can be necessary.*

Moonlight shattered on the branches overhead and lay in shards on the ground. I breathed deep of the cool darkness, tasted pot and woods and distant animals and the good crisp scents of a balanced ecology, heard the faraway hum of wind generators storing power for the work yet to be done. And I thought of a man gone mad with a dream of a better, simpler world; a man who, Heaven help him, meant well. And I thought of the tape recording I planned to leave behind me, explaining what I had done to the Council and the world.

CHAPTER SIX

*Transcript of a Tape Recording Made by Isham Stone (Fresh Start Judicial Archives).*

I might as well address this tape to you, Collaci—I'll bet my Musky gun that you're the first one to notice and play it. I hope you'll listen to it as well, but that might be too much to ask, the first time around. Just keep playing it.

The story goes back a couple of months, to when I was in the city. By now you've no doubt found my journal, with its account of my day in New York, and you've probably noticed the missing ending. Well, there are two endings to that story. There's the ending I told my father, and then there's the one you're about to hear. The true one.

I drifted in the darkness for a thousand years, helpless as a Musky in a hurricane, caroming off the inside of my skull. Memories swept by like drifting blimps, and I clutched at them as I sailed past, but the ones tangible enough to grasp burned my fingers. Vaguely, I sensed distant daylight on either side, decided those must be my ears and tried to steer for the right one, which seemed a bit closer. I singed my arm banking off an adolescent trauma, but it did the trick—I sailed out into daylight and landed on my face with a hell of a crash. I thought about getting up, but I couldn't remember whether I'd brought my legs with me, and they weren't talking. My arm hurt even more than my face, and something stank.

"Help?" I suggested faintly, and a pair of hands got me by the armpits. I rose in the air and closed my eyes against a sudden wave of vertigo. When it passed, I decided I was on my back in the bed I had just contrived to fall out of. High in my chest, a dull but insistent pain advised me to breathe shallowly.

*I'll be damned,* I thought weakly. *Collaci must have come along to back me up without telling me. Canny old son of a bitch, I should have thought to pick him up some toothpicks.*

"Hey, Teach'," I croaked, and opened my eyes.

Wendell Morgan Carlson leaned over me, concern in his gaze.

Curiously enough, I didn't try to reach up and crush his larynx. I closed my eyes, relaxed all over, counted to ten very slowly, shook my head to clear it, and opened my eyes again. Carlson was still there.

*Then* I tried to reach up and crush his larynx. I failed, of course, not so much because I was too weak to *reach* his larynx as because only one arm even acknowledged the command. My brain said that my left arm was straining upwards for Carlson's throat, and complaining like hell about it too, but I didn't see the arm anywhere. I looked down and saw the neatly bandaged stump and lifted it up absently to see if my arm was underneath it and it wasn't. It dawned on me then that the stump was all the left arm I was ever going to find, and whacko: I was back inside my skull, safe in the friendly dark, ricocheting off smoldering recollections again.

The second time I woke up was completely different. One minute I was wrestling with a phantom, and then a switch was thrown and I was lucid. *Play for time* was my first thought, *the tactical situation sucks.* I opened my eyes.

Carlson was nowhere in sight. Or smell—but then my plugs were back in place.

I looked around the room. It was a room. Four walls, ceiling, floor, the bed I was in and assorted ugly furniture. Not a weapon in sight, nor anything I could make one from. A look out the window in the opposite wall confirmed my guess that I was in Butler Hall, apparently on the ground floor, not far from the main entrance. The great curved dome of Low Library was nearly centered in the window frame, its great stone steps partly obscured by overgrown shrubbery in front of Butler. The shadows said it was morning, getting on toward noon. I closed my eyes, firmly.

Next I took stock of myself. My head throbbed a good deal, but it was easily drowned out by the ache in my chest. Unquestionably some ribs had broken, and it felt as though the ends were mismatched. But as near as I could tell the lung was intact—it didn't hurt more when I inhaled. Not much more, anyway. My legs both moved when I asked them to, with a minimum of back talk, and the ankles appeared sound. No need to open my eyes again, was there?

I stopped the inventory for a moment. In the back of my skull a clawed lizard yammered for release, and I devoted a few minutes to reinforcing the walls of its prison. When I could no longer hear the shrieking, I switched on my eyes again and quite dispassionately considered the stump on my left arm.

It looked like a good, clean job. The placement of the cut said it was a surgical procedure rather than the vengeful hostility I'd assumed first— it seemed as though the gangrene had been beaten. *Oh fine,* I thought, *a benevolent madman I have to kill.* Then I was ashamed. My mother had been benevolent, as I remembered her; and Israfel never got much chance to be anything. All men knew Carlson's intentions had been good. I could kill him with one hand.

I wondered where he was.

A fly buzzed mournfully around the room. Hedges rustled outside the window, and somewhere birds sang, breathless trills that hung sparkling on the morning air. It was a beautiful day, just warm enough to be comfortable, no clouds evident, just enough breeze and the best part of the day yet to come. It made me want to go down by the stream and poke frogs with a stick, or go pick strawberries for Mr. Fletcher, red-stained hands and a bellyful of sweet and the trots next morning. It was a great day for an assassination.

I thought about it, considered the possibilities. Carlson was . . . somewhere. I was weaker than a Musky in a pressure cooker and my most basic armament was down by twenty-five percent. I was on unfamiliar territory, and the only objects in the room meaty enough to constitute weaponry were too heavy for me to lift. Break the windowpane and acquire a knife? How would I hold it? My sneakers were in sight across the room, under a chair holding the rest of my clothes, and I wondered if I could hide behind the door until Carlson entered, then strangle him with the laces.

I brought up short. How was I going to strangle Carlson with one hand?

Things swam then for a bit, as I got the first of an endless series of flashes of just how drastically my life was altered now by the loss of my arm. *You'll never use a chain saw again, or a shovel, or a catcher's mitt, or . . .*

I buried the lizard again and forced myself to concentrate. Perhaps I could fashion a noose from my sneaker laces. With one hand? *Could* I? Maybe if I fastened one end of the lace to something, then looped the other end around his neck and pulled? I needn't be strong, it could be arranged so that my weight did the killing. . . .

Just in that one little instant I think I decided not to die, decided to keep on living with one arm, and the question never really arose in my mind again. I was too busy to despair, and by the time I could afford to —much later—the urge was gone.

All of my tentative plans, therapeutic as they were, hinged on one important question: could I stand up? It seemed essential to find out.

Until then I had moved only my eyes—now I tried sitting up. It was no harder than juggling bulldozers, and I managed to cut the scream down to an explosive, "Uh *huh!*" My ribs felt like glass, broken glass ripping through the muscle sheathing and pleural tissue. Sweat broke out on my forehead and I fought down dizziness and nausea, savagely commanding my body to obey me like a desperate rider digging spurs into a dying horse. I locked my right arm behind me and leaned on it, swaying but upright, and waited for the room to stop spinning. I spent the time counting to one thousand by eighths. Finally it stopped, leaving me with the feeling that a stiff breeze could start it spinning again.

All right then. *Let's get this show on the road, Stone.* I swung a leg over the side of the bed, discovered with relief that my foot reached the floor. That would make it easier to balance upright on the edge of the bed before attempting to stand. Before I could lose my nerve I swung the other leg over, pushed off with my arm, and was sitting upright. The floor was an incredible distance below—had I really fallen that far and lived? Perhaps I should just wait for Carlson to return, get him to come close, and sink my teeth into his jugular.

I stood up.

A staggering crescendo in the symphony of pain, ribs still carrying the melody. I locked my knees and tottered, moaning piteously like a kitten trapped on a cornice. It was the closest I could come to stealthy silence, and all things considered it was pretty damn close. My right shoulder was discernibly heavier than the left one, and it played hob with my balance. The floor, which had been steadily receding, was now so far away I stopped worrying about it—surely there would be time for the chute to open.

Well then, why not try a step or two?

My left leg was as light as a helium balloon—once peeled off the floor it tried to head for the ceiling, and it took an enormous effort to force it down again. The right leg fared no better. Then the room started spinning again, just as I'd feared, and it was suddenly impossible to keep either leg beneath my body, which began losing altitude rapidly. The chute didn't open. There was a jarring crash, and a ghastly *bounce*. Many pretty lights appeared, and one of the screams fenced in behind closed teeth managed to break loose. The pretty lights gave way to flaking ceiling, and the ceiling gave way to blackness. I remembered a line from an old song Dr. Mike used to sing, something about ". . . road maps in a well-cracked ceiling . . ." and wished I'd had time to read the map. . . .

I came out of it almost at once, I think. It *felt* as though the room was still spinning, but I was now spinning with it at the same velocity. By great good fortune I had toppled backward, across the bed. I took a tentative breath, and it still felt like my lung was intact. I was drenched with sweat, and I seemed to be lying on someone's rock collection.

*Okay*, I decided, *if you're too weak to kill Carlson now, pretend you're even weaker. Get back under the sheets and play dead, until your position improves.* Isham Machiavelli, that's me. You'd've been proud of me, Teach'.

The rock collection turned out to be wrinkled sheets. Getting turned around and back to where I'd started was easier than reeling a whale into a rowboat, and I had enough strength to arrange the sheets plausibly before all my muscles turned into peanut butter. Then I just lay there breathing as shallowly as I could manage, wondering why my left . . . why my stump didn't seem to hurt enough. I hated to look a gift horse in the mouth; the psychological burden was quite heavy enough, thanks. But it made me uneasy.

I began composing a square-dance tune in time to the throbbing of my ribs. The room reeled to it, slightly out of synch at first but then so rhythmically that it actually seemed to stumble when the snare drummer out in the hall muffed a paradiddle. The music stopped, but the drummer staggered on off-rhythm, faint at first but getting louder. Footsteps.

It had to be Carlson.

He was making a hell of a racket. Feverishly I envisioned him dragging a bazooka into the room and lining it up on me. Crazy. A flyswatter would have more than sufficed. But what the hell *was* he carrying then?

The answer came through the doorway: a large carton filled with things that clanked and rattled. Close behind it came Wendell Morgan Carlson himself, and it was as well that the square-dance music had stopped—the acceleration of my pulse would have made the tune undanceable. My nostrils tried to flare around the plugs, and the hair on the back of my neck might have bristled in atavistic reflex if there hadn't been a thousand pounds of head lying on it.

*The Enemy!*

He had no weapons visible. He looked much older than his picture on the Carlson Poster—but the craggy brow, thin pinched nose, and high cheeks were unmistakable, even if the lantern jaw was obscured by an inordinate amount of gray beard. He was a bit taller than I had pictured him, with more hair and narrower shoulders. I hadn't expected the potbelly. He wore baggy jeans and a plaid flannel shirt, both ineptly patched here and there, and a pair of black sandals.

His face held more intelligence than I like in an antagonist—he would not be easy to fool. *Wendell who? Never heard of him. Just got back from Pellucidar myself, and I was wondering if you could tell me where all the people went? Sorry I took a shot at you, and oh yeah, thanks for cutting off my arm; you're a brick.*

He put the carton down on an ancient brown desk, crushing a faded photograph of someone's children, turned at once to meet my gaze, and said an incredible thing.

"I'm sorry I woke you."

I don't know what I'd expected. But in the few fevered moments I'd had to prepare myself for this moment, my first exchange of words with Wendell Morgan Carlson, I had never imagined such an opening gambit. I had no riposte prepared.

"You're welcome," I croaked insanely, and tried to smile. Whatever it was I actually did seemed to upset him; his face took on that look of concern I had glimpsed once before—when? Yesterday? *How long had I been here?*

"I'm glad you are awake," he went on obligingly. "You've been unconscious for nearly a week." No wonder I felt constructed of inferior materials. I decided I must be a pretty tough mothafucka. It was nice to know I wasn't copping out.

"What's in the box?" I asked, with a little less fuzz tone.

"Box?" He looked down. "Oh yes, I thought . . . you see, it's intravenous feeding equipment. I studied the literature, and I . . ." he trailed off. His voice was a reedy but pleasant alto, with rusting brass edges. He appeared unfamiliar with its use.

"You were going to . . ." An ice cube formed in my bowels. Needle into sleeping arm, suck my life from a tube; have a hit of old Isham. *Steady, boy, steady.*

"Perhaps it might still be a good idea," he mused. "All I have to offer you at the moment is bread and milk. Not real milk of course . . . but then you could have honey with the bread. I suppose that's as good as glucose."

"Fine with me, Doctor," I said hastily. "I have a thing about needles." And other sharp instruments. "But where do you get your honey?"

He frowned quizzically. "How did you know I have a Ph.D.?"

*Think quick.* "I didn't. I assumed you were a Healer. It was you who amputated my arm?" I kept my voice even.

His frown deepened, a striking expression on that craggy face. "Young man," he said reluctantly, "I have no formal medical training of any sort. Perhaps your arm could have stayed on—but it seemed to me . . ." He was, to my astonishment, mortally embarrassed.

"Doctor, it needed extensive cutting the last time I saw it, and I'm sure it got worse while I was under. Don't . . . worry about it. I'm sure you did the best you could." If he was inclined to forget my attempt to blow his head off, who was *I* to hold a grudge? Let bygones be bygones—I didn't need a new reason to kill him.

"I read all I could find on field amputation," he went on, still apologetic, "but of course I'd never done one before." On anything smaller than a race. I assured him that it looked to me like a textbook job. It was inexpressibly weird to have this man seek my pardon for saving my life when I planned to take his at the earliest possible opportunity. It upset me, made me irritable. My wounds provided a convenient distraction, and I moved enough to justify a moan.

Carlson was instantly solicitous. From his cardboard carton he produced a paper package which, torn open, revealed a plastic syringe. Taking a stoppered jar from the carton, he drew off a small amount of clear fluid.

"What's that?" I said, trying to keep the suspicion from my voice.

"Demerol."

I shook my head. "No, thanks, Doc. I told you I don't like needles."

He nodded, put down the spike, and took another object from the carton. "Here's oral Demerol, then. I'll leave it where you can reach it." He put it on a bedside table. I picked up the jar, gave it a quick glance. It said it was Demerol. I could not break the seal around the cap with one hand—Carlson had to open it for me. *Thank you, my enemy.* Weird, weird, weird! I palmed a pill, pretending to swallow it. He looked satisfied.

"Thanks, Doc."

"Please don't call me Doc," he asked. "My name is Wendell Carlson."

If he was expecting a reaction, he was disappointed. "Sure thing, Wendell. I'm Tony Latimer. Pleased to meet you." It was the first name that entered my head.

There was a lull in the conversation. We studied each other with the frank curiosity of men who have not known human company for a while. At last he looked embarrassed again and tore his gaze from mine. "I'd better see about that food. You must be terribly hungry."

I thought about it. It seemed to me that I could put away a quarter horse. Raw. With my fingers. "I could eat."

Carlson left the room, looking at his sandals.

I thought of loading the hypo with an overdose and ambushing him when he returned, but it was just a thought. That hypo was mighty far away. I returned my attention to the jar on the table. It still said it was Demerol—and it *had* been sealed, with white plastic. But Carlson could have soaked off and replaced a skull-and-crossbones label—I decided to live with the pain a while longer.

It seemed like a long time before he returned, but my time sense was not too reliable. He fetched a half loaf of brown bread, a mason jar of soya milk, and some thick, crystallized honey. They say that smell is essential to taste, and I couldn't unplug, but it tasted better than food ever had before.

"You never told me where you get honey, Wendell."

"I have a small hive down in Central Park. Only a few supers, but adequate for my needs. Wintering the bees is quite a trick, but I manage."

"I'll bet it is." Small talk in the slaughterhouse. I ate what he gave me and drank soya milk until I was full. My body still hurt, but not as much.

We talked for about half an hour, mostly inconsequentialities, and it seemed that a tension grew up between us, because of the very inconsequentiality of our words. There were things of which we did not speak, of which innocent men should have spoken. In my dazed condition I could concoct no plausible explanation for my presence in New York, nor for the shot I had fired at him. Somehow he accepted this, but in return I was not to ask him how he came to be living in New York City,

I was not supposed to have any idea who Wendell Morgan Carlson was. It was an absurd bargain, a truth level impossible to maintain, but it suited both of us. I couldn't imagine what he thought of my own conversational omissions, but I was convinced that his silence was an admission of guilt, and my resolve was firmed. He left me at last, advising me to sleep if I could and promising to return the next day.

I didn't sleep. Not at first. I lay there looking at the Demerol bottle for a hundred years, explaining to myself how unlikely it was that the bottle wasn't genuine. I could not help it—hatred and distrust of Carlson were ingrained in me.

But enough pain will break through the strongest conditioning. About sundown I ate the pill I'd palmed, and in a very short time I was unconscious.

The next few days passed slowly.

Woops—I'm out of tape. Time to flip over the re—

## CHAPTER SEVEN

*Stone Tape Transcript, Side Two*

The days passed slowly, but not so slowly as the pain. Lucidity returned slowly, but no faster than physical strength.

You've got to understand how it was, Teach'.

The Demerol helped—but not by killing pain. What it did was keep me so stoned that I often forgot the pain was there. In a warm, creative glow I would devise a splendidly subtle and poetic means of Killing Carlson—then half an hour later the same plan would seem hopelessly crackbrained. An imperfection of the glass in the window across the room, warping the clean proud curve of the Low dome, held me fascinated for hours—yet I could not seem to concentrate for five minutes on practical matters.

Carlson came and went, asking few questions and answering fewer, and in my stupor I tried to fire my hate to the killing point, and—Collaci, my instructor and mentor and (I hope) friend—I failed.

You must understand me—I spent hours trying to focus on the hatred my father had passed on to me, to live up to the geas that fate had laid upon me, to do my duty. But it was damned hard work. Carlson was an absurd combination: so absentminded as to remind me of Dad—and as thoughtful, in his way, as you. He would forget his coat when he left at night—but be back on time with a hot breakfast, shivering and failing to notice. He would forget my name, but never my chamber pot. He would search, blinking, in all directions for the coffee cup that sat perched on his lap, but he never failed to put mine where I could reach it without strain on my ribs. I discovered quite by accident that I slept in the only bed Carlson had ever hauled into Butler, that he himself dossed on a makeshift bed out in the hall, so as to be near if I cried out in the night.

He offered no clue to his motivations, no insight into what kept him entombed in New York City. He spoke of his life of exile as a simple fact, requiring no explanation. It seemed more and more obvious that his silence was an admission of guilt: that he could not explain his survival and continued presence in this smelly mausoleum without admitting his crime. I tried, how I tried, to hate him.

But it was damnably difficult. He supplied my needs before I could voice them, wants before I could form them. He sensed when I craved company and when to leave me be, when I needed to talk and when I needed to be talked to. He suffered my irritability and occasional rages in a way that somehow allowed me to keep my self-respect.

He was gone for long periods of time during the day and night, and never spoke of his activities. I never pressed him for information; as a recuperating assassin it behooved me to display no undue curiosity. I could not risk arousing his suspicions.

We never, for instance, chanced to speak of my weapons or their whereabouts.

And so the subconscious tension of our first conversation stayed with us, born of the things of which we did not speak. It was obvious to both of us—and yet it was a curious kind of kinship, too: both of us lived with something we could not share, and recognized the condition in the other. Even as I planned his death I felt a kind of empathy between Wendell Morgan Carlson and myself. It bothered hell out of me. If Carlson was what I *knew* he was, what his guilty silence only proved him to be, then his death was necessary and just—for my father had taught me that debts are always paid. But I could not help but like the absent-minded old man.

Yet that tension was there. We spoke only of neutral things: where he got gasoline to feed the generator that powered wall sockets in the ground-floor rooms (we did not discuss what he would store it in now that I'd ruined his two-hundred-gallon tank). How far he had to walk these days to find scavengeable flour, beans, and grains. The trouble he had encountered in maintaining the University's hydroponics cultures by himself. What he did with sewage and compost. The probability of tomatoes growing another year in the miserable sandy soil of Central Park. What a turkey he'd been to not think of using the pure-grain alky in Organic Chem for fuel. Never did we talk of why he undertook all the complex difficulty of living in New York, nor why I had sought him here. He . . . diverted the patient with light conversation, and the patient allowed him to do so.

I had the hate part all ready to go, but I couldn't superimpose my lifetime picture of Carlson over this fuzzy, pleasant old academic and make it fit. And so the hate boiled in my skull and made convalescence an aimless, confused time. It got much worse when Carlson, explaining that few things on earth are more addictive than oral Demerol, cut me off cold turkey in my second week. Less potent analgesics, Talwin, aspirin, all had decayed years ago, and if I sent Carlson rummaging through the rucksack I had left under a station wagon on 114th Street for the remaining weed, he would in all likelihood come across the annotated map of New York given me by Collaci, and the mimeo'd Carlson Poster. Besides, my ribs hurt too much to smoke.

One night I woke in a sweat-soaked agony to find the room at a crazy angle, the candle flame slanting out of the dark like a questing tongue. I had half fallen out of bed, and my right arm kept me from falling the rest of the way, but I could not get back up without another arm. I didn't seem to have one. Ribs began to throb as I considered the dilemma, and I cried out from the pain.

From out in the hallway came a honking snore that broke off in a grunted "Whazzat? Wha?" and then a series of gasps as Carlson dutifully rolled from his bed to assist me. There came a crash, then a greater one attended by a splash, then a really tremendous crash that echoed and reechoed. Carlson lurched into view, a potbellied old man in yellow pajamas, eyes three-quarters closed and unfocused, one foot trapped in a galvanized wastebasket, gallantly coming to my rescue. He hit the doorframe a glancing blow with his shoulder, overbalanced, and went down on his face. I believe he came fully awake a second after he hit the floor; his eyes opened wide and he saw me staring at him in dazed disbelief from a few inches away. And for one timeless moment the absurdity of our respective positions hit us, and we broke up, simultaneous whoops of laughter at ourselves that cut off at once, and a second later he was helping me back into bed with strong, gentle hands, and I was trying not to groan aloud.

Dammit, I liked him.

Then one day while he was away I rose from the bed all by myself, quite gratified to find that I could, and hobbled like an old, old man composed of glass to the window that looked out on the entrance area of Butler and the hedge-hidden quadrangle beyond. It was a chill, slightly off-white day, but to me even the meager colors of shrub and tree seemed unaccountably vivid. From the overfamiliar closeness of the sickroom, the decaying campus had a magnificent depth. Everything was so *far away*. It was a little overwhelming. Moving closer to the window, I looked to the right.

Carlson stood before the front doors, staring up at the sky over the quadrangle with his back to me. On his head was the same curious helmet I had seen once before, days ago, framed in the cross hairs of my rifle. The odd-looking machine was before him, wired to his helmet and his arms. I wondered again what it could be, and then I saw something that made me freeze, made me forget the pain and the dizziness and stare with full attention.

Carlson was staring down the row between two greatly overgrown hedges that ran parallel to each other and perpendicular to Butler, facing toward Low's mighty cascade of steps. But he stared as a man watching something *near* him, and its position followed that of the wind-tossed upper reaches of the hedges.

Intuitively I knew that he was using the strange machine to communicate with a Musky, and all the hatred and rage for which I had found no outlet boiled over, contorting my face with fury.

It seemed an enormous effort not to cry out some primal challenge; I believe I bared my teeth. *You bastard,* I thought savagely, *you set us up for them, made them our enemies, and now you're hand in glove with them.* I was stupefied by such incredible treachery, could not make any sense of it, did not care. As I watched from behind and to the left I saw his lips move silently, but I did not care what they said, what kind of deal Carlson had worked out with the murderous gas clouds. He had one. He dealt with the creatures that had killed my mother, that he had virtually created. He would soon die.

I shuffled with infinite care back to bed, and planned.

I was ready to kill him within a week. My ribs were mostly healed now—I came to realize that my body's repair process had been waiting only for me to decide to heal, to leave the safe haven of convalescence. My strength returned to me and soon I could walk easily, and even dress myself with care, letting the left sleeve dangle. Most of the pain was gone from the stump, leaving only the many annoying tactile phenomena of severed nerves, the classic "phantom arm," and the flood of sweat which seemed to pour from my left armpit but could not be found on my side. Thanks to Carlson's tendency toward sound sleep, I was familiar with the layout of the main floor—and had recovered the weapons he was too absentminded to destroy. He had "hidden" them in the broom closet.

I wanted to take him in a time and place where his Musky pals couldn't help him; it seemed to me certain that the ones I had destroyed were bodyguards. A blustery cold night obliged by occurring almost immediately, breezes too choppy to be effectively used by a windrider.

The kind of night which, in my childhood, we chose for a picnic or a hayride.

We ate together in my room, a bean and lentil dish with tamari and fresh bread, and as he was finishing his last sip of coffee I brought the rifle out from under the blanket and drew a bead on his face.

"End of the line, Wendell."

He sat absolutely still, cup still raised to his lips, gazing gravely over it at me, for a long moment. Then he put the cup down very slowly, and sighed. "I didn't think you'd do it so soon. You're not well enough, you know."

I grinned. "You were expecting this, huh?"

"Ever since you discovered your weapons the night before last, Tony."

My grin faded. "And you let me live? Wendell, have you a death wish?"

"I cannot kill," he said sadly, and I roared with sudden laughter.

"Maybe not anymore, Wendell. Certainly not in another few minutes." *But you have killed before, killed more than anyone in history. Hell, Hitler, Attila, they're all punks beside you!*

He grimaced. "So you know who I am."

"The whole world knows. What's left of it."

Pain filled his eyes, and he nodded. "The last few times I tried to leave the city, to find others to help me in my work, they shot at me. Two years ago I found a man down in the Bowery who had been attacked by a dog pack. He had a tooth missing. He said he had come to kill me, for the price on my head, and he died, cursing me, in my arms as I brought him here. The price he named was high, and I knew there would be others."

"And you nursed me back to health? You must know that you deserve to die." I sneered. "Musky-lover."

"You know even that, then?"

"I saw you talking with them, with that crazy helmet of yours. The ones who attacked me were your bodyguards, weren't they?"

"The windriders came to me almost twenty years ago," he said softly, eyes far away. "They did not harm me. Since then I have slowly learned to speak with them, after a fashion, using the undermind. We might yet have understood one another."

The gun was becoming heavy on my single arm, difficult to aim properly. I rested the barrel on my knee, and shifted my grip slightly. My hands were sweaty.

"Well?" he said gruffly. "Why haven't you killed me already?"

A good question. I swept it aside irritably. "Why did you do it?" I barked.

"Why did I create the Hyperosmic Virus?" His weathered face saddened even more, and he tugged at his beard. "Because I was a damned fool, I suppose. Because it was a pretty problem in biochemistry. Because no one else could have done it, and because I wasn't certain that I could. I never suspected when I began that it would be used as it was."

"Its release was a spur-of-the-moment decision, is that it?" I snarled, tightening my grip on the trigger.

"I suppose so," he said quietly. "Only Jacob could say, of course."

"*Who?*"

"Jacob Stone," he said, startled by my violence. "My assistant. I thought you said you . . ."

"So you knew who I was all the time," I growled.

He blinked at me, plainly astounded. Then understanding flooded his craggy features. "Of course," he murmured. "Of *course*. You're young Isham—I should have recognized you. I smelled your hate, of course, but I never . . ."

"You *what?*"

"Smelled the scent of hate upon you," he repeated, puzzled. "Not much of a trick—you've been reeking with it lately."

*How could he? . . .* Impossible, sweep it aside.

"And now I imagine you'll want to discharge that hate and avenge your father's death. That was his own doing, but no matter: it was I who made it possible. Go ahead, pull the trigger." He closed his eyes.

"My father is not dead," I said, drowning now in confusion.

Carlson opened his eyes at once. "No? I assumed he perished when he released the Virus."

My ears roared; the rifle was suddenly impossible to aim. I wanted to cry out, to damn Carlson for a liar, but I knew the fuzzy professor was no actor and all at once I sprang up out of the bed and burst from the room, through wrought-iron lobby doors and out of the great empty hall, out into blackness and howling wind and a great swirling kaleidoscope of stars that reeled drunkenly overhead. Ribs pulsing, I walked for a hundred years, clutching my idiot rifle, heedless of danger from Musky or hungry Doberman, pursued by a thousand howling demons. Dimly I heard Carlson calling out behind me for a time, but I lost him easily and continued, seeking oblivion. The city, finding its natural prey for the first time in two decades, obligingly swallowed me up.

More than a day later I had my next conscious thought. I became aware that I had been staring at my socks for at least an hour, trying to decide what color they were.

My second coherent thought was that my ass hurt.

I looked around: beyond smashed observation windows, the great steel-and-stone corpse of New York City was laid out below me like some incredible three-dimensional jigsaw. I was at the top of the Empire State Building.

I had no memory of the long climb, nor of the flight downtown from Columbia University, and it was only after I had worked out how tired I must be that I realized how tired I was. My ribs felt sand-blasted and the winds that swept the observation tower were very very cold.

I was higher from the earth than I had ever been before in my life, facing south toward the empty World Trade Center, toward that part of the Atlantic into which this city had once dumped five hundred cubic feet of human shit every day; but I saw neither city nor sea. Instead I saw a frustrated, ambitious black man, obsessed with a scheme for quick-and-easy world salvation, conning a fuzzy-headed genius whose eminence he could never hope to attain. I saw that man, terrified by the ghastly results of his folly, fashioning a story to shift blame from himself and repeating it until all men believed it—and perhaps he himself as well. I saw at last the true face of that story's villain: a tormented, guilt-driven old man, exiled for the high crime of gullibility, befriended only by his race's bitterest enemies, nursing his assassin back to health. And I saw as though for the first time that assassin, trained and schooled to complete a cover-up, the embittered black man's last bucket of white-wash.

My father had loaded me with all the hatred and anger he felt for himself, aimed me toward a scapegoat and fired me like a cannon.

But I would ricochet.

I became aware of noise below me, in the interior of the building. I waited incuriously, not even troubling to lift my rifle from my lap. The noise became weary footsteps on the floor below me. They shuffled slowly up the iron stairway nearest me, and paused at the top. I heard hoarse, wheezing breath, struggling to slow itself, succeeding. I did not turn.

"Hell of a view," I said, squinting at it.

"View of a hell," Carlson wheezed behind me.

"How'd you find me, Wendell?"

"I followed your spoor."

I spun, stared at him. "You—"

"Followed your spoor."

I turned around again, and giggled. The giggle became a chuckle, and then I sat on it. "Still got your adenoids, eh, Doc? Sure. Twenty years in this rotten graveyard and I'll bet you've never owned a set of nose plugs. Punishment to fit the crime—and then some."

He did not reply. His breathing was easier now.

"My father, Wendell, now there's an absentminded man for you," I went on conversationally. "Always doing some sort of Civilized work, always forgetting to remove his plugs when he comes home—he surely does take a lot of kidding. Our security chief, Phil Collaci, quietly makes sure Dad has a Guard with him at all times when he goes out-doors—just can't depend on Dad's sense of smell, Teach' says. Dad always was a terrible cook, you know? He always puts too much garlic in the soup. Am I boring you, Wendell? Would you like to hear a lovely death I just dreamed? I am the last assassin on earth, and I have just created a brand-new death, a unique one. It convicts as it kills—if you die, you deserve to." My voice was quite shrill now, and a part of me clinically diagnosed hysteria. Carlson said something I did not hear as I raved of toilet bowls and brains splashing on a sidewalk and impossible thousands of chittering gray rats and my eyes went nova and a carillon shattered in my skull and when the world came back I realized that the exhausted old man had slapped my head near off my shoulders. He crouched beside me, holding his hand and wincing.

"Why have no Muskies attacked me, here in the heights?" My voice was soft now, wind-tossed.

"The windriders project and receive emotions. Those who sorrow as you and I engender respect and fear in them. You are protected now, as I have been these twenty years. An expensive shield."

I blinked at him and burst into tears.

He held me then in his frail old arms, as my father had never done, and rocked me while I wept. I wept until I was exhausted, and when I had not cried for a time he said softly, "You will put away your new death, unused. You are his son, and you love him."

I shivered then, and he held me closer, and did not see me smile.

So there you have it, Teach'. Stop thinking of Jacob Stone as the Father of Fresh Start, and see him as a man—and you will not only realize that his sense of smell was a hoax, but like me will wonder how you were ever taken in by so transparent a fiction. There are a dozen blameless explanations for Dad's anosmia—none of which would have required pretense.

So look at the method of his dying. The lid of the septic tank will be found ajar—the bathroom will surely smell of chlorine. Ask yourself how a chemist could possibly walk into such a trap—*if he had any sense of smell at all?*

Better yet, examine the corpse for adenoids.

When you've put it all together, come look me up. I'll be at Columbia University, with my good friend Wendell Morgan Carlson. We have a lot of work to do, and I suspect we'll need the help of you and the Council before long. We're learning to talk with Muskies, you see.

If you come at night, I've got a little place of my own set up in the lobby of the Waldorf-Astoria. You can't miss me. But be sure to knock: I'm Musky-proof these days, but I've still got those subconscious sentries you gave me.

And I'm scared of the dark.

# James Tiptree, Jr.

A few years ago, Theodore Sturgeon, writing a review column in the New York *Times,* listed the new great science fiction writers of the 1970s, and pointed out that, except for James Tiptree, Jr., they were all women.

What Ted didn't know, and what no one knew till 1977 (a year after "Houston, Houston, Do You Read?" was published), was that James Tiptree, Jr., was a woman, too. Her real name is Alice Sheldon.

Tiptree appears also in Volume Three. In the introduction to the earlier tale, written in 1976, I used the male pronoun six times. How was I to know?

So what do I call her? I can't say "Sheldon," and certainly not "Alice." Her literary name is "James Tiptree, Jr.," and as long as I'm dealing with her in her literary persona, I ought to use her literary name. (You say "Lewis Carroll" when speaking of the author of *Alice in Wonderland.* You say "Charles Lutwidge Dodgson" when speaking of the mathematician and dean.)

And yet I can't say "James" or "Jim," either, even though I have exchanged friendly letters with her (not knowing she was a "her"). It seems silly to refer to a known woman that way, especially since I strongly suspect that no one has ever called her "James" or "Jim" to her face in her whole life.

So I'm afraid I am going to have to say "Tiptree."

Tiptree is a psychologist by profession and has a doctorate in the field, which she obtained in 1967.

The doctorate is never mentioned in the literary context, and rightly so. I remember that back in the 1920s, when magazine science fiction was just born, Hugo Gernsback was terribly anxious to give it what respectability he could. When he found that one of his authors had an academic degree, he used it. Thus Miles J. Breuer appeared always as Miles J. Breuer, M.D., and David H. Keller, as David H. Keller, M.D.

The prize example, however, was Edward Elmer Smith, who had a Ph.D. in chemistry. When his first story, "The Skylark of Space," was published, Gernsback featured him on the cover as "E. E. Smith, Ph.D."

Men like Breuer and Keller, however worthy, faded out in the 1930s, but E. E. Smith was a major force in science fiction for twenty years, and E. E. Smith, Ph.D., he was to the end. No one resented it, or thought it presumptuous or self-aggrandizing, because "Doc" Smith (as he was universally called) was the sweetest, most unassuming character ever invented, and everyone loved him.

I don't think anyone else could get away with it. When, in 1948, I got my own Ph.D., for one wild moment I thought of putting "Isaac Asimov, Ph.D." on my next submission. Just one! It may have even been a half moment. Then sanity swept over me like a great healing wave.

I simply do not use the degree at all in a literary context, not even on my stationery. A friend, I remember, urged me to use it.

"No," I said. "It would seem arrogant."

"It would seem more arrogant," he said, "if you didn't. You would be implying that your name required no artificial additions to make it important."

"True," I said.

I suspect Tiptree feels the same way—and should.

# HOUSTON, HOUSTON, DO YOU READ?

Lorimer gazes around the crowded cabin, trying to listen to the voices, trying to ignore the twitch in his insides that means he is about to remember something bad. No help; he lives it again, that long-ago moment. Himself running blindly—or was he pushed?—into the strange toilet at Evanston Junior High. His fly open, his dick in his hand, he can still see the gray zipper edge of his jeans around his pale exposed pecker. The hush. The sickening wrongness of shapes, faces turning. The first blaring giggle. *Girls.* He was in the *girls' can.*

He flinches now wryly, so many years later, not looking at the women's faces. The big cabin surrounds him with their alien things, curved around over his head: the beading rack, the twins' loom, Andy's leatherwork, the damned kudzu vine wriggling everywhere, the chickens. So cozy. . . . Trapped, he is. Irretrievably trapped for life in everything he does not enjoy. Structurelessness. Personal trivia, unmeaning intimacies. The claims he can somehow never meet. Ginny: *You never talk to me* . . . Ginny, love, he thinks involuntarily. The hurt doesn't come.

Bud Geirr's loud chuckle breaks in on him. Bud is joking with some of them, out of sight around a bulkhead. Dave is visible, though. Major Norman Davis on the far side of the cabin, his bearded profile bent toward a small dark woman Lorimer can't quite focus on. But Dave's head seems oddly tiny and sharp, in fact the whole cabin looks unreal. A cackle bursts out from the "ceiling"—the bantam hen in her basket.

At this moment Lorimer becomes sure he has been drugged.

Curiously, the idea does not anger him. He leans or rather tips back, perching cross-legged in the zero gee, letting his gaze go to the face of the woman he has been talking with. Connie. Constantia Morelos. A tall moon-faced woman in capacious green pajamas. He has never really cared for talking to women. Ironic.

"I suppose," he says aloud, "it's possible that in some sense we are not here."

That doesn't sound too clear, but she nods interestedly. She's watching my reactions, Lorimer tells himself. Women are natural poisoners. Has he said that aloud, too? Her expression doesn't change. His vision is taking on a pleasing local clarity. Connie's skin strikes him as quite fine, healthy-looking. Olive tan even after two years in space. She was a farmer, he recalls. Big pores, but without the caked look he associates with women her age.

"You probably never wore makeup," he says. She looks puzzled. "Face paint, powder. None of you have."

"Oh!" Her smile shows a chipped front tooth. "Oh yes, I think Andy has."

"Andy?"

"For plays. Historical plays, Andy's good at that."

"Of course. Historical plays."

Lorimer's brain seems to be expanding, letting in light. He is understanding actively now, the myriad bits and pieces linking into patterns. Deadly patterns, he perceives; but the drug is shielding him in some way. Like an amphetamine high without the pressure. Maybe it's something they use socially? No, they're watching, too.

"Space bunnies, I still don't dig it," Bud Geirr laughs infectiously. He has a friendly buoyant voice people like; Lorimer still likes it after two years.

"You chicks have kids back home, what do your folks think about you flying around out here with old Andy, h'mm?" Bud floats into view, his arm draped around a twin's shoulders. The one called Judy Paris, Lorimer decides; the twins are hard to tell. She drifts passively at an angle to Bud's big body: a jut-breasted plain girl in flowing yellow pajamas, her black hair raying out. Andy's red head swims up to them. He is holding a big green spaceball, looking about sixteen.

"Old Andy." Bud shakes his head, his grin flashing under his thick dark mustache. "When I was your age folks didn't let their women fly around with me."

Connie's lips quirk faintly. In Lorimer's head the pieces slide toward pattern. I know, he thinks. Do you know I know? His head is vast and crystalline, very nice really. Easier to think. Women. . . . No compact generalization forms in his mind, only a few speaking faces on a matrix of pervasive irrelevance. Human, of course. Biological necessity. Only so, so . . . diffuse? Pointless? . . . His sister Amy, *soprano con tremulo: Of course women could contribute as much as men if you'd treat us as equals.*

*You'll see!* And then marrying that idiot the second time. Well, now he can see.

"Kudzu vines," he says aloud. Connie smiles. How they all smile.

"How 'boot that?" Bud says happily. "Ever think we'd see chicks in zero gee, hey, Dave? Artits-stico. Woo-ee!" Across the cabin Dave's bearded head turns to him, not smiling.

"And ol' Andy's had it all to hisself. Stunt your growth, lad." He punches Andy genially on the arm, Andy catches himself on the bulkhead. Bud can't be drunk, Lorimer thinks; not on that fruit cider. But he doesn't usually sound so much like a stage Texan either. A drug.

"Hey, no offense," Bud is saying earnestly to the boy, "I mean that. You have to forgive one underprilly, underprivileged brother. These chicks are good people. Know what?" he tells the girl. "You could look stu-pen-dous if you fix yourself up a speck. Hey, I can show you, old Buddy's a expert. I hope you don't mind my saying that. As a matter of fact you look real stupendous to me right now."

He hugs her shoulders, flings out his arm and hugs Andy, too. They float upwards in his grasp, Judy grinning excitedly, almost pretty.

"Let's get some more of that good stuff." Bud propels them both toward the serving rack which is decorated for the occasion with sprays of greens and small real daisies.

"Happy New Year! Hey, Happy New Year, y'all!"

Faces turn, more smiles. Genuine smiles, Lorimer thinks, maybe they really like their New Years. He feels he has infinite time to examine every event, the implications evolving in crystal facets. I'm an echo chamber. Enjoyable, to be the observer. But others are observing, too. They've started something here. Do they realize? So vulnerable, three of us, five of them in this fragile ship. They don't know. A dread unconnected to action lurks behind his mind.

"By God, we made it," Bud laughs. "You space chickies, I have to give it to you. I commend you, by God, I say it. We wouldn't be here, wherever we are. Know what, I jus' might decide to stay in the service after all. Think they have room for old Bud in your space program, sweetie?"

"Knock that off, Bud," Dave says quietly from the far wall. "I don't want to hear us use the name of the Creator like that." The full chestnut beard gives him a patriarchal gravity. Dave is forty-six, a decade older than Bud and Lorimer. Veteran of six successful missions.

"Oh, my apologies, Major Dave, old buddy." Bud chuckles intimately to the girl. "Our commanding ossifer. Stupendous guy. Hey, Doc!" he calls. "How's your attitude? You making out dinko?"

"Cheers," Lorimer hears his voice reply, the complex stratum of his feelings about Bud rising like a kraken in the moonlight of his mind. The submerged silent thing he has about them all, all the Buds and Daves and big, indomitable cheerful, able, disciplined slow-minded mesomorphs he has cast his life with. Meso-ectos, he corrected himself; astronauts aren't muscleheads. They like him, he has been careful about that. Liked him well enough to get him on *Sunbird,* to make him the official scientist on the first circumsolar mission. That little Doc Lorimer, he's cool, he's on the team. No shit from Lorimer, not like those other scientific assholes. He does the bit well with his small neat build and his dead-pan remarks. And the years of turning out for the bowling, the volleyball, the tennis, the skeet, the skiing that broke his ankle, the touch football that broke his collarbone. Watch that Doc, he's a sneaky one. And the big men banging him on the back, accepting him. Their token scientist . . . The trouble is, he isn't any kind of scientist anymore. Living off his postdoctoral plasma work, a lucky hit. He hasn't really been into the math for years, he isn't up to it now. Too many other interests, too much time spent explaining elementary stuff. I'm a half jock, he thinks. A foot taller and a hundred pounds heavier and I'd be just like them. One of them. An alpha. They probably sense it underneath, the beta bile. Had the jokes worn a shade thin in *Sunbird,* all that year going out? A year of Bud and Dave playing gin. That damn exercycle, gearing it up too tough for me. They didn't mean it, though. We were a team.

The memory of gaping jeans flicks at him, the painful end part—the grinning faces waiting for him when he stumbled out. The howls, the dribble down his leg. Being cool, pretending to laugh, too. You shitheads, I'll show you. I am not a girl.

Bud's voice rings out, chanting. "And a Hap-pee New Year to you-all down there!" Parody of the oily NASA tone. "Hey, why don't we shoot 'em a signal? Greetings to all you Earthlings, I mean, all you little Lunies. Hap-py New Year in the good year whatsis." He snuffles comically. "There is a Santy Claus, Houston, ye-ew nevah saw nothin' like this! Houston, wherever you are," he sings out. "Hey, Houston! Do you read?"

In the silence Lorimer sees Dave's face set into Major Norman Davis, commanding.

And without warning he is suddenly back there, back a year ago in the cramped, shook-up command module of *Sunbird,* coming out from behind the sun. It's the drug doing this, he thinks as memory closes around him, it's so real. Stop. He tries to hang on to reality, to the sense of trouble building underneath.

—But he can't, he is *there,* hovering behind Dave and Bud in the triple couches, as usual avoiding his official station in the middle, seeing beside them their reflections against blackness in the useless port window. The outer layer has been annealed, he can just make out a bright smear that has to be Spica floating through the image of Dave's head, making the bandage look like a kid's crown.

"Houston, Houston, *Sunbird,*" Dave repeats; *"Sunbird* calling Houston. Houston, do you read? Come in, Houston."

The minutes start by. They are giving it seven out, seven back; seventy-eight million miles, ample margin.

"The high gain's shot, that's what it is," Bud says cheerfully. He says it almost every day.

"No way." Dave's voice is patient, also as usual. "It checks out. Still too much crap from the sun, isn't that right, Doc?"

"The residual radiation from the flare is just about in line with us," Lorimer says. "They could have a hard time sorting us out." For the thousandth time he registers his own faint, ridiculous gratification at being consulted.

"Shit, we're outside Mercury." Bud shakes his head. "How we gonna find out who won the Series?"

He often says that, too. A ritual, out here in eternal night. Lorimer watches the sparkle of Spica drift by the reflection of Bud's curly face-bush. His own whiskers are scant and scraggly, like a blond Fu Manchu. In the aft corner of the window is a striped glare that must be the remains of their port energy accumulators, fried off in the solar explosion that hit them a month ago and fused the outer layers of their windows. That was when Dave cut his head open on the sexlogic panel. Lorimer had been banged in among the gravity wave experiment, he still doesn't trust the readings. Luckily the particle stream has missed one piece of the front window; they still have about twenty degrees of clear vision straight ahead. The brilliant web of the Pleiades shows there, running off into a blur of light.

Twelve minutes . . . thirteen. The speaker sighs and clicks emptily. Fourteen. Nothing.

*"Sunbird* to Houston, *Sunbird* to Houston. Come in, Houston. *Sunbird* out." Dave puts the mike back in its holder. "Give it another twenty-four."

They wait ritually. Tomorrow Packard will reply. Maybe.

"Be good to see old Earth again," Bud remarks.

"We're not using any more fuel on attitude," Dave reminds him. "I trust Doc's figures."

It's not my figures, it's the elementary facts of celestial mechanics, Lorimer thinks; in October there's only one place for Earth to be. He never says it. Not to a man who can fly two-body solutions by intuition once he knows where the bodies are. Bud is a good pilot and a better engineer; Dave is the best there is. He takes no pride in it. "The Lord helps us, Doc, if we let Him."

"Going to be a bitch docking if the radar's screwed up," Bud says idly. They all think about that for the hundredth time. It will be a bitch. Dave will do it. That was why he is hoarding fuel.

The minutes tick off.

"That's it," Dave says—and a voice fills the cabin, shockingly.

"Judy?" It is high and clear. A girl's voice.

"Judy, I'm so glad we got you. What are you doing on this band?"

Bud blows out his breath; there is a frozen instant before Dave snatches up the mike.

"*Sunbird*, we read you. This is Mission *Sunbird* calling Houston, ah, *Sunbird One* calling Houston Ground Control. Identify, who are you? Can you relay our signal? Over."

"Some skip," Bud says. "Some incredible ham."

"Are you in trouble, Judy?" the girl's voice asks. "I can't hear, you sound terrible. Wait a minute."

"This is United States Space Mission *Sunbird One*," Dave repeats. "Mission *Sunbird* calling Houston Space Center. You are dee-exxing our channel. Identify, repeat identify yourself and say if you can relay to Houston. Over."

"Dinko, Judy, try it again," the girl says.

Lorimer abruptly pushes himself up the Lurp, the Long-Range Particle Density Cumulator experiment, and activates its shaft motor. The shaft whines, jars; lucky it was retracted during the flare, lucky it hasn't fused shut. He sets the probe pulse on max and begins a rough manual scan.

"You are intercepting official traffic from the United States space mission to Houston Control," Dave is saying forcefully. "If you cannot relay to Houston get off the air, you are committing a federal offense. Say again, can you relay our signal to Houston Space Center? Over."

"You still sound terrible," the girl says. "What's Houston? Who's talking, anyway? You know we don't have much time." Her voice is sweet but very nasal.

"Jesus, that's close," Bud says. "That is close."

"Hold it." Dave twists around to Lorimer's improvised radarscope.

"There." Lorimer points out a tiny stable peak at the extreme edge of the read-out slot, in the transcoronal scatter. Bud cranes too.

"A bogey!"

"Somebody else out here."

"Hello, hello? We have you now," the girl says. "Why are you so far out? Are you dinko, did you catch the flare?"

"Hold it," warns Dave. "What's the status, Doc?"

"Over three hundred thousand kilometers, guesstimated. Possibly headed away from us, going around the sun. Could be cosmonauts, a Soviet mission?"

"Out to beat us. They missed."

"With a *girl?*" Bud objects.

"They've done that. You taping this, Bud?"

"Roger-r-r." He grins. "That sure didn't sound like a Russky chick. Who the hell's Judy?"

Dave thinks for a second, clicks on the mike. "This is Major Norman Davis commanding United States spacecraft *Sunbird One.* We have you on scope. Request you identify yourself. Repeat, who are you? Over."

"Judy, stop joking," the voice complains. "We'll lose you in a minute, don't you realize we worried about you?"

"*Sunbird* to unidentified craft. This is not Judy. I say again, this is not Judy. Who are you? Over."

"What—" the girl says, and is cut off by someone saying, "Wait a minute, Ann." The speaker squeals. Then a different woman says, "This is Lorna Bethune in *Escondita.* What is going on here?"

"This is Major Davis commanding United States Mission *Sunbird* on course for Earth. We do not recognize any spacecraft *Escondita.* Will you identify yourself? Over."

"I just did." She sounds older with the same nasal drawl. "There is no spaceship *Sunbird* and you're not on course for Earth. If this is an andy joke it isn't any good."

"This is no joke, madam!" Dave explodes. "This is the American circumsolar mission and we are American astronauts. We do not appreciate your interference. Out."

The woman starts to speak and is drowned in a jibber of static. Two voices come through briefly. Lorimer thinks he hears the words *"Sunbird* program" and something else. Bud works the squelcher; the interference subsides to a drone.

"Ah, Major Davis?" The voice is fainter. "Did I hear you say you are on course for Earth?"

Dave frowns at the speaker and then says curtly, "Affirmative."

"Well, we don't understand your orbit. You must have very unusual flight characteristics, our readings show you won't node with anything on your present course. We'll lose the signal in a minute or two. Ah, would you tell us where you see Earth now? Never mind the coordinates, just tell us the constellation."

Dave hesitates and then holds up the mike. "Doc."

"Earth's apparent position is in Pisces," Lorimer says to the voice. "Approximately three degrees from P. Gamma."

"It is not," the woman says. "Can't you see it's in Virgo? Can't you see out at all?"

Lorimer's eyes go to the bright smear in the port window. "We sustained some damage—"

"Hold it," snaps Dave.

"—to one window during a disturbance we ran into at perihelion. Naturally we know the relative direction of Earth on this date, October nineteen."

"October? It's March, March fifteen. You must—" Her voice is lost in a shriek.

"E-M front," Bud says, tuning. They are all leaning at the speaker from different angles, Lorimer is head-down. Space noise wails and crashes like surf, the strange ship is too close to the coronal horizon. "—Behind you," they hear. More howls. "Band, try . . . ship . . . if you can, your signal—" Nothing more comes through.

Lorimer pushes back, staring at the spark in the window. It has to be Spica. But is it elongated, as if a second point-source is beside it? Impossible. An excitement is trying to flare out inside him, the women's voices resonate in his head.

"Playback," Dave says. "Houston will really like to hear this."

They listen again to the girl calling Judy, the woman saying she is Lorna Bethune. Bud holds up a finger. "Man's voice in there." Lorimer listens hard for the words he thought he heard. The tape ends.

"Wait till Packard gets this one." Dave rubs his arms. "Remember what they pulled on Howie? Claiming they rescued him."

"Seems like they want us on their frequency." Bud grins. "They must think we're fa-a-ar gone. Hey, looks like this other capsule's going to show up, getting crowded out here."

"If it shows up," Dave says. "Leave it on voice alert, Bud. The batteries will do that."

Lorimer watches the spark of Spica, or Spica-plus-something, wondering if he will ever understand. The casual acceptance of some trick or ploy out here in this incredible loneliness. Well, if these strangers are from the same mold, maybe that is it. Aloud he says, *"Escondita* is an odd name for a Soviet mission. I believe it means 'hidden' in Spanish."

"Yeah," says Bud. "Hey, I know what that accent is, it's Australian. We had some Aussie bunnies at Hickam. Or-stryle-ya, woo-ee! You s'pose Woomara is sending up some kind of com-bined do?"

Dave shakes his head. "They have no capability whatsoever."

"We ran into some fairly strange phenomena back there, Dave," Lorimer says thoughtfully. "I'm beginning to wish we could take a visual check."

"Did you goof, Doc?"

"No. Earth is where I said, if it's October. Virgo is where it would appear in March."

"Then that's it." Dave grins, pushing out of the couch. "You been asleep five months, Rip van Winkle? Time for a hand before we do the roadwork."

"What I'd like to know is what that chick looks like," says Bud, closing down the transceiver. "Can I help you into your space suit, miss? Hey, miss, pull that in, psst-psst-psst! You going to listen, Doc?"

"Right." Lorimer is getting out his charts. The others go aft through the tunnel to the small dayroom, making no further comment on the presence of the strange ship or ships out here. Lorimer himself is more shaken than he likes; it was that damn phrase.

The tedious exercise period comes and goes. Lunchtime: They give the containers a minimum warm to conserve the batteries. Chicken à la king again; Bud puts ketchup on his and breaks their usual silence with a funny anecdote about an Australian girl, laboriously censoring himself to conform to *Sunbird*'s unwritten code on talk. After lunch Dave goes forward to the command module. Bud and Lorimer continue their current task of checking out the suits and packs for a damage-assessment EVA to take place as soon as the radiation count drops.

They are just clearing away when Dave calls them. Lorimer comes through the tunnel to hear a girl's voice blare, "—dinko trip. What did Lorna say? *Gloria* over!"

He starts up the Lurp and begins scanning. No results this time. "They're either in line behind us or in the sunward quadrant," he reports finally. "I can't isolate them."

Presently the speaker holds another thin thread of sound.

"That could be their ground control," says Dave. "How's the horizon, Doc?"

"Five hours; Northwest Siberia, Japan, Australia."

"I told you the high gain is fucked up." Bud gingerly feeds power to his antenna motor. "Easy, eas-ee. The frame is twisted, that's what it is."

"Don't snap it," Dave says, knowing Bud will not.

The squeaking fades, pulses back. "Hey, we can really use this," Bud says. "We can calibrate on them."

A hard soprano says suddenly "—should be outside your orbit. Try around Beta Aries."

"Another chick. We have a fix," Bud says happily. "We have a fix now. I do believe our troubles are over. That monkey was torqued one hundred forty-nine degrees. Woo-ee!"

The first girl comes back. "We see them, Margo! But they're so small, how can they live in there? Maybe they're tiny aliens! Over."

"That's Judy." Bud chuckles. "Dave, this is screwy, it's all in English. It has to be some UN thingie."

Dave massages his elbows, flexes his fists; thinking. They wait. Lorimer considers a hundred and forty-nine degrees from Gamma Piscium.

In thirteen minutes the voice from Earth says, "Judy, call the others, will you? We're going to play you the conversation, we think you should all hear. Two minutes. Oh, while we're waiting, Zebra wants to tell Connie the baby is fine. And we have a new cow."

"Code," says Dave.

The recording comes on. The three men listen once more to Dave calling Houston in a rattle of solar noise. The transmission clears up rapidly and cuts off with the woman saying that another ship, the *Gloria*, is behind them, closer to the sun.

"We looked up history," the Earth voice resumes. "There was a Major Norman Davis on the first *Sunbird* flight. Major was a military title. Did you hear them say 'Doc'? There was a scientific doctor on board, Dr. Orren Lorimer. The third member was Captain—that's another title —Bernhard Geirr. Just the three of them, all males of course. We think they had an early reaction engine and not too much fuel. The point is, the first *Sunbird* mission was lost in space. They never came out from behind the sun. That was about when the big flares started. Jan thinks they must have been close to one, you heard them say they were damaged."

Dave grunts. Lorimer is fighting excitement like a brush discharge sparking in his gut.

"Either they are who they say they are or they're ghosts; or they're aliens pretending to be people. Jan says maybe the disruption in those super-flares could collapse the local time dimension. Pluggo. What did you observe there, I mean the highlights?"

*Time dimension . . . never come back . . .* Lorimer's mind narrows onto the reality of the two unmoving bearded heads before him, refuses to admit the words he thought he heard: *Before the year two thousand.* The language, he thinks. The language would have to have changed. He feels better.

A deep baritone voice says, "Margo?" In *Sunbird* eyes come alert.

"—like the big one fifty years ago." The man has the accent, too. "We were really lucky being right there when it popped. The most interesting part is that we confirmed the gravity turbulence. Periodic but not waves. It's violent, we got pushed around some. Space is under monster stress in those things. We think France's theory that our system is passing through a micro-black-hole cluster looks right so long as one doesn't plonk us."

"France?" Bud mutters. Dave looks at him speculatively.

"It's hard to imagine anything being kicked out in time. But they're here, whatever they are, they're over eight hundred kays outside us scooting out toward Aldebaran. As Lorna said, if they're trying to reach Earth they're in trouble unless they have a lot of spare gees. Should we try to talk to them? Over. Oh, great about the cow. Over again."

"Black holes." Bud whistles softly. "That's one for you, Doc. Was we in a black hole?"

"Not in one or we wouldn't be here." If we are here, Lorimer adds to himself. A micro-black-hole cluster . . . what happens when fragments of totally collapsed matter approach each other, or collide, say in the photosphere of a star? Time disruption? Stop it. Aloud he says, "They could be telling us something, Dave."

Dave says nothing. The minutes pass.

Finally the Earth voice comes back, saying that it will try to contact the strangers on their original frequency. Bud glances at Dave, tunes the selector.

"Calling *Sunbird One?*" the girl says slowly through her nose. "This is Luna Central calling Major Norman Davis of *Sunbird One.* We have picked up your conversation with our ship *Escondita.* We are very puzzled as to who you are and how you got here. If you really are *Sunbird One* we think you must have been jumped forward in time when you passed the solar flare." She pronounces it Cockney style, "toime."

"Our ship *Gloria* is near you, they see you on their radar. We think you may have a serious course problem because you told Lorna you were headed for Earth and you think it is now October with Earth in Pisces. It is not October. It is March fifteen. I repeat, the Earth date"— she says "dyte"—"is March fifteen, time twenty hundred hours. You should be able to see Earth very close to Spica in Virgo. You said your window is damaged. Can't you go out and look? We think you have to make a big course correction. Do you have enough fuel? Do you have a computer? Do you have enough air and water and food? Can we help you? We're listening on this frequency. Luna to *Sunbird One,* come in."

On *Sunbird* nobody stirs. Lorimer struggles against internal eruptions. *Never came back. Jumped forward in time.* The cyst of memories he has schooled himself to suppress bulges up in the lengthening silence. "Aren't you going to answer?"

"Don't be stupid," Dave says.

"Dave. A hundred and forty-nine degrees is the difference between Gamma Piscium and Spica. That transmission is coming from where they say Earth is."

"You goofed."

"I did not goof. It has to be March."

Dave blinks as if a fly is bothering him.

In fifteen minutes the Luna voice runs through the whole thing again, ending, "Please, come in."

"Not a tape." Bud unwraps a stick of gum, adding the plastic to the neat wad back of the gyro leads. Lorimer's skin crawls, watching the ambiguous dazzle of Spica. Spica-plus-Earth? Unbelief grips him, rocks him with a complex pang compounded of faces, voices, the sizzle of bacon frying, the creak of his father's wheelchair, chalk on a sunlit blackboard, Ginny's bare legs on the flowered couch, Jenny and Penny running dangerously close to the lawn mower. The girls will be taller now, Jenny is already as tall as her mother. His father is living with Amy in Denver, determined to last till his son gets home. *When I get home.* This has to be insanity, Dave's right; it's a trick, some crazy trick. The language.

Fifteen minutes more; the flat, earnest female voice comes back and repeats it all, putting in more stresses. Dave wears a remote frown, like a man listening to a lousy sports program. Lorimer has the notion he might switch off and propose a hand of gin; wills him to do so. The voice says it will now change frequencies.

Bud tunes back, chewing calmly. This time the voice stumbles on a couple of phrases. It sounds tired.

Another wait; an hour, now. Lorimer's mind holds only the bright point of Spica digging at him. Bud hums a bar of "Yellow Ribbons," falls silent again.

"Dave," Lorimer says finally, "our antenna is pointed straight at Spica. I don't care if you think I goofed, if Earth is over there we have to change course soon. Look, you can see it could be a double light source. We have to check this out."

Dave says nothing. Bud says nothing but his eyes rove to the port window, back to his instrument panel, to the window again. In the corner of the panel is a polaroid snap of his wife. Patty: a tall, giggling, rump-switching redhead; Lorimer has occasional fantasies about her. Little-girl voice, though. And so tall. . . . Some short men chase tall women; it strikes Lorimer as undignified. Ginny is an inch shorter than he. Their girls will be taller. And Ginny insisted on starting a pregnancy before he left, even though he'll be out of commo. Maybe, maybe a boy, a son—*stop it.* Think about anything. Bud. . . . Does Bud love Patty? Who knows? He loves Ginny. At seventy million miles. . . .

"Judy?" Luna Central or whoever it is says. "They don't answer. You want to try? But listen, we've been thinking. If these people really are from the past this must be very traumatic for them. They could be just realizing they'll never see their world again. Myda says these males had children and women they stayed with, they'll miss them terribly. This is exciting for us but it may seem awful to them. They could be too shocked to answer. They could be frightened, maybe they think we're aliens or hallucinations even. See?"

Five seconds later the nearby girl says, "Da, Margo, we were into that, too. Dinko. Ah, *Sunbird?* Major Davis of *Sunbird,* are you there? This is Judy Paris in the ship *Gloria,* we're only about a million kay from you, we see you on our screen." She sounds young and excited. "Luna Central has been trying to reach you, we think you're in trouble and we want to help. Please don't be frightened, we're people just like you. We think you're way off course if you want to reach Earth. Are you in trouble? Can we help? If your radio is out can you make any sort of signal? Do you know Old Morse? You'll be off our screen soon, we're truly worried about you. Please reply somehow if you possibly can, *Sunbird,* come in!"

Dave sits impassive. Bud glances at him, at the port window, gazes stolidly at the speaker, his face blank. Lorimer has exhausted surprise, he wants only to reply to the voices. He can manage a rough signal by heterodyning the probe beam. But what then, with them both against him?

The girl's voice tries again determinedly. Finally she says, "Margo, they won't peep. Maybe they're dead? I think they're aliens."

Are we not? Lorimer thinks. The Luna station comes back with a different, older voice.

"Judy, Myda here, I've had another thought. These people had a very rigid authority code. You remember your history, they peck-ordered everything. You notice Major Davis repeated about being commanding. That's called dominance-submission structure, one of them gave orders and the others did whatever they were told, we don't know quite why. Perhaps they were frightened. The point is that if the dominant one is in shock or panicked, maybe the others can't reply unless this Davis lets them.''

Jesus Christ, Lorimer thinks. Jesus H. Christ in colors. It is his father's expression for the inexpressible. Dave and Bud sit unstirring.

"How weird," the Judy voice says. "But don't they know they're on a bad course? I mean, could the dominant one make the others fly right out of the system? Truly?"

It's happened, Lorimer thinks; it has happened. I have to stop this. I have to act now, before they lose us. Desperate visions of himself defying Dave and Bud loom before him. Try persuasion first.

Just as he opens his mouth he sees Bud stir slightly, and with immeasurable gratitude hears him say, "Dave-o, what say we take an eyeball look? One little old burp won't hurt us."

Dave's head turns a degree or two.

"Or should I go out and see, like the chick said?" Bud's voice is mild.

After a long minute Dave says neutrally, "All right. . . . Attitude change." His arm moves up as though heavy; he starts methodically setting in the values for the vector that will bring Spica in line with their functional window.

Now why couldn't I have done that? Lorimer asks himself for the thousandth time, following the familiar check sequence. Don't answer. . . . And for the thousandth time he is obscurely moved by the rightness of them. The authentic ones, the alphas. Their bond. The awe he had felt first for the absurd jocks of his school ball team.

"That's go, Dave, assuming nothing got creamed."

Dave throws the ignition safety, puts the computer on real time. The hull shudders. Everything in the cabin drifts sidewise while the bright point of Spica swims the other way, appears on the front window as the retros cut in. When the star creeps out onto clear glass Lorimer can clearly see its companion. The double light steadies there; a beautiful job. He hands Bud the telescope.

"The one on the left."

Bud looks. "There she is, all right. Hey, Dave, look at that!"

He puts the scope in Dave's hand. Slowly, Dave raises it and looks. Lorimer can hear him breathe. Suddenly Dave pulls up the mike.

"Houston!" he says harshly. *"Sunbird* to Houston, *Sunbird* calling Houston. Houston, come in!"

Into the silence the speaker squeals, "They fired their engines—wait, she's calling!" And shuts up.

In *Sunbird's* cabin nobody speaks. Lorimer stares at the twin stars ahead, impossible realities shifting around him as the minutes congeal. Bud's reflected face looks downwards, grin gone. Dave's beard moves silently; praying, Lorimer realizes. Alone of the crew Dave is deeply religious; at Sunday meals he gives a short, dignified grace. A shocking pity for Dave rises in Lorimer; Dave is so deeply involved with his family, his four sons, always thinking about their training, taking them hunting, fishing, camping. And Doris his wife so incredibly active and sweet, going on their trips, cooking and doing things for the community. Driving Penny and Jenny to classes while Ginny was sick that time. Good people, the backbone. . . . This can't be, he thinks; Packard's voice is going to come through in a minute, the antenna's beamed right now. Six minutes now. This will all go away. *Before the year two thousand* —stop it, the language would have changed. Think of Doris. . . . She has that glow, feeding her five men; women with sons are different. But Ginny, but his dear woman, his *wife,* his *daughters*—grandmothers now? All dead and dust? *Quit that.* Dave is still praying. . . . Who knows what goes on inside those heads? Dave's cry. . . . Twelve minutes, it has to be right. The second sweep is stuck, no, it's moving. Thirteen. It's all insane, a dream. Thirteen plus . . . fourteen. The speaker hissing and clicking vacantly. Fifteen now. A dream. . . . Or are those women staying off, letting us see? Sixteen. . . .

At twenty Dave's hand moves, stops again. The seconds jitter by, space crackles. Thirty minutes coming up.

"Calling Major Davis in *Sunbird?"* It is the older woman, a gentle voice. "This is Luna Central. We are the service and communication facility for space flight now. We're sorry to have to tell you that there is no space center at Houston anymore. Houston itself was abandoned when the shuttle base moved to White Sands, over two centuries ago."

A cool dust-colored light enfolds Lorimer's brain, isolating it. He will remain so a long time.

The woman is explaining it all again, offering help, asking if they were hurt. A nice dignified speech. Dave still sits immobile, gazing at Earth. Bud puts the mike in his hand.

"Tell them, Dave-o."

Dave looks at it, takes a deep breath, presses the send button.

*"Sunbird* to Luna Control," he says quite normally. (It's "Central"

Lorimer thinks.) "We copy. Ah, negative on life support, we have no problems. We copy the course change suggestion and are proceeding to recompute. Your offer of computer assistance is appreciated. We suggest you transmit position data so we can get squared away. Ah, we are economizing on transmission until we see how our accumulators have held up. *Sunbird* out."

And so it had begun.

Lorimer's mind floats back to himself now floating in *Gloria,* nearly a year, or three hundred years, later; watching and being watched by them. He still feels light, contented; the dread underneath has come no nearer. But it is so silent. He seems to have heard no voices for a long time. Or was it a long time? Maybe the drug is working on his time sense, maybe it was only a minute or two.

"I've been remembering," he says to the woman Connie, wanting her to speak.

She nods. "You have so much to remember. Oh, I'm sorry— that wasn't good to say." Her eyes speak sympathy.

"Never mind." It is all dreamlike now, his lost world and this other which he is just now seeing plain. "We must seem like very strange beasts to you."

"We're trying to understand," she says. "It's history, you learn the events but you don't really feel what the people were like, how it was for them. We hope you'll tell us."

The drug, Lorimer thinks, that's what they're trying. Tell them . . . how can he? Could a dinosaur tell how it was? A montage flows through his mind, dominated by random shots of Operations' north parking lot and Ginny's yellow kitchen telephone with the sickly ivy vines. . . . Women and vines. . . .

A burst of laughter distracts him. It's coming from the chamber they call the gym. Bud and the others must be playing ball in there. Bright idea, really, he muses: Using muscle power, sustained mild exercise. That's why they are all so fit. The gym is a glorified squirrel wheel; when you climb or pedal up the walls it revolves and winds a gear train, which among other things rotates the sleeping drum. A real Woolagong. . . . Bud and Dave usually take their shifts together, scrambling the spinning gym like big pale apes. Lorimer prefers the easy rhythm of the women, and the cycle here fits him nicely. He usually puts in his shift with Connie, who doesn't talk much, and one of the Judys, who do.

No one is talking now, though. Remotely uneasy, he looks around the big cylinder of the cabin, sees Dave and Lady Blue by the forward window. Judy Dakar is behind them, silent for once. They must be looking at Earth; it has been a beautiful expanding disk for some weeks now. Dave's beard is moving, he is praying again. He has taken to doing that, not ostentatiously, but so obviously sincere that Lorimer, a life atheist, can only sympathize.

The Judys have asked Dave what he whispers, of course. When Dave understood that they had no concept of prayer and had never seen a Christian Bible, there had been a heavy silence.

"So you have lost all faith," he said finally.

"We have faith," Judy Paris protested.

"May I ask in what?"

"We have faith in ourselves, of course," she told him.

"Young lady, if you were my daughter I'd tan your britches," Dave said, not joking. The subject was not raised again.

But he came back so well after that first dreadful shock, Lorimer thinks. A personal God, a father-model, man needs that. Dave draws strength from it and we lean on him. Maybe leaders have to believe. Dave was so great; cheerful, unflappable, patiently working out alternatives, making his decisions on the inevitable discrepancies in the position readings in a way Lorimer couldn't do. A bitch. . . .

Memory takes him again; he is once again back in *Sunbird,* gritty-eyed, listening to the women's chatter, Dave's terse replies. God, how they chattered. But their computer work checks out. Lorimer is suffering also from a quirk of Dave's, his reluctance to transmit their exact thrust and fuel reserve. He keeps holding out a margin and making Lorimer compute it back in.

But the margins don't help; it is soon clear that they are in big trouble. Earth will pass too far ahead of them on her next orbit, they don't have the acceleration to catch up with her before they cross her path. They can carry out an ullage maneuver, they can kill enough velocity to let Earth catch them on the second go-by; but that would take an extra year and their life support would be long gone. The grim question of whether they have enough to enable a single man to wait it out pushes into Lorimer's mind. He pushes it back; that one is for Dave.

There is a final possibility: Venus will approach their trajectory three months hence and they may be able to gain velocity by swinging by it. They go to work on that.

Meanwhile Earth is steadily drawing away from them and so is *Gloria,* closer toward the sun. They pick her out of the solar interference and then lose her again. They know her crew now: the man is Andy Kay, the senior woman is Lady Blue Parks; they appear to do the navigating.

Then there is a Connie Morelos and the two twins, Judy Paris and Judy Dakar, who run the communications. The chief Luna voices are women too, Margo and Azella. The men can hear them talking to the *Escondita,* which is now swinging in toward the far side of the sun. Dave insists on monitoring and taping everything that comes through. It proves to be largely replays of their exchanges with Luna and *Gloria,* mixed with a variety of highly personal messages. As references to cows, chickens, and other livestock multiply Dave reluctantly gives up his idea that they are code. Bud counts a total of five male voices.

"Big deal," he says. "There were more chick drivers on the road when we left. Means space is safe now, the girlies have taken over. Let them sweat their little asses off." He chuckles. "When we get this bird down, the stars ain't gonna study old Buddy no more, no, ma'm. A nice beach and about a zillion steaks and ale and all those sweet things. Hey, we'll be living history, we can charge admission."

Dave's face takes on the expression that means an inappropriate topic has been breached. Much to Lorimer's impatience, Dave discourages all speculation as to what may await them on this future Earth. He confines their transmissions strictly to the problem in hand; when Lorimer tries to get him at least to mention the unchanged-language puzzle Dave only says firmly, "Later." Lorimer fumes; inconceivable that he is three centuries in the future, unable to learn a thing.

They do glean a few facts from the women's talk. There have been nine successful *Sunbird* missions after theirs and one other casualty. And the *Gloria* and her sister ship are on a long-planned fly-by of the two inner planets.

"We always go along in pairs," Judy says. "But those planets are no good. Still, it was worth seeing."

"For Pete's sake, Dave, ask them how many planets have been visited," Lorimer pleads.

"Later."

But about the fifth meal break Luna suddenly volunteers.

"Earth is making up a history for you, *Sunbird,*" the Margo voice says. "We know you don't want to waste power asking, so we thought we'd send you a few main points right now." She laughs. "It's much harder than we thought, nobody here does history."

Lorimer nods to himself; he has been wondering what he could tell a man from 1690 who would want to know what happened to Cromwell —was Cromwell then?—and who had never heard of electricity, atoms, or the U.S.A.

"Let's see, probably the most important is that there aren't as many people as you had, we're just over two million. There was a world epidemic not long after your time. It didn't kill people but it reduced the population. I mean there weren't any babies in most of the world. Ah, sterility. The country called Australia was affected least." Bud holds up a finger.

"And North Canada wasn't too bad. So the survivors all got together in the south part of the American states, where they could grow food and the best communications and factories were. Nobody lives in the rest of the world but we travel there sometimes. Ah, we have five main activities, was 'industries' the word? Food, that's farming and fishing. Communications, transport, and space—that's us. And the factories they need. We live a lot simpler than you did, I think. We see your things all over, we're very grateful to you. Oh, you'll be interested to know we use zeppelins just like you did, we have six big ones. And our fifth thing is the children. Babes. Does that help? I'm using a children's book we have here."

The men have frozen during this recital; Lorimer is holding a cooling bag of hash. Bud starts chewing again and chokes.

"Two million people and a space capability?" He coughs. "That's incredible."

Dave gazes reflectively at the speaker. "There's a lot they're not telling us."

"I gotta ask them," Bud says. "Okay?"

Dave nods. "Watch it."

"Thanks for the history, Luna," Bud says. "We really appreciate it. But we can't figure out how you maintain a space program with only a couple of million people. Can you tell us a little more on that?"

In the pause Lorimer tries to grasp the staggering figures. From eight billion to two million . . . Europe, Asia, Africa, South America, America itself—wiped out. *There weren't any more babies.* World sterility, from what? The Black Death, the famines of Asia—those had been decimations. This is magnitudes worse. No, it is all the same: beyond comprehension. An empty world, littered with junk.

*"Sunbird?"* says Margo, "Da, I should have thought you'd want to know about space. Well, we have only the four real spaceships and one building. You know the two here. Then there's *Indira* and *Pech,* they're on the Mars run now. Maybe the Mars dome was since your day. You had the satellite stations, though, didn't you? And the old Luna dome, of course—I remember now, it was during the epidemic. They tried to set up colonies to, ah, breed children, but the epidemic got there, too. They struggled terribly hard. We owe a lot to you really, you men I

mean. The history has it all, how you worked out a minimal viable program and trained everybody and saved it from the crazies. It was a glorious achievement. Oh, the marker here has one of your names on it. Lorimer. We love to keep it all going and growing, we all love traveling. Man is a rover, that's one of our mottoes."

"Are you hearing what I'm hearing?" Bud asks, blinking comically.

Dave is still staring at the speaker. "Not one word about their government," he says slowly. "Not a word about economic conditions. We're talking to a bunch of monkeys."

"Should I ask them?"

"Wait a minute . . . Roger, ask the name of their chief of state and the head of the space program. And—no, that's all."

"President?" Margo echoes Bud's query. "You mean like queens and kings? Wait, here's Myda. She's been talking about you with Earth."

The older woman they hear occasionally says *"Sunbird?* Da, we realize you had a very complex activity, your governments. With so few people we don't have that type of formal structure at all. People from the different activities meet periodically and our communications are good, everyone is kept informed. The people in each activity are in charge of doing it while they're there. We rotate, you see. Mostly in five-year hitches; for example, Margo here was on the zeppelins and I've been on several factories and farms and of course the, well, the education, we all do that. I believe that's one big difference from you. And of course we all work. And things are basically far more stable now, I gather. We change slowly. Does that answer you? Of course, you can always ask Registry, they keep track of us all. But we can't, ah, take you to our leader, if that's what you mean." She laughs, a genuine, jolly sound. "That's one of our old jokes. I must say," she goes on seriously, "it's been a joy to us that we can understand you so well. We make a big effort not to let the language drift, it would be tragic to lose touch with the past."

Dave takes the mike. "Thank you, Luna. You've given us something to think about. *Sunbird* out."

"How much of that is for real, Doc?" Bud rubs his curly head. "They're giving us one of your science fiction stories."

"The real story will come later," says Dave. "Our job is to get there."

"That's a point that doesn't look too good."

By the end of the session it looks worse. No Venus trajectory is any good. Lorimer reruns all the computations; same result.

"There doesn't seem to be any solution to this one, Dave," he says at last. "The parameters are just too tough. I think we've had it."

Dave massages his knuckles thoughtfully. Then he nods. "Roger. We'll fire the optimum sequence on the Earth heading."

"Tell them to wave if they see us go by," says Bud.

They are silent, contemplating the prospect of a slow death in space eighteen months hence. Lorimer wonders if he can raise the other question, the bad one. He is pretty sure what Dave will say. What will he himself decide, what will he have the guts to do?

"Hello, *Sunbird?*" the voice of *Gloria* breaks in. "Listen, we've been figuring. We think if you use all your fuel you could come back in close enough to our orbit so we could swing out and pick you up. You'd be using solar gravity that way. We have plenty of maneuver but much less acceleration than you do. You have suits and some kind of propellants, don't you? I mean, you could fly across a few kays?"

The three men look at each other; Lorimer guesses he had not been the only one to speculate on that.

"That's a good thought, *Gloria,*" Dave says. "Let's hear what Luna says."

"Why?" asks Judy. "It's our business, we wouldn't endanger the ship. We'd only miss another look at Venus, who cares? We have plenty of water and food and if the air gets a little smelly we can stand it."

"Hey, the chicks are all right," Bud says. They wait.

The voice of Luna comes on. "We've been looking at that, too, Judy. We're not sure you understand the risk. Ah, *Sunbird,* excuse me. Judy, if you manage to pick them up you'll have to spend nearly a year in the ship with these three male persons from a *very different culture.* Myda says you should remember history and it's a risk no matter what Connie says. *Sunbird,* I hate to be so rude. Over."

Bud is grinning broadly, they all are. "Cavemen." He chuckles. "All the chicks land preggers."

"Margo, they're human beings," the Judy voice protests. "This isn't just Connie, we're all agreed. Andy and Lady Blue say it would be very interesting. If it works, that is. We can't let them go without trying."

"We feel that way, too, of course," Luna replies. "But there's another problem. They could be carrying diseases. *Sunbird,* I know you've been isolated for fourteen months, but Murti says people in your day were immune to organisms that aren't around now. Maybe some of ours could harm you, too. You could all get mortally sick and lose the ship."

"We thought of that, Margo," Judy says impatiently. "Look, if you have contact with them at all somebody has to test, true? So we're ideal.

By the time we get home you'll know. And how could we get sick so fast we couldn't put *Gloria* in a stable orbit where you could get her later on?"

They wait. "Hey, what about that epidemic?" Bud pats his hair elaborately. "I don't know if I want a career in gay lib."

"You rather stay out here?" Dave asks.

"Crazies," says a different voice from Luna. *"Sunbird,* I'm Murti, the health person here. I think what we have to fear most is the meningitis-influenza complex, they mutate so readily. Does your Dr. Lorimer have any suggestions?"

"Roger, I'll put him on," says Dave. "But as to your first point, madam, I want to inform you that at the time of takeoff the incidence of rape in the United States space cadre was zero point zero. I guarantee the conduct of my crew provided you can control yours. Here is Dr. Lorimer."

But Lorimer cannot, of course, tell them anything useful. They discuss the men's polio shots, which luckily have used killed virus, and various childhood diseases which still seem to be around. He does not mention their epidemic.

"Luna, we're going to try it," Judy declares. "We couldn't live with ourselves. Now, let's get the course figured before they get any farther away."

From there on, there is no rest on *Sunbird* while they set up and refigure and rerun the computations for the envelope of possible intersecting trajectories. The *Gloria's* drive, they learn, is indeed low-thrust, although capable of sustained operation. *Sunbird* will have to get most of the way to the rendezvous on her own if they can cancel their outward velocity.

The tension breaks once during the long session, when Luna calls *Gloria* to warn Connie to be sure the female crew members wear concealing garments at all times if the men came aboard.

"Not suit liners, Connie, they're much too tight." It is the older woman, Myda. Bud chuckles.

"Your light sleepers, I think. And when the men unsuit, your Andy is the only one who should help them. You others stay away. The same for all body functions and sleeping. This is very important, Connie, you'll have to watch it the whole way home. There are a great many complicated taboos. I'm putting an instruction list on the bleeper. Is your receiver working?"

"Da, we used it for France's black hole paper."

"Good. Tell Judy to stand by. Now listen, Connie, listen carefully.

Tell Andy he has to read it all. I repeat, *he* has to read every word. Did you hear that?"

"Ah, dinko," Connie answers. "I understand, Myda. He will."

"I think we just lost the ball game, fellas," Bud laments. "Old mother Myda took it all away."

Even Dave laughs. But later when the modulated squeal that is a whole text comes through the speaker, he frowns again. "There goes the good stuff."

The last factors are cranked in; the revised program spins, and Luna confirms them. "We have a payout, Dave," Lorimer reports. "It's tight but there are at least two viable options. Provided the main jets are fully functional."

"We're going EVA to check."

That is exhausting; they find a warp in the deflector housing of the port engines and spend four sweating hours trying to wrestle it back. It is only Lorimer's third sight of open space but he is soon too tired to care.

"Best we can do," Dave pants finally. "We'll have to compensate in the psychic mode."

"You can do it, Dave-o," says Bud. "Hey, I gotta change those suit radios, don't let me forget."

In the psychic mode . . . Lorimer surfaces back to his real self, co-cooned in *Gloria*'s big cluttered cabin, seeing Connie's living face. It must be hours, how long has he been dreaming?

"About two minutes." Connie smiles.

"I was thinking of the first time I saw you."

"Oh yes. We'll never forget that, ever."

Nor will he . . . He lets it unroll again in his head. The interminable hours after the first long burn, which has sent *Sunbird* yawing so they all have to gulp nausea pills. Judy's breathless voice reading down their approach: "Oh, very good, four hundred thousand . . . Oh great, *Sunbird,* you're almost three, you're going to break a hundred for sure—" Dave has done it, the big one.

Lorimer's probe is useless in the yaw, it isn't until they stabilize enough for the final burst that they can see the strange blip bloom and vanish in the slot. Converging, hopefully, on a theoretical near-intersection point.

"Here goes everything."

The final burn changes the yaw into a sickening tumble with the star field looping past the glass. The pills are no more use and the fuel feed to the attitude jets goes sour. They are all vomiting before they manage to hand-pump the last of the fuel and slow the tumble.

"That's it, *Gloria.* Come and get us. Lights on, Bud. Let's get those suits up."

Fighting nausea, they go through the laborious routine in the fouled cabin. Suddenly Judy's voice sings out, "We see you, *Sunbird!* We see your light! Can't you see us?"

"No time," Dave says. But Bud, half suited, points at the window. "Fellas, oh, hey, look at that."

Lorimer stares, thinks he sees a faint spark between the whirling stars before he has to retch.

"Father, we thank you," says Dave quietly. "All right, move it on, Doc. Packs."

The effort of getting themselves plus the propulsion units and a couple of cargo nets out of the rolling ship drives everything else out of mind. It isn't until they are floating linked together and stabilized by Dave's hand jet that Lorimer has time to look.

The sun blanks out their left. A few meters below them *Sunbird* tumbles empty, looking absurdly small. Ahead of them, infinitely far away, is a point too blurred and yellow to be a star. It creeps: *Gloria,* on her approach tangent.

"Can you start, *Sunbird?*" says Judy in their helmets. "We don't want to brake any more on account of our exhaust. We estimate fifty kay in an hour, we're coming out on a line."

"Roger. Give me your jet, Doc."

"Goodbye, *Sunbird,*" says Bud. "Plenty of lead, Dave-o."

Lorimer finds it restful in a childish way, being towed across the abyss tied to the two big men. He has total confidence in Dave, he never considers the possibility that they will miss, sail by and be lost. Does Dave feel contempt? Lorimer wonders; that banked-up silence, is it partly contempt for those who can manipulate only symbols, who have no mastery of matter? . . . He concentrates on mastering his stomach.

It is a long, dark trip. *Sunbird* shrinks to a twinkling light, slowly accelerating on the spiral course that will end her ultimately in the sun with their precious records that are three hundred years obsolete. With, also, the packet of photos and letters that Lorimer has twice put in his suit pouch and twice taken out. Now and then he catches sight of *Gloria,* growing from a blur to an incomprehensible tangle of lighted crescents.

"Woo-ee, it's big," Bud says. "No wonder they can't accelerate, that thing is a flying trailer park. It'd break up."

"It's a spaceship. Got those nets tight, Doc?"

Judy's voice suddenly fills their helmets. "I see your lights! Can you see me? Will you have enough left to brake at all?"

"Affirmative to both, *Gloria,*" says Dave.

At that moment Lorimer is turned slowly forward again and he sees —will see it forever: the alien ship in the star field and on its dark side the tiny lights that are women in the stars, waiting for them. Three—no, four; one suit light is way out, moving. If that is a tether it must be over a kilometer.

"Hello, I'm Judy Dakar!" The voice is close. "Oh, mother, you're big! Are you all right? How's your air?"

"No problem."

They are in fact stale and steaming wet; too much adrenaline. Dave uses the jets again and suddenly she is growing, is coming right at them, a silvery spider on a trailing thread. Her suit looks trim and flexible; it is mirror-bright, and the pack is quite small. Marvels of the future, Lorimer thinks; Paragraph One.

"You made it, you made it! Here, tie in. Brake!"

"There ought to be some historic words," Bud murmurs. "If she gives us a chance."

"Hello, Judy," says Dave calmly. "Thanks for coming."

"Contact!" She blasts their ears. "Haul us in, Andy! Brake, brake—the exhaust is back there!"

And they are grabbed hard, deflected into a great arc toward the ship. Dave uses up the last jet. The line loops.

"Don't jerk it," Judy cries. "Oh, I'm *sorry.*" She is clinging on them like a gibbon, Lorimer can see her eyes, her excited mouth. Incredible. "Watch out, it's slack."

"Teach me, honey," says Andy's baritone. Lorimer twists and sees him far back at the end of a heavy tether, hauling them smoothly in. Bud offers to help, is refused. "Just hang loose, please," a matronly voice tells them. It is obvious Andy has done this before. They come in spinning slowly, like space fish. Lorimer finds he can no longer pick out the twinkle that is *Sunbird.* When he is swung back, *Gloria* has changed to a disorderly cluster of bulbs and spokes around a big central cylinder. He can see pods and miscellaneous equipment stowed all over her. Not like science fiction.

Andy is paying the line into a floating coil. Another figure floats beside him. They are both quite short, Lorimer realizes as they near.

"Catch the cable," Andy tells them. There is a busy moment of shifting inertial drag.

"Welcome to *Gloria,* Major Davis, Captain Geirr, Dr. Lorimer. I'm Lady Blue Parks. I think you'll like to get inside as soon as possible. If you feel like climbing go right ahead, we'll pull all this in later."

"We appreciate it, ma'am."

They start hand over hand along the catenary of the main tether. It has a good rough grip. Judy coasts up to peer at them, smiling broadly, towing the coil. A taller figure waits by the ship's open airlock.

"Hello, I'm Connie. I think we can cycle in two at a time. Will you come with me, Major Davis?"

It is like an emergency on a plane, Lorimer thinks as Dave follows her in. Being ordered about by supernaturally polite little girls.

"Space-going stews." Bud nudges him. "How 'bout that?" His face is sprouting sweat. Lorimer tells him to go next, his own LSP has less load.

Bud goes in with Andy. The woman named Lady Blue waits beside Lorimer while Judy scrambles on the hull securing their cargo nets. She doesn't seem to have magnetic soles; perhaps ferrous metals aren't used in space now. When she begins hauling in the main tether on a simple hand winch Lady Blue looks at it critically.

"I used to make those," she says to Lorimer. What he can see of her features looks compressed, her dark eyes twinkle. He has the impression she is part black.

"I ought to get over and clean that aft antenna." Judy floats up. "Later," says Lady Blue. They both smile at Lorimer. Then the hatch opens and he and Lady Blue go in. When the toggles seat there comes a rising scream of air and Lorimer's suit collapses.

"Can I help you?" She has opened her faceplate, the voice is rich and live. Eagerly Lorimer catches the latches in his clumsy gloves and lets her lift the helmet off. His first breath surprises him, it takes an instant to identify the gas as fresh air. Then the inner hatch opens, letting in greenish light. She waves him through. He swims into a short tunnel. Voices are coming from around the corner ahead. His hand finds a grip and he stops, feeling his heart shudder in his chest.

When he turns that corner the world he knows will be dead. Gone, rolled up, blown away forever with *Sunbird.* He will be irrevocably in the future. A man from the past, a time traveler. In the future. . . .

He pulls himself around the bend.

The future is a vast bright cylinder, its whole inner surface festooned with unidentifiable objects, fronds of green. In front of him floats an odd tableau: Bud and Dave, helmets off, looking enormous in their bulky white suits and packs. A few meters away hang two bareheaded figures in shiny suits and a dark-haired girl in flowing pink pajamas.

They are all simply staring at the two men, their eyes and mouths open in identical expressions of pleased wonder. The face that has to be Andy's is grinning openmouthed like a kid at the zoo. He is a surprisingly young boy, Lorimer sees, in spite of his deep voice; blond, downy-cheeked, compactly muscular. Lorimer finds he can scarcely bear to look at the pink woman, can't tell if she really is surpassingly beautiful or plain. The taller suited woman has a shiny, ordinary face.

From overhead bursts an extraordinary sound which he finally recognizes as a chicken cackling. Lady Blue pushes past him.

"All right, Andy, Connie, stop staring and help them get their suits off. Judy, Luna is just as eager to hear about this as we are."

The tableau jumps to life. Afterwards Lorimer can recall mostly eyes, bright curious eyes tugging his boots, smiling eyes upside down over his pack—and always that light, ready laughter. Andy is left alone to help them peel down, blinking at the fittings which Lorimer still finds embarrassing. He seems easy and nimble in his own half-open suit. Lorimer struggles out of the last lacings, thinking: A boy! A boy and four women orbiting the sun, flying their big junky ships to Mars. Should he feel humiliated? He only feels grateful, accepting a short robe and a bulb of tea somebody—Connie?—gives him.

The suited Judy comes in with their nets. The men follow Andy along another passage, Bud and Dave clutching at the small robes. Andy stops by a hatch.

"This greenhouse is for you, it's your toilet. Three's a lot but you have full sun."

Inside is a brilliant jungle, foliage everywhere, glittering water droplets, rustling leaves. Something whirs away—a grasshopper.

"You crank that handle." Andy points to a seat on a large cross-duct. "The piston rams the gravel and waste into a compost process and it ends up in the soil core. That vetch is a heavy nitrogen user and a great oxidator. We pump $CO_2$ in and oxy out. It's a real Woolagong."

He watches critically while Bud tries out the facility.

"What's a Woolagong?" asks Lorimer dazedly.

"Oh, she's one of our inventors. Some of her stuff is weird. When we have a pluggy-looking thing that works we call it a Woolagong." He grins. "The chickens eat the seeds and the hoppers, see, and the hoppers and iguanas eat the leaves. When a greenhouse is going darkside we turn them in to harvest. With this much light I think we could keep a goat, don't you? You didn't have any life at all on your ship, true?"

"No," Lorimer says, "not a single iguana."

"They promised us a Shetland pony for Christmas," says Bud, rattling gravel. Andy joins perplexedly in the laugh.

Lorimer's head is foggy; it isn't only fatigue, the year in *Sunbird* has atrophied his ability to take in novelty. Numbly he uses the Woolagong and they go back out and forward to *Gloria*'s big control room, where Dave makes a neat short speech to Luna and is answered graciously.

"We have to finish changing course now," Lady Blue says. Lorimer's impression has been right, she is a small light part-Negro in late middle age. Connie is part something exotic, too, he sees; the others are European types.

"I'll get you something to eat." Connie smiles warmly. "Then you probably want to rest. We saved all the cubbies for you." She says "syved"; their accents are all identical.

As they leave the control room Lorimer sees the withdrawn look in Dave's eyes and knows he must be feeling the reality of being a passenger in an alien ship; not in command, not deciding the course, the communications going on unheard.

That is Lorimer's last coherent observation, that and the taste of the strange, good food. And then being led aft through what he now knows is the gym, to the shaft of the sleeping drum. There are six irised ports like dog doors; he pushes through his assigned port and finds himself facing a roomy mattress. Shelves and a desk are in the wall.

"For your excretions." Connie's arm comes through the iris, pointing at bags. "If you have a problem stick your head out and call. There's water."

Lorimer simply drifts toward the mattress, too sweated out to reply. His drifting ends in a curious heavy settling and his final astonishment: the drum is smoothly, silently starting to revolve. He sinks gratefully onto the pad, growing "heavier" as the minutes pass. About a tenth gee, maybe more, he thinks, it's still accelerating. And falls into the most restful sleep he has known in the long weary year.

It isn't till next day that he understands that Connie and two others have been on the rungs of the gym chamber, sending it around hour after hour without pause or effort and chatting as they went.

How they talk, he thinks, again floating back to real present time. The bubbling irritant pours through his memory, the voices of Ginny and Jenny and Penny on the kitchen telephone, before that his mother's voice, his sister Amy's. Interminable. What do they always have to talk, talk, talk of?

"Why, everything," says the real voice of Connie beside him now, "it's natural to share."

"Natural. . . ." Like ants, he thinks. They twiddle their antennae together every time they meet. Where did you go, what did you do? Twiddle-twiddle. How do you *feel?* Oh, I feel this, I feel that, blah blah twiddle-twiddle. Total coordination of the hive. Women have no self-respect. Say anything, no sense of the strategy of words, the dark danger of naming. Can't hold in.

"Ants, beehives." Connie laughs, showing the bad tooth. "You truly see us as insects, don't you? Because they're females?"

"Was I talking aloud? I'm sorry." He blinks away dreams.

"Oh, please don't be. It's so sad to hear about your sister and your children and your, your wife. They must have been wonderful people. We think you're very brave."

But he has only thought of Ginny and them all for an instant—what has he been babbling? What is the drug doing to him?

"What are you doing to us?" he demands, lanced by real alarm now, almost angry.

"It's all right, truly." Her hand touches his, warm and somehow shy. "We all use it when we need to explore something. Usually it's pleasant. It's a laevonoramine compound, a disinhibitor, it doesn't dull you like alcohol. We'll be home so soon, you see. We have the responsibility to understand and you're so locked in." Her eyes melt at him. "You don't feel sick, do you? We have the antidote."

"No . . ." His alarm has already flowed away somewhere. Her explanation strikes him as reasonable enough. "We're not locked in," he says or tries to say. "We talk . . ." He gropes for a word to convey the judiciousness, the adult restraint. Objectivity, maybe? "We talk when we have something to say." Irrelevantly he thinks of a mission coordinator named Forrest, famous for his blue jokes. "Otherwise it would all break down," he tells her. "You'd fly right out of the system." That isn't quite what he means; let it pass.

The voices of Dave and Bud ring out suddenly from opposite ends of the cabin, awakening the foreboding of evil in his mind. They don't know us, he thinks. They should look out, stop this. But he is feeling too serene, he wants to think about his own new understanding, the pattern of them all he is seeing at last.

"I feel lucid," he manages to say, "I want to think."

She looks pleased. "We call that the ataraxia effect. It's so nice when it goes that way."

Ataraxia, philosophical calm. Yes. But there are monsters in the deep, he thinks or says. The night side. The night side of Orren Lorimer, a self hotly dark and complex, waiting in leash. They're so vulnerable.

They don't know we can take them. Images rush up: a Judy spread-eagled on the gym rungs, pink pajamas gone, open to him. Flash sequence of the three of them taking over the ship, the women tied up, helpless, shrieking, raped and used. The team—get the satellite station, get a shuttle down to Earth. Hostages. Make them do anything, no defense whatever . . . Has Bud actually said that? But Bud doesn't know, he remembers. Dave knows they're hiding something, but he thinks it's socialism or sin. When they find out . . .

How has he himself found out? Simply listening, really, all these months. He listens to their talk much more than the others; "fraternizing," Dave calls it. . . . They all listened at first, of course. Listened and looked and reacted helplessly to the female bodies, the tender bulges so close under the thin, tantalizing clothes, the magnetic mouths and eyes, the smell of them, their electric touch. Watching them touch each other, touch Andy, laughing, vanishing quietly into shared bunks. *What goes on? Can I? My need, my need—*

The power of them, the fierce resentment. . . . Bud muttered and groaned meaningfully despite Dave's warnings. He kept needling Andy until Dave banned all questions. Dave himself was noticeably tense and read his Bible a great deal. Lorimer found his own body pointing after them like a famished hound, hoping to Christ the cubicles are as they appeared to be, unwired.

All they learn is that Myda's instructions must have been ferocious. The atmosphere has been implacably antiseptic, the discretion impenetrable. Andy politely ignored every probe. No word or act has told them what, if anything, goes on; Lorimer was irresistibly reminded of the weekend he spent at Jenny's Scout camp. The men's training came presently to their rescue, and they resigned themselves to finishing their mission on a super-*Sunbird*, weirdly attended by a troop of Boy and Girl Scouts.

In every other way their reception couldn't be more courteous. They have been given the run of the ship and their own dayroom in a cleaned-out gravel storage pod. They visit the control room as they wish. Lady Blue and Andy give them specs and manuals and show them every circuit and device of *Gloria*, inside and out. Luna has bleeped up a stream of science texts and the data on all their satellites and shuttles and the Mars and Luna dome colonies.

Dave and Bud plunged into an orgy of engineering. *Gloria* is, as they suspected, powered by a fission plant that uses a range of Lunar materials. Her ion drive is only slightly advanced over the experimental models of their own day. The marvels of the future seem so far to consist mainly of ingenious modifications.

"It's primitive," Bud tells him. "What they've done is sacrifice everything to keep it simple and easy to maintain. Believe it, they can hand-feed fuel. And the backups, brother! They have redundant redundancy."

But Lorimer's technical interest soon flags. What he really wants is to be alone a while. He makes a desultory attempt to survey the apparently few developments in his field, and finds he can't concentrate. What the hell, he tells himself, I stopped being a physicist three hundred years ago. Such a relief to be out of the cell of *Sunbird;* he has given himself up to drifting solitary through the warren of the ship, using their excellent 400 mm telescope, noting the odd life of the crew.

When he finds that Lady Blue likes chess they form a routine of biweekly games. Her personality intrigues him; she has reserve and an aura of authority. But she quickly stops Bud when he calls her "Captain."

"No one here commands in your sense. I'm just the oldest." Bud goes back to "ma'am."

She plays a solid positional game, somewhat more erratic than a man but with occasional elegant traps. Lorimer is astonished to find that there is only one new chess opening, an interesting queen-side gambit called the Dagmar. One new opening in three centuries? He mentions it to the others when they come back from helping Andy and Judy Paris overhaul a standby converter.

"They haven't done much anywhere," Dave says. "Most of your new stuff dates from the epidemic, Andy, if you'll pardon me. The program seems to be stagnating. You've been gearing up this Titan project for eighty years."

"We'll get there." Andy grins.

"C'mon, Dave," says Bud. "Judy and me are taking on you two for the next chicken dinner, we'll get a bridge team here yet. Woo-ee, I can taste that chicken! Losers get the iguana."

The food is so good. Lorimer finds himself lingering around the kitchen end, helping whoever is cooking, munching on their various seeds and chewy roots as he listens to them talk. He even likes the iguana. He begins to put on weight, in fact they all do. Dave decrees double exercise shifts.

"You going to make us *climb* home, Dave-o?" Bud groans. But Lorimer enjoys it, pedaling or swinging easily along the rungs while the women chat and listen to tapes. Familiar music: he identifies a strange spectrum from Handel, Brahms, Sibelius, through Strauss to ballad tunes and intricate light jazz rock. No lyrics. But plenty of informative texts doubtless selected for his benefit.

From the promised short history he finds out more about the epidemic. It seems to have been an airborne quasi-virus escaped from Franco-Arab military labs, possibly potentiated by pollutants.

"It apparently damaged only the reproductive cells," he tells Dave and Bud. "There was little actual mortality, but almost universal sterility. Probably a molecular substitution in the gene code in the gametes. And the main effect seems to have been on the men. They mention a shortage of male births afterwards, which suggests that the damage was on the Y-chromosome where it would be selectively lethal to the male fetus."

"Is it still dangerous, Doc?" Dave asks. "What happens to us when we get back home?"

"They can't say. The birthrate is normal now, about two percent and rising. But the present population may be resistant. They never achieved a vaccine."

"Only one way to tell," Bud says gravely. "I volunteer."

Dave merely glances at him. Extraordinary how he still commands, Lorimer thinks. Not submission, for Pete's sake. A team.

The history also mentions the riots and fighting which swept the world when humanity found itself sterile. Cities bombed, and burned, massacres, panics, mass rapes and kidnapping of women, marauding armies of biologically desperate men, bloody cults. The crazies. But it is all so briefly told, so long ago. Lists of honored names. "We must always be grateful to the brave people who held the Denver Medical Laboratories—" And then on to the drama of building up the helium supply for the dirigibles.

In three centuries it's all dust, he thinks. What do I know of the hideous Thirty Years' War that was three centuries back for me? *Fighting devastated Europe for two generations.* Not even names.

The description of their political and economic structure is even briefer. They seem to be, as Myda had said, almost ungoverned.

"It's a form of loose social-credit system run by consensus," he says to Dave. "Somewhat like a permanent frontier period. They're building up slowly. Of course they don't need an army or air force. I'm not sure if they even use cash money or recognize private ownership of land. I did notice one favorable reference to early Chinese communalism," he adds to see Dave's mouth set. "But they aren't tied to a community. They travel about. When I asked Lady Blue about their police and legal system she told me to wait and talk with real historians. This Registry seems to be just that, it's not a policy organ."

"We've run into a situation here, Lorimer," Dave says soberly. "Stay away from it. They're not telling the story."

"You notice they never talk about their husbands?" Bud laughs. "I asked a couple of them what their husband did and I swear they had to think. And they all have kids. Believe me, it's a swinging scene down there, even if old Andy acts like he hasn't found out what it's for."

"I don't want any prying into their personal family lives while we're on this ship, Geirr. None whatsoever. That's an order."

"Maybe they don't have families. You ever hear 'em mention anybody getting married? That has to be the one thing on a chick's mind. Mark my words, there's been some changes made."

"The social mores are bound to have changed to some extent," Lorimer says. "Obviously you have women doing more work outside the home, for one thing. But they have family bonds; for instance, Lady Blue has a sister in an aluminum mill and another in health. Andy's mother is on Mars and his sister works in Registry. Connie has a brother or brothers on the fishing fleet near Biloxi, and her sister is coming out to replace her here next trip, she's making yeast now."

"That's the top of the iceberg."

"I doubt the rest of the iceberg is very sinister, Dave."

But somewhere along the line the blandness begins to bother Lorimer, too. So much is missing. Marriage, love affairs, children's troubles, jealousy squabbles, status, possessions, money problems, sicknesses, funerals even—all the daily minutiae that occupied Ginny and her friend seems to have been edited out of these women's talk. *Edited.* . . . Can Dave be right? Is some big, significant aspect being deliberately kept from them?

"I'm still surprised your language hasn't changed more," he says one day to Connie during their exertions in the gym.

"Oh, we're very careful about that." She climbs at an angle beside him, not using her hands. "It would be a dreadful loss if we couldn't understand the books. All the children are taught from the same original tapes, you see. Oh, there's faddy words we use for a while, but our communicators have to learn the old texts by heart, that keeps us together."

Judy Paris grunts from the pedicycle. "You, my dear children, will never know the oppression we suffered," she declaims mockingly.

"Judys talk too much," says Connie.

"We do, for a fact." They both laugh.

"So you still read our so-called great books, our fiction and poetry?" asks Lorimer. "Who do you read, H. G. Wells? Shakespeare? Dickens, ah, Balzac, Kipling, Brian?" He gropes; Brian had been a bestseller Ginny liked. When had he last looked at Shakespeare or the others?

"Oh, the historicals," Judy says. "It's interesting, I guess. Grim. They're not very realistic. I'm sure it was to you," she adds generously.

And they turn to discussing whether the laying hens are getting too much light, leaving Lorimer to wonder how what he supposes are the eternal verities of human nature can have faded from a world's reality. Love, conflict, heroism, tragedy—all "unrealistic"? Well, flight crews are never great readers; still, women read more. . . . Something *has* changed, he can sense it. Something basic enough to affect human nature. A physical development perhaps; a mutation? What is really under those floating clothes?

It is the Judys who give him part of it.

He is exercising alone with both of them, listening to them gossip about some legendary figure named Dagmar.

"The Dagmar who invented the chess opening?" he asks.

"Yes. She does anything, when she's good she's great."

"Was she bad sometimes?"

A Judy laughs. "The Dagmar problem, you can say. She has this tendency to organize everything. It's fine when it works but every so often it runs wild, she thinks she's queen or what. Then they have to get out the butterfly nets."

All in present tense—but Lady Blue has told him the Dagmar gambit is over a century old.

*Longevity,* he thinks; by God, that's what they're hiding. Say they've achieved a doubled or tripled life span, that would certainly change human psychology, affect their outlook on everything. Delayed maturity, perhaps? We were working on endocrine cell juvenescence when I left. How old are these girls, for instance?

He is framing a question when Judy Dakar says, "I was in the crèche when she went pluggo. But she's good, I loved her later on."

Lorimer thinks she has said "crash" and then realizes she means a communal nursery. "Is that the same Dagmar?" he asks. "She must be very old."

"Oh no, her sister."

"A sister a hundred years apart?"

"I mean, her daughter. Her, her *grand*daughter." She starts pedaling fast.

"Judys," says her twin, behind them.

Sister again. Everybody he learns of seems to have an extraordinary number of sisters, Lorimer reflects. He hears Judy Paris saying to her twin, "I think I remember Dagmar at the crèche. She started uniforms for everybody. Colors and numbers."

"You couldn't have, you weren't born," Judy Dakar retorts.

There is a silence in the drum.

Lorimer turns on the rungs to look at them. Two flushed cheerful faces stare back warily, make identical head-dipping gestures to swing the black hair out of their eyes. Identical. . . . But isn't the Dakar girl on the cycle a shade more mature, her face more weathered?

"I thought you were supposed to be twins."

"Ah, Judys talk a lot," they say together—and grin guiltily.

"You aren't sisters," he tells them. "You're what we called clones."

Another silence.

"Well, yes," says Judy Dakar. "We call it sisters. Oh, mother! We weren't supposed to tell you, Myda said you would be frightfully upset. It was illegal in your day, true?"

"Yes. We considered it immoral and unethical, experimenting with human life. But it doesn't upset me personally."

"Oh, that's beautiful, that's great," they say together. "We think of you as different," Judy Paris blurts, "you're more hu— more like us. Please, you don't have to tell the others, do you? Oh, *please* don't."

"It was an accident there were two of us here," says Judy Dakar. "Myda *warned* us. Can't you wait a little while?" Two identical pairs of dark eyes beg him.

"Very well," he says slowly. "I won't tell my friends for the time being. But if I keep your secret you have to answer some questions. For instance, how many of your people are created artificially this way?"

He begins to realize he *is* somewhat upset. Dave is right, damn it, they are hiding things. Is this brave new world populated by subhuman slaves, run by master brains? Decorticate zombies, workers without stomachs or sex, human cortexes wired into machines, monstrous experiments rush through his mind. He had been naïve again. These normal-looking women can be fronting for a hideous world.

"How many?"

"There's only about eleven thousand of us," Judy Dakar says. The two Judys look at each other, transparently confirming something. They're unschooled in deception, Lorimer thinks; is that good? And is diverted by Judy Paris exclaiming, "What we can't figure out is why did you think it was wrong?"

Lorimer tries to tell them, to convey the horror of manipulating human identity, creating abnormal life. The threat to individuality, the fearful power it would put in a dictator's hand.

"Dictator?" one of them echoes blankly. He looks at their faces and can only say, "Doing things to people without their consent. I think it's sad."

"But that's just what we think about you," the younger Judy bursts out. "How do you know who you *are?* Or who anybody is? All alone, no sisters to share with! You don't know what you can do, or what would be interesting to try. All you poor singletons, you—why, you just have to blunder along and die, all for nothing!"

Her voice trembles. Amazed, Lorimer sees both of them are misty-eyed.

"We better get this m-moving," the other Judy says.

They swing back into the rhythm and in bits and pieces Lorimer finds out how it is. Not bottled embryos, they tell him indignantly. Human mothers like everybody else, young mothers, the best kind. A somatic cell nucleus is inserted in an enucleated ovum and reimplanted in the womb. They have each borne two "sister" babies in their late teens and nursed them a while before moving on. The crèches always have plenty of mothers.

His longevity notion is laughed at; nothing but some rules of healthy living have as yet been achieved. "We should make ninety in good shape," they assure him. "A hundred and eight, that was Judy Eagle, she's our record. But she was pretty blah at the end."

The clone strains themselves are old, they date from the epidemic. They were part of the first effort to save the race when the babies stopped and they've continued ever since.

"It's so perfect," they tell him. "We each have a book, it's really a library. All the recorded messages. The Book of Judy Shapiro, that's us. Dakar and Paris are our personal names, we're doing cities now." They laugh, trying not to talk at once about how each Judy adds her individual memoir, her adventures and problems and discoveries in the genotype they all share.

"If you make a mistake it's useful for the others. Of course you try not to—or at least make a *new* one."

"Some of the old ones aren't so realistic," her other self puts in. "Things were so different, I guess. We make excerpts of the parts we like best. And practical things, like Judys should watch out for skin cancer."

"But we have to read the whole thing every ten years," says the Judy called Dakar. "It's inspiring. As you get older you understand some of the ones you didn't before."

Bemused, Lorimer tries to think how it would be, hearing the voices of three hundred years of Orren Lorimers. Lorimers who were mathematicians or plumbers or artists or bums or criminals, maybe. The continuing exploration and completion of self. And a dozen living doubles; aged Lorimers, infant Lorimers. And other Lorimers' women and children . . . would he enjoy it or resent it? He doesn't know.

"Have you made your records yet?"

"Oh, we're too young. Just notes in case of accident."

"Will we be in them?"

"You can say!" They laugh merrily, then sober. "Truly you won't tell?" Judy Paris asks. "Lady Blue, we have to let her know what we did. Oof. But *truly* you won't tell your friends?"

He hadn't told on them, he thinks now, emerging back into his living self. Connie beside him is drinking cider from a bulb. He has a drink in his hand, too, he finds. But he hasn't told.

"Judys will talk." Connie shakes her head, smiling. Lorimer realizes he must have gabbled out the whole thing.

"It doesn't matter," he tells her. "I would have guessed soon anyhow. There were too many clues . . . Woolagongs invent, Mydas worry, Jans are brains, Billy Dees work so hard. I picked up six different stories of hydroelectric stations that were built or improved or are being run by one Lala Singh. Your whole way of life. I'm more interested in this sort of thing than a respectable physicist should be," he says wryly. "You're all clones, aren't you? Every one of you. What do Connies do?"

"You really do know." She gazes at him like a mother whose child has done something troublesome and bright. "Whew! Oh, well, Connies farm like mad, we grow things. Most of our names are plants. I'm Veronica, by the way. And of course the crèches, that's our weakness. The runt mania. We tend to focus on anything smaller or weak."

Her warm eyes focus on Lorimer, who draws back involuntarily.

"We control it." She gives a hearty chuckle. "We aren't all that way. There's been engineering Connies, and we have two young sisters who love metallurgy. It's fascinating what the genotype can do if you try. The original Constantia Morelos was a chemist, she weighed ninety pounds and never saw a farm in her life." Connie looks down at her own muscular arms. "She was killed by the crazies, she fought with weapons. It's so hard to understand . . . And I had a sister Timothy who made dynamite and dug two canals and she wasn't even an andy."

*"An* andy," he says.

"Oh, dear."

"I guessed that, too. Early androgen treatments."

She nods hesitantly. "Yes. We need the muscle power for some jobs. A few. Kays are quite strong anyway. Whew!" She suddenly stretches her back, wriggles as if she'd been cramped. "Oh, I'm glad you know. It's been such a strain. We couldn't even sing."

"Why not?"

"Myda was sure we'd make mistakes, all the words we'd have had to change. We sing a lot." She softly hums a bar or two.

"What kinds of songs do you sing?"

"Oh, every kind. Adventure songs, work songs, mothering songs, roaming songs, mood songs, trouble songs, joke songs—everything."

"What about love songs?" he ventures. "Do you still have, well, love?"

"Of course, how could people not love?" But she looks at him doubtfully. "The love stories I've heard from your time are so, I don't know, so weird. Grim and pluggy. It doesn't seem like love. . . . Oh, yes, we have famous love songs. Some of them are partly sad, too. Like Tamil and Alcmene O., they're fated together. Connies are fated, too, a little." She grins bashfully. "We love to be with Ingrid Anders. It's more one-sided. I hope there'll be an Ingrid on my next hitch. She's so exciting, she's like a little diamond."

Implications are exploding all about him, sparkling with questions. But Lorimer wants to complete the darker pattern beyond.

"Eleven thousand genotypes, two million people: that averages two hundred of each of you alive now." She nods. "I suppose it varies? There's more of some?"

"Yes, some types aren't as viable. But we haven't lost any since early days. They tried to preserve all the genes they could, we have people from all the major races and a lot of small strains. Like me, I'm the Carib Blend. Of course, we'll never know what was lost. But eleven thousand is a lot, really. We all try to know everyone, it's a life hobby."

A chill penetrates his ataraxia. Eleven thousand, period. That is the true population of Earth now. He thinks of two hundred tall olive-skinned women named after plants, excited by two hundred little bright Ingrids; two hundred talkative Judys, two hundred self-possessed Lady Blues, two hundred Margos and Mydas and the rest. He shivers. The heirs, the happy pallbearers of the human race.

"So evolution ends," he says somberly.

"No, why? It's just slowed down. We do everything much slower

than you did, I think. We like to experience things *fully*. We have time."
She stretches again, smiling. "There's all the time."

"But you have no new genotypes. It is the end."

"Oh but there are, now. Last century they worked out the way to
make haploid nuclei combine. We can make a stripped egg cell function
like pollen," she says proudly. "I mean sperm. It's tricky, some don't
come out too well. But now we're finding both X's viable we have over
a hundred new types started. Of course it's hard for them, with no
sisters. The donors try to help."

Over a hundred, he thinks. Well. Maybe. . . . But "both X's viable," what does that mean? She must be referring to the epidemic. But
he had figured it primarily affected the men. His mind goes happily to
work on the new puzzle, ignoring a sound from somewhere that is
trying to pierce his calm.

"It was a gene or genes on the X chromosome that was injured," he
guesses aloud. "Not the Y. And the lethal trait had to be recessive,
right? Thus there would have been no births at all for a time, until some
men recovered or were isolated long enough to manufacture undamaged X-bearing gametes. But women carry their lifetime supply of ova,
they could never regenerate reproductively. When they mated with the
recovered males only female babies would be produced, since the female carries two X's and the mother's defective gene would be com-
pensated by a normal X from the father. But the male is XY, he re-
ceives only the mother's defective X. Thus the lethal defect would be
expressed, the male fetus would be finished. . . . A planet of girls and
dying men. The few odd viables died off."

"You truly do understand," she says admiringly.

The sound is becoming urgent; he refuses to hear it, there is significance here.

"So we'll be perfectly all right on Earth. No problem. In theory we
can marry again and have families, daughters anyway."

"Yes," she says. "In theory."

The sound suddenly broaches his defenses, becomes the loud voice of
Bud Geirr raised in song. He sounds plain drunk now. It seems to be
coming from the main garden pod, the one they use to grow vegetables, not sanitation. Lorimer feels the dread alive again, rising closer.
Dave ought to keep an eye on him. But Dave seems to have vanished,
too, he recalls seeing him go toward Control with Lady Blue.

"OH, THE SUN SHINES BRIGHT ON PRET-TY RED WI-I-ING,"
carols Bud.

Something should be done, Lorimer decides painfully. He stirs; it is an effort.

"Don't worry," Connie says. "Andy's with them."

"You don't know, you don't know what you've started." He pushes off toward the garden hatchway.

"—AS SHE LAY SLE-EEPING, A COWBOY CREE-E-EEPING—" General laughter from the hatchway. Lorimer coasts through into the green dazzle. Beyond the radial fence of snap beans he sees Bud sailing in an exaggerated crouch after Judy Paris. Andy hangs by the iguana cages, laughing.

Bud catches one of Judy's ankles and stops them both with a flourish, making her yellow pajamas swirl. She giggles at him upside down, making no effort to free herself.

"I don't like this," Lorimer whispers.

"Please don't interfere." Connie has hold of his arm, anchoring them both to the tool rack. Lorimer's alarm seems to have ebbed; he will watch, let serenity return. The others have not noticed them.

"Oh, there once was an Indian maid," Bud sings more restrainedly, "who never was a-fraid, that some buckaroo would slip it up her, ahem, ahem." He coughs ostentatiously, laughing. "Hey, Andy, I hear them calling you."

"What?" says Judy. "I don't hear anything."

"They're calling you, lad. Out there."

"Who?" asks Andy, listening.

"*They* are, for Crissake." He lets go of Judy and kicks over to Andy. "Listen, you're a great kid. Can't you see me and Judy have some business to discuss in private?" He turns Andy gently around and pushes him at the bean stakes. "It's New Year's Eve, dummy."

Andy floats passively away through the fence of vines, raising a hand at Lorimer and Connie. Bud is back with Judy.

"Happy New Year, kitten." He smiles.

"Happy New Year. Did you do special things on New Year?" she asks curiously.

"What we did on New Year's." He chuckles, taking her shoulders in his hands. "On New Year's Eve, yes we did. Why don't I show you some of our primitive Earth customs, h'mm?"

She nods, wide-eyed.

"Well, first we wish each other well, like this." He draws her to him and lightly kisses her cheek. "Kee-rist, what a dumb bitch," he says in a totally different voice. "You can tell you've been out too long when the geeks start looking good. Knockers, ahhh—" His hand plays with her blouse. The man is unaware, Lorimer realizes. He doesn't know he's drugged, he's speaking his thoughts. I must have done that. Oh, God. . . . He takes shelter behind his crystal lens, an observer in the protective light of eternity.

"And then we smooch a little." The friendly voice is back, Bud holds the girl closer, caressing her back. "Fat ass." He puts his mouth on hers; she doesn't resist. Lorimer watches Bud's arms tighten, his hands working on her buttocks, going under her clothes. Safe in the lens, his own sex stirs. Judy's arms are waving aimlessly.

Bud breaks for breath, a hand at his zipper.

"Stop staring," he says hoarsely. "One fucking more word, you'll find out what that big mouth is for. Oh, man, a flagpole. Like steel. . . . Bitch, this is your lucky day." He is baring her breasts now, big breasts. Fondling them. "Two fucking years in the ass end of noplace," he mutters, "shit on me, will you? Can't wait, watch it—titty-titty-titties—"

He kisses her again quickly and smiles down at her. "Good?" he asks in his tender voice, and sinks his mouth on her nipples, his hand seeking in her thighs. She jerks and says something muffled. Lorimer's arteries are pounding with delight, with dread.

"I, I think this should stop," he makes himself say falsely, hoping he isn't saying more. Through the pulsing tension he hears Connie whisper back, it sounds like "Don't worry, Judy's very athletic." Terror stabs him, they don't know. But he can't help.

"Cunt," Bud grunts, "you have to have a cunt in there, is it froze up? You dumb cunt—" Judy's face appears briefly in her floating hair, a remote part of Lorimer's mind notes that she looks amused and uncomfortable. His being is riveted to the sight of Bud expertly controlling her body in midair, peeling down the yellow slacks. Oh, God—her dark pubic mat, the thick white thighs—a perfectly normal woman, no mutation. Ohhh, God. . . . But there is suddenly a drifting shadow in the way: Andy again floating over them with something in his hands.

"You dinko, Jude?" the boy asks.

Bud's face comes up red and glaring. "Bug out, you!"

"Oh, I won't bother."

"Jee-sus Christ." Bud lunges up and grabs Andy's arm, his legs still hooked around Judy. "This is man's business, boy, do I have to spell it out?" He shifts his grip. "Shoo!"

In one swift motion he has jerked Andy close and backhanded his face hard, sending him sailing into the vines.

Bud gives a bark of laughter, bends back to Judy. Lorimer can see his erection poking through his fly. He wants to utter some warning, tell them their peril, but he can only ride the hot pleasure surging through him, melting his crystal shell. Go on, more—avidly he sees Bud mouth her breasts again and then suddenly flip her whole body over, holding her wrists behind her in one fist, his legs pinning hers. Her bare buttocks bulge up helplessly, enormous moons. "Ass-s-s," Bud groans. "Up, you bitch, ahhh-hh—" He pulls her butt onto him.

Judy gives a cry, begins to struggle futilely. Lorimer's shell boils and bursts. Amid the turmoil ghosts outside are trying to rush in. And something *is* moving, a real ghost—to his dismay he sees it is Andy again, floating toward the joined bodies, holding a whirring thing. Oh, no—a camera. The fools.

"Get away!" he tries to call to the boy.

But Bud's head turns, he has seen. "You little pissass." His long arm shoots out and captures Andy's shirt, his legs still locked around Judy.

"I've had it with you." His fist slams into Andy's mouth, the camera goes spinning away. But this time Bud doesn't let him go, he is battering the boy, all of them rolling in a tangle in the air.

"Stop!" Lorimer hears himself shout, plunging at them through the beans. "Bud, stop it! You're hitting a woman."

The angry face comes around, squinting at him.

"Get lost, Doc, you little fart. Get your own ass."

"Andy is a *woman*, Bud. You're hitting a girl. She's not a man."

"Huh?" Bud glances at Andy's bloody face. He shakes the shirtfront. "Where's the boobs?"

"She doesn't have breasts, but she's a woman. Her real name is Kay. They're all women. Let her go, Bud."

Bud stares at the androgyne, his legs still pinioning Judy, his penis poking the air. Andy put up his/her hands in a vaguely combative way.

"A dyke?" says Bud slowly. "A goddam little bull dyke? This I gotta see."

He feints casually, thrusts a hand into Andy's crotch.

"No balls!" he roars. "No balls at all!" Convulsing with laughter, he lets himself tip over in the air, releasing Andy, his legs letting Judy slip free. "Na-ah." He interrupts himself to grab her hair and goes on guffawing. "A dyke! Hey, dykey!" He takes hold of his hard-on, waggles it at Andy. "Eat your heart out, little dyke." Then he pulls up Judy's head. She has been watching unresisting all along.

"Take a good look, girlie. See what old Buddy has for you? Tha-a-at's what you want, say it. How long since you saw a real man, hey, dogface?"

Maniacal laughter bubbles up in Lorimer's gut, farce too strong for fear. "She never saw a man in her life before, none of them has. You imbecile, don't you get it? There aren't any other men, they've all been dead three hundred years."

Bud slowly stops chuckling, twists around to peer at Lorimer.

"What'd I hear you say, Doc?"

"The men are all gone. They died off in the epidemic. There's nothing but women left alive on Earth."

"You mean there's, there's two million women down there and no men?" His jaw gapes. "Only little bull dykes like Andy. . . . Wait a minute. Where do they get the kids?"

"They grow them artificially. They're all girls."

"Gawd. . . ." Bud's hand clasps his drooping penis, jiggles it absently. It stiffens. "Two million hot little cunts down there, waiting for old Buddy. Gawd. The last man on Earth. . . . You don't count, Doc. And old Dave, he's full of crap."

He begins to pump himself, still holding Judy by the hair. The motion sends them slowly backward. Lorimer sees that Andy—Kay—has the camera going again. There is a big star-shaped smear of blood on the boyish face; cut lip, probably. He himself feels globed in thick air, all action spent. Not lucid.

"Two million cunts," Bud repeats. "Nobody home, nothing but pussy everywhere. I can do anything I want, anytime. No more shit." He pumps faster. "They'll be spread out for miles begging for it. Clawing each other for it. All for me, King Buddy. . . . I'll have strawberries and cunt for breakfast. Hot buttered boobies, man. 'N' head, there'll be a couple little twats licking whip cream off my cock all day long. . . . Hey, I'll have contests! Only the best for old Buddy now. Not you, cow." He jerks Judy's head. "Li'l teenies, tight li'l holes. I'll make the old broads hot 'em up while I watch." He frowns slightly, working on himself. In a clinical corner of his mind Lorimer guesses the drug is retarding ejaculation. He tells himself that he should be relieved by Bud's self-absorption, is instead obscurely terrified.

"King, I'll be their god," Bud is mumbling. "They'll make statues of me, my cock a mile high, all over. . . . His Majesty's sacred balls. They'll worship it. . . . Buddy Geirr, the last cock on Earth. Oh man, if old George could see that. When the boys hear that they'll really shit themselves, woo-ee!"

He frowns harder. "They can't all be gone." His eyes rove, find Lorimer. "Hey, Doc, there's some men left someplace, aren't there? Two or three, anyway?"

"No." Effortfully Lorimer shakes his head. "They're all dead, all of them."

"Balls." Bud twists around, peering at them. "There has to be some left. Say it." He pulls Judy's head up. "Say it, cunt."

"No, it's true," she says.

"No men," Andy/Kay echoes.

"You're lying." Bud scowls, frigs himself faster, thrusting his pelvis. "There has to be some men, sure there are. . . . They're hiding out in the hills, that's what it is. Hunting, living wild. . . . Old wild men, I knew it."

"Why do there have to be men?" Judy asks him, being jerked to and fro.

"Why, you stupid bitch." He doesn't look at her, thrusts furiously. "Because, dummy, otherwise nothing counts, that's why. . . . There's some men, some good old buckaroos—Buddy's a good old buckaroo—"

"Is he going to emit sperm now?" Connie whispers.

"Very likely," Lorimer says, or intends to say. The spectacle is of merely clinical interest, he tells himself, nothing to dread. One of Judy's hands clutches something: a small plastic bag. Her other hand is on her hair that Bud is yanking. It must be painful.

"Uhhh, ahh," Bud pants distressfully, "fuck away, fuck—" Suddenly he pushes Judy's head into his groin, Lorimer glimpses her nonplussed expression.

"You have a mouth, bitch, get working! . . . Take it, for shit's sake, *take* it! Uh, uh—" A small oyster jets limply from him. Judy's arm goes after it with the bag as they roll over in the air.

"*Geirr!*"

Bewildered by the roar, Lorimer turns and sees Dave—Major Norman Davis—looming in the hatchway. His arms are out, holding back Lady Blue and the other Judy.

"Geirr! I said there would be no misconduct on this ship and I mean it. Get away from that woman!"

Bud's legs only move vaguely, he does not seem to have heard. Judy swims through them bagging the last drops.

"You, what the hell are you doing?"

In the silence Lorimer hears his own voice say, "Taking a sperm sample, I should think."

"Lorimer? Are you out of your perverted mind? Get Geirr to his quarters."

Bud slowly rotates upright. "Ah, the reverend Leroy," he says tone-lessly.

"You're drunk, Geirr. Go to your quarters."

"I have news for you, Dave-o," Bud tells him in the same flat voice. "I bet you don't know we're the last men on Earth. Two million twats down there."

"I'm aware of that," Dave says furiously. "You're a drunken dis-grace. Lorimer, get that man out of here."

But Lorimer feels no nerve of action stir. Dave's angry voice has pushed back the terror, created a strange hopeful stasis encapsulating them all.

"I don't have to take that anymore. . . ." Bud's head moves back and forth, silently saying no, no, as he drifts toward Lorimer. "Nothing counts anymore. All gone. What for, friends?" His forehead puckers. "Old Dave, he's a man. I'll let him have some. The dummies. . . . Poor old Doc, you're a creep but you're better'n nothing, you can have some, too. . . . We'll have places, see, big spreads. Hey, we can run drags, there has to be a million good old cars down there. We can go hunting. And then we find the wild men."

Andy, or Kay, is floating toward him, wiping off blood.

"Ah, no you don't!" Bud snarls and lunges for her. As his arm stretches out Judy claps him on the triceps.

Bud gives a yell that dopplers off, his limbs thrash—and then he is floating limply, his face suddenly serene. He is breathing, Lorimer sees, releasing his own breath, watching them carefully straighten out the big body. Judy plucks her pants out of the vines, and they start towing him out through the fence. She has the camera and the specimen bag.

"I put this in the freezer, dinko?" she says to Connie as they come by. Lorimer has to look away.

Connie nods. "Kay, how's your face?"

"I felt it!" Andy/Kay says excitedly through puffed lips. "I felt physi-cal anger, I wanted to hit him. Woo-ee!"

"Put that man in my wardroom," Dave orders as they pass. He has moved into the sunlight over the lettuce rows. Lady Blue and Judy Dakar are back by the wall, watching. Lorimer remembers what he wanted to ask.

"Dave, do you really know? Did you find out they're all women?"

Dave eyes him broodingly, floating erect with the sun on his chestnut beard and hair. The authentic features of man. Lorimer thinks of his own father, a small pale figure like himself. He feels better.

"I always knew they were trying to deceive us, Lorimer. Now that this woman has admitted the facts I understand the full extent of the tragedy."

It is his deep, mild Sunday voice. The women look at him interestedly.

"They are lost children. They have forgotten He who made them. For generations they have lived in darkness."

"They seem to be doing all right," Lorimer hears himself say. It sounds rather foolish.

"Women are not capable of running anything. You should know that, Lorimer. Look what they've done here, it's pathetic. Marking time, that's all. Poor souls." Dave sighs gravely. "It is not their fault. I recognize that. Nobody has given them any guidance for three hundred years. Like a chicken with its head off."

Lorimer recognizes his own thought; the structureless, chattering, trivial, two-million-celled protoplasmic lump.

"The head of the woman is the man," Dave says crisply. "Corinthians one eleven three. No discipline whatsoever." He stretches out his arm, holding up his crucifix as he drifts toward the wall of vines. "Mockery. Abominations." He touches the stakes and turns, framed in the green arbor.

"We were sent here, Lorimer. This is God's plan. *I* was sent here. Not you, you're as bad as they are. My middle name is Paul," he adds in a conversational tone. The sun gleams on the cross, on his uplifted face, a strong, pure, apostolic visage. Despite some intellectual reservations Lorimer feels a forgotten nerve respond.

"Oh, Father, send me strength," Dave prays quietly, his eyes closed. "You have spared us from the void to bring Your light to this suffering world. I shall lead Thy erring daughters out of the darkness. I shall be a stern but merciful father to them in Thy name. Help me to teach the children Thy holy law and train them in the fear of Thy righteous wrath. Let the women learn in silence and all subjection; Timothy two eleven. They shall have sons to rule over them and glorify Thy name."

He could do it, Lorimer thinks, a man like that really could get life going again. Maybe there is some mystery, some plan. I was too ready to give up. No guts. . . . He becomes aware of women whispering.

"This tape is about through." It is Judy Dakar. "Isn't that enough? He's just repeating."

"Wait," murmurs Lady Blue.

"And she brought forth a man-child to rule the nations with a rod of iron, Revelations twelve five," Dave says, louder. His eyes are open now, staring intently at the crucifix. *"For God so loved the world that he sent his only begotten son."*

Lady Blue nods; Judy pushes off toward Dave. Lorimer understands, protest rising in his throat. They mustn't do that to Dave, treating him like an animal, for Christ's sake, a man—

"Dave! Look out, don't let her get near you!" he shouts.

"May I look, Major? It's beautiful, what is it?" Judy is coasting close, her hand out toward the crucifix.

"She's got a hypo, watch it!"

But Dave has already wheeled round. "Do not profane, woman!"

He thrusts the cross at her like a weapon, so menacing that she recoils in midair and shows the glinting needle in her hand.

"Serpent!" He kicks her shoulder away, sending himself upward. "Blasphemer. All right," he snaps in his ordinary voice, "there's going to be some order around here starting now. Get over by that wall, all of you."

Astounded, Lorimer sees that Dave actually has a weapon in his other hand, a small gray handgun. He must have had it since Houston. Hope and ataraxia shrivel away, he is shocked into desperate reality.

"Major Davis," Lady Blue is saying. She is floating right at him, they all are, right at the gun. Oh God, do they know what it is?

"Stop!" he shouts at them. "Do what he says, for God's sake. That's a ballistic weapon, it can kill you. It shoots metal slugs." He begins edging toward Dave along the vines.

"Stand back." Dave gestures with the gun. "I am taking command of this ship in the name of the United States of America under God."

"Dave, put that gun away. You don't want to shoot people."

Dave sees him, swings the gun around. "I warn you, Lorimer, get over there with them. Geirr's a man, when he sobers up." He looks at the women still drifting puzzledly toward him and understands. "All right, lesson one. Watch this."

He takes deliberate aim at the iguana cages and fires. There is a pinging crack. A lizard explodes bloodily, voices cry out. A loud mechanical warble starts up and overrides everything.

"A leak!" Two bodies go streaking toward the far end, everybody is moving. In the confusion Lorimer sees Dave calmly pulling himself back to the hatchway behind them, his gun ready. He pushes frantically across the tool rack to cut him off. A spray canister comes loose in his grip, leaving him kicking in the air. The alarm warble dies.

"You will stay here until I decide to send for you," Dave announces.

He has reached the hatch, is pulling the massive lock door around. It will seal off the pod, Lorimer realizes.

"Don't do it, Dave! Listen to me, you're going to kill us all." Lorimer's own internal alarms are shaking him, he knows now what all that damned volleyball has been for and he is scared to death. "Dave, listen to me!"

"Shut up." The gun swings toward him. The door is moving. Lorimer gets a foot on solidity.

"Duck! It's a bomb!" With all his strength he hurls the massive canister at Dave's head and launches himself after it.

"Look out!" And he is sailing helplessly in slow motion, hearing the gun go off again, voices yelling. Dave must have missed him, overhead shots are tough—and then he is doubling downwards, grabbing hair. A hard blow strikes his gut, it is Dave's leg kicking past him but he has his arm under the beard, the big man bucking like a bull, throwing him around.

"Get the gun, get it!" People are bumping him, getting hit. Just as his hold slips, a hand snakes by him onto Dave's shoulder and they are colliding into the hatch door in a tangle. Dave's body is suddenly no longer at war.

Lorimer pushes free, sees Dave's contorted face tip slowly backward looking at him.

"Judas—"

The eyes close. It is over.

Lorimer looks around. Lady Blue is holding the gun, sighting down the barrel.

"Put that down," he gasps, winded. She goes on examining it.

"Hey, thanks!" Andy—Kay—grins lopsidedly at him, rubbing his jaw. They are all smiling, speaking warmly to him, feeling themselves, their torn clothes. Judy Dakar has a black eye starting, Connie holds a shattered iguana by the tail.

Beside him Dave drifts breathing stertorously, his blind face pointing at the sun. *Judas . . .* Lorimer feels the last shield break inside him, desolation flooding in. *On the deck my captain lies.*

Andy-who-is-not-a-man comes over and matter-of-factly zips up Dave's jacket, takes hold of it, and begins to tow him out. Judy Dakar stops them long enough to wrap the crucifix chain around his hand. Somebody laughs, not unkindly, as they go by.

For an instant Lorimer is back in that Evanston toilet. But they are gone, all the little giggling girls. All gone forever, gone with the big boys waiting outside to jeer at him. Bud is right, he thinks. Nothing counts anymore. Grief and anger hammer at him. He knows now what he has been dreading: not their vulnerability, his.

"They were good men," he says bitterly. "They aren't bad men. You don't know what bad means. You did it to them, you broke them down. You made them do crazy things. Was it interesting? Did you learn enough?" His voice is trying to shake. "Everybody has aggressive fantasies. They didn't act on them. Never. Until you poisoned them."

They gaze at him in silence. "But nobody does," Connie says finally. "I mean, the fantasies."

"They were good men," Lorimer repeats elegiacally. He knows he is speaking for it all, for Dave's Father, for Bud's manhood, for himself, for Cro-Magnon, for the dinosaurs, too, maybe. "I'm a man. By God yes, I'm angry. I have a right. We gave you all this, we made it all. We built your precious civilization and your knowledge and comfort and medicines and your dreams. All of it. We protected you, we worked our balls off keeping you and your kids. It was hard. It was a fight, a bloody fight all the way. We're tough. We had to be, can't you understand? Can't you for Christ's sake understand that?"

Another silence.

"We're trying." Lady Blue sighs. "We are trying, Dr. Lorimer. Of course we enjoy your inventions and we do appreciate your evolutionary role. But you must see there's a problem. As I understand it, what you protected people from was largely other males, wasn't it? We've just had an extraordinary demonstration. You have brought history to life for us." Her wrinkled brown eyes smile at him; a small, tea-colored matron holding an obsolete artifact.

"But the fighting is long over. It ended when you did, I believe. We can hardly turn you loose on Earth, and we simply have no facilities for people with your emotional problems."

"Besides, we don't think you'd be very happy," Judy Dakar adds earnestly.

"We could clone them," says Connie. "I know there's people who would volunteer to mother. The young ones might be all right, we could try."

"We've been *over* all that." Judy Paris is drinking from the water tank. She rinses and spits into the soil bed, looking worriedly at Lorimer. "We ought to take care of that leak now, we can talk tomorrow. And tomorrow and tomorrow." She smiles at him, unselfconsciously rubbing her crotch. "I'm sure a lot of people will want to meet you."

"Put us on an island," Lorimer says wearily. "On three islands." That look; he knows that look of preoccupied compassion. His mother and sister had looked just like that the time the diseased kitten came in the yard. They had comforted it and fed it and tenderly taken it to the vet to be gassed.

An acute, complex longing for the women he has known grips him. Ginny . . . dear God. His sister Amy. Poor Amy, she was good to him when they were kids. His mouth twists.

"Your problem is," he says, "if you take the risk of giving us equal rights, what could we possibly contribute?"

"Precisely," says Lady Blue. They all smile at him relievedly, not understanding that he isn't.

"I think I'll have that antidote now," he says.

Connie floats toward him, a big, warmhearted, utterly alien woman. "I thought you'd like yours in a bulb." She smiles kindly.

"Thank you." He takes the small, pink bulb. "Just tell me," he says to Lady Blue, who is looking at the bullet gashes, "what do you call yourselves? Women's World? Liberation? Amazonia?"

"Why, we call ourselves human beings." Her eyes twinkle absently at him, go back to the bullet marks. "Humanity, mankind." She shrugs. "The human race."

The drink tastes cool going down, something like peace and freedom, he thinks. Or death.

# Isaac Asimov

At last! At last! At long last!

There were nine stories in Volume One, fourteen stories in Volume Two, fifteen stories in Volume Three, and five stories so far in Volume Four. That's forty-three Hugo Winners in the short categories, before I finally made it in forty-fourth place. (Of course, I had won three Hugos previously in other categories—and a fourth one since—so this is not the tragedy I'm trying to make it sound like.)

The story was originally written for an anthology that was being planned for 1976 and was to be entitled *The Bicentennial Man.* Every story written for the anthology was to be inspired by that title, but in the broadest possible way. I was asked for 7,500 words, but the story got away from me and it became 15,000 words. The anthologist took it anyway.

Unfortunately, the anthology fell apart for a variety of reasons that had nothing to do with my story. I didn't know it fell apart, but Judy-Lynn del Rey, of Ballantine Books, who knows everything, knew. She was annoyed with me, in any case, because I hadn't done a story for one of *her* anthologies, and Judy-Lynn, when annoyed, is a formidable personage.

"I want to see the story," she said. "Show it to me!"

What could I do? I gave her a carbon of the story.

The next day she called me. "I did my best not to like the story," she said, "but I didn't succeed. I want it. Get it back."

I had to write to the original anthologist and return the money paid me. I received a reversion of the rights and Judy-Lynn published the story in her anthology *Stellar Science Fiction #2* in February 1976. Later that year I included it in my collection *The Bicentennial Man and Other Stories.*

The first hint I got that something unusual had taken place was in the reviews that began to appear in the fan magazines. My favorite review line of all time (for one of my s.f. stories) showed up. It went like this: "I read 'Bicentennial Man' and, for a time, I found myself back in the Golden Age."

And then I found I was nominated for a Hugo in the novelette category. That was bittersweet news. Sweet, for obvious reasons, but bitter because the 1977 convention at which the award was to be given out was to be held at Miami Beach and it was out of reach for me.

But was it? Could I not take a train? I had taken a train to Miami Beach in 1976, and back, too, and had survived (not by much). Wasn't a possible Hugo worth a repeat of the effort? I decided it was.

And then, in May 1977, I had a mild coronary, and I decided I had better not subject myself to the stress of long travel. There was nothing to do but wait. (Again this is not quite the tragedy that I'm trying to make it sound like. Shortly before my coronary, "The Bicentennial Man" won the Nebula Award and I was there to collect *that*—but I'm not here to plug the competition. This is a book of *Hugo* Winners.)

At 11 p.m. on Sunday, September 4, 1977, immediately after the award banquet, Barbara Bova (Ben's beautiful and vivacious wife) called with the good news. "The Bicentennial Man" had won the Hugo as well.

*6*

# THE BICENTENNIAL MAN

*The Three Laws of Robotics:*
  1. *A robot may not injure a human being or, through inaction, allow a human being to come to harm.*
  2. *A robot must obey the orders given it by human beings except where such orders would conflict with the First Law.*
  3. *A robot must protect its own existence as long as such protection does not conflict with the First or Second Law.*

1

Andrew Martin said, "Thank you," and took the seat offered him. He didn't look driven to the last resort, but he had been.

He didn't, actually, look anything, for there was a smooth blankness to his face, except for the sadness one imagined one saw in his eyes. His hair was smooth, light brown, rather fine, and there was no facial hair. He looked freshly and cleanly shaved. His clothes were distinctly old-fashioned, but neat and predominantly a velvety red-purple in color.

Facing him from behind the desk was the surgeon, and the nameplate on the desk included a fully identifying series of letters and numbers, which Andrew didn't bother with. To call him Doctor would be quite enough.

"When can the operation be carried through, Doctor?" he asked.

The surgeon said softly, with that certain inalienable note of respect that a robot always used to a human being, "I am not certain, sir, that I understand how or upon whom such an operation could be performed."

There might have been a look of respectful intransigence on the surgeon's face, if a robot of his sort, in lightly bronzed stainless steel, could have such an expression, or any expression.

Andrew Martin studied the robot's right hand, his cutting hand, as it lay on the desk in utter tranquillity. The fingers were long and shaped into artistically metallic looping curves so graceful and appropriate that one could imagine a scalpel fitting them and becoming, temporarily, one piece with them.

There would be no hesitation in his work, no stumbling, no quivering, no mistakes. That came with specialization, of course, a specialization so fiercely desired by humanity that few robots were, any longer, independently brained. A surgeon, of course, would have to be. And this one, though brained, was so limited in his capacity that he did not recognize Andrew—had probably never heard of him.

Andrew said, "Have you ever thought you would like to be a man?"

The surgeon hesitated a moment as though the question fitted nowhere in his allotted positronic pathways. "But I am a robot, sir."

"Would it be better to be a man?"

"It would be better, sir, to be a better surgeon. I could not be so if I were a man, but only if I were a more advanced robot. I would be pleased to be a more advanced robot."

"It does not offend you that I can order you about? That I can make you stand up, sit down, move right or left, by merely telling you to do so?"

"It is my pleasure to please you, sir. If your orders were to interfere with my functioning with respect to you or to any other human being, I would not obey you. The First Law, concerning my duty to human safety, would take precedence over the Second Law relating to obedience. Otherwise, obedience is my pleasure. . . . But upon whom am I to perform this operation?"

"Upon me," said Andrew.

"But that is impossible. It is patently a damaging operation."

"That does not matter," said Andrew calmly.

"I must not inflict damage," said the surgeon.

"On a human being, you must not," said Andrew, "but I, too, am a robot."

2

Andrew had appeared much more a robot when he had first been—manufactured. He had then been as much a robot in appearance as any that had ever existed, smoothly designed and functional.

He had done well in the home to which he had been brought in those days when robots in households, or on the planet altogether, had been a rarity.

There had been four in the home: Sir and Ma'am and Miss and Little Miss. He knew their names, of course, but he never used them. Sir was Gerald Martin.

His own serial number was NDR— He forgot the numbers. It had been a long time, of course, but if he had wanted to remember, he could not forget. He had not wanted to remember.

Little Miss had been the first to call him Andrew because she could not use the letters, and all the rest followed her in this.

Little Miss— She had lived ninety years and was long since dead. He had tried to call her Ma'am once, but she would not allow it. Little Miss she had been to her last day.

Andrew had been intended to perform the duties of a valet, a butler, a lady's maid. Those were the experimental days for him and, indeed, for all robots anywhere but in the industrial and exploratory factories and stations off Earth.

The Martins enjoyed him, and half the time he was prevented from doing his work because Miss and Little Miss would rather play with him.

It was Miss who understood first how this might be arranged. She said, "We order you to play with us and you must follow orders."

Andrew said, "I am sorry, Miss, but a prior order from Sir must surely take precedence."

But she said, "Daddy just said he hoped you would take care of the cleaning. That's not much of an order. I *order* you."

Sir did not mind. Sir was fond of Miss and of Little Miss, even more than Ma'am was, and Andrew was fond of them, too. At least, the effects they had upon his actions were those which in a human being would have been called the result of fondness. Andrew thought of it as fondness, for he did not know any other word for it.

It was for Little Miss that Andrew had carved a pendant out of wood. She had ordered him to. Miss, it seemed, had received an ivorite pendant with scrollwork for her birthday and Little Miss was unhappy over it. She had only a piece of wood, which she gave Andrew together with a small kitchen knife.

He had done it quickly and Little Miss said, "That's *nice*, Andrew. I'll show it to Daddy."

Sir would not believe it. "Where did you really get this, Mandy?" Mandy was what he called Little Miss. When Little Miss assured him she was really telling the truth, he turned to Andrew. "Did you do this, Andrew?"

"Yes, Sir."

"The design, too?"

"Yes, Sir."

"From what did you copy the design?"

"It is a geometric representation, Sir, that fit the grain of the wood."

The next day, Sir brought him another piece of wood, a larger one, and an electric vibro-knife. He said, "Make something out of this, Andrew. Anything you want to."

Andrew did so and Sir watched, then looked at the product a long time. After that, Andrew no longer waited on tables. He was ordered to read books on furniture design instead, and he learned to make cabinets and desks.

Sir said, "These are amazing productions, Andrew."

Andrew said, "I enjoy doing them, Sir."

"Enjoy?"

"It makes the circuits of my brain somehow flow more easily. I have heard you use the word 'enjoy' and the way you use it fits the way I feel. I enjoy doing them, Sir."

3

Gerald Martin took Andrew to the regional offices of United States Robots and Mechanical Men, Inc. As a member of the Regional Legislature he had no trouble at all in gaining an interview with the Chief Robopsychologist. In fact, it was only as a member of the Regional Legislature that he qualified as a robot owner in the first place—in those early days when robots were rare.

Andrew did not understand any of this at the time, but in later years, with greater learning, he could re-view that early scene and understand it in its proper light.

The robopsychologist, Merton Mansky, listened with a gathering frown and more than once managed to stop his fingers at the point beyond which they would have irrevocably drummed on the table. He had drawn features and a lined forehead and looked as though he might be younger than he looked.

He said, "Robotics is not an exact art, Mr. Martin. I cannot explain it to you in detail, but the mathematics governing the plotting of the positronic pathways is far too complicated to permit of any but approximate solutions. Naturally, since we build everything about the Three

Laws, those are incontrovertible. We will, of course, replace your robot—"

"Not at all," said Sir. "There is no question of failure on his part. He performs his assigned duties perfectly. The point is, he also carves wood in exquisite fashion and never the same twice. He produces works of art."

Mansky looked confused. "Strange. Of course, we're attempting generalized pathways these days. . . . Really creative, you think?"

"See for yourself." Sir handed over a little sphere of wood on which there was a playground scene in which the boys and girls were almost too small to make out, yet they were in perfect proportion and blended so naturally with the grain that that, too, seemed to have been carved.

Mansky said, *"He* did that?" He handed it back with a shake of his head. "The luck of the draw. Something in the pathways."

"Can you do it again?"

"Probably not. Nothing like this has ever been reported."

"Good! I don't in the least mind Andrew's being the only one."

Mansky said, "I suspect that the company would like to have your robot back for study."

Sir said with sudden grimness, "Not a chance. Forget it." He turned to Andrew, "Let's go home now."

"As you wish, Sir," said Andrew.

4

Miss was dating boys and wasn't about the house much. It was Little Miss, not as little as she was, who filled Andrew's horizon now. She never forgot that the very first piece of wood carving he had done had been for her. She kept it on a silver chain about her neck.

It was she who first objected to Sir's habit of giving away the productions. She said, "Come on, Dad, if anyone wants one of them, let him pay for it. It's worth it."

Sir said, "It isn't like you to be greedy, Mandy."

"Not for us, Dad. For the artist."

Andrew had never heard the word before and when he had a moment to himself he looked it up in the dictionary. Then there was another trip, this time to Sir's lawyer.

Sir said to him, "What do you think of this, John?"

The lawyer was John Feingold. He had white hair and a pudgy belly, and the rims of his contact lenses were tinted a bright green. He looked at the small plaque Sir had given him. "This is beautiful. . . . But I've heard the news. This is a carving made by your robot. The one you've brought with you."

"Yes, Andrew does them. Don't you, Andrew?"

"Yes, Sir," said Andrew.

"How much would you pay for that, John?" asked Sir.

"I can't say. I'm not a collector of such things."

"Would you believe I have been offered two hundred and fifty dollars for that small thing? Andrew has made chairs that have sold for five hundred dollars. There's two hundred thousand dollars in the bank out of Andrew's products."

"Good heavens, he's making you rich, Gerald."

"Half rich," said Sir. "Half of it is in an account in the name of Andrew Martin."

"The robot?"

"That's right, and I want to know if it's legal."

"Legal?" Feingold's chair creaked as he leaned back in it. "There are no precedents, Gerald. How did your robot sign the necessary papers?"

"He can sign his name and I brought in the signature. I didn't bring him in to the bank himself. Is there anything further that ought to be done?"

"Um." Feingold's eyes seemed to turn inward for a moment. Then he said, "Well, we can set up a trust to handle all finances in his name and that will place a layer of insulation between him and the hostile world. Further than that, my advice is you do nothing. No one is stopping you so far. If anyone objects, let *him* bring suit."

"And will you take the case if suit is brought?"

"For a retainer, certainly."

"How much?"

"Something like that," and Feingold pointed to the wooden plaque.

"Fair enough," said Sir.

Feingold chuckled as he turned to the robot. "Andrew, are you pleased that you have money?"

"Yes, sir."

"What do you plan to do with it?"

"Pay for things, sir, which otherwise Sir would have to pay for. It would save him expense, sir."

5

The occasions came. Repairs were expensive, and revisions were even more so. With the years, new models of robots were produced and

Sir saw to it that Andrew had the advantage of every new device until he was a paragon of metallic excellence. It was all at Andrew's expense. Andrew insisted on that.

Only his positronic pathways were untouched. Sir insisted on that.

"The new ones aren't as good as you are, Andrew," he said. "The new robots are worthless. The company has learned to make the pathways more precise, more closely on the nose, more deeply on the track. The new robots don't shift. They do what they're designed for and never stray. I like you better."

"Thank you, Sir."

"And it's your doing, Andrew, don't you forget that. I am certain Mansky put an end to generalized pathways as soon as he had a good look at you. He didn't like the unpredictability. . . . Do you know how many times he asked for you so he could place you under study? Nine times! I never let him have you, though, and now that he's retired, we may have some peace."

So Sir's hair thinned and grayed and his face grew pouchy, while Andrew looked rather better than he had when he first joined the family.

Ma'am had joined an art colony somewhere in Europe and Miss was a poet in New York. They wrote sometimes, but not often. Little Miss was married and lived not far away. She said she did not want to leave Andrew and when her child, Little Sir, was born, she let Andrew hold the bottle and feed him.

With the birth of a grandson, Andrew felt that Sir had someone now to replace those who had gone. It would not be so unfair to come to him with the request.

Andrew said, "Sir, it is kind of you to have allowed me to spend my money as I wished."

"It was your money, Andrew."

"Only by your voluntary act, Sir. I do not believe the law would have stopped you from keeping it all."

"The law won't persuade me to do wrong, Andrew."

"Despite all expenses, and despite taxes, too, Sir, I have nearly six hundred thousand dollars."

"I know that, Andrew."

"I want to give it to you, Sir."

"I won't take it, Andrew."

"In exchange for something you can give me, Sir."

"Oh? What is that, Andrew?"

"My freedom, Sir."

"Your—"

"I wish to buy my freedom, Sir."

## 6

It wasn't that easy. Sir had flushed, had said "For God's sake!" had turned on his heel, and stalked away.

It was Little Miss who brought him around, defiantly and harshly—and in front of Andrew. For thirty years, no one had hesitated to talk in front of Andrew, whether the matter involved Andrew or not. He was only a robot.

She said, "Dad, why are you taking it as a personal affront? He'll still be here. He'll still be loyal. He can't help that. It's built in. All he wants is a form of words. He wants to be called free. Is that so terrible? Hasn't he earned it? Heavens, he and I have been talking about it for years."

"Talking about it for years, have you?"

"Yes, and over and over again, he postponed it for fear he would hurt you. I *made* him put it up to you."

"He doesn't know what freedom is. He's a robot."

"Dad, you don't know him. He's read everything in the library. I don't know what he feels inside but I don't know what *you* feel inside. When you talk to him you'll find he reacts to the various abstractions as you and I do, and what else counts? If someone else's reactions are like your own, what more can you ask for?"

"The law won't take that attitude," Sir said angrily. "See here, you!" He turned to Andrew with a deliberate grate in his voice. "I can't free you except by doing it legally, and if it gets into the courts, you not only won't get your freedom but the law will take official cognizance of your money. They'll tell you that a robot has no right to earn money. Is this rigmarole worth losing your money?"

"Freedom is without price, Sir," said Andrew. "Even the chance of freedom is worth the money."

## 7

The court might also take the attitude that freedom was without price, and might decide that for no price, however great, could a robot buy its freedom.

The simple statement of the regional attorney who represented those who had brought a class action to oppose the freedom was this: The word "freedom" had no meaning when applied to a robot. Only a human being could be free.

He said it several times, when it seemed appropriate; slowly, with his hand coming down rhythmically on the desk before him to mark the words.

Little Miss asked permission to speak on behalf of Andrew. She was recognized by her full name, something Andrew had never heard pronounced before:

"Amanda Laura Martin Charney may approach the bench."

She said, "Thank you, your honor. I am not a lawyer and I don't know the proper way of phrasing things, but I hope you will listen to my meaning and ignore the words.

"Let's understand what it means to be free in Andrew's case. In some ways, he *is* free. I think it's at least twenty years since anyone in the Martin family gave him an order to do something that we felt he might not do of his own accord.

"But we can, if we wish, give him an order to do anything, couch it as harshly as we wish, because he is a machine that belongs to us. Why should we be in a position to do so, when he has served us so long, so faithfully, and earned so much money for us? He owes us nothing more. The debt is entirely on the other side.

"Even if we were legally forbidden to place Andrew in involuntary servitude, he would still serve us voluntarily. Making him free would be a trick of words only, but it would mean much to him. It would give him everything and cost us nothing."

For a moment the Judge seemed to be suppressing a smile. "I see your point, Mrs. Charney. The fact is that there is no binding law in this respect and no precedent. There is, however, the unspoken assumption that only a man can enjoy freedom. I can make new law here, subject to reversal in a higher court, but I cannot lightly run counter to that assumption. Let me address the robot. Andrew!"

"Yes, your honor."

It was the first time Andrew had spoken in court and the Judge seemed astonished for a moment at the human timbre of the voice. He said, "Why do you want to be free, Andrew? In what way will this matter to you?"

Andrew said, "Would you wish to be a slave, your honor?"

"But you are not a slave. You are a perfectly good robot, a genius of a robot I am given to understand, capable of an artistic expression that can be matched nowhere. What more can you do if you were free?"

"Perhaps no more than I do now, your honor, but with greater joy. It has been said in this courtroom that only a human being can be free. It seems to me that only someone who wishes for freedom can be free. I wish for freedom."

And it was that that cued the Judge. The crucial sentence in his decision was: "There is no right to deny freedom to any object with a mind advanced enough to grasp the concept and desire the state."

It was eventually upheld by the World Court.

## 8

Sir remained displeased and his harsh voice made Andrew feel almost as though he were being short-circuited.

Sir said, "I don't want your damned money, Andrew. I'll take it only because you won't feel free otherwise. From now on, you can select your own jobs and do them as you please. I will give you no orders, except this one—that you do as you please. But I am still responsible for you; that's part of the court order. I hope you understand that."

Little Miss interrupted. "Don't be irascible, Dad. The responsibility is no great chore. You know you won't have to do a thing. The Three Laws still hold."

"Then how is he free?"

Andrew said, "Are not human beings bound by their laws, Sir?"

Sir said, "I'm not going to argue." He left, and Andrew saw him only infrequently after that.

Little Miss came to see him frequently in the small house that had been built and made over for him. It had no kitchen, of course, nor bathroom facilities. It had just two rooms; one was a library and one was a combination storeroom and workroom. Andrew accepted many commissions and worked harder as a free robot than he ever had before, till the cost of the house was paid for and the structure legally transferred to him.

One day Little Sir came. . . . No, George! Little Sir had insisted on that after the court decision. "A free robot doesn't call anyone Little Sir," George had said. "I call you Andrew. You must call me George."

It was phrased as an order, so Andrew called him George—but Little Miss remained Little Miss.

The day George came alone, it was to say that Sir was dying. Little Miss was at the bedside but Sir wanted Andrew as well.

Sir's voice was quite strong, though he seemed unable to move much. He struggled to get his hand up. "Andrew," he said, "Andrew— Don't help me, George. I'm only dying; I'm not crippled. . . . Andrew, I'm glad you're free. I just wanted to tell you that."

Andrew did not know what to say. He had never been at the side of someone dying before, but he knew it was the human way of ceasing to function. It was an involuntary and irreversible dismantling, and Andrew did not know what to say that might be appropriate. He could only remain standing, absolutely silent, absolutely motionless.

When it was over, Little Miss said to him, "He may not have seemed friendly to you toward the end, Andrew, but he was old, you know, and it hurt him that you should want to be free."

And then Andrew found the words to say. He said, "I would never have been free without him, Little Miss."

## 9

It was only after Sir's death that Andrew began to wear clothes. He began with an old pair of trousers at first, a pair that George had given him.

George was married now, and a lawyer. He had joined Feingold's firm. Old Feingold was long since dead but his daughter had carried on and eventually the firm's name became Feingold and Martin. It remained so even when the daughter retired and no Feingold took her place. At the time Andrew put on clothes for the first time, the Martin name had just been added to the firm.

George had tried not to smile, the first time Andrew put on the trousers, but to Andrew's eyes the smile was clearly there.

George showed Andrew how to manipulate the static charge so as to allow the trousers to open, wrap about his lower body, and move shut. George demonstrated on his own trousers, but Andrew was quite aware that it would take him awhile to duplicate that one flowing motion.

George said, "But why do you want trousers, Andrew? Your body is so beautifully functional it's a shame to cover it—especially when you needn't worry about either temperature control or modesty. And it doesn't cling properly, not on metal."

Andrew said, "Are not human bodies beautifully functional, George? Yet you cover yourselves."

"For warmth, for cleanliness, for protection, for decorativeness. None of that applies to you."

Andrew said, "I feel bare without clothes. I feel different, George."

"Different! Andrew, there are millions of robots on Earth now. In this region, according to the last census, there are almost as many robots as there are men."

"I know, George. There are robots doing every conceivable type of work."

"And none of them wear clothes."

"But none of them are free, George."

Little by little, Andrew added to the wardrobe. He was inhibited by George's smile and by the stares of the people who commissioned work.

He might be free, but there was built into him a carefully detailed program concerning his behavior toward people, and it was only by the tiniest steps that he dared advance. Open disapproval would set him back months.

Not everyone accepted Andrew as free. He was incapable of resenting that and yet there was a difficulty about his thinking process when he thought of it.

Most of all, he tended to avoid putting on clothes—or too many of them—when he thought Little Miss might come to visit him. She was old now and was often away in some warmer climate, but when she returned the first thing she did was visit him.

On one of her returns, George said ruefully, "She's got me, Andrew. I'll be running for the Legislature next year. Like grandfather, she says, like grandson."

"Like grandfather—" Andrew stopped, uncertain.

"I mean that I, George, the grandson, will be like Sir, the grandfather, who was in the Legislature once."

Andrew said, "It would be pleasant, George, if Sir were still—" He paused, for he did not want to say, "in working order." That seemed inappropriate.

"Alive," said George. "Yes, I think of the old monster now and then, too."

It was a conversation Andrew thought about. He had noticed his own incapacity in speech when talking with George. Somehow the language had changed since Andrew had come into being with an innate vocabulary. Then, too, George used a colloquial speech, as Sir and Little Miss had not. Why should he have called Sir a monster when surely that word was not appropriate?

Nor could Andrew turn to his own books for guidance. They were old and most dealt with woodworking, with art, with furniture design. There were none on language, none on the way of human beings.

It was at that moment it seemed to him that he must seek the proper books; and as a free robot, he felt he must not ask George. He would go to town and use the library. It was a triumphant decision and he felt his electropotential grow distinctly higher until he had to throw in an impedance coil.

He put on a full costume, even including a shoulder chain of wood. He would have preferred the glitter plastic but George had said that wood was much more appropriate and that polished cedar was considerably more valuable as well.

He had placed a hundred feet between himself and the house before gathering resistance brought him to a halt. He shifted the impedance coil out of circuit, and when that did not seem to help enough, he returned to his home and on a piece of notepaper wrote neatly, "I have gone to the library," and placed it in clear view on his worktable.

## 10

Andrew never quite got to the library. He had studied the map. He knew the route, but not the appearance of it. The actual landmarks did not resemble the symbols on the map and he would hesitate. Eventually he thought he must have somehow gone wrong, for everything looked strange.

He passed an occasional field robot, but at the time he decided he should ask his way, there were none in sight. A vehicle passed and did not stop. He stood irresolute, which meant calmly motionless, and then coming across the field toward him were two human beings.

He turned to face them, and they altered their course to meet him. A moment before, they had been talking loudly; he had heard their voices; but now they were silent. They had the look that Andrew associated with human uncertainty, and they were young, but not very young. Twenty perhaps? Andrew could never judge human age.

He said, "Would you describe to me the route to the town library, sirs?"

One of them, the taller of the two, whose tall hat lengthened him still farther, almost grotesquely, said, not to Andrew, but to the other, "It's a robot."

The other had a bulbous nose and heavy eyelids. He said, not to Andrew, but to the first, "It's wearing clothes."

The tall one snapped his fingers. "It's the free robot. They have a robot at the Martins who isn't owned by anybody. Why else would it be wearing clothes?"

"Ask it," said the one with the nose.

"Are you the Martin robot?" asked the tall one.

"I am Andrew Martin, sir," said Andrew.

"Good. Take off your clothes. Robots don't wear clothes." He said to the other, "That's disgusting. Look at him."

Andrew hesitated. He hadn't heard an order in that tone of voice in so long that his Second Law circuits had momentarily jammed.

The tall one said, "Take off your clothes. I order you."

Slowly, Andrew began to remove them.

"Just drop them," said the tall one.

The nose said, "If it doesn't belong to anyone, he could be ours as much as someone else's."

"Anyway," said the tall one, "who's to object to anything we do? We're not damaging property. . . . Stand on your head." That was to Andrew.

"The head is not meant—" began Andrew.

"That's an order. If you don't know how, try anyway."

Andrew hesitated again, then bent to put his head on the ground. He tried to lift his legs and fell, heavily.

The tall one said, "Just lie there." He said to the other, "We can take him apart. Ever take a robot apart?"

"Will he let us?"

"How can he stop us?"

There was no way Andrew could stop them, if they ordered him not to resist in a forceful enough manner. Second Law of obedience took precedence over the Third Law of self-preservation. In any case, he could not defend himself without possibly hurting them and that would mean breaking the First Law. At that thought, every motile unit contracted slightly and he quivered as he lay there.

The tall one walked over and pushed at him with his foot. "He's heavy. I think we'll need tools to do the job."

The nose said, "We could order him to take himself apart. It would be fun to watch him try."

"Yes," said the tall one thoughtfully, "but let's get him off the road. If someone comes along—"

It was too late. Someone had indeed come along and it was George. From where he lay, Andrew had seen him topping a small rise in the middle distance. He would have liked to signal him in some way, but the last order had been "Just lie there!"

George was running now and he arrived somewhat winded. The two young men stepped back a little and then waited thoughtfully.

George said anxiously, "Andrew, has something gone wrong?"

Andrew said, "I am well, George."

"Then stand up. . . . What happened to your clothes?"

The tall young man said, "That your robot, mac?"

George turned sharply. "He's no one's robot. What's been going on here?"

"We politely asked him to take his clothes off. What's that to you if you don't own him?"

George said, "What were they doing, Andrew?"

Andrew said, "It was their intention in some way to dismember me. They were about to move me to a quiet spot and order me to dismember myself."

George looked at the two and his chin trembled. The two young men retreated no further. They were smiling. The tall one said lightly, "What are you going to do, pudgy? Attack us?"

George said, "No. I don't have to. This robot has been with my family for over seventy years. He knows us and he values us more than he values anyone else. I am going to tell him that you two are threatening my life and that you plan to kill me. I will ask him to defend me. In choosing between me and you two, he will choose me. Do you know what will happen to you when he attacks you?"

The two were backing away slightly, looking uneasy.

George said sharply, "Andrew, I am in danger and about to come to harm from these young men. Move toward them!"

Andrew did so, and the two young men did not wait. They ran fleetly.

"All right, Andrew, relax," said George. He looked unstrung. He was far past the age where he could face the possibility of a dustup with one young man, let alone two.

Andrew said, "I couldn't have hurt them, George. I could see they were not attacking you."

"I didn't order you to attack them; I only told you to move toward them. Their own fears did the rest."

"How can they fear robots?"

"It's a disease of mankind, one of which it is not yet cured. But never mind that. What the devil are you doing here, Andrew? I was on the point of turning back and hiring a helicopter when I found you. How did you get it into your head to go to the library? I would have brought you any books you needed."

"I am a—" began Andrew.

"Free robot. Yes, yes. All right, what did you want in the library?"

"I want to know more about human beings, about the world, about everything. And about robots, George. I want to write a history about robots."

George said, "Well, let's walk home. . . . And pick up your clothes first. Andrew, there are a million books on robotics and all of them include histories of the science. The world is growing saturated not only with robots but with information about robots."

Andrew shook his head, a human gesture he had lately begun to make. "Not a history of robotics, George. A history of *robots,* by a robot. I want to explain how robots feel about what has happened since the first ones were allowed to work and live on Earth."

George's eyebrows lifted, but he said nothing in direct response.

## 11

Little Miss was just past her eighty-third birthday, but there was nothing about her that was lacking in either energy or determination. She gestured with her cane oftener than she propped herself up with it.

She listened to the story in a fury of indignation. She said, "George, that's horrible. Who were those young ruffians?"

"I don't know. What difference does it make? In the end they did no damage."

"They might have. You're a lawyer, George, and if you're well off, it's entirely due to the talent of Andrew. It was the money *he* earned that is the foundation of everything we have. He provides the continuity for this family and I will *not* have him treated as a wind-up toy."

"What would you have me do, Mother?" asked George.

"I said you're a lawyer. Don't you listen? You set up a test case somehow, and you force the regional courts to declare for robot rights and get the Legislature to pass the necessary bills, and carry the whole thing to the World Court, if you have to. I'll be watching, George, and I'll tolerate no shirking."

She was serious, and what began as a way of soothing the fearsome old lady became an involved matter with enough legal entanglement to make it interesting. As senior partner of Feingold and Martin, George plotted strategy but left the actual work to his junior partners, with much of it a matter for his son, Paul, who was also a member of the firm and who reported dutifully nearly every day to his grandmother. She, in turn, discussed it every day with Andrew.

Andrew was deeply involved. His work on his book on robots was delayed again, as he pored over the legal arguments and even, at times, made very diffident suggestions.

He said, "George told me that day that human beings have always been afraid of robots. As long as they are, the courts and the legislatures are not likely to work hard on behalf of robots. Should there not be something done about public opinion?"

So while Paul stayed in court, George took to the public platform. It gave him the advantage of being informal and he even went so far sometimes as to wear the new, loose style of clothing which he called drapery. Paul said, "Just don't trip over it on stage, Dad."

George said despondently, "I'll try not to."

He addressed the annual convention of holo-news editors on one occasion and said, in part:

"If, by virtue of the Second Law, we can demand of any robot unlimited obedience in all respects not involving harm to a human being, then any human being, *any* human being, has a fearsome power over any robot, *any* robot. In particular, since Second Law supersedes Third Law, *any* human being can use the law of obedience to overcome the law of self-protection. He can order any robot to damage itself or even destroy itself for any reason, or for no reason.

"Is this just? Would we treat an animal so? Even an inanimate object which has given us good service has a claim on our consideration. And a robot is not insensible; it is not an animal. It can think well enough to enable it to talk to us, reason with us, joke with us. Can we treat them as friends, can we work together with them, and not give them some of the fruit of that friendship, some of the benefit of co-working?

"If a man has the right to give a robot any order that does not involve harm to a human being, he should have the decency never to give a robot any order that involves harm to a robot, unless human safety absolutely requires it. With great power goes great responsibility, and if the robots have Three Laws to protect men, is it too much to ask that men have a law or two to protect robots?"

Andrew was right. It was the battle over public opinion that held the key to courts and Legislature and in the end a law passed which set up conditions under which robot-harming orders were forbidden. It was endlessly qualified and the punishments for violating the law were totally inadequate, but the principle was established. The final passage by the World Legislature came through on the day of Little Miss's death.

That was no coincidence. Little Miss held on to life desperately during the last debate and let go only when word of victory arrived. Her last smile was for Andrew. Her last words were: "You have been good to us, Andrew."

She died with her hand holding his, while her son and his wife and children remained at a respectful distance from both.

## 12

Andrew waited patiently while the receptionist disappeared into the inner office. It might have used the holographic chatterbox, but unquestionably it was unmanned (or perhaps unroboted) by having to deal with another robot rather than with a human being.

Andrew passed the time revolving the matter in his mind. Could "unroboted" be used as an analogue of "unmanned," or had "unmanned" become a metaphoric term sufficiently divorced from its original literal meaning to be applied to robots—or to women for that matter?

Such problems came frequently as he worked on his book on robots. The trick of thinking out sentences to express all complexities had undoubtedly increased his vocabulary.

Occasionally, someone came into the room to stare at him and he did not try to avoid the glance. He looked at each calmly, and each in turn looked away.

Paul Martin finally came out. He looked surprised, or he would have if Andrew could have made out his expression with certainty. Paul had taken to wearing the heavy makeup that fashion was dictating for both sexes and though it made sharper and firmer the somewhat bland lines of his face, Andrew disapproved. He found that disapproving of human beings, as long as he did not express it verbally, did not make him very uneasy. He could even write the disapproval. He was sure it had not always been so.

Paul said, "Come in, Andrew. I'm sorry I made you wait but there was something I *had* to finish. Come in. You had said you wanted to talk to me, but I didn't know you meant here in town."

"If you are busy, Paul, I am prepared to continue to wait."

Paul glanced at the interplay of shifting shadows on the dial on the wall that served as timepiece and said, "I can make some time. Did you come alone?"

"I hired an automatobile."

"Any trouble?" Paul asked, with more than a trace of anxiety.

"I wasn't expecting any. My rights are protected."

Paul looked the more anxious for that. "Andrew, I've explained that the law is unenforceable, at least under most conditions. . . . And if you insist on wearing clothes, you'll run into trouble eventually—just like that first time."

"And only time, Paul. I'm sorry you are displeased."

"Well, look at it this way; you are virtually a living legend, Andrew, and you are too valuable in many different ways for you to have any right to take chances with yourself. . . . How's the book coming?"

"I am approaching the end, Paul. The publisher is quite pleased."

"Good!"

"I don't know that he's necessarily pleased with the book as a book. I think he expects to sell many copies because it's written by a robot and it's that that pleases him."

"Only human, I'm afraid."

"I am not displeased. Let it sell for whatever reason since it will mean money and I can use some."

"Grandmother left you—"

"Little Miss was generous, and I'm sure I can count on the family to help me out further. But it is the royalties from the book on which I am counting to help me through the next step."

"What next step is that?"

"I wish to see the head of U. S. Robots and Mechanical Men, Inc. I have tried to make an appointment, but so far I have not been able to reach him. The corporation did not cooperate with me in the writing of the book, so I am not surprised, you understand."

Paul was clearly amused. "Cooperation is the last thing you can expect. They didn't cooperate with us in our great fight for robot rights. Quite the reverse and you can see why. Give a robot rights and people may not want to buy them."

"Nevertheless," said Andrew, "if you call them, you may obtain an interview for me."

"I'm no more popular with them than you are, Andrew."

"But perhaps you can hint that by seeing me they may head off a campaign by Feingold and Martin to strengthen the rights of robots further."

"Wouldn't that be a lie, Andrew?"

"Yes, Paul, and I can't tell one. That is why you must call."

"Ah, you can't lie, but you can urge me to tell a lie, is that it? You're getting more human all the time, Andrew."

13

It was not easy to arrange, even with Paul's supposedly weighted name.

But it was finally carried through and, when it was, Harley Smythe-Robertson, who, on his mother's side, was descended from the original founder of the corporation and who had adopted the hyphenation to indicate it, looked remarkably unhappy. He was approaching retirement age and his entire tenure as president had been devoted to the matter of robot rights. His gray hair was plastered thinly over the top of his scalp, his face was not made up, and he eyed Andrew with brief hostility from time to time.

Andrew said, "Sir, nearly a century ago, I was told by a Merton Mansky of this corporation that the mathematics governing the plotting of the positronic pathways was far too complicated to permit of any but approximate solutions and that therefore my own capacities were not fully predictable."

"That was a century ago." Smythe-Robertson hesitated, then said icily, "*Sir.* It is true no longer. Our robots are made with precision now and are trained precisely to their jobs."

"Yes," said Paul, who had come along, as he said, to make sure that the corporation played fair, "with the result that my receptionist must be guided at every point once events depart from the conventional, however slightly."

Smythe-Robertson said, "You would be much more displeased if it were to improvise."

Andrew said, "Then you no longer manufacture robots like myself which are flexible and adaptable."

"No longer."

"The research I have done in connection with my book," said Andrew, "indicates that I am the oldest robot presently in active operation."

"The oldest presently," said Smythe-Robertson, "and the oldest ever. The oldest that will ever be. No robot is useful after the twenty-fifth year. They are called in and replaced with newer models."

"No robot *as presently manufactured* is useful after the twenty-fifth year," said Paul pleasantly. "Andrew is quite exceptional in this respect."

Andrew, adhering to the path he had marked out for himself, said,

"As the oldest robot in the world and the most flexible, am I not unusual enough to merit special treatment from the company?"

"Not at all," said Smythe-Robertson freezingly. "Your unusualness is an embarrassment to the company. If you were on lease, instead of having been a sale outright through some mischance, you would long since have been replaced."

"But that is exactly the point," said Andrew. "I am a free robot and I own myself. Therefore I come to you and ask you to replace me. You cannot do this without the owner's consent. Nowadays, that consent is extorted as a condition of the lease, but in my time this did not happen."

Smythe-Robertson was looking both startled and puzzled, and for a moment there was silence. Andrew found himself staring at the holograph on the wall. It was a death mask of Susan Calvin, patron saint of all roboticists. She was dead nearly two centuries now, but as a result of writing his book Andrew knew her so well he could half persuade himself that he had met her in life.

Smythe-Robertson said, "How can I replace you for you? If I replace you as robot, how can I donate the new robot to you as owner since in the very act of replacement you cease to exist?" He smiled grimly.

"Not at all difficult," interposed Paul. "The seat of Andrew's personality is his positronic brain and it is the one part that cannot be replaced without creating a new robot. The positronic brain, therefore, is Andrew the owner. Every other part of the robotic body can be replaced without affecting the robot's personality, and those other parts are the brain's possessions. Andrew, I should say, wants to supply his brain with a new robotic body."

"That's right," said Andrew calmly. He turned to Smythe-Robertson. "You have manufactured androids, haven't you? Robots that have the outward appearance of humans complete to the texture of the skin?"

Smythe-Robertson said, "Yes, we have. They worked perfectly well, with their synthetic fibrous skins and tendons. There was virtually no metal anywhere except for the brain, yet they were nearly as tough as metal robots. They were tougher, weight for weight."

Paul looked interested. "I didn't know that. How many are on the market?"

"None," said Smythe-Robertson. "They were much more expensive than metal models and a market survey showed they would not be accepted. They looked too human."

Andrew said, "But the corporation retains its expertise, I assume.

Since it does, I wish to request that I be replaced by an organic robot, an android."

Paul looked surprised. "Good Lord," he said.

Smythe-Robertson stiffened. "Quite impossible!"

"Why is it impossible?" asked Andrew. "I will pay any reasonable fee, of course."

Smythe-Robertson said, "We do not manufacture androids."

"You do not *choose* to manufacture androids," interposed Paul quickly. "That is not the same as being unable to manufacture them."

Smythe-Robertson said, "Nevertheless, the manufacture of androids is against public policy."

"There is no law against it," said Paul.

"Nevertheless, we do not manufacture them, and we will not."

Paul cleared his throat. "Mr. Smythe-Robertson," he said, "Andrew is a free robot who is under the purview of the law guaranteeing robot rights. You are aware of this, I take it?"

"Only too well."

"This robot, as a free robot, chooses to wear clothes. This results in his being frequently humiliated by thoughtless human beings despite the law against the humiliation of robots. It is difficult to prosecute vague offenses that don't meet with the general disapproval of those who must decide on guilt and innocence."

"U. S. Robots understood that from the start. Your father's firm unfortunately did not."

"My father is dead now," said Paul, "but what I see is that we have here a clear offense with a clear target."

"What are you talking about?" said Smythe-Robertson.

"My client, Andrew Martin—he has just become my client—is a free robot who is entitled to ask U. S. Robots and Mechanical Men, Inc., for the right of replacement, which the corporation supplies anyone who owns a robot for more than twenty-five years. In fact, the corporation insists on such replacement."

Paul was smiling and thoroughly at his ease. He went on, "The positronic brain of my client is the owner of the body of my client—which is certainly more than twenty-five years old. The positronic brain demands the replacement of the body and offers to pay any reasonable fee for an android body as that replacement. If you refuse the request, my client undergoes humiliation and we will sue.

"While public opinion would not ordinarily support the claim of a robot in such a case, may I remind you that U. S. Robots is not popular with the public generally. Even those who most use and profit from robots are suspicious of the corporation. This may be a hangover from the days when robots were widely feared. It may be resentment against the power and wealth of U. S. Robots, which has a worldwide monopoly. Whatever the cause may be, the resentment exists and I think you will find that you would prefer not to withstand a lawsuit, particularly since my client is wealthy and will live for many more centuries and will have no reason to refrain from fighting the battle forever."

Smythe-Robertson had slowly reddened. "You are trying to force me to . . ."

"I force you to do nothing," said Paul. "If you wish to refuse to accede to my client's reasonable request, you may by all means do so and we will leave without another word. . . . But we will sue, as is certainly our right, and you will find that you will eventually lose."

Smythe-Robertson said, "Well—" and paused.

"I see that you are going to accede," said Paul. "You may hesitate but you will come to it in the end. Let me assure you, then, of one further point. If, in the process of transferring my client's positronic brain from his present body to an organic one, there is any damage, however slight, then I will never rest till I've nailed the corporation to the ground. I will, if necessary, take every possible step to mobilize public opinion against the corporation if one brain path of my client's platinum-iridium essence is scrambled." He turned to Andrew and said, "Do you agree to all this, Andrew?"

Andrew hesitated a full minute. It amounted to the approval of lying, of blackmail, of the badgering and humiliation of a human being. But not physical harm, he told himself, not physical harm.

He managed at last to come out with a rather faint "Yes."

## 14

It was like being constructed again. For days, then for weeks, finally for months, Andrew found himself not himself somehow, and the simplest actions kept giving rise to hesitation.

Paul was frantic. "They've damaged you, Andrew. We'll have to institute suit."

Andrew spoke very slowly. "You mustn't. You'll never be able to prove—something—m-m-m-m—"

"Malice?"

"Malice. Besides, I grow stronger, better. It's the tr-tr-tr—"

"Tremble?"

"Trauma. After all, there's never been such an op—op—op— before."

Andrew could feel his brain from the inside. No one else could. He knew he was well and during the months that it took him to learn full coordination and full positronic interplay, he spent hours before the mirror.

Not quite human! The face was stiff—too stiff—and the motions were too deliberate. They lacked the careless free flow of the human being, but perhaps that might come with time. At least he could wear clothes without the ridiculous anomaly of a metal face going along with it.

Eventually he said, "I will be going back to work."

Paul laughed and said, "That means you are well. What will you be doing? Another book?"

"No," said Andrew seriously. "I live too long for any one career to seize me by the throat and never let me go. There was a time when I was primarily an artist and I can still turn to that. And there was a time when I was a historian and I can still turn to that. But now I wish to be a robobiologist."

"A robopsychologist, you mean."

"No. That would imply the study of positronic brains and at the moment I lack the desire to do that. A robobiologist, it seems to me, would be concerned with the working of the body attached to that brain."

"Wouldn't that be a roboticist?"

"A roboticist works with a metal body. I would be studying an organic humanoid body, of which I have the only one, as far as I know."

"You narrow your field," said Paul thoughtfully. "As an artist, all conception is yours; as a historian, you dealt chiefly with robots; as a robobiologist, you will deal with yourself."

Andrew nodded. "It would seem so."

Andrew had to start from the very beginning, for he knew nothing of ordinary biology, almost nothing of science. He became a familiar sight in the libraries, where he sat at the electronic indices for hours at a time, looking perfectly normal in clothes. Those few who knew he was a robot in no way interfered with him.

He built a laboratory in a room which he added to his house, and his library grew, too.

Years passed, and Paul came to him one day and said, "It's a pity you're no longer working on the history of robots. I understand U. S. Robots is adopting a radically new policy."

Paul had aged, and his deteriorating eyes had been replaced with photoptic cells. In that respect, he had drawn closer to Andrew. Andrew said, "What have they done?"

"They are manufacturing central computers, gigantic positronic brains, really, which communicate with anywhere from a dozen to a thousand robots by microwave. The robots themselves have no brains at all. They are the limbs of the gigantic brain, and the two are physically separate."

"Is that more efficient?"

"U. S. Robots claims it is. Smythe-Robertson established the new direction before he died, however, and it's my notion that it's a backlash at you. U. S. Robots is determined that they will make no robots that will give them the type of trouble you have, and for that reason they separate brain and body. The brain will have no body to wish changed; the body will have no brain to wish anything.

"It's amazing, Andrew," Paul went on, "the influence you have had on the history of robots. It was your artistry that encouraged U. S. Robots to make robots more precise and specialized; it was your freedom that resulted in the establishment of the principle of robotic rights; it was your insistence on an android body that made U. S. Robots switch to brain-body separation."

Andrew said, "I suppose in the end the corporation will produce one vast brain controlling several billion robotic bodies. All the eggs will be in one basket. Dangerous. Not proper at all."

"I think you're right," said Paul, "but I don't suspect it will come to pass for a century at least and I won't live to see it. In fact, I may not live to see next year."

"Paul!" said Andrew, in concern.

Paul shrugged. "We're mortal, Andrew. We're not like you. It doesn't matter too much, but it does make it important to assure you on one point. I'm the last of the human Martins. There are collaterals descended from my great-aunt, but they don't count. The money I control personally will be left to the trust in your name and as far as anyone can foresee the future, you will be economically secure."

"Unnecessary," said Andrew, with difficulty. In all this time, he could not get used to the deaths of the Martins.

Paul said, "Let's not argue. That's the way it's going to be. What are you working on?"

"I am designing a system for allowing androids—myself—to gain energy from the combustion of hydrocarbons, rather than from atomic cells."

Paul raised his eyebrows. "So that they will breathe and eat?"

"Yes."

"How long have you been pushing in that direction?"

"For a long time now, but I think I have designed an adequate combustion chamber for catalyzed controlled breakdown."

"But why, Andrew? The atomic cell is surely infinitely better."

"In some ways, perhaps, but the atomic cell is inhuman."

### 15

It took time, but Andrew had time. In the first place, he did not wish to do anything till Paul had died in peace.

With the death of the great-grandson of Sir, Andrew felt more nearly exposed to a hostile world and for that reason was the more determined to continue the path he had long ago chosen.

Yet he was not really alone. If a man had died, the firm of Feingold and Martin lived, for a corporation does not die any more than a robot does. The firm had its directions and it followed them soullessly. By way of the trust and through the law firm, Andrew continued to be wealthy. And in return for their own large annual retainer, Feingold and Martin involved themselves in the legal aspects of the new combustion chamber.

When the time came for Andrew to visit U. S. Robots and Mechanical Men, Inc., he did it alone. Once he had gone with Sir and once with Paul. This time, the third time, he was alone and manlike.

U. S. Robots had changed. The production plant had been shifted to a large space station, as had grown to be the case with more and more industries. With them had gone many robots. The Earth itself was becoming parklike, with its one-billion-person population stabilized and perhaps not more than thirty percent of its at least equally large robot population independently brained.

The Director of Research was Alvin Magdescu, dark of complexion and hair, with a little pointed beard and wearing nothing above the waist but the breastband that fashion dictated. Andrew himself was well covered in the older fashion of several decades back.

Magdescu said, "I know you, of course, and I'm rather pleased to see you. You're our most notorious product and it's a pity old Smythe-Robertson was so set against you. We could have done a great deal with you."

"You still can," said Andrew.

"No, I don't think so. We're past the time. We've had robots on

Earth for over a century, but that's changing. It will be back to space with them and those that stay here won't be brained."

"But there remains myself, and I stay on Earth."

"True, but there doesn't seem to be much of the robot about you. What new request have you?"

"To be still less a robot. Since I am so far organic, I wish an organic source of energy. I have here the plans—"

Magdescu did not hasten through them. He might have intended to at first, but he stiffened and grew intent. At one point he said, "This is remarkably ingenious. Who thought of all this?"

"I did," said Andrew.

Magdescu looked up at him sharply, then said, "It would amount to a major overhaul of your body, and an experimental one, since it has never been attempted before. I advise against it. Remain as you are."

Andrew's face had limited means of expression, but impatience showed plainly in his voice. "Dr. Magdescu, you miss the entire point. You have no choice but to accede to my request. If such devices can be built into my body, they can be built into human bodies as well. The tendency to lengthen human life by prosthetic devices has already been remarked on. There are no devices better than the ones I have designed and am designing.

"As it happens, I control the patents by way of the firm of Feingold and Martin. We are quite capable of going into business for ourselves and of developing the kind of prosthetic devices that may end by producing human beings with many of the properties of robots. Your own business will then suffer.

"If, however, you operate on me now and agree to do so under similar circumstances in the future, you will receive permission to make use of the patents and control the technology of both robots and the prosthetization of human beings. The initial leasing will not be granted, of course, until after the first operation is completed successfully, and after enough time has passed to demonstrate that it is indeed successful." Andrew felt scarcely any First Law inhibition to the stern conditions he was setting a human being. He was learning to reason that what seemed like cruelty might, in the long run, be kindness.

Magdescu looked stunned. He said, "I'm not the one to decide something like this. That's a corporate decision that would take time."

"I can wait a reasonable time," said Andrew, "but only a reasonable time." And he thought with satisfaction that Paul himself could not have done it better.

## 16

It took only a reasonable time, and the operation was a success.

Magdescu said, "I was very much against the operation, Andrew, but not for the reasons you might think. I was not in the least against the experiment, if it had been on someone else. I hated risking *your* positronic brain. Now that you have the positronic pathways interacting with simulated nerve pathways, it might be difficult to rescue the brain intact if the body went bad."

"I had every faith in the skill of the staff at U. S. Robots," said Andrew. "And I can eat now."

"Well, you can sip olive oil. It will mean occasional cleanings of the combustion chamber, as we have explained to you. Rather an uncomfortable touch, I should think."

"Perhaps, if I did not expect to go further. Self-cleaning is not impossible. In fact, I am working on a device that will deal with solid food that may be expected to contain incombustible fractions—indigestible matter, so to speak, that will have to be discarded."

"You would then have to develop an anus."

"The equivalent."

"What else, Andrew?"

"Everything else."

"Genitalia, too?"

"Insofar as they will fit my plans. My body is a canvas on which I intend to draw—"

Magdescu waited for the sentence to be completed, and when it seemed that it would not be, he completed it himself. "A man?"

"We shall see," said Andrew.

Magdescu said, "It's a puny ambition, Andrew. You're better than a man. You've gone downhill from the moment you opted for organicism."

"My brain has not suffered."

"No, it hasn't. I'll grant you that. But, Andrew, the whole new breakthrough in prosthetic devices made possible by your patents is being marketed under your name. You're recognized as the inventor and you're honored for it—as you are. Why play further games with your body?"

Andrew did not answer.

The honors came. He accepted membership in several learned societies, including one which was devoted to the new science he had established; the one he had called robobiology but had come to be termed prosthetology.

On the one hundred and fiftieth anniversary of his construction, there was a testimonial dinner given in his honor at U. S. Robots. If Andrew saw irony in this, he kept it to himself.

Alvin Magdescu came out of retirement to chair the dinner. He was himself ninety-four years old and was alive because he had prosthetized devices that, among other things, fulfilled the function of liver and kidneys. The dinner reached its climax when Magdescu, after a short and emotional talk, raised his glass to toast "the Sesquicentennial Robot."

Andrew had had the sinews of his face redesigned to the point where he could show a range of emotions, but he sat through all the ceremonies solemnly passive. He did not like to be a Sesquicentennial Robot.

## 17

It was prosthetology that finally took Andrew off the Earth. In the decades that followed the celebration of the Sesquicentennial, the Moon had come to be a world more Earth-like than Earth in every respect but its gravitational pull and in its underground cities there was a fairly dense population.

Prosthetized devices there had to take the lesser gravity into account and Andrew spent five years on the Moon working with local prosthetologists to make the necessary adaptations. When not at his work, he wandered among the robot population, every one of which treated him with the robotic obsequiousness due a man.

He came back to an Earth that was humdrum and quiet in comparison and visited the offices of Feingold and Martin to announce his return.

The current head of the firm, Simon DeLong, was surprised. He said, "We had been told you were returning, Andrew" (he had almost said "Mr. Martin"), "but we were not expecting you till next week."

"I grew impatient," said Andrew brusquely. He was anxious to get to the point. "On the Moon, Simon, I was in charge of a research team of twenty human scientists. I gave orders that no one questioned. The Lunar robots deferred to me as they would to a human being. Why, then, am I not a human being?"

A wary look entered DeLong's eyes. He said, "My dear Andrew, as you have just explained, you are treated as a human being by both robots and human beings. You are therefore a human being *de facto*."

"To be a human being *de facto* is not enough. I want not only to be treated as one, but to be legally identified as one. I want to be a human being *de jure*."

"Now that is another matter," said DeLong. "There we would run into human prejudice and into the undoubted fact that however much you may be like a human being, you are *not* a human being."

"In what way not?" asked Andrew. "I have the shape of a human being and organs equivalent to those of a human being. My organs, in fact, are identical to some of those in a prosthetized human being. I have contributed artistically, literarily, and scientifically to human culture as much as any human being now alive. What more can one ask?"

"I myself would ask nothing more. The trouble is that it would take an act of the World Legislature to define you as a human being. Frankly, I wouldn't expect that to happen."

"To whom on the Legislature could I speak?"

"To the chairman of the Science and Technology Committee perhaps."

"Can you arrange a meeting?"

"But you scarcely need an intermediary. In your position, you can—"

"No. *You* arrange it." (It didn't even occur to Andrew that he was giving a flat order to a human being. He had grown accustomed to that on the Moon.) "I want him to know that the firm of Feingold and Martin is backing me in this to the hilt."

"Well, now—"

"To the hilt, Simon. In one hundred and seventy-three years I have in one fashion or another contributed greatly to this firm. I have been under obligation to individual members of the firm in times past. I am not now. It is rather the other way around now and I am calling in my debts."

DeLong said, "I will do what I can."


18


The chairman of the Science and Technology Committee was of the East Asian region and she was a woman. Her name was Chee Li-Hsing and her transparent garments (obscuring what she wanted obscured only by their dazzle) made her look plastic-wrapped.

She said, "I sympathize with your wish for full human rights. There have been times in history when segments of the human population fought for full human rights. What rights, however, can you possibly want that you do not have?"

"As simple a thing as my right to life. A robot can be dismantled at any time."

"A human being can be executed at any time."

"Execution can only follow due process of law. There is no trial needed for my dismantling. Only the word of a human being in authority is needed to end me. Besides—besides—" Andrew tried desperately to allow no sign of pleading, but his carefully designed tricks of human expression and tone of voice betrayed him here. "The truth is, I want to be a man. I have wanted it through six generations of human beings."

Li-Hsing looked up at him out of darkly sympathetic eyes. "The Legislature can pass a law declaring you one—they could pass a law declaring a stone statue to be defined as a man. Whether they will actually do so is, however, as likely in the first case as the second. Congresspeople are as human as the rest of the population and there is always that element of suspicion against robots."

"Even now?"

"Even now. We would all allow the fact that you have earned the prize of humanity and yet there would remain the fear of setting an undesirable precedent."

"What precedent? I am the only free robot, the only one of my type, and there will never be another. You may consult U. S. Robots."

" 'Never' is a long time, Andrew—or, if you prefer, Mr. Martin— since I will gladly give you my personal accolade as man. You will find that most Congresspeople will not be willing to set the precedent, no matter how meaningless such a precedent might be. Mr. Martin, you have my sympathy, but I cannot tell you to hope. Indeed—"

She sat back and her forehead wrinkled. "Indeed, if the issue grows too heated, there might well arise a certain sentiment, both inside the Legislature and outside, for that dismantling you mentioned. Doing away with you could turn out to be the easiest way of resolving the dilemma. Consider that before deciding to push matters."

Andrew said, "Will no one remember the technique of prosthetology, something that is almost entirely mine?"

"It may seem cruel, but they won't. Or if they do, it will be remembered against you. It will be said you did it only for yourself. It will be said it was part of a campaign to roboticize human beings, or to humanify robots; and in either case evil and vicious. You have never been part of a political hate campaign, Mr. Martin, and I tell you that you will be the object of vilification of a kind neither you nor I would credit and there would be people who'll believe it all. Mr. Martin, let your life be." She rose and, next to Andrew's seated figure, she seemed small and almost childlike.

Andrew said, "If I decide to fight for my humanity, will you be on my side?"

She thought, then said, "I will be—insofar as I can be. If at any time such a stand would appear to threaten my political future, I may have to abandon you, since it is not an issue I feel to be at the very root of my beliefs. I am trying to be honest with you."

"Thank you, and I will ask no more. I intend to fight this through whatever the consequences, and I will ask you for your help only for as long as you can give it."

## 19

It was not a direct fight. Feingold and Martin counseled patience and Andrew muttered grimly that he had an endless supply of that. Feingold and Martin then entered on a campaign to narrow and restrict the area of combat.

They instituted a lawsuit denying the obligation to pay debts to an individual with a prosthetic heart on the grounds that the possession of a robotic organ removed humanity, and with it the constitutional rights of human beings.

They fought the matter skillfully and tenaciously, losing at every step but always in such a way that the decision was forced to be as broad as possible, and then carrying it by way of appeals to the World Court.

It took years, and millions of dollars.

When the final decision was handed down, DeLong held what amounted to a victory celebration over the legal loss. Andrew was, of course, present in the company offices on the occasion.

"We've done two things, Andrew," said DeLong, "both of which are good. First of all, we have established the fact that no number of artifacts in the human body causes it to cease being a human body. Secondly, we have engaged public opinion in the question in such a way as to put it fiercely on the side of a broad interpretation of humanity since there is not a human being in existence who does not hope for prosthetics if that will keep him alive."

"And do you think the Legislature will now grant me my humanity?" asked Andrew.

DeLong looked faintly uncomfortable. "As to that, I cannot be optimistic. There remains the one organ which the World Court has used as the criterion of humanity. Human beings have an organic cellular brain and robots have a platinum-iridium positronic brain if they have one at all—and you certainly have a positronic brain. . . . No, Andrew, don't get that look in your eye. We lack the knowledge to duplicate the work of a cellular brain in artificial structures close enough to the organic type to allow it to fall within the Court's decision. Not even you could do it."

"What ought we do, then?"

"Make the attempt, of course. Congresswoman Li-Hsing will be on our side and a growing number of other Congresspeople. The President will undoubtedly go along with a majority of the Legislature in this matter."

"Do we have a majority?"

"No, far from it. But we might get one if the public will allow its desire for a broad interpretation of humanity to extend to you. A small chance, I admit, but if you do not wish to give up, we must gamble for it."

"I do not wish to give up."

20

Congresswoman Li-Hsing was considerably older than she had been when Andrew had first met her. Her transparent garments were long gone. Her hair was now close-cropped and her coverings were tubular. Yet still Andrew clung, as closely as he could within the limits of reasonable taste, to the style of clothing that had prevailed when he had first adopted clothing over a century before.

She said, "We've gone as far as we can, Andrew. We'll try once more after recess, but, to be honest, defeat is certain and the whole thing will have to be given up. All my most recent efforts have only earned me a certain defeat in the coming congressional campaign."

"I know," said Andrew, "and it distresses me. You said once you would abandon me if it came to that. Why have you not done so?"

"One can change one's mind, you know. Somehow, abandoning you became a higher price than I cared to pay for just one more term. As it is, I've been in the Legislature for over a quarter of a century. It's enough."

"Is there no way we can change minds, Chee?"

"We've changed all that are amenable to reason. The rest—the majority—cannot be moved from their emotional antipathies."

"Emotional antipathy is not a valid reason for voting one way or the other."

"I know that, Andrew, but they don't advance emotional antipathy as their reason."

Andrew said cautiously, "It all comes down to the brain, then, but must we leave it at the level of cells versus positrons? Is there no way of forcing a functional definition? Must we say that a brain is made of this or that? May we not say that a brain is something—anything—capable of a certain level of thought?"

"Won't work," said Li-Hsing. "Your brain is man-made, the human brain is not. Your brain is constructed, theirs developed. To any human being who is intent on keeping up the barrier between himself and a robot, those differences are a steel wall a mile high and a mile thick."

"If we could get at the source of their antipathy—the very source of—"

"After all your years," said Li-Hsing sadly, "you are still trying to reason out the human being. Poor Andrew, don't be angry, but it's the robot in you that drives you in that direction."

"I don't know," said Andrew. "If I could bring myself—"


## 1   (reprise)

If he could bring himself—

He had known for a long time it might come to that, and in the end he was at the surgeon's. He found one, skillful enough for the job at hand, which meant a robot surgeon, for no human surgeon could be trusted in this connection, either in ability or in intention.

The surgeon could not have performed the operation on a human being, so Andrew, after putting off the moment of decision with a sad line of questioning that reflected the turmoil within himself, put the First Law to one side by saying, "I, too, am a robot."

He then said, as firmly as he had learned to form the words even at human beings over these past decades, "I *order* you to carry through the operation on me."

In the absence of the First Law, an order so firmly given from one who looked so much like a man activated the Second Law sufficiently to carry the day.


## 21

Andrew's feeling of weakness was, he was sure, quite imaginary. He had recovered from the operation. Nevertheless, he leaned, as unobtrusively as he could manage, against the wall. It would be entirely too revealing to sit.

Li-Hsing said, "The final vote will come this week, Andrew. I've been able to delay it no longer, and we must lose. . . . And that will be it, Andrew."

Andrew said, "I am grateful for your skill at delay. It gave me the time I needed, and I took the gamble I had to."

"What gamble is this?" asked Li-Hsing with open concern.

"I couldn't tell you, or the people at Feingold and Martin. I was sure I would be stopped. See here, if it is the brain that is at issue, isn't the greatest difference of all the matter of immortality? Who really cares what a brain looks like or is built of or how it was formed? What matters is that brain cells die; *must* die. Even if every other organ in the body is maintained or replaced, the brain cells, which cannot be replaced without changing and therefore killing the personality, must eventually die.

"My own positronic pathways have lasted nearly two centuries without perceptible change and can last for centuries more. Isn't *that* the fundamental barrier? Human beings can tolerate an immortal robot, for it doesn't matter how long a machine lasts. They cannot tolerate an immortal human being, since their own mortality is endurable only so long as it is universal. And for that reason they won't make me a human being."

Li-Hsing said, "What is it you're leading up to, Andrew?"

"I have removed that problem. Decades ago, my positronic brain was connected to organic nerves. Now, one last operation has arranged that connection in such a way that slowly—quite slowly—the potential is being drained from my pathways."

Li-Hsing's finely wrinkled face showed no expression for a moment. Then her lips tightened. "Do you mean you've arranged to die, Andrew? You can't have. That violates the Third Law."

"No," said Andrew, "I have chosen between the death of my body and the death of my aspirations and desires. To have let my body live at the cost of the greater death is what would have violated the Third Law."

Li-Hsing seized his arm as though she were about to shake him. She stopped herself. "Andrew, it won't work. Change it back."

"It can't be. Too much damage was done. I have a year to live—more or less. I will last through the two hundredth anniversary of my construction. I was weak enough to arrange that."

"How can it be worth it? Andrew, you're a fool."

"If it brings me humanity, that will be worth it. If it doesn't, it will bring an end to striving and that will be worth it, too."

And Li-Hsing did something that astonished herself. Quietly, she began to weep.


## 22

It was odd how that last deed caught at the imagination of the world. All that Andrew had done before had not swayed them. But he had finally accepted even death to be human and the sacrifice was too great to be rejected.

The final ceremony was timed, quite deliberately, for the two hundredth anniversary. The World President was to sign the act and make it law and the ceremony would be visible on a global network and would be beamed to the Lunar state and even to the Martian colony.

Andrew was in a wheelchair. He could still walk, but only shakily.

With mankind watching, the World President said, "Fifty years ago, you were declared a Sesquicentennial Robot, Andrew." After a pause, and in a more solemn tone, he said, "Today we declare you a Bicentennial Man, Mr. Martin."

And Andrew, smiling, held out his hand to shake that of the President.


## 23

Andrew's thoughts were slowly fading as he lay in bed.

Desperately he seized at them. Man! He was a man! He wanted that to be his last thought. He wanted to dissolve—die—with that.

He opened his eyes one more time and for one last time recognized Li-Hsing waiting solemnly. There were others, but those were only shadows, unrecognizable shadows. Only Li-Hsing stood out against the deepening gray. Slowly, inchingly, he held out his hand to her and very dimly and faintly felt her take it.

She was fading in his eyes, as the last of his thoughts trickled away.

But before she faded completely, one last fugitive thought came to him and rested for a moment on his mind before everything stopped.

"Little Miss," he whispered, too low to be heard.

# Joe Haldeman

Joe Haldeman is a member of the Vietnam generation. He fought in Vietnam and was wounded there, and used his experiences there for his first big success, *The Forever War,* which appeared first in the magazines, beginning in 1972, but then came out in book form in 1974. As a novel, it won the Hugo in 1976, and the very next year he won the short story award, with which he makes his first appearance in these volumes. We can't give you the novel to read, but here is the short story.

I can't say I envy Joe his wartime experiences. A warrior I'm not. I was in the Army, yes, but I think I must have been the most inadequate member of the armed forces ever invented. I am certain the military establishment itself must have had a presentiment of this fact, for I was not drafted until immediately after the Japanese surrendered. (The word flew through the corridors of the Pentagon: "The Japanese have surrendered. The war is over. —It's safe to draft Asimov.")

Then after I had completed Basic Training, I was told in confidence (by a kindly and amused lieutenant) that everyone had been warned away from me by the captain. "With his peculiar background," he said, "no one's ever going to send him to fight anyone, and he doesn't know his left foot from his right, anyway, so ignore him." Of course, no one told me this at the time and I went through Basic Training constantly convinced that I would be court-martialed and shot for various (totally involuntary) examples of misfeasance, malfeasance, and nonfeasance of soldierly duties.

(No, I don't know what that means either.)

I've met Joe at several of the conventions I have attended; also, once, quite unexpectedly, on the *Queen Elizabeth 2,* a meeting which greatly improved the ambience of that trip. The *QE2* is a beautiful ship and we are always happy on it, but I must admit that it never crawls with fellow science fiction writers, and what is as great as a fellow science fiction writer?

Joe is a very quiet and gentle soul, but he has hidden depths.

Let me explain. I am a professional after-dinner speaker and I have the infinite gall to charge high fees and the infinite luck to get them. I think well of myself as a speaker and have no hesitation in telling people that I'm the best off-the-cuff speaker in the world. (I don't know if that's true or not, but saying it is what supplies most of the luck in getting high fees. That, and a ruthless lecture agent.)

So, generally, I don't worry about who I follow on the convention program. Once I followed Joe Haldeman. "Poor guy," I thought. "He's so quiet and gentle. I'll pull my punches afterward. I don't want him to look bad."

Hah! That quiet, gentle guy got up and gave one of the best and funniest talks I ever heard. Pull my punches? When I got up, I had to sweat out my very best just to stay even. You-all watch out for these quiet and gentle guys, you hear?

I must say one more thing about Joe, perhaps because I have a prejudice in favor of the fair sex (as many people have noticed, especially the fair sex). The very nicest thing about Joe is his wife, Gay, who is ever sweet and cheerful. Personally, I think they're both lucky.

# TRICENTENNIAL

### December 1975

Scientists pointed out that the Sun could be part of a double star system. For its companion to have gone undetected, of course, it would have to be small and dim, and thousands of astronomical units distant.

They would find it eventually; "it" would turn out to be "them"; they would come in handy.

### January 2075

The office was opulent even by the extravagant standards of 21st-century Washington. Senator Connors had a passion for antiques. One wall was lined with leatherbound books; a large brass telescope symbolized his role as Liaison to the Science Guild. An intricately woven Navajo rug from his home state covered most of the parquet floor. A grandfather clock. Paintings, old maps.

The computer terminal was discreetly hidden in the top drawer of his heavy teak desk. On the desk: a blotter, a precisely centered fountain pen set, and a century-old sound-only black Bell telephone. It chimed.

His secretary said that Dr. Leventhal was waiting to see him. "Keep answering me for thirty seconds," the Senator said. "Then hang it and send him right in."

He cradled the phone and went to a wall mirror. Straightened his tie and cape; then with a fingernail evened out the bottom line of his lip pomade. Ran a hand through long, thinning white hair and returned to stand by the desk, one hand on the phone.

The heavy door whispered open. A short thin man bowed slightly. "Sire."

The Senator crossed to him with both hands out. "Oh, blow that, Charlie. Give ten." The man took both his hands, only for an instant. "When was I ever 'Sire' to you, heyfool?"

"Since last week," Leventhal said, "Guild members have been calling you worse names than 'Sire.'"

The Senator bobbed his head twice. "True, and true. And I sympathize. Will of the people, though."

"Sure." Leventhal pronounced it as one word: "Willathapeeble."

Connors went to the bookcase and opened a chased panel. "Drink?"

"Yeah, Bo." Charlie sighed and lowered himself into a deep sofa. "Hit me. Sherry or something."

The Senator brought the drinks and sat down beside Charlie. "You shoulda listened to me. Shoulda got the Ad Guild to write your proposal."

"We have good writers."

"Begging to differ. Less than two percent of the electorate bothered to vote; most of them for the administration advocate. Now you take the Engineering Guild—"

"*You* take the engineers. And—"

"They used the Ad Guild." Connors shrugged. "They got their budget."

"It's easy to sell bridges and power plants and shuttles. Hard to sell pure science."

"The more reason for you to—"

"Yeah, sure. Ask for double and give half to the Ad boys. Maybe next year. That's not what I came to talk about."

"That radio stuff?"

"Right. Did you read the report?"

Connors looked into his glass. "Charlie, you know I don't have time to—"

"Somebody read it, though."

"Oh, righty-o. Good astronomy boy on my staff; he gave me a boil-down. Mighty interesting, that."

"There's an intelligent civilization eleven light-years away—that's 'mighty interesting'?"

"Sure. Real breakthrough." Uncomfortable silence. "Uh, what are you going to do about it?"

"Two things. First, we're trying to figure out what they're saying. That's hard. Second, we want to send a message back. That's easy. And that's where you come in."

The Senator nodded and looked somewhat wary.

"Let me explain. We've sent messages to this star, 61 Cygni, before. It's a double star, actually, with a dark companion."

"Like us."

"Sort of. Anyhow, they never answered. They aren't listening, evidently; they aren't sending."

"But we got—"

"What we're picking up is about what you'd pick up eleven light-years from Earth. A confused jumble of broadcasts, eleven years old. Very faint. But obviously not generated by any sort of natural source."

"Then we're already sending a message back. The same kind they're sending us."

"That's right, but—"

"So what does all this have to do with me?"

"Bo, we don't want to whisper at them—we want to *shout!* Get their attention." Leventhal sipped his wine and leaned back. "For that, we'll need one hell of a lot of power."

"Uh, righty-o. Charlie, power's money. How much are you talking about?"

"The whole show. I want to shut down Death Valley for twelve hours."

The Senator's mouth made a silent O. "Charlie, you've been working too hard. Another Blackout? On purpose?"

"There won't be any Blackout. Death Valley has emergency storage for fourteen hours."

"At half capacity." He drained his glass and walked back to the bar, shaking his head. "First you say you want power. Then you say you want to turn off the power." He came back with the burlap-covered bottle. "You aren't making sense, boy."

"Not turn it off, really. Turn it around."

"Is that a riddle?"

"No, look. You know the power doesn't really come from the Death Valley grid; it's just a way station and accumulator. Power comes from the orbital—"

"I know all that, Charlie. I've got a Science Certificate."

"Sure. So what we've got is a big microwave laser in orbit that shoots down a tight beam of power. Enough to keep North America running. Enough—"

"That's what I mean. You can't just—"

"So we turn it around and shoot it at a power grid on the Moon. Relay the power around to the big radio dish at Farside. Turn it into radio waves and point it at 61 Cygni. Give 'em a blast that'll fry their fillings."

"Doesn't sound neighborly."

"It wouldn't actually be that powerful—but it would be a hell of a lot more powerful than any natural 21-centimeter source."

"I don't know, boy." He rubbed his eyes and grimaced. "I could maybe do it on the sly, only tell a few people what's on. But that'd only work for a few minutes . . . What do you need twelve hours for, anyway?"

"Well, the thing won't aim itself at the Moon automatically, the way it does at Death Valley. Figure as much as an hour to get the thing turned around and aimed.

"Then, we don't want to just send a blast of radio waves at them. We've got a five-hour program that first builds up a mutual language, then tells them about us, and finally asks them some questions. We want to send it twice."

Connors refilled both glasses. "How old were you in '47, Charlie?"

"I was born in '45."

"You don't remember the Blackout. Ten thousand people died . . . and you want me to suggest—"

"Come on, Bo, it's not the same thing. We know the accumulators work now—besides, the ones who died, most of them had faulty failsafes on their cars. If we warn them the power's going to drop, they'll check their fail-safes or damn well stay out of the air."

"And the media? They'd have to take turns broadcasting. Are you going to tell the People what they can watch?"

"Fuzz the media. They'll be getting the biggest story since the Crucifixion."

"Maybe." Connors took a cigarette and pushed the box toward Charlie. "You don't remember what happened to the Senators from California in '47, do you?"

"Nothing good, I suppose."

"No, indeed. They were impeached. Lucky they weren't lynched. Even though the real trouble was way up in orbit.

"Like you say: people pay a grid tax to California. They think the power comes from California. If something fuzzes up, they get pissed at California. I'm the Lib Senator from California, Charlie; ask me for the Moon, maybe I can do something. Don't ask me to fuzz around with Death Valley."

"All right, all right. It's not like I was asking you to wire it for me, Bo. Just get it on the ballot. We'll do everything we can to educate—"

"Won't work. You barely got the Scylla probe voted in—and that was no skin off nobody, not with L-5 picking up the tab."

"Just get it on the ballot."

"We'll see. I've got a quota, you know that. And the Tricentennial coming up, hell, everybody wants on the ballot."

"Please, Bo. This is bigger than that. This is bigger than anything. Get it on the ballot."

"Maybe as a rider. No promises."

### March 1992

From *Fax & Pix,* 12 March 1992:

#### ANTIQUE SPACE PROBE ZAPPED BY NEW STARS

1. Pioneer 10 sent first Jupiter pix Earthward in 1973 (see pix upleft, upright).

2. Left solar system 1987. First man-made thing to leave solar system.

3. Yesterday, reports NSA, Pioneer 10 begins a.m. to pick up heavy radiation. Gets more and more to max about 3 p.m. Then goes back down. Radiation has to come from outside solar system.

4. NSA and Hawaii scientists say Pioneer 10 went through disk of synchrotron (sin-kro-tron) radiation that comes from two stars we didn't know about before.

A. The stars are small "black dwarfs."

B. They are going around each other once every forty seconds, and take 350,000 years to go around the Sun.

C. One of the stars is made of *antimatter.* This is stuff that blows up if it touches real matter. What the Hawaii scientists saw was a dim circle of invisible (infrared) light that blinks on and off every twenty seconds. This light comes from where the atmospheres of the two stars touch (see pic downleft).

D. The stars have a big magnetic field. Radiation comes from stuff spinning off the stars and trying to get through the field.

E. The stars are about 5,000 times as far away from the Sun as we are. They sit at the wrong angle, compared to the rest of the solar system (see pic downright).

5. NSA says we aren't in any danger from the stars. They're too far away, and besides, nothing in the solar system ever goes through the radiation.

6. The woman who discovered the stars wants to call them Scylla (*skill*-a) and Charybdis (ku-*rib*-dus).

7. Scientists say they don't know where the hell those two stars came from. Everything else in the solar system makes sense.

## February 2075

When the docking phase started, Charlie thought, that was when it was easy to tell the scientists from the baggage. The scientists were the ones who looked nervous.

Superficially, it seemed very tranquil—nothing like the bone-hurting skin-stretching acceleration when the shuttle lifted off. The glittering transparent cylinder of L-5 simply grew larger, slowly, then wheeled around to point at them.

The problem was that a space colony big enough to hold 4,000 people has more inertia than God. If the shuttle hit the mating dimple too fast, it would fold up like an accordion. A spaceship is made to take stress in the *other* direction.

Charlie hadn't paid first-class, but they let him up into the observation dome anyhow; professional courtesy. There were only two other people there, standing on the Velcro rug, strapped to one bar and hanging on to another.

They were a young man and woman, probably new colonists. The man was talking excitedly. The woman stared straight ahead, not listening. Her knuckles were white on the bar and her teeth were clenched. Charlie wanted to say something in sympathy, but it's hard to talk while you're holding your breath.

The last few meters are the worst. You can't see over the curve of the ship's hull, and the steering jets make a constant stutter of little bumps: left, right, forward, back. If the shuttle folded, would the dome shatter? Or just pop off.

It was all controlled by computers, of course. The pilot just sat up there in a mist of weightless sweat.

Then the low moan, almost subsonic, shuddering as the shuttle's smooth hull complained against the friction pads. Charlie waited for the ringing *spang* that would mean they were a little too fast: friable alloy plates under the friction pads crumbling to absorb the energy of their forward motion; last-ditch stand.

If that didn't stop them, they would hit a two-meter wall of solid steel, which would . . . It had happened once. But not this time.

"Please remain seated until pressure is equalized," a recorded voice said. "It's been a pleasure having you aboard."

Charlie crawled down the pole, back to the passenger area. He walked *rip-rip-rip* back to his seat and obediently waited for his ears to pop. Then the side door opened and he went with the other passengers through the tube that led to the elevator. They stood on the ceiling. Someone had laboriously scratched a graffito on the metal wall:

> *Stuck on this lift for hours, perforce:*
> *This lift that cost a million bucks.*
> *There's no such thing as centrifugal force:*
> *L-5 sucks.*

Thirty more weightless seconds as they slid to the ground. There were a couple of dozen people waiting on the loading platform.

Charlie stepped out into the smell of orange blossoms and newly mown grass. He was home.

"Charlie! Hey, over here." Young man standing by a tandem bicycle. Charlie squeezed both his hands and then jumped on the back seat. "Drink."

"Did you get—"

"Drink. Then talk." They glided down the smooth macadam road toward town.

The bar was just a rain canopy over some tables and chairs overlooking the lake in the center of town. No bartender: you went to the service table and punched in your credit number, then chose wine or fruit juice, with or without vacuum-distilled raw alcohol. They talked about shuttle nerves a while, then:

"What you get from Connors?"

"Words, not much. I'll give a full report at the meeting tonight. Looks like we won't even get on the ballot, though."

"Now isn't that what we said was going to happen? We shoulda gone with François Pétain's idea."

"Too risky." Pétain's plan had been to tell Death Valley they had to shut down the laser for repairs. Not tell the groundhogs about the signal at all, just answer it. "If they found out they'd sue us down to our teeth."

The man shook his head. "I'll never understand groundhogs."

"Not your job." Charlie was an Earth-born, Earth-trained psychologist. "Nobody born here ever could."

"Maybe so." He stood up. "Thanks for the drink; I've gotta get back to work. You know to call Dr. Bemis before the meeting?"

"Yeah. There was a message at the Cape."

"She has a surprise for you."

"Doesn't she always? You clowns never do anything around here until I leave."

All Abigail Bemis would say over the phone was that Charlie should come to her place for dinner; she'd prep him for the meeting.

"That was good, Ab. Can't afford real food on Earth."

She laughed and stacked the plates in the cleaner, then drew two cups of coffee. She laughed again when she sat down. Stocky, white-haired woman with bright eyes in a sea of wrinkles.

"You're in a jolly mood tonight."

"Yep. It's expectation."

"Johnny said you had a surprise."

"Hoo-boy, he doesn't know half. So you didn't get anywhere with the Senator."

"No. Even less than I expected. What's the secret?"

"Connors is a nice-hearted boy. He's done a lot for us."

"Come on, Ab. What is it?"

"He's right. Shut off the groundhogs' TV for twenty minutes and they'd have another Revolution on their hands."

"Ab . . ."

"We're going to send the message."

"Sure, I figured we would. Using Farside at whatever wattage we've got. If we're lucky—"

"Nope. Not enough power."

Charlie stirred a half spoon of sugar into his coffee. "You plan to . . . defy Connors?"

"Fuzz Connors. We're not going to use radio at all."

"Visible light? Infra?"

"We're going to hand-carry it. In *Daedalus.*"

Charlie's coffee cup was halfway to his mouth. He spilled a great deal.

"Here, have a napkin."

## June 2040

From *A Short History of the Old Order* (Freeman Press, 2040):

". . . and if you think *that* was a waste, consider Project Daedalus.

"This was the first big space thing after L-5. Now L-5 worked out all right, because it was practical. But *Daedalus* (named from a Greek god who could fly)—that was a clear-cut case of throwing money down the rathole.

"These scientists in 2016 talked the bourgeoisie into paying for a trip to another *star!* It was going to take over a hundred years—but the scientists were going to have babies along the way, and train *them* to be scientists (whether they wanted to or not!).

"They were going to use all the old H-bombs for fuel—as if we might not need the fuel someday right here on Earth. What if L-5 decided they didn't like us, and shut off the power beam?

"*Daedalus* was supposed to be a spaceship almost a kilometer long! Most of it was manufactured in space, from Moon stuff, but a lot of it— the most expensive part, you bet—had to be boosted from Earth.

"They almost got it built, but then came the Breakup and the People's Revolution. No way in hell the People were going to let them have those H-bombs, not sitting right over our heads like that.

"So we left the H-bombs in Helsinki and the space freaks went back to doing what they're supposed to do. Every year they petition to get those H-bombs, but every year the Will of the People says no.

"That spaceship is still up there, a sky-trillion-dollar boondoggle. As a monument to bourgeoisie folly, it's worse than the Pyramids!!"

## February 2075

"So the Scylla probe is just a ruse, to get the fuel—"

"Oh no, not really." She slid a blue-covered folder to him. "We're still going to Scylla. Scoop up a few megatons of degenerate antimatter. And a similar amount of degenerate matter from Charybdis.

"We don't plan a generation ship, Charlie. The hydrogen fuel will get us out there; once there, it'll power the magnetic bottles to hold the real fuel."

"Total annihilation of matter," Charlie said.

"That's right. Em cee squared to the ninth decimal place. We aren't talking about centuries to get to 61 Cygni. Nine years, there and back."

"The groundhogs aren't going to like it. All the bad feeling about the original *Daedalus*—"

"Fuzz the groundhogs. We'll do everything we said we'd do with their precious H-bombs: go out to Scylla, get some antimatter, and bring it back. Just taking a long way back."

"You don't want to just tell them that's what we're going to do? No skin off . . ."

She shook her head and laughed again, this time a little bitterly. "You didn't read the editorial in *Peoplepost* this morning, did you?"

"I was too busy."

"So am I, boy; too busy for that drik. One of my staff brought it in, though."

"It's about *Daedalus?*"

"No . . . it concerns 61 Cygni. How the crazy scientists want to let those boogers know there's life on Earth."

"They'll come make peopleburgers out of us."

"Something like that."

Over three thousand people sat on the hillside, a "natural" amphitheater fashioned of moon dirt and Earth grass. There was an incredible din, everyone talking at once: Dr. Bemis had just told them about the 61 Cygni expedition.

On about the tenth "Quiet, please," Bemis was able to continue. "So you can see why we didn't simply broadcast this meeting. Earth would pick it up. Likewise, there are no groundhog media on L-5 right now. They were rotated back to Earth and the shuttle with their replacements needed repairs at the Cape. The other two shuttles are here.

"So I'm asking all of you—and all of your brethren who had to stay at their jobs—to keep secret the biggest thing since Isabella hocked her jewels. Until we lift.

"Now Dr. Leventhal, who's chief of our social sciences section, wants to talk to you about selecting the crew."

Charlie hated public speaking. In this setting, he felt like a Christian on the way to being cat food. He smoothed out his damp notes on the podium.

"Uh, basic problem." A thousand people asked him to speak up. He adjusted the microphone.

"The basic problem is, we have space for about a thousand people. Probably more than one out of four want to go."

Loud murmur of assent. "And we don't want to be despotic about choosing . . . but I've set up certain guidelines, and Dr. Bemis agrees with them.

"Nobody should plan on going if he or she needs sophisticated medical care, obviously. Same toke, few very old people will be considered."

Almost inaudibly, Abigail said, "Sixty-four isn't very old, Charlie. I'm going." She hadn't said anything earlier.

He continued, looking at Bemis. "Second, we must leave behind those people who are absolutely necessary for the maintenance of L-5. Including the power station." She smiled at him.

"We don't want to split up mating pairs, not for, well, nine years plus . . . but neither will we take children." He waited for the commotion to die down. "On this mission, children are baggage. You'll have to find foster parents for them. Maybe they'll go on the next trip.

"Because we can't afford baggage. We don't know what's waiting for us at 61 Cygni—a thousand people sounds like a lot, but it isn't. Not when you consider that we need a cross section of all human knowledge, all human abilities. It may turn out that a person who can sing madrigals will be more important than a plasma physicist. No way of knowing ahead of time."

The 4,000 people did manage to keep it secret, not so much out of strength of character as from a deep-seated paranoia about Earth and Earthlings.

And Senator Connors' Tricentennial actually came to their aid.

Although there was "One World," ruled by "The Will of the People," some regions had more clout than others, and nationalism was by no means dead. This was one factor.

Another factor was the way the groundhogs felt about the thermonuclear bombs stockpiled in Helsinki. All antiques; mostly a century or more old. The scientists said they were perfectly safe, but you know how that goes.

The bombs still technically belonged to the countries that had surrendered them, nine out of ten split between North America and Russia. The tenth remaining was divided among forty-two other countries. They all got together every few years to argue about what to do with the damned things. Everybody wanted to get rid of them in some useful way, but nobody wanted to put up the capital.

Charlie Leventhal's proposal was simple. L-5 would provide bankroll, materials, and personnel. On a barren rock in the Norwegian Sea they would take apart the old bombs, one at a time, and turn them into uniform fuel capsules for the *Daedalus* craft.

The Scylla/Charybdis probe would be timed to honor both the major spacefaring countries. Renamed the *John F. Kennedy,* it would leave Earth orbit on America's Tricentennial. The craft would accelerate halfway to the double star system at one gee, then flip and slow down at the same rate. It would use a magnetic scoop to gather antimatter from Scylla. On May Day, 2077, it would again be renamed, being the *Leonid I. Brezhnev* for the return trip. For safety's sake, the antimatter would be delivered to a lunar research station near Farside. L-5 scientists claimed that harnessing the energy from total annihilation of matter would make a heaven on Earth.

Most people doubted that, but looked forward to the fireworks.

## January 2076

"The *hell* with that!" Charlie was livid. "I—I just won't do it. Won't!"

"You're the only one—"

"That's not true, Ab, you know it." Charlie paced from wall to wall of her office cubicle. "There are dozens of people who can run L-5. Better than I can."

"Not better, Charlie."

He stopped in front of her desk, leaned over. "Come on, Ab. There's only one logical person to stay behind and run things. Not only has she proven herself in the position, but she's too old to—"

"That kind of drik I don't have to listen to."

"Now, Ab . . ."

"No, you listen to me. I was an infant when we started building *Daedalus;* worked on it as a girl and a young woman.

"I could take you out there in a shuttle and show you the rivets that I put in myself. A half century ago."

"That's my—"

"I earned my ticket, Charlie." Her voice softened. "Age is a factor, yes. This is only the first trip of many—and when it comes back, I *will* be too old. You'll just be in your prime . . . and with over twenty years of experience as Coordinator, I don't doubt they'll make you captain of the next—"

"I don't want to be captain. I don't want to be Coordinator. I just want to *go!*"

"You and three thousand other people."

"And of the thousand that don't want to go, or can't, there isn't one person who could serve as Coordinator? I could name you—"

"That's not the point. There's no one on L-5 who has anywhere near the influence, the connections, you have on Earth. No one who understands groundhogs as well."

"That's racism, Ab. Groundhogs are just like you and me."

"Some of them. I don't see you going Earthside every chance you can get . . . what, you like the view up here? You like living in a can?"

He didn't have a ready answer for that. Ab continued: "Whoever's Coordinator is going to have to do some tall explaining, trying to keep things smooth between L-5 and Earth. That's been your life's work, Charlie. And you're also known and respected here. You're the only logical choice."

"I'm not arguing with your logic."

"I know." Neither of them had to mention the document, signed by Charlie, among others, that gave Dr. Bemis final authority in selecting the crew for *Daedalus/Kennedy/Brezhnev.* "Try not to hate me too much, Charlie. I have to do what's best for my people. All of my people."

Charlie glared at her for a long moment and left.

## June 2076

From *Fax & Pix,* 4 June 2076:

### SPACE FARM LEAVES FOR STARS NEXT MONTH

1. The *John F. Kennedy,* which goes to Scylla/Charybdis next month, is like a little L-5 with bombs up its tail (see pix upleft, upright).

A. The trip's twenty months. They could either take a few people and fill the thing up with food, air, and water—or take a lot of people inside a closed ecology, like L-5.

B. They could've gotten by with only a couple hundred people, to run the farms and stuff. But almost all the space freaks wanted to go. They're used to living that way, anyhow (and they never get to go anyplace).

C. When they get back, the farms will be used as a starter for L-4, like L-5 but smaller at first, and on the other side of the Moon (pic downleft).

2. For other Tricentennial fax & pix, see bacover.

## July 2076

Charlie was just finishing up a week on Earth the day the *John F. Kennedy* was launched. Tired of being interviewed, he slipped away from the media lounge at the Cape shuttleport. His white clearance card got him out onto the landing strip, alone.

The midnight shuttle was being fueled at the far end of the strip, gleaming pink-white in the last light from the setting sun. Its image twisted and danced in the shimmering heat that radiated from the tarmac. The smell of the soft tar was indelibly associated in his mind with leave-taking, relief.

He walked to the middle of the strip and checked his watch. Five minutes. He lit a cigarette and threw it away. He rechecked his mental calculations: the flight would start low in the southwest. He blocked out the sun with a raised hand. What would 150 bombs per second look like? For the media they were called fuel capsules. The people who had carefully assembled them and gently lifted them to orbit and installed them in the tanks, they called them bombs. Ten times the brightness of a full moon, they had said. On L-5 you weren't supposed to look toward it without a dark filter.

No warm-up: it suddenly appeared, impossibly brilliant rainbow speck just over the horizon. It gleamed for several minutes, then dimmed slightly with the haze, and slipped away.

Most of the United States wouldn't see it until it came around again, some two hours later, turning night into day, competing with local pyrotechnic displays. Then every couple of hours after that, Charlie would see it once more, then get on the shuttle. And finally stop having to call it by the name of a dead politician.

## September 2076

There was a quiet celebration on L-5 when *Daedalus* reached the midpoint of its journey, flipped, and started decelerating. The progress report from its crew characterized the journey as "uneventful." At that time they were going nearly two tenths of the speed of light. The laser beam that carried communications was red-shifted from blue light down to orange; the message that turnaround had been successful took two weeks to travel from *Daedalus* to L-5.

They announced a slight course change. They had analyzed the polarization of light from Scylla/Charybdis as their phase angle increased, and were pretty sure the system was surrounded by flat rings of debris, like Saturn. They would "come in low" to avoid collision.

## January 2077

*Daedalus* had been sending back recognizable pictures of the Scylla/Charybdis system for three weeks. They finally had one that was dramatic enough for groundhog consumption.

Charlie set the holo cube on his desk and pushed it around with his finger, marveling.

"This is incredible. How did they do it?"

"It's a montage, of course." Johnny had been one of the youngest adults left behind: heart murmur, trick knees, a surfeit of astrophysicists.

"The two stars are a strobe snapshot in infrared. Sort of. Some ten or twenty thousand exposures taken as the ship orbited around the system, then sorted out and enhanced." He pointed, but it wasn't much help, since Charlie was looking at the cube from a different angle.

"The lamina of fire where the atmospheres touch, that was taken in ultraviolet. Shows more fine structure that way.

"The rings were easy. Fairly long exposures in visible light. Gives the star background, too."

A light tap on the door and an assistant stuck his head in. "Have a second, Doctor?"

"Sure."

"Somebody from a Russian May Day committee is on the phone. She wants to know whether they've changed the name of the ship to *Brezhnev* yet."

"Yeah. Tell her we decided on *Leon Trotsky* instead, though."

He nodded seriously. "Okay." He started to close the door.

*"Wait!"* Charlie rubbed his eyes. "Tell her, uh . . . the ship doesn't have a commemorative name while it's in orbit there. They'll rechristen it just before the start of the return trip."

"Is that true?" Johnny asked.

"I don't know. Who cares? In another couple of months they won't *want* it named after anybody." He and Ab had worked out a plan— admittedly rather shaky—to protect L-5 from the groundhogs' wrath: nobody on the satellite knew ahead of time that the ship was headed for 61 Cygni. It was a decision the crew arrived at on the way to Scylla/ Charybdis; they modified the drive system to accept matter-antimatter destruction while they were orbiting the double star. L-5 would first hear of the mutinous plan via a transmission sent as *Daedalus* left Scylla/ Charybdis. They'd be a month on their way by the time the message got to Earth.

It was pretty transparent, but at least they had been careful that no record of *Daedalus'* true mission be left on L-5. Three thousand people did know the truth, though, and any competent engineer or physical scientist would suspect it.

Ab had felt that, although there was a better than even chance they would be exposed, surely the groundhogs couldn't stay angry for twenty-three years—even if they were unimpressed by the antimatter and other wonders . . .

Besides, Charlie thought, it's not their worry anymore.

As it turned out, the crew of *Daedalus* would have bigger things to worry about.

## June 2077

The Russians had their May Day celebration—Charlie watched it on TV and winced every time they mentioned the good ship *Leonid I. Brezhnev*—and then things settled back down to normal. Charlie and three thousand others waited nervously for the "surprise" message. It came in early June, as expected, scrambled in a data channel. But it didn't say what it was supposed to:

> *This is Abigail Bemis, to Charles Leventhal.*
>
> *Charlie, we have real trouble. The ship has been damaged, hit in the stern by a good chunk of something. It punched right through the main drive reflector. Destroyed a set of control sensors and one attitude jet.*
>
> *As far as we can tell, the situation is stable. We're maintaining acceleration at just a tiny fraction under one gee. But we can't steer, and we can't shut off the main drive.*
>
> *We didn't have any trouble with ring debris when we were orbiting, since we were inside Roche's limit. Coming in, as you know, we'd managed to take advantage of natural divisions in the rings. We tried the same going back, but it was a slower, more complicated process, since we mass so goddamn much now. We must have picked up a piece from the fringe of one of the outer rings.*
>
> *If we could turn off the drive, we might have a chance at fixing it. But the work pods can't keep up with the ship, not at one gee. The radiation down there would fry the operator in seconds, anyway.*
>
> *We're working on it. If you have any ideas, let us know. It occurs to me that this puts you in the clear—we were headed back to Earth, but got clobbered. Will send a transmission to that effect on the regular comm channel. This message is strictly burn-before-reading.*
>
> *Endit.*

It worked perfectly, as far as getting Charlie and L-5 off the hook—and the drama of the situation precipitated a level of interest in space travel unheard-of since the 1960s.

They even had a hero. A volunteer had gone down in a heavily shielded work pod, lowered on a cable, to take a look at the situation. She'd sent back clear pictures of the damage, before the cable snapped.

### *Daedalus:* A.D. 2081
### Earth: A.D. 2101

The following news item was killed from *Fax & Pix*, because it was too hard to translate into the "plain English" that made the paper so popular:

## SPACESHIP PASSES 61 CYGNI—SORT OF

### (L-5 Stringer)

A message received today from the spaceship *Daedalus* said that it had just passed within 400 astronomical units of 61 Cygni. That's about ten times as far as the planet Pluto is from the Sun.

Actually, the spaceship passed the star some eleven years ago. It's taken all that time for the message to get back to us.

We don't know for sure where the spaceship actually is now. If they still haven't repaired the runaway drive, they're about eleven light-years past the 61 Cygni system (their speed when they passed the double star was better than 99% the speed of light).

The situation is more complicated if you look at it from the point of view of a passenger on the spaceship. Because of relativity, time seems to pass more slowly as you approach the speed of light. So only about four years passed for them on the eleven-light-year journey.

L-5 Coordinator Charles Leventhal points out that the spaceship has enough antimatter fuel to keep accelerating to the edge of the Galaxy. The crew then would be only some twenty years older—but it would be twenty *thousand* years before we heard from them. . . .

*(Kill this one. There's more stuff about what the ship looked like to the people on 61 Cygni, and howcum we could talk to them all the time even though time was slower there, but it's all as stupid as this.)*

### Daedalus: A.D. 2083
### Earth: A.D. 2144

Charlie Leventhal died at the age of ninety-nine, bitter. Almost a decade earlier it had been revealed that they'd planned all along for *Daedalus* to be a starship. Few people had paid much attention to the news. Among those who did, the consensus was that anything that got rid of a thousand scientists at once was a good thing. Look at the mess they got us in.

*Daedalus:* Sixty-seven light-years out, and still accelerating.

### Daedalus: A.D. 2085
### Earth: A.D. 3578

After over seven years of shipboard research and development—and some 1,500 light-years of travel—they managed to shut down the engine. With sophisticated telemetry, the job was done without endangering another life.

Every life was precious now. They were no longer simply explorers; almost half their fuel was gone. They were colonists, with no ticket back.

The message of their success would reach Earth in fifteen centuries. Whether there would be an infrared telescope around to detect it, that was a matter of some conjecture.

*Daedalus:* **A.D. 2093**
**Earth: ca. A.D. 5000**

While decelerating, they had investigated several systems in their line of flight. They found one with an Earth-type planet around a Sun-type sun, and aimed for it.

The season they began landing colonists, the dominant feature in the planet's night sky was a beautiful blooming cloud of gas that astronomers had named the North American Nebula.

Which was an irony that didn't occur to any of these colonists from L-5—give or take a few years, it was America's Trimillennial.

America itself was a little the worse for wear, this three thousandth anniversary. The seas that lapped its shores were heavy with a crimson crust of anaerobic life; the mighty cities had fallen and their remains nearly ground away by the never-ceasing sandstorms.

No fireworks were planned, for lack of an audience, for lack of planners; bacteria just don't care. May Day too would be ignored.

The only humans in the Solar System lived in a glass and metal tube. They tended their automatic machinery, and turned their backs on the dead Earth, and worshipped the constellation Cygnus, and had forgotten why.

# Spider and Jeanne Robinson

Well, well, here's Spider again, as he wins a Hugo for the second year in a row (and to make it worse, with a second novella—though Fritz Leiber did the same in 1970 and 1971).

You will notice that he has a co-author with the same surname and you might guess from that that they are related. I will end the suspense. Jeanne is Spider's wife, they having been married in 1975.

Spider explains the co-authorship. Jeanne read the story as it was typed and argued it out with Spider. The conclusion was, said Spider, that "although she never set finger to typewriter, the resulting novella was at least as much hers as mine."

I'm not sure about the justification of that. I'm thinking of the times when John Campbell helped me a great deal with one story or another, to say nothing of the help I received from other editors, such as Horace Gold and Fred Pohl. Ought I to have given them bylines? Tight-fisted credit-grabbing me? Never. I'm not as generous as Spider.

To be sure, I have collaborated with my wife, Janet, on an anthology, and on two juvenile s.f. novels, but in each case, dear Janet set all ten fingers to typewriter, so to speak. She did the collecting and arranging of the stories in the anthology, and she did the first draft, complete, in the case of the juveniles. That made it difficult for me to keep her name off. (She has also published two novels of her own and has a collection of her short stories in press, so I'm lucky she didn't decide to keep *my* name out of it.)

We can look at the matter from another standpoint, however.

When I was young and naïve (as opposed to being older and naïve) I thought the thing to know, if you wanted to write science fiction, was science. Brush up on your physics and paleontology and plane geometry and you were all set.

All that science stuff is in the background, however. The social milieu of the story is what requires the technological razzle-dazzle. In the foreground is the plot, and that can deal with anything at all. Science fiction is universal.

This means that the widest cultural knowledge can be useful. Joe

Haldeman's military experience, James Tiptree's psychological expertise, Roger Zelazny's knowledge of contemporary literature and Hindu mythology, all come in useful, and lead those fine people in directions where, for instance, I can't follow.

But choreography! If I were awakened in the middle of the night and asked to name something a science fiction writer didn't have to know, I would say, "Choreography."

And I would be wrong. Spider has written here a piece of choreographic science fiction and it won the Hugo. You can't remove the choreography and still have the story. Apparently, most of the choreography was supplied by Jeanne. Under those circumstances, even I would have seen the justice of giving her half the byline.

# 8

# *STARDANCE*

I can't really say that I knew her, certainly not the way Seroff knew Isadora. All I know of her childhood and adolescence are the anecdotes she chanced to relate in my hearing—just enough to make me certain that all three of the contradictory biographies on the current best-seller list are fictional. All I know of her adult life are the hours she spent in my presence and on my monitors—more than enough to tell me that every newspaper account I've seen is fictional. Carrington probably believed he knew her better than I, and in a limited sense he was correct —but he would never have written of it, and now he is dead.

But I was her video man, since the days when you touched the camera with your hands, and I knew her backstage: a type of relationship like no other on Earth or off it. I don't believe it can be described to anyone not of the profession—you might think of it as somewhere between co-workers and combat buddies. I was with her the day she came to Skyfac, terrified and determined, to stake her life upon a dream. I watched her work and worked with her for that whole two months, through endless rehearsals, and I have saved every tape and they are not for sale.

And, of course, I saw the Stardance. I was there; I taped it.

I guess I can tell you some things about her.

To begin with, it was not, as Cahill's *Shara* and Von Derski's *Dance Unbound: The Creation of New Modern* suggest, a lifelong fascination with space and space travel that led her to become the race's first zero-gravity dancer. Space was a means to her, not an end, and its vast empty immensity scared her at first. Nor was it, as Melberg's hardcover tabloid *The Real Shara Drummond* claims, because she lacked the talent to make it as a dancer on Earth. If you think free-fall dancing is easier than conventional dance, you try it. Don't forget your dropsickness bag.

But there is a grain of truth in Melberg's slander, as there is in all the best slanders. She could *not* make it on Earth—but not through lack of talent.

I first saw her in Toronto in July of 1984. I headed Toronto Dance Theater's video department at that time, and I hated every minute of it. I hated everything in those days. The schedule that day called for spending the entire afternoon taping students, a waste of time and tape which I hated more than anything except the phone company. I hadn't seen the year's new crop yet, and was not eager to. I love to watch dance done well—the efforts of a tyro are usually as pleasing to me as a first-year violin student in the next apartment is to you.

My leg was bothering me even more than usual as I walked into the studio. Norrey saw my face and left a group of young hopefuls to come over. "Charlie . . . ?"

"I know, I know. They're tender fledglings, Charlie, with egos as fragile as an Easter egg in December. Don't bite them, Charlie. Don't even bark at them if you can help it, Charlie."

She smiled. "Something like that. Leg?"

"Leg."

Norrey Drummond is a dancer who gets away with looking like a woman because she's small. There's about a hundred and fifteen pounds of her, and most of it is heart. She stands about five four, and is perfectly capable of seeming to tower over the tallest student. She has more energy than the North American Grid, and uses it as efficiently as a vane pump (have you ever studied the principle of a standard piston-type pump? Go look up the principle of a vane pump. I wonder what the original conception of *that* notion must have been like, as an emotional experience). There's a signaturelike uniqueness to her dance, the only reason I can see why she got so few of the really juicy parts in company productions until Modern gave way to New Modern. I liked her because she didn't pity me.

"It's not only the leg," I admitted. "I hate to see the tender fledglings butcher your choreography."

"Then you needn't worry. The piece you're taping today is by . . . one of the students."

"Oh, fine. I knew I should have called in sick." She made a face. "What's the catch?"

"Eh?"

"Why did the funny thing happen to your voice just as you got to 'one of the students'?"

She blushed. "Dammit, she's my sister."

Norrey and I are the very oldest and closest of friends, but I'd never chanced to meet a sister—not unusual these days, I suppose.

My eyebrows rose. "She must be good, then."

"Why, thank you, Charlie."

"Bullshit. I give compliments right-handed or not at all—I'm not talking about heredity. I mean that you're so hopelessly ethical you'd bend over backward to avoid nepotism. For you to give your own sister a feature like that, she must be *terrific.*"

"Charlie, she is," Norrey said simply.

"We'll see. What's her name?"

"Shara." Norrey pointed her out, and I understood the rest of the catch. Shara Drummond was ten years younger than her sister—and seven inches taller, with thirty or forty more pounds. I noted absently that she was stunningly beautiful, but it didn't deter my dismay—in her best years, Sophia Loren could never have become a modern dancer. Where Norrey was small, Shara was big, and where Norrey was big, Shara was bigger. If I'd seen her on the street I might have whistled appreciatively—but in the studio I frowned.

"My God, Norrey, she's enormous."

"Mother's second husband was a football player," she said mournfully. "She's awfully good."

"If she *is* good, that *is* awful. Poor girl. Well, what do you want me to do?"

"What makes you think I want you to do anything?"

"You're still standing here."

"Oh. I guess I am. Well . . . have lunch with us, Charlie?"

"Why?" I knew perfectly well why, but I expected a polite lie.

Not from Norrey Drummond. "Because you two have something in common, I think."

I paid her honesty the compliment of not wincing. "I suppose we do."

"Then you will?"

"Right after the session."

She twinkled and was gone. In a remarkably short time she had organized the studioful of wandering, chattering young people into something that resembled a dance ensemble if you squinted. They warmed up during the twenty minutes it took me to set up and check out my equipment. I positioned one camera in front of them, one behind, and kept one in my hands for walk-around close-up work. I never triggered it.

There's a game you play in your mind. Every time someone catches or is brought to your attention, you begin making guesses about them. You try to extrapolate their character and habits from their appearance. Him? Surly, disorganized—leaves the cap off the toothpaste and drinks boilermakers. Her? Art-student type, probably uses a diaphragm and writes letters in a stylized calligraphy of her own invention. Them? They look like schoolteachers from Miami, probably here to see what snow looks like, attend a convention. Sometimes I come pretty close. I don't know how I typecast Shara Drummond in those first twenty minutes. The moment she began to dance, all preconceptions left my mind. She became something elemental, something unknowable, a living bridge between our world and the one the Muses live in.

I know, on an intellectual and academic level, all there is to know about dance, and I could not categorize or classify or even really comprehend the dance she danced that afternoon. I saw it, I even appreciated it, but I was not equipped to understand it. My camera dangled from the end of my arm, next to my jaw. Dancers speak of their "center," the place their motion centers around, often quite near the physical center of gravity. You strive to "dance from your center," and the "contraction and release" idea which underlies much of Modern dance depends on the center for its focus of energy. Shara's center seemed to move about the room under its own power, trailing limbs that attached to it by choice rather than necessity. What's the word for the outermost part of the sun, the part that still shows in an eclipse? Corona? That's what her limbs were: four lengthy tongues of flame that followed the center in its eccentric, whirling orbit, writhing fluidly around its surface. That the lower two frequently contacted the floor seemed coincidental —indeed, the other two touched the floor nearly as regularly.

There were other students dancing. I know this because the two automatic video cameras, unlike me, did their job and recorded the piece as a whole. It was called *Birthing,* and depicted the formation of a galaxy that ended up resembling Andromeda. It was only vaguely accurate, literally, but it wasn't intended to be. Symbolically, it felt like the birth of a galaxy.

In retrospect. At the time I was aware only of the galaxy's heart: Shara. Students occluded her from time to time, and I simply never noticed. It hurt to watch her.

If you know anything about dance, this must all sound horrid to you. A dance about a *nebula?* I know, I know. It's a ridiculous notion. And it worked. In the most gut-level, cellular way it worked—save only that Shara was too good for those around her. She did not belong in that eager crew of awkward, half-trained apprentices. It was like listening to the late Stephen Wonder trying to work with a pickup band in a Montreal bar.

But that wasn't what hurt.

Le Maintenant was shabby, but the food was good and the house brand of grass was excellent. Show a Diner's Club card in there and they'd show you a galley full of dirty dishes. It's gone now. Norrey and Shara declined a toke, but in my line of work it helps. Besides, I needed a few hits. How to tell a lovely lady her dearest dream is hopeless?

I didn't need to ask Shara to know that her dearest dream was to dance. More: to dance professionally. I have often speculated on the motives of the professional artist. Some seek the narcissistic assurance that others will actually pay cash to watch or hear them. Some are so incompetent or disorganized that they can support themselves in no other way. Some have a message which they feel needs expressing. I suppose most artists combine elements of all three. This is no complaint —what they do for us is necessary. We should be grateful that there *are* motives.

But Shara was one of the rare ones. She danced because she needed to. She needed to say things which could be said in no other way, and she needed to take her meaning and her living from the saying of them. Anything else would have demeaned and devalued the essential statement of her dance. I know this, from watching that one dance.

Between toking up and keeping my mouth full and then toking again (a mild amount to offset the slight down that eating brings), it was over half an hour before I was required to say anything, beyond an occasional grunted response to the luncheon chatter of the ladies. As the coffee arrived, Shara looked me square in the eye and said, "Do you talk, Charlie?"

She was Norrey's sister, all right.

"Only inanities."

"No such thing. Inane people, maybe."

"Do you enjoy dancing, Miss Drummond?"

She answered seriously. "Define 'enjoy.'"

I opened my mouth and closed it, perhaps three times. You try it.

"And for God's sake tell me why you're so intent on not talking to me. You've got me worried."

"Shara!" Norrey looked dismayed.

"Hush. I want to know."

I took a crack at it. "Shara, before he died I had the privilege of meeting Bertram Ross. I had just seen him dance. A producer who knew and liked me took me backstage, the way you take a kid to see Santa Claus. I had expected him to look even older off stage, at rest. He looked younger, as if that incredible motion of his was barely in check. He talked to me. After a while I stopped opening my mouth, because nothing ever came out."

She waited, expecting more. Only gradually did she comprehend the compliment and its dimension. I had assumed it would be obvious. Most artists *expect* to be complimented. When she did twig, she did not blush or simper. She did not cock her head and say "Oh, come on." She did not say "You flatter me." She did not look away.

She nodded slowly and said, "Thank you, Charlie. That's worth a lot more than idle chatter." There was a suggestion of sadness in her smile, as if we shared a bitter joke.

"You're welcome."

"For heaven's sake, Norrey, what are you looking so upset about?" The cat now had Norrey's tongue.

"She's disappointed in me," I said. "I said the wrong thing."

"That was the wrong thing?"

"It should have been 'Miss Drummond, I think you ought to give up dancing.' "

"It should have been '*Shara,* I think you ought' . . . *what?*"

"Charlie," Norrey began.

"I was supposed to tell you that we can't all be professional dancers, that they also surf who only sand and wade. Shara, I was supposed to tell you to dump the dance—before it dumps you."

In my need to be honest with her, I had been more brutal than was necessary, I thought. I was to learn that bluntness never dismayed Shara. She demanded it.

"Why you?" was all she said.

"We're inhabiting the same vessel, you and I. We've both got an itch that our bodies just won't let us scratch."

Her eyes softened. "What's your itch?"

"The same as yours."

"Eh?"

"The man was supposed to come and fix the phone on Thursday. My roommate, Karen, and I had an all-day rehearsal. We left a note. Mister telephone man, we had to go out, and we sure couldn't call you, heh heh. Please get the key from the concierge and come on in; the phone's in the bedroom. The phone man never showed up. They never do." My hands seemed to be shaking. "We came home up the back stairs from the alley. The phone was still dead, but I never thought to take down the note on the front door. I got sick the next morning. Cramps. Vomiting. Karen and I were just friends, but she stayed home to take care of me. I suppose on a Friday night the note seemed even more plausible. He slipped the lock with a piece of plastic, and Karen came out of the kitchen as he was unplugging the stereo. He was so indignant he shot her. Twice. The noise scared him; by the time I got there he was halfway out the door. He just had time to put a slug through my hip joint, and then he was gone. They never got him. They never even came to fix the phone." My hands were under control now. "Karen was a damned good dancer, but I was better. In my head, I still am."

Her eyes were round. "You're not Charlie . . . Charles *Armstead*." I nodded.

"Oh my God. So *that's* where you went."

I was shocked by how she looked. It brought me back from the cold and windy border of self-pity. I began a little to pity her. I should have guessed the depth of her empathy. And in the way that really mattered, we were too damned alike—we *did* share the same bitter joke. I wondered why I had wanted to shock her.

"They couldn't repair the joint?" she asked softly.

"I can walk splendidly. Given a strong enough motivation, I can even run short distances. I can't dance worth a damn."

"So you became a video man."

"Three years ago. People who know both video and dance are about as common as garter belts these days. Oh, they've been taping dance since the seventies—with the imagination of a network news cameraman. If you film a stage play with two cameras in the orchestra pit, is it a movie?"

"You do for dance what the movie camera did for drama?"

"Pretty fair analogy. Where it breaks down is that dance is more analogous to music than to drama. You can't stop and start it, or go back and retake a scene that didn't go in the can right, or reverse the chronology to get a tidy shooting schedule. The event happens and you record it. What I am is what the record industry pays top dollar for—a mix man with savvy enough to know which ax is wailing at the moment and mike it high—and the sense to have given the heaviest dudes the best mikes. There are a few others like me. I'm the best."

She took it the way she had the compliment to herself—at face value. Usually when I say things like that I don't give a damn what reaction I get, or I'm being salty and hoping for outrage. But I was pleased at her acceptance, pleased enough for it to bother me. A faint irritation made me go brutal again, *knowing* it wouldn't work. "So what all this leads to is that Norrey was hoping I'd suggest some similar form of sublimation for you. Because I'll make it in dance before you will."

She stubborned up. "I don't buy that, Charlie. I know what you're talking about, I'm not a fool, but I think I can beat it."

"Sure you will. *You're too damned big, lady.* You've got tits like both halves of a prize honeydew melon and an ass that any actress in Hollywood would sell her parents for, and in Modern dance that makes you d-e-d dead, you haven't got a chance. Beat it? You'll beat your head in first. How'm I doing, Norrey?"

"For Christ's sake, Charlie!"

I softened. I can't work Norrey into a tantrum—I like her too much. "I'm sorry, hon. My leg's giving me the mischief, and I'm stinkin' mad. She *ought* to make it—and she won't. She's your sister, and so it saddens you. Well, I'm a total stranger, and it enrages me."

"How do you think it makes me feel?" Shara blazed, startling us both. I hadn't known she had so much voice. "So you want me to pack it in and rent me a camera, huh, Charlie? Or maybe sell apples outside the studio?" A ripple ran up her jaw. "Well, I will be damned by all the gods in Southern California before I'll pack it in. God gave me the large economy size, but there is not a surplus pound on it and it fits me like a glove and I can by Jesus *dance* it and I will. You may be right—I may beat my head in first. But I will get it done." She took a deep breath. "Now I thank you for your kind intentions, Char—Mr. Armst— Oh shit." The tears came and she left hastily, spilling a quarter cup of cold coffee on Norrey's lap.

"Charlie," Norrey said through clenched teeth, "why do I like you so much?"

"Dancers are dumb." I gave her my handkerchief.

"Oh." She patted at her lap a while. "How come you like me?"

"Video men are smart."

"Oh."

I spent the afternoon in my apartment, reviewing the footage I'd shot that morning, and the more I watched, the madder I got.

Dance requires intense motivation at an extraordinarily early age—a blind devotion, a gamble on the as-yet-unrealized potentials of heredity and nutrition. You can begin, say, classical ballet training at age six— and at fourteen find yourself broad-shouldered, the years of total effort utterly wasted. Shara had set her sights on Modern dance—and found out too late that God had dealt her the body of a woman.

She was not fat—you have seen her. She was tall, big-boned tall, and on that great frame was built a rich, ripely female body. As I ran and reran the tapes of *Birthing,* the pain grew in me until I even forgot the ever-present aching of my own leg. It was like watching a supremely gifted basketball player who stood four feet tall.

To make it in Modern dance, it is essential to get into a company. You cannot be seen unless you are visible. Norrey had told me, on the walk back to the studio, of Shara's efforts to get into a company—and I could have predicted nearly every word.

"Merce *Cunningham* saw her dance, Charlie. Martha Graham saw her dance, just before she died. Both of them praised her warmly, for her choreography as much as for her technique. Neither offered her a position. I'm not even sure I blame them—I can sort of understand."

Norrey could understand all right. It was her own defect magnified a hundredfold: uniqueness. A company member must be capable of excellent solo work—but she must also be able to blend into group effort, in ensemble work. Shara's very uniqueness made her virtually useless as a company member. She could not help but draw the eye.

And, once drawn, the male eye at least would never leave. Modern dancers must sometimes work nude these days, and it is therefore meet that they have the body of a fourteen-year-old boy. We may have ladies dancing with few or no clothes on up here, but by God it is Art. An actress or a musician or a singer or a painter may be lushly endowed, deliciously rounded—but a dancer must be nearly as sexless as a high-fashion model. Perhaps God knows why. Shara could not have purged her dance of her sexuality even if she had been interested in trying, and as I watched her dance on my monitor and in my mind's eye, I knew she was not.

Why did her genius have to lie in the only occupation besides model and nun in which sexiness is a liability? It broke my heart, by empathic analogy.

"It's no good at all, is it?"

I whirled and barked. "Dammit, you made me bite my tongue."

"I'm sorry." She came from the doorway into my living room. "Norrey told me how to find the place. The door was ajar."

"I forgot to shut it when I came home."

"You leave it open?"

"I've learned the lesson of history. No junkie, no matter how strung out he is, will enter an apartment with the door ajar and the radio on. Obviously there's someone home. And you're right, it's no damn good at all. Sit down."

She sat on the couch. Her hair was down now, and I liked it better that way. I shut off the monitor and popped the tape, tossing it on a shelf.

"I came to apologize. I shouldn't have blown up at you at lunch. You were trying to help me."

"You had it coming. I imagine by now you've built up quite a head of steam."

"Five years' worth. I figured I'd start in the States instead of Canada. Go farther faster. Now I'm back in Toronto and I don't think I'm going to make it here either. You're right, Mr. Armstead—I'm too damned big. Amazons don't dance."

"It's still Charlie. Listen, something I want to ask you. That last gesture, at the end of *Birthing*—what was that? I thought it was a beckoning, Norrey says it was a farewell, and now that I've run the tape it looks like a yearning, a reaching out."

"Then it worked."

"Pardon?"

"It seemed to me that the birth of a galaxy called for all three. They're so close together in spirit it seemed silly to give each a separate movement."

"Mmm." Worse and worse. Suppose Einstein had had aphasia. "Why couldn't you have been a rotten dancer? That'd just be irony. This"—I pointed to the tape—"is high tragedy."

"Aren't you going to tell me I still dance for myself?"

"No. For you that'd be worse than not dancing at all."

"My God, you're perceptive. Or am I that easy to read?"

I shrugged.

"Oh, Charlie," she burst out, "what am I going to do?"

"You'd better not ask me that." My voice sounded funny.

"Why not?"

"Because I'm already two thirds in love with you. And because you're not in love with me and never will be. And so that is the sort of question you shouldn't ask me."

It jolted her a little, but she recovered quickly. Her eyes softened, and she shook her head slowly. "You even know why I'm not, don't you?"

"And why you won't be."

I was terribly afraid she was going to say "Charlie, I'm sorry." But she surprised me again. What she said was "I can count on the fingers of one foot the number of grown-up men I've ever met. I'm grateful for you. I guess ironic tragedies come in pairs?"

"Sometimes."

"Well, now all I have to do is figure out what to do with my life. That should kill the weekend."

"Will you continue your classes?"

"Might as well. It's never a waste of time to study. Norrey's teaching me things."

All of a sudden my mind started to percolate. Man is a rational animal, right? Right? "What if I had a better idea?"

"If you've got another idea, it's better. Speak."

"Do you have to have an audience? I mean, does it have to be *live?*"

"What do you mean?"

"Maybe there's a back way in. Look, they're building tape facilities into all the TVs nowadays, right? And by now everybody has collected all the old movies and Ernie Kovacs programs and such that they always wanted, and now they're looking for new stuff. Exotic stuff, too esoteric for network or local broadcast, stuff that—"

"The independent video companies, you're talking about."

"Right. TDT is thinking of entering the market, and the Graham company already has."

"So?"

"So suppose we go freelance? You and me? You dance it and I'll tape it: a straight business deal. I've got a few connections, and maybe I can get more. I could name you ten acts in the music business right now that never go on tour—just record and record. Why don't you bypass the structure of the dance companies and take a chance on the public? Maybe word of mouth could . . ."

Her face was beginning to light up like a jack-o'-lantern. "Charlie, do you think it could work? Do you really think so?"

"I don't think it has a snowball's chance." I crossed the room, opened up the beer fridge, took out the snowball I keep there in the summer, and tossed it at her. She caught it, but just barely, and when she realized what it was, she burst out laughing. "I've got just enough faith in the idea to quit working for TDT and put my time into it. I'll invest my time, my tape, my equipment, and my savings. Ante up."

She tried to get sober, but the snowball froze her fingers and she broke up again. "A snowball in July. You madman. Count me in. I've got a little money saved. And . . . and I guess I don't have much choice, do I?"

"I guess not."

The next three years were some of the most exciting years of my life, of both our lives. While I watched and taped, Shara transformed herself from a potentially great dancer into something truly awesome. She did something I'm not sure I can explain.

She became dance's analogy of the jazzman.

Dance was, for Shara, self-expression, pure and simple, first, last and always. Once she freed herself of the attempt to fit into the world of company dance, she came to regard choreography per se as an *obstacle* to her self-expression, as a preprogrammed rut, inexorable as a script and as limiting. And so she devalued it.

A jazzman may blow *Night in Tunisia* for a dozen consecutive nights, and each evening will be a different experience, as he interprets and reinterprets the melody according to his mood of the moment. Total unity of artist and his art: spontaneous creation. The melodic starting point distinguishes the result from pure anarchy.

In just this way Shara devalued preperformance choreography to a starting point, a framework on which to build whatever the moment demanded, and then jammed around it. She learned in those three busy years to dismantle the interface between herself and her dance. Dancers have always tended to sneer at improv dancing, even while they practiced it, in the studio, for the looseness it gave. They failed to see that *planned* improv, improv around a theme fully thought out in advance, was the natural next step in dance. Shara took the step. You must be very, very good to get away with that much freedom. She was good enough.

There's no point in detailing the professional fortunes of Drumstead Enterprises over those three years. We worked hard, we made some magnificent tapes, and we couldn't sell them for paperweights. A home video cassette industry indeed existed—and they knew as much about Modern dance as the record industry knew about the blues when *they* started. The big outfits wanted credentials, and the little outfits wanted cheap talent. Finally we even got desperate enough to try the schlock houses—and learned what we already knew. They didn't have the distribution, the prestige, or the technical specs for the critics to pay any attention to them. Word-of-mouth advertising is like a gene pool—if it isn't a certain minimum size to start with, it doesn't get anywhere. "Spider" John Koerner is an incredibly talented musician and songwriter who has been making and selling his own records since 1972. How many of you have ever heard of him?

In May of 1987 I opened my mailbox in the lobby and found the letter from VisuEnt Inc., terminating our option with deepest sorrow and no severance. I went straight over to Shara's apartment, and my leg felt as if the bone marrow had been replaced with thermite and ignited. It was a very long walk.

She was working on *Weight Is a Verb* when I got there. Converting her big living room into a studio had cost time, energy, skull sweat, and a fat bribe to the landlord, but it was cheaper than renting time in a studio, considering the sets we wanted. It looked like high mountain country that day, and I hung my hat on a fake alder when I entered.

She flashed me a smile and kept moving, building up to greater and greater leaps. She looked like the most beautiful mountain goat I ever saw. I was in a foul mood and I wanted to kill the music (McLaughlin and Miles together, leaping some themselves), but I never could interrupt Shara when she was dancing. She built it gradually, with directional counterpoint, until she seemed to hurl herself into the air, stay there until she was damned good and ready, and then hurl herself down again. Sometimes she rolled when she hit and sometimes she landed on her hands, and always the energy of falling was transmuted into something instead of being absorbed. It was total energy output, and by the time she was done I had calmed down enough to be almost philosophical about our mutual professional ruin.

She ended up collapsed in upon herself, head bowed, exquisitely humbled in her attempt to defy gravity. I couldn't help applauding. It felt corny, but I couldn't help it.

"Thank you, Charlie."

"I'll be damned. Weight *is* a verb. I thought you were crazy when you told me the title."

"It's one of the strongest verbs in dance—and you can make it do *anything.*"

"Almost anything."

"Eh?"

"VisuEnt gave us our contract back."

"Oh." Nothing showed in her eyes, but I knew what was behind them. "Well, who's next on the list?"

"There is no one left on the list."

"*Oh.*" This time it showed. "Oh."

"We should have remembered. Great artists are never honored in their own lifetime. What we ought to do is drop dead—then we'd be all set."

In my way I was trying to be strong for her, and she knew it and tried to be strong for me.

"Maybe what we should do is go into death insurance, for artists," she said. "We pay the client premiums against a controlling interest in his estate, and we insure that he'll die."

"We can't lose. And if he becomes famous in his lifetime he can buy out."

"Terrific. Let's stop this before I laugh myself to death."

"Yeah."

She was silent for a long time. My own mind was racing efficiently, but the transmission seemed to be blown—it wouldn't *go* anywhere. Finally she got up and turned off the music machine, which had been whining softly ever since the tape ended. It made a loud *click*.

"Norrey's got some land in Prince Edward Island," she said, not meeting my eyes. "There's a house."

I tried to head her off with the punch line from the old joke about the kid shoveling out the elephant cage in the circus whose father offers to take him back and set him up with a decent job. "What? And leave show business?"

"Screw show business," she said softly. "If I went out to PEI now, maybe I could get the land cleared and plowed in time to get a garden in." Her expression changed. "How about you?"

"Me? I'll be okay. TDT asked me to come back."

"That was six months ago."

"They asked again. Last week."

"And you said no. Moron."

"Maybe so, maybe so."

"The whole damn thing was a waste of time. All that time. All that energy. All that work. I might as well have been farming in PEI—by now the soil'd be starting to bear well. What a waste, Charlie, what a stinking waste."

"No, I don't think so, Shara. It sounds glib to say that 'nothing is wasted,' but—well, it's like that dance you just did. Maybe you can't beat gravity—but it surely is a beautiful thing to *try.*"

"Yeah, I know. Remember the Light Brigade. Remember the Alamo. They tried." She laughed, a bitter laugh.

"Yes, and so did Jesus of Nazareth. Did you do it for material reward, or because it needed doing? If nothing else, we now have several hundred thousand feet of the most magnificent dance recordings on tape, commercial value zero, real value incalculable, and by me that is no waste. It's over now, and we'll both go do the next thing, but it was *not a waste.*" I discovered that I was shouting, and stopped.

She closed her mouth. After a while she tried a smile. "You're right, Charlie. It wasn't waste. I'm a better dancer than I ever was."

"Damn right. You've transcended choreography."

She smiled ruefully. "Yeah. Even Norrey thinks it's a dead end."

"It is *not* a dead end. There's more to poetry than haiku and sonnets. Dancers don't *have* to be robots, delivering memorized lines with their bodies."

"They do if they want to make a living."

"We'll try again in a few years. Maybe they'll be ready then."

"Sure. Let me get us some drinks."

I slept with her that night, for the first and last time. In the morning I broke down the set in the living room while she packed. I promised to write. I promised to come and visit when I could. I carried her bags down to the car, and stowed them inside. I kissed her and waved good-bye. I went looking for a drink, and at four o'clock the next morning a mugger decided I looked drunk enough and I broke his jaw, his nose, and two ribs, and then sat down on him and cried. On Monday morning I showed up at the studio with my hat in my hand and a mouth like a bus-station ashtray and crawled back into my old job. Norrey didn't ask any questions. What with rising food prices, I gave up eating anything but bourbon, and in six months I was fired. It went like that for a long time.

I never did write to her. I kept getting bogged down after "Dear Shara . . ."

When I got to the point of selling my video equipment for booze, a relay clicked somewhere and I took stock of myself. The stuff was all the life I had left, and so I went to the local Al-Anon instead of the pawn-shop and got sober. After a while my soul got numb, and I stopped flinching when I woke up. A hundred times I began to wipe the tapes I still had of Shara—she had copies of her own—but in the end I could not. From time to time I wondered how *she* was doing, and I could not bear to find out. If Norrey heard anything, she didn't tell me about it. She even tried to get me my job back a third time, but it was hopeless. Reputation can be a terrible thing once you've blown it. I was lucky to land a job with an educational TV station in New Brunswick.

It was a long couple of years.

Vidphones were coming out by 1990, and I had breadboarded one of my own without the knowledge or consent of the phone company, which I still hated more than anything. When the peanut bulb I had replaced the damned bell with started glowing softly on and off one evening in June, I put the receiver on the audio pickup and energized the tube, in case the caller was also equipped. "Hello?"

She was. When Shara's face appeared, I got a cold cube of fear in the pit of my stomach, because I had quit seeing her face everywhere when I quit drinking, and I had been thinking lately of hitting the sauce again. When I blinked and she was still there, I felt a little better and tried to speak. It didn't work.

"Hello, Charlie. It's been a long time."

The second time it worked. "Seems like yesterday. Somebody else's yesterday."

"Yes, it does. It took me *days* to find you. Norrey's in Paris, and no one else knew where you'd gone."

"Yeah. How's farming?"

"I . . . I've put that away, Charlie. It's even more creative than dancing, but it's not the same."

"Then what *are* you doing?"

"Working."

*"Dancing?"*

"Yes. Charlie, I need you. I mean, I have a job for you. I need your cameras and your eye."

"Never mind the qualifications. Any kind of need will do. *Where are you?* When's the next plane there? Which cameras do I pack?"

"New York, an hour from now, and none of them. I didn't mean 'your cameras' literally—unless you're using GLX-5000s and a Hamilton Board lately."

I whistled. It hurt my mouth. "Not on my budget. Besides, I'm old-fashioned—I like to hold 'em with my hands."

"For this job you'll use a Hamilton, and it'll be a twenty-input Masterchrome, brand new."

"You grew poppies on that farm? Or just struck diamonds with the rototiller?"

"You'll be getting paid by Bryce Carrington."

I blinked.

"Now will you catch that plane so I can tell you about it? The New Age, ask for the Presidential Suite."

"The hell with the plane, I'll walk. Quicker." I hung up.

According to the *Time* magazine in my dentist's waiting room, Bryce Carrington was the genius who had become a multimillionaire by convincing a number of giants of industry to underwrite Skyfac, the great orbiting complex that kicked the bottom out of the crystals market. As I recalled the story, some rare poliolike disease had wasted both his legs and put him in a wheelchair. But the legs had lost strength, not function —in lessened gravity, they worked well enough. So he created Skyfac, establishing mining crews on Luna to supply it with cheap raw materials, and lived in orbit under reduced gravity. His picture made him look like a reasonably successful author (as opposed to writer). Other than that I knew nothing about him. I paid little attention to news and none at all to space news.

The New Age was *the* hotel in New York in those days, built on the ruins of the Sheraton. Ultra-efficient security, bulletproof windows, carpet thicker than the outside air, and a lobby of an architectural persuasion that John D. MacDonald once called "Early Dental Plate." It stank of money. I was glad I'd made the effort to locate a necktie, and I wished I'd shined my shoes. An incredible man blocked my way as I came in through the air lock. He moved and was built like the toughest, fastest bouncer I ever saw, and he dressed and acted like God's butler. He said his name was Perry. He asked if he could help me as though he didn't think so.

"Yes, Perry. Would you mind lifting up one of your feet?"

"Why?"

"I'll bet twenty dollars you've shined your soles."

Half his mouth smiled, and he didn't move an inch. "Whom did you wish to see?"

"Shara Drummond."

"Not registered."

"The Presidential Suite."

"Oh." Light dawned. "Mr. Carrington's lady. You should have said so. Wait here, please." While he phoned to verify that I was expected, keeping his eye on me and his hand near his pocket, I swallowed my heart and rearranged my face. It took some time. So that was how it was. All right then. That was how it was.

Perry came back and gave me the little button transmitter that would let me walk the corridors of the New Age without being cut down by automatic laser fire, and explained carefully that it would blow a largish hole in me if I attempted to leave the building without returning it. From his manner I gathered that I had just skipped four grades in social standing. I thanked him, though I'm damned if I knew why.

I followed the green fluorescent arrows that appeared on the bulbless ceiling, and came after a long and scenic walk to the Presidential Suite. Shara was waiting at the door, in something like an angel's pajamas. It made all that big body look delicate. "Hello, Charlie."

I was jovial and hearty. "Hi, babe. Swell joint. How've you been keeping yourself?"

"I haven't been."

"Well, how's Carrington been keeping you, then?" Steady, boy.

"Come in, Charlie."

I went in. It looked like where the Queen stayed when she was in town, and I'm sure she enjoyed it. You could have landed an airplane in the living room without waking anyone in the bedroom. It had two pianos. Only one fireplace, barely big enough to barbecue a buffalo—you have to scrimp somewhere, I guess. Roger Kellaway was on the quadio, and for a wild moment I thought he was actually in the suite, playing some unseen third piano. So this was how it was.

"Can I get you something, Charlie?"

"Oh, sure. Hash oil, Tangier Supreme. Dom Pérignon for the pipe."

Without cracking a smile she went to a cabinet, which looked like a midget cathedral, and produced precisely what I had ordered. I kept my own features impassive and lit up. The bubbles tickled my throat, and the rush was exquisite. I felt myself relaxing, and when we had passed the narghile's mouthpiece a few times I felt her relax. We looked at each other then—really looked at each other—then at the room around us and then at each other again. Simultaneously we roared with laughter, a laughter that blew all the wealth out of the room and let in richness. Her laugh was the same whooping, braying belly laugh I remembered so well, an unselfconscious and lusty laugh, and it reassured me tremendously. I was so relieved I couldn't stop laughing myself, and that kept *her* going, and just as we might have stopped she pursed her lips and blew a stuttered arpeggio. There's an old recording called the *Spike Jones Laughing Record,* where the tuba player tries to play "The Flight of the Bumblebee" and falls down laughing, and the whole band breaks up and horse-laughs for a full two minutes, and every time they run out of air the tuba player tries another flutter and roars and they all break up again, and once when Shara was blue I bet her ten dollars that she couldn't listen to that record without at least giggling and I won. When I understood now that she was quoting it, I shuddered and dissolved into great whoops of new laughter, and a minute later we had reached the stage where we literally laughed ourselves out of our chairs and lay on the floor in agonies of mirth, weakly pounding the floor and howling. I take that laugh out of my memory now and then and rerun it —but not often, for such records deteriorate drastically with play.

At last we Dopplered back down to panting grins, and I helped her to her feet.

"What a perfectly dreadful place," I said, still chuckling.

She glanced around and shuddered. "Oh God, it *is,* Charlie. It must be awful to need this much front."

"For a horrid while I thought *you* did."

She sobered, and met my eyes. "Charlie, I wish I could resent that. In a way I do need it."

My eyes narrowed. "Just what do you mean?"

"I need Bryce Carrington."

"This time you can trot out the qualifiers. *How* do you need him?"

"I need his money," she cried.

How can you relax and tense up at the same time? "Oh, *damn* it, Shara! Is *that* how you're going to get to dance? Buy your way in? What does a critic go for these days?"

"Charlie, stop it. I need Carrington to get seen. He's going to rent me a hall, that's all."

"If that's all, let's get out of the dump right now. I can bor . . . get enough cash to rent you any hall in the world, and I'm just as willing to risk my money."

"Can you get me Skyfac?"

"*Uh?*"

I couldn't for the life of me imagine why she proposed to go to Skyfac to dance. Why not Antarctica?

"Shara, you know even less about space than I do, but you must know that a satellite broadcast doesn't have to be made from a satellite?"

"Idiot. It's the setting I want."

I thought about it. "Moon'd be better, visually. Mountains. Light. Contrast."

"The visual aspect is secondary. I don't want one-sixth g, Charlie. I want zero gravity."

My mouth hung open.

"And I want you to be my video man."

God, she was a rare one. What I needed then was to sit there with my mouth open and think for several minutes. She let me do just that, waiting patiently for me to work it all out.

"Weight isn't a verb anymore, Charlie," she said finally. "That dance ended on the assertion that you can't beat gravity—you said so yourself. Well, that statement is incorrect—obsolete. The dance of the twenty-first century will have to acknowledge that."

"And it's just what you need to make it. A new kind of dance for a new kind of dancer. Unique. It'll catch the public eye, and you should have the field entirely to yourself for years. I like it, Shara. I like it. But can you pull it off?"

"I thought about what you said: that you can't beat gravity but it's beautiful to try. It stayed in my head for months, and then one day I was visiting a neighbor with a TV and I saw newsreels of the crew working on Skyfac Two. I was up all night thinking, and the next morning I came up to the States and got a job in Skyfac One. I've been up there for nearly a year, getting next to Carrington. I can do it, Charlie, I can make it work." There was a ripple in her jaw that I had seen before—when she told me off in Le Maintenant. It was a ripple of determination.

Still I frowned. "With Carrington's backing."

Her eyes left mine. "There's no such thing as a free lunch."

"What does he charge?"

She failed to answer, for long enough to answer me. In that instant, I began believing in God again, for the first time in years, just to be able to hate Him.

But I kept my mouth shut. She was old enough to manage her own finances. The price of a dream gets higher every year. Hell, I'd half expected it from the moment she'd called me.

But only half.

"Charlie, don't just sit there with your face all knotted up. Say something. Cuss me out, call me a whore, *something.*"

"Nuts. You be your own conscience, I have trouble enough being my own. You want to dance, you've got a patron. So now you've got a video man."

I hadn't intended to say that last sentence at all.

Strangely, it almost seemed to disappoint her at first. But then she relaxed and smiled. "Thank you, Charlie. Can you get out of whatever you're doing right away?"

"I'm working for an educational station in Shediac. I even got to shoot some dance footage. A dancing bear from the London Zoo. The amazing thing was how well he danced." She grinned. "I can get free."

"I'm glad. I don't think I could pull this off without you."

"I'm working for you. Not for Carrington."

"All right."

"Where is the great man, anyway? Scuba diving in the bathtub?"

"No," came a quiet voice from the doorway. "I've been sky diving in the lobby."

His wheelchair was a mobile throne. He wore a four-hundred-dollar suit the color of strawberry ice cream, a powder-blue turtleneck, and one gold earring. The shoes were genuine leather. The watch was that newfangled bandless kind that literally tells you the time. He wasn't tall enough for her, and his shoulders were absurdly broad, although the suit tried hard to deny both. His eyes were like twin blueberries. His smile was that of a shark wondering which part will taste best. I wanted to crush his head between two boulders.

Shara was on her feet. "Bryce, this is Charles Armstead. I told you . . ."

"Oh yes. The video chap." He rolled forward and extended an impeccably manicured hand. "I'm Bryce Carrington, Armstead."

I remained seated, hands in my lap. "Oh yes. The rich chap."

One eyebrow rose an urbane quarter inch. "Oh, my. Another rude one. Well, if you're as good as Shara says you are, you're entitled."

"I'm rotten."

The smile faded. "Let's stop fencing, Armstead. I don't expect manners from creative people, but I have far more significant contempt than yours available if I need any. Now I'm tired of this damned gravity and I've had a rotten day testifying for a friend and it looks like they're going to recall me tomorrow. Do you want the job or don't you?"

He had me there. I did. "Yeah."

"All right, then. Your room is 2772. We'll be going up to Skyfac in two days. Be here at eight A.M."

"I'll want to talk with you about what you'll be needing, Charlie," Shara said. "Give me a call tomorrow."

I whirled to face her, and she flinched from my eyes.

Carrington failed to notice. "Yes, make a list of your requirements by tomorrow, so it can go up with us. Don't scrimp—if you don't fetch it, you'll do without. Good night, Armstead."

I faced him. "Good night, Mr. Carrington." Suh.

He turned toward the narghile, and Shara hurried to refill the chamber and bowl. I turned away hastily and made for the door. My leg hurt so much I nearly fell on the way, but I set my jaw and made it. When I reached the door I said to myself, You will now open the door and go through it, and then I spun on my heel. "Carrington!"

He blinked, surprised to discover I still existed. "Yes?"

"Are you *aware* that she doesn't love you in the slightest? Does that matter to you in any way?" My voice was high, and my fists were surely clenched.

"Oh," he said, and then again, "Oh. So that's what it is. I didn't *think* success alone merited that much contempt." He put down the mouthpiece and folded his fingers together. "Let me tell you something, Armstead. No one has ever loved me, to my knowledge. This suite does not love me." His voice took on human feeling for the first time. "But it is *mine*. Now get out."

I opened my mouth to tell him where to put his job, and then I saw

Shara's face, and the pain in it suddenly made me deeply ashamed. I left at once, and when the door closed behind me I vomited on a rug that was worth slightly less than a Hamilton Masterchrome board. I was sorry then that I'd worn a necktie.

The trip to Pike's Peak Spaceport, at least, was aesthetically pleasurable. I enjoy air travel, gliding among stately clouds, watching the rolling procession of mountains and plains, vast jigsaws of farmland and intricate mosaics of suburbia unfolding below.

But the jump to Skyfac in Carrington's personal shuttle, *That First Step*, might as well have been an old *Space Commando* rerun. I *know* they can't put portholes in space ships—but dammit, a shipboard video relay conveys no better resolution, color values, or presence than you get on your living-room tube. The only differences are that the stars don't "move" to give the illusion of travel, and there's no director editing the POV to give you dramatically interesting shots.

Aesthetically speaking. The *experiential* difference is that they do not, while you are watching the Space Commando sell hemorrhoid remedies, strap you into a couch, batter you with thunders, make you weigh better than half a ton for an unreasonably long time, and then drop you off the edge of the world into weightlessness. I had been half expecting nausea, but what I got was even more shocking: the sudden, unprecedented, total absence of pain in my leg. At that, Shara was hit worse than I was, barely managing to deploy her dropsickness bag in time. Carrington unstrapped and administered an antinausea injection with sure movements. It seemed to take forever to hit her, but when it did there was an enormous change—color and strength returned rapidly, and she was apparently fully recovered by the time the pilot announced that we were commencing docking and would everyone please strap in and shut up. I half expected Carrington to bark manners into him, but apparently the industrial magnate was not that sort of fool. He shut up and strapped himself down.

My leg didn't hurt in the slightest. Not at all.

The Skyfac complex looked like a disorderly heap of bicycle tires and beach balls of various sizes. The one our pilot made for was more like a tractor tire. We matched course, became its axle, and matched spin, and the damned thing grew a spoke that caught us square in the air lock. The air lock was "overhead" of our couches, but we entered and left it feet first. A few yards into the spoke, the direction we traveled became "down," and handholds became a ladder. Weight increased with every step, but even when we had emerged in a rather large cubical compartment it was far less than Earth normal. Nonetheless, my leg resumed biting me.

The room tried to be a classic reception room, high-level ("Please be seated. His Majesty will see you shortly"), but the low g and the p-suits racked along two walls spoiled the effect. Unlike the Space Commando's armor, a real pressure suit looks like nothing so much as a people-shaped baggie, and they look particularly silly in repose. A young dark-haired man in tweed rose from behind a splendidly gadgeted desk and smiled. "Good to see you, Mr. Carrington, I hope you had a pleasant jump."

"Fine, thanks, Tom. You remember Shara, of course. This is Charles Armstead. Tom McGillicuddy." We both displayed our teeth and said we were delighted to meet each other. I could see that beneath the pleasantries McGillicuddy was upset about something.

"Nils and Mr. Longmire are waiting in your office, sir. There's . . . there's been another sighting."

"God *damn* it," Carrington began, and cut himself off. I stared at him. The full force of my best sarcasm had failed to anger this man. "All right. Take care of my guests while I go hear what Longmire has to say." He started for the door, moving like a beach ball in slow motion but under his own power. "Oh yes—the *Step* is loaded to the gun'ls with bulky equipment, Tom. Have her brought around to the cargo bays. Store the equipment in Six." He left, looking worried. McGillicuddy activated his desk and gave the necessary orders.

"What's going on, Tom?" Shara asked when he was through.

He looked at me before replying. "Pardon my asking, Mr. Armstead, but—are you a newsman?"

"Charlie. No, I'm not. I am a video man, but I work for Shara."

"Mmmm. Well, you'll hear about it sooner or later. About two weeks ago, an object appeared within the orbit of Neptune, just appeared out of nowhere. There were . . . certain other anomalies. It stayed put for half a day and then vanished again. The Space Command slapped a hush on it, but it's common knowledge on board Skyfac."

"And the thing has been sighted again?" Shara asked.

"Just beyond the orbit of Jupiter."

I was only mildly interested. No doubt there was an explanation for the phenomenon, and since Isaac Asimov wasn't around I would doubtless never understand a word of it. Most of us gave up on intelligent nonhuman life when the last intersystem probe came back empty. "Little green men, I suppose. Can you show us the lounge, Tom? I understand it's just like the one we'll be working in."

He seemed to welcome the change of subject. "Sure thing."

McGillicuddy led us through a p-door opposite the one Carrington had used, through long halls whose floors curved up ahead of and behind us. Each was outfitted differently, each was full of busy, purposeful people, and each reminded me somehow of the lobby of the New Age, or perhaps of the old movie *2001*. Futuristic Opulence, so understated as to fairly shriek. Wall Street lifted bodily into orbit—the *clocks* were on Wall Street time. I tried to make myself believe that cold, empty space lay a short distance away in any direction, but it was impossible. I decided it was a good thing spacecraft didn't have portholes— once he got used to the low gravity, a man might forget and open one to throw out a cigar.

I studied McGillicuddy as we walked. He was immaculate in every respect, from necktie down to nail polish, and he wore no jewelry at all. His hair was short and black, his beard inhibited, and his eyes surprisingly warm in a professionally sterile face. I wondered what he had sold his soul for. I hoped he had gotten his price.

We had to descend two levels to get to the lounge. The gravity on the upper level was kept at one-sixth normal, partly for the convenience of the lunar personnel who were Skyfac's only regular commuters, and mostly (of course) for the convenience of Carrington. But descending brought a subtle increase in weight, to perhaps a fifth or a quarter normal. My leg complained bitterly, but I found to my surprise that I preferred the pain to its absence. It's a little scary when an old friend goes away like that.

The lounge was a larger room than I had expected, quite big enough for our purposes. It encompassed all three levels, and one whole wall was an immense video screen, across which stars wheeled dizzily, joined with occasional regularity by a slice of mother Terra. The floor was crowded with chairs and tables in various groupings, but I could see that, stripped, it would provide Shara with entirely adequate room to dance; equally important, my feet told me that it would make a splendid dancing surface. Then I remembered how little use the floor was liable to get.

"Well," Shara said to me with a smile, "this is what home will look like for the next six months. The Ring Two lounge is identical to this one."

"Six?" McGillicuddy said. "Not a chance."

"*What do you mean?*" Shara and I said together.

He blinked at our combined volume. "Well, *you'll* probably be good for that long, Charlie. But Shara's already had over a year of low **g**, while she was in the typing pool."

"So what?"

"Look, you expect to be in free fall for long periods of time, if I understand this correctly?"

"Twelve hours a day," Shara agreed.

He grimaced. "Shara, I hate to say this . . . but I'll be surprised if you last a month. A body designed for a one-g environment doesn't work properly in zero g."

"But it will adapt, won't it?"

He laughed mirthlessly. "Sure. That's why we rotate all personnel Earthside every fourteen months. Your body will adapt. One way. No return. Once you've fully adapted, returning to Earth will stop your heart—if some other major systemic failure doesn't occur first. Look, you were just Earthside for three days—did you have any chest pains? Dizziness? Bowel trouble? Dropsickness on the way up?"

"All of the above," she admitted.

"There you go. You were close to the nominal fourteen-month limit when you left. And your body will adapt even faster under no gravity at all. The successful free-fall endurance record of about eight months was set by a Skyfac construction gang with bad deadline problems—and they hadn't spent a year in one-sixth g first, *and* they weren't straining their hearts the way you will be. Hell, there are four men on Luna now, from the original dozen in the first mining team, who will never see Earth again. Eight of their teammates tried. Don't you two know *any-thing* about space?"

"But I've got to have at least four months. Four months of solid work, every day. I *must.*" She was dismayed, but fighting hard for control.

McGillicuddy started to shake his head, and then thought better of it. His warm eyes were studying Shara's face. I knew exactly what he was thinking, and I liked him for it.

He was thinking, *How to tell a lovely lady her dearest dream is hopeless?*

He didn't know the half of it. I *knew* how much Shara had already—irrevocably—invested in this dream, and something in me screamed.

And then I saw her jaw ripple and I dared to hope.

Dr. Panzarella was a wiry old man with eyebrows like two fuzzy caterpillars. He wore a tight-fitting jumpsuit which would not foul a p-suit's seals should he have to get into one in a hurry. His shoulder-length hair, which should have been a mane on that great skull, was clipped securely back against a sudden absence of gravity. A cautious man. To employ an obsolete metaphor, he was a suspenders-*and*-belt type. He looked Shara over, ran tests, and gave her just under a month and a half. Shara said some things. I said some things. McGillicuddy said some things. Panzarella shrugged, made further, very careful tests, and reluctantly cut loose of the suspenders. Two months. Not a day over. Possibly less, depending on subsequent monitoring of her body's reactions to extended weightlessness. Then a year Earthside before risking it again. Shara seemed satisfied.

I didn't see how we could do it.

McGillicuddy had assured us that it would take Shara at least a month simply to learn to handle herself competently in zero g, much less dance. Her familiarity with one-sixth g would, he predicted, be a liability rather than an asset. Then figure three weeks of choreography and rehearsal, a week of taping, and just maybe we could broadcast one dance before Shara had to return to Earth. Not good enough. She and I had calculated that we would need three successive shows, each well received, to make a big enough dent in the dance world for Shara to squeeze into it. A year was far too big a spacing—*and who knew how soon Carrington would tire of her?* So I hollered at Panzarella.

"Mr. Armstead," he said hotly, "I am specifically contractually forbidden to allow this young lady to commit suicide." He grimaced sourly. "I'm told it's terrible public relations."

"Charlie, it's okay," Shara insisted. "I can fit in three dances. We may lose some sleep, but we can do it."

"I once told a man nothing was impossible. He asked me if I could ski through a revolving door. You haven't got . . ."

My brain slammed into hyperdrive, thought about things, kicked itself in the ass a few times, and returned to real time in time to hear my mouth finish without a break: ". . . much choice, though. Okay, Tom, have that damned Ring Two lounge cleaned out, I want it naked and spotless, and have somebody paint over that damned video wall, the same shade as the other three, and I mean *the same.* Shara, get out of those clothes and into your leotard. Doctor, we'll be seeing you in twelve hours. Quit gaping and *go,* Tom—we'll be going over there at once; *where the hell are my cameras?*"

McGillicuddy sputtered.

"Get me a torch crew—I'll want holes cut through the walls, cameras behind them, one-way glass, six locations, a room adjacent to the lounge for a mixer console the size of a jetliner cockpit, and bolt a Norelco coffee machine next to the chair. I'll need another room for editing, complete privacy, and total darkness, size of an efficiency kitchen, another Norelco."

McGillicuddy finally drowned me out. "Mr. *Armstead,* this is the Main Ring of the Skyfac One complex, the administrative offices of one of the wealthiest corporations in existence. If you think this whole Ring is going to stand on its head for you . . ."

So we brought the problem to Carrington. He told McGillicuddy that henceforth Ring Two was *ours,* as well as any assistance whatsoever that we requested. He looked rather distracted. McGillicuddy started to tell him by how many weeks all this would put off the opening of the Skyfac Two complex. Carrington replied very quietly that he could add and subtract quite well, thank you, and McGillicuddy got white and quiet.

I'll give Carrington that much. He gave us a free hand.

Panzarella ferried over to Skyfac Two with us. We were chauffeured by lean-jawed astronaut types, on vehicles looking, for all the world, like pregnant broomsticks. It was as well that we had the doctor with us —Shara fainted on the way over. I nearly did myself, and I'm sure that broomstick has my thigh-prints on it yet—falling through space is a scary experience the first time. Shara responded splendidly once we had her inboard again, and fortunately her dropsickness did not return— nausea can be a nuisance in free fall, a disaster in a p-suit. By the time my cameras and mixer had arrived, she was on her feet and sheepish. And while I browbeat a sweating crew of borrowed techs into installing them faster than was humanly possible, Shara began learning how to move in zero g.

We were ready for the first taping in three weeks.

Living quarters and minimal life support were rigged for us in Ring Two so that we could work around the clock if we chose, but we spent nearly half of our nominal "off-hours" in Skyfac One. Shara was required to spend half of three days a week there with Carrington, and spent a sizable portion of her remaining putative sack time out in space, in a p-suit. At first it was a conscious attempt to overcome her gut-level fear of all that emptiness. Soon it became her meditation, her retreat, her artistic reverie, an attempt to gain from contemplation of the cold black depths enough insight into the meaning of extraterrestrial existence to dance of it.

I spent my own time arguing with engineers and electricians and technicians and a damn fool union legate who insisted that the second lounge, finished or not, belonged to the hypothetical future crew and administrative personnel. Securing his permission to work there wore the lining off my throat and the insulation off my nerves. Far too many nights I spent slugging instead of sleeping. Minor example: Every interior wall in the whole damned second Ring was painted the identical shade of turquoise—and they couldn't duplicate it to cover that godforsaken video wall in the lounge. It was McGillicuddy who saved me from gibbering apoplexy—at his suggestion, I washed off the third latex job, unshipped the outboard camera that fed the wall screen, brought it inboard, and fixed it to scan an interior wall in an adjoining room. That made us friends again.

It was all like that: jury-rig, improvise, file to fit and paint to cover. If a camera broke down, I spent sleep time talking with off-shift engineers, finding out what parts in stock could be adapted. It was simply too expensive to have anything shipped up from Earth's immense gravity well, and Luna didn't have what I needed.

At that, Shara worked harder than I did. A body must totally recoordinate itself to function in the absence of weight—she had to forget literally everything she had ever known or learned about dancing and acquire a whole new set of skills. This turned out to be even harder than we had expected. McGillicuddy had been right: What Shara had learned in her year of one-sixth g was an exaggerated attempt to *retain* terrestrial patterns of coordination—rejecting them altogether was actually easier for *me*.

But I couldn't keep up with her—I had to abandon any thought of handheld camera work and base my plans solely on the six fixed cameras. Fortunately GLX-5000s have a ball-and-socket mount; even behind that damned one-way glass I had about forty degrees of traverse on each one. Learning to coordinate all six simultaneously on the Hamilton Board did a truly extraordinary thing to me—it lifted me that one last step to unity with my art. I found that I could learn to be aware of all six monitors with my mind's eye, to perceive almost spherically, to—not share my attention among the six—to *encompass* them all, seeing like a six-eyed creature from many angles at once. My mind's eye became holographic, my awareness multilayered. I began to really understand, for the first time, three-dimensionality.

It was that fourth dimension that was the kicker. It took Shara two days to decide that she could not possibly become proficient enough in free-fall maneuvering to sustain a half-hour piece in the time required. So she rethought her work plan too, adapting her choreography to the demands of exigency. She put in six hard days under normal Earth weight.

And for her, too, the effort brought her that one last step toward apotheosis.

On Monday of the fourth week we began taping *Liberation.*

Establishing shot:

A great turquoise box, seen from within. Dimensions unknown, but the color somehow lends an impression of immensity, of vast distances. Against the far wall, a swinging pendulum attests that this is a standard-gravity environment; but the pendulum swings so slowly and is so featureless in construction that it is impossible to estimate its size and so extrapolate that of the room.

Because of this *trompe l'oeil* effect, the room seems rather smaller than it really is when the camera pulls back and we are wrenched into proper perspective by the appearance of Shara, prone, inert, face down on the floor, facing us.

She wears beige leotard and tights. Hair the color of fine mahogany is pulled back into a loose ponytail which fans across one shoulder blade. She does not appear to breathe. She does not appear to be alive.

Music begins. The aging Mahavishnu, on obsolete nylon acoustic, establishes a Minor E in no hurry at all. A pair of small candles in simple brass holders appear inset on either side of the room. They are larger than life, though small beside Shara. Both are unlit.

Her body . . . there is no word. It does not move, in the sense of motor activity. One might say that a ripple passes through it, save that the motion is clearly all outward from her center. She *swells,* as if the first breath of life were being taken by her whole body at once. She lives.

The twin wicks begin to glow, oh, softly. The music takes on quiet urgency.

Shara raises her head to us. Her eyes focus somewhere beyond the camera yet short of infinity. Her body writhes, undulates, and the glowing wicks are coals (that this brightening takes place in slow motion is not apparent).

A violent contraction raises her to a crouch, spilling the ponytail across her shoulder. Mahavishnu begins a cyclical cascade of runs, in increasing tempo. Long, questing tongues of yellow-orange flame begin to blossom *downward* from the twin wicks, whose coals are turning to blue.

The contraction's release flings her to her feet. The twin skirts of flame about the wicks curl up over themselves, writhing furiously, to become conventional candle flames, flickering now in normal time.

Tablas, tambouras, and a bowed string bass join the guitar, and they segue into an energetic interplay around a minor seventh that keeps trying, fruitlessly, to find resolution in the sixth. The candles stay in perspective, but dwindle in size until they vanish.

Shara begins to explore the possibilities of motion. First she moves only perpendicular to the camera's line of sight, exploring that dimension. Every motion of arms or legs or head is clearly seen to be a defiance of gravity, of a force as inexorable as radioactive decay, as entropy itself. The most violent surges of energy succeed only for a time—the outflung leg falls, the outthrust arm drops. She must struggle or fall. She pauses in thought.

Her hands and arms reach out toward the camera, and at the instant they do we cut to a view from the left-hand wall. Seen from the right side, she reaches out into this new dimension, and soon begins to move in it. (As she moves backward out of the camera's field, its entire image shifts right on our screen, butted out of the way by the incoming image of a second camera, which picks her up as the first loses her without a visible seam.)

The new dimension too fails to fulfill Shara's desire for freedom from gravity. Combining the two, however, presents so many permutations of movement that for a while, intoxicated, she flings herself into experimentation. In the next fifteen minutes, Shara's entire background and history in dance are recapitulated, in a blinding tour de force that incorporates elements of jazz, Modern, and the more graceful aspects of Olympic-level mat gymnastics. Five cameras come into play, singly and in pairs on split screen, as the "bag of tricks" amassed in a lifetime of study and improvisation are rediscovered and performed by a superbly trained and versatile body, in a pyrotechnic display that would shout of joy if her expression did not remain aloof, almost arrogant. *This is the offering,* she seems to say, *which you would not accept. This, by itself, was not good enough.*

And it is not. Even in its raging energy and total control, her body returns again and again to the final compromise of mere erectness, that last simple refusal to fall.

Clamping her jaw, she works into a series of leaps, ever longer, ever higher. She seems at last to hang suspended for full seconds, straining to fly. When, inevitably, she falls, she falls reluctantly, only at the last possible instant tucking and rolling back onto her feet. The musicians are in a crescendoing frenzy. We see her now only with the single original camera, and the twin candles have returned, small but burning fiercely.

The leaps begin to diminish in intensity and height, and she takes longer to build to each one. She has been dancing flat out for nearly twenty minutes; as the candle flames begin to wane, so does her strength. At last she retreats to a place beneath the indifferent pendulum, gathers herself with a final desperation, and races forward toward us. She reaches incredible speed in a short space, hurls herself into a double roll, and bounds up into the air off one foot, seeming a full second later to push off against empty air for a few more inches of height. Her body goes rigid, her eyes and mouth gape wide, the flames reach maximum brilliance, the music peaks with the tortured wail of an electric guitar, and—she falls, barely snapping into a roll in time, rising only as far as a crouch. She holds there for a long moment, and gradually her head and shoulders slump, defeated, toward the floor. The candle flames draw in upon themselves in a curious way and appear to go out. The string bass saws on, modulating down to D.

Muscle by muscle, Shara's body gives up the struggle. The air seems to tremble around the wicks of the candles, which have now grown nearly as tall as her crouching form.

Shara lifts her face to the camera with evident effort. Her face is anguished, her eyes nearly shut. A long beat.

All at once she opens her eyes wide, squares her shoulders, and contracts. It is the most exquisite and total contraction ever dreamed of, filmed in real time but seeming almost to be in slow motion. She holds it. Mahavishnu comes back in on guitar, building in increasing tempo from a down-tuned bass string to a D with a flatted fourth. Shara holds.

We shift for the first time to an overhead camera, looking down on her from a great height. As Mahavishnu's picking increases to the point where the chord seems a sustained drone, Shara slowly lifts her head, still holding the contraction, until she is staring directly up at us. She poises there for an eternity, like a spring wound to the bursting point . . .

. . . and explodes upward toward us, rising higher and faster than she possibly can in a soaring flight that *is* slow motion now, coming closer and closer until her hands disappear off either side and her face fills the screen, flanked by two candles which have bloomed into gouts of yellow flame in an instant. The guitar and bass are submerged in an orchestra.

Almost at once she whirls away from us, and the POV switches to the original camera, on which we see her fling herself down ten meters to the floor, reversing her attitude in mid-flight and twisting. She comes out of her roll in an absolutely flat trajectory that takes her the length of the room. She hits the far wall with a crash audible even over the music, shattering the still pendulum. Her thighs soak up the kinetic energy and then release it, and once again she is racing toward us, hair streaming straight out behind her, a broad smile of triumph growing larger in the screen.

In the next five minutes all six cameras vainly try to track her as she caroms around the immense room like a hummingbird trying to batter its way out of a cage, using the walls, floor, and ceiling the way a jai alai master does, *existing in three dimensions.* Gravity is defeated. The basic assumption of all dance is transcended.

Shara is transformed.

She comes to rest at last at vertical center in the forefront of the turquoise cube, arms-legs-fingers-toes-face straining *outward,* turning gently end over end. All four cameras that bear on her join in a four-way split screen, the orchestra resolves into its final E Major, and—fade-out.

I had neither the time nor the equipment to create the special effects that Shara wanted. So I found ways to warp reality to my need. The first candle segment was a twinned shot of a candle being blown out from above—in ultra-slow-motion, and in reverse. The second segment was a simple recording of reality. I had lit the candle, started taping—and had the Ring's spin killed. A candle behaves oddly in zero g. The low-density combustion gases do not rise up from the flame, allowing air to reach it from beneath. The flame does not go out: It becomes dormant. Restore gravity within a minute or so, and it blooms back to life again. All I did was monkey with speeds a bit to match in with the music and Shara's dance. I got the idea from Harry Stein, Skyfac's construction foreman, who was helping me design the next dance.

I set up a screen in the Ring One lounge, and everyone in Skyfac who could cut work crowded in for the broadcast. They saw exactly what was being sent out over worldwide satellite hookup (Carrington had sufficient pull to arrange twenty-five minutes without commercial interruption) almost a full half second before the world did.

I spent the broadcast in the Communications Room, chewing my fingernails. But it went without a hitch, and I slapped my board dead and made it to the lounge in time to see the last half of the standing ovation. Shara stood before the screen, Carrington sitting beside her, and I found the difference in their expressions instructive. Her face showed no surprise or modesty. She had had faith in herself throughout, had approved this tape for broadcast—she was aware, with that incredible detachment of which so few artists are capable, that the wild applause was only what she deserved. But her face showed that she was deeply surprised—and deeply grateful—to be given what she deserved.

Carrington, on the other hand, registered a triumph strangely mingled with relief. He too had had faith in Shara, backing it with a large investment—but his faith was that of a businessman in a gamble he believes will pay off, and as I watched his eyes and the glisten of sweat on his forehead, I realized that no businessman ever takes an expensive gamble without worrying that it may be the fiasco that will begin the loss of his only essential commodity: face.

Seeing his kind of triumph next to hers spoiled the moment for me, and instead of thrilling for Shara I found myself almost hating her. She spotted me, and waved me to join her before the cheering crowd, but I turned and literally flung myself from the room. I borrowed a bottle from Harry Stein and got stinking.

The next morning my head felt like a fifteen-amp fuse on a forty-amp circuit, and I seemed to be held together only by surface tension. Sudden movements frightened me. It's a long fall off that wagon, even at one-sixth g.

The phone chimed—I hadn't had time to rewire it—and a young man I didn't know politely announced that Mr. Carrington wished to see me in his office. At once, I spoke of a barbed-wire suppository and what Mr. Carrington might do with it, at once. Without changing expression, he repeated his message and disconnected.

So I crawled into my clothes, decided to grow a beard, and left. Along the way I wondered what I had traded my independence for, and why.

Carrington's office was oppressively tasteful, but at least the lighting was subdued. Best of all, its filter system would handle smoke—the sweet musk of pot lay on the air. I accepted a macrojoint of "Maoi-Zowie" from Carrington with something approaching gratitude, and began melting my hangover.

Shara sat next to his desk, wearing a leotard and a layer of sweat. She had obviously spent the morning rehearsing for the next dance. I felt ashamed, and consequently snappish, avoiding her eyes and her hello. Panzarella and McGillicuddy came in on my heels, chattering about the latest sighting of the mysterious object from deep space, which had appeared this time in the neighborhood of Mercury. They were arguing over whether it displayed signs of sentience or not, and I wished they'd shut up.

Carrington waited until we had all seated ourselves and lit up, then rested a hip on his desk and smiled. "Well, Tom?"

McGillicuddy beamed. "Better than we expected, sir. All the ratings agree we had about seventy-four percent of the world audience—"

"The hell with the Nielsons," I snapped. *"What did the critics say?"*

McGillicuddy blinked. "Well, the general reaction so far is that Shara was a smash. The *Times*—"

I cut him off again. "What was the less-than-general reaction?"

"Well, nothing is ever unanimous."

"Specifics. The dance press? Liz Zimmer? Migdalski?"

"Uh. Not as good. Praise, yes—only a blind man could've panned that show. But guarded praise. Uh, Zimmer called it a magnificent dance spoiled by a gimmicky ending."

"And Migdalski?" I insisted.

"He headed his review, 'But What Do You Do for an Encore?'" McGillicuddy admitted. "His basic thesis was that it was a charming one-shot. But the *Times*—"

"Thank you, Tom," Carrington said quietly. "About what we expected, isn't it, my dear? A big splash, but no one's willing to call it a tidal wave yet."

She nodded. "But they will, Bryce. The next two dances will sew it up."

Panzarella spoke up. "Ms. Drummond, may I ask why you played it the way you did? Using the null-g interlude only as a brief adjunct to conventional dance—surely you must have expected the critics to call it gimmickry."

Shara smiled and answered, "To be honest, Doctor, I had no choice. I'm learning to use my body in free fall, but it's still a conscious effort, almost a pantomime. I need another few weeks to make it second nature, and it *has* to be if I'm to sustain a whole piece in it. So I dug a conventional dance out of the trunk, tacked on a five-minute ending that used every zero-g move I knew, and found to my extreme relief that they made thematic sense together. I told Charlie my notion, and he made it work visually and dramatically—that whole business of the candles was his, and it underlined what I was trying to say better than any set we could have built."

"So you have not yet completed what you came here to do?" Panzarella asked Shara.

"Oh, no. Not by any means. The next dance will show the world that dance is more than controlled falling. And the third . . . the third will be what this has all been for." Her face lit, became animated. "The third dance will be the one I have wanted to dance all my life. I can't entirely picture it yet—but I know that when I become capable of dancing it, I will create it, and it will be my greatest dance."

Panzarella cleared his throat. "How long will it take you?"

"Not long," she said. "I'll be ready to tape the next dance in two weeks, and I can start on the last one almost at once. With luck, I'll have it in the can before my month is up."

"Ms. Drummond," Panzarella said gravely, "I'm afraid you don't have another month."

Shara went white as snow, and I half rose from my seat. Carrington looked intrigued.

"How much time?" Shara asked.

"Your latest tests have not been encouraging. I had assumed that the sustained exercise of rehearsal and practice would tend to slow your system's adaptation. But most of your work has been in total weightlessness, and I failed to realize the extent to which your body is accustomed to sustained exertion—in a terrestrial environment."

*"How much time?"*

"Two weeks. Possibly three, if you spend three separate hours a day at hard exercise in two gravities."

"That's ridiculous," I burst out. "Don't you understand about dancers' spines? She could ruin herself in two gees."

"I've got to have four weeks," Shara said.

"Ms. Drummond, I am sorry."

"I've got to have four weeks."

Panzarella had that same look of helpless sorrow that McGillicuddy and I had had in our turn, and I was suddenly sick to death of a universe in which people had to keep looking at Shara that way. "Dammit," I roared, "she needs four weeks."

Panzarella shook his shaggy head. "If she stays in zero g for four working weeks, she may die."

Shara sprang from her chair. "Then I'll die," she cried. "I'll take that chance. I *have* to."

Carrington coughed. "I'm afraid I can't permit you to, darling."

She whirled on him furiously.

"This dance of yours is excellent PR for Skyfac," he said calmly, "but if it were to kill you it might boomerang, don't you think?"

Her mouth worked, and she fought desperately for control. My own head whirled. Die? Shara?

"Besides," he added, "I've grown quite fond of you."

"Then I'll stay up here in space," she burst out.

"Where? The only areas of sustained weightlessness are factories, and you're not qualified to work in one."

"Then for God's sake give me one of the new pods, the small spheres. Bryce, I'll give you a higher return on your investment than a factory pod, and I'll . . ." Her voice changed. "I'll be available to you always."

He smiled lazily. "Yes, but I might not *want* you always, darling. My mother warned me strongly against making irrevocable decisions about women. Especially informal ones. Besides, I find zero-g sex rather too exhausting as a steady diet."

I had almost found my voice, and now I lost it again. I was glad Carrington was turning her down—but the way he did it made me yearn to drink his blood.

Shara too was speechless for a time. When she spoke, her voice was low, intense, almost pleading. "Bryce, it's a matter of timing. If I broadcast two more dances in the next four weeks, I'll have a world to return to. If I have to go Earthside and wait a year or two, that third dance will sink without a trace—no one'll be looking, and they won't have the memory of the first two. This is my only option, Bryce—*let me take the chance.* Panzarella can't guarantee four weeks will kill me."

"I can't guarantee your survival," the doctor said.

"You can't guarantee that any one of us will live out the day," she snapped. She whirled back to Carrington, held him with her eyes. "Bryce, *let me risk it.*" Her face underwent a massive effort, produced a smile that put a knife through my heart. "I'll make it worth your while."

Carrington savored that smile and the utter surrender in her voice like a man enjoying a fine claret. I wanted to slay him with my hands and teeth, and I prayed that he would add the final cruelty of turning her down. But I had underestimated his true capacity for cruelty.

"Go ahead with your rehearsal, my dear," he said at last. "We'll make a final decision when the time comes. I shall have to think about it."

I don't think I've ever felt so hopeless, so . . . impotent in my life. Knowing it was futile, I said, "Shara, I can't let you risk your life—"

"I'm going to do this, Charlie," she cut me off, "with or without you. No one else knows my work well enough to tape it properly, but if you want out I can't stop you." Carrington watched me with detached interest. "Well?"

I said a filthy word. "You know the answer."

"Then let's get to work."

Tyros are transported on the pregnant broomsticks. Old hands hang outside the air lock, dangling from handholds on the outer surface of the spinning Ring. They face in the direction of the spin, and when their destination comes under the horizon, they just drop off. Thruster units built into gloves and boots supply the necessary course corrections. The distances involved are small. Shara and I, having spent more weightless hours than some technicians who'd been in Skyfac for years, were old hands. We made scant and efficient use of our thrusters, chiefly in canceling the energy imparted to us by the spin of the Ring we left. We had throat mikes and hearing-aid-sized receivers, but there was no conversation on the way across the void. I spent the journey appreciating the starry emptiness through which I fell—I had come, perforce, to understand the attraction of sky diving—and wondering whether I would ever get used to the cessation of pain in my leg. It even seemed to hurt less under spin those days.

We grounded, with much less force than a sky diver does, on the surface of the new studio. It was an enormous steel globe, studded with sunpower screens and heat-losers, tethered to three more spheres in various stages of construction, on which p-suited figures were even now working. McGillicuddy had told me that the complex when completed would be used for "controlled density processing," and when I said, "How nice," he added, "Dispersion foaming and variable density casting," as if that explained everything. Perhaps it did. Right at the moment, it was Shara's studio.

The air lock led to a rather small working space around a smaller interior sphere some fifty meters in diameter. It too was pressurized, intended to contain a vacuum, but its locks stood open. We removed our p-suits, and Shara unstrapped her thruster bracelets from a bracing strut and put them on, hanging by her ankles from the strut while she did so. The anklets went on next. As jewelry they were a shade bulky—but they had twenty minutes' continuous use each, and their operation was not visible in normal atmosphere and lighting. Indoor zero-gee dance without them would have been enormously more difficult.

As she was fastening the last strap I drifted over in front of her and grabbed the strut. "Shara . . ."

"Charlie, I can beat it. I'll exercise in *three* gravities, and I'll sleep in two, and I'll make this body last. I know I can."

"You could skip *Mass Is a Verb* and go right to the *Stardance.*"

She shook her head. "I'm not ready yet—and neither is the audience. I've got to lead myself and them through dance in a sphere first—in a contained space—before I'll be ready to dance in empty space, or for them to appreciate it. I have to free my mind, and theirs, from just about every preconception of dance, change the postulates. Even two stages is too few—but it's the irreducible minimum." Her eyes softened. "Charlie—I must."

"I know," I said gruffly, and turned away. Tears are a nuisance in free fall—they don't *go* anywhere. I began hauling myself around the surface of the inner sphere toward the camera emplacement I was working on, and Shara entered the inner sphere to begin rehearsal.

I prayed as I worked on my equipment, snaking cables among the bracing struts and connecting them to drifting terminals. For the first time in years I prayed, prayed that Shara would make it. That we both would.

The next twelve days were the toughest of my life. Shara worked twice as hard as I did. She spent half of every day working in the studio, half of the rest in exercise under two and a quarter gravities (the most Dr. Panzarella would permit), and half of the rest in Carrington's bed, trying to make him contented enough to let her stretch her time limit. Perhaps she slept in the few hours left over. I only know that she never looked tired, never lost her composure or her dogged determination. Stubbornly, reluctantly, her body lost its awkwardness, took on grace even in an environment where grace required enormous concentration. Like a child learning to walk, Shara learned how to fly.

I even began to get used to the absence of pain in my leg.

What can I tell you of *Mass,* if you have not seen it? It cannot be described, even badly, in mechanistic terms, the way a symphony could be written out in words. Conventional dance terminology is, by its built-in assumptions, worse than useless, and if you are at all familiar with the new nomenclature you *must* be familiar with *Mass Is a Verb,* from which it draws *its* built-in assumptions.

Nor is there much I can say about the technical aspects of *Mass.* There were no special effects; not even music. Brindle's superb score was composed *from the dance,* and added to the tape with my permission two years later, but it was for the original, silent version that I was given the Emmy. My entire contribution, aside from editing and installing the two trampolines, was to camouflage batteries of wide-dispersion light sources in clusters around each camera eye, and wire them so that they energized only when they were out-of-frame with respect to whichever camera was on at the time—ensuring that Shara was always lit from the front, presenting two (not always congruent) shadows. I made no attempt to employ flashy camera work; I simply recorded what Shara danced, changing POV only as she did.

No. *Mass Is a Verb* can be described only in symbolic terms, and then poorly. I can say that Shara demonstrated that mass and inertia are as able as gravity to supply the dynamic conflict essential to dance. I can tell you that from them she distilled a kind of dance that could have been imagined only by a group-head consisting of an acrobat, a stunt diver, a skywriter, and an underwater ballerina. I can tell you that she dismantled the last interface between herself and utter freedom of motion, subduing her body to her will and space itself to her need.

And still I will have told you next to nothing. For Shara sought more than freedom—she sought meaning. *Mass* was, above all, a spiritual event—its title pun paralleling its thematic ambiguity between the technological and the theological. Shara made the human confrontation with existence a transitive act, literally meeting God halfway. I do not mean to imply that her dance at any time addressed an exterior God, a discrete entity with or without white beard. Her dance addressed reality, gave successive expression to the Three Eternal Questions asked by every human being who ever lived.

Her dance observed her *self,* and asked, *How have I come to be here?*

Her dance observed the universe in which self existed, and asked, *How did all this come to be here with me?*

And at last, observing her self in relation to its universe, *Why am I so alone?*

And, having asked these questions, having earnestly asked them with every muscle and sinew she possessed, she paused, hung suspended in the center of the sphere, her body and soul open to the universe, and when no answer came, she contracted. Not in a dramatic, ceiling-spring sense as she had in *Liberation,* a compressing of energy and tension. This was physically similar, but an utterly different phenomenon. It was a focusing inward, an act of introspection, a turning of the mind's (soul's?) eye in upon itself, to seek answers that lay nowhere else. Her body too, therefore, seemed to fold in upon itself, compacting her mass, so evenly that her position in space was not disturbed.

And reaching within herself, she closed on emptiness. The camera faded out, leaving her alone, rigid, encapsulated, yearning. The dance ended, leaving her three questions unanswered, the tension of their asking unresolved. Only the expression of patient waiting on her face blunted the shocking edge of the non-ending, made it bearable, a small, blessed sign whispering, "To be continued."

By the eighteenth day we had it in the can, in rough form. Shara put it immediately out of her mind and began choreographing *Stardance*, but I spent two hard days of editing before I was ready to release the tape for broadcast. I had four days until the half hour of prime time Carrington had purchased—but that wasn't the deadline I felt breathing down the back of my neck.

McGillicuddy came into my workroom while I was editing, and although he saw the tears running down my face he said no word. I let the tape run, and he watched in silence, and soon his face was wet too. When the tape had been over for a long time he said, very softly, "One of these days I'm going to have to quit this stinking job."

I said nothing.

"I used to be a karate instructor. I was pretty good. I could teach again, maybe do exhibition work, make ten percent of what I do now."

I said nothing.

"The whole damned Ring's bugged, Charlie. The desk in my office can activate and tap any vidphone in Skyfac. Four at a time, actually."

I said nothing.

"I saw you both in the air lock when you came back the last time. I saw her collapse. I saw you bringing her around. I heard her make you promise not to tell Dr. Panzarella."

I waited. Hope stirred.

He dried his face. "I came in here to tell you I was going to Panzarella, to tell him what I saw. He'd bully Carrington into sending her home right away."

"And now?" I said.

"I've seen that tape."

"And you know the *Stardance* will probably kill her?"

"Yes."

"And you know we have to let her do it?"

"Yes."

Hope died. I nodded. "Then get out of here and let me work."

He left.

On Wall Street and aboard Skyfac it was late afternoon when I finally had the tape edited to my satisfaction. I called Carrington, told him to expect me in half an hour, showered, shaved, dressed, and left.

A major of the Space Command was there with him when I arrived, but he was not introduced and so I ignored him. Shara was there too, wearing a thing made of orange smoke that left her breasts bare. Carrington had obviously made her wear it, as an urchin writes filthy words on an altar, but she wore it with a perverse and curious dignity that I sensed annoyed him. I looked her in the eye and smiled. "Hi, kid. It's a good tape."

"Let's see," Carrington said. He and the major took seats behind the desk, and Shara sat beside it.

I fed the tape into the video rig built into the office wall, dimmed the lights, and sat across from Shara. It ran twenty minutes, uninterrupted, no sound track, stark naked.

It was terrific.

"Aghast" is a funny word. To make you aghast, a thing must hit you in a place you haven't armored over with cynicism yet. I seem to have been born cynical; I have been aghast three times that I can remember. The first was when I learned, at the age of three, that there were people who could deliberately hurt kittens. The second was when I learned, at age seventeen, that there were people who could actually take LSD and then hurt other people for fun. The third was when *Mass Is a Verb* ended and Carrington said in perfectly conversational tones, "Very pleasant; very graceful. I like it," when I learned, at age forty-five, that there were men, not fools or cretins but intelligent men, who could watch Shara Drummond dance and fail to *see*. We all, even the most cynical of us, always have some illusion which we cherish.

Shara simply let it bounce off her somehow, but I could see that the major was as aghast as I, controlling his features with a visible effort.

Suddenly welcoming a distraction from my horror and dismay, I studied him more closely, wondering for the first time what he was doing here. He was my age, lean and more hard-bitten than I am, with silver fuzz on top of his skull and an extremely tidy mustache on the front. I'd taken him for a crony of Carrington's, but three things changed my mind. Something indefinable about his eyes told me that he was a military man of long combat experience. Something equally indefinable about his carriage told me that he was on duty at the moment. And something quite definable about the line his mouth made told me that he was disgusted with the duty he had drawn.

When Carrington went on, "What do you think, Major?" in polite tones, the man paused for a moment, gathering his thoughts and choosing his words. When he did speak, it was not to Carrington.

"Ms. Drummond," he said quietly, "I am Major William Cox, commander of S.C. *Champion,* and I am honored to meet you. That was the most profoundly moving thing I have ever seen."

Shara thanked him most gravely. "This is Charles Armstead, Major Cox. He made the tape."

Cox regarded me with new respect. "A magnificent job, Mr. Armstead." He stuck out his hand, and I shook it.

Carrington was beginning to understand that we three shared a thing which excluded him. "I'm glad you enjoyed it, Major," he said with no visible trace of sincerity. "You can see it again on your television tomorrow night, if you chance to be off duty. And eventually, of course, cassettes will be made available. Now perhaps we can get to the matter at hand."

Cox's face closed as if it had been zipped up, became stiffly formal. "As you wish, sir."

Puzzled, I began what I thought was the matter at hand. "I'd like your own Comm Chief to supervise the actual transmission this time, Mr. Carrington. Shara and I will be too busy to—"

"My Comm Chief will supervise the broadcast, Armstead," Carrington interrupted, "but I don't think you'll be particularly busy."

I was groggy from lack of sleep; my uptake was rather slow.

He touched his desk delicately. "McGillicuddy, report at once," he said, and released it. "You see, Armstead, you and Shara are both returning to Earth. At once."

"*What?*"

"Bryce, you *can't,*" Shara cried. "You *promised.*"

"I promised I would think about it, my dear," he corrected.

"The hell you say. That was weeks ago. Last night you *promised.*"

"Did I? My dear, there were no witnesses present last night. Altogether for the best, don't you agree?"

I was speechless with rage.

McGillicuddy entered. "Hello, Tom," Carrington said pleasantly. "You're fired. You'll be returning to Earth at once, with Ms. Drummond and Mr. Armstead, aboard Major Cox's vessel. Departure in one hour, and don't leave anything you're fond of." He glanced from McGillicuddy to me. "From Tom's desk you can tap any vidphone in Skyfac. From my desk you can tap Tom's desk."

Shara's voice was low. "Bryce, two days. God damn you, name your price."

He smiled slightly. "I'm sorry, darling. When informed of your collapse, Dr. Panzarella became most specific. Not even one more day. Alive you are a distinct plus for Skyfac's image—you are my gift to the world. Dead you are an albatross around my neck. I cannot allow you to die on my property. I anticipated that you might resist leaving, and so I spoke to a friend in the"—he glanced at Cox—"*higher* echelons of the Space Command, who was good enough to send the Major here to escort you home. You are not under arrest in the legal sense—but I assure you that you have no choice. Something like protective custody applies. Goodbye, Shara." He reached for a stack of reports on his desk, and I surprised myself considerably.

I cleared the desk entirely, tucked head catching him squarely in the sternum. His chair was belted to the deck and so it snapped clean. I recovered so well that I had time for one glorious right. Do you know how, if you punch a basketball squarely, it will bounce up from the floor? That's what his head did, in low-g slow motion.

Then Cox had hauled me to my feet and shoved me into the far corner of the room. "Don't," he said to me, and his voice must have held a lot of that "habit of command" they talk about, because it stopped me cold. I stood breathing in great gasps while Cox helped Carrington to his feet.

The millionaire felt his smashed nose, examined the blood on his fingers, and looked at me with raw hatred. "You'll never work in video again, Armstead. You're through. Finished. Un-em-ployed, you get that?"

Cox tapped him on the shoulder, and Carrington spun on him. "What the hell do you want?" he barked.

Cox smiled. "Carrington, my late father once said, 'Bill, make your enemies by choice, not by accident.' Over the years I have found that to be excellent advice. You suck."

"And not particularly well," Shara agreed.

Carrington blinked. Then his absurdly broad shoulders swelled and he roared, "Out, all of you! *Off my property at once!*"

By unspoken consent, we waited for McGillicuddy, who knew his cue. "Mr. Carrington, it is a rare privilege and a great honor to have been fired by you. I shall think of it always as a Pyrrhic defeat." And he half bowed and we left, each buoyed by a juvenile feeling of triumph that must have lasted ten seconds.

The sensation of falling that comes with zero g is literal truth, but your body quickly learns to treat it as an illusion. Now, in zero g for the last time, for the half hour before I would be back in Earth's own gravitational field, I felt I was falling. Plummeting into some bottomless gravity well, dragged down by the anvil that was my heart, the scraps of a dream that should have held me aloft fluttering overhead.

The *Champion* was three times the size of Carrington's yacht, which childishly pleased me until I recalled that he had summoned it here without paying for either fuel or crew. A guard at the air lock saluted as we entered. Cox led us to a compartment aft of the air lock where we were to strap in. He noticed along the way that I used only my left hand to pull myself along, and when we stopped he said, "Mr. Armstead, my late father also told me, 'Hit the soft parts with your hand. Hit the hard parts with a utensil.' Otherwise I can find no fault with your technique. I wish I could shake your hand."

I tried to smile, but I didn't have it in me. "I admire your taste in enemies, Major."

"A man can't ask for more. I'm afraid I can't spare time to have your hand looked at until we've grounded. We begin reentry immediately."

"Forget it."

He bowed to Shara, did *not* tell her how deeply sorry he was to et cetera, wished us all a comfortable journey, and left. We strapped into our acceleration couches to await ignition. There ensued a long and heavy silence, compounded of a mutual sadness that bravado could only have underlined. We did not look at each other, as though our combined sorrow might achieve some kind of critical mass. Grief struck us dumb, and I believe that remarkably little of it was self-pity.

But then a whole lot of time seemed to have gone by. Quite a bit of intercom chatter came faintly from the next compartment, but ours was not in circuit. At last we began to talk, desultorily, discussing the probable critical reaction to *Mass Is a Verb*, whether analysis was worthwhile or the theater really dead, anything at all except future plans. Eventually there was nothing else to talk about, so we shut up again. I guess I'd say we were in shock.

For some reason I came out of it first. "What in hell is taking them so long?" I barked irritably.

McGillicuddy started to say something soothing, then glanced at his watch and yelped. "You're right. It's been nearly an hour."

I looked at the wall clock, got hopelessly confused until I realized it was on Greenwich time rather than Wall Street, and realized he was correct. "Chrissakes," I shouted, "the whole bloody *point* of this exercise is to protect Shara from overexposure to free fall! I'm going forward."

"Charlie, hold it." McGillicuddy, with two good hands, unstrapped faster than I. "Dammit, stay right there and cool off. I'll go find out what the holdup is."

He was back in a few minutes, and his face was slack. "We're not going anywhere. Cox has orders to sit tight."

"What? Tom, what the *hell* are you talking about?"

His voice was all funny. "Red fireflies. More like bees, actually. In a balloon."

He simply *could not* be joking with me, which meant he flat out *had* to have gone completely round the bend, which meant that somehow I had blundered into my favorite nightmare where everyone but me goes crazy, and begins gibbering at me. So I lowered my head like an enraged bull, and charged out of the room so fast the door barely had time to get out of my way.

It just got worse. When I reached the door to the bridge I was going much too fast to be stopped by anything short of a body block, and the crewmen present were caught flatfooted. There was a brief flurry at the door, and then I was on the bridge, and then I decided that I had gone crazy too, which somehow made everything all right.

The forward wall of the bridge was one enormous video tank—and just enough off center to faintly irritate me, standing out against the black deep as clearly as cigarettes in a darkroom, there truly did swarm a multitude of red fireflies.

The conviction of unreality made it okay. But then Cox snapped me back to reality with a bellowed *"Off this bridge, mister."* If I'd been in a normal frame of mind it would have blown me out the door and into the farthest corner of the ship; in my current state it managed to jolt me into acceptance of the impossible situation. I shivered like a wet dog and turned to him.

"Major," I said desperately, "What is going on?"

As a king may be amused by an insolent varlet who refuses to kneel, he was bemused by the phenomenon of someone failing to obey him. It bought me an answer. "We are confronting intelligent alien life," he said concisely. "I believe them to be sentient plasmoids."

I had never for a moment believed that the mysterious object which had been leapfrogging around the solar system since I came to Skyfac was *alive.* I tried to take it in, then abandoned the task and went back to my main priority. "I don't care if they're eight tiny reindeer; you've got to get this can back to Earth *now.*"

"Sir, this vessel is on Emergency Red Alert and on Combat Standby. At this moment the suppers of everyone in North America are getting cold. I will consider myself fortunate if I ever see Earth again. Now get off my bridge."

"But you don't *understand.* Sustained free fall might kill Shara. That's what you came up here to prevent, dammit—"

*"MR. ARMSTEAD!* This is a military vessel. We are facing nearly a

dozen intelligent beings who appeared out of hyperspace near here twenty minutes ago, beings who therefore use a drive beyond my conception with no visible parts. If it makes you feel any better, I am aware that I have a passenger aboard of greater intrinsic value to my species than this ship and everyone else on her, and if it is any comfort to you this knowledge already provides a distraction I need like an auxiliary anus, and I can no more leave this orbit than I can grow horns. Now will you get off this bridge or will you be dragged?"

I didn't get a chance to decide: They dragged me.

On the other hand, by the time I got back to our compartment Cox had put our vidphone screen in circuit with the tank on the bridge. Shara and McGillicuddy were studying it with rapt attention. Having nothing better to do, I did too.

McGillicuddy had been right. They *did* act more like bees, in the swarming rapidity of their movement. It was a while before I could get an accurate count: ten of them. And they *were* in a balloon—a faint, barely tangible thing on the fine line between transparency and translucency. Though they darted like furious red gnats, it was only within the confines of the spheroid balloon—they never left it or seemed to touch its inner surface.

As I watched, the last of the adrenaline rinsed out of my kidneys, but it left a sense of frustrated urgency. I tried to grapple with the fact that these *Space Commando* special effects represented something that was— more important than Shara. It was a primevally disturbing notion, but I could not reject it.

In my mind were two voices, each hollering questions at the top of their lungs, each ignoring the other's questions. One yelled: *Are those things friendly? Or hostile? Or do they even use those concepts? How big are they? How far away? From where?* The other voice was less ambitious but just as loud: all it said, over and over again, was: *How much longer can Shara remain in free fall without dooming herself?*

Shara's voice was full of wonder. "They're . . . they're *dancing.*"

I looked closer. If there was a pattern to the flies-on-garbage swarm they made, I couldn't detect it. "Looks random to me."

"Charlie, look. All that furious activity, and they never bump into each other or the walls of that envelope they're in. They must be in orbits as carefully choreographed as those of electrons."

"Do atoms dance?"

She gave me an odd look. "Don't they, Charlie?"

"Laser beam," McGillicuddy said.

We looked at him.

"Those things have to be plasmoids—the man I talked to said they were first spotted on radar. That means they're ionized gases of some kind—the kind of thing that used to cause UFO reports." He giggled, then caught himself. "If you could slice through that envelope with a laser, I'll bet you could deionize them pretty good—besides, that envelope has to hold their life support, whatever it is they metabolize."

I was dizzy. "Then we're not defenseless?"

"You're both talking like soldiers," Shara burst out. "I tell you they're dancing. Dancers aren't fighters."

"Come on, Shara," I barked. "Even if those things happen to be remotely like us, that's not true. Samurai, karate, kung fu—they're dance." I nodded to the screen. "All we know about these animated embers is that they travel interstellar space. That's enough to scare me."

"Charlie, look at them," she commanded.

I did.

By God, they didn't look threatening. They did, the more I watched, seem to move in a dancelike way, whirling in mad adagios just too fast for the eye to follow. Not like conventional dance—more analogous to what Shara had begun with *Mass Is a Verb*. I found myself wanting to switch to another camera for contrast of perspective, and that made my mind start to wake up at last. Two ideas surfaced, the second one necessary in order to sell Cox the first.

"How far do you suppose we are from Skyfac?" I asked McGillicuddy.

He pursed his lips. "Not far. There hasn't been much more than maneuvering acceleration. The damn things were probably attracted to Skyfac in the first place—it must be the most easily visible sign of intelligent life in this system." He grimaced. "Maybe they don't *use* planets."

I reached forward and punched the audio circuit. "Major Cox."

*"Get off this circuit."*

"How would you like a closer view of those things?"

"We're staying put. Now stop jiggling my elbow and get off this circuit or I'll—"

"Will you listen to me? I have four mobile cameras in space, remote-control, self-contained power source and light, and better resolution than you've got. They were set up to tape Shara's next dance."

He shifted gears at once. "Can you patch them into my ship?"

"I think so. But I'll have to get back to the master board in Ring One."

"No good, then. I can't tie myself to a top—what if I have to fight or run?"

"Major—how far a walk is it?"

It startled him a bit. "A mile or two, as the crow flies. But you're a groundlubber."

"I've been in free fall for most of two months. Give me a portable radar and I can ground on Phobos."

"Mmmm. You're a civilian—but dammit, I need better video. Permission granted."

Now for the first idea. "Wait—one thing more. Shara and Tom must come with me."

"Nuts. This isn't a field trip."

"Major Cox—Shara *must* return to a gravity field as quickly as possible. Ring One'll do—in fact, it'd be ideal, if we can enter through the 'spoke' in the center. She can descend very slowly and acclimatize gradually, the way a diver decompresses in stages, but in reverse. McGillicuddy will have to come along to stay with her—if she passes out and falls down the tube, she could break a leg even in one-sixth g. Besides, he's better at EVA than either of us."

He thought it over. "Go."

We went.

The trip back to Ring One was far longer than any Shara or I had ever made, but under McGillicuddy's guidance we made it with minimal maneuvering. Ring, *Champion,* and aliens formed an equiangular triangle about a mile and a half on a side. Seen in perspective, the aliens took up about as much volume as Shea Stadium. They did not pause or slacken in their mad gyration, but somehow they seemed to watch us cross the gap to Skyfac. I got an impression of a biologist studying the strange antics of a new species. We kept our suit radios off to avoid distraction, and it made me just a little bit more susceptible to suggestion.

I left McGillicuddy with Shara and dropped down the tube six rings at a time. Carrington was waiting for me in the reception room, with two flunkies. It was plain to see that he was scared silly, and trying to cover it with anger. "Goddammit, Armstead, those are my bloody cameras."

"Shut up, Carrington. If you put those cameras in the hands of the best technician available—me—and if I put their data in the hands of the best strategic mind in space—Cox—we *might* be able to save your damned factory for you. And the human race for the rest of us." I moved forward, and he got out of my way. It figured. Putting all humanity in danger might just be bad PR.

After all the practicing I'd done, it wasn't hard to direct four mobile cameras through space simultaneously by eye. The aliens ignored their approach. The Skyfac comm crew fed my signals to the *Champion* and patched me in to Cox on audio. At his direction I bracketed the balloon with the cameras, shifting POV at his command. Space Command Headquarters must have recorded the video, but I couldn't hear their conversation with Cox, for which I was grateful. I gave him slow-motion replay, close-ups, split screens—everything at my disposal. The movements of individual fireflies did not appear particularly symmetrical, but patterns began to repeat. In slow motion they looked more than ever as though they were dancing, and although I couldn't be sure, it seemed to me that they were increasing their tempo. Somehow the dramatic tension of their dance seemed to build.

And then I shifted POV to the camera which included Skyfac in the background, and my heart turned to hard vacuum and I screamed in pure primal terror—halfway between Ring One and the swarm of aliens, coming up on them slowly but inexorably, was a p-suited figure that had to be Shara.

With theatrical timing, McGillicuddy appeared in the doorway, leaning heavily on the chief engineer, his face drawn with pain. He stood on one foot, the other leg plainly broken.

"Guess I can't . . . go back to exhibition work . . . after all," he gasped. "Said . . . 'I'm sorry, Tom' . . . knew she was going to swing on me . . . wiped me out anyhow. Oh, dammit, Charlie, I'm sorry." He sank into an empty chair.

Cox's voice came urgently. "What the hell is going on? Who is that?"

She *had* to be on our frequency. "Shara!" I screamed. "Get your ass back in here!"

"I can't, Charlie." Her voice was startlingly loud, and very calm. "Halfway down the tube my chest started to hurt like hell."

"Ms. Drummond," Cox rapped, "if you approach any closer to the aliens I will destroy you."

She laughed, a merry sound that froze my blood. "Bullshit, Major. You aren't about to get gay with laser beams near those things. Besides, you need me as much as you do Charlie."

"What do you mean?"

"These creatures communicate by dance. It's their equivalent of speech, it has to be a sophisticated kind of sign language, like hula."

"You can't know that."

"I *feel* it. I know it. Hell, how else do you communicate in airless space? Major Cox, I am the only qualified interpreter the human race has at the moment. Now will you kindly shut up so I can try to learn their 'language'?"

"I have no authority to—"

I said an extraordinary thing. I should have been gibbering, pleading with Shara to come back, even racing for a p-suit to *bring* her back. Instead I said, "She's right. Shut up, Cox."

"What are you trying to do?"

"Damn you, *don't waste her last effort.*"

He shut up.

Panzarella came in, shot McGillicuddy full of painkiller, and set his leg right there in the room, but I was oblivious. For over an hour I watched Shara watch the aliens. I watched them myself, in the silence of utter despair, and for the life of me I could not follow their dance. I strained my mind, trying to suck meaning from their crazy whirling, and failed. The best I could do to aid Shara was to record everything that happened, for a hypothetical posterity. Several times she cried out softly, small muffled exclamations, and I ached to call out to her in reply, but did not. With the last exclamation, she used her thrusters to bring her closer to the alien swarm, and hung there for a long time.

At last her voice came over the speaker, thick and slurred at first, as though she were talking in her sleep. "God, Charlie. Strange. So strange. I'm beginning to read them."

"How?"

"Every time I begin to understand a part of the dance, it . . . it brings us closer. Not telepathy, exactly. I just . . . know them better. Maybe it is telepathy, I don't know. By dancing what they feel, they give it enough intensity to make me understand. I'm getting about one concept in three. It's stronger up close."

Cox's voice was gentle but firm. "What have you learned, Shara?"

"That Tom and Charlie were right. They are warlike. At least there's a flavor of arrogance to them—conviction of superiority. Their dance is a challenging, a dare. Tell Tom they *do* use planets."

"What?"

"I think at one stage of their development they're corporeal, planetbound. Then when they have matured sufficiently, they . . . become these fireflies, like caterpillars becoming butterflies, and head out into space."

"Why?" from Cox.

"To find spawning grounds. They want Earth."

There was a silence lasting perhaps ten seconds. Then Cox spoke up quietly. "Back away, Shara. I'm going to see what lasers will do to them."

"No!" she cried, loud enough to make a really first-rate speaker distort.

"Shara, as Charlie pointed out to me, you are not only expendable, you are for all practical purposes expended."

"No!" This time it was me shouting.

"Major," Shara said urgently, "that's not the way. Believe me, they can dodge or withstand anything you or Earth can throw at them. I *know*."

"Hell and damnation, woman," Cox said, "what do you want me to do? Let them have the first shot? There are vessels from four countries on their way right now."

"Major, wait. Give me time."

He began to swear, then cut off. "How much time?"

She made no direct reply. "If only this telepathy thing works in reverse . . . it must. I'm no more strange to them than they are to me. Probably less so; I get the idea they've been around. Charlie?"

"Yeah."

"This is a take."

I knew. I had known since I first saw her in open space on my monitor. And I knew what she needed now, from the faint trembling of her voice. It took everything I had, and I was only glad I had it to give. With extremely realistic good cheer, I said, "Break a leg, kid," and killed my mike before she could hear the sob that followed.

And she danced.

It began slowly, the equivalent of one-finger exercises, as she sought to establish a vocabulary of motion that the creatures could comprehend. *Can you see,* she seemed to say, *that* this *movement is a reaching, a yearning? Do you see that* this *is a spurning,* this *an unfolding, that a graduated elision of energy? Do you feel the ambiguity in the way I distort this arabesque, or that the tension can be resolved* so?

And it seemed that Shara was right, that they had infinitely more experience with disparate cultures than we, for they were superb linguists of motion. It occurred to me later that perhaps they had selected motion for communication because of its very universality. At any rate, as Shara's dance began to build, their own began to slow down perceptibly in speed and intensity, until at last they hung motionless in space, watching her.

Soon after that Shara must have decided that she had sufficiently defined her terms, at least well enough for pidgin communication—for now she began to dance in earnest. Before, she had used only her own muscles and the shifting masses of her limbs. Now she added thrusters, singly and in combination, moving within as well as in space. Her dance became a true dance: more than a collection of motions, a thing of substance and meaning. It was unquestionably the *Stardance,* just as she had choreographed it, as she had always intended to dance it. That it had something to say to utterly alien creatures, of man and his nature, was not at all a coincidence: It was the essential and ultimate statement of the greatest artist of her age, and it had something to say to God himself.

The camera lights struck silver from her p-suit, gold from the twin air tanks on her shoulders. To and fro against the black backdrop of space, she wove the intricacies of her dance, a leisurely movement that seemed somehow to leave echoes behind it. And the meaning of these great loops and whirls slowly became clear, drying my throat and clamping my teeth.

For her dance spoke of nothing more and nothing less than the tragedy of being alive, and being human. It spoke, most eloquently, of pain. It spoke, most knowingly, of despair. It spoke of the cruel humor of limitless ambition yoked to limited ability, of eternal hope invested in an ephemeral lifetime, of the driving need to try and create an inexorably predetermined future. It spoke of fear, and of hunger, and, most clearly, of the basic loneliness and alienation of the human animal. It described the universe through the eyes of man: a hostile environment, the embodiment of entropy, into which we are all thrown alone, forbidden by our nature to touch another mind save secondhand, by proxy. It spoke of the blind perversity which forces man to strive hugely for a peace which, once attained, becomes boredom. And it spoke of folly, of the terrible paradox by which man is simultaneously capable of reason and unreason, forever unable to cooperate even with himself.

It spoke of Shara and her life.

Again and again, cyclical statements of hope began, only to collapse into confusion and ruin. Again and again, cascades of energy strove for resolution, and found only frustration. All at once she launched into a pattern that seemed familiar, and in moments I recognized it: the closing movement of *Mass Is a Verb* recapitulated—not repeated but reprised, echoed, the Three Questions given a more terrible urgency by this new altar on which they were piled. And as before, it segued into that final relentless contraction, that ultimate drawing-inward of all energies. Her body became derelict, abandoned, drifting in space, the essence of her being withdrawn to her center and invisible.

The quiescent aliens stirred for the first time.

And suddenly she exploded, blossoming from her contraction not as a spring uncoils, but as a flower bursts from a seed. The force of her release flung her through the void as though she were tossed like a gull in a hurricane by galactic winds. Her center appeared to hurl itself through space and time, yanking her body into a new dance.

And the new dance said, *This is what it is to be human: to see the essential existential futility of all action, all striving—and to act, to strive. This is what it is to be human: to reach forever beyond your grasp. This is what it is to be human: to live forever or die trying. This is what it is to be human: to perpetually ask the unanswerable questions, in the hope that the asking of them will somehow hasten the day when they will be answered. This is what it is to be human: to strive in the face of the certainty of failure.*

*This is what it is to be human: to persist.*

It said all this with a soaring series of cyclical movements that held all the rolling majesty of grand symphony, as uniquely different from each other as snowflakes, and as similar. And the new dance *laughed,* and it laughed as much at tomorrow as it did at yesterday, and it laughed most of all at today.

*For this is what it means to be human: to laugh at what another would call tragedy.*

The aliens seemed to recoil from the ferocious energy, startled, awed, and faintly terrified by Shara's indomitable spirit. They seemed to wait for her dance to wane, for her to exhaust herself, and her laughter sounded on my speaker as she redoubled her efforts, became a pinwheel, a Catherine wheel. She changed the focus of her dance, began to dance *around* them, in pyrotechnic spatters of motion that came ever closer to the intangible spheroid which contained them. They cringed inward from her, huddling together in the center of the envelope, not so much physically threatened as cowed.

*This,* said her body, *is what it means to be human: to commit hara-kiri, with a smile, if it becomes needful.*

And before that terrible assurance, the aliens broke. Without warning fireflies and balloon vanished, gone, *elsewhere.*

I know that Cox and McGillicuddy were still alive, because I saw them afterward, and that means they were probably saying and doing things in my hearing and presence, but I neither heard nor saw them then; they were as dead to me as everything except Shara. I called out her name, and she approached the camera that was lit, until I could make out her face behind the plastic hood of her p-suit.

"We may be puny, Charlie," she puffed, gasping for breath. "But by Jesus we're tough."

"Shara—come on in now."

"You know I can't."

"Carrington'll *have* to give you a free-fall place to live now."

"A life of exile? For what? To dance? Charlie, *I haven't got anything more to say.*"

"Then I'll come out there."

"Don't be silly. Why? So you can hug a p-suit? Tenderly bump hoods one last time? Balls. It's a good exit so far—let's not blow it."

"*Shara!*" I broke completely, just caved in on myself and collapsed in great racking sobs.

"Charlie, listen now," she said softly, but with an urgency that reached me even in my despair. "Listen now, for I haven't much time. I have something to give you. I hoped you'd find it for yourself, but . . . will you listen?"

"Y—yes."

"Charlie, zero-g dance is going to get awful popular all of a sudden. I've opened the door. But you know how fads are, they'll bitch it all up unless you move fast. I'm leaving it in your hands."

"What . . . what are you talking about?"

"About you, Charlie. You're going to dance again."

Oxygen starvation, I thought. But she can't be that low on air already. "Okay. Sure thing."

"For God's sake stop humoring me—I'm straight, I tell you. You'd have seen it yourself if you weren't so damned stupid. Don't you understand? *There's nothing wrong with your leg in free fall!*"

My jaw dropped.

"Do you hear me, Charlie? You can dance again!"

"No," I said, and searched for a reason why not. "I . . . you can't . . . it's . . . dammit, the leg's not strong enough for inside work."

"Forget for the moment that inside work'll be less than half of what you do. Forget it and remember that smack in the nose you gave Carrington. Charlie, when you leaped over the desk, *you pushed off with your right leg.*"

I sputtered for a while and shut up.

"There you go, Charlie. My farewell gift. You know I've never been in love with you . . . but you must know that I've always loved you. Still do."

"I love you, Shara."

"So long, Charlie. Do it right."

And all four thrusters went off at once. I watched her go down. A while after she was too far to see, there was a long golden flame that arced above the face of the globe, waned, and then flared again as the air tanks went up.

There's a tired old hack plot about the threat of alien invasion unifying mankind overnight. It's about as realistic as Love Will Find a Way— if those damned fireflies ever come back, they'll find us just as disorganized as we were the last time. There you go.

Carrington, of course, tried to grab all the tapes and all the money— but neither Shara nor I had ever signed a contract, and her will was most explicit. So he tried to buy the judge, and he picked the wrong judge, and when it hit the papers and he saw how public and private opinion were going, he left Skyfac in a p-suit with no thrusters. I think he wanted to go the same way she had, but he was unused to EVA and let go too late. He was last seen heading in the general direction of Betelgeuse. The Skyfac board of directors picked a new man who was most anxious to wash off the stains, and he offered me continued use of all facilities.

And so I talked it over with Norrey, and she was free, and that's how the Shara Drummond Company of New Modern Dance was formed. We specialize in good dancers who couldn't cut it on Earth for one reason or another, and there are a surprising hell of a lot of them.

I enjoy dancing with Norrey. Together we're not as good as Shara was alone—but we mesh well. In spite of the obvious contraindications, I think our marriage is going to work.

That's the thing about us humans: We persist.

# Joan D. Vinge

Maybe it's time to talk about women. (When isn't it time?)

In Hugo Winners, Volume One, the nine stories that were included were written by nine males, and I don't remember, at the time, being surprised at that. Sure, there were competent and well-thought-of women writers—Judith Merril springs to mind—but somehow such was the casual sexist attitude within science fiction that the field was accepted by one and all as primarily of interest to males. Women who wrote science fiction, or even merely read it, were considered somewhat anomalous.

Of the fourteen stories in Volume Two, one was written by a woman, Anne McCaffrey. Of the fifteen stories in Volume Three, two were written by Ursula K. Le Guin and one was written by James Tiptree, Jr., who, it turned out, was a woman.

Le Guin was, in my opinion, the breakthrough. For the first time, people began to speak of a woman as a first-magnitude star without any trace of condescension whatever. She could bear comparison with any male writer whatever. For a while there, I could actually feel the foundations of the Big Three tremble as she moved up to fourth place in some reader polls, and I covered my eyes waiting for the crash.

In Volume Four, we already have three women represented, three different women—James Tiptree, Jr. (again), Jeanne Robinson, and now Joan D. Vinge, making her first appearance. I promise you that before this volume is done there will be a fourth woman.

Mind you, we are not talking merely about the increasing number of women writers of science fiction; we are talking about the increasing number of Hugo-winning women writers of science fiction.

All this is a consummation devoutly to be wished (to put it in my own words).

For one thing, I have a personal sin I can never adequately atone for. One of my most embarrassing memories concerns my anti-feminist stance as a teenager. (Many teenage boys, especially those who feel totally inadequate with respect to teenage girls—as I did—compensate by developing a feeling of lordly superiority to these creatures they both long for and fear.) I remember writing teenage letters to *Astounding Science Fiction* denouncing the mere appearance of women in science fiction stories, and I even think that John Campbell may have carelessly printed one.

I have changed since. My fear of women vanished abruptly with my teens. I now get along with them easily and well, and I am a convinced feminist. I believe that the entrance of more and more women writers into the field will broaden and strengthen science fiction, give it added dimensions and delight, and be, in every way, a good thing.

To be sure, there are still differences. Women writers, I think, tend to avoid hard science fiction more than men do, but that is the same cultural phenomenon that pushes professional women into law and real estate rather than into science; and women who *do* enter science go into biology rather than into physics. It arises out of a supposed feminine distaste for mathematics, which I firmly believe is culturally induced and can be made to vanish with time.

# EYES OF AMBER

The beggar woman shuffled up the silent evening street to the rear of Lord Chwiul's town house. She hesitated, peering up at the softly glowing towers, then clawed at the watchman's arm. "A word with you, master—"

"Don't touch me, hag!" The guard raised his spear butt in disgust.

A deft foot kicked free of the rags and snagged him off balance. He found himself sprawled on his back in the spring melt, the spear tip dropping toward his belly, guided by a new set of hands. He gaped, speechless. The beggar tossed an amulet onto his chest.

"Look at it, fool! I have business with your lord." The beggar woman stepped back, the spear tip tapped him impatiently.

The guard squirmed in the filth and wet, holding the amulet up close to his face in the poor light. "You . . . you are the one? You may pass—"

"Indeed!" Muffled laughter. "Indeed I may pass—for many things, in many places. The Wheel of Change carries us all." She lifted the spear. "Get up, fool . . . and no need to escort me, I'm expected."

The guard climbed to his feet, dripping and sullen, and stood back while she freed her wing membranes from the folds of cloth. He watched them glisten and spread as she gathered herself to leap effortlessly to the tower's entrance, twice his height above. He waited until she had vanished inside before he even dared to curse her.

"Lord Chwiul?"

"T'uupieh, I presume." Lord Chwiul leaned forward on the couch of fragrant mosses, peering into the shadows of the hall.

"*Lady* T'uupieh." T'uupieh strode forward into light, letting the ragged hood slide back from her face. She took a fierce pleasure in making no show of obeisance, in coming forward directly as nobility to nobility. The sensuous ripple of a hundred tiny *miih* hides underfoot made her callused feet tingle. *After so long, it comes back too easily . . .*

She chose the couch across the low, waterstone table from him, stretching languidly in her beggar's rags. She extended a finger claw and picked a juicy *kelet* berry from the bowl in the table's scroll-carven surface; let it slide into her mouth and down her throat, as she had done so often, so long ago. And then, at last, she glanced up, to measure his outrage.

"You dare to come to me in this manner—"

Satisfactory. *Yes, very . . .* "I did not come to you. You came to me . . . you sought my services." Her eyes wandered the room with affected casualness, taking in the elaborate frescoes that surfaced the waterstone walls even in this small, private room . . . particularly in this room? she wondered. How many midnight meetings, for what varied intrigues, were held in this room? Chwiul was not the wealthiest of his family or clan: and appearances of wealth and power counted in this city, in this world—for wealth and power were everything.

"I sought the services of T'uupieh the Assassin. I'm surprised to find that the Lady T'uupieh dared to accompany her here." Chwiul had regained his composure; she watched his breath frost, and her own, as he spoke.

"Where one goes, the other follows. We are inseparable. You should know that better than most, my lord." She watched his long, pale arm extend to spear several berries at once. Even though the nights were chill he wore only a body-wrapping tunic, which let him display the intricate scaling of jewels that danced and spiraled over his wing surfaces.

He smiled; she saw the sharp fangs protrude slightly. "Because my brother made the one into the other, when he seized your lands? I'm surprised you would come at all—how did you know you could trust me?" His movements were ungraceful; she remembered how the jewels dragged down fragile, translucent wing membranes and slender arms, until flight was impossible. Like every noble, Chwiul was normally surrounded by servants who answered his every whim. Incompetence, feigned or real, was one more trapping of power, one more indulgence that only the rich could afford. She was pleased that the jewels were not of high quality.

"I don't trust you," she said, "I trust only myself. But I have friends, who told me you were sincere enough—in this case. And of course, I did not come alone."

"Your outlaws?" Disbelief. "That would be no protection."

Calmly she separated the folds of cloth that held her secret companion at her side.

"It is true," Chwiul trilled softly. "They call you Demon's Consort!"

She turned the amber lens of the demon's precious eye so that it could see the room, as she had seen it, and then settled its gaze on Chwiul. He drew back slightly, fingering moss.

" 'A demon has a thousand eyes, and a thousand thousand torments for those who offend it.' " She quoted from the Book of Ngoss, whose rituals she had used to bind the demon to her.

Chwiul stretched nervously, as if he wanted to fly away. But he only said, "Then I think we understand each other. And I think I have made a good choice: I know how well you have served the Overlord, and other court members . . . I want you to kill someone for me."

"Obviously."

"I want you to kill Klovhiri."

T'uupieh started, very slightly. "You surprise me in return, Lord Chwiul. Your own brother?" *And the usurper of my lands. How I have ached to kill him, slowly, so slowly, with my own hands. . . . But always he is too well guarded.*

"And your sister too—my lady." Faint overtones of mockery. "I want his whole family eliminated; his mate, his children . . ."

Klovhiri . . . and Ahtseet. Ahtseet, her own younger sister, who had been her closest companion since childhood, her only family since their parents had died. Ahtseet, whom she had cherished and protected; dear, conniving, traitorous little Ahtseet—who could forsake pride and decency and family honor to mate willingly with the man who had robbed them of everything . . . Anything to keep the family lands, Ahtseet had shrilled; anything to keep her position. But that was not the way! Not by surrendering; but by striking back—T'uupieh became aware that Chwiul was watching her reaction with unpleasant interest. She fingered the dagger at her belt.

"Why?" She laughed, wanting to ask, *"How?"*

"That should be obvious. I'm tired of coming second. I want what he has—your lands, and all the rest. I want him out of my way, and I don't want anyone else left with a better claim to his inheritance than I have."

"Why not do it yourself? Poison them, perhaps . . . it's been done before."

"No. Klovhiri has too many friends, too many loyal clansmen, too much influence with the Overlord. It has to be an 'accidental' murder. And no one would be better suited than you, my lady, to do it for me."

T'uupieh nodded vaguely, assessing. No one could be better chosen for a desire to succeed than she . . . and also, for a position from which to strike. All she had lacked until now was the opportunity. From the time she had been dispossessed, through the fading days of autumn and the endless winter—for nearly a third of her life now—she had haunted the wild swamp and fenland of her estate. She had gathered a few faithful servants, a few malcontents, a few cutthroats, to harry and murder Klovhiri's retainers, ruin his phib nets, steal from his snares and poach her own game. And for survival, she had taken to robbing whatever travelers took the roads that passed through her lands.

Because she was still nobility, the Overlord had at first tolerated, and then secretly encouraged, her banditry: Many wealthy foreigners traveled the routes that crossed her estate, and for a certain commission, he allowed her to attack them with impunity. It was a sop, she knew, thrown to her because he had let his favorite, Klovhiri, have her lands. But she used it to curry what favor she could, and after a time the Overlord had begun to bring her more discreet and profitable business —the elimination of certain enemies. And so she had become an assassin as well—and found that the calling was not so very different from that of noble: both required nerve, and cunning, and an utter lack of compunction. And because she was T'uupieh, she had succeeded admirably. But because of her vendetta, the rewards had been small . . . until now.

"You do not answer," Chwiul was saying. "Does that mean your nerve fails you, in kith-murder, where mine does not?"

She laughed sharply. "That you say it proves twice that your judgment is poorer than mine. . . . No, my nerve does not fail me. Indeed, my blood burns with desire! But I hadn't thought to lay Klovhiri under the ice just to give my lands to his brother. Why should I do that favor for you?"

"Because obviously you cannot do it alone. Klovhiri hasn't managed to have you killed, in all the time you've plagued him; which is a testament to your skill. But you've made him too wary—you can't get near him, when he keeps himself so well protected. You need the cooperation of someone who has his trust—someone like myself. I can make him yours."

"And what will be my reward, if I accept? Revenge is sweet; but revenge is not enough."

"I will pay what you ask."

"My estate." She smiled.

"Even you are not so naïve—"

"No." She stretched a wing toward nothing in the air. "I am not so naïve. I know its value . . ." The memory of a golden-clouded summer's day caught her—of soaring, soaring, on the warm updrafts above the streaming lake . . . seeing the fragile rose-red of the manor towers spearing light far off above the windswept tide of the trees . . . the saffron and crimson and aquamarine of ammonia pools, bright with dissolved metals, that lay in the gleaming melt-surface of her family's land, the land that stretched forever, like the summer . . . "I know its value." Her voice hardened. "And that Klovhiri is still the Overlord's pet. As you say, Klovhiri has many powerful friends, and they will become your friends when he dies. I need more strength, more wealth, before I can buy enough influence to hold what is mine again. The odds are not in my favor—now."

"You are carved from ice, T'uupieh. I like that." Chwiul leaned forward. His amorphous red eyes moved along her outstretched body; trying to guess what lay concealed beneath the rags in the shadowy foxfire-light of the room. His eyes came back to her face.

She showed him neither annoyance nor amusement. "I like no man who likes that in me."

"Not even if it meant regaining your estate?"

"As a mate of yours?" Her voice snapped like a frozen branch. "My lord—I have just about decided to kill my sister for doing as much. I would sooner kill myself."

He shrugged, lying back on the couch. "As you wish . . ." He waved a hand in dismissal. "Then what will it take to be rid of my brother—and of you as well?"

"Ah." She nodded, understanding more. "You wish to buy my services, and to buy me off, too. That may not be so easy to do. But—" *But I will make the pretense, for now.* She speared berries from the bowl in the tabletop, watched the silky sheet of emerald-tinted ammonia water that curtained one wall. It dropped from heights within the tower into a tiny plunge basin, with a music that would blur conversation for anyone who tried to listen outside. Discretion, and beauty. . . . The musky fragrance of the mossy couch brought back her childhood suddenly, disconcertingly: the memory of lying in a soft bed, on a soft spring night. . . . "But as the seasons change, change moves me in new directions. Back into the city, perhaps. I like your tower, Lord Chwiul. It combines discretion and beauty."

"Thank you."

"Give it to me, and I'll do what you ask."

Chwiul sat up, frowning. "My town house!" Recovering, "Is that all you want?"

She spread her fingers, studied the vestigial webbing between them. "I realize it is rather modest." She closed her hand. "But considering what satisfaction will come from earning it, it will suffice. And you will not need it, once I succeed."

"No . . ." He relaxed somewhat. "I suppose not. I will scarcely miss it after I have your lands."

She let it pass. "Well then, we are agreed. Now, tell me, where is the key to Klovhiri's lock? What is your plan for delivering him—and his family—into my hands?"

"You are aware that your sister and the children are visiting here, in my house, tonight? And that Klovhiri will return before the new day?"

"I am aware." She nodded, with more casualness than she felt; seeing that Chwiul was properly, if silently, impressed at her nerve in coming here. She drew her dagger from its sheath beside the demon's amber eye and stroked the serrated blade of waterstone-impregnated wood. "You wish me to slit their throats, while they sleep under your very roof?" She managed the right blend of incredulity.

"No!" Chwiul frowned again. "What sort of fool do you—" He broke off. "With the new day, they will be returning to the estate by the usual route. I have promised to escort them, to ensure their safety along the way. There will also be a guide, to lead us through the bogs. But the guide will make a mistake . . ."

"And I will be waiting." T'uupieh's eyes brightened. During the winter the wealthy used sledges for travel on long journeys—preferring to be borne over the frozen melt by membranous sails, or dragged by slaves where the surface of the ground was rough and crumpled. But as spring came and the surface of the ground began to dissolve, treacherous sinks and pools opened like blossoms to swallow the unwary. Only an experienced guide could read the surfaces, tell sound waterstone from changeable ammonia-water melt. "Good," she said softly. "Yes, very good. . . . Your guide will see them safely foundered in some slushhole, and then I will snare them like changeling phibs."

"Exactly. But I want to be there when you do; I want to watch. I'll make some excuse to leave the group, and meet you in the swamp. The guide will mislead them only if he hears my signal."

"As you wish. You've paid well for the privilege. But come alone. My followers need no help, and no interference." She sat up, let her long, webbed feet down to rest again on the sensuous hides of the rug.

"And if you think that I'm a fool, and playing into your hands myself, consider this. You will be the obvious suspect when Klovhiri is murdered. I'll be the only witness who can swear to the Overlord that your outlaws weren't the attackers. Keep that in mind."

She nodded. "I will."

"How will I find you, then?"

"You will not. My thousand eyes will find you." She rewrapped the demon's eye in its pouch of rags.

Chwiul looked vaguely disconcerted. "Will—*it* take part in the attack?"

"It may, or it may not; as it chooses. Demons are not bound to the Wheel of Change like you and me. But you will surely meet it face to face—although it has no face—if you come." She brushed the pouch at her side. "Yes—do keep in mind that I have my safeguards too in this agreement. A demon never forgets."

She stood up at last, gazing once more around the room. "I shall be comfortable here." She glanced back at Chwiul. "I will look for you, come the new day."

"Come the new day." He rose, his jeweled wings catching light.

"No need to escort me. I shall be discreet." She bowed, as an equal, and started toward the shadowed hall. "I shall definitely get rid of your watchman. He doesn't know a lady from a beggar."

"The Wheel turns once more for me, my demon. My life in the swamps will end with Klovhiri's life. I shall move into town . . . and I shall be lady of my manor again, when the fishes sit in the trees!"

T'uupieh's alien face glowed with malevolent joy as she turned away, on the display screen above the computer terminal. Shannon Wyler leaned back in his seat, finished typing his translation, and pulled off the wire headset. He smoothed his long, blond, slicked-back hair, the habitual gesture helping him reorient to his surroundings. When T'uupieh spoke he could never maintain the objectivity he needed to help him remember he was still on Earth, and not really on Titan, orbiting Saturn, some fifteen hundred million kilometers away. *T'uupieh, whenever I think I love you, you decide to cut somebody's throat. . . .*

He nodded vaguely at the congratulatory murmurs of the staff and technicians, who literally hung on his every word waiting for new information. They began to thin out behind him, as the computer reproduced copies of the transcript. Hard to believe he'd been doing this for over a year now. He looked up at his concert posters on the wall, with nostalgia but no regret.

Someone was phoning Marcus Reed: he sighed, resigned.

" 'Ven the fishes sit in the trees'? Are you being sarcastic?"

He looked over his shoulder at Dr. Garda Bach's massive form. "Hi, Garda. Didn't hear you come in."

She glanced up from a copy of the translation, tapped him lightly on the shoulder with her forked walking stick. "I know, dear boy. You never hear anything when T'uupieh speaks. But what do you mean by this?"

"On Titan that's summer—when the triphibians metamorphose for the third time. So she means maybe five years from now, our time."

"Ah! Of course. The old brain is not what it was . . ." She shook her gray-white head; her black cloak swirled out melodramatically.

He grinned, knowing she didn't mean a word of it. "Maybe learning Titanese on top of fifty other languages is the straw that breaks the camel's back."

"*Ja . . . ja . . .* maybe it is . . ." She sank heavily into the next seat over, already lost in the transcript. He had never, he thought, expected to like the old broad so well. He had become aware of her Presence while he studied linguistics at Berkeley—she was the *grande dame* of linguistic studies, dating back to the days when there had still been unrecorded languages here on Earth. But her skill at getting her name in print and her face on television, as an expert on what everybody "really meant," had convinced him that her true talent lay in merchandising. Meeting her at last, in person, hadn't changed his mind about that; but it had convinced him forever that she knew her stuff about cultural linguistics. And that, in turn, had convinced him her accent was a total fraud. But despite the flamboyance, or maybe even because of it, he found that her now-archaic views on linguistics were much closer to his own feelings about communication than the views of either one of his parents.

Garda sighed. "Remarkable, Shannon! You are simply remarkable—your feel for a wholly alien language amazes me. Whatever vould ve have done if you had not come to us?"

"Done without, I expect." He savored the special pleasure that came of being admired by someone he respected. He looked down again at the computer console, at the two shining green-lit plates of plastic thirty centimeters on a side that together gave him the versatility of a virtuoso violinist and a typist with a hundred thousand keys: His link to T'uupieh, his voice—the new IBM synthesizer, whose touch-sensitive control plates could be manipulated to re-create the impossible complexities of her language. God's gift to the world of linguistics . . . except that it required the sensitivity and inspiration of a musician to fully use its range.

He glanced up again and out the window, at the now familiar fog-shrouded skyline of Coos Bay. Since very few linguists were musicians, their resistance to the synthesizer had been like a brick wall. The old guard of the aging New Wave—which included His Father the Professor and His Mother the Communications Engineer—still clung to a fruitless belief in mathematical computer translation. They still struggled with ungainly programs weighed down by endless morpheme lists that supposedly would someday generate any message in a given language. But even after years of refinement, computer-generated translations were still uselessly crude and sloppy.

At graduate school there had been no new languages to seek out, and no permission for him to use the synthesizer to explore the old ones. And so—after a final, bitter family argument—he had quit graduate school. He had taken his belief in the synthesizer into the world of his second love, music; into a field where, he hoped, real communication still had some value. Now, at twenty-four, he was Shann the Music Man, the musician's musician, a hero to an immense generation of aging fans and a fresh new generation that had inherited their love for the ever-changing music called "rock." And neither of his parents had willingly spoken to him in years.

"No false modesty," Garda was chiding. "What could we have done without you? You yourself have complained enough about your mother's methods. You know we would not have a tenth of the information about Titan we've gained from T'uupieh if she had gone on using that damned computer translation."

Shannon frowned faintly, at the sting of secret guilt. "Look, I know I've made some cracks—and I meant most of them—but I'd never have gotten off the ground if she hadn't done all the preliminary analysis before I even came." His mother had already been on the mission staff, having worked for years at NASA on the esoterics of computer communication with satellites and space probes; and because of her linguistic background, she had been made head of the newly pulled-together staff of communications specialists by Marcus Reed, the Titan project director. She had been in charge of the initial phonic analysis, using the computer to compress the alien voice range into one audible to humans, then breaking up the complex sounds into more, and simpler, human phones . . . she had identified phonemes, separated morphemes, fitted them into a grammatical framework, and assigned English sound equivalents to it all. Shannon had watched her on the early TB interviews, looking unhappy and ill at ease while Reed held court for the spellbound press. But what Dr. Wyler the Communications Engineer had had to say, at last, had held them on the edge of his seat; and unable to resist, he had taken the next plane to Coos Bay.

"Vell, I meant no offense," Garda said. "Your mother is obviously a skilled engineer. But she needs a little more—flexibility."

"You're telling me." He nodded ruefully. "She'd still love to see the synthesizer drop through the floor. She's been out of joint ever since I got here. At least Reed appreciates my 'value.' " Reed had welcomed him like a long-lost son when he first arrived at the institute. . . . Wasn't he a skilled linguist as well as an inspired musician, didn't he have some time between gigs, wouldn't he like to extend his visit, and get an insider's view of his mother's work? He had agreed, modestly, to all three—and then the television cameras and reporters had sprung up as if on cue, and he understood clearly enough that they were not there to record the visit of Dr. Wyler's kid, but Shann the Music Man.

But he had gotten his first session with a voice from another world. And with one hearing, he had become an addict . . . because their speech was music. Every phoneme was formed of two or three super-posed sounds, and every morpheme was a blend of phonemes, flowing together like water. They spoke in chords, and the result was a choir, crystal bells ringing, the shattering of glass chandeliers . . .

And so he had stayed on and on, at first only able to watch his mother and her assistants with agonized frustration: His mother's computer-analysis methods had worked well in the initial transphonemicizing of T'uupieh's speech, and they had learned enough very quickly to send back clumsy responses using the probe's echo-locating device, to keep T'uupieh's interest from wandering. But typing input at a keyboard, and expecting even the most sophisticated programming to transform it into another language, still would not work even for known human languages. And he knew, with an almost religious fervor, that the syn-thesizer had been designed for just this miracle of communication; and that he alone could use it to capture directly the nuances and subtleties machine translation could never supply. He had tried to approach his mother about letting him use it, but she had turned him down flat: "This is a research center, not a recording studio."

And so he had gone over her head to Reed, who had been delighted. And when at last he felt his hands moving across the warm, faintly tingling plates of light, tentatively re-creating the speech of another world, he had known that he had been right all along. He had let his music commitments go to hell, without a regret, almost with relief, as he slid back into the field that had always come first.

Shannon watched the display, where T'uupieh had settled back with comfortable familiarity against the probe's curving side, half obscuring his view of the camp. Fortunately both she and her followers treated the probe with obsessive care, even when they dragged it from place to place as they constantly moved to camp. He wondered what would have happened if they had inadvertently set off its automatic defense system—which had been designed to protect it from aggressive animals; which delivered an electric shock that varied from merely painful to fatal. And he wondered what would have happened if the probe and its "eyes" hadn't fit so neatly into T'uupieh's beliefs about demons. The idea that he might never have known her, or heard her voice. . . .

More than a year had passed already since he, and the rest of the world, had heard the remarkable news that intelligent life existed on Saturn's major moon. He had no memory at all of the first two flybys to Titan, back in '79 and '81—although he could clearly remember the 1990 orbiter that had caught fleeting glimpses of the surface through Titan's swaddling of opaque, golden clouds. But the handful of miniprobes it had dropped had proved that Titan profited from the same "greenhouse effect" that made Venus a boiling hell. And even though the seasonal temperatures never rose above two hundred degrees Kelvin, the few photographs had shown, unquestionably, that life existed there. The discovery of life, after so many disappointments throughout the rest of the solar system, had been enough to initiate another probe mission, one designed to actually send back data from Titan's surface.

That probe had discovered a life form with human intelligence . . . or rather, the life form had discovered the probe. And T'uupieh's discovery had turned a potentially ruined mission into a success: The probe had been designed with a main, immobile data processing unit, and ten "eyes," or subsidiary units, that were to be scattered over Titan's surface to relay information. The release of the subsidiary probes during landing had failed, however, and all of the "eyes" had come down within a few square kilometers of its own landing in the uninhabited marsh. But T'uupieh's self-interested fascination and willingness to appease her "demon" had made up for everything.

Shannon looked up at the flat wall-screen again, at T'uupieh's incredible, unhuman face—a face that was as familiar now as his own in the mirror. She sat waiting with her incredible patience for a reply from her "demon": She would have been waiting for over an hour by the time her transmission reached him across the gap between their worlds; and she would have to wait as long again, while they discussed a response and he created the new translation. She spent more time now with the probe than she did with her own people. *The loneliness of command* . . . he smiled. The almost flat profile of her moon-white face turned slightly toward him—toward the camera lens; her own fragile mouth smiled gently, not quite revealing her long, sharp teeth. He could see one red pupilless eye, and the crescent nose-slit that half ringed it; her frosty cyanide breath shone blue-white, illuminated by the ghostly haloes of St. Elmo's fire that wreathed the probe all through Titan's interminable eight-day nights. He could see balls of light hanging like Japanese lanterns on the drooping snarl of icebound branches in a distant thicket.

It was unbelievable . . . or perfectly logical; depending on which biological expert was talking . . . that the nitrogen- and ammonia-based life on Titan should have so many analogs with oxygen- and water-based life on Earth. But T'uupieh was not human, and the music of her words time and again brought him messages that made a mockery of any ideals he tried to harbor about her and their relationship. So far in the past year she had assassinated eleven people, and with her outlaws had murdered God knew how many more, in the process of robbing them. The only reason she cooperated with the probe, she had as much as said, was because only a demon had a more bloody reputation; only a demon could command her respect. And yet, from what little she had been able to show them and tell them about the world she lived in, she was no better or no worse than anyone else—only more competent. Was she a prisoner of an age, a culture, where blood was something to be spilled instead of shared? Or was it something biologically innate that let her philosophize brutality, and brutalize philosophy—

Beyond T'uupieh, around the nitrogen campfire, some of her outlaws had begun to sing—the alien folk melodies that in translation were no more than simple, repetitious verse. But heard in their pure, untranslated form, they layered harmonic complexity on complexity: musical speech in a greater pattern of song. Shannon reached out and picked up the headset again, forgetting everything else. He had had a dream, once, where he had been able to sing in chords—

Using the long periods of waiting between their communications, he had managed, some months back, to record a series of the alien songs himself, using the synthesizer. They had been spare and uncomplicated versions compared to the originals, because even now his skill with the language couldn't help wanting to make them his own. Singing was a part of religious ritual, T'uupieh had told him. "But they don't sing because they're religious; they sing because they like to sing." Once, privately, he had played one of his own human compositions for her on the synthesizer, and transmitted it. She had stared at him (or into the probe's golden eye) with stony, if tolerant, silence. She never sang herself, although he had sometimes heard her softly harmonizing. He wondered what she would say if he told her that her outlaws' songs had already earned him his first Platinum Record. Nothing, probably . . . but knowing her, if he could make the concepts clear, she would probably be heartily in favor of the exploitation.

He had agreed to donate the profits of the record to NASA (and although he had intended that all along, it had annoyed him to be asked by Reed), with the understanding that the gesture would be kept quiet. But somehow, at the next press conference, some reporter had known just what question to ask, and Reed had spilled it all. And his mother, when asked about her son's sacrifice, had murmured, "Saturn is becoming a three-ring circus," and left him wondering whether to laugh or swear.

Shannon pulled a crumpled pack of cigarettes out of the pocket of his caftan and lit one. Garda glanced up, sniffing, and shook her head. She didn't smoke, or anything else (although he suspected she ran around with men), and she had given him a long, wasted lecture about it, ending with "Vell, at least they're not tobacco." He shook his head back at her.

"What do you think about T'uupieh's latest victims, then?" Garda flourished the transcript, pulling his thoughts back. "Vill she kill her own sister?"

He exhaled slowly around the words "Tune in tomorrow, for our next exciting episode! I think Reed will love it; that's what I think." He pointed at the newspaper lying on the floor beside his chair. "Did you notice we've slipped to page three?" T'uupieh had fed the probe's hopper some artifacts made of metal—a thing she had said was only known to the "Old Ones"; and the scientific speculation about the existence of a former technological culture had boosted interest in the probe to front-page status again. But even news of that discovery couldn't last forever . . . "Gotta keep those ratings up, folks. Keep those grants and donations rolling in."

Garda clucked. "Are you angry at Reed, or at T'uupieh?"

He shrugged dispiritedly. "Both of 'em. I don't see why she won't kill her own sister—" He broke off, as the subdued noise of the room's numerous project workers suddenly intensified, and concentrated: Marcus Reed was making an entrance, simultaneously solving everyone else's problems, as always. Shannon marveled at Reed's energy, even while he felt something like disgust at the way he spent it. Reed exploited everyone, and everything, with charming cynicism, in the ultimate hype for Science—and watching him at work had gradually drained away whatever respect and goodwill Shannon had brought with him to the project. He knew that his mother's reaction to Reed was close to his own, even though she had never said anything to him about it; it surprised him that there was something they could still agree on.

"Dr. Reed—"

"Excuse me, Dr. Reed, but—"

His mother was with Reed now as they all came down the room; looking tight-lipped and resigned, her lab coat buttoned up as if she was trying to avoid contamination. Reed was straight out of *Manstyle* magazine, as usual. Shannon glanced down at his own loose gray caftan and jeans, which had led Garda to remark, "Are you planning to enter a monastery?"

". . . we'd really like to—"

"Senator Foyle wants you to call him back—"

". . . yes, all right; and tell Dinocci he can go ahead and have the probe run another sample. Yes, Max, I'll get to that . . ." Reed gestured for quiet as Shannon and Garda turned in their seats to face him. "Well, I've just heard the news about our 'Robin Hood's' latest hard contract."

Shannon grimaced quietly. He had been the one who had first, facetiously, called T'uupieh "Robin Hood." Reed had snapped it up and dubbed her ammonia swamps "Sherwood Forest" for the press: After the facts of her bloodthirsty body counts began to come out, and it even began to look like she was collaborating with "the Sheriff of Nottingham," some reporter had pointed out that T'uupieh bore no more resemblance to Robin Hood than she did to Rima the Bird-Girl. Reed had said, laughing, "Well, after all, the only reason Robin Hood stole from the rich was because the poor didn't have any money!" That, Shannon thought, had been the real beginning of the end of his tolerance.

". . . this could be used as an opportunity to show the world graphically the harsh realities of life on Titan—"

*"Ein Moment,"* Garda said. "You're telling us you want to let the public watch this atrocity, Marcus?" Up until now they had never released to the media the graphic tapes of actual murders; even Reed had not been able to argue that that would have served any real scientific purpose.

"No, he's not, Garda." Shannon glanced up as his mother began to speak. "Because we all agreed that we would *not* release any tapes just for purposes of sensationalism."

"Carly, you know that the press has been after me to release those other tapes, and that I haven't, because we all voted against it. But I feel this situation is different—a demonstration of a unique, alien sociocultural condition. What do you think, Shann?"

Shannon shrugged, irritated and not covering it up. "I don't know what's so damn unique about it: a snuff flick is a snuff flick, wherever you film it. I think the idea stinks." Once, at a party while he was still in college, he had watched a film of an unsuspecting victim being hacked to death. The film, and what all films like it said about the human race, had made him sick to his stomach.

"*Ach*—there's more truth than poetry in that!" Garda said.

Reed frowned, and Shannon saw his mother raise her eyebrows.

"I have a better idea." He stubbed out his cigarette in the ashtray under the panel. "Why don't you let me try to talk her out of it?" As he said it, he realized how much he wanted to try; and how much success could mean, to his belief in communication—to his image of T'uupieh's people and maybe his own.

They both showed surprise this time. "How?" Reed said.

"Well . . . I don't know yet. Just let me talk to her, try to really communicate with her, find out how she thinks and what she feels; without all the technical garbage getting in the way for a while."

His mother's mouth thinned, he saw the familiar worry crease form between her brows. "Our job here is to collect that 'garbage.' Not to begin imposing moral values on the universe. We have too much to do as it is."

"What's 'imposing' about trying to stop a murder?" A certain light came into Garda's faded blue eyes. "Now that has real . . . social implications. Think about it, Marcus—"

Reed nodded, glancing at the patiently attentive faces that still ringed him. "Yes—it does. A great deal of human interest . . ." Answering nods and murmurs. "All right, Shann. There are about three days left before morning comes again in Sherwood Forest. You can have them to yourself, to work with T'uupieh. The press will want reports on your progress . . ." He glanced at his watch, and nodded toward the door, already turning away. Shannon looked away from his mother's face as she moved past him.

"Good luck, Shann." Reed threw it back at him absently. "I wouldn't count on reforming Robin Hood; but you can still give it a good try."

Shannon hunched down in his chair, frowning, and turned back to the panel. "In your next incarnation may you come back as a toilet."

T'uupieh was confused. She sat on the hummock of clammy water-stone beside the captive demon, waiting for it to make a reply. In the time that had passed since she'd found it in the swamp, she had been surprised again and again by how little its behavior resembled all the demon lore she knew. And tonight. . . .

She jerked, startled, as its grotesque, clawed arm came to life suddenly and groped among the icy-silver spring shoots pushing up through the melt at the hummock's foot. The demon did many incomprehensible things (which was fitting) and it demanded offerings of meat and vegetation and even stone—even, sometimes, some part of the loot she had taken from passersby. She had given it those things gladly, hoping to win its favor and its aid . . . she had even, somewhat grudgingly, given it precious metal ornaments of Old Ones which she had stripped from a whining foreign lord. The demon had praised her effusively for that; all demons hoarded metal, and she supposed that it must need metals to sustain its strength: its domed carapace—gleaming now with the witch-fire that always shrouded it at night—was an immense metal jewel the color of blood. And yet she had always heard that demons preferred the flesh of men and women. But when she had tried to stuff the wing of the foreign lord into its maw it had spit him out with a few dripping scratches, and told her to let him go. Astonished, she had obeyed, and let the fool run off screaming to be lost in the swamp.

And then, tonight—"You are going to kill your sister, T'uupieh," it had said to her tonight, "and two innocent children. How do you feel about that?" She had spoken what had come first, and truthfully, into her mind: "That the new day cannot come soon enough for me! I have waited so long—too long—to take my revenge on Klovhiri! My sister and her brats are a part of his foulness, better slain before they multiply." She had drawn her dagger and driven it into the mushy melt, as she would drive it into their rotten hearts.

The demon had been silent again, for a long time; as it always was. (The lore said that demons were immortal, and so she had always supposed that it had no reason to make a quick response, she had wished, sometimes, it would show more consideration for her own mortality.) Then at last it had said, in its deep voice filled with alien shadows, "But the children have harmed no one. And Ahtseet is your only sister, she and the children are your only blood kin. She has shared your life. You say that once you"—the demon paused, searching its limited store of words—"cherished her for that. Doesn't what she once meant to you mean anything now? Isn't there any love left to slow your hand as you raise it against her?"

"Love!" she had said, incredulous. "What speech is that, O Soulless One? You mock me—" Sudden anger had bared her teeth. "Love is a toy, my demon, and I have put my toys behind me. And so has Ahtseet . . . she is no kin of mine. Betrayer, betrayer!" The word hissed like the dying embers of the campfire; she had left the demon in disgust, to rake in the firepit's insulating layer of sulphury ash, and lay on a few more soggy branches. Y'lirr, her second-in-command, had smiled at her from where he lay in his cloak on the ground, telling her that she should sleep. But she had ignored him, and gone back to her vigil on the hill.

Even though this night was chill enough to recrystallize the slowly thawing limbs of the *safilil* trees, the equinox was long past, and now the fine mist of golden polymer rain presaged the golden days of the approaching summer. T'uupieh had wrapped herself more closely in her own cloak and pulled up the hood, to keep the clinging, sticky mist from fouling her wings and ear membranes; and she had remembered last summer, her first summer, which she would always remember . . . Ahtseet had been a clumsy, flapping infant as that first summer began, and T'uupieh the child had thought her new sister was silly and useless. But summer slowly transformed the land, and filled her wondering eyes with miracles; and her sister was transformed too, into a playful, easily led companion who could follow her into adventure. Together they learned to use their wings, and to use the warm updrafts to explore the boundaries and the freedoms of their heritage.

And now, as spring moved into summer once again, T'uupieh clung fiercely to the vision, not wanting to lose it, or to remember that childhood's sweet, unreasoning summer would never come again, even though the seasons returned; for the Wheel of Change swept on, and there was never a turning back. No turning back . . . she had become an adult by the summer's end, and she would never soar with a child's light-winged freedom again. And Ahtseet would never do anything again. Little Ahtseet, always just behind her, like her own fair shadow . . . *No! She would not regret it! She would be glad—*

"Did you ever think, T'uupieh," the demon had said suddenly, "that it is wrong to kill anyone? You don't want to die—no one wants to die too soon. Why should they have to? Have you ever wondered what it would be like if you could change the world into one where you— where you treated everyone else as you wanted them to treat you, and they treated you the same? If everyone could—live and let live . . ." Its voice slipped into blurred overtones that she couldn't hear.

She had waited, but it said no more, as if it were waiting for her to consider what she'd already heard. But there was no need to think about what was obvious: "Only the dead 'live and let live.' I treat everyone as I expect them to treat me; or I would quickly join the peaceful dead! Death is a part of life. We die when fate wills it, and when fate wills it, we kill.

"You are immortal, you have the power to twist the Wheel, to turn destiny as you want. You may toy with idle fantasies, even make them real, and never suffer the consequences. We have no place for such things in our small lives. No matter how much I might try to be like you, in the end I die like all the rest. We can change nothing, our lives are preordained. That is the way among mortals." And she had fallen silent again, filled with unease at this strange wandering of the demon's mind. But she must not let it prey on her nerves. Day would come very soon, she must not be nervous; she must be totally in control when she led this attack on Klovhiri. No emotion must interfere . . . no matter how much she yearned to feel Klovhiri's blood spill bluely over her hands, and her sister's, and the children's . . . Ahtseet's brats would never feel the warm wind lift them into the sky; or plunge, as she had, into the depths of her rainbow-petaled pools; or see her towers spearing light far off among the trees. *Never! Never!*

She had caught her breath sharply then, as a fiery pinwheel burst through the wall of tangled brush behind her, tumbling past her head into the clearing of the camp. She had watched it circle the fire—spitting sparks, hissing furiously in the quiet air—three and a half times before it spun on into the darkness. No sleeper wakened, and only two stirred. She clutched one of the demon's hard, angular legs, shaken; knowing that the circling of the fire had been a portent . . . but not knowing what it meant. The burning silence it left behind oppressed her; she stirred restlessly, stretching her wings.

And utterly unmoved, the demon had begun to drone its strange, dark thoughts once more, "Not all you have heard about demons is true. We can suffer"—it groped for words again—"the—consequences of our acts; among ourselves we fight and die. We *are* vicious, and brutal, and pitiless: But we don't like to be that way. We want to change into something better, more merciful, more forgiving. We fail more than we win . . . but we believe we *can* change. And you are more like us than you realize. You can draw a line between—trust and betrayal, right and wrong, good and evil; you can choose never to cross that line—"

"How, then?" She had twisted to face the amber eye as large as her own head, daring to interrupt the demon's speech. "How can one droplet change the tide of the sea? It's impossible! The world melts and flows, it rises into mist, it returns again to ice, only to melt and flow once more. A wheel has no beginning, and no end; no starting place. There is no 'good,' no 'evil' . . . no line between them. Only acceptance. If you were a mortal, I would think you were mad!"

She had turned away again, her claws digging shallow runnels in the polymer-coated stone as she struggled for self-control. *Madness. . . .* Was it possible? she wondered suddenly. Could her demon have gone mad? How else could she explain the thoughts it had put into her mind? Insane thoughts, bizarre, suicidal . . . but thoughts that would haunt her.

Or, could there be a method in its madness? She knew that treachery lay at the heart of every demon. It could simply be lying to her when it spoke of trust and forgiveness—knowing she must be ready for tomorrow, hoping to make her doubt herself, make her fail. Yes, that was much more reasonable. But then, why was it so hard to believe that this demon would try to ruin her most cherished goals? After all, she held it prisoner; and though her spells kept it from tearing her apart, perhaps it still sought to tear apart her mind, to drive her mad instead. Why shouldn't it hate her, and delight in her torment, and hope for her destruction?

*How could it be so ungrateful!* She had almost laughed aloud at her own resentment, even as it formed the thought. As if a demon ever knew gratitude! But ever since the day she had netted it in spells in the swamp, she had given it nothing but the best treatment. She had fetched and carried, and made her fearful followers do the same. She had given it the best of everything—anything it desired. At its command she had sent out searchers to look for its scattered eyes, and it had allowed—even encouraged—her to use the eyes as her own, as watchers and protectors. She had even taught it to understand her speech (for it was as ignorant as a baby about the world of mortals) when she realized that it wanted to communicate with her. She had done all those things to win his favor—because she knew that it had come into her hands for a reason; and if she could gain its cooperation, there would be no one who would dare to cross her.

She had spent every spare hour in keeping it company, feeding its curiosity—and her own—as she fed its jeweled maw . . . until gradually those conversations with the demon had become an end in themselves, a treasure worth the sacrifice of even precious metals. Even the constant waiting for its alien mind to ponder her questions and answers had never tired her, she had come to enjoy sharing even the simple pleasure of its silences, and resting in the warm amber light of its gaze.

T'uupieh looked down at the finely woven fiber belt which passed through the narrow slits between her side and wing and held her tunic to her. She fingered the heavy, richly-amber beads that decorated it—metal-dyed melt trapped in polished waterstone by the jewelsmith's secret arts—that reminded her always of her demon's thousand eyes. *Her* demon—

She looked away again, toward the fire, toward the cloak-wrapped forms of her outlaws. Since the demon had come to her she had felt both the physical and emotional space that she had always kept between herself as leader and her band of followers gradually widening. She was still completely their leader, perhaps more firmly so because she had tamed the demon; and their bond of shared danger and mutual respect had never weakened. But there were other needs which her people might fill for each other, but never for her.

She watched them sleeping like the dead, as she should be sleeping now; preparing themselves for tomorrow. They took their sleep sporadically, when they could, as all commoners did—as she did now, too, instead of hibernating the night through like proper nobility. Many of them slept in pairs, man and woman; even though they mated with a commoner's chaotic lack of discrimination whenever a woman felt the season come upon her. T'uupieh wondered what they must imagine when they saw her sitting here with the demon far into the night. She knew what they believed—what she encouraged all to believe—that she had chosen it for a consort, or that it had chosen her. Y'lirr, she saw, still slept alone. She trusted and liked him as well as she did anyone; he was quick and ruthless, and she knew that he worshipped her. But he was a commoner . . . and more importantly, he did not challenge her. Nowhere, even among the nobility, had she found anyone who offered the sort of companionship she craved . . . until now, until the demon had come to her. No, she would not believe that all its words had been lies—

"T'uupieh," the demon called her name buzzingly in the misty darkness. "Maybe you can't change the pattern of fate . . . but you can change your mind. You've already defied fate, by turning outlaw, and defying Klovhiri. Your sister was the one who accepted . . ." (unintelligible words) ". . . only let the Wheel take her. Can you really kill her for that? You must understand why she did it, how she *could* do it. You don't have to kill her for that . . . you don't have to kill any of them. You have the strength, the courage, to put vengeance aside, and find another way to your goals. You can choose to be merciful—you can choose your own path through life, even if the ultimate destination of all life is the same."

She stood up resentfully, matching the demon's height, and drew her cloak tightly around her. "Even if I wished to change my mind, it is too late. The Wheel is already in motion . . . and I must get my sleep, if I am to be ready for it." She started away toward the fire; stopped, looking back. "There is nothing I can do now, my demon. I cannot change tomorrow. Only you can do that. Only you."

She heard it, later, calling her name softly as she lay sleepless on the cold ground. But she turned her back toward the sound and lay still, and at last sleep came.

Shannon slumped back into the embrace of the padded chair, rubbing his aching head. His eyelids were sandpaper, his body was a weight. He stared at the display screen, at T'uupieh's back turned stubbornly toward him as she slept beside the nitrogen campfire. "Okay, that's it. I give up. She won't even listen. Call Reed and tell him I quit."

"That you've quit trying to convince T'uupieh," Garda said. "Are you sure? She may yet come back. Use a little more emphasis on—spiritual matters. We must be certain we have done all we can to . . . change her mind."

*To save her soul,* he thought sourly. Garda had gotten her early training at an institute dedicated to translating the Bible; he had discovered in the past few hours that she still had a hidden desire to proselytize. *What soul?* "We're wasting our time. It's been six hours since she walked out on me. She's not coming back. . . . And I mean quit everything. I don't want to be around for the main event, I've had it."

"You don't mean that," Garda said. "You're tired, you need the rest too. When T'uupieh wakes, you can talk to her again."

He shook his head, pushing back his hair. "Forget it. Just call Reed." He looked out the window, at dawn separating the mist-wrapped silhouette of seaside condominiums from the sky.

Garda shrugged, disappointed, and turned to the phone.

He studied the synthesizer's touch boards again, still bright and waiting, still calling his leaden, weary hands to try one more time. At least when he made this final announcement, it wouldn't have to be direct to the eyes and ears of a waiting world: He doubted that any reporter was dedicated enough to still be up in the glass-walled observation room at this hour. Their questions had been endless earlier tonight, probing his feelings and his purpose and his motives and his plans, asking about Robin Hood's morality, or lack of it, and his own; about a hundred and one other things that were nobody's business but his own.

The music world had tried to do the same thing to him once, but then there had been buffers—agents, publicity staffs—to protect him. Now, when he'd had so much at stake, there had been no protection, only Reed at the microphone eloquently turning the room into a sideshow, with Shann the Man as chief freak; until Shannon had begun to feel like a man staked out on an anthill and smeared with honey. The reporters gazed down from on high critiquing T'uppieh's responses and criticizing his own, and filled the time gaps when he needed quiet to think with infuriating interruptions. Reed's success had been total in wringing every drop of pathos and human interest out of his struggle to prevent T'uupieh's vengeance against the innocents . . . and by that, had managed to make him fail.

*No.* He sat up straighter, trying to ease his back. No, he couldn't lay it on Reed. By the time what he'd had to say had really counted, the reporters had given up on him. The failure belonged to him, only him: his skill hadn't been great enough, his message hadn't been convincing enough—he was the one who hadn't been able to see through T'uppieh's eyes clearly enough to make her see through his own. He had had his chance to really communicate, for once in his life—to communicate something important. And he'd sunk it.

A hand reached past him to set a cup of steaming coffee on the shelf below the terminal. "One thing about this computer," a voice said quietly, "it's programmed for a good cup of coffee."

Startled, he laughed without expecting to; he glanced up. His mother's face looked drawn and tired, she held another cup of coffee in her hand. "Thanks." He picked up the cup and took a sip, felt the hot liquid slide down his throat into his empty stomach. Not looking up again, he said, "Well, you got what you wanted. And so did Reed. He got his pathos, and he gets his murders too."

She shook her head. "This isn't what I wanted. I don't want to see you give up everything you've done here, just because you don't like what Reed is doing with part of it. It isn't worth that. Your work means too much to this project . . . and it means too much to you."

He looked up.

"*Ja,* she is right, Shannon. You can't quit now—we need you too much. And T'uupieh needs you."

He laughed again, not meaning it. "Like a cement yo-yo. What are you trying to do, Garda, use my own moralizing against me?"

"She's telling you what any blind man could see tonight; if he hadn't seen it months ago . . ." His mother's voice was strangely distant. "That this project would never have had this degree of success without you. That you were right about the synthesizer. And that losing you now might—"

She broke off, turning away to watch as Reed came through the doors at the end of the long room. He was alone, this time, for once, and looking rumpled. Shannon guessed that he had been sleeping when the phone call came and was irrationally pleased at waking him up.

Reed was not so pleased. Shannon watched the frown that might be worry, or displeasure, or both, forming on his face as he came down the echoing hall toward them. "What did she mean, you want to quit? Just because you can't change an alien mind?" He entered the cubicle, and glanced down at the terminal—to be sure that the remote microphones were all switched off, Shannon guessed. "You knew it was a long shot, probably hopeless . . . you have to accept that she doesn't want to reform, accept that the values of an alien culture are going to be different from your own—"

Shannon leaned back, feeling a muscle begin to twitch with fatigue along the inside of his elbow. "I can accept that. What I can't accept is that you want to make us into a bunch of damn panderers. Christ, you don't even have a good reason! I didn't come here to play sound track for a snuff flick. If you go ahead and feed the world those murders, I'm laying it down. I don't want to give all this up, but I'm not staying for a kill-porn carnival."

Reed's frown deepened, he glanced away. "Well? What about the rest of you? Are you still privately branding me an accessory to murder, too? Carly?"

"No, Marcus—not really." She shook her head. "But we all feel that we shouldn't cheapen and weaken our research by making a public spectacle of it. After all, the people of Titan have as much right to privacy and respect as any culture on Earth."

"*Ja*, Marcus—I think we all agree about that."

"And just how much privacy does anybody on Earth have today? Good God—remember the Tasaday? And that was thirty years ago. There isn't a single mountaintop or desert island left that the all-seeing eye of the camera hasn't broadcast all over the world. And what do you call the public crime surveillance laws—our own lives are one big peep show."

Shannon shook his head. "That doesn't mean we have to—"

Reed turned cold eyes on him. "And I've had a little too much of your smartass piety, Wyler. Just what do you owe your success as a musician to, if not publicity?" He gestured at the posters on the walls. "There's more hard sell in your kind of music than any other field I can name."

"I have to put up with some publicity push, or I couldn't reach the people, I couldn't do the thing that's really important to me—communicate. That doesn't mean I like it."

"You think I enjoy this?"

"Don't you?"

Reed hesitated. "I happen to be good at it, which is all that really matters. Because you may not believe it, but I'm still a scientist, and what I care about most of all is seeing that research gets its fair slice of the pie. You say I don't have a good reason for pushing our findings: Do you realize that NASA lost all the data from our Neptune probe just because somebody in effect got tired of waiting for it to get to Neptune, and cut off our funds? The real problem on these long outer-planet missions isn't instrumental reliability, it's financial reliability. The public will pay out millions for one of your concerts, but not one cent for something they don't understand—"

"I don't make—"

"People want to forget their troubles, be entertained . . . and who can blame them? So in order to compete with movies, and sports, and people like you—not to mention ten thousand other worthy government and private causes—we have to give the public what it wants. It's my responsibility to deliver that, so that the 'real scientists' can sit in their neat, bright institutes with half a billion dollars' worth of equipment around them, and talk about 'respect for research.' "

He paused; Shannon kept his gaze stubbornly. "Think it over. And when you can tell me how what you did as a musician is morally superior to, or more valuable than, what you're doing now, you can come to my office and tell me who the real hypocrite is. But think it over, first—all of you." Reed turned and left the cubicle.

They watched in silence, until the double doors at the end of the room hung still. "Vell . . ." Garda glanced at her walking stick, and down at her cloak. "He does have a point."

Shannon leaned forward, tracing the complex beauty of the synthesizer terminal, feeling the combination of chagrin and caffeine pushing down his fatigue: "I know he does. But that isn't the point I was trying to get at! I didn't want to change T'uupieh's mind, or quit either, just because I objected to selling this project. It's the *way* it's being sold, like some kind of kill-porn show perversion, that I can't take—" When he was a child, he remembered, rock concerts had had a kind of notoriety; but they were as respectable as a symphony orchestra now, compared to the "thrill shows" that had eclipsed them as he was growing up: where "experts" gambled their lives against a million-dollar pot, in front of a crowd who came to see them lose; where masochists made a living by self-mutilation; where they ran cinema verité films of butchery and death.

"I mean, is that what everybody really wants? Does it really make everybody feel good to watch somebody else bleed? Or are they going to get some kind of moral superiority thing out of watching it happen on Titan instead of here?" He looked up at the display, at T'uupieh, who still lay sleeping, unmoving and unmoved. "If I could have changed T'uupieh's mind, or changed what happens here, then maybe I could have felt good about something. At least about myself. But who am I kidding . . ." T'uupieh had been right all along; and now he had to admit it to himself: that there had never been any way he could change either one. "T'uupieh's just like the rest of them, she'd rather cut off your hand than shake it . . . and doing it vicariously means we're no better. And none of us ever will be." The words to a song older than he was slipped into his mind, with sudden irony. " 'One man's hands can't build,' " he began to switch off the terminal, "anything."

"You need to sleep . . . ve all need to sleep." Garda rose stiffly from her chair.

" '. . . but if one and one and fifty make a million,' " his mother matched his quote softly.

Shannon turned back to look at her, saw her shake her head; she felt him looking at her, glanced up. "After all, if T'uupieh could have accepted that everything she did was morally evil, what would have become of her? She knew: It would have destroyed her—we would have destroyed her. She would have been swept away and drowned in the tide of violence." His mother looked away at Garda, back at him. "T'uupieh is a realist, whatever else she is."

He felt his mouth tighten against the resentment that sublimated a deeper, more painful emotion; he heard Garda's grunt of indignation.

"But that doesn't mean that you were wrong—or that you failed."

"That's big of you." He stood up, nodding at Garda, and toward the exit. "Come on."

"Shannon."

He stopped, still facing away.

"I don't think you failed. I think you did reach T'uupieh. The last thing she said was 'only you can change tomorrow' . . . I think she was challenging the demon to go ahead; to do what she didn't have the power to do herself. I think she was asking you to help her."

He turned, slowly. "You really believe that?"

"Yes, I do." She bent her head, freed her hair from the collar of her sweater.

He moved back to his seat, his hands brushed the dark, unresponsive touchplates on the panel. "But it wouldn't do any good to talk to her again. Somehow the demon has to stop the attack itself. If I could use the 'voice' to warn them. . . . Damn the time lag!" By the time his voice reached them, the attack would have been over for hours. How could he change anything tomorrow, if he was always two hours behind?

"I know how to get around the time-lag problem."

"How?" Garda sat down again, mixed emotions showing on her broad, seamed face. "He can't send a varning ahead of time; no one knows when Klovhiri will pass. It would come too soon, or too late."

Shannon straightened up. "Better to ask 'why?' Why are you changing your mind?"

"I never changed my mind," his mother said mildly. "I never liked this either. When I was a girl, we used to believe that our actions *could* change the world; maybe I've never stopped wanting to believe that."

"But Marcus is not going to like us meddling behind his back, anyway." Garda waved her staff. "And what about the point that perhaps we do need this publicity?"

Shannon glanced back irritably. "I thought you were on the side of the angels, not the devil's advocate."

"I am!" Garda's mouth puckered. "But—"

"Then what's such bad news about the probe making a last-minute rescue? It'll be a sensation."

He saw his mother smile, for the first time in months. "Sensational . . . if T'uupieh doesn't leave us stranded in the swamp for our betrayal."

He sobered: "Not if you really think she wants our help. And I know she wants it . . . I *feel* it. But how do we beat the time lag?"

"I'm the engineer, remember? I'll need a recorded message from you, and some time to play with that." His mother pointed at the computer terminal.

He switched on the terminal and moved aside. She sat down, and

started a program documentation on the display; he read, REMOTE OP-
ERATIONS MANUAL. "Let's see . . . I'll need feedback on the approach of Klovhiri's party."

He cleared his throat. "Did you really mean what you said, before
Reed came in?"

She glanced up, he watched one response form on her face, and then
fade into another smile. "Garda—have you met My Son, the Linguist?"

"And when did you ever pick up on that Pete Seeger song?"

"And My Son, the Musician . . ." The smile came back to him.
"I've listened to a few records, in my day." The smile turned inward,
toward a memory. "I don't suppose I ever told you that I fell in love
with your father because he reminded me of Elton John."

T'uupieh stood silently, gazing into the demon's unwavering eye. A
new day was turning the clouds from bronze to gold; the brightness
seeped down through the glistening, snarled hair of the treetops,
glanced from the green translucent cliff faces and sweating slopes to
burnish the demon's carapace with light. She gnawed the last shreds of
flesh from a bone, forcing herself to eat, scarcely aware that she did. She
had already sent out watchers in the direction of the town, to keep
watch for Chwiul . . . and Klovhiri's party. Behind her the rest of her
band made ready now, testing weapons and reflexes or feeding their
bellies.

And still the demon had not spoken to her. There had been many
times when it had chosen not to speak for hours on end; but after its
mad ravings of last night, the thought obsessed her that it might never
speak again. Her concern grew, lighting the fuse of her anger, which
this morning was already short enough; until at last she strode recklessly
forward and struck it with her open hand. "Speak to me, *mala 'ingga!*"

But as her blow landed a pain like the touch of fire shot up the
muscles of her arm. She leaped back with a curse of surprise, shaking
her hand. The demon had never lashed out at her before, never hurt
her in any way: But she had never dared to strike it before, she had
always treated it with calculated respect. *Fool!* She looked down at her
hand, half afraid to see it covered with burns that would make her a
cripple in the attack today. But the skin was still smooth and unblis-
tered, only bright with the smarting shock.

"T'uupieh! Are you all right?"

She turned to see Y'lirr, who had come up behind her looking half
frightened, half grim. "Yes." She nodded, controlling a sharper reply at
the sight of his concern. "It was nothing." He carried her double-

arched bow and quiver, she put out her smarting hand and took them from him casually, slung them at her back. "Come, Y'lirr, we must—"

"T'uupieh." This time it was the demon's eerie voice that called her name. "T'uupieh, if you believe in my power to twist fate as I like, then you must come back and listen to me again."

She turned back, felt Y'lirr hesitate behind her. "I believe truly in all your powers, my demon!" She rubbed her hand.

The amber depths of its eye absorbed her expression, and read her sincerity; or so she hoped. "T'uupieh, I know I did not make you believe what I said. But I want you to"—its words blurred unintelligibly—"in me. I want you to know my name. T'uupieh, my name is—"

She heard a horrified yowl from Y'lirr behind her. She glanced around—seeing him cover his ears—and back, paralyzed by disbelief.

"—Shang'ang."

The word struck her like the demon's fiery lash, but the blow this time struck only in her mind. She cried out, in desperate protest; but the name had already passed into her knowledge, *too late!*

A long moment passed; she drew a breath, and shook her head. Disbelief still held her motionless as she let her eyes sweep the brightening camp, as she listened to the sounds of the wakening forest, and breathed in the spicy acridness of the spring growth. And then she began to laugh. She had heard a demon speak its name, and she still lived—and was not blind, not deaf, not mad. The demon had chosen her, joined with her, surrendered to her at last!

Dazed with exultation, she almost did not realize that the demon had gone on speaking to her. She broke off the song of triumph that rose in her, listening:

". . . then I command you to take me with you when you go today. I must see what happens, and watch Klovhiri pass."

"Yes! Yes, my—Shang'ang. It will be done as you wish. Your whim is my desire." She turned away down the slope, stopped again as she found Y'lirr still prone where he had thrown himself down when the demon spoke its name. "Y'lirr?" She nudged him with her foot. Relieved, she saw him lift his head; watched her own disbelief echoing in his face as he looked up at her.

"My lady . . . it did not—?"

"No, Y'lirr," she said softly; then more roughly, "Of course it did not! I am truly the Demon's Consort now; nothing shall stand in my way." She pushed him again with her foot, harder. "Get up. What do I have, a pack of sniveling cowards to ruin the morning of my success?"

Y'lirr scrambled to his feet, brushing himself off. "Never that,

T'uupieh! We're ready for any command . . . ready to deliver your revenge." His hand tightened on his knife hilt.

"And my demon will join us in seeking it out!" The pride she felt rang in her voice. "Get help to fetch a sledge here, and prepare it. And tell them to move it *gently.*"

He nodded, and for a moment as he glanced at the demon she saw both fear and envy in his eyes. "Good news." He moved off then with his usual brusqueness, without glancing back at her.

She heard a small clamor in the camp, and looked past him, thinking that word of the demon had spread already. But then she saw Lord Chwiul, come as he had promised, being led into the clearing by her escorts. She lifted her head slightly, in surprise—he had indeed come alone, but he was riding a *bliell.* They were rare and expensive mounts, being the only beast she knew of large enough to carry so much weight, and being vicious and difficult to train, as well. She watched this one snapping at the air, its fangs protruding past slack, dribbling lips, and grimaced faintly. She saw that the escort kept well clear of its stumplike webbed feet, and kept their spears ready to prod. It was an amphibian, being too heavy ever to make use of wings, but buoyant and agile when it swam. T'uupieh glanced fleetingly at her own webbed fingers and toes, at the wings that could only lift her body now for bare seconds at a time; she wondered, as she had so many times, what strange turns of fate had formed, or transformed, them all.

She saw Y'lirr speak to Chwiul, pointing her out, saw his insolent grin and the trace of apprehension that Chwiul showed looking up at her; she thought that Y'lirr had said, "She knows its name."

Chwiul rode forward to meet her, with his face under control as he endured the demon's scrutiny. T'uupieh put out a hand to casually— gently—stroke its sensuous jewel-faceted side. Her eyes left Chwiul briefly, drawn by some instinct to the sky directly above him—and for half a moment she saw the clouds break open . . .

She blinked, to see more clearly, and when she looked again it was gone. No one else, not even Chwiul, had seen the gibbous disc of greenish gold, cut across by a line of silver and a band of shadow-black: The Wheel of Change. She kept her face expressionless, but her heart raced. The Wheel appeared only when someone's life was about to be changed profoundly—and usually the change meant death.

Chwiul's mount lunged at her suddenly as he stopped before her. She held her place at the demon's side; but some of the *bliell*'s bluish spittle landed on her cloak as Chwiul jerked at its heavy head. "Chwiul!" She let her emotion out as anger. "Keep that slobbering filth under control, or I will have it struck dead!" Her hand fisted on the demon's slick hide.

Chwiul's near-smile faded abruptly, and he pulled his mount back, staring uncomfortably at the demon's glaring eye.

T'uupieh took a deep breath, and produced a smile of her own. "So you did not quite dare to come to my camp alone, my lord."

He bowed slightly, from the saddle. "I was merely hesitant to wander in the swamp on foot, alone, until your people found me."

"I see." She kept the smile. "Well then—I assumed that things went as you planned this morning. Are Klovhiri and his party all on their way into our trap?"

"They are. And their guide is waiting for my sign, to lead them off safe ground into whatever mire you choose."

"Good. I have a spot in mind that is well ringed by heights." She admired Chwiul's self-control in the demon's presence, although she sensed that he was not as easy as he wanted her to believe. She saw some of her people coming toward them, with a sledge to carry the demon on their trek. "My demon will accompany us, by its own desire. A sure sign of our success today, don't you agree?"

Chwiul frowned, as if he wanted to question that, but didn't quite dare. "If it serves you loyally, then yes, my lady. A great honor and a good omen."

"It serves me with true devotion." She smiled again, insinuatingly. She stood back as the sledge came up onto the hummock, watched as the demon was settled onto it, to be sure her people used the proper care. The fresh reverence with which her outlaws treated it—and their leader—was not lost on either Chwiul or herself.

She called her people together then, and they set out for their destination, picking their way over the steaming surface of the marsh and through the slimy slate-blue tentacles of the fragile, thawing underbrush. She was glad that they covered this ground often, because the pungent spring growth and the ground's mushy unpredictability changed the pattern of their passage from day to day. She wished that she could have separated Chwiul from his ugly mount, but she doubted that he would cooperate, and she was afraid that he might not be able to keep up on foot. The demon was lashed securely onto its sledge, and its sweating bearers pulled it with no hint of complaint.

At last they reached the heights overlooking the main road—though it could hardly be called one now—that led past her family's manor. She had the demon positioned where it could look back along the overgrown trail in the direction of Klovhiri's approach, and sent some of her followers to secret its eyes further down the track. She stood then, gazing down at the spot below where the path seemed to fork, but did not. The false fork followed the rippling yellow bands of the cliff face below her—directly into a sink caused by ammonia-water melt seeping down and through the porous sulphide compounds of the rock. There they would all wallow, while she and her band picked them off like swatting *ngips* . . . she thoughtfully swatted a *ngip* that had settled on her hand. Unless her demon—unless her demon chose to create some other outcome . . .

"Any sign?" Chwiul rode up beside her.

She moved back slightly from the cliff's crumbly edge, watching him with more than casual interest. "Not yet. But soon." She had outlaws posted on the lower slope across the track as well; but not even her demon's eyes could pierce too deeply into the foliage along the road. It had not spoken since Chwiul's arrival, and she did not expect it to reveal its secrets now. "What livery does your escort wear, and how many of them do you want killed for effect?" She unslung her bow, and began to test its pull.

Chwiul shrugged. "The dead carry no tales; kill them all. I shall have Klovhiri's men soon. Kill the guide too—a man who can be bought once, can be bought twice."

"Ah—" She nodded, grinning. "A man with your foresight and discretion will go far in the world, my lord." She nocked an arrow in the bowstring before she turned away to search the road again. Still empty. She looked away restlessly, at the spiny silver-blue-green of the distant, fog-clad mountains; at the hollow fingers of upthrust ice, once taller than she was, stubby and diminishing now along the edge of the nearer lake. The lake where last summer she had soared . . .

A flicker of movement, a small unnatural noise, pulled her eyes back to the road. Tension tightened the fluid ease of her movement as she made the trilling call that would send her band to their places along the cliff's edge. *At last*—She leaned forward eagerly for the first glimpse of Klovhiri; spotting the guide, and then the sledge that bore her sister and the children. She counted the numbers of the escort, saw them all emerge into her unbroken view on the track. But Klovhiri . . . where was Klovhiri? She turned back to Chwiul, her whisper struck out at him, "Where is he! Where is Klovhiri?"

Chwiul's expression lay somewhere between guilt and guile. "Delayed. He stayed behind, he said there were still matters at court—"

"Why didn't you tell me that?"

He jerked sharply on the *bliell*'s rein. "It changes nothing! We can still eradicate his family. That will leave me first in line to the inheritance . . . and Klovhiri can always be brought down later."

"But it's Klovhiri I want, for myself." T'uupieh raised her bow, the arrow tracked toward his heart.

"They'll know who to blame if I die!" He spread a wing defensively. "The Overlord will turn against you for good; Klovhiri will see to that. Avenge yourself on your sister, T'uupieh—and I will still reward you well if you keep the bargain!"

"This is not the bargain we agreed to!" The sounds of the approaching party reached her clearly now from down below; she heard a child's high notes of laughter. Her outlaws crouched, waiting for her signal; and she saw Chwiul prepare for his own signal call to his guide. She looked back at the demon, its amber eye fixed on the travelers below. She started toward it. It could still twist fate for her. . . . *Or had it already?*

"*Go back, go back!*" The demon's voice burst over her, down across the silent forest, like an avalanche. "Ambush . . . trap . . . you have been betrayed!"

"—betrayal!"

She barely heard Chwiul's voice below the roaring; she looked back, in time to see the *bliell* leap forward, to intersect her own course toward the demon. Chwiul drew his sword, she saw the look of white fury on his face, not knowing whether it was for her, or the demon itself. She ran toward the demon's sledge, trying to draw her bow; but the *bliell* covered the space between them in two great bounds. Its head swung toward her, jaws gaping. Her foot skidded on the slippery melt, and she went down; the dripping jaws snapped futilely shut above her face. But one flailing leg struck her heavily and knocked her sliding through the melt to the demon's foot—

*The demon.* She gasped for the air that would not fill her lungs, trying to call its name, saw with incredible clarity the beauty of its form, and the ululating horror of the *bliell* bearing down on them to destroy them both. She saw it rear above her, above the demon—saw Chwiul, either leaping or thrown, sail out into the air—and at last her voice came back to her and she screamed the name, a warning and a plea, "Shang'ang!"

And as the *bliell* came down, lightning lashed out from the demon's carapace and wrapped the *bliell* in fire. The beast's ululations rose off the scale; T'uupieh covered her ears against the piercing pain of its cry. But not her eyes: the demon's lash ceased with the suddenness of lightning, and the *bliell* toppled back and away, rebounding lightly as it crashed to the ground, stone dead. T'uupieh sank back against the demon's foot, supported gratefully as she filled her aching lungs, and looked away—

To see Chwiul, trapped in the updrafts at the cliff's edge, gliding, gliding . . . and she saw the three arrows that protruded from his back, before the currents let his body go, and it disappeared below the rim. She smiled, and closed her eyes.

"T'uupieh! T'uupieh!"

She blinked them open again, resignedly, as she felt her people cluster around her. Y'lirr's hand drew back from the motion of touching her face as she opened her eyes. She smiled again, at him, at them all; but not with the smile she had had for Chwiul. "Y'lirr—" She gave him her own hand, and let him help her up. Aches and bruises prodded her with every small movement, but she was certain, reassured, that the only real damage was an oozing tear in her wing. She kept her arm close to her side.

"T'uupieh—"

"My lady—"

"What happened? The demon—"

"The demon saved my life." She waved them silent. "And . . . for its own reasons, it foiled Chwiul's plot." The realization, and the implications, were only now becoming real in her mind. She turned, and for a long moment gazed into the demon's unreadable eye. Then she moved away, going stiffly to the edge of the cliff to look down.

"But the contract—" Y'lirr said.

"Chwiul broke the contract! He did not give me Klovhiri." No one made a protest. She peered through the brush, guessing without much difficulty the places where Ahtseet and her party had gone to earth below. She could hear a child's whimpered crying now. Chwiul's body lay sprawled on the flat, in plain view of them all, and she thought she saw more arrows bristling from his corpse. Had Ahtseet's guard riddled him too, taking him for an attacker? The thought pleased her. And a small voice inside her dared to whisper that Ahtseet's escape pleased her much more. . . . She frowned suddenly at the thought.

But Ahtseet had escaped, and so had Klovhiri—and so she might as well make use of that fact, to salvage what she could. She paused, collecting her still-shaken thoughts. "Ahtseet!" Her voice was not the voice of the demon, but it echoed satisfactorily. "It's T'uupieh! See the traitor's corpse that lies before you—your own mate's brother, Chwiul! He hired murderers to kill you in the swamp—seize your guide, make him tell you all. It is only by my demon's warning that you still live."

"Why?" Ahtseet's voice wavered faintly on the wind.

T'uupieh laughed bitterly. "Why, to keep the roads clear of ruffians. To make the Overlord love his loyal servant more, and reward her better, dear sister! And to make Klovhiri hate me. May it eat his guts out that he owes your lives to me! Pass freely through my lands, Ahtseet; I give you leave—this once."

She drew back from the ledge and moved wearily away, not caring whether Ahtseet would believe her. Her people stood waiting, gathered silently around the corpse of the *bliell.*

"What now?" Y'lirr asked, looking at the demon, asking for them all.

And she answered, but made her answer directly to the demon's silent amber eye. "It seems I spoke the truth to Chwiul after all, my demon: I told him he would not be needing his town house after today . . . Perhaps the Overlord will call it a fair trade. Perhaps it can be arranged. The Wheel of Change carries us all; but not with equal ease. Is that not so, my beautiful Shang'ang?"

She stroked its day-warmed carapace tenderly, and settled down on the softening ground to wait for its reply.

# Harlan Ellison

Harlan is no stranger to the Hugo volumes. He didn't have one in Volume One, for though he was already writing professionally by then, he had not yet hit his stride in science fiction. In Volume Two, however, he is the author of no fewer than three of the fourteen stories, and in Volume Three he has two more. "Jeffty Is Five," in this volume, is therefore his sixth appearance in these Hugo Winner books.

Harlan is a good friend of mine. I make inordinate fun at his expense (as he does at mine), for we are both thick-skinned where friends are concerned (only friends) and we are both keenly aware that we can give as good as we get. People listening to us at conventions, however, sometimes get the idea we are deadly enemies and might at any moment come to blows. (The Fates forbid! For all that Harlan is several inches—or perhaps feet—shorter than I am, he can break me—or almost anyone—in two with his left hand.) Anyway, I'll never get tired of stressing our friendship, though I know there will always remain many who will cling to the myth of an Asimov-Ellison feud.

Harlan is a Hollywood person. He lives in Los Angeles in what I have heard is a marvelous house, which, of course, I have never seen because I don't fly. He also works with Hollywood people.

Personally, I think this is a fate worse than death. When you write books, you are boss. Your editor may make suggestions, but past a certain point you can override him and get your books published essentially as you've written them. In Hollywood, as I understand it, writing a screenplay is just an act of futility since everyone who lives in Los Angeles has the constitutional right to rewrite it at will—the producer, the director, the actors, the stenographers, the office boys, to say nothing of strangers passing by.

This kills Harlan, but then it would even kill me. Some years ago, he did a screenplay for my book *I, Robot*. It was a terrific screenplay. It was in many ways different from the book, for he added distinctive Harlanesque touches, but there were unmistakable parts of my book included, too, and what he added would have been cinematographically wonderful.

Nothing ever came of it, alas. Partly, it was Harlan's temper. "Harlan," I said to him at the beginning, "whatever they say to you, smile and say 'Yes, sir.' If they want a revision, stir it around a bit and say you've revised. If they want you to do something you don't want to do, say you'll do it, and then don't quite, but say you've done it. Understand?"

"Yes, Isaac," he said docilely.

But then came the time when the head of the studio made one dumb remark too many (which is often just one dumb remark where Harlan is concerned) and Harlan said to him in a fury, "You have the cranial capacity of an artichoke."

As soon as the studio head found out what "cranial capacity" meant, he fired Harlan, and made a great many cursory remarks about him.

Too bad, but I love Harlan as he is, thorns and all.

# 10

# JEFFTY IS FIVE

When I was five years old, there was a little kid I played with: Jeffty. His real name was Jeff Kinzer, and everyone who played with him called him Jeffty. We were five years old together, and we had good times playing together.

When I was five, a Clark Bar was as fat around as the gripping end of a Louisville Slugger, and pretty nearly six inches long, and they used real chocolate to coat it, and it crunched very nicely when you bit into the center, and the paper it came wrapped in smelled fresh and good when you peeled off one end to hold the bar so it wouldn't melt onto your fingers. Today, a Clark Bar is as thin as a credit card, they use something artificial and awful-tasting instead of pure chocolate, the thing is soft and soggy, it costs fifteen or twenty cents instead of a decent, correct nickel, and they wrap it so you think it's the same size it was twenty years ago, only it isn't; it's slim and ugly and nasty-tasting and not worth a penny, much less fifteen or twenty cents.

When I was that age, five years old, I was sent away to my Aunt Patricia's home in Buffalo, New York for two years. My father was going through "bad times" and Aunt Patricia was very beautiful, and had married a stockbroker. They took care of me for two years. When I was seven, I came back home and went to find Jeffty, so we could play together.

I was seven. Jeffty was still five. I didn't notice any difference. I didn't know: I was only seven.

When I was seven years old I used to lie on my stomach in front of our Atwater-Kent radio and listen to swell stuff. I had tied the ground wire to the radiator, and I would lie there with my coloring books and my Crayolas (when there were only sixteen colors in the big box), and listen to the NBC Red network: Jack Benny on the *Jell-O Program, Amos 'n' Andy,* Edgar Bergen and Charlie McCarthy on the *Chase and Sanborn Program, One Man's Family, First Nighter;* the NBC Blue network: *Easy Aces,* the *Jergens Program* with Walter Winchell, *Information Please, Death*

*Valley Days;* and best of all, the Mutual Network with *The Green Hornet, The Lone Ranger, The Shadow,* and *Quiet, Please.* Today, I turn on my car radio and go from one end of the dial to the other and all I get is 100 strings orchestras, banal housewives and insipid truckers discussing their kinky sex lives with arrogant talk show hosts, country and western drivel and rock music so loud it hurts my ears.

When I was ten, my grandfather died of old age and I was "a troublesome kid," and they sent me off to military school, so I could be "taken in hand."

I came back when I was fourteen. Jeffty was still five.

When I was fourteen years old, I used to go to the movies on Saturday afternoons and a matinee was ten cents and they used real butter on the popcorn and I could always be sure of seeing a western like Lash LaRue, or Wild Bill Elliott as Red Ryder with Bobby Blake as Little Beaver, or Roy Rogers, or Johnny Mack Brown; a scary picture like *House of Horrors* with Rondo Hatton as the Strangler, or *The Cat People,* or *The Mummy,* or *I Married a Witch* with Fredric March and Veronica Lake; plus an episode of a great serial like *The Shadow* with Victor Jory, or *Dick Tracy* or *Flash Gordon;* and three cartoons; a James Fitzpatrick TravelTalk; Movietone News; a singalong and, if I stayed on till evening, Bingo or Keeno; and free dishes. Today, I go to movies and see Clint Eastwood blowing people's heads apart like ripe cantaloupes.

At eighteen, I went to college. Jeffty was still five. I came back during the summers, to work at my Uncle Joe's jewelry store. Jeffty hadn't changed. Now I knew there was something different about him, something wrong, something weird. Jeffty was still five years old, not a day older.

At twenty-two I came home for keeps. To open a Sony television franchise in town, the first one. I saw Jeffty from time to time. He was five.

Things are better in a lot of ways. People don't die from some of the old diseases any more. Cars go faster and get you there more quickly on better roads. Shirts are softer and silkier. We have paperback books even though they cost as much as a good hardcover used to. When I'm running short in the bank I can live off credit cards till things even out. But I still think we've lost a lot of good stuff. Did you know you can't buy linoleum any more, only vinyl floor covering? There's no such thing as oilcloth any more; you'll never again smell that special, sweet smell from your grandmother's kitchen. Furniture isn't made to last thirty years or longer because they took a survey and found that young homemakers like to throw their furniture out and bring in all new,

color-coded borax every seven years. Records don't feel right; they're
not thick and solid like the old ones, they're thin and you can bend
them . . . that doesn't seem right to me. Restaurants don't serve
cream in pitchers any more, just that artificial glop in little plastic tubs,
and one is never enough to get coffee the right color. You can make a
dent in a car fender with only a sneaker. Everywhere you go, all the
towns look the same with Burger Kings and McDonald's and 7-Elevens
and Taco Bells and motels and shopping centers. Things may be better,
but why do I keep thinking about the past?

What I mean by five years old is not that Jeffty was retarded. I don't
think that's what it was. Smart as a whip for five years old; very bright,
quick, cute, a funny kid.

But he was three feet tall, small for his age, and perfectly formed: no
big head, no strange jaw, none of that. A nice, normal-looking five-year-
old kid. Except that he was the same age as I was: twenty-two.

When he spoke it was with the squeaking, soprano voice of a five-
year-old; when he walked it was with the little hops and shuffles of a
five-year-old; when he talked to you it was about the concerns of a five-
year-old . . . comic books, playing soldier, using a clothespin to attach
a stiff piece of cardboard to the front fork of his bike so the sound it
made when the spokes hit was like a motorboat, asking questions like
*why does that thing do like that,* how high is up, how old is old, why is
grass green, what's an elephant look like? At twenty-two, he was five.

•

Jeffty's parents were a sad pair. Because I was still a friend of Jeffty's,
still let him hang around with me, sometimes took him to the county
fair or miniature golf or the movies, I wound up spending time with
*them.* Not that I much cared for them, because they were so awfully
depressing. But then, I suppose one couldn't expect much more from
the poor devils. They had an alien thing in their home, a child who had
grown no older than five in twenty-two years, who provided the treasure of that special childlike state indefinitely, but who also denied them
the joys of watching the child grow into a normal adult.

Five is a wonderful time of life for a little kid . . . or it *can* be, if the
child is relatively free of the monstrous beastliness other children in-
dulge in. It is a time when the eyes are wide open and the patterns are
not yet set; a time when one has not yet been hammered into accepting
everything as immutable and hopeless; a time when the hands cannot
do enough, the mind cannot learn enough, the world is infinite and
colorful and filled with mysteries. Five is a special time before they take

the questing, unquenchable, quixotic soul of the young dreamer and thrust it into dreary schoolroom boxes. A time before they take the trembling hands that want to hold everything, touch everything, figure everything out, and make them lie still on desktops. A time before people begin saying "act your age" and "grow up" or "you're behaving like a baby." It is a time when a child who acts adolescent is still cute and responsive and everyone's pet. A time of delight, of wonder, of innocence.

Jeffty had been stuck in that time, just five, just so.

But for his parents it was an ongoing nightmare from which no one— not social workers, not priests, not child psychologists, not teachers, not friends, not medical wizards, not psychiatrists, no one—could slap or shake them awake. For seventeen years their sorrow had grown through stages of parental dotage to concern, from concern to worry, from worry to fear, from fear to confusion, from confusion to anger, from anger to dislike, from dislike to naked hatred, and finally, from deepest loathing and revulsion to a stolid, depressive acceptance.

John Kinzer was a shift foreman at the Balder Tool & Die plant. He was a thirty-year man. To everyone but the man living it, his was a spectacularly uneventful life. In no way was he remarkable . . . save that he had fathered a twenty-two-year-old five-year-old.

John Kinzer was a small man; soft, with no sharp angles; with pale eyes that never seemed to hold mine for longer than a few seconds. He continually shifted in his chair during conversations, and seemed to see things in the upper corners of the room, things no one else could see . . . or wanted to see. I suppose the word that best suited him was *haunted*. What his life had become . . . well, *haunted* suited him.

Leona Kinzer tried valiantly to compensate. No matter what hour of the day I visited, she always tried to foist food on me. And when Jeffty was in the house she was always at *him* about eating: "Honey, would you like an orange? A nice orange? Or a tangerine? I have tangerines. I could peel a tangerine for you." But there was clearly such fear in her, fear of her own child, that the offers of sustenance always had a faintly ominous tone.

Leona Kinzer had been a tall woman, but the years had bent her. She seemed always to be seeking some area of wallpapered wall or storage niche into which she could fade, adopt some chintz or rose-patterned protective coloration and hide forever in plain sight of the child's big brown eyes, pass her a hundred times a day and never realize she was there, holding her breath, invisible. She always had an apron tied around her waist, and her hands were red from cleaning. As if by maintaining the environment immaculately she could pay off her imagined sin: having given birth to this strange creature.

Neither of them watched television very much. The house was usually dead silent, not even the sibilant whispering of water in the pipes, the creaking of timbers settling, the humming of the refrigerator. Awfully silent, as if time itself had taken a detour around that house.

As for Jeffty, he was inoffensive. He lived in that atmosphere of gentle dread and dulled loathing, and if he understood it, he never remarked in any way. He played, as a child plays, and seemed happy. But he must have sensed, in the way of a five-year-old, just how alien he was in their presence.

Alien. No, that wasn't right. He was *too* human, if anything. But out of phase, out of sync with the world around him, and resonating to a different vibration than his parents, God knows. Nor would other children play with him. As they grew past him, they found him at first childish, then uninteresting, then simply frightening as their perceptions of aging became clear and they could see he was not affected by time as they were. Even the little ones, his own age, who might wander into the neighborhood, quickly came to shy away from him like a dog in the street when a car backfires.

Thus, I remained his only friend. A friend of many years. Five years. Twenty-two years. I liked him; more than I can say. And never knew exactly why. But I did, without reserve.

But because we spent time together, I found I was also—polite society—spending time with John and Leona Kinzer. Dinner, Saturday afternoons sometimes, an hour or so when I'd bring Jeffty back from a movie. They were grateful: slavishly so. It relieved them of the embarrassing chore of going out with him, of having to pretend before the world that they were loving parents with a perfectly normal, happy, attractive child. And their gratitude extended to hosting me. Hideous, every moment of their depression, hideous.

I felt sorry for the poor devils, but I despised them for their inability to love Jeffty, who was eminently lovable.

I never let on, of course, even during the evenings in their company that were awkward beyond belief.

We would sit there in the darkening living room—*always* dark or darkening, as if kept in shadow to hold back what the light might reveal to the world outside through the bright eyes of the house—we would sit and silently stare at one another. They never knew what to say to me.

"So how are things down at the plant?" I'd say to John Kinzer.

He would shrug. Neither conversation nor life suited him with any ease or grace. "Fine, just fine," he would say, finally.

And we would sit in silence again.

"Would you like a nice piece of coffee cake?" Leona would say. "I made it fresh just this morning." Or deep dish green apple pie. Or milk and tollhouse cookies. Or a brown betty pudding.

"No, no, thank you, Mrs. Kinzer; Jeffty and I grabbed a couple of cheeseburgers on the way home." And again, silence.

Then, when the stillness and the awkwardness became too much even for them (and who knew how long that total silence reigned when they were alone, with that thing they never talked about any more hanging between them), Leona Kinzer would say, "I think he's asleep."

John Kinzer would say, "I don't hear the radio playing."

Just so, it would go on like that, until I could politely find excuse to bolt away on some flimsy pretext. Yes, that was the way it would go on, every time, just the same . . . except once.

•

"I don't know what to do any more," Leona said. She began crying. "There's no change, not one day of peace."

Her husband managed to drag himself out of the old easy chair and went to her. He bent and tried to soothe her, but it was clear from the graceless way in which he touched her graying hair that the ability to be compassionate had been stunned in him. "Shhh, Leona, it's all right. Shhh." But she continued crying. Her hands scraped gently at the antimacassars on the arms of the chair.

Then she said, "Sometimes I wish he had been stillborn."

John looked up into the corners of the room. For the nameless shadows that were always watching him? Was it God he was seeking in those spaces? "You don't mean that," he said to her, softly, pathetically, urging her with body tension and trembling in his voice to recant before God took notice of the terrible thought. But she meant it; she meant it very much.

I managed to get away quickly that evening. They didn't want witnesses to their shame. I was glad to go.

•

And for a week I stayed away. From them, from Jeffty, from their street, even from that end of town.

I had my own life. The store, accounts, suppliers' conferences, poker with friends, pretty women I took to well-lit restaurants, my own parents, putting antifreeze in the car, complaining to the laundry about too much starch in the collars and cuffs, working out at the gym, taxes, catching Jan or David (whichever one it was) stealing from the cash register. I had my own life.

But not even *that* evening could keep me from Jeffty. He called me at the store and asked me to take him to the rodeo. We chummed it up as best a twenty-two-year-old with other interests *could* . . . with a five-year-old. I never dwelled on what bound us together; I always thought it was simply the years. That, and affection for a kid who could have been the little brother I never had. (Except I *remembered* when we had played together, when we had both been the same age; I *remembered* that period, and Jeffty was still the same.)

And then, one Saturday afternoon, I came to take him to a double feature, and things I should have noticed so many times before, I first began to notice only that afternoon.

•

I came walking up to the Kinzer house, expecting Jeffty to be sitting on the front porch steps, or in the porch glider, waiting for me. But he was nowhere in sight.

Going inside, into that darkness and silence, in the midst of May sunshine, was unthinkable. I stood on the front walk for a few moments, then cupped my hands around my mouth and yelled, "Jeffty? Hey Jeffty, come on out, let's go. We'll be late."

His voice came faintly, as if from under the ground.

"Here I am, Donny."

I could hear him, but I couldn't see him. It was Jeffty, no question about it: as Donald H. Horton, President and Sole Owner of The Horton TV & Sound Center, no one but Jeffty called me Donny. He had never called me anything else.

(Actually, it isn't a lie. I *am*, as far as the public is concerned, Sole Owner of the Center. The partnership with my Aunt Patricia is only to repay the loan she made me, to supplement the money I came into when I was twenty-one, left to me when I was ten by my grandfather. It wasn't a very big loan, only eighteen thousand, but I asked her to be a silent partner, because of when she had taken care of me as a child.)

"Where are you, Jeffty?"

"Under the porch in my secret place."

I walked around the side of the porch, and stooped down and pulled away the wicker grating. Back in there, on the pressed dirt, Jeffty had built himself a secret place. He had comics in orange crates, he had a little table and some pillows, it was lit by big fat candles, and we used to hide there when we were both . . . five.

"What'cha up to?" I asked, crawling in and pulling the grate closed behind me. It was cool under the porch, and the dirt smelled comfortable, the candles smelled clubby and familiar. Any kid would feel at home in such a secret place: there's never been a kid who didn't spend the happiest, most productive, most deliciously mysterious times of his life in such a secret place.

"Playin'," he said. He was holding something golden and round. It filled the palm of his little hand.

"You forget we were going to the movies?"

"Nope. I was just waitin' for you here."

"Your mom and dad home?"

"Momma."

I understood why he was waiting under the porch. I didn't push it any further. "What've you got there?"

"Captain Midnight Secret Decoder Badge," he said, showing it to me on his flattened palm.

I realized I was looking at it without comprehending what it was for a long time. Then it dawned on me what a miracle Jeffty had in his hand. A miracle that simply could *not* exist.

"Jeffty," I said softly, with wonder in my voice, "where'd you get that?"

"Came in the mail today. I sent away for it."

"It must have cost a lot of money."

"Not so much. Ten cents an' two inner wax seals from two jars of Ovaltine."

"May I see it?" My voice was trembling, and so was the hand I extended. He gave it to me and I held the miracle in the palm of my hand. It was *wonderful*.

You remember. *Captain Midnight* went on the radio nationwide in 1940. It was sponsored by Ovaltine. And every year they issued a Secret Squadron Decoder Badge. And every day at the end of the program, they would give you a clue to the next day's installment in a code that only kids with the official badge could decipher. They stopped making those wonderful Decoder Badges in 1949. I remember the one I had in 1945: it was beautiful. It had a magnifying glass in the center of the code dial. *Captain Midnight* went off the air in 1950, and though I understand it was a short-lived television series in the midFifties, and though they issued Decoder Badges in 1955 and 1956, as far as the *real* badges were concerned, they never made one after 1949.

The Captain Midnight Code–O–Graph I held in my hand, the one Jeffty said he had gotten in the mail for ten cents *(ten cents!!!)* and two Ovaltine labels, was brand new, shiny gold metal, not a dent or a spot of rust on it like the old ones you can find at exorbitant prices in collectible shoppes from time to time . . . it was a *new* Decoder. And the date on it was *this* year.

But *Captain Midnight* no longer existed. Nothing like it existed on the radio. I'd listened to the one or two weak imitations of old-time radio the networks were currently airing, and the stories were dull, the sound effects bland, the whole feel of it wrong, out of date, cornball. Yet I held a *new* Code–O–Graph.

"Jeffty, tell me about this," I said.

"Tell you what, Donny? It's my new Capt'n Midnight Secret Decoder Badge. I use it to figger out what's gonna happen tomorrow."

"Tomorrow how?"

"On the program."

"*What* program?!"

He stared at me as if I was being purposely stupid. "On Capt'n *Mid-night!* Boy!" I was being dumb.

I still couldn't get it straight. It was right there, right out in the open, and I still didn't know what was happening. "You mean one of those records they made of the old-time radio programs? Is that what you mean, Jeffty?"

"What records?" he asked. He didn't know what *I* meant.

We stared at each other, there under the porch. And then I said, very slowly, almost afraid of the answer, "Jeffty, how do you hear *Captain Midnight?*"

"Every day. On the radio. On my radio. Every day at five-thirty."

News. Music, dumb music, and news. That's what was on the radio every day at 5:30. Not *Captain Midnight.* The Secret Squadron hadn't been on the air in twenty years.

"Can we hear it tonight?" I asked.

"Boy!" he said. I was being dumb. I knew it from the way he said it; but I didn't know *why.* Then it dawned on me: this was Saturday. *Captain Midnight* was on Monday through Friday. Not on Saturday or Sunday.

"We goin' to the movies?"

He had to repeat himself twice. My mind was somewhere else. Nothing definite. No conclusions. No wild assumptions leapt to. Just off somewhere trying to figure it out, and concluding—as *you* would have concluded, as *any*one would have concluded rather than accepting the truth, the impossible and wonderful truth—just finally concluding there was a simple explanation I didn't yet perceive. Something mundane and dull, like the passage of time that steals all good, old things from us, packratting trinkets and plastic in exchange. And all in the name of Progress.

"We goin' to the movies, Donny?"

"You bet your boots we are, kiddo," I said. And I smiled. And I handed him the Code–O–Graph. And he put it in his side pants pocket. And we crawled out from under the porch. And we went to the movies. And neither of us said anything about *Captain Midnight* all the rest of that day. And there wasn't a ten-minute stretch, all the rest of that day, that I didn't think about it.

●

It was inventory all that next week. I didn't see Jeffty till late Thursday. I confess I left the store in the hands of Jan and David, told them I had some errands to run, and left early. At 4:00. I got to the Kinzers' right around 4:45. Leona answered the door, looking exhausted and distant. "Is Jeffty around?" She said he was upstairs in his room . . .

. . . listening to the radio.

I climbed the stairs two at a time.

All right, I had finally made that impossible, illogical leap. Had the stretch of belief involved anyone but Jeffty, adult or child, I would have reasoned out more explicable answers. But it *was* Jeffty, clearly another kind of vessel of life, and what he might experience should not be expected to fit into the ordered scheme.

I admit it: I *wanted* to hear what I heard.

Even with the door closed, I recognized the program:

*"There he goes, Tennessee! Get him!"*

There was the heavy report of a squirrel-rifle shot and the keening whine of the slug ricocheting, and then the same voice yelled triumphantly, *"Got him! D-e-a-a-a-d center!"*

He was listening to the American Broadcasting Company, 790 kilohertz, and he was hearing *Tennessee Jed,* one of my most favorite programs from the Forties, a western adventure I had not heard in twenty years, because it had not existed for twenty years.

I sat down on the top step of the stairs, there in the upstairs hall of the Kinzer home, and I listened to the show. It wasn't a rerun of an old program; I knew every one of them by heart, had never missed an episode. Further evidence that this was a new installment: there were occasional references during the integrated commercials to current cultural and technological developments, and phrases that had not existed in common usage in the Forties: aerosol spray cans, laserasing of tattoos, Tanzania, the word "uptight."

I couldn't ignore it: Jeffty was listening to a *new* segment of *Tennessee Jed.*

I ran downstairs and out the front door to my car. Leona must have been in the kitchen. I turned the key and punched on the radio and spun the dial to 790 kilohertz. The ABC station. Rock music.

I sat there for a few moments, then ran the dial slowly from one end to the other. Music, news, talk shows. No *Tennessee Jed.* And it was a Blaupunkt, the best radio I could get. I wasn't missing some perimeter station. It simply was not there!

After a few moments I turned off the radio and the ignition and went back upstairs quietly. I sat down on the top step and listened to the entire program. It was *wonderful.*

Exciting, imaginative, filled with everything I remembered as being most innovative about radio drama. But it was modern. It wasn't an antique, rebroadcast to assuage the need of that dwindling listenership who longed for the old days. It was a new show, with all the old voices, but still young and bright. Even the commercials were for currently available products, but they weren't as loud or as insulting as the screamer ads one heard on radio these days.

And when *Tennessee Jed* went off at 5:00, I heard Jeffty spin the dial on his radio till I heard the familiar voice of the announcer Glenn Riggs proclaim, *"Presenting Hop Harrigan! America's ace of the airwaves!"* There was the sound of an airplane in flight. It was a prop plane, *not* a jet! Not the sound kids today have grown up with, but the sound *I* grew up with, the *real* sound of an airplane, the growling, revving, throaty sound of the kind of airplanes G-8 and His Battle Aces flew, the kind Captain Midnight flew, the kind Hop Harrigan flew. And then I heard Hop say, *"CX–4 calling control tower. CX–4 calling control tower. Standing by!"* A pause, then, *"Okay, this is Hop Harrigan . . . coming in!"*

And Jeffty, who had the same problem all of us kids had had in the Forties with programming that pitted equal favorites against one another on different stations, having paid his respects to Hop Harrigan and Tank Tinker, spun the dial and went back to ABC, where I heard the stroke of a gong, the wild cacophony of nonsense Chinese chatter, and the announcer yelled, *"T-e-e-e-rry and the Pirates!"*

I sat there on the top step and listened to Terry and Connie and Flip Corkin and, so help me God, Agnes Moorehead as the Dragon Lady, all of them in a new adventure that took place in a Red China that had not existed in the days of Milton Caniff's 1937 version of the Orient, with river pirates and Chiang Kai-shek and warlords and the naive Imperialism of American gunboat diplomacy.

Sat, and listened to the whole show, and sat even longer to hear *Superman* and part of *Jack Armstrong, the All-American Boy* and part of *Captain Midnight,* and John Kinzer came home and neither he nor Leona came upstairs to find out what had happened to me, or where Jeffty was, and sat longer, and found I had started crying, and could not stop, just sat there with tears running down my face, into the corners of my mouth, sitting and crying until Jeffty heard me and opened his door and saw me and came out and looked at me in childish confusion as I heard the station break for the Mutual Network and they began the theme music of *Tom Mix,* "When It's Round-Up Time in Texas and the Bloom Is on the Sage," and Jeffty touched my shoulder and smiled at me, with his mouth and his big brown eyes, and said, "Hi, Donny. Wanna come in an' listen to the radio with me?"

•

Hume denied the existence of an absolute space, in which each thing has its place; Borges denies the existence of one single time, in which all events are linked.

Jeffty received radio programs from a place that could not, in logic, in the natural scheme of the space-time universe as conceived by Einstein, exist. But that wasn't all he received. He got mail-order premiums that no one was manufacturing. He read comic books that had been defunct for three decades. He saw movies with actors who had been dead for twenty years. He was the receiving terminal for endless joys and pleasures of the past that the world had dropped along the way. On its headlong suicidal flight toward New Tomorrows, the world had razed its treasurehouse of simple happinesses, had poured concrete over its playgrounds, had abandoned its elfin stragglers, and all of it was being impossibly, miraculously shunted back into the present through Jeffty. Revivified, updated, the traditions maintained but contemporaneous. Jeffty was the unbidding Aladdin whose very nature formed the magic lampness of his reality.

And he took me into his world with him.

Because he trusted me.

We had breakfast of Quaker Puffed Wheat Sparkies and warm Ovaltine we drank out of *this* year's Little Orphan Annie Shake-Up Mugs. We went to the movies and while everyone else was seeing a comedy starring Goldie Hawn and Ryan O'Neal, Jeffty and I were enjoying

Humphrey Bogart as the professional thief Parker in John Huston's brilliant adaptation of the Donald Westlake novel *Slayground*. The second feature was Spencer Tracy, Carole Lombard and Laird Cregar in the Val Lewton-produced film of *Leiningen Versus the Ants*.

Twice a month we went down to the newsstand and bought the current pulp issues of *The Shadow, Doc Savage* and *Startling Stories*. Jeffty and I sat together and I read to him from the magazines. He particularly liked the new short novel by Henry Kuttner, "The Dreams of Achilles," and the new Stanley G. Weinbaum series of short stories set in the subatomic particle universe of Redurna. In September we enjoyed the first installment of the new Robert E. Howard Conan novel, *Isle of the Black Ones*, in *Weird Tales;* and in August we were only mildly disappointed by Edgar Rice Burroughs's fourth novella in the Jupiter series featuring John Carter of Barsoom—"Corsairs of Jupiter." But the editor of *Argosy All-Story Weekly* promised there would be two more stories in the series, and it was such an unexpected revelation for Jeffty and me that it dimmed our disappointment at the lessened quality of the current story.

We read comics together, and Jeffty and I both decided—separately, before we came together to discuss it—that our favorite characters were Doll Man, Airboy, and The Heap. We also adored the George Carlson strips in *Jingle Jangle Comics*, particularly the Pie-Face Prince of Old Pretzleburg stories, which we read together and laughed over, even though I had to explain some of the esoteric puns to Jeffty, who was too young to have that kind of subtle wit.

How to explain it? I can't. I had enough physics in college to make some offhand guesses, but I'm more likely wrong than right. The laws of the conservation of energy occasionally break. These are laws that physicists call "weakly violated." Perhaps Jeffty was a catalyst for the weak violation of conservation laws we're only now beginning to realize exist. I tried doing some reading in the area—muon decay of the "forbidden" kind: gamma decay that doesn't include the muon neutrino among its products—but nothing I encountered, not even the latest readings from the Swiss Institute for Nuclear Research near Zurich, gave me an insight. I was thrown back on a vague acceptance of the philosophy that the real name for "science" is *magic*.

No explanations, but enormous good times.

The happiest time of my life.

I had the "real" world, the world of my store and my friends and my family, the world of profit&loss, of taxes and evenings with young women who talked about going shopping or the United Nations, of the rising cost of coffee and microwave ovens. And I had Jeffty's world, in which I existed only when I was with him. The things of the past he knew as fresh and new, I could experience only when in his company. And the membrane between the two worlds grew ever thinner, more luminous and transparent. I had the best of both worlds. And knew, somehow, that I could carry nothing from one to the other.

Forgetting for just a moment, betraying Jeffty by forgetting, brought an end to it all.

Enjoying myself so much, I grew careless and failed to consider how fragile the relationship between Jeffty's world and my world really was. There is a reason why the present begrudges the existence of the past. I never really understood. Nowhere in the beast books, where survival is shown in battles between claw and fang, tentacle and poison sac, is there recognition of the ferocity the present always brings to bear on the past. Nowhere is there a detailed statement of how the Present lies in wait for What-Was, waiting for it to become Now-This-Moment so it can shred it with its merciless jaws.

Who could know such a thing . . . at any age . . . and certainly not at my age . . . who could understand such a thing?

I'm trying to exculpate myself. I can't. It was my fault.

•

It was another Saturday afternoon.

"What's playing today?" I asked him, in the car, on the way downtown.

He looked up at me from the other side of the front seat and smiled one of his best smiles. "Ken Maynard in *Bullwhip Justice* an' *The Demolished Man.*" He kept smiling, as if he'd really put one over on me. I looked at him with disbelief.

"You're *kidd*ing!" I said, delighted. "Bester's *The Demolished Man?*" He nodded his head, delighted at my being delighted. He knew it was one of my favorite books. "Oh, that's super!"

"Super *duper,*" he said.

"Who's in it?"

"Franchot Tone, Evelyn Keyes, Lionel Barrymore, and Elisha Cook, Jr." He was much more knowledgeable about movie actors than I'd ever been. He could name the character actors in any movie he'd ever seen. Even the crowd scenes.

"And cartoons?" I asked.

"Three of 'em: a *Little Lulu,* a *Donald Duck* and a *Bugs Bunny.* An' a *Pete Smith Specialty* an' a Lew Lehr *Monkeys is da C-r-r-r-aziest Peoples.*"

"Oh boy!" I said. I was grinning from ear to ear. And then I looked down and saw the pad of purchase order forms on the seat. I'd forgotten to drop it off at the store.

"Gotta stop by the Center," I said. "Gotta drop off something. It'll only take a minute."

"Okay," Jeffty said. "But we won't be late, will we?"

"Not on your tintype, kiddo," I said.

•

When I pulled into the parking lot behind the Center, he decided to come in with me and we'd walk over to the theater. It's not a large town. There are only two movie houses, the Utopia and the Lyric. We were going to the Utopia and it was only three blocks from the Center.

I walked into the store with the pad of forms, and it was bedlam. David and Jan were handling two customers each, and there were people standing around waiting to be helped. Jan turned a look on me and her face was a horror-mask of pleading. David was running from the stockroom to the showroom and all he could murmur as he whipped past was "Help!" and then he was gone.

"Jeffty," I said, crouching down, "listen, give me a few minutes. Jan and David are in trouble with all these people. We won't be late, I promise. Just let me get rid of a couple of these customers." He looked nervous, but nodded okay.

I motioned to a chair and said, "Just sit down for a while and I'll be right with you."

He went to the chair, good as you please, though he knew what was happening, and he sat down.

I started taking care of people who wanted color television sets. This was the first really substantial batch of units we'd gotten in—color television was only now becoming reasonably priced and this was Sony's first promotion—and it was bonanza time for me. I could see paying off the loan and being out in front for the first time with the Center. It was business.

In my world, good business comes first.

Jeffty sat there and stared at the wall. Let me tell you about the wall.

Stanchion and bracket designs had been rigged from floor to within two feet of the ceiling. Television sets had been stacked artfully on the wall. Thirty-three television sets. All playing at the same time. Black and white, color, little ones, big ones, all going at the same time.

Jeffty sat and watched thirty-three television sets, on a Saturday afternoon. We can pick up a total of thirteen channels including the UHF educational stations. Golf was on one channel; baseball was on a second; celebrity bowling was on a third; the fourth channel was a religious seminar; a teenage dance show was on the fifth; the sixth was a rerun of a situation comedy; the seventh was a rerun of a police show; eighth was a nature program showing a man flycasting endlessly; ninth was news and conversation; tenth was a stock car race; eleventh was a man doing logarithms on a blackboard; twelfth was a woman in a leotard doing setting-up exercises; and on the thirteenth channel was a badly animated cartoon show in Spanish. All but six of the shows were repeated on three sets. Jeffty sat and watched that wall of television on a Saturday afternoon while I sold as fast and as hard as I could, to pay back my Aunt Patricia and stay in touch with my world. It was business.

I should have known better. I should have understood about the present and the way it kills the past. But I was selling with both hands. And when I finally glanced over at Jeffty, half an hour later, he looked like another child.

He was sweating. That terrible fever sweat when you have stomach flu. He was pale, as pasty and pale as a worm, and his little hands were gripping the arms of the chair so tightly I could see his knuckles in bold relief. I dashed over to him, excusing myself from the middle-aged couple looking at the new 21″ Mediterranean model.

"Jeffty!"

He looked at me, but his eyes didn't track. He was in absolute terror. I pulled him out of the chair and started toward the front door with him, but the customers I'd deserted yelled at me, "Hey!" The middle-aged man said, "You wanna sell me this thing or don't you?"

I looked from him to Jeffty and back again. Jeffty was like a zombie. He had come where I'd pulled him. His legs were rubbery and his feet dragged. The past, being eaten by the present, the sound of something in pain.

I clawed some money out of my pants pocket and jammed it into Jeffty's hand. "Kiddo . . . listen to me . . . get out of here right now!" He still couldn't focus properly. *"Jeffty,"* I said as tightly as I could, *"listen* to me!" The middle-aged customer and his wife were walking toward us. "Listen, kiddo, get out of here right this minute. Walk over to the Utopia and buy the tickets. I'll be right behind you." The middle-aged man and his wife were almost on us. I shoved Jeffty through the door and watched him stumble away in the wrong direction, then stop as if gathering his wits, turn and go back past the front of the Center and in the direction of the Utopia. "Yes sir," I said, straightening up and facing them, "yes, ma'am, that is one terrific set with some sensational features! If you'll just step back here with me . . ."

There was a terrible sound of something hurting, but I couldn't tell from which channel, or from which set, it was coming.

•

Most of it I learned later, from the girl in the ticket booth, and from some people I knew who came to me to tell me what had happened. By the time I got to the Utopia, nearly twenty minutes later, Jeffty was already beaten to a pulp and had been taken to the manager's office.

"Did you see a very little boy, about five years old, with big brown eyes and straight brown hair . . . he was waiting for me?"

"Oh, I think that's the little boy those kids beat up?"

"What!?! *Where is he?*"

"They took him to the manager's office. No one knew who he was or where to find his parents—"

A young girl wearing an usher's uniform was kneeling down beside the couch, placing a wet paper towel on his face.

I took the towel away from her and ordered her out of the office. She looked insulted and snorted something rude, but she left. I sat on the edge of the couch and tried to swab away the blood from the lacerations without opening the wounds where the blood had caked. Both his eyes were swollen shut. His mouth was ripped badly. His hair was matted with dried blood.

He had been standing in line behind two kids in their teens. They started selling tickets at 12:30 and the show started at 1:00. The doors weren't opened till 12:45. He had been waiting, and the kids in front of him had had a portable radio. They were listening to the ball game. Jeffty had wanted to hear some program, God knows what it might have been, *Grand Central Station, Let's Pretend, Land of the Lost,* God only knows which one it might have been.

He had asked if he could borrow their radio to hear the program for a minute, and it had been a commercial break or something, and the kids had given him the radio, probably out of some malicious kind of courtesy that would permit them to take offense and rag the little boy. He had changed the station . . . and they'd been unable to get it to go back to the ball game. It was locked into the past, on a station that was broadcasting a program that didn't exist for anyone but Jeffty.

They had beaten him badly . . . as everyone watched.

And then they had run away.

I had left him alone, left him to fight off the present without sufficient weaponry. I had betrayed him for the sale of a 21″ Mediterranean console television, and now his face was pulped meat. He moaned something inaudible and sobbed softly.

"Shhh, it's okay, kiddo, it's Donny. I'm here. I'll get you home, it'll be okay."

I should have taken him straight to the hospital. I don't know why I didn't. I should have. I should have done that.

•

When I carried him through the door, John and Leona Kinzer just stared at me. They didn't move to take him from my arms. One of his hands was hanging down. He was conscious, but just barely. They stared, there in the semi-darkness of a Saturday afternoon in the present. I looked at them. "A couple of kids beat him up at the theater." I raised him a few inches in my arms and extended him. They stared at me, at both of us, with nothing in their eyes, without movement. "Jesus Christ," I shouted, "he's been beaten! He's your son! Don't you even want to touch him? What the hell kind of people are you?!"

Then Leona moved toward me very slowly. She stood in front of us for a few seconds, and there was a leaden stoicism in her face that was terrible to see. It said, *I have been in this place before, many times, and I cannot bear to be in it again; but I am here now.*

So I gave him to her. God help me, I gave him over to her.

And she took him upstairs to bathe away his blood and his pain.

John Kinzer and I stood in our separate places in the dim living room of their home, and we stared at each other. He had nothing to say to me.

I shoved past him and fell into a chair. I was shaking.

I heard the bath water running upstairs.

After what seemed a very long time Leona came downstairs, wiping her hands on her apron. She sat down on the sofa and after a moment John sat down beside her. I heard the sound of rock music from upstairs.

"Would you like a piece of nice pound cake?" Leona said.

I didn't answer. I was listening to the sound of the music. Rock music. On the radio. There was a table lamp on the end table beside the sofa. It cast a dim and futile light in the shadowed living room. *Rock music from the present, on a radio upstairs?* I started to say something, and then *knew* . . . Oh, God . . . *no!*

I jumped up just as the sound of hideous crackling blotted out the music, and the table lamp dimmed and flickered. I screamed something, I don't know what it was, and ran for the stairs.

Jeffty's parents did not move. They sat there with their hands folded, in that place they had been for so many years.

I fell twice rushing up the stairs.

•

There isn't much on television that can hold my interest. I bought an old cathedral-shaped Philco radio in a second-hand store, and I replaced all the burnt-out parts with the original tubes from old radios I could cannibalize that still worked. I don't use transistors or printed circuits. They wouldn't work. I've sat in front of that set for hours sometimes, running the dial back and forth as slowly as you can imagine, so slowly it doesn't look as if it's moving at all sometimes.

But I can't find *Captain Midnight* or *Land of the Lost* or *The Shadow* or *Quiet, Please.*

So she did love him, still, a little bit, even after all those years. I can't hate them: they only wanted to live in the present world again. That isn't such a terrible thing.

It's a good world, all things considered. It's much better than it used to be, in a lot of ways. People don't die from the old diseases any more. They die from new ones, but that's Progress, isn't it?

Isn't it?

Tell me.

Somebody please tell me.

*1979*
*37th CONVENTION*
*BRIGHTON,*
*ENGLAND*

# John Varley

John Varley is two years younger than Spider Robinson, so you can see the situation grows continually worse. To make it still worse, John is of the Heinlein/van Vogt school of writers, who make it big with their very first few stories. (He published his first in 1974.) What makes it worst of all is that I met him at a regional convention in Philadelphia a few years ago and found to my horror that he is six and a half feet tall and as handsome as the day is long.

It doesn't seem right, somehow.

One of the good points of science fiction, it has always seemed to me, was that a writer could work out almost any subtlety without readers turning a hair. If you deal with the future or with a different world or with a radically different society, there is no limit to the oddities you can insert into your social background. You can deliberately violate any taboo, dislodge anything ordinarily taken for granted, and in this way have a lot of fun, to say nothing of doing a little exploring in ordinarily forbidden territory.

Alas, I'm not much good at this myself, but I did once write a story about a society in which mother love was considered obscene. I don't know that I did a very good job of it. Certainly, the story I wrote ended up being one of my most obscure.

Well, to get to the point— John, in "The Persistence of Vision," takes up a society (no, I won't tell you the details; read for yourself) which I found frightening, and in the highest degree unpleasant. In fact, I wondered if, perhaps, for my own peace of mind I ought *not* to read it —but I *had* to read it because I can't shove a story into an anthology without reading it (even though its presence is compelled by the fact of its Hugo award, whether I like it or not).

And as I read on, John won me over. In fact, he ended with a sentence (no, don't look at it now) which is one of those powerful conclusions that will stay with you forever. It will certainly stay with me forever.

This leads on to further thoughts. People ask me sometimes why so much science fiction seems to be so unpleasant these days. I know what they mean. I cut my teeth on stories of science fiction adventure in which the good guys could be told from the bad guys and you could rely on the good guys winning.

As a matter of fact, I still write stories like that. My stories are accessible. I write clearly, with a beginning, middle, and end, and you know where you are at all times.

The newer generation of writers, however, appears to set itself a harder task. They face up to more ambiguous and realistic situations; they deal with worlds in which good and bad are not conveniently compartmentalized, in which there is confusion of emotions and motives, in which understanding comes not only from words but from all kinds of symbols. The result may be more difficult to understand, but, once understood, may be found to mean more.

However, I trust you will all nevertheless continue to read my own non-obscure stories, for old times' sake (and my economic welfare) if nothing else.

# 11

# *THE PERSISTENCE OF VISION*

It was the year of the fourth non-depression. I had recently joined the ranks of the unemployed. The President had told me that I had nothing to fear but fear itself. I took him at his word, for once, and set out to backpack to California.

I was not the only one. The world's economy had been writhing like a snake on a hot griddle for the last twenty years, since the early seventies. We were in a boom-and-bust cycle that seemed to have no end. It had wiped out the sense of security the nation had so painfully won in the golden years after the thirties. People were accustomed to the fact that they could be rich one year and on the breadlines the next. I was on the breadlines in '81, and again in '88. This time I decided to use my freedom from the time clock to see the world. I had ideas of stowing away to Japan. I was forty-seven years old and might not get another chance to be irresponsible.

This was in late summer of the year. Sticking out my thumb along the interstate, I could easily forget that there were food riots back in Chicago. I slept at night on top of my bedroll and saw stars and listened to crickets.

I must have walked most of the way from Chicago to Des Moines. My feet toughened up after a few days of awful blisters. The rides were scarce, partly competition from other hitchhikers and partly the times we were living in. The locals were none too anxious to give rides to city people, who they had heard were mostly a bunch of hunger-crazed potential mass murderers. I got roughed up once and told never to return to Sheffield, Illinois.

But I gradually learned the knack of living on the road. I had started with a small supply of canned goods from the welfare and by the time they ran out, I had found that it was possible to work for a meal at many of the farmhouses along the way.

Some of it was hard work, some of it was only a token from people with a deeply ingrained sense that nothing should come for free. A few meals were gratis, at the family table, with grandchildren sitting around while grandpa or grandma told oft-repeated tales of what it had been like in the Big One back in '29, when people had not been afraid to help a fellow out when he was down on his luck. I found that the older the person, the more likely I was to get a sympathetic ear. One of the many tricks you learn. And most older people will give you anything if you'll only sit and listen to them. I got very good at it.

The rides began to pick up west of Des Moines, then got bad again as I neared the refugee camps bordering the China Strip. This was only five years after the disaster, remember, when the Omaha nuclear reactor melted down and a hot mass of uranium and plutonium began eating its way into the earth, headed for China, spreading a band of radioactivity six hundred kilometers downwind. Most of Kansas City, Missouri, was still living in plywood and sheet-metal shantytowns till the city was rendered habitable again.

The refugees were a tragic group. The initial solidarity people show after a great disaster had long since faded into the lethargy and disillusionment of the displaced person. Many of them would be in and out of hospitals for the rest of their lives. To make it worse, the local people hated them, feared them, would not associate with them. They were modern pariahs, unclean. Their children were shunned. Each camp had only a number to identify it, but the local populace called them all Geigertowns.

I made a long detour to Little Rock to avoid crossing the Strip, though it was safe now as long as you didn't linger. I was issued a pariah's badge by the National Guard—a dosimeter—and wandered from one Geigertown to the next. The people were pitifully friendly once I made the first move, and I always slept indoors. The food was free at the community messes.

Once at Little Rock, I found that the aversion to picking up strangers —who might be tainted with "radiation disease"—dropped off, and I quickly moved across Arkansas, Oklahoma, and Texas. I worked a little here and there, but many of the rides were long. What I saw of Texas was through a car window.

I was a little tired of that by the time I reached New Mexico. I decided to do some more walking. By then I was less interested in California than in the trip itself.

I left the roads and went cross-country where there were no fences to stop me. I found that it wasn't easy, even in New Mexico, to get far from signs of civilization.

Taos was the center, back in the '60's, of cultural experiments in alternative living. Many communes and cooperatives were set up in the surrounding hills during that time. Most of them fell apart in a few months, or years, but a few survived. In later years, any group with a new theory of living and a yen to try it out seemed to gravitate to that part of New Mexico. As a result, the land was dotted with ramshackle windmills, solar heating panels, geodesic domes, group marriages, nudists, philosophers, theoreticians, messiahs, hermits, and more than a few just plain nuts.

Taos was great. I could drop into most of the communes and stay for a day or a week, eating organic rice and beans and drinking goat's milk. When I got tired of one, a few hours' walk in any direction would bring me to another. There, I might be offered a night of prayer and chanting or a ritualistic orgy. Some of the groups had spotless barns with automatic milkers for the herds of cows. Others didn't even have latrines; they just squatted. In some, the members dressed like nuns, or Quakers in early Pennsylvania. Elsewhere, they went nude and shaved all their body hair and painted themselves purple. There were all-male and all-female groups. I was urged to stay at most of the former; at the latter, the responses ranged from a bed for the night and good conversation to being met at a barbed-wire fence with a shotgun.

I tried not to make judgments. These people were doing something important, all of them. They were testing ways whereby people didn't have to live in Chicago. That was a wonder to me. I had thought Chicago was inevitable, like diarrhea.

This is not to say they were all successful. Some made Chicago look like Shangri-La. There was one group who seemed to feel that getting back to nature consisted of sleeping in pigshit and eating food a buzzard wouldn't touch. Many were obviously doomed. They would leave behind a group of empty hovels and the memory of cholera.

So the place wasn't paradise, not by a long way. But there were successes. One or two had been there since '63 or '64 and were raising their third generation. I was disappointed to see that most of these were the ones that departed last from established norms of behavior, though some of the differences could be startling. I suppose the most radical experiments are the least likely to bear fruit.

I stayed through the winter. No one was surprised to see me a second time. It seems that many people came to Taos and shopped around. I seldom stayed more than three weeks at any one place, and always pulled my weight. I made many friends and picked up skills that would serve me if I stayed off the roads. I toyed with the idea of staying at one of them forever. When I couldn't make up my mind, I was advised that there was no hurry. I could go to California and return. They seemed sure I would.

So when spring came I headed west over the hills. I stayed off the roads and slept in the open. Many nights I would stay at another commune, until they finally began to get farther apart, then tapered off entirely. The country was not as pretty as before.

Then, three days' leisurely walking from the last commune, I came to a wall.

In 1964, in the United States, there was an epidemic of German measles, or rubella. Rubella is one of the mildest of infectious diseases. The only time it's a problem is when a woman contracts it in the first four months of her pregnancy. It is passed to the fetus, which usually develops complications. These complications include deafness, blindness, and damage to the brain.

In 1964, in the old days before abortion became readily available, there was nothing to be done about it. Many pregnant women caught rubella and went to term. Five thousand deaf-blind children were born in one year. The normal yearly incidence of deaf-blind children in the United States is one hundred and forty.

In 1970 these five thousand potential Helen Kellers were all six years old. It was quickly seen that there was a shortage of Anne Sullivans. Previously, deaf-blind children could be sent to a small number of special institutions.

It was a problem. Not just anyone can cope with a blind-deaf child. You can't tell them to shut up when they moan; you can't reason with them, tell them that the moaning is driving you crazy. Some parents were driven to nervous breakdowns when they tried to keep their children at home.

Many of the five thousand were badly retarded and virtually impossible to reach, even if anyone had been trying. These ended up, for the most part, warehoused in the hundreds of anonymous nursing homes and institutes for "special" children. They were put into beds, cleaned up once a day by a few overworked nurses, and generally allowed the full blessings of liberty: they were allowed to rot freely in their own dark, quiet, private universes. Who can say if it was bad for them? None of them were heard to complain.

Many children with undamaged brains were shuffled in among the retarded because they were unable to tell anyone that they were in there behind the sightless eyes. They failed the batteries of tactile tests, unaware that their fates hung in the balance when they were asked to fit round pegs into round holes to the ticking of a clock they could not see or hear. As a result, they spent the rest of their lives in bed, and none of them complained, either. To protest, one must be aware of the possibility of something better. It helps to have a language, too.

Several hundred of the children were found to have IQ's within the normal range. There were news stories about them as they approached puberty and it was revealed that there were not enough good people to properly handle them. Money was spent, teachers were trained. The education expenditures would go on for a specified period of time, until the children were grown, then things would go back to normal and everyone could congratulate themselves on having dealt successfully with a tough problem.

And indeed, it did work fairly well. There are ways to reach and teach such children. They involve patience, love, and dedication, and the teachers brought all that to their jobs. All the graduates of the special schools left knowing how to speak with their hands. Some could talk. A few could write. Most of them left the institutions to live with parents or relatives, or, if neither was possible, received counseling and help in fitting themselves into society. The options were limited, but people can live rewarding lives under the most severe handicaps. Not everyone, but most of the graduates, were as happy with their lot as could reasonably be expected. Some achieved the almost saintly peace of their role model, Helen Keller. Others became bitter and withdrawn. A few had to be put in asylums, where they became indistinguishable from the others of their group who had spent the last twenty years there. But for the most part, they did well.

But among the group, as in any group, were some misfits. They tended to be among the brightest, the top ten percent in the IQ scores. This was not a reliable rule. Some had unremarkable test scores and were still infected with hunger to do something, to change things, to rock the boat. With a group of five thousand, there were certain to be a few geniuses, a few artists, a few dreamers, hell-raisers, individualists, movers and shapers: a few glorious maniacs.

There was one among them who might have been President but for the fact that she was blind, deaf, and a woman. She was smart, but not one of the geniuses. She was a dreamer, a creative force, an innovator. It was she who dreamed of freedom. But she was not a builder of fairy castles. Having dreamed it, she had to make it come true.

The wall was made of carefully fitted stone and was about five feet high. It was completely out of context with anything I had seen in New Mexico, though it was built of native rock. You just don't build that kind of wall out there. You use barbed wire if something needs fencing in, but many people still made use of the free range and brands. Somehow it seemed transplanted from New England.

It was substantial enough that I felt it would be unwise to crawl over it. I had crossed many wire fences in my travels and had not gotten in trouble for it yet, though I had some talks with some ranchers. Mostly they told me to keep moving, but didn't seem upset about it. This was different. I set out to walk around it. From the lay of the land, I couldn't tell how far it might reach, but I had time.

At the top of the next rise I saw that I didn't have far to go. The wall made a right-angle turn just ahead. I looked over it and could see some buildings. They were mostly domes, the ubiquitous structure thrown up by communes because of the combination of ease of construction and durability. There were sheep behind the wall, and a few cows. They grazed on grass so green I wanted to go over and roll in it. The wall enclosed a rectangle of green. Outside, where I stood, it was all scrub and sage. These people had access to Rio Grande irrigation water.

I rounded the corner and followed the wall west again.

I saw a man on horseback about the same time he spotted me. He was south of me, outside the wall, and he turned and rode in my direction.

He was a dark man with thick features, dressed in denim and boots with a gray battered Stetson. Navaho, maybe. I don't know much about Indians, but I'd heard they were out here.

"Hello," I said when he'd stopped. He was looking me over. "Am I on your land?"

"Tribal land," he said. "Yeah, you're on it."

"I didn't see any signs."

He shrugged.

"It's okay, bud. You don't look like you out to rustle cattle." He grinned at me. His teeth were large and stained with tobacco. "You be camping out tonight?"

"Yes. How much farther does the, uh, tribal land go? Maybe I'll be out of it before tonight?"

He shook his head gravely. "Nah. You won't be off it tomorrow. 'S all right. You make a fire, you be careful, huh?" He grinned again and started to ride off.

"Hey, what is this place?" I gestured to the wall, and he pulled his horse up and turned around again. It raised a lot of dust.

"Why you asking?" He looked a little suspicious.

"I dunno. Just curious. It doesn't look like the other places I've been to. This wall . . ."

He scowled. "Damn wall." Then he shrugged. I thought that was all he was going to say. Then he went on.

"These people, we look out for 'em, you hear? Maybe we don't go for what they're doin'. But they got it rough, you know?" He looked at me, expecting something. I never did get the knack of talking to these laconic Westerners. I always felt that I was making my sentences too long. They use a shorthand of grunts and shrugs and omitted parts of speech, and I always felt like a dude when I talked to them.

"Do they welcome guests?" I asked. "I thought I might see if I could spend the night."

He shrugged again, and it was a whole different gesture.

"Maybe. They all deaf and blind, you know?" And that was all the conversation he could take for the day. He made a clucking sound and galloped away.

I continued down the wall until I came to a dirt road that wound up the arroyo and entered the wall. There was a wooden gate, but it stood open. I wondered why they took all the trouble with the wall only to leave the gate like that. Then I noticed a circle of narrow-gauge train tracks that came out of the gate, looped around outside it, and rejoined itself. There was a small siding that ran along the outer wall for a few yards.

I stood there a few moments. I don't know what entered into my decision. I think I was a little tired of sleeping out, and I was hungry for a home-cooked meal. The sun was getting closer to the horizon. The land to the west looked like more of the same. If the highway had been visible, I might have headed that way and hitched a ride. But I turned the other way and went through the gate.

I walked down the middle of the tracks. There was a wooden fence on each side of the road, built of horizontal planks, like a corral. Sheep grazed on one side of me. There was a Shetland sheepdog with them, and she raised her ears and followed me with her eyes as I passed, but did not come when I whistled.

It was about half a mile to the cluster of buildings ahead. There were four or five domes made of something translucent, like greenhouses, and several conventional square buildings. There were two windmills turning lazily in the breeze. There were several banks of solar water heaters. These are flat constructions of glass and wood, held off the ground so they can tilt to follow the sun. They were almost vertical now, intercepting the oblique rays of sunset. There were a few trees, what might have been an orchard.

About halfway there I passed under a wooden footbridge. It arched over the road, giving access from the east pasture to the west pasture. I wondered, What was wrong with a simple gate?

Then I saw something coming down the road in my direction. It was traveling on the tracks and it was very quiet. I stopped and waited.

It was a sort of converted mining engine, the sort that pulls loads of coal up from the bottom of shafts. It was battery-powered, and it had gotten quite close before I heard it. A small man was driving it. He was pulling a car behind him and singing as loud as he could with absolutely no sense of pitch.

He got closer and closer, moving about five miles per hour, one hand held out as if he was signaling a left turn. Suddenly I realized what was happening, as he was bearing down on me. He wasn't going to stop. He was counting fence posts with his hand. I scrambled up the fence just in time. There wasn't more than six inches of clearance between the train and the fence on either side. His palm touched my leg as I squeezed close to the fence, and he stopped abruptly.

He leaped from the car and grabbed me and I thought I was in trouble. But he looked concerned, not angry, and felt me all over, trying to discover if I was hurt. I was embarrassed. Not from the examination; because I had been foolish. The Indian had said they were all deaf and blind but I guess I hadn't quite believed him.

He was flooded with relief when I managed to convey to him that I was all right. With eloquent gestures he made me understand that I was not to stay on the road. He indicated that I should climb over the fence and continue through the fields. He repeated himself several times to be sure I understood, then held on to me as I climbed over to assure himself that I was out of the way. He reached over the fence and held my shoulders, smiling at me. He pointed to the road and shook his head, then pointed to the buildings and nodded. He touched my head and smiled when I nodded. He climbed back onto the engine and started up, all the time nodding and pointing where he wanted me to go. Then he was off again.

I debated what to do. Most of me said turn around, go back to the wall by way of the pasture, and head back into the hills. These people probably wouldn't want me around. I doubted that I'd be able to talk to them, and they might even resent me. On the other hand, I was fascinated, as who wouldn't be? I wanted to see how they managed it. I still didn't believe that they were *all* deaf and blind. It didn't seem possible.

The Sheltie was sniffing at my pants. I looked down at her and she backed away, then daintily approached me as I held out my open hand. She sniffed, then licked me. I patted her on the head, and she hustled back to her sheep.

I turned toward the buildings.

The first order of business was money.

None of the students knew much about it from experience, but the library was full of Braille books. They started reading.

One of the first things that became apparent was that when money was mentioned, lawyers were not far away. The students wrote letters. From the replies, they selected a lawyer and retained him.

They were in a school in Pennsylvania at the time. The original pupils of the special schools, five hundred in number, had been narrowed down to about seventy as people left to live with relatives or found other solutions to their special problems. Of those seventy, some had places to go but didn't want to go there; others had few alternatives. Their parents were either dead or not interested in living with them. So the seventy had been gathered from the schools around the country into this one, while ways to deal with them were worked out. The authorities had plans, but the students beat them to it.

Each of them had been entitled to a guaranteed annual income since 1980. They had been under the care of the government, so they had not received it. They sent their lawyer to court. He came back with a ruling that they could not collect. They appealed, and won. The money was paid retroactively, with interest, and came to a healthy sum. They thanked their lawyer and retained a real estate agent. Meanwhile, they read.

They read about communes in New Mexico, and instructed their agent to look for something out there. He made a deal for a tract to be leased in perpetuity from the Navaho nation. They read about the land, found that it would need a lot of water to be productive in the way they wanted it to be.

They divided into groups to research what they would need to be self-sufficient.

Water could be obtained by tapping into the canals that carried it from the reservoirs on the Rio Grande into the reclaimed land in the south. Federal money was available for the project through a labyrinthine scheme involving HEW, the Agriculture Department, and the Bureau of Indian Affairs. They ended up paying little for their pipeline.

The land was arid. It would need fertilizer to be of use in raising sheep without resorting to open-range techniques. The cost of fertilizer could be subsidized through the Rural Resettlement Program. After that, planting clover would enrich the soil with all the nitrates they could want.

There were techniques available to farm ecologically, without worrying about fertilizers or pesticides. Everything was recycled. Essentially, you put sunlight and water into one end and harvested wool, fish, vegetables, apples, honey, and eggs at the other end. You used nothing but the land, and replaced even that as you recycled your waste products back into the soil. They were not interested in agribusiness with huge combine harvesters and crop dusters. They didn't even want to turn a profit. They merely wanted sufficiency.

The details multiplied. Their leader, the one who had had the original idea and the drive to put it into action in the face of overwhelming obstacles, was a dynamo named Janet Reilly. Knowing nothing about the techniques generals and executives employ to achieve large objectives, she invented them herself and adapted them to the peculiar needs and limitations of her group. She assigned task forces to look into solutions of each aspect of their project: law, science, social planning, design, buying, logistics, construction. At any one time, she was the only person who knew everything about what was happening. She kept it all in her head, without notes of any kind.

It was in the area of social planning that she showed herself to be a visionary and not just a superb organizer. Her idea was not to make a place where they could lead a life that was a sightless, soundless imitation of their unafflicted peers. She wanted a whole new start, a way of living that was by and for the blind-deaf, a way of living that accepted no convention just because that was the way it had always been done. She examined every human cultural institution from marriage to indecent exposure to see how it related to her needs and the needs of her friends. She was aware of the peril of this approach, but was undeterred. Her Social Task Force read about every variant group that had ever tried to make it on its own anywhere, and brought her reports about how and why they had failed or succeeded. She filtered this information through her own experiences to see how it would work for her unusual group with its own set of needs and goals.

The details were endless. They hired an architect to put their ideas into Braille blueprints. Gradually the plans evolved. They spent more money. The construction began, supervised on the site by their architect, who by now was so fascinated by the scheme that she donated her services. It was an important break, for they needed someone there whom they could trust. There is only so much that can be accomplished at such a distance.

When things were ready for them to move, they ran into bureaucratic trouble. They had anticipated it, but it was a setback. Social agencies charged with overseeing their welfare doubted the wisdom of the project. When it became apparent that no amount of reasoning was going to stop it, wheels were set in motion that resulted in a restraining order, issued for their own protection, preventing them from leaving the school. They were twenty-one years old by then, all of them, but were judged mentally incompetent to manage their own affairs. A hearing was scheduled.

Luckily, they still had access to their lawyer. He also had become infected with the crazy vision, and put on a great battle for them. He succeeded in getting a ruling concerning the rights of institutionalized persons, later upheld by the Supreme Court, which eventually had severe repercussions in state and county hospitals. Realizing the trouble they were already in regarding the thousands of patients in inadequate facilities across the country, the agencies gave in.

By then, it was the spring of 1986, one year after their target date. Some of their fertilizer had washed away already for lack of erosion-preventing clover. It was getting late to start crops, and they were running short of money. Nevertheless, they moved to New Mexico and began the backbreaking job of getting everything started. There were fifty-five of them, with nine children aged three months to six years.

I don't know what I expected. I remember that everything was a surprise, either because it was so normal or because it was so different. None of my idiot surmises about what such a place might be like proved to be true. And of course I didn't know the history of the place; I learned that later, picked up in bits and pieces.

I was surprised to see lights in some of the buildings. The first thing I had assumed was that they would have no need of them. That's an example of something so normal that it surprised me.

As to the differences, the first thing that caught my attention was the fence around the rail line. I had a personal interest in it, having almost been injured by it. I struggled to understand, as I must if I was to stay even for a night.

The wood fences that enclosed the rails on their way to the gate continued up to a barn, where the rails looped back on themselves in the same way they did outside the wall. The entire line was enclosed by the fence. The only access was a loading platform by the barn, and the gate to the outside. It made sense. The only way a deaf-blind person could operate a conveyance like that would be with assurances that there was no one on the track. These people would *never* go on the tracks; there was no way they could be warned of an approaching train.

There were people moving around me in the twilight as I made my way into the group of buildings. They took no notice of me, as I had expected. They moved fast; some of them were actually running. I stood still, eyes searching all around me so no one would come crashing into me. I had to figure out how they kept from crashing into each other before I got bolder.

I bent to the ground and examined it. The light was getting bad, but I saw immediately that there were concrete sidewalks crisscrossing the area. Each of the walks was etched with a different sort of pattern in grooves that had been made before the stuff set—lines, waves, depressions, patches of rough and smooth. I quickly saw that the people who were in a hurry moved only on those walkways, and they were all barefoot. It was no trick to see that it was some sort of traffic pattern read with the feet. I stood up. I didn't need to know how it worked. It was sufficient to know what it was and stay off the paths.

The people were unremarkable. Some of them were not dressed, but I was used to that by now. They came in all shapes and sizes, but all seemed to be about the same age except for the children. Except for the fact that they did not stop and talk or even wave as they approached each other, I would never have guessed they were blind. I watched them come to intersections in the pathways—I didn't know how they knew they were there, but could think of several ways—and slow down as they crossed. It was a marvelous system.

I began to think of approaching someone. I had been there for almost half an hour, an intruder. I guess I had a false sense of these people's vulnerability; I felt like a burglar.

I walked along beside a woman for a minute. She was very purposeful in her eyes-ahead stride, or seemed to be. She sensed something, maybe my footsteps. She slowed a little, and I touched her on the shoulder, not knowing what else to do. She stopped instantly and turned toward me. Her eyes were open but vacant. Her hands were all over me, lightly touching my face, my chest, my hands, fingering my clothing. There was no doubt in my mind that she knew me for a stranger, probably from the first tap on the shoulder. But she smiled warmly at me, and hugged me. Her hands were very delicate and warm. That's funny, because they were callused from hard work. But they felt sensitive.

She made me to understand—by pointing to the building, making eating motions with an imaginary spoon, and touching a number on her watch—that supper was served in an hour, and that I was invited. I nodded and smiled beneath her hands; she kissed me on the cheek and hurried off.

Well. It hadn't been so bad. I had worried about my ability to communicate. Later I found out she learned a great deal more about me than I had told.

I put off going into the mess hall or whatever it was. I strolled around in the gathering darkness looking at their layout. I saw the little Sheltie bringing the sheep back to the fold for the night. She herded them expertly through the open gate without any instructions, and one of the residents closed it and locked them in. The man bent and scratched the dog on the head and got his hand licked. Her chores done for the night, the dog hurried over to me and sniffed my pant leg. She followed me around the rest of the evening.

Everyone seemed so busy that I was surprised to see one woman sitting on a rail fence, doing nothing. I went over to her.

Closer, I saw that she was younger than I had thought. She was thirteen, I learned later. She wasn't wearing any clothes. I touched her on the shoulder, and she jumped down from the fence and went through the same routine as the other woman had, touching me all over with no reserve. She took my hand and I felt her fingers moving rapidly in my palm. I couldn't understand it, but knew what it was. I shrugged, and tried out other gestures to indicate that I didn't speak hand talk. She nodded, still feeling my face with her hands.

She asked me if I was staying to dinner. I assured her that I was. She asked me if I was from a university. And if you think that's easy to ask with only body movements, try it. But she was so graceful and supple in her movements, so deft at getting her meaning across. It was beautiful to watch her. It was speech and ballet at the same time.

I told her I wasn't from a university, and launched into an attempt to tell her a little about what I was doing and how I got there. She listened to me with her hands, scratching her head graphically when I failed to make my meanings clear. All the time the smile on her face got broader and broader, and she would laugh silently at my antics. All this while standing very close to me, touching me. At last she put her hands on her hips.

"I guess you need the practice," she said, "but if it's all the same to you, could we talk mouthtalk for now? You're cracking me up."

I jumped as if stung by a bee. The touching, while something I could ignore for a deaf-blind girl, suddenly seemed out of place. I stepped back a little, but her hands returned to me. She looked puzzled, then read the problem with her hands.

"I'm sorry," she said. "You thought I was deaf and blind. If I'd known I would have told you right off."

"I thought everyone here was."

"Just the parents. I'm one of the children. We all hear and see quite well. Don't be so nervous. If you can't stand touching, you're not going to like it here. Relax, I won't hurt you." And she kept her hands moving over me, mostly my face. I didn't understand it at the time, but it didn't seem sexual. Turned out I was wrong, but it wasn't blatant.

"You'll need me to show you the ropes," she said, and started for the domes. She held my hand and walked close to me. Her other hand kept moving to my face every time I talked.

"Number one, stay off the concrete paths. That's where—"

"I already figured that out."

"You did? How long have you been here?" Her hands searched my face with renewed interest. It was quite dark.

"Less than an hour. I was almost run over by your train."

She laughed, then apologized and said she knew it wasn't funny to me.

I told her it *was* funny to me now, though it hadn't been at the time. She said there was a warning sign on the gate, but I had been unlucky enough to come when the gate was open—they opened it by remote control before a train started up—and I hadn't seen it.

"What's your name?" I asked her, as we neared the soft yellow lights coming from the dining room.

Her hand worked reflexively in mine, then stopped. "Oh, I don't know. I *have* one; several, in fact. But they're in bodytalk. I'm . . . Pink. It translates as Pink, I guess."

There was a story behind it. She had been the first child born to the school students. They knew that babies were described as being pink, so they called her that. She felt pink to them. As we entered the hall, I could see that her name was visually inaccurate. One of her parents had been black. She was dark, with blue eyes and curly hair lighter than her skin. She had a broad nose, but small lips.

She didn't ask my name, so I didn't offer it. No one asked my name, in speech, the entire time I was there. They called me many things in bodytalk, and when the children called me it was "Hey, you!" They weren't big on spoken words.

The dining hall was in a rectangular building made of brick. It connected to one of the large domes. It was dimly lighted. I later learned that the lights were for me alone. The children didn't need them for anything but reading. I held Pink's hand, glad to have a guide. I kept my eyes and ears open.

"We're informal," Pink said. Her voice was embarrassingly loud in the large room. No one else was talking at all; there were just the sounds of movement and breathing. Several of the children looked up. "I won't introduce you around now. Just feel like part of the family. People will feel you later, and you can talk to them. You can take your clothes off here at the door."

I had no trouble with that. Everyone else was nude, and I could easily adjust to household customs by that time. You take your shoes off in Japan, you take your clothes off in Taos. What's the difference?

Well, quite a bit, actually. There was all the touching that went on. Everybody touched everybody else, as routinely as glancing. Everyone touched my face first, then went on with what seemed like total innocence to touch me everywhere else. As usual, it was not quite what it seemed. It was *not* innocent, and it was not the usual treatment they gave others in their group. They touched each other's genitals a lot *more* than they touched mine. They were holding back with me so I wouldn't be frightened. They were very polite with strangers.

There was a long, low table, with everyone sitting on the floor around it. Pink led me to it.

"See the bare strips on the floor? Stay out of them. Don't leave anything in them. That's where people walk. Don't *ever* move anything. Furniture, I mean. That has to be decided at full meetings, so we'll all know where everything is. Small things, too. If you pick up something, put it back exactly where you found it."

"I understand."

People were bringing bowls and platters of food from the adjoining kitchen. They set them on the table, and the diners began feeling them. They ate with their fingers, without plates, and they did it slowly and lovingly. They smelled things for a long time before they took a bite. Eating was very sensual to these people.

They were *terrific* cooks. I have never, before or since, eaten as well as I did at Keller. (That's my name for it, in speech, though their bodytalk name was something very like that. When I called it Keller, everyone knew what I was talking about.) They started off with good, fresh produce, something that's hard enough to find in the cities, and went at the cooking with artistry and imagination. It wasn't like any national style I've eaten. They improvised, and seldom cooked the same thing the same way twice.

I sat between Pink and the fellow who had almost run me down earlier. I stuffed myself disgracefully. It was too far removed from beef jerky and the organic dry cardboard I had been eating for me to be able to resist. I lingered over it, but still finished long before anyone else. I watched them as I sat back carefully and wondered if I'd be sick. (I wasn't, thank God.) They fed themselves and each other, sometimes getting up and going clear around the table to offer a choice morsel to a friend on the other side. I was fed in this way by all too many of them, and nearly popped until I learned a pidgin phrase in handtalk, saying I was full to the brim. I learned from Pink that a friendlier way to refuse was to offer something myself.

Eventually I had nothing to do but feed Pink and look at the others. I began to be more observant. I had thought they were eating in solitude, but soon saw that lively conversation was flowing around the table. Hands were busy, moving almost too fast to see. They were spelling into each other's palms, shoulders, legs, arms, bellies; any part of the body. I watched in amazement as a ripple of laughter spread like falling dominoes from one end of the table to the other as some witticism was passed along the line. It was *fast*. Looking carefully, I could see the thoughts moving, reaching one person, passed on while a reply went in the other direction and was in turn passed on, other replies originating all along the line and bouncing back and forth. They were a wave form, like water.

It was messy. Let's face it; eating with your fingers and talking with your hands is going to get you smeared with food. But no one minded. *I* certainly didn't. I was too busy feeling left out. Pink talked to me, but I knew I was finding out what it's like to be deaf. These people were friendly and seemed to like me, but could do nothing about it. We couldn't communicate.

Afterwards, we all trooped outside, except the cleanup crew, and took a shower beneath a set of faucets that gave out very cold water. I told Pink I'd like to help with the dishes, but she said I'd just be in the way. I couldn't do anything around Keller until I learned their very specific ways of doing things. She seemed to be assuming already that I'd be around that long.

Back into the building to dry off, which they did with their usual puppy dog friendliness, making a game and a gift of toweling each other, and then we went into the dome.

It was warm inside, warm and dark. Light entered from the passage to the dining room, but it wasn't enough to blot out the stars through the lattice of triangular panes overhead. It was almost like being out in the open.

Pink quickly pointed out the positional etiquette within the dome. It wasn't hard to follow, but I still tended to keep my arms and legs pulled in close so I wouldn't trip someone by sprawling into a walk space.

My misconceptions got me again. There was no sound but the soft whisper of flesh against flesh, so I thought I was in the middle of an orgy. I had been at them before, in other communes, and they looked pretty much like this. I quickly saw that I was wrong, and only later found out I had been right. In a sense.

What threw my evaluations out of whack was the simple fact that group conversation among these people *had* to look like an orgy. The much subtler observation that I made later was that with a hundred naked bodies sliding, rubbing, kissing, caressing, all at the same time, what was the point in making a distinction? There was no distinction.

I have to say that I use the noun "orgy" only to get across a general idea of many people in close contact. I don't like the word, it is too ripe with connotations. But I had these connotations myself at the time, so I was relieved to see that it was not an orgy. The ones I had been to had been tedious and impersonal, and I had hoped for better from these people.

Many wormed their way through the crush to get to me and meet me. Never more than one at a time; they were constantly aware of what was going on and were waiting their turn to talk to me. Naturally, I didn't know it then. Pink sat with me to interpret the hard thoughts. I eventually used her words less and less, getting into the spirit of tactile seeing and understanding. No one felt they really knew me until they had touched every part of my body, so there were hands on me all the time. I timidly did the same.

What with all the touching, I quickly got an erection, which embarrassed me quite a bit. I was berating myself for being unable to keep sexual responses out of it, for not being able to operate on the same intellectual plane I thought they were on, when I realized with some shock that the couple next to me was making love. They had been doing it for the last ten minutes, actually, and it had seemed such a natural part of what was happening that I had known it and not known it at the same time.

No sooner had I realized it than I suddenly wondered if I was right. *Were they?* It was very slow and the light was bad. But her legs were up, and he was on top of her, that much I was sure of. It was foolish of me, but I really had to know. I had to find out *what the hell I was in.* How could I give the proper social responses if I didn't know the situation?

I was very sensitive to polite behavior after my months at the various communes. I had become adept at saying prayers before supper in one place, chanting Hare Krishna at another, and going happily nudist at still another. It's called "when in Rome," and if you can't adapt to it you shouldn't go visiting. I would kneel to Mecca, burp after my meals, toast anything that was proposed, eat organic rice and compliment the cook; but to do it right, you have to know the customs. I had thought I knew them, but had changed my mind three times in as many minutes.

They *were* making love, in the sense that he was penetrating her. They were also deeply involved with each other. Their hands fluttered like butterflies all over each other, filled with meanings I couldn't see or feel. But they were being touched by and were touching many other people around them. They were talking to all these people, even if the message was as simple as a pat on the forehead or arm.

Pink noticed where my attention was. She was sort of wound around me, without really doing anything I would have thought of as provocative. I just couldn't *decide.* It seemed so innocent, and yet it wasn't.

"That's (—) and (—)," she said, the parentheses indicating a series of hand motions against my palm. I never learned a sound word as a name for any of them but Pink, and I can't reproduce the bodytalk names they had. Pink reached over, touched the woman with her foot, and did some complicated business with her toes. The woman smiled and grabbed Pink's foot, her fingers moving.

"(—) would like to talk with you later," Pink told me. "Right after she's through talking to (—). You met her earlier, remember? She says she likes your hands."

Now this is going to sound crazy, I know. It sounded pretty crazy to me when I thought of it. It dawned on me with a sort of revelation that her word for talk and mine were miles apart. Talk, to her, meant a complex interchange involving all parts of the body. She could read words or emotions in every twitch of my muscles, like a lie detector. Sound, to her, was only a minor part of communication. It was something she used to speak to outsiders. Pink talked with her whole being.

I didn't have the half of it, even then, but it was enough to turn my head entirely around in relation to these people. They talked with their bodies. It wasn't all hands, as I'd thought. Any part of the body in contact with any other was communication, sometimes a very simple and basic sort—think of McLuhan's light bulb as the basic medium of information—perhaps saying no more than "I am here." But talk was talk, and if conversation evolved to the point where you needed to talk to another with your genitals, it was still a part of the conversation. What I wanted to know was *what were they saying?* I knew, even at that dim moment or realization, that it was much more than I could grasp. Sure, you're saying. You know about talking to your lover with your body as you make love. That's not such a new idea. Of course it isn't, but think how wonderful that talk is even when you're not primarily tactile-oriented. Can you carry the thought from there, or are you doomed to be an earthworm thinking about sunsets?

While this was happening to me, there was a woman getting acquainted with my body. Her hands were on me, in my lap, when I felt myself ejaculating. It was a big surprise to me, but to no one else. I had been telling everyone around me for many minutes, through signs they could feel with their hands, that it was going to happen. Instantly, hands were all over my body. I could almost understand them as they spelled tender thoughts to me. I got the gist, anyway, if not the words. I was terribly embarrassed for only a moment, then it passed away in the face of the easy acceptance. It was very intense. For a long time I couldn't get my breath.

The woman who had been the cause of it touched my lips with her fingers. She moved them slowly, but meaningfully I was sure. Then she melted back into the group.

"What did she say?" I asked Pink.

She smiled at me. "You know, of course. If you'd only cut loose from your verbalizing. But, generally, she meant 'How nice for you.' It also translates as 'How nice for me.' And 'me,' in this sense, means all of us. The organism."

I knew I had to stay and learn to speak.

The commune had its ups and downs. They had expected them, in general, but had not known what shape they might take.

Winter killed many of their fruit trees. They replaced them with hybrid strains. They lost more fertilizer and soil in windstorms because the clover had not had time to anchor it down. Their schedule had been thrown off by the court actions, and they didn't really get things settled in a groove for more than a year.

Their fish all died. They used the bodies for fertilizer and looked into what might have gone wrong. They were using a three-stage ecology of the type pioneered by the New Alchemists in the '70's. It consisted of three domed ponds: one containing fish, another with crushed shells and bacteria in one section and algae in another, and a third full of daphnids. The water containing fish waste from the first pond was pumped through the shells and bacteria, which detoxified it and converted the ammonia it contained into fertilizer for the algae. The algae water was pumped into the second pond to feed the daphnids. Then daphnids and algae were pumped to the fish pond as food and the enriched water was used to fertilize greenhouse plants in all of the domes.

They tested the water and the soil and found that chemicals were being leached from impurities in the shells and concentrated down the food chain. After a thorough cleanup, they restarted and all went well. But they had lost their first cash crop.

They never went hungry. Nor were they cold; there was plenty of sunlight year-round to power the pumps and the food cycle and to heat their living quarters. They had built their buildings half buried with an eye to the heating and cooling powers of convective currents. But they had to spend some of their capital. The first year they showed a loss.

One of their buildings caught fire during the first winter. Two men and a small girl were killed when a sprinkler system malfunctioned. This was a shock to them. They had thought things would operate as advertised. None of them knew much about the building trades, about estimates as opposed to realities. They found that several of their installations were not up to specifications, and instituted a program of periodic checks on everything. They learned to strip down and repair anything on the farm. If something contained electronics too complex for them to cope with, they tore it out and installed something simpler.

Socially, their progress had been much more encouraging. Janet had wisely decided that there would be only two hard and fast objectives in the realm of their relationships. The first was that she refused to be their president, chairwoman, chief, or supreme commander. She had seen from the start that a driving personality was needed to get the planning done and the land bought and a sense of purpose fostered from their formless desire for an alternative. But once at the promised land, she abdicated. From that point they would operate as a democratic communism. If that failed, they would adopt a new approach. Anything but a dictatorship with her at the head. She wanted no part of that.

The second principle was to accept nothing. There had never been a blind-deaf community operating on its own. They had no expectations to satisfy, they did not need to live as the sighted did. They were alone.

There was no one to tell them not to do something simply because it was not done.

They had no clearer idea of what their society would be than anyone else. They had been forced into a mold that was not relevant to their needs, but beyond that they didn't know. They would search out the behavior that made sense, the moral things for blind-deaf people to do. They understood the basic principles of morals: that nothing is moral always, and anything is moral under the right circumstances. It all had to do with social context. They were starting from a blank slate, with no models to follow.

By the end of the second year they had their context. They continually modified it, but the basic pattern was set. They knew themselves and what they were as they had never been able to do at the school. They defined themselves in their own terms.

I spent my first day at Keller in school. It was the obvious and necessary step. I had to learn handtalk.

Pink was kind and very patient. I learned the basic alphabet and practiced hard at it. By the afternoon she was refusing to talk to me, forcing me to speak with my hands. She would speak only when pressed hard, and eventually not at all. I scarcely spoke a single word after the third day.

This is not to say that I was suddenly fluent. Not at all. At the end of the first day I knew the alphabet and could laboriously make myself understood. I was not so good at reading words spelled into my own palm. For a long time I had to look at the hand to see what was spelled. But like any language, eventually you think in it. I speak fluent French, and I can recall my amazement when I finally reached the point where I wasn't translating my thoughts before I spoke. I reached it at Keller in about two weeks.

I remember one of the last things I asked Pink in speech. It was something that was worrying me.

"Pink, am I welcome here?"

"You've been here three days. Do you feel rejected?"

"No, it's not that. I guess I just need to hear your policy about outsiders. How *long* am I welcome?"

She wrinkled her brow. It was evidently a new question.

"Well, practically speaking, until a majority of us decide we want you to go. But that's never happened. No one's stayed here much longer than a few days. We've never had to evolve a policy about what to do, for instance, if someone who sees and hears wants to join us. No one has, so far, but I guess it could happen. My guess is that they wouldn't accept it. They're very independent and jealous of their freedom, though you might not have noticed it. I don't think you could ever be one of them. But as long as you're willing to think of yourself as a guest, you could probably stay for twenty years."

"You said 'they.' Don't you include yourself in the group?"

For the first time she looked a little uneasy. I wish I had been better at reading body language at the time. I think my hands could have told me volumes about what she was thinking.

"Sure," she said. "The children are part of the group. We like it. I sure wouldn't want to be anywhere else, from what I know of the outside."

"I don't blame you." There were things left unsaid here, but I didn't know enough to ask the right questions. "But it's never a problem, being able to see when none of your parents can? They don't . . . resent you in any way?"

This time she laughed. "Oh, no. Never that. They're much too independent for that. You've seen it. They don't *need* us for anything they can't do themselves. We're part of the family. We do exactly the same things they do. And it really doesn't matter. Sight, I mean. Hearing, either. Just look around you. Do I have any special advantages because I can see where I'm going?"

I had to admit that she didn't. But there was still the hint of something she wasn't saying to me.

"I know what's bothering you. About staying here." She had to draw me back to my original question; I had been wandering.

"What's that?"

"You don't feel a part of the daily life. You're not doing your share of the chores. You're very conscientious and you want to do your part. I can tell."

She read me right, as usual, and I admitted it.

"And you won't be able to until you can talk to everybody. So let's get back to your lessons. Your fingers are still very sloppy."

There was a lot of work to be done. The first thing I had to learn was to slow down. They were slow and methodical workers, made few mistakes, and didn't care if a job took all day so long as it was done well. When I was working by myself I didn't have to worry about it: sweeping, picking apples, weeding in the gardens. But when I was on a job that required teamwork I had to learn a whole new pace. Eyesight enables a person to do many aspects of a job at once with a few quick glances. A blind person will take each aspect of the job in turn if the job is spread out. Everything has to be verified by touch. At a bench job, though, they could be much faster than I. They could make me feel as though I was working with my toes instead of fingers.

I never suggested that I could make anything quicker by virtue of my sight or hearing. They quite rightly would have told me to mind my own business. Accepting sighted help was the first step to dependence, and after all, they would still be here with the same jobs to do after I was gone.

And that got me to thinking about the children again. I began to be positive that there was an undercurrent of resentment, maybe unconscious, between the parents and children. It was obvious that there was a great deal of love between them, but how could the children fail to resent the rejection of their talent? So my reasoning went, anyway.

I quickly fit myself into the routine. I was treated no better or worse than anyone else, which gratified me. Though I would never become part of the group, even if I should desire it, there was absolutely no indication that I was anything but a full member. That's just how they treated guests: as they would one of their own number.

Life was fulfilling out there in a way it has never been in the cities. It wasn't unique to Keller, this pastoral peace, but the people there had it in generous helpings. The earth beneath your bare feet is something you can never feel in a city park.

Daily life was busy and satisfying. There were chickens and hogs to feed, bees and sheep to care for, fish to harvest, and cows to milk. Everybody worked: men, women, and children. It all seemed to fit together without any apparent effort. Everybody seemed to know what to do when it needed doing. You could think of it as a well-oiled machine, but I never liked that metaphor, especially for people. I thought of it as an organism. Any social group is, but this one *worked.* Most of the other communes I'd visited had glaring flaws. Things would not get done because everyone was too stoned or couldn't be bothered or didn't see the necessity of doing it in the first place. That sort of ignorance leads to typhus and soil erosion and people freezing to death and invasions of social workers who take your children away. I'd seen it happen.

Not here. They had a good picture of the world as it is, not the rosy misconceptions so many other utopians labor under. They did the jobs that needed doing.

I could never detail all the nuts and bolts (there's that machine metaphor again) of how the place worked. The fish-cycle ponds alone were complicated enough to over-awe me. I killed a spider in one of the greenhouses, then found out it had been put there to eat a specific set of plant predators. Same for the frogs. There were insects in the water to kill other insects; it got to a point where I was afraid to swat a mayfly without prior okay.

As the days went by I was told some of the history of the place. Mistakes had been made, though surprisingly few. One had been in the area of defense. They had made no provision for it at first, not knowing much about the brutality and random violence that reaches even to the out-of-the-way corners. Guns were the logical and preferred choice out here, but were beyond their capabilities.

One night a carload of men who had had too much to drink showed up. They had heard of the place in town. They stayed for two days, cutting the phone lines and raping many of the women.

The people discussed all the options after the invasion was over, and settled on the organic one. They bought five German shepherds. Not the psychotic wretches that are marketed under the description of "attack dogs," but specially trained ones from a firm recommended by the Albuquerque police. They were trained as both Seeing-Eye and police dogs. They were perfectly harmless until an outsider showed overt agression, then they were trained, not to disarm, but to go for the throat.

It worked, like most of their solutions. The second invasion resulted in two dead and three badly injured, all on the other side. As a backup in case of a concerted attack, they hired an ex-marine to teach them the fundamentals of close-in dirty fighting. These were not dewy-eyed flower children.

There were three superb meals a day. And there was leisure time, too. It was not all work. There was time to take a friend out and sit in the grass under a tree, usually around sunset, just before the big dinner. There was time for someone to stop working for a few minutes, to share some special treasure. I remember being taken by the hand by one woman—whom I must call Tall-one-with-the-green-eyes—to a spot where mushrooms were growing in the cool crawl space beneath the barn. We wriggled under until our faces were buried in the patch, picked a few, and smelled them. She showed me how to smell. I would have thought a few weeks before that we had ruined their beauty, but after all it was only visual. I was already beginning to discount that sense, which is so removed from the essence of an object. She showed me that they were still beautiful to touch and smell after we had apparently destroyed them. Then she was off to the kitchen with the pick of the bunch in her apron. They tasted all the better that night.

And a man—I will call him Baldy—who brought me a plank he and one of the women had been planing in the woodshop. I touched its smoothness and smelled it and agreed with him how good it was.

And after the evening meal, the Together.

During my third week there I had an indication of my status with the group. It was the first real test of whether I meant anything to them. Anything special, I mean. I wanted to see them as my friends, and I suppose I was a little upset to think that just anyone who wandered in here would be treated the way I was. It was childish and unfair to them, and I wasn't even aware of the discontent until later.

I had been hauling water in a bucket into the field where a seedling tree was being planted. There was a hose for that purpose, but it was in use on the other side of the village. This tree was not in reach of the automatic sprinklers and it was drying out. I had been carrying water to it until another solution was found.

It was hot, around noon. I got the water from a standing spigot near the forge. I set the bucket down on the ground behind me and leaned my head into the flow of water. I was wearing a shirt made of cotton, unbuttoned in the front. The water felt good running through my hair and soaking into the shirt. I let it go on for almost a minute.

There was a crash behind me and I bumped my head when I raised it up too quickly under the faucet. I turned and saw a woman sprawled on her face in the dust. She was turning over slowly, holding her knee. I realized with a sinking feeling that she had tripped over the bucket I had carelessly left on the concrete express lane. Think of it: ambling along on ground that you trust to be free of all obstruction, suddenly you're sitting on the ground. Their system would only work with trust, and it had to be total; everybody had to be responsible all the time. I had been accepted into that trust and I had blown it. I felt sick.

She had a nasty scrape on her left knee that was oozing blood. She felt it with her hands, sitting there on the ground, and she began to howl. It was weird, painful. Tears came from her eyes, then she pounded her fists on the ground, going "Hunnnh, hunnnh, *hunnnh!*" with each blow. She was angry, and she had every right to be.

She found the pail as I hesitantly reached out for her. She grabbed my hand and followed it up to my face. She felt my face, crying all the time, then wiped her nose and got up. She started off for one of the buildings. She limped slightly.

I sat down and felt miserable. I didn't know what to do.

One of the men came out to get me. It was Big Man. I called him that because he was the tallest person at Keller. He wasn't any sort of policeman, I found out later; he was just the first one the injured woman had met. He took my hand and felt my face. I saw tears start when he felt the emotions there. He asked me to come inside with him.

An impromptu panel had been convened. Call it a jury. It was made up of anyone who was handy, including a few children. There were ten or twelve of them. Everyone looked very sad. The woman I had hurt was there, being consoled by three or four people. I'll call her Scar, for the prominent mark on her upper arm.

Everybody kept telling me—in handtalk, you understand—how sorry they were for me. They petted and stroked me, trying to draw some of the misery away.

Pink came racing in. She had been sent for to act as a translator if needed. Since this was a formal proceeding it was necessary that they be sure I understood everything that happened. She went to Scar and cried with her for a bit, then came to me and embraced me fiercely, telling me with her hands how sorry she was that this had happened. I was already figuratively packing my bags. Nothing seemed to be left but the formality of expelling me.

Then we all sat together on the floor. We were close, touching on all sides. The hearing began.

Most of it was in handtalk, with Pink throwing in a few words here and there. I seldom knew who said what, but that was appropriate. It was the group speaking as one. No statement reached me without already having become a consensus.

"You are accused of having violated the rules," said the group, "and of having been the cause of an injury to (the one I called Scar). Do you dispute this? Is there any fact that we should know?"

"No," I told them. "I was responsible. It was my carelessness."

"We understand. We sympathize with you in your remorse, which is evident to all of us. But carelessness is a violation. Do you understand this? This is the offense for which you are (—)." It was a set of signals in shorthand.

"What was that?" I asked Pink.

"Uh . . . 'brought before us'? 'Standing trial'?" She shrugged, not happy with either interpretation.

"Yes. I understand."

"The facts not being in question, it is agreed that you are guilty."

(" 'Responsible,' " Pink whispered in my ear.) "Withdraw from us a moment while we come to a decision."

I got up and stood by the wall, not wanting to look at them as the debate went back and forth through the joined hands. There was a burning lump in my throat that I could not swallow. Then I was asked to rejoin the circle.

"The penalty for your offense is set by custom. If it were not so, we would wish we could rule otherwise. You now have the choice of accepting the punishment designated and having the offense wiped away, or of refusing our jurisdiction and withdrawing your body from our land. What is your choice?"

I had Pink repeat this to me, because it was so important that I know what was being offered. When I was sure I had read it right, I accepted their punishment without hesitation. I was very grateful to have been given an alternative.

"Very well. You have elected to be treated as we would treat one of our own who had done the same act. Come to us."

Everyone drew in closer. I was not told what was going to happen. I was drawn in and nudged gently from all directions.

Scar was sitting with her legs crossed more or less in the center of the group. She was crying again, and so was I, I think. It's hard to remember. I ended up face down across her lap. She spanked me.

I never once thought of it as improbable or strange. It flowed naturally out of the situation. Everyone was holding on to me and caressing me, spelling assurances into my palms and legs and neck and cheeks. We were all crying. It was a difficult thing that had to be faced by the whole group. Others drifted in and joined us. I understood that this punishment came from everyone there, but only the offended person, Scar did the actual spanking. That was one of the ways I had wronged her, beyond the fact of giving her a scraped knee. I had laid on her the obligation of disciplining me and that was why she had sobbed so loudly, not from the pain of her injury, but from the pain of knowing she would have to hurt me.

Pink later told me that Scar had been the staunchest advocate of giving me the option to stay. Some had wanted to expel me outright, but she paid me the compliment of thinking I was a good enough person to be worth putting herself and me through the ordeal. If you can't understand that, you haven't grasped the feeling of community I felt among these people.

It went on for a long time. It was very painful, but not cruel. Nor was it primarily humiliating. There was some of that, of course. But it was essentially a practical lesson taught in the most direct terms. Each of them had undergone it during the first months, but none recently. You *learned* from it, believe me.

I did a lot of thinking about it afterward. I tried to think of what else they might have done. Spanking grown people is really unheard of, you know, though that didn't occur to me until long after it had happened. It seemed so natural when it was going on that the thought couldn't even enter my mind that this was a weird situation to be in.

They did something like this with the children, but not as long or as hard. Responsibility was lighter for the younger ones. The adults were willing to put up with an occasional bruise or scraped knee while the children learned.

But when you reached what they thought of as adulthood—which was whenever a majority of the adults thought you had or when you assumed the privilege yourself—that's when the spanking really got serious.

They had a harsher punishment, reserved for repeated or malicious offenses. They had not had to invoke it often. It consisted of being sent to Coventry. No one would touch you for a specified period of time. By the time I heard of it, it sounded like a very tough penalty. I didn't need it explained to me.

I don't know how to explain it, but the spanking was administered in such a loving way that I didn't feel violated. *This hurts me as much as it hurts you. I'm doing this for your own good. I love you, that's why I'm spanking you.* They made me understand those old clichés by their actions.

When it was over, we all cried together. But it soon turned to happiness. I embraced Scar and we told each other how sorry we were that it had happened. We talked to each other—made love if you like—and I kissed her knee and helped her dress it.

We spent the rest of the day together, easing the pain.

As I became more fluent in handtalk, "the scales fell from my eyes." Daily, I would discover a new layer of meaning that had eluded me before; it was like peeling the skin of an onion to find a new skin beneath it. Each time I thought I was at the core, only to find that there was another layer I could not yet see.

I had thought that learning handtalk was the key to communication with them. Not so. Handtalk was baby talk. For a long time I was a baby who could not even say goo-goo clearly. Imagine my surprise when, having learned to say it, I found that there were syntax, conjunctions, parts of speech, nouns, verbs, tense, agreement, and the subjunctive mood. I was wading in a tide pool at the edge of the Pacific Ocean.

By handtalk I mean the International Manual Alphabet. Anyone can learn it in a few hours or days. But when you talk to someone in speech, do you spell each word? Do you read each letter as you read this? No, you grasp words as entities, hear groups of sounds and see groups of letters as a gestalt full of meaning.

Everyone at Keller had an absorbing interest in language. They each knew several languages—spoken languages—and could read and spell them fluently.

While still children they had understood the fact that handtalk was a way for blind-deaf people to talk to *outsiders*. Among themselves it was much too cumbersome. It was like Morse Code: useful when you're limited to on-off modes of information transmission, but not the preferred mode. Their ways of speaking to each other were much closer to our type of written or verbal communication, and—dare I say it?—better.

I discovered this slowly, first by seeing that though I could spell rapidly with my hands, it took *much* longer for me to say something than it took anyone else. It could not be explained by differences in dexterity. So I asked to be taught their shorthand speech. I plunged in, this time taught by everyone, not just Pink.

It was hard. They could say any word in any language with no more than two moving hand positions. I knew this was a project for years, not days. You learn the alphabet and you have all the tools you need to spell any word that exists. That's the great advantage in having your written and spoken speech based on the same set of symbols. Shorthand was not like that at all. It partook of none of the linearity or commonality of handtalk; it was not code for English or any other language; it did not share construction or vocabulary with any other language. It was wholly constructed by the Kellerites according to their needs. Each word was something I had to learn and memorize separately from the handtalk spelling.

For months I sat in the Togethers after dinner saying things like "Me love Scar much much well," while waves of conversation ebbed and flowed and circled around me, touching me only at the edges. But I kept at it, and the children were endlessly patient with me. I improved gradually. Understand that the rest of the conversations I will relate took place in either handtalk or shorthand, limited to various degrees by my fluency. I did not speak nor was I spoken to orally from the day of my punishment.

I was having a lesson in bodytalk from Pink. Yes, we were making love. It had taken me a few weeks to see that she was a sexual being, that her caresses, which I had persisted in seeing as innocent—as I had defined it at the time—both were and weren't innocent. She understood it as perfectly natural that the result of her talking to my penis with her hands might be another sort of conversation. Though still in the middle flush of puberty, she was regarded by all as an adult and I accepted her as such. It was cultural conditioning that had blinded me to what she was saying.

So we talked a lot. With her, I understood the words and music of the body better than with anyone else. She sang a very uninhibited song with her hips and hands, free of guilt, open and fresh with discovery in every note she touched.

"You haven't told me much about yourself," she said. "What did you do on the outside?" I don't want to give the impression that this speech was in sentences, as I have presented it. We were bodytalking, sweating and smelling each other. The message came through from hands, feet, mouth.

I got as far as the sign for pronoun, first person singular, and was stopped.

How could I tell her of my life in Chicago? Should I speak of my early ambition to be a writer, and how that didn't work out? And why hadn't it? Lack of talent, or lack of drive? I could tell her about my profession, which was meaningless shuffling of papers when you got down to it, useless to anything but the Gross National Product. I could talk of the economic ups and downs that had brought me to Keller when nothing else could dislodge me from my easy sliding through life. Or the loneliness of being forty-seven years old and never having found someone worth loving, never having been loved in return. Of being a permanently displaced person in a stainless-steel society. One-night stands, drinking binges, nine-to-five, Chicago Transit Authority, dark movie houses, football games on television, sleeping pills, the John Hancock Tower where the windows won't open so you can't breathe the smog or jump out. That was me, wasn't it?

"I see," she said.

"I travel around," I said, and suddenly realized that it was the truth.

"I see," she repeated. It was a different sign for the same thing. Context was everything. She had heard and understood both parts of me, knew one to be what I had been, the other to be what I hoped I was.

She lay on top of me, one hand lightly on my face to catch the quick interplay of emotions as I thought about my life for the first time in years. And she laughed and nipped my ear playfully when my face told her that for the first time I could remember, I was happy about it. Not just telling myself I was happy, but truly happy. You cannot lie in bodytalk any more than your sweat glands can lie to a polygraph.

I noticed that the room was unusually empty. Asking around in my fumbling way, I learned that only the children were there.

"Where is everybody?" I asked.

"They are all out***," she said. It was like that: three sharp slaps on the chest with the fingers spread. Along with the finger configuration for "verb form, gerund," it meant that they were all out ***ing. Needless to say, it didn't tell me much.

What did tell me something was her bodytalk as she said it. I read her better than I ever had. She was upset and sad. Her body said something like "Why can't I join them? Why can't I (smell-taste-touch-hear-see) *sense* with them?" That is exactly what she said. Again, I didn't trust my understanding enough to accept that interpretation. I was still trying to force my conceptions on the things I experienced there. I was determined that she and the other children be resentful of their parents in some way, because I was sure they had to be. They *must* feel superior in some way, they *must* feel held back.

I found the adults, after a short search of the area, out in the north pasture. All the parents, none of the children. They were standing in a group with no apparent pattern. It wasn't a circle, but it was almost round. If there was any organization, it was in the fact that everybody was about the same distance from everybody else.

The German shepherds and the Sheltie were out there, sitting on the cool grass facing the group of people. Their ears were perked up, but they were not moving.

I started to go up to the people. I stopped when I became aware of the concentration. They were touching, but their hands were not moving. The silence of seeing all those permanently moving people standing that still was deafening to me.

I watched them for at least an hour. I sat with the dogs and scratched them behind the ears. They did that choplicking thing that dogs do when they appreciate it, but their full attention was on the group.

It gradually dawned on me that the group was moving. It was very slow, just a step here and another there, over many minutes. It was expanding in such a way that the distance between any of the individuals was the same. Like the expanding universe, where all galaxies move away from all others. Their arms were extended now; they were touching only with fingertips, in a crystal lattice arrangement.

Finally they were not touching at all. I saw their fingers straining to cover distances that were too far to bridge. And still they expanded equilaterally. One of the shepherds began to whimper a little. I felt the hair on the back of my neck stand up. Chilly out here, I thought.

I closed my eyes, suddenly sleepy.

I opened them, shocked. Then I forced them shut. Crickets were chirping in the grass around me.

There was something in the darkness behind my eyeballs. I felt that if I could turn my eyes around I would see it easily, but it eluded me in a way that made peripheral vision seem like reading headlines. If there was ever anything impossible to pin down, much less describe, that was it. It tickled at me for a while as the dogs whimpered louder, but I could make nothing of it. The best analogy I could think of was the sensation a blind person might feel from the sun on a cloudy day.

I opened my eyes again.

Pink was standing there beside me. Her eyes were screwed shut, and she was covering her ears with her hands. Her mouth was open and working silently. Behind her were several of the older children. They were all doing the same thing.

Some quality of the night changed. The people in the group were about a foot away from each other now, and suddenly the pattern broke. They all swayed for a moment, then laughed in that eerie, un-selfconscious noise deaf people use for laughter. They fell in the grass and held their bellies, rolled over and over and roared.

Pink was laughing, too. To my surprise, so was I. I laughed until my face and sides were hurting, like I remembered doing sometimes when I'd smoked grass.

And that was ***ing.

I can see that I've only given a surface view of Keller. And there are some things I should deal with, lest I foster an erroneous view.

Clothing, for instance. Most of them wore something most of the time. Pink was the only one who seemed temperamentally opposed to clothes. She never wore anything.

No one ever wore anything I'd call a pair of pants. Clothes were loose: robes, shirts, dresses, scarves, and such. Lots of men wore things that would be called women's clothes. They were simply more comfortable.

Much of it was ragged. It tended to be made of silk or velvet or something else that felt good. The stereotyped Kellerite would be wearing a Japanese silk robe, hand-embroidered with dragons, with many gaping holes and loose threads and tea and tomato stains all over it while she sloshed through the pigpen with a bucket of slop. Wash it at the end of the day and don't worry about the colors running.

I also don't seem to have mentioned homosexuality. You can mark it down to my early conditioning that my two deepest relationships at Keller were with women: Pink and Scar. I haven't said anything about it simply because I don't know how to present it. I talked to men and women equally, on the same terms. I had surprisingly little trouble being affectionate with the men.

I could not think of the Kellerites as bisexual, though clinically they were. It was much deeper than that. They could not even recognize a concept as poisonous as a homosexuality taboo. It was one of the first things they learned. If you distinguish homosexuality from heterosexuality you are cutting yourself off from communication—*full* communication—with half the human race. They were pansexual; they could not separate sex from the rest of their lives. They didn't even have a word in shorthand that could translate directly into English as *sex.* They had words for male and female in infinite variation, and words for degrees and varieties of physical experience that would be impossible to express in English, but all those words included other parts of the world of experience also; none of them walled off what we call *sex* into its own discrete cubbyhole.

There's another question I haven't answered. It needs answering, because I wondered about it myself when I first arrived. It concerns the necessity for the commune in the first place. Did it really have to be like this? Would they have been better off adjusting themselves to our ways of living?

All was not a peaceful idyll. I've already spoken of the invasion and rape. It could happen again, especially if the roving gangs that operate around the cities start to really rove. A touring group of motorcyclists could wipe them out in a night.

There were also continuing legal hassles. About once a year the social workers descended on Keller and tried to take their children away. They had been accused of everything possible from child abuse to contributing to delinquency. It hadn't worked so far, but it might someday.

And after all, there are sophisticated devices on the market that allow a blind and deaf person to see and hear a little. They might have been helped by some of those.

I met a blind-deaf woman living in Berkeley once. I'll vote for Keller.

As to those machines . . .

In the library at Keller there is a seeing machine. It uses a television camera and a computer to vibrate a closely set series of metal pins. Using it, you can feel a moving picture of whatever the camera is pointed at. It's small and light, made to be carried with the pinpricker touching your back. It cost about thirty-five thousand dollars.

I found it in the corner of the library. I ran my finger over it and left a gleaming streak behind as the thick dust came away.

Other people came and went, and I stayed on.

Keller didn't get as many visitors as the other places I had been. It was out of the way.

One man showed up at noon, looked around, and left without a word.

Two girls, sixteen-year-old runaways from California, showed up one night. They undressed for dinner and were shocked when they found out I could see. Pink scared the hell out of them. Those poor kids had a lot of living to do before they approached Pink's level of sophistication. But then Pink might have been uneasy in California. They left the next day, unsure if they had been to an orgy or not. All that touching and no getting down to business, very strange.

There was a nice couple from Santa Fe who acted as a sort of liaison between Keller and their lawyer. They had a nine-year-old boy who chattered endlessly in handtalk to the other kids. They came up about every other week and stayed a few days, soaking up sunshine and participating in the Together every night. They spoke halting shorthand and did me the courtesy of not speaking to me in speech.

Some of the Indians came around at odd intervals. Their behavior was almost aggressively chauvinistic. They stayed dressed at all times in their Levi's and boots. But it was evident that they had a respect for the people, though they thought them strange. They had business dealings with the commune. It was the Navahos who trucked away the produce that was taken to the gate every day, sold it, and took a percentage. They would sit and powwow in sign language spelled into hands. Pink said they were scrupulously honest in their dealings.

And about once a week all the parents went out in the field and ***ed.

I got better and better at shorthand and bodytalk. I had been breez-ing along for about five months and winter was in the offing. I had not examined my desires as yet, not really thought about what it was I wanted to do with the rest of my life. I guess the habit of letting myself drift was too ingrained. I was there, and constitutionally unable to de-cide whether to go or to face up to the problem if I wanted to stay for a long, long time.

Then I got a push.

For a long time I thought it had something to do with the economic situation outside. They were aware of the outside world at Keller. They knew that isolation and ignoring problems that could easily be dis-missed as not relevant to them was a dangerous course, so they sub-scribed to the Braille *New York Times* and most of them read it. They had a television set that got plugged in about once a month. The kids would watch it and translate for their parents.

So I was aware that the non-depression was moving slowly into a more normal inflationary spiral. Jobs were opening up, money was flow-ing again. When I found myself on the outside again shortly afterward, I thought that was the reason.

The real reason was more complex. It had to do with peeling off the onion layer of shorthand and discovering another layer beneath it.

I had learned handtalk in a few easy lessons. Then I became aware of shorthand and bodytalk, and of how much harder they would be to learn. Through five months of constant immersion, which is the only way to learn a language, I had attained the equivalent level of a five- or six-year-old in shorthand. I knew I could master it, given time. Bodytalk was another matter. You couldn't measure progress as easily in bodytalk. It was a variable and highly interpersonal language that evolved according to the person, the time, the mood. But I was learn-ing.

Then I became aware of Touch. That's the best I can describe it in a single, unforced English noun. What *they* called this fourth-stage lan-guage varied from day to day, as I will try to explain.

I first became aware of it when I tried to meet Janet Reilly. I now knew the history of Keller, and she figured very prominently in all the stories. I knew everyone at Keller, and I could find her nowhere. I knew everyone by names like Scar, and She-with-the-missing-front-tooth, and Man-with-wiry-hair. These were shorthand names that I had given them myself, and they all accepted them without question. They had abolished their outside names within the commune. They meant nothing to them; they told nothing and described nothing.

At first I assumed that it was my imperfect command of shorthand that made me unable to clearly ask the right question about Janet Reilly. Then I saw that they were not telling me on purpose. I saw why, and I approved, and thought no more about it. The name Janet Reilly described what she had been *on the outside,* and one of her conditions for pushing the whole thing through in the first place had been that she be no one special on the inside. She melted into the group and disappeared. She didn't want to be found. All right.

But in the course of pursuing the question I became aware that each of the members of the commune had no specific name at all. That is, Pink, for instance, had no less than one hundred and fifteen names, one from each of the commune members. Each was a contextual name that told the story of Pink's relationship to a particular person. My simple names, based on physical descriptions, were accepted as the names a child would apply to people. The children had not yet learned to go beneath the outer layers and use names that told of themselves, their lives, and their relationships to others.

What is even more confusing, the names evolved from day to day. It was my first glimpse of Touch, and it frightened me. It was a question of permutations. Just the first simple expansion of the problem meant there were no less than thirteen thousand names in use, and they wouldn't stay still so I could memorize them. If Pink spoke to me of Baldy, for instance, she would use her Touch name for him, modified by the fact that she was speaking to me and not Short-chubby-man.

Then the depths of what I had been missing opened beneath me and I was suddenly breathless with fear of heights.

Touch was what they spoke to each other. It was an incredible blend of all three other modes I had learned, and the essence of it was that it never stayed the same. I could listen to them speak to me in shorthand, which was the real basis for Touch, and be aware of the currents of Touch flowing just beneath the surface.

It was a language of inventing languages. Everyone spoke their own dialect because everyone spoke with a different instrument: a different body and set of life experiences. It was modified by everything. *It would not stand still.*

They would sit at the Together and invent an entire body of Touch responses in a night; idiomatic, personal, totally naked in its honesty. And they used it only as a building block for the next night's language.

I didn't know if I wanted to be that naked. I had looked into myself a little recently and had not been satisfied with what I found. The realization that every one of them knew more about it than I, because my honest body had told what my frightened mind had not wanted to reveal, was shattering. I was naked under a spotlight in Carnegie Hall, and all the no-pants nightmares I had ever had came out to haunt me. The fact that they all loved me with all my warts was suddenly not enough. I wanted to curl up in a dark closet with my ingrown ego and let it fester.

I might have come through this fear. Pink was certainly trying to help me. She told me that it would only hurt for a while, that I would quickly adjust to living my life with my darkest emotions written in fire across my forehead. She said Touch was not as hard as it looked at first, either. Once I learned shorthand and bodytalk, Touch would flow naturally from it like sap rising in a tree. It would be unavoidable, something that would happen to me without much effort at all.

I almost believed her. But she betrayed herself. No, no, no. Not that, but the things in her concerning ***ing convinced me that if I went through this I would only bang my head hard against the next step up the ladder.

   \*\*\*

I had a little better definition now. Not one that I can easily translate into English, and even that attempt will only convey my hazy concept of what it was.

"It is the mode of touching without touching," Pink said, her body going like crazy in an attempt to reach me with her own imperfect concept of what it was, handicapped by my illiteracy. Her body denied the truth of her shorthand definition, and at the same time admitted to me that she did not know what it was herself.

"It is the gift whereby one can expand oneself from the eternal quiet and dark into something else." And again her body denied it. She beat on the floor in exasperation.

"It is an attribute of being in the quiet and dark all the time, touching others. All I know for sure is that vision and hearing preclude it or obscure it. I can make it as quiet and dark as I possibly can and be aware of the edges of it, but the visual orientation of the mind persists. That door is closed to me, and to all the children."

Her verb "to touch" in the first part of that was a Touch amalgam, one that reached back into her memories of me and what I had told her of my experiences. It implied and called up the smell and feel of broken mushrooms in soft earth under the barn with Tall-one-with-green-eyes, she who taught me to feel the essence of an object. It also contained references to our bodytalking while I was penetrating into the dark and wet of her, and her running account to me of what it was like to receive me into herself. This was all one word.

I brooded on that for a long time. What was the point of suffering through the nakedness of Touch, only to reach the level of frustrated blindness enjoyed by Pink?

What was it that kept pushing me away from the one place in my life where I had been happiest?

One thing was the realization, quite late in coming, that can be summoned up as "What the hell am I *doing* here?" The question that should have answered that question was "What the hell would I do if I *left?*"

I was the only visitor, the only one in *seven years,* to stay at Keller for longer than a few days. I brooded on that. I was not strong enough or confident enough in my opinion of myself to see it as anything but a flaw in *me,* not in those others. I was obviously too easily satisfied, too complacent to see the flaws that those others had seen.

It didn't have to be flaws in the people of Keller, or in their system. No, I loved and respected them too much to think that. What they had going certainly came as near as anyone ever has in this imperfect world to a sane, rational way for people to exist without warfare and with a minimum of politics. In the end, those two old dinosaurs are the only ways humans have yet discovered to be social animals. Yes, I do see war as a way of living with another; by imposing your will on another in terms so unmistakable that the opponent has to either knuckle under to you, die, or beat your brains out. And if that's a solution to anything, I'd rather live without solutions. Politics is not much better. The only thing going for it is that it occasionally succeeds in substituting talk for fists.

Keller *was* an organism. It was a new way of relating, and it seemed to work. I'm not pushing it as a solution for the world's problems. It's possible that it could only work for a group with a common self-interest as binding and rare as deafness and blindness. I can't think of another group whose needs are so interdependent.

The cells of the organism cooperated beautifully. The organism was strong, flourishing, and possessed of all the attributes I've ever heard used in defining life except the ability to reproduce. That might have been its fatal flaw, if any. I certainly saw the seeds of something developing in the children.

The strength of the organism was communication. There's no way around it. Without the elaborate and impossible-to-falsify mechanisms for communication built into Keller, it would have eaten itself in pettiness, jealousy, possessiveness, and any dozen other "innate" human defects.

The nightly Together was the basis of the organism. Here, from after dinner till it was time to fall asleep, everyone talked in a language that was incapable of falsehood. If there was a problem brewing, it presented itself and was solved almost automatically. Jealousy? Resentment? Some little festering wrong that you're nursing? You couldn't conceal it at the Together, and soon everyone was clustered around you and loving the sickness away. It acted like white corpuscles, clustering around a sick cell, not to destroy it, but to heal it. There seemed to be no problem that couldn't be solved if it was attacked early enough, and with Touch, your neighbors knew about it before you did and were already laboring to correct the wrong, heal the wound, to make you feel better so you could laugh about it. There was a lot of laughter at the Togethers.

I thought for a while that I was feeling possessive about Pink. I know I had done so a little at first. Pink was my special friend, the one who had helped me out from the first, who for several days was the only one I could talk to. It was her hands that had taught me handtalk. I know I felt stirrings of territoriality the first time she lay in my lap while another man made love to her. But if there was any signal the Kellerites were adept at reading, it was that one. It went off like an alarm bell in Pink, the man, and the women and men around me. They soothed me, coddled me, told me in every language that it was all right, not to feel ashamed. Then the man in question began loving *me*. Not Pink, but the man. An observational anthropologist would have had subject matter for a whole thesis. Have you seen the films of baboons' social behavior? Dogs do it, too. Many male mammals do it. When males get into dominance battles, the weaker can defuse the aggression by submitting, by turning tail and surrendering. I have never felt so defused as when that man surrendered the object of our clash of wills—Pink—and turned his attention to me. What could I do? What I did was laugh, and he laughed, and soon we were all laughing, and that was the end of territoriality.

That's the essence of how they solved most "human nature" problems at Keller. Sort of like an oriental martial art; you yield, roll with the blow so that your attacker takes a pratfall with the force of the aggression. You do that until the attacker sees that the initial push wasn't worth the effort, that it was a pretty silly thing to do when no one was resisting you. Pretty soon he's not Tarzan of the Apes, but Charlie Chaplin. And he's laughing.

So it wasn't Pink and her lovely body and my realization that she could never be all mine to lock away in my cave and defend with a gnawed-off thighbone. If I'd persisted in that frame of mind she would have found me about as attractive as an Amazonian leech, and that was a great incentive to confound the behaviorists and overcome it.

So I was back to those people who had visited and left, and what did they see that I didn't see?

Well, there was something pretty glaring. I was not part of the organism, no matter how nice the organism was to me. I had no hopes of ever becoming a part, either. Pink had said it in the first week. She felt it herself, to a lesser degree. She could not \*\*\*, though that fact was not going to drive her away from Keller. She had told me that many times in shorthand and confirmed it in bodytalk. If I left, it would be without her.

Trying to stand outside and look at it, I felt pretty miserable. What was I trying to *do*, anyway? Was my goal in life *really* to become a part of a blind-deaf commune? I was feeling so low by that time that I actually thought of that as denigrating, in the face of all the evidence to the contrary. I should be out in the real world where the real people lived, not these freakish cripples.

I backed off from that thought very quickly. I was not totally out of my mind, just on the lunatic edges. These people were the best friends I'd ever had, maybe the only ones. That I was confused enough to think that of them even for a second worried me more than anything else. It's possible that it's what pushed me finally into a decision. I saw a future of growing disillusion and unfulfilled hopes. Unless I was willing to put out my eyes and ears, I would always be on the outside. *I* would be the blind and deaf one. I would be the freak. I didn't want to be a freak.

They knew I had decided to leave before I did. My last few days turned into a long goodbye, with a loving farewell implicit in every word touched to me. I was not really sad, and neither were they. It was nice, like everything they did. They said goodbye with just the right mix of wistfulness and life-must-go-on, and hope-to-touch-you-again.

Awareness of Touch scratched on the edges of my mind. It was not bad, just as Pink had said. In a year or two I could have mastered it.

But I was set now. I was back in the life groove that I had followed for so long. Why is it that once having decided what I must do, I'm afraid to reexamine my decision? Maybe because the original decision cost me so much that I didn't want to go through it again.

I left quietly in the night for the highway and California. They were out in the fields, standing in that circle again. Their fingertips were farther apart than ever before. The dogs and children hung around the edges like beggars at a banquet. It was hard to tell which looked more hungry and puzzled.

The experiences at Keller did not fail to leave their mark on me. I was unable to live as I had before. For a while I thought I could not live at all, but I did. I was too used to living to take the decisive step of ending my life. I would wait. Life had brought one pleasant thing to me; maybe it would bring another.

I became a writer. I found I now had a better gift for communicating than I had before. Or maybe I had it now for the first time. At any rate, my writing came together and I sold. I wrote what I wanted to write, and was not afraid of going hungry. I took things as they came.

I weathered the non-depression of '97, when unemployment reached twenty percent and the government once more ignored it as a temporary downturn. It eventually upturned, leaving the jobless rate slightly higher than it had been the time before, and the time before that. Another million useless persons had been created with nothing better to do than shamble through the streets looking for beatings in progress, car smash-ups, heart attacks, murders, shootings, arson, bombings, and riots: the endlessly inventive street theater. It never got dull.

I didn't become rich, but I was usually comfortable. That is a social disease, the symptoms of which are the ability to ignore the fact that your society is developing weeping pustules and having its brains eaten out by radioactive maggots. I had a nice apartment in Marin County, out of sight of the machine-gun turrets. I had a car, at a time when they were beginning to be luxuries.

I had concluded that my life was not destined to be all I would like it to be. We all make some sort of compromise, I reasoned, and if you set your expectations too high you are doomed to disappointment. It did occur to me that I was settling for something far from "high," but I didn't know what to do about it. I carried on with a mixture of cynicism and optimism that seemed about the right mix for me. It kept my motor running, anyway.

I even made it to Japan, as I had intended in the first place.

I didn't find someone to share my life. There was only Pink for that, Pink and all her family, and we were separated by a gulf I didn't dare cross. I didn't even dare think about her too much. It would have been very dangerous to my equilibrium. I lived with it, and told myself that it was the way I was. Lonely.

The years rolled on like a Caterpillar tractor at Dachau, up to the penultimate day of the millennium.

San Francisco was having a big bash to celebrate the year 2000. Who gives a shit that the city is slowly falling apart, that civilization is disintegrating into hysteria? Let's have a party!

I stood on the Golden Gate Dam on the last day of 1999. The sun was setting in the Pacific, on Japan, which had turned out to be more of the same but squared and cubed with neo-samurai. Behind me the first bombshells of a firework celebration of holocaust tricked up to look like festivity competed with the flare of burning buildings as the social and economic basket cases celebrated the occasion in their own way. The city quivered under the weight of misery, anxious to slide off along the fracture lines of some subcortical San Andreas Fault. Orbiting atomic bombs twinkled in my mind, up there somewhere, ready to plant mushrooms when we'd exhausted all the other possibilities.

I thought of Pink.

I found myself speeding through the Nevada desert, sweating, gripping the steering wheel. I was crying aloud but without sound, as I had learned to do at Keller.

Can you go back?

I slammed the citicar over the potholes in the dirt road. The car was falling apart. It was not built for this kind of travel. The sky was getting light in the east. It was the dawn of a new millennium. I stepped harder on the gas pedal and the car bucked savagely. I didn't care. I was not driving back down that road, not ever. One way or another, I was here to stay.

I reached the wall and sobbed my relief. The last hundred miles had been a nightmare of wondering if it had been a dream. I touched the cold reality of the wall and it calmed me. Light snow had drifted over everything, gray in the early dawn.

I saw them in the distance. All of them, out in the field where I had left them. No, I was wrong. It was only the children. Why had it seemed like so many at first?

Pink was there. I knew her immediately, though I had never seen her in winter clothes. She was taller, filled out. She would be nineteen years old. There was a small child playing in the snow at her feet, and she cradled an infant in her arms. I went to her and talked to her hand.

She turned to me, her face radiant with welcome, her eyes staring in a way I had never seen. Her hands flitted over me and her eyes did not move.

"I touch you, I welcome you," her hands said. "I wish you could have been here just a few minutes ago. Why did you go away, darling? Why did you stay away so long?" Her eyes were stones in her head. She was blind. She was deaf.

All the children were. No, Pink's child sitting at my feet looked up at me with a smile.

"Where is everybody?" I asked when I got my breath. "Scar? Baldy? Green-eyes? And what's happened? What's happened to you?" I was tottering on the edge of a heart attack or nervous collapse or something. My reality felt in danger of dissolving.

"They've gone," she said. The word eluded me, but the context put it with the *Mary Celeste* and Roanoke, Virginia. It was complex, the way she used the word *gone.* It was like something she had said before; unattainable, a source of frustration like the one that had sent me running from Keller. But now her word told of something that was not hers yet, but was within her grasp. There was no sadness in it.

"Gone?"

"Yes. I don't know where. They're happy. They ***ed. It was glorious. We could only touch a part of it."

I felt my heart hammering to the sound of the last train pulling away from the station. My feet were pounding along the ties as it faded into the fog. Where are the Brigadoons of yesterday? I've never yet heard of a fairy tale where you can go back to the land of enchantment. You wake up, you find that your chance is gone. You threw it away. *Fool!* You only get one chance; that's the moral, isn't it?

Pink's hands laughed along my face.

"Hold this part-of-me-who-speaks-mouth-to-nipple," she said, and handed me her infant daughter. "I will give you a gift."

She reached up and lightly touched my ears with her cold fingers. The sound of the wind was shut out, and when her hands came away it never came back. She touched my eyes, shut out all the light, and I saw no more.

We live in the lovely quiet and dark.

# Poul Anderson

Here's Poul, one top-ranking science fiction writer who comes ahead of me in the alphabetical listing. You didn't think you'd miss him, did you? He is the only writer who has appeared in every one of the four Hugo Winner volumes. He has one in the first, two in the second, two in the third, and now one in the fourth. That gives him six appearances, which ties him with Harlan Ellison. And if you would like to have a little peep into the future, I can assure you that Poul will appear in the forthcoming fifth volume as well.

Poul has been writing steadily and quite prolifically for nearly forty years now, and has clearly won his share of awards, and yet somehow I have always felt that he was underrated. In fact, it's my idea that he is the most highly rated author in the field who manages to be underrated just the same.

Sometimes I speculate idly on why that should be.

It may be a matter of charisma. I remember a top-notch s.f. writer (*not* Poul) once saying to me bitterly that he was of a mind to quit the field because he felt unappreciated.

He said, "Good writing isn't enough. You have to put on a show. If I were willing to make a fool of myself the way you and Harlan do, and jump around like a madman at conventions and chase the girls and yell at people and turn handsprings, then everyone would notice me and decide my books were good. But just because I behave like a quiet, civilized person, they ignore me."

Well, perhaps there's something to that. Certainly Poul is among the most civilized people I know. He is extremely quiet and soft-spoken and, as far as I know, has never offended anyone, but is unfailingly polite, and thoughtful, and considerate. His reward is that people tend to overlook him, which is Not Right.

Of course, I have to defend the charismatics. I don't think for one minute that Harlan, for instance, behaves as he does out of a calculated intention of attracting attention and selling books. I know that *I* don't.

When Harlan loses his temper and lets loose a stream of colorful invective, it's because he can't help it. He sometimes does himself infinite harm in this way, and he would *not* do it if only he knew how not to do it. As for myself, when I kiss the girls that is not because I think to myself that a reputation as a "lovable lecher" (I have a plaque that was awarded to me at a convention with that phrase upon it as my reason for getting it) will lend color to my otherwise colorless stories. I do it because I enjoy kissing girls.

If Harlan or I were forced to attend a convention, or any gathering, and act quiet and civilized, the chances are that we would explode through internal combustion. On the other hand, I don't think that even threats of imminent torture could force Poul Anderson to do some of the crazy things that Harlan and I do as a matter of course.

It's the way it is—but don't worry, Poul, you have more Hugos than I have and we all love you, too.

# 12

# *HUNTER'S MOON*

We do not perceive reality, we conceive it. To suppose otherwise is to invite catastrophic surprises. The tragic nature of history stems in large part from this endlessly recurrent mistake.

—Oskar Haeml, *Betrachtungen über die menschliche Verlegenheit*

\*\*\* Both suns were now down. The western mountains had become a wave of blackness, unstirring, as though the cold of Beyond had touched and frozen it even as it crested, a first sea barrier on the flightway to the Promise; but heaven stood purple above, bearing the earliest stars and two small moons, ocher edged with silvery crescents, like the Promise itself. Eastward, the sky remained blue. There, just over the ocean, Ruii was almost fully lighted, Its bands turned luminous across Its crimson glow. Beneath the glade that It cast, the waters shivered, wind made visible.

A'i'ach felt the wind too, cool and murmurous. Each finest hair on his body responded. He needed but little thrust to hold his course, enough effort to give him a sense of his own strength and of being at one, in travel and destination, with his Swarm. Their globes surrounded him, palely iridescent, well-nigh hiding from him the ground over which they passed; he was among the highest up. Their life-scents overwhelmed all else which the air bore, sweet, heady, and they were singing together, hundreds of voices in chorus, so that their spirits might mingle and become Spirit, a foretaste of what awaited them in the far west. Tonight, when P'a crossed the face of Ruii, there would return the Shining Time. Already they rejoiced in the raptures ahead.

A'i'ach alone did not sing, nor did he lose more than a part of himself in dreams of feast and love. He was too aware of what he carried. The thing that the human had fastened to him weighed very little, but what it was putting into his soul was heavy and harsh. The whole Swarm knew about the dangers of attack, of course, and many clutched weapons—stones to drop or sharp-pointed branches shed by ü trees—in the tendrils that streamed under their globes. A'i'ach had a steel knife, his price for letting the human burden him. Yet it was not in the nature of the People to dread what might sink down upon them out of the future. A'i'ach was strangely changed by that which went on inside him.

The knowledge had come, he knew not how, slowly enough that he was not astonished by it. Instead, a grimness had meanwhile congealed. Somewhere in those hills and forests, a Beast ran that bore the same thing he did, that was also in ghostly Swarm-touch with a human. He could not guess what this might portend, save trouble of some kind for the People. He might well be unwise to ask. Therefore he had come to a resolve he realized was alien to his race: he would end the menace.

Since his eyes were set low on his body, he could not see the object secured on top, nor the radiance beaming upward from it. His companions could, though, and he had gotten a demonstration before he agreed to carry it. The beam was faint, faint, visible only at night and then only against a dark background. He would look for a shimmer among shadows on the land. Sooner or later, he would come upon it. The chance was not bad now at this, the Shining Time, when the Beasts would seek to kill People they knew would be gathered in vast numbers to revel.

A'i'ach had wanted the knife as a curiosity of possible usefulness. He meant to keep it in the boughs of a tree; when the mood struck him, he would experiment with it. A Person did once in a while employ a chance-found object, such as a sharp pebble, for some fleeting purpose, such as scooping open a crestflower pod to release its delicious seedlets upon the air. Perhaps with a knife he could shape wood into tools and have a stock of them always ready.

Given his new insight, A'i'ach saw what the blade was truly for. He could smite from above till a Beast was dead—no, *the* Beast.

A'i'ach was hunting. ✱✱✱

Several hours before sundown, Hugh Brocket and his wife, Jannika Rezek, had been preparing for their night's work when Chrisoula Gryparis arrived, much overdue. A storm had first grounded aircraft at Enrique and then, perversely moving west, forced her into a long detour on her way to Hansonia. She didn't even see the Ring Ocean until she had traversed a good thousand kilometers of mainland, whereafter she must bend southward an equal distance to reach the big island.

"How lonely Port Kato looks from the air," she remarked. Though accented, her English—the agreed-upon common language at this particular station—was fluent: one reason she had come here to investigate the possibility of taking a post.

"Because it is," Jannika answered in her different accent. "A dozen scientists, twice as many juniors, and a few support personnel. That makes you extra welcome."

"What, do you feel isolated?" Chrisoula wondered. "You can call to anywhere on Nearside that there is a holocom, can you not?"

"Yeah, or flit to a town on business or vacation or whatever," Hugh said. "But no matter how stereo an image is and sounds, it's only an image. You can't go out with it for a drink after your conference is finished, can you? As for an actual visit, well, you're soon back here among the same old faces. Outposts get pretty ingrown socially. You'll find out, if you sign on." In haste: "Not that I'm trying to discourage you. Jan's right, we'd be more than happy to have somebody fresh join us."

His own accent was due to history. English was his mother tongue, but he was third-generation Medean, which meant that his grandparents had left North America so long ago that speech back there had changed like everything else. To be sure, Chrisoula wasn't exactly up-to-date, when a laser beam took almost fifty years to go from Sol to Colchis and the ship in which she had fared, unconscious and unaging, was considerably slower than that . . .

"Yes, from Earth!" Jannika's voice glowed.

Chrisoula winced. "It was not happy on Earth when I left. Maybe things got better afterward. Please, I will talk about that later, but now I would like to look forward."

Hugh patted her shoulder. She was fairly pretty, he thought: not in a class with Jan, which few women were, but still, he'd enjoy it if acquaintance developed bedward. Variety is the spice of wife.

"You really have had bad luck today, haven't you?" he murmured. "Getting delayed till Roberto—uh, Dr. Venosta went out in the field—and Dr. Feng back to the Center with a batch of samples—" He referred to the chief biologist and the chief chemist. Chrisoula's training was in biochemistry; it was hoped that she, lately off the latest of the rare starcraft, would contribute significantly to an understanding of life on Medea.

She smiled. "Well, then I will know others first, starting with you two nice people."

Jannika shook her head. "I am sorry," she said. "We are busy ourselves, soon to leave, and may not return until sunrise."

"That is—how long? About thirty-six hours? Yes. Is that not long to be away in . . . what do you say? . . . this weird an environment?"

Hugh laughed. "It's the business of a xenologist, which we both are," he said. "Uh, I think I, at least, can spare a little time to show you around and introduce you and make you feel sort of at home." Arriving as she did at a point in the cycle of watches when most folk were still asleep, Chrisoula had been conducted to his and Jannika's quarters. They were early up, to make ready for their expedition.

Jannika gave him a hard glance. She saw a big man who reckoned his age at forty-one Terrestrial years: burly, a trifle awkward in his movements, beginning to show a slight paunch; craggy-featured, sandy-haired, blue-eyed; close-cropped, clean-shaven, but sloppily clad in tunic, trousers, and boots, the style of the miners among whom he had grown up. *"I* have not time," she stated.

Hugh made an expansive gesture. "Sure, you just continue, dear." He took Chrisoula under the elbow. "Come on, let's wander."

Bewildered, she accompanied him out of the cluttered hut. In the compound, she halted and stared about her as if this were her first sight of Medea.

Port Kato was indeed tiny. Not to disturb regional ecology with things like ultraviolet lamps above croplands and effluents off them, it drew its necessities from older and larger settlements on the Nearside mainland. Moreover, while close to the eastern edge of Hansonia, it stood a few kilometers inland, on high ground, as a precaution against Ring Ocean tides, which could get monstrous. Thus nature walled and roofed and weighed on the huddle of structures, wherever she looked—

—or listened, smelled, touched, tasted, moved. In slightly lesser gravity than Earth's, she had a bound to her step. The extra oxygen seemed to lend energy likewise, though her mucous membranes had not yet quite stopped smarting. Despite a tropical location, the air was balmy and not overly humid, for the island lay close enough to Farside to be cooled. It was full of pungencies, only a few of which she could remotely liken to anything familiar, such as musk or iodine. Foreign too were sounds—rustlings, trills, croakings, mumbles—which the dense atmosphere made loud in her ears.

The station itself had an outlandish aspect. Buildings were made of local materials to local design; even a radiant energy converter resembled nothing at home. Multiple shadows carried peculiar tints; in fact, every color was changed in this ruddy light. The trees that reared above the roof were of odd shapes, their foliage in hues of orange, yellow, and brown. Small things flitted among them or scuttled along their branches. Occasional glittery drifts in the breeze did not appear to be dust.

The sky was deep-toned. A few clouds were washed with faint pink and gold. The double sun Colchis—Castor C was suddenly too dry a name—was declining westward, both members so dim that she could safely gaze at them for a short while, Phrixus at close to its maximum angular separation from Helle.

Opposite them, Argo dominated heaven, as always on the inward-facing hemisphere of Medea. Here the primary planet hung low; tree-tops hid part of the great flattened disc. Daylight paled the redness of its heat, which would be lurid after dark. Nonetheless it was a colossus, as broad to the eye as fifteen or sixteen Lunas above Earth. The subtly chromatic bands and spots upon its face, ever-changing, were clouds more huge than continents and hurricane vortices that could have swallowed whole this moon upon which she stood.

Chrisoula shivered. "It . . . strikes me," she whispered, "more than anywhere around Enrique or—or approaching from space . . . I have come elsewhere in the universe."

Hugh laid an arm around her waist. Not being a glib man otherwise, he merely said, "Well this *is* different. That's why Port Kato exists, you know. To study in depth an area that's been isolated a while; they tell me the isthmus between Hansonia and the mainland disappeared fifteen thousand years ago. The local dromids, at least, never heard of humans before we arrived. The ouranids did get rumors, which may have influenced them a little, but surely not much."

"Dromids—ouranids—oh." Being Greek, she caught his meanings at once. "Fuxes and balloons, correct?"

Hugh frowned. "Please. Those are pretty cheap jokes, aren't they? I know you hear them a lot in town, but I think both races deserve more dignified names from us. They are intelligent, remember."

"I am sorry."

He squeezed a trifle. "No harm done, Chris. You're new. With a century needed for question and answer, between here and Earth—"

"Yes. I have wondered if it is really worth the cost, planting colonies beyond the Solar System just to send back scientific knowledge that slowly."

"You've got more recent information about that than I do."

"Well . . . the planetology, biology, chemistry, they were still giving new insights when I left, and this was good for everything from medicine to volcano control." The woman straightened. "Perhaps the next step is in your field, xenology? If we can come to understand a nonhuman mind—no, two, on this world—maybe three, if there really are two quite unlike sorts of ouranid as I have heard theorized—" She drew breath. "Well, then we might have a chance of understanding ourselves." He thought she was genuinely interested, not merely trying to please him, when she went on: "What is it you and your wife do? They mentioned to me in Enrique it is quite special."

"Experimental, anyway." Not to overdo things, he released her. "A complicated story. Wouldn't you rather take the grand tour of our metropolis?"

"Later I can by myself, if you must go back to work. But I am fascinated by what I have heard of your project. Reading the minds of aliens!"

"Hardly that." Seeing his opportunity, he indicated a bench outside a machine shed. "If you really would like to hear, sit down."

As they did, Piet Marais, botanist, emerged from his cabin. To Hugh's relief, he simply greeted them before hurrying off. Certain Hansonian plants did odd things at this time of day. Everyone else was still indoors, the cook and bull cook making breakfast, the rest washing and dressing for their next wakeful period.

"I suppose you are surprised," Hugh commenced. "Electronic neuranalysis techniques were in their infancy on Earth when your ship left. They took a spurt soon afterward, and of course the information reached us before you did. The use there had been on lower animals as well as humans, so it wasn't too hard for us—given a couple of geniuses in the Center—to adapt the equipment for both dromids and ouranids. Both those species have nervous systems too, after all, and the signals are electrical. Actually, it's been more difficult to develop the software, the programs, than the hardware. Jannika and I are working on that, collecting empirical data for the psychologists and semanticians and computer people to use.

"Uh, don't misunderstand, please. To *us,* this is nearly incidental. Mindscan—bad word, but we seem to be stuck with it—mindscan should eventually be a valuable tool in our real job, which is to learn how local natives live, what they think and feel, everything about them. However, at present it's very new, very limited, and very unpredictable."

Chrisoula tugged her chin. "Let me tell you what I imagine I know," she suggested, "then you tell me how wrong I am."

"Sure."

She grew downright pedantic: "Synapse patterns can be identified and recorded which correspond to motor impulses, sensory inputs, their processing—and at last, theoretically, to thoughts themselves. But the study is a matter of painfully accumulating data, interpreting them, and correlating the interpretations with verbal responses. Whatever results one gets, they can be stored in a computer program as an $n$-dimensional map off which readings can be made. More readings can be gotten by interpolation."

"Whe-ew!" the man exclaimed. "Go on."

"I am right this far? I did not expect to be."

"Well, naturally, you're trying to sketch in a few words what needs volumes of math and symbolic logic to describe halfway properly. Still, you're doing better than I could myself."

"I continue. Now recently there are systems which can make correspondences between different maps. They can transform the patterns that constitute thought in one mind into the thought-patterns of another. Also, direct transmission between nervous systems is possible. A pattern can be detected, passed through a computer for translation, and electromagnetically induced in a receiving brain. Does this not amount to telepathy?"

Hugh started to shake his head, but settled for: "M-m-m, of an extremely crude sort. Even two humans who think in the same language and know each other inside out, even they get only partial information —simple messages, burdened with distortion, low signal-to-noise ratio, and slow transmission. How much worse when you try with a different life form! The variations in speech alone, not to mention neurological structure, chemistry—"

"Yet you are attempting it, with some success, I hear."

"Well, we made a certain amount of progress on the mainland with both dromids and ouranids. But believe me, 'certain amount' is a gross overstatement."

"Next you are trying it on Hansonia, where the cultures must be entirely strange to you. In fact, the species of ouranid— Why? Do you not add needlessly to your difficulties?"

"Yes—that is, we do add countless problems, but it is not needless. You see, most cooperating natives have spent their whole lives around humans. Many of them are professional subjects of study: dromids for material pay, ouranids for psychological satisfaction, amusement, I suppose you could say. They're deracinated; they themselves often don't have any idea why their 'wild' kinfolk do something. We wanted to find out if mindscan can be developed into a tool for learning about more than neurology. For that, we needed beings who're relatively, uh, uncontaminated. Lord knows Nearside is full of virgin areas. But here Port Kato already was, set up for intensive study of a region that's both isolated and sharply defined. Jan and I decided we might as well include mindscan in our research program."

Hugh's glance drifted to the immensity of Argo and lingered. "As far as we're concerned," he said low, "it's incidental—one more way for us to try and find out why the dromids and ouranids here are at war."

"They kill each other elsewhere too, do they not?"

"Yes, in a variety of ways, for a larger variety of reasons, as nearly as we can determine. Let me remark for the record, I myself don't hold with the theory that information on this planet can be acquired by eating its possessor. For one thing, I can show you more areas than not where dromids and ouranids seem to coexist perfectly peacefully." Hugh shrugged. "Nations on Earth never were identical. Why should we expect Medea to be the same everywhere?"

"On Hansonia, however—you say war?"

"Best word I can think of. Oh, neither group has a government to issue a formal declaration. But the fact is that more and more, for the past couple of decades—as long as humans have been observing, if not longer—dromids on this island have been hell-bent to kill ouranids. Wipe them out! The ouranids are pacifistic, but they do defend themselves, sometimes with active measures like ambushes." Hugh grimaced. "I've glimpsed several fights, and examined the results of a lot more. Not pleasant. If we in Port Kato could mediate—bring peace— well, I'd think that alone might justify man's presence on Medea."

While he sought to impress her with his kindliness, he was not hypocritical. A pragmatist, he had nevertheless wondered occasionally if humans had a right to be here. Long-range scientific study was impossible without a self-supporting colony, which in turn implied a minimum population, most of whose members were not scientists. He, for example, was the son of a miner and had spent his boyhood in the outback. True, settlement was not supposed to increase beyond its present level, and most of this huge moon was hostile enough to his breed that further growth did seem unlikely. But—if nothing else, simply by their presence, Earthlings had already done irreversible things to both native races.

"You cannot ask them why they fight?" Chrisoula wondered.

Hugh smiled wryly. "Oh, sure, we can ask. By now we've mastered local languages for everyday purposes. Except, how deep does our understanding go?

"Look, I'm the dromid specialist, she's the ouranid specialist, and we've both worked hard trying to win the friendship of specific individuals. It's worse for me, because dromids won't come into Port Kato as long as ouranids might show up anytime. They admit they'd be duty bound to try and kill the ouranids—and eat them, too, by the way; that's a major symbolic act. The dromids agree this would be a violation of our hospitality. Therefore I have to go meet them in their camps and dens. In spite of this handicap, she doesn't feel she's progressed any further than me. We're equally baffled."

"What do the autochthons *say?*"

"Well, either species admits they used to live together amicably . . . little or no direct contact, but with considerable interest in each other. Then, twenty or thirty years back, more and more dromids started failing to reproduce. Oftener and oftener, castoff segments don't come to term, they die. The leaders have decided the ouranids are at fault and must be exterminated."

"Why?"

"An article of faith. No rationale that I can untangle, though I've guessed at motivations, like the wish for a scapegoat. We've got pathologists hunting for the real cause, but imagine how long that might take. Meanwhile, the attacks and killings go on."

Chrisoula regarded the dusty ground. "Have the ouranids changed in any way? The dromids might then jump to a conclusion of *post hoc, propter hoc.*"

"Huh?" When she had explained, Hugh laughed. "I'm not a cultivated type, I'm afraid," he said. "The rock rats and bush rangers I grew up amongst do respect learning—we wouldn't survive on Medea without learning—but they don't claim to have a lot of it themselves. I got interested in xenology because as a kid I acquired a dromid friend and followed her-him through the whole cycle, female to male to postsexual. It grabbed hold of my imagination—a life that exotic."

His attempt to turn the conversation into personal channels did not succeed. "What have the ouranids done?" she persisted.

"Oh . . . they've acquired a new—no, not a new religion. That implies a special compartment of life, doesn't it? And ouranids don't compartmentalize their lives. Call it a new Way, a new *Tao.* It involves eventually riding an east wind off across the ocean, to die in the Farside cold. Somehow, that's transcendental. Please don't ask me how, or why. Nor can I understand—or Jan—why the dromids consider this is such a terrible thing for the ouranids to do. I have some guesses, but they're only guesses. She jokes that they're born fanatics."

Chrisoula nodded. "Cultural abysses. Suppose a modern materialist with little empathy had a time machine, and went back to the Middle Ages on Earth, and tried to find out what drove a Crusade or Jihad. It would appear senseless to him. Doubtless he would conclude everybody concerned was crazy, and the sole possible way to peace was total victory of one side or the other. Which was not true, we know today."

The man realized that this woman thought a good deal like his wife. She continued: "Could it be that human influences have brought about these changes, perhaps indirectly?"

"It could," he admitted. "Ouranids travel widely, of course, so those on Hansonia may well have picked up, at second or third hand, stories about Paradise which originated with humans. I suppose it'd be natural to think Paradise lies in the direction of sunset. Not that anybody has ever tried to convert a native. But natives have occasionally inquired what our ideas are. And ouranids are compulsive mythmakers, who might seize on any concept. They're ecstatics, too. Even about death."

"While dromids are prone to develop militant new religions overnight, I have heard. On this island, then, a new one happens to have turned against the ouranids, no? Tragic—though not unlike persecutions on Earth, I expect."

"Anyhow, we can't help till we have a lot more knowledge. Jan and I are trying for that. Mostly, we follow the usual procedures, field studies, observations, interviews, et cetera. We're experimenting with mindscan as well. Tonight it gets our most thorough test yet."

Chrisoula sat upright, gripped. "What will you do?"

"We'll draw a blank, probably. You're a scientist yourself, you know how rare the real breakthroughs are. We're only slogging along."

When she remained silent, Hugh filled his lungs for talk. "To be exact," he proceeded, "Jan's been cultivating a 'wild' ouranid, I a 'wild' dromid. We've persuaded them to wear miniaturized mindscan transmitters, and have been working with them to develop our own capability. What we can receive and interpret isn't much. Our eyes and ears give us a lot more information. Still, this is special information. Supplementary.

"The actual layout? Oh, our native wears a button-sized unit glued onto the head, if you can talk about the head of an ouranid. A mercury cell gives power. The unit broadcasts a recognition signal on the radio band—microwatts, but ample to lock onto. Data transmission naturally requires plenty of bandwidth, so that's on an ultraviolet beam."

"What?" Chrisoula was startled. "Isn't that dangerous to the dromids? I was taught they, most animals, have to take shelter when a sun flares."

"This is safely weak, also because of energy limitations," Hugh replied. "Obviously, it's limited to line-of-sight and a few kilometers through air. At that, natives of either kind tell us they can spot the fluorescence of gas along the path. Not that they describe it in such terms!

"So Jan and I go out in our separate aircraft. We hover too high to be seen, activate the transmitters by a signal, and 'tune in' on our individual subjects through our amplifiers and computers. As I said, to date we've gotten extremely limited results; it's a mighty poor kind of telepathy. This night we're planning an intensive effort, because an important thing will be happening."

She didn't inquire immediately what that was, but asked instead: "Have you ever tried sending to a native, rather than receiving?"

"What? No, nobody has. For one thing, we don't want them to know they're being scanned. That would likely affect their behavior. For another thing, no Medeans have anything like a scientific culture. I doubt they could comprehend the idea."

"Really? With their high metabolic rate, I should guess they think faster than us."

"They seem to, though we can't measure that till we've improved mindscan to the point of decoding verbal thought. All we've identified thus far is sensory impressions. Come back in a hundred years and maybe someone can tell you."

The talk had gotten so academic that Hugh positively welcomed the diversion when an ouranid appeared. He recognized the individual in spite of her being larger than usual, her globe distended with hydrogen to a full four meters of diameter. This made her fur sparse across the skin, taking away its mother-of-pearl sheen. Just the same, she was a handsome sight as she passed the treetops, crosswind and then downward. Prehensile tendrils streaming below in variable configurations, to help pilot a jet-propelled swim through the air, she hardly deserved the name "flying jellyfish"—though he had seen pictures of Earthside Portuguese men-of-war and thought them beautiful. He could sympathize with Jannika's attraction to this race.

He rose. "Meet a local character," he invited Chrisoula. "She has a little English. However, don't expect to understand her pronunciation at once. Probably she's come to make a quick swap before she rejoins her group for the big affair tonight."

The woman got up. "Swap? Exchange?"

"Yeah. Niallah answers questions, tells legends, sings songs, demonstrates maneuvers, whatever we request. Afterward we have to play human music for her. Schönberg, usually; she dotes on Schönberg."

—Loping along a clifftop, Erakoum spied Sarhouth clearly against Mardudek. The moon was waxing toward solar fullness as it crossed that coal-glow. Its disc was dwarfed by the enormous body behind, was actually smaller to the eye than the spot which also passed in view, and its cold luminance had well-nigh been drowned earlier when it moved over one of the belts which changeably girded Mardudek. They grew bright after dark, those belts; thinkers like Yasari believed they cast back the light of the suns.

For an instant, Erakoum was captured by the image, spheres traveling through unbounded spaces in circles within circles. She hoped to become a thinker herself. But it could not be soon. She still had her second breeding to go through, her second segment to shed and guard, the young that it presently brought forth to help rear; and then she would be male, with begetting of her own to do—before that need faded out likewise and there was time for serenity.

She remembered in a stab of pain how her first birthing had been for naught. The segment staggered about weakly for a short while, until it lay down and died as so many were doing, so many. The Flyers had brought that curse. It had to be them, as the Prophet Illdamen preached. Their new way of faring west when they grew old, never to return, instead of sinking down and rotting back into the soil as Mardudek intended, surely angered the Red Watcher. Upon the People had been laid the task of avenging this sin against the natural order of things. Proof lay in the fact that females who slew and ate a Flyer shortly before mating always shed healthy segments which brought forth live offspring.

Erakoum swore that tonight she was going to be such a female.

She stopped for breath and to search the landscape. These precipices rimmed a fjord whose waters lay more placid than the sea beyond, brilliant under the radiance from the east. A dark patch bespoke a mass of floating weed. Might it be plants of the kind from which the Flyers budded in their abominable infancy? Erakoum could not tell at her distance. Sometimes valiant members of her race had ventured out on logs, trying to reach those beds and destroy them; but they had failed, and often drowned, in treacherous great waves.

Westward rose rugged, wooded hills where darkness laired. Athwart their shadows, sparks danced glittering golden, by the thousands—the millions, across the land. They were firemites. Through more than a hundred days and nights, they had been first eggs, then worms, deep down in forest mold. Now Sarhouth was passing across Mardudek in the exact path that mysteriously summoned them. They crept to the surface, spread wings which they had been growing, and went aloft, agleam, to mate.

Once it had meant no more to the People than a pretty sight. Then the need came into being, to kill Flyers . . . and Flyers gathered in hordes to feed on yonder swarms. Hovering low, careless in their glee, they became more vulnerable to surprise than they commonly were. Erakoum hefted an obsidian-headed javelin. She had five more lashed across her back. A number of the People had spent the day setting out nets and snares, but she considered that impractical; the Flyers were not ordinary winged quarry. Anyhow, she wanted to fling a spear, bring down a victim, sink fangs into its thin flesh, herself!

The night muttered around her. She drank odors of soil, growth, decay, nectar, blood, striving. Warmth from Mardudek streamed through a chill breeze to lave her pelt. Half-glimpsed flitting shapes, half-heard as they rustled the brush, were her fellows. They were not gathered into a single company, they coursed as each saw fit, but they kept more or less within earshot, and whoever first saw or winded a Flyer would signal it with a whistle.

Erakoum was farther separated from her nearest comrade than any of them were. The others feared that the light-beam reaching upward from the little shell on her head would give them away. She deemed it unlikely, as faint as the bluish gleam was. The human called Hugh paid her well in trade goods to wear the talisman whenever he asked and afterward discuss her experiences with him. For her part, she knew a darkling thrill at such times, akin to nothing else in the world, and knowledge came into her, as if through dreams but more real. These gains were worth a slight handicap on an occasional hunt . . . even tonight's hunt.

Moreover—there was something she had not told Hugh, because he had not told her earlier. It was among the things she learned without words from the gleam-shell. A certain Flyer also carried one, which also kept it in eldritch contact with a human.

The big grotesque creatures were frank about being neutral in the strife between People and Flyers. Erakoum did not hold that against them. This was not their home, and they could not be expected to care if it grew desolate. Yet she had shrewdly deduced that they would try to keep in its burrow their equal intimacy with members of both breeds.

If Hugh had been anxious for her to be soul-tied to him this night, doubtless another human wanted the same for a Flyer. It would be a special joy to her to bring that one down. Besides, looking as she fared for a pale ray among firemites and stars might lead her toward a whole pack of enemies. Rested, she began to trot inland.

Erakoum was hunting.—

Jannika Rezek was forever homesick for a land where she had never lived.

Her parents had politically offended the government of the Danubian Federation. It informed them they need not enter a reindoctrination hospice if they would volunteer to represent their country in the next shipful of personnel to Medea. That was scarcely a choice. Nevertheless, her father told her afterward that his last thought, as he sank down into suspended animation, was of the irony that when he awakened, none of his judges would be alive and nobody would remember what his opinions had been, let alone care. As a matter of fact, he learned at his goal that there was no longer a Danubian Federation.

The rule remained in force that, except for crewfolk, no person went in the opposite direction. A trip was too expensive for a passenger to be carried who would land on Earth as a useless castaway out of past history. Husband and wife made the best they could of their exile. Both physicians, they were eagerly received in Armstrong and its agricultural hinterland. By the modest standards of Medea, they prospered, finally winning a rare privilege. The human population had now been legally stabilized. More would overcrowd the limited areas suitable for settlement, as well as wreaking havoc on environments which the colony existed to study. To balance reproductive failures, a few couples per generation were allowed three children. Jannika's folk were among these.

Thus everybody, herself perforce included, reckoned hers a happy childhood. It was a highly civilized one, too. In the molecules of reels kept at the Center was stored most of mankind's total culture. Industry was, at last, sufficiently developed that well-to-do families could have sets which retrieved the data in as full hologrammic and stereophonic detail as desired. Her parents took advantage of this to ease their nostalgia, never thinking what it might do to younger hearts. Jannika grew up among vivid ghosts: old towers in Prague, springtime in the Böhmerwald, Christmas in a village which centuries had touched only lightly, a concert hall where music rolled in glory across a festive-clad audience which outnumbered the dwellers in Armstrong, replications of events which once made Earth tremble, songs, poetry, books, legends, fairy tales. . . . She sometimes wondered if she had gone into xenology because the ouranids were light, bright, magical beings in a fairy tale.

Today, when Hugh led Chrisoula outside, she had stood for a moment staring after them. Abruptly the room pressed in as if to choke her. She had done what she could in the way of brightening it with drapes, pictures, keepsakes. At present, however, it was bestrewn with field gear; and she hated disorder. He cared naught.

The question rose afresh: How much did he care at all, any longer? They were in love when they married, yes, of course, but even then she recognized it was in high degree a marriage of convenience. Both were after appointments to an outpost station where they would maximize their chances of doing really significant, original research. Wedded couples were preferred, on the theory that they would be less distracted from their work than singletons. When they had their first babies, they were customarily transferred to a town.

She and Hugh quarreled about that. Social pressure—remarks, hints, embarrassed avoidance of the subject—was mounting on them to reproduce. Within population limits, it was desirable to keep the gene pool as large as possible. She was getting along in age, a bit, for motherhood. He was more than willing. But he took for granted that *she* would maintain the home, hold down the desk job, while *he* continued in the field. . . .

She must not reprove him when he came back from his flirtatious little stroll. She lost her temper too often these days, grew outright shrewish, till he stormed from the hut or else grabbed the whiskey and started glugging. He was not a bad man—at the core, he was a good man, she amended hastily—thoughtless in many ways but well-meaning. At her time of life, she couldn't likely do any better.

Although— She felt the heat in her cheeks, made a gesture as if to fend off the memory, and failed. It was two days old.

Having learned from A'i'ach about the Shining Time, she wanted to gather specimens of the glitterbug larvae. Hitherto humans had merely known that the adult insectoids swarmed aloft at intervals of approximately a year. If that was important to the inhabitants of Hansonia, she ought to know more. Observe for herself, enlist the aid of biologists, ecologists, chemists— She asked Piet Marais where to go, and he offered to come along. "The idea should have occurred to me before," he said. "Living in humus, the worms must influence plant growth."

Moister soil was required than existed at Port Kato. They went several kilometers to a lake. The walking was easy, for dense foliage overhead inhibited underbrush. Softness muffled footfalls, trees formed high-arched naves, multiple rays of light passed through dusk and fragrances to fleck the ground or glance off small wings, a sound as of lyres rippled from an unseen throat.

"How delightful," Piet said after a while.

He was looking at her, not ahead. She became very conscious of his blond handsomeness. And his youth, she reminded herself; he was her junior by well-nigh a decade, though mature, considerate, educated, wholly a man. "Yes," she blurted. "I wish I could appreciate it as you do."

"It is not Earth," he discerned. She realized that her answer had been less noncommittal than intended.

"I wasn't pitying myself," she said fast. "Please don't think that. I do see beauty here, and fascination, and freedom, oh, yes, we're lucky on Medea." Attempting to laugh: "Why, on Earth, what would I have done for ouranids?"

"You love them, don't you?" he asked gravely. She nodded. He laid a hand on her bare arm. "You have a great deal of love in you, Jannika."

She made a confused effort to see herself through his eyes. Medium-sized, with a figure she knew was stunning; dark hair worn shoulder length, with gray streaks that she wished Hugh would insist were premature; high cheekbones, tilted nose, pointed chin, large brown eyes, ivory complexion. Still, though Piet was a bachelor, someone that attractive needn't be desperate, he could meet girls in town and keep up acquaintance by holocom. He shouldn't be this appreciative of her. She shouldn't respond. True, she'd had other men a few times, before and after she married. But never in Port Kato; too much likelihood of complications, and she'd been furious when Hugh got involved locally. Worse yet, she suspected Piet saw her as more than a possible partner in a frolic. That could break lives apart.

"Oh, look," she said, and disengaged from his touch in order to point at a cluster of seed pyramids. Meanwhile her mind came to the rescue. "I quite forgot, I meant to tell you, I got a call today from Professor al-Ghazi. We think we've found what makes the glitterbugs metamorphose and swarm."

"Eh?" He blinked. "I didn't realize anybody was working on that."

"Well, it was a, a notion that occurred to me after my special ouranid started me speculating about them. He, A'i'ach, I mean, he told me the time is not strictly seasonal—that is not necessary here in the tropics—but set by Jason—the moon," she added, because the name that humans had bestowed on the innermost of the larger satellites happened to resemble a word which humans had adopted, given by dromids in the Enrique area to an analog of the sirocco wind.

"He says the metamorphoses come during particular transits of Jason across Argo," she continued. "Roughly, every four hundredth. To be exact, the figure is every hundred and twenty-seven Medean days, plus or minus a trifle. The natives here are as keenly conscious of heavenly bodies as everywhere else. The ouranids make a festival of the swarming; they find glitterbugs delicious. Well, this gave me an idea, and I called the Center and requested an astronomical computation. It seems I was right."

"Astronomical cues, for a worm underground?" Marais exclaimed.

"Well, you doubtless recall how Jason excites electrical activity in the atmosphere of Argo, like Io with Jupiter"—the solar system, where Earth has her dwelling! "In this case, there's a beaming effect on one of the radio frequencies that are generated, a kind of natural maser. Therefore those waves only reach Medea when the two moons are on their line of nodes. And that is the exact period my friend was describing. The phase is right, too."

"But can the worms detect so weak a signal?"

"I think it is clear that they do. How, I cannot tell without help from specialists. Remember, though, Phrixus and Helle create little interference. Organisms can be fantastically sensitive. Did you know that it takes less than five photons to activate the visual purple in your eye? I suppose the waves from Argo penetrate the soil to a few centimeters' depth and trigger a chain of biochemical reactions. No doubt it is an evolutionary relic from a time when the orbits of Jason and Medea gave an exact match to the seasons. Perturbation does keep changing the movements of the moons, you know."

He was silent a while before he said: "I do know you are a most extraordinary person, Jannika."

She had regained enough equilibrium to control their talk until they reached the lake. There, for a moment, she felt herself shaken again.

A canebrake screened it from them till they had passed through, to halt on a beach carpeted with mosslike amber-hued turf. Untouched by man in its chalice of forest, the water lay scummy, bubbling, and odorous. The sight of soft colors and the smell of living things were not unpleasant; they were normal to Medea—yet how clear and silver-blue the Neusiedler See gleamed in Danubia. Breath hissed between her teeth.

"What's wrong?" Piet followed her gaze. "The dromids?"

A party of them had arrived to drink, some distance off. Jannika stared as if she had never seen their kind before.

Nearest was a young adult, presumably virgin, since she had six legs. From the slender, long-tailed body rose a two-armed centauroid torso, up to the oddly vulpine head, which would reach to Jannika's chest. Her pelt shimmered blue-black under the suns; Argo was hidden by trees.

Four-legged, a trio of mothers kept watch on the eight cubs they had between them. One set of young showed by their size that their parent would soon ovulate again, be impregnated by a mating, shortly thereafter shed her second segment, and attend it until it gave birth. Another member of this group was at that stage of life, walking on two legs, no longer a functional female but with the male gonads still undeveloped.

No male of breeding age was present. Such a creature was too driven, lustful, impatient, violent, for sociability. There were three postsexual beings, grizzled but strong, protective, their biped movements fast by human standards though laggard compared to the lightning fluidity of their companions.

All adults were armed with stone-age spears, hatchets, and daggers, plus the carnivore teeth in their jaws.

They were gone almost as soon as Jannika had seen them, not out of fear but because they were Medean animals whose chemistry and living went swifter than hers.

"The dromids," she got out.

Piet regarded her a while before he said gently: "They pursue your dear ouranids. You tell me that will get worse than ever on the night when the glitterbugs rise. But you must not hate them. They are caught in a tragedy."

"Yes, the sterility problem, yes. Why should they drag the ouranids down with them?" She struck fist into palm. "Let's get to work, let's collect our samples and go home, can we, please?"

He was fully understanding.

—She cast the memory out and flung herself back into preparations for the night.

Hugh Brocket and his wife departed a while after sunset. Their flitters jetted off in a whisper, reached an intermediate altitude, and circled for a minute while the riders got bearings and exchanged radioed farewells. Observed from below, catching the last gleam of sunken Colchis on their flanks, they resembled a pair of teardrops.

"Good hunting, Jan."

"Ugh! Don't say that."

"Sorry," he apologized in a stiff tone, and cut out the sender. Sure, it had been tactless of him, but why must she be so goddamn touchy?

Never mind. He'd plenty to do. Erakoum had promised to be on Shipwreck Cliffs about this time, since her gang meant to proceed north along the coast from its camp before turning inland. Thereafter her location would be unpredictable. He must lock onto her transmitter soon. Jannika's craft dwindled in sight, bound on her own quest. Hugh set his inertial pilot and settled back in his safety harness to double-check his instruments. That was mechanical, since he knew quite well everything was in order. Most of his attention roamed free.

The canopy gave a titanic vista. Below, hills lay in dappled masses of shadow, here and there relieved by an argent thread that was a river or by the upheaving of precipices and scarps. The hemisphere-dividing Ring Ocean turned the eastern horizon to quicksilver. Westward in heaven, the double sun had left a Tyrian wake. Overhead reached a velvety dark, becoming more starry with each of his heartbeats. He saw a pair of moons, close enough to show discs lighted from two sides, rusty and white; he recognized more, which were mere bright points to his eyes, by their positions as they went on sentry-go among the constellations. Low above the sea smoldered Argo—no, shone, because its upper clouds were in full daylight, bands of brilliance splashed over sullen red. Jason was close to transit, with angular diameter exceeding twenty minutes of arc, and nevertheless Hugh had trouble finding it amidst that glare.

The shore came in view. He activated the detector and set his craft to hovering. An indicator light flashed green; he had his contact. He sent the vehicle aloft, a full three kilometers. Partly this was because he would be concentrating on encephalic input and wanted plenty of room for piloting error; partly it was to keep beyond sight or hearing of the natives, lest his presence affect their actions. Having taken station, he connected and secured the receiver helmet to his head—it didn't weigh much—and switched it on. Transmitted, amplified, transformed, re-layed, reinduced, the events in Erakoum's nervous system merged with the events in his.

By no means did he acquire the dromid's full awareness. Conveyance and translation were far too primitive. He had spent his professional lifetime gaining sufficient fellow-feeling with the species that, after as much patience as both individuals could maintain over a span of years, he could barely begin to interpret the signals he gathered. The speed of native mental processes was less of a help—through repetition and reinforcement—than an added hindrance. As a rough analogy, imagine trying to follow a rapid and nearly inaudible conversation, missing many a word, in a language you do not know well. Actually, none of what Hugh perceived was verbal; it was sight, sound, a complex of senses, including those interior like balance and hunger, including dream-hints of senses that he did not think he possessed.

He saw the land go by, bush, branch, slope, stars and moons above shaggy ridges; he felt its varying contours and textures as feet went pacing; he heard its multitudinous low noises; he smelled richness; the impressions were endless, most of them vague and fleeting, the best of them strong enough to take him out of himself, draw him groundward toward oneness with the creature below.

Clearest, perhaps because his glands were stimulated thereby, was emotion, determination. Erakoum was out to get herself a Flyer.

It was going to be a long night, quite possibly a harrowing one. Hugh expected he'd need a dose or two of sleep surrogate. Humans had never gotten away from the ancient rhythms of Earth. Dromids catnapped; ouranids went—daydreamy? contemplative?

As often before, he wondered briefly what Jan's rapport with her native felt like. They would never be able to describe their sharings to each other.

***Well into the hills, A'i'ach's Swarm found a grand harvest of starwings. The heights were less densely wooded than the lowlands, which was good, for the bright prey never went far up, and below a forest crown, the People were vulnerable to Beast attack. Here was a fair amount of open ground, turf-begrown and boulder-strewn, scattered through the shadowing timber. A narrow ravine crossed the largest of those glades, a gash abrim with blackness.

Like an endless shower of sparks, the starwings danced, dashed, dodged about, beyond counting, meant for naught save the ecstasy of their mating and of the People who fed upon them. Despite the wariness in him, A'i'ach could resist no more than anyone else. He did refrain from valving out gas in his haste to descend, as many did. That would make ascent slow. Instead, he contracted his globe and sank, letting it reexpand slightly as varying air densities demanded. Nor did he release gas to propel himself. Rhythmically pumping, his siphon worked together with the breezes to zigzag him about at low speed. There was no hurry. The starwings numbered more than the Swarm could eat. Plenty would go free to lay their eggs for the next crop.

Among the motes, A'i'ach inhaled his first swallow of them. The sweet hot flavor sang in his flesh. Thickly gathered around him, bobbing, spinning, rippling, and flailing their corybantic tendrils, filling the sky with music, the People forgot caution. Love began. It was not purposeless, though without water to fall into, the pollinated seeds would not germinate. It united everyone. Life-dust drifted like smoke in the radiance of Ruii; the sight, smell, taste made feverish that joy which the starwing feast awakened. Again and again A'i'ach ejaculated. He went past his skin, he became a cell of a single divine being which was itself a tornado of love. Sometimes when he felt age upon him, he would drift westward across the sea, into the cold Beyond. There, yielding up the last warmth of his body, his spirit would take its reward, the Promise that forever and ever it would be what it was now in this brief night. . . .

A howl smote. Shapes bounded from under trees, out into the open. A'i'ach saw a shaft pierce the globe next to his. Blood spurted, gas hissed forth, the shriveling form fell as a dead leaf falls. Tendrils still writhed when a Beast snatched it the last way down and fangs rent it asunder.

In the crowd and chaos, he could not know how many others died. The greatest number were escaping, rising above missile reach. Those who were armed began to drop their stones and ü boughs. It was not likely that any killed a Beast.

A'i'ach had relaxed the muscles in his globe and shot instantly upward. Safe, he might have joined the rest of the Swarm, to wander off in search of a place to renew festival. But rage and grief seethed too high. A far-off part of him wondered at that; the People did not take hard the death of a Person. This thing he wore, that somehow whispered mysteries—

And he carried a knife!

Recklessly spending gas, he swung about, downward. Most of the Beasts had vanished back into the woods. A few remained, devouring. He cruised at a height near the limits of prudence and peered after his chance. Since he could not drop like a rock, he must feint at one individual, then quickly jet at another, stab, rise, and attack again.

A wan beam of light struck toward him. It came from the head of a Beast which emerged from shadow, halted, and glared upward.

His will blazed forth in A'i'ach. Yonder was the monster which had his kind of bond to humans. If he had already gained a knife thereby, what might that being have gotten, what might it get, to wreak worse harm? If nothing else, killing it ought to shock its companions, make them think twice about their murderousness.

A'i'ach moved to battle. About him, the starwings happily danced and mated.***

Jannika must search for an hour before she made her contact. An ouranid could not undertake to be at an exact spot at a given time. Hers had simply informed her, while she fastened the transmitter on him, that his group was currently in the neighborhood of Mount MacDonald. She flew there and cast about in ever-deepening darkness until her indicator shone green. Having established linkage, she rose to three kilometers and set the autopilot to make slow circles. From time to time, as her subject passed northeast, she moved the center of her path.

Otherwise she was engaged in trying to be her ouranid. It was impossible, of course, but from the effort she was learning what could never have come to her through spoken language. Answers to factual questions she would not have thought to ask. Folkways, beliefs, music, poetry, aerial ballet, which she could not have known for what they were, observing from outside. Lower down in her, dimmer, but more powerful—nothing she could write into a scientific report: a sense of delights, yearnings, wind, shiningness, perfumes, clouds, rain, immense distances, a sense of what it was to be a heaven-dweller. Not complete, no, a few wavery glimpses, hard to remember afterward; yet taking her out of herself into a new world agleam with wonder.

The thrill was redoubled tonight by A'i'ach's excitement. Her impressions of what he was experiencing had never been stronger or sharper. She floated on airstreams, life-scents and song possessed her, she was a drop in an ocean beneath Ruii the mighty, there was no home to hopelessly long for because everywhere was home.

The Swarm came at last upon a cloud of glitterbugs, and Jannika's cosmos went wild.

For a moment, half terrified, she started to switch off her helmet. Reason checked her hand. What was happening was just an extreme of what she had partaken in before. Ouranids seldom took much nourishment at a single time; when they did, it had an intoxicating effect. She had also felt their sexuality; A'i'ach's maleness was too unearthly to disturb her, as his dromid's femaleness had disturbed Hugh when she mated and later shed her hindquarters. Tonight the ouranids held high revel.

She surrendered to it, crescendo after crescendo, oh, if she only had a man here, but no, that would be different, would blur the sacred splendor, the Promise, the Promise!

Then the Beasts arrived. Horror erupted. Somewhere a strange voice screamed for the avenging of her shattered bliss.

—As she trotted along a bare ridge, Erakoum had thought, with a leap of her pulse, that she spied afar a faint blue ray of light in the air. She could not be certain, through the brilliance cast by Mardudek, but she altered her course in hopes. When she had scrambled a long while among stones and thorns, the glimmer disappeared. It must have been a trick of the night, perhaps moonglow on rising mists. That conclusion did nothing to ease her temper. Everything about the Flyers was unlucky!

Because of this, she was behind the rest of the pack. Her first news of quarry came through their yells. *"Hai-ay, hai-ay, hai-ay!"* echoed around, and she snarled in bafflement. Surely she would arrive too late for a kill. Nonetheless she bounded in that direction. If the Flyers did not get a good wind, she could overtake them and follow along from cover to cover, unseen. Maybe they would not go further than she had strength for, before they chanced on a fresh upswelling of firemites and descended anew. Breath rasped in her gullet, the hillside struck at her feet with unseen rocks, but eagerness flung her on till she reached the place.

It was a glade, brightly lit though crisscrossed by shadows, cut in half by a small ravine. The firemites swirled about against the forest murk, like a glinting dustcloud. Several females crouched on the turf and ripped at the remnants of their prey. The rest had departed, to trail the escaped Flyers as Erakoum planned.

She stopped at the edge of trees to pant, looked up, and froze. The mass of Flyers was slowly and chaotically streaming west, but a few lingered to cast down their pitiful weapons. From the top of one, dim light beamed aloft. She had found what she sought.

*"Ee-hah!"* she screamed, sprang forward, shook her javelin. "Come, evilworker, come and be slain! By your blood shall you give to my next brood the life you reaved from my first!"

There was no surprise, there was fate, when the eerie shape spiraled about and drew nearer. More would be settled this night than which of them was to survive. She, Erakoum, had been seized by a Power, had become an instrument of the Prophet.

Crouched, she cast her spear. The effort surged through her muscles. She saw it fly straight as the damnation it carried—but her foe swerved, it missed him by a fingerbreadth, and then all at once he was coming directly at her.

They never did that! What sheened in his seaweed grip?

Erakoum grabbed after a new javelin off her back. Each knot in the lashing was supposed to give way at a jerk, but this jammed, she must tug again, and meanwhile the enemy loomed ever more big. She recognized what he held, a human-made knife, sharp as a fresh obsidian blade and more thin and strong. She retreated. Her spear was now loose. No room for a throw. She thrust.

With crazy glee, she saw the head strike. The Flyer rolled aside before it could pierce, but blood and gas together foamed darkly from a slash across his paleness.

He spurted forward, was inside her guard. The knife smote and smote. Erakoum felt the stabs, but not yet the pain. She dropped her shaft, batted her arms, snapped jaws together. Teeth closed in flesh. Through her mouth and down her throat poured a rush of strength.

Abruptly the ground was no more beneath her hind feet. She fell over, clawed with forefeet and hands for a hold, lost it, and toppled. When she hit the side of the ravine, she rolled down across cruel snags. She had an instant's glimpse of sky above, stars and firemites, the Mardudek-lighted Flyer drifting by and bleeding. Then nothingness snatched her to itself.—

Folk at Port Kato asked what brought Jannika Rezek and Hugh Brocket home so early, so shaken. They evaded questions and hastened to their place. The door slammed behind them. A minute later, they blanked their windows.

For a time they stared at each other. The familiar room held no comfort. Illumination meant for human eyes was brass-harsh, air shut away from the forest was lifeless, faint noises from the settlement outside thickened the silence within.

He shook his head finally, blindly, and turned from her. "Erakoum gone," he mumbled. "How'm I ever going to understand that?"

"Are you sure?" she whispered.

"I . . . I felt her mind shut off . . . damn near like a blow to my own skull . . . but you were making such a fuss about your precious ouranid—"

"A'i'ach's *hurt!* His people know nothing of medicine. If you hadn't been raving till I decided I must talk you back with me before you crashed your flitter—"

Jannika broke off, swallowed hard, unclenched her fists, and became able to say: "Well, the harm is done and here we are. Shall we try to reason about it, try to find out what went wrong and how to stop another such horror, or not?"

"Yeah, of course." He went to the pantry. "You want a drink?" he called.

She hesitated. "Wine."

He fetched her a glassful. His right hand clutched a tumbler of straight whiskey, which he began on at once. "I felt Erakoum die," he said.

Jannika took a chair. "Yes, and I felt A'i'ach take wounds that may well prove mortal. Sit down, will you?"

He did, heavily, opposite her. She sipped from her glass, he gulped from his. Newcomers to Medea always said wine and distilled spirits there tasted more peculiar than the food. A poet had made that fact the takeoff point for a chilling verse about isolation. When it was sent to Earth as part of the news, the reply came after a century that nobody could imagine what the colonists saw in it.

Hugh hunched his shoulders. "Okay," he growled. "We should compare notes before we start forgetting, and maybe repeat tomorrow when we've had a chance to think." He reached across to their recorder and flicked it on. As he entered an identification phrase, his tone stayed dull.

"That is best for us too," Jannika reminded him. "Work, logical thought, those hold off the nightmares."

"Which this absolutely was— All right!" He regained a little vigor. "Let's try to reconstruct what did happen.

"The ouranids were out after glitterbugs and the dromids were out after ouranids. You and I witnessed an encounter. Naturally, we'd hoped we wouldn't—I suppose you prayed for that, hm?—but we knew there'd be hostilities in a lot of places. What shocked the wits out of us was when our personal natives got into a fight, with us in rapport."

Jannika bit her lip. "Worse than that," she said. "They were seeking it, those two. It was not a random encounter, it was a duel." She raised her eyes. "You never told Erakoum, any dromid, that we were linking with an ouranid too, did you?"

"No, certainly not. Nor did you tell your ouranid about my liaison. We both know better than to throw that kind of variable into a program like this."

"And the rest of the station personnel have vocabularies too limited, in either language. Very well. But I can tell you that A'i'ach knew. I was not aware he did until the fight began. Then it reached the forefront of his mind, it shouted at me, not in words but not to be mistaken about."

"Yeah, same thing for me with Erakoum, more or less."

"Let's admit what we don't want to, my dear. We have not simply been receiving from our natives. We have been transmitting. Feedback."

He lifted a helpless fist. "What the devil might convey a return message?"

"If nothing else, the radio beam that locks us onto our subjects. Induced modulation. We know from the example of the glitterbug larvae—and no doubt other cases you and I never heard of—how shall we know everything about a whole world? We know Medean organisms can be extremely radio-sensitive."

"M-m, yeah, the terrific speed of Medean animals, key molecules more labile than the corresponding compounds in us. . . . Hey, wait! Neither Erakoum nor A'i'ach had more than a smattering of English. Certainly no Czech, which you've told me you usually think in. Besides, look what an effort we had to make before we could tune them in at all, in spite of everything learned on the mainland. They'd no reason to do the same, no idea of scientific method. They surely assumed it was only a whim or a piece of magic or something that made us want them to carry those objects around."

Jannika shrugged. "Perhaps when we are in rapport, we think more in their languages than we ourselves realize. And both kinds of Medeans think faster than humans, observe, learn. Anyway, I do not say their contact with us was as good as our contact with them. If nothing else, radio has much less bandwidth. I think probably what they picked up from us was subliminal."

"I guess you're right," Hugh sighed. "We'll have to sic the electronicians and neurologists into the problem, but I sure can't think of any better explanation than yours."

He leaned forward. The energy which now vibrated in his voice turned cold: "But let's try to see this thing in context, so we can maybe get a hint of what kind of information the natives have been receiving from us. Let's lay out once more why the Hansonian dromids and ouranids are at war. Basically, the dromids are dying off, and blame the ouranids. Could we, Port Kato, be at fault?"

"Why, hardly," Jannika said in astonishment. "You know what precautions we take."

Hugh smiled without mirth. "I'm thinking of psychological pollution."

"What? Impossible! Nowhere else on Medea—"

"Be quiet, will you?" he shouted. "I'm trying to bring back to my mind what I got from my friend that your friend killed."

She half rose, white-faced, sat down again, and waited. The wineglass trembled in her fingers.

"You've always babbled about how kind and gentle and esthetic the ouranids are," he said, at her rather than to her. "You swoon over this beautiful new local faith they've acquired—the windborne flight to Farside, the death in dignity, the Nirvana, I forget what else. To hell with the grubby dromids. Dromids don't do anything but make tools and fires, hunt, care for their young, live in communities, create art and philosophy, same as humans. What's interesting to you in that?

"Well, let me tell you what I've told you before, dromids are believers too. If we could compare, I'd give long odds their faiths are stronger and more meaningful than the ouranids'. They keep trying to make sense of the world. Can't you sympathize the least bit?

"Okay, they have a tremendous respect for the fitness of things. When something goes seriously wrong—when a great crime or sin or shame happens—the whole world hurts. If the wrong isn't set right, everything will go bad. That's what they believe on Hansonia, and I don't know but what they've got hold of a truth.

"The lordly ouranids never paid much attention to the groundling dromids, but that was not symmetrical. The ouranids are as conspicuous as Argo, Colchis, any part of nature. In dromid eyes, they too have their ordained place and cycle.

"All at once the ouranids change. They don't give themselves back to the soil when they die, the way life is supposed to—no, they head west, over the ocean, toward that unknown place where the suns go down every evening. Can't you see how unnatural that might seem? As if a tree should walk or a corpse rise. And not an isolated incident; no, year after year after year.

"Psychosomatic abortion? How can I tell? What I can tell is that the dromids are shocked to the guts by this thing the ouranids are doing. No matter how ridiculous the thing is, it hurts them!"

She sprang to her feet. Her glass hit the floor. "Ridiculous?" she yelled. "That *Tao,* that vision? No, ridiculous, that's what your . . . your fuxes believe—except that it makes them attack innocent beings and, and eat them—I can't wait till those creatures are extinct!"

He had risen likewise. "You don't care about children dying, no, of course not," he answered. "What sense of motherhood have you got, for hell's sake? About like a balloon's. Drift free, scatter seed, forget it, it'll bud and break loose and the Swarm will adopt it, never mind anything except your pleasure."

"Why, you— Are you wishing you could be a mother?" she jeered.

His empty hand swung at her. She barely evaded the blow. Appalled, they stiffened where they stood.

He tried to speak, failed, and drank. After a full minute she said, quite low: "Hugh, our natives were getting messages from us. Not verbal. Unconscious. Through them"—she choked—"were you and I seeking to kill each other?"

He gaped until, in a single clumsy gesture, he set his own glass down and held out his arms to her. "Oh, no, oh, no," he stammered. She came to him.

Presently they went to bed. And then he could do nothing. The medicine cabinet held a remedy for that, but what followed might have happened between a couple of machines. At last she lay quietly crying and he went out to drink some more.

The wind awakened her. She lay for a time listening to it boom around the walls. Sleep drained out of her. She opened her eyes and looked at the clock. Its luminous dial said three hours had passed. She might as well get up. Maybe she could make Hugh feel better.

The main room was still lighted. He was asleep himself, sprawled in an armchair, a bottle beside it. How deep the lines were in his face.

How loud the wind was. Probably a storm front which the weather service had reported at sea had taken a quick, unexpected swing this way. Medean meteorology was not yet an exact science. Poor ouranids, their festival disrupted, they themselves blown about and scattered, even endangered. Normally they could ride out a gale, but a few might be carried to disaster, hit by lightning or dashed against a cliff or hopelessly entangled in a tree. The sick and injured would suffer most.

A'i'ach.

Jannika squeezed her lids together and struggled to recall how badly wounded he was. But everything had been too confused and terrible; Hugh had diverted her attention; before long she had flitted out of transmission range. Besides, A'i'ach himself could hardly have ascertained his own condition at once. It might not be grave. Or it might. He could be dead by now, or dying, or doomed to die if he didn't get help.

She was responsible—perhaps not guilty, by a moralistic definition, but responsible.

Resolution crystallized. If the weather didn't preclude, she would go search for him.

Alone? Yes. Hugh would protest, delay her, perhaps actually restrain her by force. She recorded a few words to him, wondered if they were overly impersonal, decided against composing something more affectionate. Yes, she wanted a reconciliation, and supposed he did, but she would not truckle. She redonned her field garb, added a jacket into whose pockets she stuffed some food bars, and departed.

The wind rushed bleak around her, *whoo-oo-oo,* a torrent she must breast. Clouds scudded low and thick, tinged red where Argo shone between them. The giant planet seemed to fly among ragged veils. Dust whirled in the compound, gritty on her skin. Nobody else was outdoors.

At the hangar, she punched for the latest forecast. It looked bad but not, she thought, frightening. (And if she did crash, was that such an enormous loss, to herself or anyone else?) "I am going back to my study area," she told the mechanic. When he attempted to dissuade her, she pulled rank. She never liked that, but from the Danubian ghosts she had learned how. "No further discussion. Stand by to open the way and give me assistance if required. That is an order."

The little craft shivered and drummed on the ground. Takeoff took skill—with a foul moment when a gust nearly upset her—but once aloft her vehicle flew sturdily. Risen above the cloud deck, she saw it heave like a sea, Argo a mountain rearing out of it, stars and companion moons flickery overhead. Northward bulked a darkness more deep and high, the front. The weather would really stiffen in the next few hours. If she wasn't back soon, she'd better stay put till it cleared.

The flight was quick to the battleground. When the inertial pilot had brought her there, she circled, put on her helmet, activated the system. Her pulse fluttered and her mouth had dried. "A'i'ach," she breathed, "be alive, please be alive."

The green light went on. At least his transmitter existed on the site. He? She must will herself toward rapport.

Weakness, pain, a racket of soughing leaves, tossing boughs— "A'i'ach, hang on, I'm coming down!"

A leap of gladness. Yes, he did perceive her.

Landing would be risky indeed. The aircraft had a vertical capability, excellent radar and sonar, a computer and effectors to handle most of the work. However, the clear space below was not large, it was cleft in twain, and while the surrounding forest was a fair windbreak, there would be vile drafts and eddies. "God, into Your hands I give myself," she said, and wondered as often before how Hugh endured his atheism.

Nevertheless, if she waited she would lose courage. Down!

Her descent was wilder still than she had expected. First the clouds were a maelstrom, then she was through them but into a raving blast, then she saw treetops grab at her. The vehicle rolled, pitched, yawed. Had she been an utter fool? She didn't truly want to leave this life. . . .

She made it, and for minutes sat strengthless. When she stirred, she felt her entire body ache from tension. But A'i'ach's hurt was in her. Called by that need, she unharnessed and went forth.

The noise was immense in the black palisade of trees around her, their branches groaned, their crowns foamed; but down on the ground the air, though restless, was quieter, nearly warm. Unseen Argo reddened the clouds, which cast enough glow that she didn't need her flashlight. She found no trace of the slain ouranids. Well, they had no bones; the dromids must have eaten every scrap. What a ghastly superstition— Where was A'i'ach?

She found him after a search. He lay behind a spiny bush, in which he had woven his tendrils to secure himself. His body was deflated to the minimum, an empty sack; but his eyes gleamed, and he could speak, in the shrill, puffing language of his people, which she had come to know was melodious.

"May joy blow upon you. I never hoped for your advent. Welcome you are. Here it has been lonely." A shudder was in that last word. Ouranids could not long stand being parted from their Swarm. Some xenologists believed that with them consciousness was more collective than individual. Jannika rejected that idea, unless perhaps it applied to the different species found in parts of Nearside. A'i'ach had a soul of his own!

She knelt. "How are you?" She could not render his sounds any better than he could hers, but he had learned to interpret.

"It is not overly ill with me, now that you are nigh. I lost blood and gas, but those wounds have closed. Weak, I settled in a tree until the Beasts left. Meanwhile the wind rose. I thought best not to ride it in my state. Yet I could not stay in the tree, I would have been blown away. So I valved out the rest of my gas and crept to this shelter."

The speech held far more than such a bare statement. The denotation was laconic and stoical, the connotations not. A'i'ach would need at least a day to regenerate sufficient hydrogen for ascent—how long depended on how much food he could reach in his crippled condition—unless a carnivore found him first, which was quite likely. Jannika imagined what a flood of suffering, dread, and bravery would have come over her had she been wearing her helmet.

She gathered the flaccid form into her arms. It weighed little. It felt warm and silky. He cooperated as well as he was able. Just the same, part of him dragged on the ground, which must have been painful.

She must be rougher still, hauling on folds of skin, when she brought him inside the aircraft. It had scant room to spare; he was practically bundled into the rear section. Rather than apologizing when he moaned, or saying anything in particular, she sang to him. He didn't know the ancient Terrestrial words, but he liked the tunes and realized what she meant by them.

She had equipped her vehicle for basic medical help to natives, and had given it on past occasions. A'i'ach's injuries were not deep, because most of him was scarcely more than a bag; however, the bag had been torn in several places and, though it was self-sealing, flight would re-open it unless it got reinforcement. Applying local anesthetics and an-tibiotics—that much had been learned about Medean biochemistry—she stitched the gashes.

"There, you can rest," she said when, cramped, sweat-soaked, and shaky, she was done. "Later I will give you an injection of gas and you can rise immediately if you choose. I think, though, we would both be wisest to wait out the gale."

A human would have groaned: "It is *tight* in here."

"Yes, I know what you mean, but— A'i'ach, let me put my helmet on." She pointed. "That will join our spirits as they were joined before. It may take your mind off your discomfort. And at this short range, given our new knowledge—" A thrill went through her. "What may we not find out?"

"Good," he agreed. "We may enjoy unique experiences." The con-cept of discovery for its own sake was foreign to him . . . but his search for pleasures went far beyond hedonism.

Eager despite her weariness, she moved into her seat and reached for the apparatus. The radio receiver, always open to the standard carrier band, chose that moment to buzz.

Argo in the east glowered at the nearing, lightning-shot wall of storm in the north. Below, the clouds already present roiled in reds and dark-nesses. Wind wailed. Hugh's aircraft lurched and bucked. Despite a heater, chill seeped through the canopy, as if brought by the light of stars and moons.

"Jan, are you there?" he called. "Are you all right?"

Her voice was a swordstroke of deliverance. "Hugh? Is that you, darling?"

"Yes, sure, who the hell else did you expect? I woke up, played your message, and— Are you all right?"

"Quite safe. But I don't dare take off in this weather. And you mustn't try to land, that would be too dangerous by now. You shouldn't stay, either. Darling, *rostomily,* that you came!"

"Judas priest, sweetheart, how could I not? Tell me what's happened."

She explained. At the end, he nodded a head which still ached a bit from liquor in spite of a nedolor tablet. "Fine," he said. "You wait for calm air, pump up your friend, and come on home." An idea he had been nursing nudged him. "Uh, I wonder. Do you think he could go down into that gulch and recover Erakoum's unit? Those things are scarce, you know." He paused. "I suppose it'd be too much to ask him to throw a little soil over her."

Jannika's tone held pity. "I can do that."

"No, you can't. I got a clear impression from Erakoum as she was falling, before she cracked her skull apart or whatever she did. Nobody can climb down without a rope secured on top. It'd be impossible to return. Even with a rope, it'd be crazy dangerous. Her companions didn't attempt anything, did they?"

Reluctance: "I'll ask him. It may be asking a lot. Is the unit functional?"

"Hm, yes, I'd better check on that first. I'll report in a minute or three. Love you."

He did, he knew, no matter how often she enraged him. The idea that, somewhere in the abysses of his being, he might have wished her death, was not to be borne. He'd have followed her through a heavier tempest than this, merely to deny it.

Well, he could go home with a satisfied conscience and wait for her arrival, after which—what? The uncertainty made a hollowness in him.

His instrument flashed green. Okay, Erakoum's button was transmitting, therefore unharmed and worth salvaging. If only she herself—

He tensed. The breath rattled in his lungs. Did he *know* she was dead?

He lowered the helmet over his temples. His hands shook, giving him trouble in making the connections. He pressed the switch. He willed to perceive—

Pain twisted like white-hot wires, strength ebbed and ebbed, soft waves of nothingness flowed ever more often, but still Erakoum defied. The slit of sky that she could see, from where she lay unable to creep further, was full of wind. . . . She shocked to complete awareness. Again she sensed Hugh's presence.

"Broken bones, feels like. Heavy blood loss. She'll die in a few more hours. Unless you give her first aid, Jan. Then she ought to last till we can fly her to Port Kato for complete attention."

"Oh, I can do sewing and bandaging and splinting, whatever, yes. And nedolor's an analgesic stimulant for dromids too, isn't it? And simply a drink of water could make the whole difference; she must be dehydrated. But how to reach her?"

"Your ouranid can lift her up, after you've inflated him."

"You can't be serious! A'i'ach's hurt, convalescent—and Erakoum tried to kill him!"

"That was mutual, right?"

"Well—"

"Jan, I'm not going to abandon her. She's down in a grave, who used to run free, and the touch of me she's getting is more to her than I could have imagined. I'll stay till she's rescued, or else I'll stay till she dies."

"No, Hugh, you mustn't. The storm."

"I'm not trying to blackmail you, dearest. In fact, I won't blame your ouranid much if he refuses. But I can't leave Erakoum. I just plain can't."

"I . . . I have learned something about you. . . . I will try."

***A'i'ach had not understood his Jannika. It was not believable that helping a Beast could help bring peace. That creature was what it was, a slaughterer. And yet, yet, once there had been no trouble with the Beasts, once they had been the animals which most interested and entertained the People. He himself remembered songs about their fleetness and their fires. In those lost days they had been called the Flame Dancers.

What made him yield to her plea was unclear in his spirit. She had probably saved his life, at hazard to her own, and this was an overpowering new thought to him. He wanted greatly to maintain his union with her, which enriched his world, and therefore hesitated to deny a request that seemed as urgent as hers. Through the union, she helmeted, he believed he felt what she did when she said, with water running from her eyes, "I want to heal what *I* have done—" and that kind of feeling was transcendent, like the Shining Time, and was what finally decided him.

She assisted him from the thing-which-bore-her and payed out a tube. Through the latter he drank gas, a wind-rush of renewed life. His injuries twinged when his globe expanded, but he could ignore that.

He needed her anchoring weight to get across the ground to the ravine. Fingers and tendrils intertwined, they nevertheless came near being carried away. Had he let himself swell to full size, he could have lifted her. Air harried and hooted, snatched at him, wanted to cast him among thorns—how horrible the ground was!

How much worse to descend below it. He throbbed to an emotion he scarcely recognized. Had she been in rapport, she could have told him that the English word for it was "terror." A human or a dromid who felt it in that degree would have recoiled from the drop. A'i'ach made it a force blowing him onward, because this too raised him out of himself.

At the edge, she threw her arms around him as far as they would go, laid her mouth to his pelt, and said, "Good luck, dear A'i'ach, dear brave A'i'ach, good luck, God keep you." Those were the noises she made in her language. He did not recognize the gesture either.

A cylinder she had given him to hold threw a strong beam of light. He saw the jagged slope tumble downward underneath him, and thought that if he was cast against that, he was done for. Then his spirit would have a fearful journey, with no body to shelter it, before it reached Beyond—if it did, if it was not shredded and scattered first. Quickly, before the churning airs could take full hold of him, he jetted across the brink. He contracted. He sank.

The dread as gloom and walls closed in was like no other carouse in his life. At its core, he felt incandescently aware. Yes, the human had brought him into strange skies.

Through the dankness he caught an odor more sharp. He steered that way. His flash picked out the Beast, sprawled on sharp talus, gasping and glaring. He used jets and siphon to position himself out of reach and said in what English he had, "I haff ch'um say-aff ee-you."***

—From the depths of her death-place, Erakoum looked up at the Flyer. She could barely make him out, a big pale moon behind a glare of light. Amazement heaved her out of a drowse. Had her enemy pursued her down here in his ill-wishing?

Good! She would die in battle, not the torment which ripped her. "Come on and fight," she called hoarsely. If she could sink teeth in him, get a last lick of his blood— The memory of that taste was like sweet lightning. During the time afterward which refused to end, she had thought she would be dead already if she had not swallowed those drops.

Their wonder-working had faded out. She stirred, seeking a defensive posture. Agony speared through her, followed by night.

When she roused, the Flyer still waited. Amidst a roaring in her ears, she heard, over and over, "I haff ch'um say-aff ee-you."

Human language? This *was* the being that the humans favored as they did her. It had to be, though the ray from its head was hidden by the ray from its tendrils. *Could Hugh have been bound all the while to both?*

Erakoum strove to form syllables never meant for her mouth and throat. "Ha-watt-tt you ha-wannit? Gho, no bea haiar, gho."

The Flyer made a response. She could no more follow that than he appeared to have followed hers. He must have come down to make sure of her, or simply to mock her while she died. Erakoum scrabbled weakly after a spear. She couldn't throw one, but—

From the unknownness wherein dwelt the soul of Hugh, she suddenly knew: He wants to save you.

Impossible. But . . . but there the Flyer was. Half delirious, Erakoum could yet remember that Flyers were seldom that patient.

What else could befall but death? Nothing. She lay back on the rock shards. Let the Flyer be her doom or be her Mardudek. She had found the courage to surrender.

The shape hovered. Her hair sensed tiny gusts, and she thought dimly that this must be a difficult place for him too. Speech burst and skirled. He was trying to explain something, but she was too hurt and tired to listen. She folded her hands around her muzzle. Would he appreciate that gesture?

Maybe. Hesitant, he neared. She kept motionless. Even when his tendrils brushed her, she kept motionless.

They slipped across her body, got a purchase, tightened. Through the haze of pain, she saw him swelling. He meant to lift her—up to Hugh?

When he did, her knife wounds opened and she shrieked before she swooned.

Her next knowledge was of lying on turf under a hasty, red-lit sky. A human crouched above her, talking to a small box that replied in the voice of Hugh. Behind, the Flyer lay shrunken, clutching a bush. Storm brawled; the first stinging raindrops fell.

In the hidden way of hunters, she knew that she was dying. The human might staunch those cuts and stabs, but could not give back what was lost.

Memory—what she had heard tell, what she had briefly tasted herself

—"Blood of the Flyer. It will save me. Blood of the Flyer, if he will give." She was not sure whether she spoke or dreamed it. She sank back into the darkness.

When she surfaced anew, the Flyer was beside her, embracing her against the wind. The human was carefully using a knife on a tendril. The Flyer brought the tendril in between Erakoum's fangs. As the rain's full violence began, she drank.—

A double sunrise was always lovely.

Jannika had delayed telling Hugh her news. She wanted to surprise him, preferably after his anxiety about his dromid was past. Well, it was; Erakoum would be hospitalized several days in Port Kato, which ought to be an interesting experience for all concerned, but she would get well. A'i'ach had already rejoined his Swarm.

When Hugh wakened from the sleep of exhaustion which followed his bedside vigil, Jannika proposed a dawn picnic, and was touched at how fast he agreed. They flitted to a place they knew on the sea cliffs, spread out their food, and sat down to watch.

At first Argo, the stars, and a pair of moons were the only lights. Slowly heaven brightened, the ocean shimmered silver beneath blue, Phrixus and Helle wheeled by the great planet. Wild songs went trilling through air drenched with an odor of roanflower, which is like violets.

"I got the word from the Center," she declared while she held his hand. "It's definite. The chemistry was soon unraveled, given the extra clue we had from the reviving effect of blood."

He turned about. "What?"

"Manganese deficiency," she said. "A trace element in Medean biology, but vital, especially to dromids and their reproduction—and evidently to something else in ouranids, since they concentrate it to a high degree. Hansonia turns out to be poorly supplied with it. Ouranids, going west to die, were removing a significant percentage from the ecology. The answer is simple. We need not try to change the ouranid belief. Temporarily, we can have a manganese supplement made up and offer it to the dromids. In the long run, we can mine the ore where it's plentiful and scatter it as a dust across the island. Your friends will live, Hugh."

He was quiet for a time. Then—he could surprise her, this son of an outback miner—he said: "That's terrific. The engineering solution. But the bitterness won't go away overnight. We won't see any quick happy ending. Maybe not you and me, either." He seized her to him. "Damnation, though, let's try!"

# C. J. Cherryh

Here is the fourth woman writer of the book. You may not be able to tell from the initials alone, but they stand for Carolyn Janice.

Actually, I disapprove of the use of initials in identification. For one thing, they mask sex. This may seem to be a matter of indifference. After all, does it matter if a writer is a man or a woman any more than if he/she had yellow hair or brown or black? No, of course not. Still, what if you get a letter from A. B. Smith and have to answer. Do you address him/her as Mr., Mrs., Miss, or Ms. (or Dr. or Prof. or Rev., for that matter.)

I think it is a matter of common courtesy, if your name is ambiguous, either because you use initials or because you have an epicene first name (suitable for either sex), that you indicate how you prefer to be addressed.

In fact, I have just made up my mind. From now on, from this very moment on, if I ever get a letter from A. B. Smith, or from Leslie Smith, with no indication of sex or preferred mode of address, I intend to answer with a Dear Smith.

To be sure, my wife had her first books appear under her maiden name, with initials, so that the author was J. O. Jeppson. There was a reason for that, however. She *was* hiding herself in a way because she did not want to give any indication that she was Mrs. Isaac Asimov, lest anyone accuse her of nepotism or of trying to use me to get ahead. (People, of course, found out, and in her most recent books, she appears as Janet Asimov.)

The use of the name Cherryh is, on the other hand, a masterstroke. Carolyn's real surname is Cherry, but she added an "h" for use in her fiction as a minimal pseudonym.

This is good because it virtually guarantees name recognition. A glance at the author and you say to yourself, " 'H'? How the hell did an 'h' get in there? How do you pronounce the name except Cherry?"

It's possible you may get quite indignant at this, and turn red, and mutter "Damn fool writer" under your breath, but the important thing is that you're not going to forget that name. The next time you see it you will say, "There's that 'h' again." If you happen to read the story and like it, you will decide that this "h" writer is pretty good. You start watching for his/her stories and you never fail to recognize them because there's just no way you can miss an author with that peculiar spelling. In no time at all, Cherryh would become a household word.

I know this because it happened to me. My name, Asimov, is a funny-looking word and a funny-sounding name, until you get used to it. People who saw it on a magazine page would nudge each other and say, "How do you suppose you pronounce that, Joe?" "Good heavens, Bill, never saw anything like it." "You suppose it's a Russian name, Joe?" "Could be anything with that spelling."

So they puzzle it out and by the time they've finished, there's nothing left of the name, but such as it was—they never forget it.

Of course, I didn't know that my name was laughable. I always thought of it as noble and patrician, and born of a heritage of kings.

# 13

# CASSANDRA

*Fires.*

They grew unbearable here.

Alis felt for the door of the flat and knew that it would be solid. She could feel the cool metal of the knob amid the flames . . . saw the shadow-stairs through the roiling smoke outside, clearly enough to feel her way down them, convincing her senses that they would bear her weight.

Crazy Alis. She made no haste. The fires burned steadily. She passed through them, descended the insubstantial steps to the solid ground—she could not abide the elevator, that closed space with the shadow-floor, that plummeted down and down; she made the ground floor, averted her eyes from the red, heatless flames.

A ghost said good morning to her . . . old man Willis, thin and transparent against the leaping flames. She blinked, bade it good morning in return—did not miss old Willis' shake of the head as she opened the door and left. Noon traffic passed, heedless of the flames, the hulks that blazed in the street, the tumbling brick.

The apartment caved in—black bricks falling into the inferno, Hell amid the green, ghostly trees. Old Willis fled, burning, fell—turned to jerking, blackened flesh—died, daily. Alis no longer cried, hardly flinched. She ignored the horror spilling about her, forced her way through crumbling brick that held no substance, past busy ghosts that could not be troubled in their haste.

Kingsley's Cafe stood, whole, more so than the rest. It was refuge for the afternoon, a feeling of safety. She pushed open the door, heard the tinkle of a lost bell. Shadowy patrons looked, whispered.

*Crazy Alis.*

The whispers troubled her. She avoided their eyes and their presence, settled in a booth in the corner that bore only traces of the fire.

WAR, the headline in the vender said in heavy type. She shivered, looked up into Sam Kingsley's wraithlike face.

"Coffee," she said. "Ham sandwich." It was constantly the same. She varied not even the order. Mad Alis. Her affliction supported her. A check came each month, since the hospital had turned her out. Weekly she returned to the clinic, to doctors who now faded like the others. The building burned about them. Smoke rolled down the blue, antiseptic halls. Last week a patient ran—burning—

A rattle of china. Sam set the coffee on the table, came back shortly and brought the sandwich. She bent her head and ate, transparent food on half-broken china, a cracked, fire-smudged cup with a transparent handle. She ate, hungry enough to overcome the horror that had become ordinary. A hundred times seen, the most terrible sights lost their power over her: she no longer cried at shadows. She talked to ghosts and touched them, ate the food that somehow stilled the ache in her belly, wore the same too-large black sweater and worn blue shirt and gray slacks because they were all she had that seemed solid. Nightly she washed them and dried them and put them on the next day, letting others hang in the closet. They were the only solid ones.

She did not tell the doctors these things. A lifetime in and out of hospitals had made her wary of confidences. She knew what to say. Her half-vision let her smile at ghost-faces, cannily manipulate their charts and cards, sitting in the ruins that had begun to smolder by late afternoon. A blackened corpse lay in the hall. She did not flinch when she smiled good-naturedly at the doctor.

They gave her medicines. The medicines stopped the dreams, the siren screams, the running steps in the night past her apartment. They let her sleep in the ghostly bed, high above ruin, with the flames crackling and the voices screaming. She did not speak of these things. Years in hospitals had taught her. She complained only of nightmares, and restlessness, and they let her have more of the red pills.

WAR, the headline blazoned.

The cup rattled and trembled against the saucer as she picked it up. She swallowed the last bit of bread and washed it down with coffee, tried not to look beyond the broken front window, where twisted metal hulks smoked on the street. She stayed, as she did each day, and Sam grudgingly refilled her cup, which she would nurse as far as she could and then order another one. She lifted it, savoring the feel of it, stopping the trembling of her hands.

The bell jingled faintly. A man closed the door, settled at the counter.

Whole, clear in her eyes. She stared at him, startled, heart pounding. He ordered coffee, moved to buy a paper from the vender, settled again and let the coffee grow cold while he read the news. She had view only of his back while he read, scuffed brown leather coat, brown hair a little over his collar. At last he drank the cooled coffee all at one draught, shoved money onto the counter, and left the paper lying, headlines turned face down.

A young face, flesh and bone among the ghosts. He ignored them all and went for the door.

Alis thrust herself from her booth.

"Hey!" Sam called at her.

She rummaged in her purse as the bell jingled, flung a bill onto the counter, heedless that it was a five. Fear was coppery in her mouth; he was gone. She fled the cafe, edged round debris without thinking of it, saw his back disappearing among the ghosts.

She ran, shouldering them, braving the flames—cried out as debris showered painlessly on her, and kept running.

Ghosts turned and stared, shocked—*he* did likewise, and she ran to him, stunned to see the same shock on his face, regarding her.

"What is it?" he asked.

She blinked, dazed to realize he saw her no differently than the others. She could not answer. In irritation he started walking again, and she followed. Tears slid down her face, her breath hard in her throat. People stared. He noticed her presence and walked the faster, through debris, through fires. A wall began to fall and she cried out despite herself.

He jerked about. The dust and the soot rose up as a cloud behind him. His face was distraught and angry. He stared at her as the others did. Mothers drew children away from the scene. A band of youths stared, cold-eyed and laughing.

"Wait," she said. He opened his mouth as if he would curse her; she flinched, and the tears were cold in the heatless wind of the fires. His face twisted in an embarrassed pity. He thrust a hand into his pocket and began to pull out money, hastily, tried to give it to her. She shook her head furiously, trying to stop the tears—stared upward, flinching, as another building fell into flames.

"What's wrong?" he asked her. "What's wrong with you?"

"Please," she said. He looked about at the staring ghosts, then began to walk slowly. She walked with him, nerving herself not to cry out at the ruin, the pale moving figures that wandered through burned shells of buildings, the twisted corpses in the street, where traffic moved.

"What's your name?" he asked. She told him. He gazed at her from time to time as they walked, a frown creasing his brow. He had a face well-worn for youth, a tiny scar beside the mouth. He looked older than she. She felt uncomfortable in the way his eyes traveled over her: she decided to accept it—to bear with anything that gave her this one solid presence. Against every inclination she reached her hand into the bend of his arm, tightened her fingers on the worn leather. He accepted it.

And after a time he slid his arm behind her and about her waist, and they walked like lovers.

WAR, the headline at the newsstand cried.

He started to turn into a street by Tenn's Hardware. She balked at what she saw there. He paused when he felt it, faced her with his back to the fires of that burning.

"Don't go," she said.

"Where do you want to go?"

She shrugged helplessly, indicated the main street, the other direction.

He talked to her then, as he might talk to a child, humoring her fear. It was pity. Some treated her that way. She recognized it, and took even that.

His name was Jim. He had come into the city yesterday, hitched rides. He was looking for work. He knew no one in the city. She listened to his rambling awkwardness, reading through it. When he was done, she stared at him still, and saw his face contract in dismay at her.

"I'm not crazy," she told him, which was a lie, that everyone in Sudbury would have known, only *he* would not, knowing no one. His face was true and solid, and the tiny scar by the mouth made it hard when he was thinking; at another time she would have been terrified of him. Now she was terrified of losing him amid the ghosts.

"It's the war," he said.

She nodded, trying to look at him and not at the fires. His fingers touched her arm, gently. "It's the war," he said again. "It's all crazy. Everyone's crazy."

And then he put his hand on her shoulder and turned her back the other way, toward the park, where green leaves waved over black, skeletal limbs. They walked along the lake, and for the first time in a long time she drew breath and felt a whole, sane presence beside her.

They bought corn, and sat on the grass by the lake, and flung it to the spectral swans. Wraiths of passersby were few, only enough to keep a feeling of occupancy about the place—old people, mostly, tottering about the deliberate tranquillity of their routine despite the headlines.

"Do you see them," she ventured to ask him finally, "all thin and gray?"

He did not understand, did not take her literally, only shrugged. Warily, she abandoned that questioning at once. She rose to her feet and stared at the horizon, where the smoke bannered on the wind.

"Buy you supper?" he asked.

She turned, prepared for this, and managed a shy, desperate smile. "Yes," she said, knowing what else he reckoned to buy with that—willing, and hating herself, and desperately afraid that he would walk away, tonight, tomorrow. She did not know men. She had no idea what she could say or do to prevent his leaving, only that he would when someday he realized her madness.

Even her parents had not been able to bear with that—visited her only at first in the hospitals, and then only on holidays, and then not at all. She did not know where they were.

There was a neighbor boy who drowned. She had said he would. She had cried for it. All the town said it was she who pushed him.

Crazy Alis.

Fantasizes, the doctors said. Not dangerous.

They let her out. There were special schools, state schools.

And from time to time—hospitals.

Tranquilizers.

She had left the red pills at home. The realization brought sweat to her palms. They gave sleep. They stopped the dreams. She clamped her lips against the panic and made up her mind that she would not need them—not while she was not alone. She slipped her hand into his arm and walked with him, secure and strange, up the steps from the park to the streets.

And stopped.

The fires were out.

Ghost-buildings rose above their jagged and windowless shells. Wraiths moved through masses of debris, almost obscured at times. He tugged her on, but her step faltered, made him look at her strangely and put his arm about her.

"You're shivering," he said. "Cold?"

She shook her head, tried to smile. The fires were out. She tried to take it for a good omen. The nightmare was over. She looked up into his solid, concerned face, and her smile almost became a wild laugh.

"I'm hungry," she said.

They lingered long over a dinner in Graben's—he in his battered jacket, she in her sweater that hung at the tails and elbows: the spectral patrons were in far better clothes, and stared at them, and they were set in a corner nearest the door, where they would be less visible. There was cracked crystal and broken china on insubstantial tables, and the stars winked coldly in gaping ruin above the wan glittering of the broken chandeliers.

Ruins, cold, peaceful ruin.

Alis looked about her calmly. One could live in ruins, only so the fires were gone.

And there was Jim, who smiled at her without any touch of pity, only a wild, fey desperation that she understood—who spent more than he could afford in Graben's, the inside of which she had never hoped to see—and told her—predictably—that she was beautiful. Others had said it. Vaguely she resented such triteness from him, from him whom she had decided to trust. She smiled sadly, when he said it, and gave it up for a frown and, fearful of offending him with her melancholies, made it a smile again.

Crazy Alis. He would learn and leave tonight if she were not careful. She tried to put on gaiety, tried to laugh.

And then the music stopped in the restaurant, and the noise of the other diners went dead, and the speaker was giving an inane announcement.

*Shelters . . . shelters . . . shelters.*

Screams broke out. Chairs overturned.

Alis went limp in her chair, felt Jim's cold, solid hand tugging at hers, saw his frightened face mouthing her name as he took her up into his arms, pulled her with him, started running.

The cold air outside hit her, shocked her into sight of the ruins again, wraith figures pelting toward that chaos where the fires had been worst.

And she knew.

"No!" she cried, pulling at his arm. "No!" she insisted, and bodies half-seen buffeted them in a rush to destruction. He yielded to her sudden certainty, gripped her hand and fled with her against the crowds as the sirens wailed madness through the night—fled with her as she ran her sighted way through the ruin.

And into Kingsley's, where safe tables stood abandoned with food still on them, doors ajar, chairs overturned. Back they went into the kitchens and down and down into the cellar, the dark, the cold safety from the flames.

No others found them there. At last the earth shook, too deep for sound. The sirens ceased and did not come on again.

They lay in the dark and clutched each other and shivered, and above them for hours raged the sound of fire, smoke sometimes drifting in to sting their eyes and noses. There was the distant crash of brick, rumblings that shook the ground, that came near, but never touched their refuge.

And in the morning, with the scent of fire still in the air, they crept up into the murky daylight.

The ruins were still and hushed. The ghost-buildings were solid now, mere shells. The wraiths were gone. It was the fires themselves that were strange, some true, some not, playing above dark, cold brick, and most were fading.

Jim swore softly, over and over again, and wept.

When she looked at him she was dry-eyed, for she had done her crying already.

And she listened as he began to talk about food, about leaving the city, the two of them. "All right," she said.

Then clamped her lips, shut her eyes against what she saw in his face. When she opened them it was still true, the sudden transparency, the wash of blood. She trembled, and he shook at her, his ghost-face distraught.

"What's wrong?" he asked. "What's wrong?"

She could not tell him, would not. She remembered the boy who had drowned, remembered the other ghosts. Of a sudden she tore from his hands and ran, dodging the maze of debris that, this morning, was solid.

"Alis!" he cried and came after her.

"No!" she cried suddenly, turning, seeing the unstable wall, the cascading brick. She started back and stopped, unable to force herself. She held out her hands to warn him back, saw them solid.

The brick rumbled, fell. Dust came up, thick for a moment, obscuring everything.

She stood still, hands at her sides, then wiped her sooty face and turned and started walking, keeping to the center of the dead streets.

Overhead, clouds gathered, heavy with rain.

She wandered at peace now, seeing the rain spot the pavement, not yet feeling it.

In time the rain did fall, and the ruins became chill and cold. She visited the dead lake and the burned trees, the ruin of Graben's, out of which she gathered a string of crystal to wear.

She smiled when, a day later, a looter drove her from her food supply. He had a wraith's look, and she laughed from a place he did not dare to climb and told him so.

And recovered her cache later when it came true, and settled among the ruined shells that held no further threat, no other nightmares, with her crystal necklace and tomorrows that were the same as today.

One could live in ruins, only so the fires were gone.

And the ghosts were all in the past, invisible.